THE *Homestead* BRIDES COLLECTION

9 Pioneering Couples Risk All for Love and Land

Mary Connealy

Darlene Franklin, Carla Olson Gade,
Ruth Logan Herne, Pam Hillman,
DiAnn Mills, Erica Vetsch,
Becca Whitham, Kathleen Y'Barbo

BARBOUR BOOKS
An Imprint of Barbour Publishing, Inc.

Print ISBN 978-1-64352-175-6

eBook Editions:
Adobe Digital Edition (.epub) 978-1-63058-688-1
Kindle and MobiPocket Edition (.prc) 978-1-63058-687-4

Published by Barbour Books, an imprint of Barbour Publishing, Inc., 1810 Barbour Drive, Uhrichsville, Ohio 44683, www.barbourbooks.com

Our mission is to inspire the world with the life-changing message of the Bible.

Member of the
Evangelical Christian
Publishers Association

Printed in the United States of America.

Contents

HOMESTEAD ON THE RANGE

by Mary Connealy

Chapter 1

Lone Tree, Nebraska, 1875

Do you want a needle and a spool of thread, Mr. Samuelson?"
Elle glanced up at the question, asked to a man. Mere curiosity because needles and thread usually were sold to women.

She saw a man with eyes as wide as a scared horse. She could swear she saw white all the way around the blue center. Biting back a smile, she felt an urge to go help him. Or at least she could advise him to find his wife and let her take over such business.

Being neighborly, she walked to his side. The Lone Tree General Store was bustling on a Saturday morning, and a line had formed to buy supplies while Myrtle talked to Mr. Samuelson.

"Good morning, Myrtle." Elle had known Myrtle Garvey for years. The older woman helped her husband run the only general store in the small northeast Nebraska frontier town.

"Mornin', Elle." Myrtle's eyes sparked with her good nature, but it was a busy morning for her and Elle could tell the woman was fretting about Mr. Samuelson's questions. "Have you met Colin Samuelson? He just claimed a homestead out by yours. Wouldn't be surprised if you shared a property line."

Colin turned to Elle, as if looking away from the spool of black thread in Myrtle's hand was a pardon from a hanging.

"Welcome to Lone Tree, Mr. Samuelson." Elle nodded. "Myrtle, if you need to see to your customers, I can help with the thread selection."

"Mr. Samuelson, this is Eleanor Winter. She is just the one to help you." Myrtle set the notions down quickly and hurried to her front counter as if afraid Elle would change her mind.

Myrtle wove through her store, packed with shelves and barrels and people, leaving Elle to deal with the clearly overwhelmed Mr. Samuelson.

"I'd appreciate the help, Miss Winter." He doffed his wide-brimmed hat and smiled at her, the nicest smile. He seemed to really look at her in a way no man had in years. "I have fabric on my list, but it appears that there is more to a shirt than just fabric."

He had overly long dark curls under that hat. The shirt he was wearing now was so threadbare it would shred in a high wind.

"It's Mrs. Winter. I assure you, I'm no Miss." Though many people thought it. She was short and slight. Her cheeks were quite round and her hair thin and blond and flyaway. She'd always looked younger than her age. She kept waiting to get old enough to count youthful looks as a blessing.

"I apologize, Mrs. Winter."

"That's fine. You do need these things, unless your wife didn't ask you to buy thread and needles and buttons because she already has them."

"I'm not married, and I just moved in with only the barest of supplies."

Elle hated to ask, but the condition of his shirt and his lack of knowledge about sewing forced her to. "Have you ever made a shirt before?"

Sadness seemed to dim the light in his vivid blue eyes. "Nope, my wife used to handle that for me. I'm afraid I'm near to useless."

"You're a widower?" Elle immediately felt such empathy for him. She reached out and rested her fingertips on his wrist. She felt the solid muscles flex under his poor shirt.

His eyes went to where she touched him as if a magnet had drawn them. She pulled away quickly, shocked at her boldness.

She cleared her throat then cleared it again and went on. "I'm a widow, and I remember well how much I had to learn when my husband died."

Five years now and the grief had faded until thinking of Jerome brought happy memories rather than tearing grief.

"Do you really have time to help me?" His smile was so genuine and so eager that it warmed something in Elle that had been cold for years. Exactly five years.

"I'm in no hurry." She was enjoying this visit immensely.

Chapter 2

Colin reached into the pocket of his pants—of course there was a hole big enough he could reach all the way through and scratch his thigh. Here he was talking with the prettiest woman he'd seen in an age, the first one he'd even noticed since Priscilla died. Her bright blue eyes matched her crisp blue-and-white gingham dress, while his clothing was nearly in rags. These were his good pants, too, and they were nearly worn through at the knees. He needed all new clothes, and he had no idea how he would get them.

He produced a piece of paper that unfolded, then unfolded again, and again. "My list. And there are more things on it I don't quite understand."

Elle covered her mouth, but a chuckle still escaped. The spark in those light blue eyes drew him. Shocking, when his thoughts had been for no one but Priscilla even with her gone now for a solid year. It felt like a betrayal of his love to notice how pretty Elle Winter was, but notice he did.

Colin shrugged one shoulder sheepishly. "Well, you did ask."

Elle let the laugh escape. Colin laughed, too, and the moment stretched. It was surprisingly pleasant.

"I'd be glad to help. Let me see your list."

She'd said yes. They spent the next half hour stacking things on the counter, off to the side, so they didn't interfere with the lady running the store. Neither of them talked much about themselves, just the list. He was busy worrying what to buy, and she was busy teasing him.

And they were both busy laughing.

Colin had done little laughing in the last year.

It turned out his land did abut hers.

"You should build right along the property line on the west side of your homestead. I'm right up against my own line on the east. My husband built there because there's an artesian well that has cold water pouring out year-round; even in winter it keeps running. It bubbles up right on the border of our land. You have as much right to that water as I do, and you wouldn't have to dig a well. It would be nice to have a close neighbor."

Colin's shoulders lifted. "I was worried about water. I've never dug a well before. I drove out to my land, picked a likely spot with no idea what I was doing, unloaded my wagon and took off the canvas, then came straight to town for supplies. Yes, having a well already there sounds wonderful." He had a lot in front of him to settle a homestead. Most of what lay ahead of him came as a shock. "I'd just planned to hire someone to build a house and dig a well."

"Most folks are mighty busy trying to work their own homesteads. Chances are you can find help with your soddy, but you'll have to work hard alongside whoever steps in."

"A soddy?" Colin had just taken off from St. Louis, so tired of his home and the painful memories. He'd heard he could homestead, which would be so different from his city life there should be nothing to remind him of Priscilla. He'd made the decision in a rush and was just learning what it meant to "stake a claim" to land on Nebraska's vast prairie.

"Well, yes. That's the only building material, unless you ship in the wood for a board house, but that takes months."

"Shipped in?" Colin felt the shock of that to his toes. "It takes months? Why is that?"

"Well, there aren't trees anywhere around. We call this town Lone Tree for a reason." She gestured out the front window to the massive cottonwood that stood just outside of town. "The closest trees are along the Missouri River, straight east nearly twenty miles away, and even those we do have are heavily picked over, leaving only sparse and spindly trees. They don't make good log cabins. So the boards have to be shipped in to the nearest railhead then loaded into a wagon and hauled out here. You'll need to build a sod house to get you through the spring and summer. There is a bit of lumber to be had in town, enough to frame the house, but not enough for walls."

Colin ran one hand into his hair and knocked his hat off.

Elle caught it.

"I don't know how to build a sod house."

"I have a sod-busting plow you can borrow." Surely she'd just said that to torment him.

"I'm a doctor. I wanted property of my own. But I've never built a house. I'd planned to hire it done."

"A doctor? Lone Tree needs one desperately. And I think I can name a man or two who would be willing to help you."

She gave directions to the well and said a bit about his property lines, while Myrtle sent a hired boy out with box after box of supplies to his team standing in their traces out front.

Looking at the team reminded him he was taking too long with this. It had just been so nice to talk to a pretty woman. As much as she'd thrown a few surprises his way, he didn't want it to end. But it had to.

Or did it?

"I've had a wonderful time, Mrs. Winter. Uh. . ." His eyes locked on hers, his smile faded, and he was sorely afraid his face was heating up with a blush. Well, it was the plain truth he had no experience talking to women.

He forced out the words he had in mind. "Would you be interested in taking a. . . a. . .a. . ." He swallowed hard. "That is going on a. . .a. . .a, well, um. . .a drive with me sometime?"

Elle's eyes widened, and since Colin was looking right at her, quite intently, he noticed.

"I think that would be lovely, Mr. Samuelson."

"Call me Colin, please." He decided to get moving before she changed her mind. Then he noticed she had his hat. He reached for it and she handed it over, rather unsteadily. He finally managed to be the one surprising her.

"All right, Colin. And I'm Elle." She gestured toward the door. "I'm running late myself."

Walking with her, he reached past and opened the door. "I'll be a few days getting settled. How about Sunday, after services? Maybe I can see you home, Elle."

Nodding, Elle stepped out on the boardwalk. "I'd like that. Thank you, Colin."

They turned and faced each other, and the world seemed to fade away. Colin didn't hear if horses or wagons passed. If anyone walked by them, he didn't notice. Only Elle was real.

"Ma! You're late!"

Chapter 3

Turning, she saw her four children running up, along with quite a few other young'uns she'd never seen before.

"I'm sorry." Honestly, what she was sorry for was the interruption, but she'd been a mother for a long time. She was used to it.

She noticed her son, Tim, whispering to a girl who seemed close to his age. The pair seemed awfully friendly for just having met.

Hers swarmed around her, and the three others yelled, "Pa."

As they ran up to Colin.

"Yours?"

Colin was staring at her children. "You have four children?" He sounded strange.

"Yes, and yours? I guess we didn't get that much talking done. You've got three?"

"Seven children," Colin said, sounding a bit faint. His eyes were wide open, and they jumped from child to child.

Tim, fifteen, taller than she was. Her only boy and the image of Jerome, with his shining brown curls that peeked out around the edges of his broad-brimmed hat. Mercifully he had none of Jerome's dark moods.

Martha, twelve, looked more like Elle every day and was nearing her in height. Petite and fair haired. The twins, Barbara and Betty, were identical and very small for six and a match for Martha and Elle. They'd been one year old when Jerome had died, and just surviving had been a struggle with two infants and all the work of running her homestead.

Elle quickly introduced them to Colin.

"We met at the church school party, Ma." Tim gave a raven-haired girl a long look. "We were coming to look for you. We found out we're living next door to each other."

The brunette, Sarah, had a full woman's height and was probably an inch taller than Elle. The girl had beautiful, bright green eyes and a wide smile, a complexion burned from the sun, and a few coiling ringlets that had escaped from a bun. "My name is Sarah, Mrs. Winter. Tim, this is my pa, Dr. Samuelson."

Sarah gave her father a bright smile, which he didn't notice because Colin was still looking from child to child to child.

Her son, Tim, was skinny, and he hadn't gotten his growing on yet, but he was a serious boy whose hard work at Elle's side had gotten her through the last five years. He extended a hand as if he were an adult.

"Nice to meet you, Doc Samuelson." Colin managed to shake, but there was something wrong with him.

Elle wasn't sure what, but there was a dazed expression, and his eyes were so wide, she could see white all around them. Like a frightened horse—much as he'd looked when she'd first noticed him.

Well, they could talk more after services on Sunday.

Sarah quickly introduced her two little brothers, who hadn't stood still for a second. Russell with chocolate-brown hair, who resembled Colin, and Frank as dark haired as Sarah.

"We need to be going, Mr. Samuelson." She realized she'd started calling him Colin in the store, but now, somehow, with the children at hand, that seemed overly familiar. "We will see you at services on Sunday and maybe before that if we're neighbors. In fact, if you'd like help settling in, come by our place. And I strongly hope you build close to us. It would be good to have neighbors."

She shooed her children into the wagon. Tim climbed up and took the reins.

Colin's children ran to climb into their wagon.

"Well, good-bye then."

Colin's hand whipped out and caught her wrist. He leaned very close to her and whispered, "About that ride."

He faltered, cleared his throat, and went on. "I won't be coming."

"What?" Elle probably had that frightened horse expression now.

"Elle, I really thought we got along well in that store but. . .but seven children between us?" Colin shook his head, tiny frantic moves surely hoping the children wouldn't notice. "That is just out of the question. I can't even take care of the ones I have."

He smiled weakly. "I'm sorry. Good-bye, Elle."

Elle's mouth gaped open, and she stood, shocked, as he turned and nearly threw himself up onto his high seat. All three of his children were there, Sarah holding the littlest boy, Frank, on her lap; Russell squashed between Colin and Sarah on a seat clearly built for two. But the back end was so full of supplies they had to fit.

It dawned on Elle that he'd bought so much because he had three children to feed and clothe.

He shook the reins and yelled at his horses to move with far too much enthusiasm. They took off. His children waved, and hers waved back. Stunned as she was, Elle managed to raise one hand.

Colin never looked back.

Finally, with his horses picking up speed with every step, Elle came out of her shock enough to be annoyed. Her children were too much for him, then? He liked her, but he didn't like her children, whom he'd only met for about two minutes? Annoyance grew into anger as she marched to her wagon and climbed up beside Tim.

Her son gave her such a sunny smile she forced herself to ignore her anger. "I liked the Samuelson family, Ma. I'm hoping we can all be good friends."

"They seemed nice." Elle managed a smile and said no more because it served no purpose to let her children know Colin Samuelson had been horrified by their very existence. How could she say, "Don't you dare be friends with them. At least not if their skunk of a father is anywhere around"?

Besides, she thought as she calmed a bit, seven children. Though she controlled it outwardly, inside she shook to think of all those children. That was an incredible number of children, and half grown. . .that seemed like more than if they'd come one at a time and started as tiny babies.

Of course Tim acted like most growing boys and was always starving, but add two more boys? And did Sarah give Tim a flirtatious look? How could brother and sister also have romantic notions about each other?

It was still annoying to have her children make a man run for the hills, but good heavens. She pictured her house and his lack of a house. Seven children! He was right. It was just as well not to start something that had no chance to go on.

That didn't stop her from wanting to kick Colin Samuelson in the backside.

Chapter 4

"Ma, we've got to go, fast." Tim came in with an unusually frantic look on his face.

"What's wrong?" Elle straightened away from the bread she was kneading.

"It's the Samuelsons, they need help."

"We just saw them at church yesterday." Tim and Sarah had talked, the rest of the children had played together. Elle hadn't gone near Colin, and he certainly hadn't come near her.

"I just saw Sarah. We've got to go, hurry."

"You saw Sarah? You mean you rode over there? Just now? I thought you were doing chores." As she said it, she realized the morning had been getting on. Tim had brought in milk and eggs, and he'd gone back out at least two hours ago. Her son was so mature and dependable she hadn't thought to notice his long absence and question what he was doing.

"Yes, and we have to stop him."

"Stop him from what?" Stop him from moving away was her first thought. Moving away so he never had to be near Elle and all her children again.

"He's going to build his house right in a waterway. He's turning up the dirt for a foundation right now. Floodwater will run right through his house, but all he sees is a smooth place. Easy to build on. You know that old Logan Creek bottom."

"Why didn't you just tell him not to build there?"

Tim rolled his eyes. "I tried, but he hired two men from town." Tim named the two biggest layabouts in Lone Tree. "And they told the doctor to pay me no mind. He took their word over mine. But he'll listen to you. We've got to go fast because if he gets any further along in building, he'll decide moving the house is more trouble than it's worth."

"And it could flood and do them harm and destroy their supplies." Elle grabbed a towel and started wiping her hands, yanked her white bibbed apron off over her head, and tossed it over a chair. She had a dark yellow housedress on and her hair was in an unkempt knot on her head, but she wasn't going to take time to change when time was of the essence.

"Yes, and there hasn't been any flooding for a couple of years, so some grass has grown and it doesn't look like a bad spot. And the creek is close by and so deep and the water so low, I can see why he doesn't believe me that it could ever jump its banks."

"Why is he even building over there? I thought he was going to build close over here and use the artesian well." But Elle knew exactly why the moment she asked the question. To avoid her and, more so, her children.

"I wondered that, too." Tim gave her a strange look, like he was wondering how she'd managed to scare Colin to the far side of his claim.

"Hitch up the wagon. I'll get the girls."

Tim jerked his chin in satisfaction. In fact, he seemed more than satisfied, he seemed delighted. It wasn't the first time that Elle had wondered if he was sweet on Sarah. They were too young of course, but they were at the age when youngsters had thoughts of the future. And Elle had known Jerome from childhood, and they'd already planned a future together, in their childish way, by this age.

She abandoned her bread. The girls abandoned their cleaning. Tim abandoned his chores. All to save a man horrified by her children.

Colin Samuelson was a trial.

Chapter 5

I 've got the team hitched up, Lou, now how do I cut bricks of sod?" Colin was exhausted from the morning's work. Lou and Dutch had come out as planned, with sturdy timbers for a house frame. Then Colin, mostly by himself, had cut a trench in the dirt as a foundation, and his hired men helped seat the heaviest logs, then they'd settled in to give orders.

It had been hard, heavy work. Russell and Frank had pitched in with good spirits. Were long hours of hard labor the answer to controlling his overactive sons?

Of course Sarah was so grown up, Colin trusted her with everything. He worried sometimes his sweet girl was being forced to grow up too fast, but he couldn't figure out how to ask less of her, because he couldn't manage without her.

Colin had no idea in the world how to build a sod house, which put him completely at the mercy of these two men, and he wasn't a bit impressed with either of them.

They'd seemed decent and eager for work when he'd met them after church yesterday. Someone had mentioned them and told Colin where to look; neither man had been to services. The only two men in town who had time to hire out for work.

Colin now wondered if the reason they were available was because they were lazy slugs and none too bright.

Dutch, short and stout, probably just about Colin's age, rose from where he sat on the ground and ambled over. To point.

Colin listened with near desperate concentration as he held the two tall, curved handles of the plow the two men had brought with them. A sod-busting plow. Elle had mentioned having such a thing and being willing to share.

These two were charging Colin to rent it.

When Colin found his mind wandering to that pretty neighbor of his, he shook his head and focused hard on what Dutch was saying.

He had to hold on to the plow handles and slap the horses with the reins to make them go.

His horses were blooded stock and had never been hitched to a plow before. They kept looking behind them nervously. And the plow wasn't sunk into the ground. Did it just go down when the horses started moving forward? And how did he hold the plow with two hands and slap the horses on the back at the same time?

"Dutch, I—"

"It's just something you have to practice at, Dr. Samuelson, like any other skill, I reckon. You'll get onto it. Me 'n' Lou left some supplies we'll need in town. There wasn't room to bring them along with the plow and timbers. Can we have our pay for today now? We'll eat lunch in town."

"My daughter is making lunch, and I'm sure any supplies will wait until tomorrow. Surely I'll be all day cutting sod." All day? Try all year!

"Nope, we need them now, and it takes both of us. We'd prefer to eat at the diner in town."

Dutch held out his hand and waited. Colin knew with a sinking stomach that if he paid this man anything, he'd never be back, at least not until the money was gone. And while he might not be knowledgeable in the building of sod houses, he was far from a fool.

He released the heavy plow and reached into his pocket for two bits. He'd offered them two bits each for a day's work, which was a good wage for a hired man. He thrust the coin at Dutch.

"Here's for half a day for the two of you. I'll pay you for the afternoon's work at day's end."

Dutch hesitated. Something unpleasant, even dangerous crossed the man's face. Colin braced himself in case the man swung a fist. It was one thing to hire a man who didn't work hard—it was another to have someone violent around the place.

Colin waited, praying nothing ugly would happen in front of the children. He didn't fool himself that in a fight with these two he'd escape unscathed.

With a grunt of disgust, Dutch reached out and snatched the coin and stormed off toward his horse. Lou caught up to him, the fastest he'd moved all morning.

As the men swung up on horseback, Colin called out, trying to sound casual, "I think I can handle this now. I won't be needing you anymore after this morning. Thanks for coming out."

Dutch threw a furious look over his shoulder but then faced forward, and the two rode off.

Most likely they weren't willing to protest being dismissed from a job they had no plans to return to anyway, but it was clear they'd hoped to ride off with two bits apiece.

They might have even come back to get it. Colin was glad now they wouldn't.

He turned to grab the plow again. He saw the heavy blade of the plowshare and the sod before him. The harnesses seemed twisted at several points, but Dutch had said they were okay. This couldn't be that hard.

"Sarah, you keep the boys back while I cut a row of sod." He asked too much of his daughter.

She caught the boys' hands, and they jumped and hollered, playing, laughing.

Smiling at his children, Colin turned back to the plow. Might as well get on with it. He let go of one handle and lifted the leathers to slap the horses.

A gunshot blasted at a distance, and he whirled around, afraid Dutch and Lou had returned to rob him.

✹

Elle lowered the rifle she'd just fired into the air as soon as Colin turned to look.

After his first jump of surprise, he relaxed and dropped the reins he'd been about to slap on his horses' backs.

"We stopped him in time." Elle heaved a sigh of relief to Tim. "You got us here fast. Good driving. Thank God I had the rifle."

"You always carry it, Ma. It'd only be worth mentioning if you didn't."

Her son wasn't a big talker. Being surrounded by women seemed to have developed the most manly possible side of him.

Barbara and Betty both poked their heads between Elle and Tim.

"Why'd you shoot, Mama?" Barbara did most of the talking for the two of them. "It was loud."

Elle smiled down at her girls. "I wanted Mr. Samuelson's attention, that's why."

Betty gave her an impish smile. "Okay."

Martha, from where she sat calmly in the back, said, "At least you weren't trying to kill him."

Her oldest daughter was always a bit sarcastic and used to caring for her little sisters. She was a child who was handy in a crisis, though Elle tried to avoid ever having a crisis by planning ahead.

Which only led to a crisis two or three times a week.

Brushing the flyaway white hair back on Barbara's forehead, Elle said, "Sit back, girls. We're almost there."

Colin came and helped Elle down from the high buckboard. He caught her around the waist as she jumped. It was a novelty not climbing down by herself. Tim was lifting the twins out of the back, and Martha had hopped out all by herself. The children ran straight for Colin's children, and the chattering and giggling began. It gave Elle a moment of privacy with Colin in the bevy of children.

"Why did you shoot the gun?" Colin's hands were solid and strong, and he didn't remove them from her waist with any great hurry.

"I—I—uh, well, you were about to whip your horses, and I had to stop you."

He let go with what looked like reluctance. A furrow appeared on his smooth brow. "Why? I'm cutting sod to build a house."

Elle turned to the team and almost shuddered to think what would have happened if she'd been even a minute later.

"Tim, help me get these horses out of the harness."

Colin caught Elle's arm but with no force, his hands were very gentle. She could well imagine him having healing skills. "But why? We're all ready to go."

Closing her eyes for a second, Elle remembered how Jerome had acted if she'd ever corrected him. He wasn't nice about it. In fact, he could be rude and surly, sometimes for hours after she'd tried to tell him something was wrong. It had gotten to the point she'd just stopped talking to him in those instances, even though she'd lived on the frontier for a long time and Jerome was a newcomer.

But his irritation at being corrected, even when he was blatantly wrong, made it more trouble than just letting him learn from his own mistakes. Elle remembered now clearly why she'd done absolutely nothing to encourage a man since Jerome died. She'd found marriage to be a trying business.

Bracing herself for Colin to take offense, Elle knew she had no choice. She'd have even spoken up to Jerome. "The plow is sure to tip if the horses move it even an inch. And that sod-busting plow is heavy enough to pull the horses along with it when it falls. It could cut them, hock them even. You could hurt them enough they'd have to be put down."

Colin looked at his horses in shock. "Put down?" Colin rushed to their sides and began frantically unhitching them.

Relieved, Elle went to the far side to help. She could have showed him how to do it right, but what she had to do was convince him to move. Another chance of unleashing his temper.

Once the horses were led a safe distance from the plow, Elle had a chance to look at the camp the Samuelsons had set up, and shuddered.

It was chaos.

Clothing and food and household supplies were all scattered everywhere. A fire that was far too big to cook over smoldered, and it had to be hours after breakfast.

A big tarp—most likely it was the canvas they'd used for their covered wagon—draped over another mountain of. . .something.

Elle turned to watch Colin tie his team of beautiful brown Belgians to a tree in such a way that they couldn't graze. Did he not know they should be staked out differently? Or was he planning to get right back to work? Either was bad.

He dragged a broad-brimmed Stetson off his head and came up to her. "I hired two men to help me. They let me hitch the team up that way."

"I heard." Elle flinched. "That's why we hurried. Dutch and Lou are known men in Lone Tree. They aren't men you want around your children. They sneak a bit of liquor all day long, and they have foul mouths. And they aren't hard workers." Elle looked around. "Where are they?"

Quickly, Colin told her what happened. The children weren't paying attention; in fact, they'd all vanished over the creek bank. Her last glimpse of them was of Sarah and Tim talking rapidly. Yes, her quiet son was talking, and Elle was struck that the two youngsters didn't look like children. Tim was still lean, like any kid, and he had some height yet to gain, but he wasn't a child any longer. And Sarah, well, a girl of fourteen was full grown, and she had a woman's curves.

They probably needed to be carefully chaperoned, but then they were walking with five other children, better than a chaperone any day.

Tearing her eyes away from the shocking realization that her son was becoming a man, Elle turned to the other man she had to worry about. She cleared her throat. There was no way to say what needed saying except just plain speaking.

Quietly, so the children couldn't overhear, she said, "I understand that when you decided we shouldn't go riding together it was because of all our children. Honestly, I understand that. But there's no reason we have to avoid each other like we did yesterday at church."

Colin was tanned and strong and probably very intelligent, being a doctor and all. She was surprised when a flush darkened his cheeks. He rubbed the back of his neck.

"I'm sorry about that. Yes, I acted like a fool yesterday."

"And that's why you're getting ready to build a house all the way over on this side of the property, to stay away from me." She wasn't asking a question, she knew the truth.

"There's water here and a smooth place to build."

"It's smooth because you're building on a flood plain."

Colin jerked around and stared at the digging they'd done. "That's why it's so perfectly level?"

Elle nodded.

"But the creek is deep. Are you saying it can rain enough to jump its banks?"

He hadn't started growling yet, and she knew from the flush that she'd upset him. That was usually when Jerome got grouchy.

"Yes, it not only can, it does, almost every spring and often a time or two during the summer and fall. Your sod cabin would have been washed away before you'd been here a year. And the creek water is muddy most of the year. It would be fine if you had no choice, but you do have a choice, Colin—my artesian well. Come and build closer to me." Elle managed a small smile. "Seven children is overwhelming and no sod house could hold them, and my house certainly couldn't. I haven't set my cap for you, but I do think we. . .we could be friends, don't you?"

Shifting his eyes back to Elle, Colin stared for a few seconds too long. His blue gaze was intense. Elle had to force herself to remember she was proposing a friendship and absolutely nothing more.

"That really could have ended in me having to shoot my horses?" Colin shuddered.

"I know how to hitch up a sod-busting plow, Colin. Tim does, too." Elle didn't tell him Martha was also fully capable. And the twins couldn't do it alone, but they'd be a big help if asked. She thought that might be a bit too much for Colin to handle. "We would be glad to help you. This is even a mile farther from town. You're adding quite a bit to your drive to Lone Tree just to avoid me."

That jolted a smile out of him. "I'm sorry about that, Elle." Colin gave her another one of those deep looks. "It hasn't been that long since Priscilla died. It's just that no woman has so much as gotten my attention, not in the way you did. But I just can't imagine taking on seven children. I'm sorry, they seem like wonderful young'uns, but—"

Unable to stand hearing it, Elle reached up and touched Colin's mouth to stop the words. When she touched his lips, the heat of them made her draw back fast. "Let's not talk of it. We agree that we aren't a match for each other. As long as we remember that, we can be friends and neighbors. You can even leave the children home alone when you do your doctoring, knowing I can help if need be."

"I'm not leaving them home alone." Colin's expression darkened for the first time. She'd finally offended him. "Sarah does a good job."

If she wasn't mistaken, she saw a flash of worry. "You ask a lot of Sarah. I do the same with Tim. I'm sure she is perfectly able to watch the children. It's not a criticism, just an offer of help."

A shout from the depths of the creek drew both their attention. Then laughter followed, so Elle didn't go check.

"The truth is, I ask too much of her." Colin looked at the creek bank, treeless of course. "She's a good cook, and she chases after Russ and Frank all day, does the laundry and mending, though she's never done much of that. We lived in St. Louis, and I could hire someone for that. But we need new clothes, and she's told me to let her figure it out. She's such a good girl, and I depend on her. Priscilla took her parents' deaths hard, and in her grief she took sick and didn't have the will to fight it off, I suppose. Sarah was already taking care of us a year ago."

"Jerome's been gone five years. Tim was nine when he died, and he had to grow up fast. All my children did, though maybe the twins less so because Martha did so much caring for them they might be confused who their mother is."

A smile slipped across Colin's face. "She'd have been what, eight?"

"Seven, actually."

"Mercy, I can't imagine how you got by. And seven years old? That's a mighty young mother."

"Well, I helped some." Elle smiled back. "We managed to stay alive, that was about it."

Their eyes met again, and Elle felt as if she were looking deep inside him. His pain was there, his worry, his kindness.

Silence stretched between them. A breeze hushed around them and the prairie grass bent and swayed, dancing as if God drew His fingers across it.

The day was warm. Early June was about the best time of the year out here. She was glad Colin was seeing Nebraska at its most beautiful.

Another shout from the creek broke the connection.

"So, do you mind moving closer to me, Colin?"

He took a step, erasing the space between them. A thrill of pleasure rushed through her before she laughed.

"No, I mean moving your house site closer to mine."

This time Colin laughed. They'd laughed together in the store.

"We'll be friends, Elle. Just friends. I'm barely surviving now with three children to care for and spend time with. I can't add anything to that."

Nodding, Elle ignored the pinch of disappointment. "That's fine. Let's get your supplies loaded and your team hitched. It looks like it will take at least a couple of trips, but it isn't far."

Colin turned to the creek and raised his voice. "Sarah, Russ, all of you kids, come up here. We need help."

The shouting fell silent, and Colin added, "We're moving across the claim to live nearer to the Winters."

A shout of joy tore loose from the depths of the creek, followed by laughter and pounding footsteps. The children rushed over the lip of the bank and began loading.

Chapter 6

Colin clutched his lower back as he straightened from setting down his last crate of supplies. They'd loaded and unloaded the wagon twice. He was within fifty feet of Elle's home, a pretty white clapboard building that made him almost sinfully envious. Her home would have fit inside his St. Louis house twice over, but they weren't in St. Louis, were they?

Elle buzzed around the campsite making orderly piles of his supplies. She wore a dress as yellow as goldenrod, and her smile gleamed nearly as bright as sunlight. She lifted and arranged and sorted, bending and reaching until she danced like the flowers waving amid the prairie grass. And everything she did was with a riveting feminine grace.

He really needed to get over being riveted.

It had been a poor excuse for an idea to move over here. She was too pretty and sweet. The pull he felt toward her was so strong it shocked him. And marrying her was out of the question. As a friend, though, he thought they could deal well with each other. He hoped, because he had no intention of marrying again, and that made the ideas that rippled through his head lacking in honor.

Even with the Winters's help, Colin and his family were looking at a long stretch sleeping outdoors. Just as they'd slept outdoors while the wagon train had made its way here. So far the children seemed to take it in stride. Colin, on the other hand, was heartily sick of sleeping on the ground.

All the children had worked with a good spirit, even his rambunctious boys seemed to tag after Tim and imitate his hard work. Elle had taken charge and done a good job of marshalling their youthful forces.

Once the wagon was empty, Elle got busy organizing. Tim hooked up the plow and started cutting the prairie sod. Sarah had talked quietly with Elle, then she'd taken all the children into the Winters's house to get an evening meal.

He could already imagine his home taking shape. Water burbled out of the artesian well, and the wind seemed a bit broken by a swell of land to the north.

Elle's property was a prime example of what could be made of this endless grassland with years of hard work. She had a few hundred sturdy little trees growing as straight as soldiers standing at attention, their leaves fluttering in the breeze. One row was of shorter trees, and he wondered if they were apple. It would make a fine windbreak. . .in about thirty years.

She had a barn, and a door sloping up out of the ground looked like a root cellar. A well-tilled garden stretched between the house and the cellar door. There were long lines of barbed wire stretching to the east, and a herd of cattle grazed placidly while calves frolicked in the tall grass.

She'd returned her team to a second corral with three more horses in it, including a foal so young it must have been born this spring. Chickens pecked and scratched in the shorter grass in a small pen behind her house. Beyond that were tidy rows of corn. Each plant was about a foot tall, and they stood in neat, precise rows, stretching away to the west. There was even a little sod house standing near the well—no doubt what they'd built when they first homesteaded. It was closed up tight, and Colin had no doubt that the ever-efficient Mrs. Winters was putting it to some extraordinarily brilliant use.

He needed to think about something other than Elle. "Where's the shovel? I can get started digging the foundation trenches."

Elle straightened from where she'd been folding a crate of clothes. She winced a bit. "You don't need trenches."

"What?" Colin thought of his blistered hands and sore back. "Dutch and Lou had me spend all morning digging."

"I know. I saw. I'm sorry. I could have told you those two were worse than nothing. You could have saved yourself a lot of aching muscles, not to mention two bits if you'd unbent enough to talk to me yesterday in church."

She really was a snippy little thing. Colin appreciated that she didn't slip the word *stubborn* into her politely delivered news. Or for that matter, *stupid*.

"Your place is beautiful, Elle. You've done so much work. The house has a settled look to it. Did you build it before your husband died?"

"Yes, it had just gone up. We homesteaded right after the law was passed. We got married, moved out here. Jerome got the sod house up." Actually he'd had a lot of help, including from Elle. "And he went off to fight in the war. Tim was born five months after he left, and we were all alone in the soddy when he came."

Colin gasped. "You had your baby alone, not a doctor, or even a neighbor?"

Elle gave her head a sassy little tilt. "There were no neighbors for ten miles. Lone Pine wasn't even a settlement yet. It was winter, there was just no possible way for someone to come and help. It was frightening to be so alone, but everything was fine. And then I had a baby to care for and finally some company out here. Jerome didn't come home until Tim was two years old. Then Martha came along. We proved up on our claim and our crops started to yield, so we built the board house, then the twins were born. A year later Jerome was dead from something. We don't know what, just a terrible pain in his belly that lasted a week before he died."

"I've seen folks with an inflammation like that. It happens sometimes just out of nowhere. I'm sorry."

"It was awful at the time, so shocking. But the children kept me going and we learned to get on, and the truth is, Jerome was gone almost as much as he was here, with the war. Some days I can't quite remember what it was like when he was here."

"Priscilla has just been gone a year now. Maybe in five years it will be less of a gap in our lives." Priscilla had always been delicate. She'd gone to bed with each child on the doctor's orders, and she'd stayed in bed for months after the baby's birth. They'd had a nanny and a wet nurse for each baby, and a personal maid for Priscilla. Besides a housekeeper and a cook and a few downstairs maids. Colin had made a point of stopping in to spend time with Priscilla each night in her bedroom—they each had their own—or he'd have gone days without seeing her. He told Elle none of this. It felt disloyal to poor sweet Priscilla.

∞

Elle saw Colin's eye look into the past. He was still in love with his wife. That was the kind of thing that only time could heal, and if he was deeply in love with his Priscilla even time might not set things right. It was as well that they hadn't taken that ride.

"Dinner!" A call from the house turned her around to see her Martha and Colin's Sarah stepping out of the house, chattering, each with a twin at their side. The boys stuck their heads out of the door then dodged between the girls and came sprinting toward their pa.

"They did that fast." Elle smiled at Colin, glad for the interruption. "Let's call it a good day's work and go eat."

Martha started clanking the triangle that hung from the porch roof. Tim stopped turning sod, unhooked the plow from the team, and came walking in behind the horses.

He hollered, "I'll let the horses have a bit of grain and a drink, but I can work another couple of hours after supper."

Elle started for the house, and Colin came behind her. "I should be doing that. He doesn't need to cut all my sod."

Smiling, Elle said, "If you were going to do it all the time I'd agree, but cutting sod is tricky and we only need to do it once to get your house built. Tim can get enough sod in a few days. We can start bringing in slabs after the evening meal. Tomorrow I'll help you get a frame up for the house. At least Dutch and Lou brought you the right supplies for that. Then we'll build while Tim cuts."

Colin nodded.

Elle hated his grief, but he didn't act hurt or offended by her taking charge. It would be foolish to when she knew what she was doing and he didn't, but that wouldn't stop most men.

They walked into the house side by side.

Chapter 7

I think Sarah and Tim are sweet on each other," Elle whispered through the window gap they'd left in the wall of the soddy. After a week of hard work, the walls were up to the roof level.

Today they'd start the roof. Tomorrow was Sunday and they wouldn't work. But if things went well, Monday night Colin could sleep in his house.

"Sweet?" Colin's eyes went blank, as if she's spoken to him in Pawnee or something. Nodding, Elle said, "Yes, they're always together. They whisper—"

"We're whispering and we're not sweet on each other."

There was no use responding to that. "I just thought you might have noticed."

Colin's brows slammed down. "My daughter is a child."

"No, she's not, Colin." Elle couldn't control a smile. "She's only three years younger than I was when I married Jerome—and I was already sweet on him when I was fourteen."

Elle looked left and right to make sure they were still alone. The children were carrying sod slabs, about three feet long and two wide, toward the house. Not the twins, they couldn't lift the slabs, but they tagged after the other children. Frank and Russ had to carry one together. Tim had cut enough of them to use for the roof, too. Elle didn't especially like the idea of a sod roof, it was too prone to leaking, but there were no choices. And Colin had ordered wood for a house, so this soddy would be a stable by the time winter winds blew.

"You're going to have to get used to the idea that your little girl is growing up."

A look crossed Colin's face. He seemed so stunned it made Elle's heart hurt for him. Poor guy. She was a little shocked herself, but she'd had a week to get used to the idea.

"I do not have to—"

"Ma, we're gonna need a little more wood to frame this door. You left too big a gap." Tim smiled at her.

She didn't bother to tell anyone she'd deliberately made it oversized so Colin's Belgians could get in. This soddy was going to be a stable before long.

Well, now she had to pay for that decision. "I can drive into town—"

"I'll go. And Sarah wants to ride along. We'll go straight in and back." Tim looked sideways at Sarah, and she smiled at him.

"Sarah needs to stay here." Colin's voice was gruff to the point of rudeness. "Someone's got to watch the youngsters."

Sarah's face fell at her father's tone. She quietly nodded. "That's fine, Pa. I'll stay. I guess I wanted a break from watching the little ones, and that's selfish of me. I'm sorry."

Tim threw Colin an angry look, then he turned and stormed toward Elle's house.

He'd hitch up his own team to the Winters's wagon.

"You can take my team, Tim," Colin called after him.

"I handle mine better." Then Tim was out of earshot.

Colin looked back at his daughter, who was walking toward the children and their heavy task. Her shoulders were slumped.

"I'm sorry I spoke of her and Tim. You'd have let them go off together if I hadn't said anything, and she's a good, hardworking girl. She doesn't ask for much."

Colin turned to look at Elle. Helplessly, he said, "I don't know how to raise children."

"Your wife did everything? That's the usual way, I suppose."

"No, they had a nanny. Priscilla wasn't. . .wasn't well a good part of the time. I played with them, but I never taught them anything, I never disciplined them, I never was a real father to them. I was too busy with work. We lived in her parents' house in St. Louis, a grand old house. We lived with them during our marriage, and I loved her folks. Her father was so generous and welcoming. Her mother had the gift of making that house into a warm, welcoming home. They were so good to all of us."

Elle noticed he gave that credit to his in-laws. He didn't mention Priscilla making the house a home. That seemed strange.

"Then they passed away and we inherited it. Then Priscilla died. I felt like I'd stolen that house from Priscilla's family. There was no one, Priscilla was an only child. I couldn't stay there with every room a reminder of a family that was all gone. The children were so devastated when their grandparents died. The whole town of St. Louis seemed to be a reminder. I sold out and moved west before the ice broke on the Mississippi this spring."

He gave the small sod house a disgusted look. "I didn't think it through. I didn't know what I was getting into. I only knew I needed to get away from all that grief."

She was ridiculously hurt to have him give that sneering look to the house. Of course it was humble, it was made of sod for heaven's sake. But she'd been the one who directed the building. She'd worked until every muscle ached as she lay in bed at night, only to wake up and go right back to work. She'd neglected her own home, her garden, her livestock, giving all that a lick and a promise while she poured her time and energy into getting a roof over Colin's head before a rainstorm passed over.

And for all that work, he sneered. She was tempted to wrap a slab of sod around his neck and tell him to go cook his own supper.

Chapter 8

Elle and Colin sat in rocking chairs to eat.

Holding her plate in her lap was awkward, but Elle didn't know quite how else to manage it. Her table was full, and that included having the twins in one chair and Colin's boys in one.

The boys behaved fairly well. Instead of their usual constant wrestling, their focus was all on their food. They'd worked hard all day, and they were tired and starving.

Tim and Sarah sat one at the head of the table and one at the foot, which was so symbolic of their coming adulthood it twisted Elle's stomach.

Martha sat between the twins and Sarah so she and Tim could cut the girls' food. Russ and Frank sat across from the twins and Martha. Sarah and Tim helped the boys when it was called for.

Elle's kitchen was bursting at the seams. She liked her house and had always found it spacious, but the Samuelson family had filled it to the limit.

Which made it easier to rock beside Colin and not be annoyed with him. There wasn't room for them in the kitchen, though the rockers, set up in front of her fireplace, were situated so they could both watch the children.

"Sarah and Martha are fine cooks." Colin ate salt pork and sliced potatoes with a good appetite. Elle realized the chairs were a bit too close together. She hadn't moved them, but someone had, and she'd simply sat down and started eating, as hungry as everyone else.

They discussed the day and what lay ahead. As they finished eating and set their plates aside—the floor was the only place available—Elle asked, "Would you like to ride into church together tomorrow?"

Dear heavens, she'd asked him to go for a drive.

Colin didn't respond. Surely he didn't think she'd been flirting.

Then after what seemed much too long, he said, "Thank you, yes, we'd appreciate the ride." Colin turned to her. "You've done so much for us this week."

That tug she'd felt between them from the very first was there when he turned those blue eyes on her.

"I've been glad to help. We're looking forward to having neighbors."

Colin turned to the table full of children. "My boys watch Tim and copy him. And he's a better example of how a man should act than I am."

"No, he's not." Elle rested a hand on his forearm. He was so close it was simple. "The boys are just tagging after an older boy. It's just different than a father."

"And Martha and Sarah work so well together, it's like they've been friends for years." Colin rocked silently for a minute before he added, "I've asked so much of my daughter."

"Maybe." Elle patted his arm. "But it's made her into a mature young woman. It's done her no harm."

"Ma, we're going back to work." Tim stood from the table.

"We'll be right along." Elle quickly removed her hand from Colin's arm and smiled at her son. Then she saw him circle the table and meet Sarah. The two stood just within view through the doorway between her kitchen and the living room with the fireplace. They whispered together, then both gave Elle and Colin a sharp glance and looked away too fast. There was definitely something between those two.

Tim said something quietly to the table full of children, and they all stood like their chairs had been jolted by lightning.

Tim walked out with Colin's boys.

"We'll get on with the dishes." Martha sounded rather falsely chipper as she began clearing the table with Sarah and the twins.

In just seconds her kitchen table full of children was empty, and they'd all vanished from sight. She heard the clinking of dishes and utensils and girlish voices whispering. One of the boys—she thought Frank—shouted and laughed from outside.

She and Colin were alone.

His gaze turned to her. He reached across and rested his hand on her shoulder. "You have this crowd overflowing your kitchen. You've as good as built a house. You've taught Sarah more about mending and sewing in one week than I have in a year. And your shoulders, bearing so much weight, are relaxed. You don't seem to be tied up in knots, inside or out. And meanwhile I have both. Knots in my muscles, unaccustomed to this kind of heavy work, and knots in my belly from worrying about every decision I make with my young'uns."

His touch was so solid, his words so kind, that she set aside how he'd sneered at the soddy. His hand massaged her shoulders for a bit, then they stopped. Their gaze locked. He leaned closer, or maybe she did. Maybe both. His eyes flickered to her lips, and it was almost as warm as a touch.

His hand on her shoulder became a caress, and she liked it.

She blinked and reached to move his hand. "Colin, we agreed to be friends. You insisted, and you were right to do it. But there can't be moments like this between us if friendship is going to survive. Please, it was your decision, and I don't want to confuse things."

Colin straightened away from her. "You're right. I apologize." With a sigh he let his head rest on the tall back of the rocker.

It occurred to Elle that from the first minute they'd discovered how big their families were, they'd begun thinking in terms of how a marriage wouldn't work. Even though they were avoiding a romance, their thoughts had gone to a very serious relationship immediately.

As if a man and woman taking a ride inevitably led to *someone* and his children moving in.

They rocked in silence for a bit longer, enjoying this rare moment without the demands of the children. "They're going to start growing up and moving out before we know it. Right now they are the center of my life, but Tim could be on his own in a year or two. Martha not long after that if she marries young. The same for Sarah. Your boys and my twins have a few more years to wait, but it will go fast."

She gave Colin a rueful smile. "Maybe you can lean back close to me in about five years."

A startled laugh escaped Colin's lips, and he nodded. "Yep, maybe I can."

He heaved himself to his feet and reached out a hand. She took it and let him help her stand. He said, "In the meantime I've got a house to build."

They got back to work.

Chapter 9

A crack of thunder jerked Colin awake. Thunder? He lurched to his feet in the roofless soddy and rushed toward the wagon where his children slept.

A bolt of lightning split the air. It hit the ground not a hundred yards away. The thunder sounded at the same moment as the flash of lightning.

And the children were sleeping in the wagon with the cover on it. The highest thing around, save the unfinished house.

Shouting, he raced toward them. "Wake up. Get out of the wagon!"

He was a doctor. He'd seen the damage lightning did to a human body. "Hurry. Sarah, Russ, Frank!"

Then Sarah poked her head out the back; the boys dove past her and raced to Colin's side. Sarah caught up just as another lightning bolt flashed. Another and another lit up the countryside like daylight. In the maniacal light, Colin saw something so ugly he wanted to drop to the ground and cover his head.

"It's a tornado!" he roared. The spinning funnel lit up in the raging storm. It was coming straight for them. He grabbed the boys by the hands. "Sarah, run! Come on."

But come on to where? Nothing was safe from one of these deadly storms. He saw Elle's house only a hundred feet away and sprinted for it.

"Tornado! Elle, Tim! Wake up!"

Out of the dark, Elle emerged, running toward them. She saw them and shouted over the roar, "Get in the cellar, now!"

Elle took Sarah's hand, turned, and ran. Colin followed, and the lightning showed Tim fighting the howling wind to hold the sloping door open. Martha scampered down with both twins in tow.

A lightning bolt exploded behind them, and Colin turned to see his wagon being blown apart. The whirling demon stormed right for the fire.

The first drop of cold rain hit the back of his neck. He kept moving. They had to survive this night first, then they'd worry about what they lost.

Colin herded everyone down the steps. He stayed above to get the door. He grabbed the handle and fought against the wind to hold it while everyone got down the stairs. Tim stayed with him and grabbed the edge of the door, dragging with all his weight.

Colin yelled over the storm to Tim. "Get down there!"

"I've got it. Go." Tim clung to the door.

A blast of thunder seemed to shake the whole earth. Colin grabbed Tim by the shirtfront with one hand while he wrestled with the door with the other. "Go. Now!"

Tim looked past Colin, and pure horror shone in his eyes. He let go of the door and dashed down the steps.

Getting around the door was a trick. Colin managed it barely and started down the steps, pulling the door closed behind him. Suddenly something tugged on him. He felt himself being lifted off the ground.

Then Elle was hanging from one leg, Tim from another—they threw all their weight against the power of the storm and dragged him down, the door slamming over his head. Elle reached past him and rammed home an iron bar to latch it.

"Get down," Elle shouted over the deafening noise of the raging storm. "Crouch in the farthest back corner. Keep your heads down, eyes closed."

Her children were already there. They were so clearly experienced at this madness. Colin's family rushed to huddle with the others. Elle sat down, her back to the cellar door, and she spread her arms wide to protect the children, as if she planned to hold her children against the force of this storm with her bare hands. Colin dropped down behind her. She felt his arms, also spread, but he was sheltering her. She wanted to scold him to get closer, to move up beside her rather than sit behind. Every inch they could get from that door could make a difference.

But his arm was so solid on her back. And his other arm was wrapped around Sarah, who held one of Elle's twins. Tim had both boys tucked behind him, crowded against the dirt wall in the back. Martha clung to the other twin. Everyone huddled together to protect the others.

The roar outside grew louder and more terrible with each passing moment. Time dragged on. Seconds passed like hours. Colin's strong arms seemed like a haven she'd never known. She shifted her body, and his arm tightened. Maybe to hold her in place, but it didn't feel like that. It felt like a hug.

And then the screaming storm lessened. Still loud, the worst of that deafening roar eased, replaced with thunder that shook the earth. Elle looked over her shoulder; lightning flared in a gap in the door.

"Is it over?" Colin asked.

"I think so. But sometimes there can be more than one tornado in a storm."

"There can?" Sarah sounded horrified.

"Yep," Elle said, patting the girl on the shoulder. "We'll stay down awhile. Anyway, do you hear the rain? We'd get soaked walking to the house."

Colin groaned quietly. "The house. I wonder if I have one anymore."

"So do I." In the pitch dark, Elle said, "If we don't, well, there's plenty more sod where that came from."

Colin choked, then he coughed, and next he laughed. In the terror that had just passed, with all of them wound up tight as a pocket watch, his laugh set them all off. Soon they were laughing wildly. Elle knew it was reaction to the madness of the storm, but it felt good to let some of it go in laughter.

By the time the laughter died, Elle felt that the storm was easing enough she could at least get some light down here. And of course the cellar was well equipped.

"Let me light the lantern."

Colin's hand tightened on her shoulder. "You took the time to grab a lantern?"

"No, we keep one down here. I know right where it is, too, so I can find it and the matches in the pitch dark." Elle thought Colin's strong hand let loose of her shoulder rather reluctantly.

"So you're saying you plan for this? You've come down here before?" He sounded stunned.

"Yes, of course we plan for it. We have a storm cellar for just this reason. Tim was going to start digging yours as soon as the roof went on your soddy."

"I thought it was a root cellar."

"I keep potatoes and beets down here through the winter, and pumpkins and squash. I have canning jars, and it's cool, so in the summer we can keep milk down here, and butter and eggs and cheese. But its primary use is as a place to go during a tornado."

"People know about a storm like that, and they still live out here?"

Silence fell over the cellar. Elle stood and found the lantern. With moves she'd practiced out of necessity in the pitch dark, she found the matches and lit the wick. The flare of bright light lifted her spirits, and she set the lantern on a shelf built just for that and turned to look at her crowded shelter.

"Didn't anyone mention tornadoes when you were claiming a homestead, Colin? That seems like information they should share with you. It's not safe to let people build their homes without a warning about the occasional need to take shelter."

Colin slapped himself in the face and kept his hand there, covering his eyes. "Why do you stay here?"

Elle smiled. "The storms haven't gotten us yet, and no place is without its troubles. Some land floods, mountains are steep enough a child can roll right off a cliff. There are grizzlies in the Rockies, too, and mountain lions. We have blizzards, but down south they have such terrible heat it's all a body can do to survive the summer." Elle shrugged. "No place on earth is perfect, and I've decided my little corner of Nebraska is as close as I'm going to get."

Colin shook his head rather frantically. It reminded Elle of a dog she'd once seen shaking off water.

"Our wagon burned, Pa," Sarah said. "But it was mostly empty except for blankets. I hope the house is still there, and our supplies."

The howling of the wind had dropped until all was silent outside. The children asked fretful questions about the possible damage until Elle decided she couldn't hear rain pounding on the cellar door anymore.

"Let's stop worrying about what might be and go see for ourselves." Quietly she added, "There is loss in life, children. Colin and I are your parents, and we love you and will always do our very best to take care of you. But we don't have to tell you that terrible things happen. You've all known great loss already. Whatever we find when we go out there, we will go to work fixing. What we've lost can be replaced as long as we survived. God will carry us through. You all know that, don't you? He's with us, in all the storms of life. And that includes this one."

Her children stood. They'd been through this many times before and had learned to accept it. Colin's children were slower to get to their feet.

Rising beside her, Colin's deep voice seemed to fill the little cellar. "That's very wise, Elle. Thank you for remembering that. And thank you for saving us. We are very likely alive because you were prepared and you came for us when you should have run for cover. God bless you for that."

Elle went to the cellar door and threw the latch.

Colin came up beside her. "Let me get the door." He reached past her without waiting for her to step aside, and again they were close, pressed together. The sense of protection and strength almost made her light-headed.

Then Colin pushed the door wide and went on up the steps.

Dreading what she'd find, Elle followed him to see. . .

Chapter 10

Both houses are still standing." Only the lightning, fading in the distance, made it possible to see.

Colin couldn't believe it. He froze in amazement.

Elle poked him in the spine, and he flipped the door all the way open and surged out of the cellar. His half-built soddy. Elle's house and barn. All still there.

"Put out the lantern, Martha," Elle called over her shoulder. She added, "I don't want to take it out of the cellar. I learned a hard lesson once when I took it to the house and we had a second storm come through and had to spend hours down there in complete darkness. It's hard to endure the storm without light."

"A second storm?" Colin tried to think where he could move to. Where were things perfect? Surely he could get closer than this.

The light behind them blinked out and left them in a night as dark as pitch.

"My wagon burned from that lightning bolt, but that's all. And there's even some of it still there, the rain must have put out the fire before it consumed everything." And the fire was long out. Colin couldn't see it, but if there'd been flames he would have.

All the children came boiling out of the cellar. Except for the now-distant lightning that showed the storm racing onward to the east, it was a coal-black night. Not a star in the sky. There'd been a bright moon, but the sky was heavy with black clouds even after the storm.

Colin saw Elle flash a bright smile, her white teeth visible when precious else was.

The children started talking and laughing. Russ and Frank were wrestling, like always, and the twins giggled and caught hands together and spun in a circle.

The older children talked loudly, full of high spirits, like they'd just had a great adventure.

Elle and Colin had moved forward to let the youngsters out of the cellar, and they'd kept walking until they stood a bit apart. The ground was soaked, but the rain had passed.

Elle said, "You'd better sleep with me tonight."

Colin had most unfortunately been inhaling at just that moment, and his gasp made him start choking.

"Oh no." Elle looked behind her. "I meant I'd like you to spend the night with me."

Colin started laughing.

"Hush up." Elle's extremely poorly worded invitation and her embarrassed order were too much, and the laughter almost bent him double. He knew it was simple joy at being alive.

She slapped him on the shoulder and in a harsh whisper, made things even worse, "Settle down or I'm not sharing my bed. Uh. . .I mean letting you sleep over. No! I mean. . ."

She was furious at him, but she was also overreacting, just as he was, from relief. She shoved him hard and hissed, "Your children are welcome, but you can sleep outside in the mud for all I care."

In the pitch dark, even with the voices of the children near, Colin could barely see a foot in front of him. It was pure delight, pure high spirits that made him wrap one arm around Elle's waist and haul her up against him.

"I accept your very tempting offer." He kissed the living daylights out of her.

She wacked him on the side of the head. She was so full of energy and life and strength. So sturdy. She struggled and fought back. Priscilla would have gone limp, maybe fainted, certainly pleaded for him to let her go. Of course he'd have never treated Priscilla like this. They'd had three children together and never spent a moment as passionately as this one right here, right now.

He'd never felt so vitally alive in his life.

And then her arms came hard around his neck, and she raised up on her tiptoes and kissed him back.

Ten seconds ago, he hadn't known what being vitally alive meant. He deepened the kiss and lifted her right off the ground.

Then her arms were gone. "Stop!" She wrested herself away and backed up so fast she stumbled.

Colin reached out and grabbed her to keep her on her feet. He absolutely knew they had to stop. He agreed with her completely. Then he reeled her back in and kissed her again.

The next time she stepped away she was more nimble, and he missed her when he tried to keep ahold.

Elle turned and stomped right into the midst of the children. Colin realized she was wearing a nightgown. Barefoot. He aimed directly for her like he was a magnet and she was true north. The children surrounded her, chattering, laughing, wrestling, dancing.

He felt as if he'd kissed Elle forever, but it must have only been moments.

And in her nightgown, too. There could hardly be anything more improper than that. And then a whole long list of more improper things cascaded through his mind, and he forgot to breathe.

"Now, let's all go inside." She clapped her hands and waved them a bit as if she were shooing a flock of chickens. "The Samuelsons will be sleeping with us tonight. Some of you children will have to sleep on the floor, but there's no help for it.

"We have church in the morning," she went on. "Then we may have to break the Sabbath and try to get a roof on their house so they have shelter by tomorrow night."

He saw nerves in every move of her hands. Her voice was a bit husky, and her words tumbled out too fast.

The children seemed thrilled with the invitation and acted as if they were throwing a party. They all turned toward the house and Elle was right behind them, trying to avoid even a second alone with him.

He didn't blame her because if they had been alone he wasn't sure how firm a grip he'd be able to cling to. All he could really think of was that pretty white nightgown and the bundle of strength and energy within.

Chapter 11

Elle had the twins in bed with her. Martha and Sarah were in the bedroom Martha usually shared with the twins. The Samuelson boys were together in Tim's room, which wasn't really a room: her house had a small attic that was really just space between the ceiling and the peaked roof. Tim couldn't stand upright, not even in the center, which was highest. But he'd declared it his room even before Jerome had died, and he willingly crawled up there to sleep, happy to have any space of his own in this two-bedroom house. The three boys would be lying side by side like strips of sod.

Colin was downstairs on some blankets in front of her fireplace. She could swear she heard him breathing.

The storm had come late in the night, and she'd resigned herself almost immediately to lying awake the rest of the night.

As she contemplated Colin and his noisy breathing, she realized it was good that they were all jam-packed into her house. It helped her see just how impossible it was for their families to be together.

Every time her mind veered to that kiss, she pictured this house packed literally to the rafters with children.

And what if they had more? Elle had shown no sign of difficulty having babies. Clearly, Colin was also up to the job.

When that notion popped into her mind, she couldn't breathe for fighting off that tantalizing vision, having Colin's baby. Conceiving Colin's baby.

Maybe she needed to go outside and sleep in the mud. It might calm her down.

She lay there and listened to the clock downstairs tick away the minutes, wrangling with all that darted through her unruly mind. Finally the black night gave way to dark gray then finally dawn.

Her rooster crowed. She really needed to get up and go outside and assess any damage.

Footsteps downstairs told her Colin was up. Had he slept at all? Maybe he had. Maybe that kiss hadn't bothered him one speck. Or maybe he'd lain awake, tormented with regrets. Scared to death Elle would come downstairs expecting him to propose.

After the way he'd kissed her that would be the proper thing to do, but proper wasn't always right.

She forced herself to stay in bed. If she didn't and she went down there, she'd end up in his arms again.

❧

Colin got out of the house the first possible minute. He knew that if Elle came down she'd end up in his arms again.

He hurried out to see what was left of his wagon and his house. He'd seen the walls still standing in the lightning, but he needed a closer look. Or at least he needed to get away from Elle. Sleeping on the hard floor, which was actually harder than the ground where he'd been sleeping, had been a strong reminder of why he couldn't think of marrying her.

Well, that wasn't true. He could think of it all right. And think and think and think.

He headed for the soddy first. There was no damage he could see on the outside. Then he stepped inside and it was like a haven, like the world closed around him, blocking certain pretty blond ladies out.

They'd stored most of their supplies in there once the walls were up, and covered them with heavy blankets and the wagon tarp. So, though things were wet, he hadn't lost anything.

Then he went to inspect his wagon, and his first action was to reach under the charred frame near the front on the left side. He found the metal box he'd fastened under there and made sure it was tightly closed. He wasn't worried about fire because the box contained only gold coins. His entire wealth. His St. Louis home and all its lavish furnishings and artwork, the building he owned that housed his doctor's office. Some other real estate and a stable full of thoroughbreds, to name the big things. He'd cashed in a lifetime of stock-market dabbling Priscilla's father had amassed, and it was considerable.

He'd left everything personal that would remind him of his life with Priscilla. Even the money was a reminder of her, and he intended to leave it to his children.

He could use it to build a grand house out here that had plenty of room for two good-sized families, but he didn't want to live in a house funded by Priscilla's family. He'd bought and paid for his doctor's office building himself. That money was his, and he'd worked hard for it. He'd used that money to pay for their journey west and had enough left to buy a humble home, possibly as nice as Elle's. But they'd just proved that both families wouldn't fit in hers.

He knew one thing, he liked being near her too much.

He had to get out of her house before he found them all crowded into that small home without room to breathe. . .and another baby on the way soon enough. Maybe he could make a bedroom out of the cellar.

"Colin, breakfast!" Elle called out the back door, but she didn't stand there and let him look at her. In fact, she kept her head down and swung the door shut as fast as she'd opened it.

He'd bet his whole box of gold she'd waited to call him until the children were up. Elle Winter didn't want to be alone with him any more than he wanted to be alone with her.

It was far too tempting.

Chapter 12

Elle was determined to stay as far away from Colin as she could. And he seemed to be in complete agreement. He sat in the back with the children on the ride to church, even though Tim offered to let him drive.

At church, they sat in two rows, just because they wouldn't fit in one, but Elle went in ahead of her four children. And one row behind, Colin went in after his.

If he looked at her she didn't know because she never took so much as one peek.

They rode home together, never speaking.

An almost frantic haste went into their building, even though Sarah complained of working on the Lord's Day and Tim insisted the Samuelsons sleeping in the Winters's house was fun.

There was no door yet and no windows, but it was a warm summer night and the roof was on. The Samuelsons slept at home.

The days took on a different shape than before. Colin started riding into town to run his doctor's practice.

Sarah stepped in and cared for her brothers, though Elle insisted they eat together. She hoped that took some of the weight off Sarah's slender shoulders.

The three Samuelson children spent a lot of time with Elle, and she welcomed them. Their lives were so much richer with some company. But once Colin came riding home, his children went to his home and he closed the door without a word to Elle. She could have invited him to supper, but she never did, knowing he'd turn her down if she asked.

Of course she nearly ran the other way when she saw him coming, so who was to know if he'd've been friendly, given a chance.

She thought not.

They'd gone on in that rather chilly fashion for two weeks. Tim and Sarah spent long hours together, doing chores and riding out to check the herd.

Elle worried about how close the two were growing, and then one day she looked out and saw Tim and Sarah talking in a way that seemed almost frantic. Sarah waved her hands around. Tim nodded. He didn't speak as much as Sarah but more than he ever did when Elle tried to talk to him.

The two took frequent furtive glances at the house. The sun must have been shining to reflect the windows rather than let the two see inside, because though they seemed worried about being seen, they kept talking.

Then Sarah clapped. A huge smile broke out on Tim's face, and he reached over to rest one hand on her shoulder.

They both nodded firmly, as if whatever they'd been discussing had been settled.

It struck Elle as a very serious nod. As firm as any vow sworn between two adults.

And her children. . .she was counting Sarah amid them for this purpose. . .were not adults, though they both looked it.

The two split up, and Elle went back to her housework, wondering what exactly they had just agreed to.

∞

"Elle, wake up!" Colin, shouting. A fist hammered on the front door, and Elle leaped out of bed and ran.

She rushed down and flung the door open just as she realized she was meeting him in her nightgown. . .again.

"Sarah's gone. And I've got a note." He lifted up a small square of paper. "She's run off with Tim to elope."

"Elope! They're just children."

"It looks like they think they're mighty grown-up." Colin waved the note in her face.

Elle spun around and charged up her stairs. Martha had her head out of her bedroom door. Elle kept going up the slender flight of stairs to Tim's attic room. She only poked her head into the low-ceilinged place. "Tim, wake up."

No sound. There was enough moonlight coming from two small windows on each end of the house to tell her Tim wasn't there. A closer look revealed a square of paper on his pillow. She crawled forward, almost landing on her face when her nightgown caught under her knees and tripped her. She grabbed the note and scooted backward to the doorway. She rammed into Colin. He'd followed right behind her.

"Tim's gone. There's a note." Elle wondered what in the world she looked like crawling about, but Colin whirled and was gone down the stairs. He was beyond looking at her legs.

Elle rushed down the stairs. Martha was in the hallway with a lantern by this time. She held the light so Elle could read the note.

I ran off with Sarah. Tim.

"Well, he was to the point."

Colin stuck his note up close to the lantern; it covered an entire page with writing.

Elle's eyes scanned it, and she saw the words *ran off* and *please forgive me, Daddy, but I know what I'm doing. . .*

Elle quit trying to read sideways. She got the message. "We have to stop them."

Then she remembered the talk they'd been having just that day. "I saw them planning this."

Like a hungry wolf, Colin turned on her. He looked for all the world like he wanted someone to chew up. "And you didn't stop them?"

"We don't have time to talk. Where would they go?"

Colin looked into space. "They need a parson. There's one in Lone Tree, but Parson O'Flaugherty wouldn't perform a ceremony for them. He knows them. They can probably convince a stranger they're old enough to get married. But Parson wouldn't do it without talking to us."

Elle knew how things worked in the West. "He would if he believed they had a. . . a. . ." She glanced at Martha and couldn't say *baby on the way.*

Instead, she said, "We've got to go. Martha, you're in charge of the twins."

"If we're not back by morning, bring the boys over here." Colin gave the order as if Martha was as much his to boss around as she was Elle's. There was no time to object.

"I'll be dressed in two minutes." Elle rushed toward her room. "Colin, go hitch up—"

She skidded to a stop. "Is the wagon gone? Did they ride horses? Colin, check on that. We may need to saddle horses instead of taking the buckboard."

"We'll take horses anyway." Colin thundered down the stairs. "It's faster."

He was out the door, and Elle rushed into her room, threw on her clothes, and headed out.

"We'll be back as soon as we can, Martha."

"Ma!" Martha's plaintive cry stopped Elle's headlong rush. She realized they'd been throwing orders at the girl without any explanation. Of course Martha was standing right there, so she knew what had happened.

Elle forced herself to stop and turn back. Martha came downstairs. Elle saw tears in her daughter's eyes.

Martha didn't stop, she rushed into Elle's arms and they held on tight.

Finally, Martha whispered, "Would it be so bad, Ma? If two people love each other, is it so bad to marry young?"

Forcing herself to hold on to the daughter right in front of her, Elle drew in a long breath. "Sarah is fourteen, honey. That's so young for marriage. And where will they live? Tim might find work, but most likely he'll have to come back home and bring Sarah with him."

"Then they can just move in here."

"But the only room Tim has is that attic, and Colin lives in a one-room soddy. That's not how a married couple lives, so crowded, no privacy."

"They can live in our old soddy."

"I've been storing tools in it for years. The roof leaks, and—"

"We'll fix the roof and clean it out, or we'll build them a new one. Or Sarah's pa has ordered boards for a house. They can get by living in a crowd then move into Sarah's soddy when her pa gets the new house up." A strange tone came into Martha's voice. Elle was too frantic to understand it, but suddenly her daughter didn't sound all that upset when she said, "I like the idea of our families joining together. I thought at first you and Mr. Samuelson might be interested."

"No, honey. I mean, Mr. Samuelson is very nice, but we have seven children between us. And we live in these little houses. We wouldn't fit."

"If you loved each other you could find a way to fit, Ma." Martha sniffed, and Elle pulled back to see her daughter crying quietly. "Love always fits, Ma. Family always fits. I'd love to have Sarah in our family. She's the best friend I ever had."

"Sarah is a fine young woman, Martha. I'm not saying she wouldn't make Tim a good wife. They're just too young."

Martha pulled away and stormed up the stairs. "Don't worry about the five of us, Ma. We'll manage, just like Sarah and Tim will manage and just like you and Mr. Samuelson could manage if you wanted to."

Then her daughter was gone into the tiny room she shared with her twin sisters. Her door closed with a sharp slap.

For a second, Elle wasn't quite sure what had just happened. In a childish sort of way, sweet little Martha had just given her quite a scolding.

"Elle, hurry up," Colin called from outside. "Your wagon is still there, they must've ridden."

Shaking her head to focus on what was important, Elle turned and rushed out of the house. Colin was on horseback with a second saddled horse close behind.

She was on horseback and they were galloping toward Lone Tree and still Martha's words haunted her. *You and Mr. Samuelson could manage if you wanted to.*

Forcing herself to pay attention on the wild ride, she wondered how far they'd have to go to find those troublesome children. They couldn't be off together for even a single night or it would be too late and marriage would be the only choice.

Chapter 13

In the dead of night, Colin galloped into Lone Tree. He'd pushed his horse beyond reason, to find. . .nothing.

He reined in his horse in the dark town, and Elle caught up to him in just seconds.

They rode at a walk, side by side, their horses blowing hard.

"What do we do? There's not a light on anywhere."

Elle said, "I can't believe the parson would bless a union between them. But let's ride to the church and look."

The parson's house sat in darkness.

They swung off their horses in front of the silent church. "Let's go in. They might be hiding there, trying to decide what to do."

"There are no horses, Elle." Colin swung down despite his words. He was absolutely right. There wasn't a horse tied to a hitching post anywhere in town. The livery sat at the end of Lone Pine, doors closed, no lantern light.

Elle led the way into the church with Colin behind her. It was a small building. An altar that was a simple table. A Bible and a cross resting on top. No cloakrooms or closets. Nowhere for two reckless children to hide.

Colin came in behind her, and they stood, thinking. It occurred to Elle that they might have been better served to do more thinking earlier.

Moonlight streamed in the window, casting shadows in the building. "Let's look very carefully, in case they're ducked behind something."

There were rows of benches. With no better notion, Elle walked up along one wall while Colin went to the other wall and walked up front. They met before the altar.

"What do we do next, Elle?" Colin whispered in the dark.

She turned to face him, and he looked so devastated that despite his standoffish ways the last two weeks, she couldn't stop from reaching across and taking his hands.

The way he grabbed hold of her made her feel like she was saving a drowning man.

"The worst that can happen is they end up married." Elle thought of Martha. "And if they do get married, well, we'll figure something out. You're going to build a house, so they can live in your soddy when the house is done, or I can clean my soddy out. It needs repairs, but I reckon if we build one from the ground up, we can fix one."

"But my little girl." Colin raised his eyes to meet hers. "It's not your son, you know that, don't you? Tim is a fine young man, and I'd be proud to have him marry Sarah, but I can't help feeling like if I'd just been a better father—"

His voice broke, and Elle couldn't withhold comfort from him. She wrapped her arms around him, and his snapped around her waist and pulled her hard against him, his face buried in her shoulder.

"You're a fine father, Colin."

"No, I've made her do too much. Why wouldn't a girl acting like an adult decide she was grown-up enough to marry? Maybe she even agreed to elope to escape from me. From the life I've dropped on her young shoulders."

"I've done the same with Tim. Treated him as an adult almost from birth, long before Jerome died. Given him chores then left him the responsibility to carry them out." Elle's voice dropped to a whisper. "And what am I going to do without him?" She swallowed hard. "That may be the most selfish thing a mother ever said."

Her throat closed, and they stood in the holy place, holding each other. Elle let her mind go to God, to His will.

It helped ease her regrets. Finally she straightened to find her arms around Colin's neck. His around her waist. When she lifted her head, he did the same, and they looked into each other's eyes.

"God will see us through, Colin. If we stop the marriage, they will no doubt try again. If we don't stop it, then we'll. . .we'll. . ."

Martha's words came to her. *"Love always fits, Ma. Family always fits. You and Mr. Samuelson could manage if you wanted to."*

"Elle," Colin said quietly, reverently.

"What?"

"I failed my children."

"No you didn't, you—"

"Shh. Let me just—" Colin touched her mouth with his fingertips. "When Priscilla died—" He acted as if the words hurt. "She was so beautiful, so delicate. I shouldn't have wanted children with her, and certainly not three. But it seemed so natural that I did. I'm a doctor, but I just. . .I did stop. . .stop. . .going to her after Frank was born."

Frank was five years old. What a lonely sort of marriage.

"She spent nearly her entire pregnancy in bed, then after each one she was a year recovering. The children and I hardly knew her. She was like a shadow living in her room. We would visit her, but she never joined in our family after a child would come, and with the nursemaids and nanny, she didn't need to. Then she'd gather her strength and be up and about more. And then another baby would come."

Shaking his head, he said, "I was a fool."

"And a baby. . .is that what happened to finally break her health and lead to her death?"

"No, when her parents died it was like the last source of her strength went with them. Her mother particularly had taken diligent care of her all through our marriage. But when her mother died, Priscilla took to her bed in grief and never recovered. A fever was too much for her, and she died a year after her parents."

Elle thought of surviving Jerome's death. It had been shocking, and the weight of all that was left to her could have crushed her. But she just hadn't had time to curl up and die. Of course she hadn't adored Jerome like Colin did Priscilla.

He ran one finger along her lips then closed his fist like he was hanging on to the feel of her. "And here you are, so strong. Up to the task of raising your own children, doing so much for mine, helping me build a house, for heaven's sake. Even birthing Tim with no one there."

Shaking his head as if it was unthinkable, he looked at her, and she waited, wanting him to talk about his wife and how much he loved her and how much he admired that delicate feminine woman, and how lacking he found Elle. She wanted him to get on with breaking her heart so she could get on with living without him.

"Do you have any idea how much it hurts to have a woman give up on life when she's got a husband and children who need her? The children barely knew to mourn her because she'd spent so much time ailing. And as I doctor I knew. . ." His jaw clenched until she hoped he didn't break his teeth. "I knew it was mostly just nonsense. There was nothing really wrong with her. There are sound medical reasons why a woman needs to stay off her feet for some difficult pregnancies, none of those reasons applied to Priscilla."

Elle heard something in his voice that she hadn't before. She'd thought he was so sad over his wife's death, but that wasn't it. He was sad over her life. Over their marriage.

"And I've seen women who, after a child was born, need to be very carefully treated. Some of them seem emotionally devastated in a way no one understands. Some have done damage during the birthing that takes time to heal. Priscilla had nothing like that. She was simply a spoiled, selfish woman who wanted to be waited on hand and foot, and her mother indulged her to a ridiculous degree. Once her mother was gone and Priscilla no longer had that slavish devotion, she seemed to lose interest in life. And not a husband nor three beautiful children could hold her to this world."

Then he whispered, "Elle, I never thought I'd find a woman as strong and wise as you. As good a mother. As good a partner. You're wonderful. I've fought it every way I know how. I've avoided you because I couldn't see how our lives would mesh. But I'm through fighting it now." He pulled her close. "I've fallen in love with you." His lips descended on hers, and she was back in his arms.

From being ready to have her heart broken to his declaration of love was such a swoop, such a change in her thoughts, she was dizzy from it. She clung to him to keep from falling over in a heap.

When at last he lifted his head, she said, "We'll still have seven children, Colin. That problem remains."

He smiled. His handsome face and dark brown hair washed blue in the moonlight. "Somehow the children don't seem like a problem anymore, not if we work together to handle them. We'll find a place for them all to sleep."

"We can manage if we want to." Elle quoted Martha's words, but they were pure truth.

"And do you want to, Elle? Will you marry me?"

"Yes."

A shout spun them both around to see children pouring into the church. Seven children. Tim and Sarah were with them.

Frank shouted, "It's about time!"

They started to laugh, and before they knew it the entire church was in an uproar. Hugs and chatter and enough laughter to keep them happy even in a crowded house.

Chapter 14

When the racket died down, Colin looked at Tim, with Russ and Frank clinging to his legs and Sarah holding one of the twins while Martha had the other. Colin still wasn't sure how to tell those little girls apart.

"I thought you two ran off?"

"We did run off." Sarah giggled.

"B–but you were running off to *elope*." Colin flexed his hand around Elle's waist, glad she was there for support.

"We never used the word elope." Tim rolled his eyes. "She's my sister."

Sarah gave Tim a firm nod. Tim smiled and went to a lantern hanging from a nail on the church wall and lit it. There were three others, and in moments the room was glowing in the firelight.

"Then where were you?"

"We took two horses and hid them behind the barn, then the two of us stayed in there until we heard you ride off."

"But why?" Elle sounded bewildered. Colin knew exactly how that felt.

"Because," Martha spoke up, "we have been trying to get the two of you to just spend a bit of time together for the last two weeks."

"We knew you were in love." Sarah patted either Betty or Barbara on the shoulder and set her down. "But we also knew you weren't doing a thing about it."

"Martha is the one who came up with this plan. Sarah and I would've never thought of it." Tim sounded bewildered by the whole notion of him and Sarah together. Which Colin thought proved the boy was still real young.

"We knew you'd finally do something together when you went to search for us."

Elle narrowed her eyes at Martha. "You came up with the idea of staging an elopement?"

Martha grinned, and Colin was struck by how much the girl looked like her pretty ma, right down to the gleam of intelligence in her blue eyes.

"Martha decided a fake runaway marriage was the right way to manage you two." Sarah slung one arm around Martha. The two were a study. Sarah so dark and tall, Martha so fair and petite. Both beautiful girls. Colin was going to have his hands full for the next few years when men came courting.

"We were even real careful not to lie when we left a note. We never said anything about eloping, we said we were running away together. And that's just what we did."

"We didn't run far," Tim interjected.

"It wasn't my first plan." Martha grinned without an ounce of repentance. "But I couldn't figure out how to let the twins get lost on the prairie."

"Martha!" Elle shouted in horror.

"And the creek is running fast, so I thought about letting one of the boys get swept away by floodwaters, but that seemed risky."

"Swept away by floodwaters?" Colin slapped one hand on his face over his eyes as if he could see it in his imagination and couldn't stand it. "You could have died."

"Well, that's why we didn't do it." Martha sounded as if she were speaking to a pair of slow students.

Russ smirked. "We went to see if we could jump in the water and float away, but it looked mighty dangerous."

"You're just tormenting me now," Colin growled.

His son giggled and added, "The land where you'd dug the trench for our soddy is under water since the rain that came with that tornado."

"You boys aren't ever to go in that creek for any reason." Colin shuddered to think of the chances they'd nearly taken. And his first homesite was flooded? What a disaster that would have been. The Winters family had saved him from that.

"And now you and Ma finally admit you love each other, right? And you're ready to get married?" Martha crossed her arms. "We want a pa, and Sarah and her brothers want a ma. I expect you two would have figured that out in time, but we were tired of waiting."

Dead silence fell over the room. Colin noticed the church was overly crowded, and their homes would be worse. And he didn't care one speck. "Yep, we've admitted it." He turned to look at Elle.

She lifted both hands as if she was giving up, surrendering, which meant he'd caught her. "I do think I need help raising these children."

"I need more help than you." Colin reached for those hands, so strong, so competent. Rough with calluses and chapped from long hours of hard work. He'd never felt anything more perfect. "I love you, Elle. Will you marry me? Will you join your family with mine and help me take care of this crowd?"

The smile on her face grew with every word he uttered.

"I would be honored and thrilled to marry you, Colin. I love you, and I have no doubt we'll"—she turned to look at all the children and added with some spunk—"we'll find a way to manage."

The children sent up a cheer that shook some dust out of the rafters. They rushed to Colin and Elle. The hugging and laughter was contagious. It was the happiest his children had been since Priscilla died. Maybe the happiest they'd ever been in their lives.

"What is going on in here?" Parson O'Flaugherty came in, dressed in an untucked white shirt and black pants. He was barefoot, and his thinning white hair stood nearly straight up on his head. His wife peeked over his shoulder from behind him.

Colin looked at Elle, who gave him a firm nod of her chin.

"We'd like to get married, Parson. Elle and I would like you to perform the ceremony right now."

The parson's brow furrowed as he looked from one joyous face to the next. . .which took him a fair amount of time, considering the crowd.

He cleared his throat. "You're sure about this?" He sounded wary, like he knew if they just took a bit of time they'd come to their senses.

Well, Colin had no intention of coming to his senses. "We're sure."

Elle said, "As sure as can be, Parson. And we'd like you to say the vows right now, please. We're all here. We might as well get on with the ceremony."

Colin reached out his hand, and she laid hers firmly in it. They shared a smile and turned to face the parson. He shrugged and came forward, tucking in his shirt.

He squeezed through them and took his place in the front of the church. His wife came up the side so she didn't need to make them all step back in the limited space.

"Tim, you and the boys come and stand at my side." Colin waved them over. "Is that all right, if I claim your son to stand up with me, Elle?"

"If I can have Sarah."

Sarah clapped her hands, and she and Martha lined up to Elle's left, the two older girls had their hands resting firmly on the shoulders of the twins between them.

Tim took Russ and Frank's hands, and the three of them lined up on Colin's right.

The parson didn't get a prayer book, he didn't open his Bible, he didn't even run home to put on his shoes. "Dearly beloved. . ."

Chapter 15

My house came in," Colin said as he entered the bedroom he'd been sharing with Elle for the last two months. "I hired men to haul it out tomorrow and build it."

"Not Dutch and Lou?" Elle looked up, alarmed. She really wished he'd talk with her before he made plans.

"Nope, the men who delivered the wood said they were willing to put up the house. They claim to do it a lot, and they'll have the house done in a couple of weeks."

"Good, because we need the space."

Colin laughed. "That is so true. We can't keep letting the boys sleep alone in my soddy. It's just not a good idea to let Russ and Frank have that much freedom, nor is it good to make Tim shoulder so much responsibility."

The boys slept on pallets on the floor at Colin's house. The girls slept all four in the second bedroom in Elle's house.

"And I explained the situation, that the house wasn't really big enough. I should have ordered more lumber to be shipped, but it was already on the way and I didn't want to wait for more." He'd ordered the lumber before he'd faced up to getting married.

"I've figured out how we'll manage." That was starting to be one of Elle's favorite words. They'd found a way to manage meals together. They'd found they could manage seven children. They'd even figured out how to very discreetly manage intimacy in the night, which was no small trick in Elle's tiny house.

"How?"

"Your house is the same size as mine, isn't it?"

"Yep, I explained to the men who sell lumber I wanted one just like yours, and let them do the ordering."

"My house is close to the border of my land but not quite close enough to attach a second house. You have to live on your property to keep your claim. If we build your house on my land, it will reach just a few feet past the edge of your property line. You and I can sleep there."

"Is that legal?"

"Yep. I asked at the land office just this morning when I went into town for supplies."

Colin knew she'd been in. She'd come to the doctor's office, mercifully alone, and the two of them had eaten lunch together in the hotel in Lone Tree.

"The agent knows men who've done it," Elle went on. "Built a one-room soddy like yours, right on top of the property line, then slept on opposite walls to fulfill the homestead requirements. He said it's completely legal."

With a smile lighting up his face, Colin said, "My house is laid out just like yours, but if we attach them we can open up the kitchen and attach it to mine. It'll be big enough for a table that will hold us all. Then we can use the part that's a sitting room in your house for a bedroom in ours. I was thinking we'd have four bedrooms, but if we change the sitting room to a bedroom, we'll have five."

"If we use one wall of my house that will give us leftover lumber, and we can use it to add another bedroom on the main floor. I think we should get the boys down out of the attic, if they are willing. That's not a decent space up there. So still five bedrooms, but we'll store things in the attic instead of sleep there."

Colin came close and drew her into his arms. They were alone in the house because the children were doing chores while Elle got supper. He'd tracked her down in their room.

Elle enjoyed the moment. They'd had lunch and now this bit of time. It was always rare and wonderful to be alone together.

He whispered in her ear, "And that will give us a bit more privacy than we have now."

"Hush." Elle looked past him. They were definitely alone.

And yes, they had the nights together, but right now they had one very thin wall between themselves and the girls. A bit more space would be welcome.

She decided she'd wait another month or two to tell him about the baby. Let him enjoy that feeling of privacy for a bit longer.

He bent his head, and she raised her lips to meet his kiss.

The kiss deepened and grew heated, and Elle could only think of just how wonderfully alone they were.

The back door crashed open. "Ma, Betty got stung by a bee. Ma, where are you?"

Martha hollering. Betty sobbing.

Elle broke the kiss and rested her forehead on his shoulder, laughing.

"Yes, Colin, I think a bit more privacy would be a blessing."

Colin laughed. "No more of a blessing than our crowd of children."

They smiled.

Colin took her hand, and together they headed down to manage—as they always did when they faced the challenges of seven children living in their little homestead on the range.

Mary Connealy writes romantic comedy with cowboys always with a strong suspense thread. She is a two-time Carol Award winner, and a Rita, Christy and Inspirational Reader's Choice finalist. She is the bestselling author of over 60 books and novellas.

Her most recent book series are: Brides of Hope Mountain, Garrison's Law, High Sierra Sweethearts, Cimarron Legacy, Wild at Heart, Trouble in Texas, and Kincaid Bride for Bethany House Publishing. She's also written four other series for Barbour Publishing and many novellas. Mary has nearly a million books in print.

PRICELESS PEARL

by Darlene Franklin

Dedication

To my ancestors, Harriett America Barton and Richard Eady,
whose names I borrowed for this story.
This book is also dedicated to my grandmother, Winifred Bremner,
who left me the heritage of faith, needlework, and music.

*And the twelve gates were twelve pearls; every several gate was of one pearl:
and the street of the city was pure gold, as it were transparent glass.*
REVELATION 21:21

Chapter 1

Cherokee Strip, Oklahoma, 1893

America Barton had never seen such a crowd. Oh, she had seen a lot of people in St. Louis. On any given day, she might encounter horses snorting, merchants barking their wares, bells ringing, arguments, the pounding of feet on streets. After all those years watching the crowds in front of her father's store, she thought she had seen it all.

Nothing in St. Louis had prepared for the multitude poised on the border of the Cherokee Strip on Saturday morning, September 16, 1893.

"America." Father scanned the crowd. "Your brothers are running around. We need you to keep an eye on them. It'll be time to saddle up soon." He pointed through the crowd. "They went in search of that man on the tall bicycle."

With one wheel as high as a wagon, the bicycle was easy to follow. America picked up the edge of her skirts and walked as quickly as she could. As the bicyclist moved, the wheel created a wide swath, pushing him closer to the starting line. The boys ran behind him as fast as they could.

"Bert! Freddy!" America called, but the boys kept running. With all the commotion, they must not have heard her. She lifted her skirts and ran a few steps. Her shoe caught on a rock, and she tilted forward.

A hand on her back kept her erect. When she looked over her shoulder, a worn leather boot in a stirrup swam in front of her face. As she lifted her head, she saw long legs, a plain belt, a scruffy shirt, and the biggest smile she had seen all day underneath a dark ten-gallon hat.

Once she was settled, the man removed his hand from her back. Tipping his hat with a smile, he steered the horse away from her.

"Thanks." The word came out with a squeak, and she didn't know if he heard her. The bicycle had disappeared, along with her brothers. "Oh no."

The stranger turned back. "What happened?"

"My brothers—I can't see them. They were following the man on the bicycle. Do you see him anywhere?"

"I see the bicycle, and several boys following." The man leaned forward. "Your brothers?"

She nodded.

"Let me help." Before she could answer, he slipped off the horse and lifted her to the saddle. "You can see much better from here." He jumped back on, and the horse moved.

Startled, America swallowed a shriek. The horse shifted, and she grabbed the saddle horn.

He leaned over her shoulder. "We're moving forward. Tell me when you see them."

A few feet farther on, she spotted a familiar green shirt. "That's Bert."

"Hold on." The horse moved with a steady purpose, moving forward without disturbing the crowds in the way. Bert looked around, bewildered, as they drew closer.

"Bert! Freddy!" America called, but the din swallowed her shout.

"Bert, Freddy!" The unknown man's voice boomed from behind her ear.

Bert's head swiveled, a confused look on his face, as the horse nudged its way toward the boys. When America called their names again, Bert spotted her and waved his cap.

They closed the gap in a few seconds. America said, "Dad wants the two of you back at the wagon. Now."

"Who's he?" Freddy pointed at the stranger, touched the nose of the horse, who snorted.

"His name is Prince," the stranger said. "And my name is Rick Eady."

Mr. Eady loosened his hold on America's waist. "Who wants to ride with me?"

Bert's enthusiastic "yes!" came a moment before Freddy's.

"Do you mind?" Mr. Eady asked. At her nod, he helped her to the ground.

"But you don't even know where our wagon is." From this distance, America had a hard time picking out their conveyance among all the others.

Mr. Eady smiled, revealing a cleft in his chin. "I couldn't help but notice a lovely young lady as yourself. You are in a wagon hitched to two oxen, with boxes marked from St. Louis and a pair of piebald gelding waiting for the run. Your father has a black gelding with a white star. Good horseflesh, which is more than can be said for some of these poor souls."

Mr. Eady helped Bert onto the horse and promised to come back for Freddy. They had walked about half the distance when Mr. Eady returned. By the time they all returned to the wagon, the time had slid to ten minutes until noon. The boys clambered into the back of the wagon and took their seats, as securely as they could on two strong wooden boxes. Their excitement made it doubtful they would remain quiet for long.

"Behave." Father's glare silenced Freddy. Bert settled down with a sigh.

"Are you riding on the wagon?" Mr. Eady asked America. At her nod, he assisted her onto the seat. He smiled at her, and America tucked the memory into all the special events of the day.

"Thank you for helping me find my brothers."

"I have younger brothers myself; I know what it's like."

Father thanked Mr. Eady. "Are you ready?" Father asked Mother.

"Of course." If Mother's smile looked forced, America could understand. She, too, had mixed feelings about today.

Mr. Eady waited for Father to join him, and together they maneuvered deeper into the crowd, closer to the starting line. That's why Father had chosen his horse. Their heavy-loaded wagon didn't stand a chance. They would follow behind.

Mother's lips moved in a quiet prayer. Noise lessened to near quiet as the seconds ticked away until twelve noon.

A single gunshot fired, and the Cherokee Strip Land Rush began.

∞

At the gunshot, Prince's ears flattened back, and he ran with the urgency of a horse seeking to reach the head of the pack.

The crowd fanned out. Soon the fastest horses left the wagons, bicycles, and ordinary runners behind. Within a quarter of an hour, Rick spotted two men in the pack jump down and plant their flag at the plot marker. Rick wanted to hold out for the perfect spot—one with running water and good farmland.

Somewhat to his surprise, Mr. Barton kept pace, not far behind Rick. They both headed in the same general direction—Black Bear Creek, near the Pawnee Nation's land. They should be coming close.

Prince's nostrils flared seconds before Rick saw his goal, glittering in the close distance. He leaned over Prince's neck, urging him faster, and they splashed through the water on flying feet. He saw movement in the rainbow of the water as they flew to the plot marker and staked his flag.

Rick lifted his arms in the air and howled. Today was the fulfillment not only of his dreams but of the family he had left behind. Many had tried, but only a few would succeed.

Mr. Barton. The man was clearly no farmer, but many came to the land rush hoping for a new start. *Lord, if it's Your will, give him success as well.*

Dismounting, Rick ground-tied Prince and drank water from his canteen. His chuckle turned into unstoppable laughter. His heart full of joy, he decided to ride the borders of his property before he prepared his campsite. First of all, he returned to the creek to refill his canteen.

Rick swung onto Prince's back and headed for the creek. Prince wasted no time in burying his nose in the water. Rick took his kerchief from his neck, dipped it in the water, and soaked his hair and face with it. As he shook the water from his head, he spotted a figure approaching the creek—Mr. Barton.

"Hallo over there, Barton," Rick called. He scooped up a handful of water and drank it, as satisfying as he expected.

Barton reined in his horse, which immediately drank the water. His smile widened as broad as a Texas sunset. "Mr. Eady. Are we to be neighbors, then?"

"It appears so."

So Rick would most likely see America again, perhaps often. The thought made him grin.

In the distance a coyote howled, and Barton looked around, frightened.

"When will your family be joining you?"

Barton stroked his chin, where bristle from a couple of days' growth showed. "I'm hoping they'll find me tonight. I'd go fetch them myself, but what's to keep someone else from claiming the land while I'm gone? I'll light a fire and fix me some supper. If they're not here by noon tomorrow, I'll figure something else out."

Visions of the family traveling across plots claimed by others made Rick uneasy. He sent up a quick prayer.

"How are you getting your equipment here?" Barton asked.

Did the man think Rick had a wagonful of supplies waiting for him somewhere? No need to unload all his secrets. "I travel light." He extended his arm and shook Barton's hand, a surprisingly strong grip. In spite of his strength, Barton's hands were lily-white, like a banker's. If Rick's suspicions were true, his new neighbors would need all his prayers—and hands-on help—he could offer.

"I'll mosey by tomorrow, if that's okay with you." Maybe he would see the raven-haired beauty as well.

"I'll look forward to it."

Prince splashed through the water. Rick drew a deep breath of the fresh air, tall grass, water, birds, sunshine, and flowers. A scissortail bird flew high overhead, bringing his attention to God in His heaven. When God promised to make all things new, He had done exactly that for Rick in giving him land in Oklahoma.

Oklahoma would change from a territory to a full-fledged state before too many more years passed. Rick praised the Lord for being born in the United States. Thinking of America, how had Miss Barton come by such an interesting name?

As Prince paced the boundaries of Rick's land, he thanked God for every detail he noticed. The clump of trees near the creek would provide shelter for the home he hoped to build someday. For now, he would build a sod house and see if a garden of hardy vegetables, like carrots, beets, turnips, would mature before the first frost.

He reached the first corner. Kitty-corner from his lot was the communal lot, where the school and church would someday stand. Maybe not this Sunday, the day after tomorrow, but next week he would visit among the others, invite them to a service of thanksgiving and a communal meal. Maybe somebody could even preach. Not him, not when the only scriptures he could preach from were the ones he had memorized.

He finished his survey of the land, locating some wild onions and a rabbit hole. His stomach growled at the thought of a savory stew. One sheltered spot looked ideal for a fall garden, close by an overhang to expand for his soddy. Those two priorities would take his time, sunup to sundown, for weeks to come.

He looked across the creek, where he saw smoke from Barton's campfire. As busy as the coming weeks would be, maybe God would give him the opportunity to see more of Miss America Barton.

∞

The Bartons hadn't found Father by sundown. Whoever planned the opening of the Cherokee Strip for a Saturday hadn't chosen very well. The Lord would have to forgive them for moving ahead on the Sabbath. The family who had allowed them to spend the night must be eager for the Bartons to leave.

Father hadn't returned. She trusted the Lord that he had claimed a plot, on which their futures depended.

They made their way down Black Bear Creek, asking for news of Father. Most of them had noticed a cowboy on a black horse—Rick?—and a couple had noticed Father on the piebald.

After a single stop to refill their canteens, the hour approached noon when Bert pointed straight ahead. "There's Father!"

Father must have seen them about the same time, for he waved his arms wildly. America flicked the reins, and the oxen increased their speed. "I'm going to run," Freddy said. Without waiting for an answer, both boys jumped from the wagon and dashed through the tall grass, their heads barely visible over the waving prairie.

A second man stood with Father, wearing a familiar black ten-gallon hat. Hundreds of men dressed like that had made the run. She had no reason to assume it was Mr. Eady, or to let her heart gallop in hopes he was their neighbor. Her heart didn't listen to common sense, racing as the two men spotted the boys and ran toward them.

Looking at their neighbor straight-on, America saw the cleft on his chin and his well-tanned skin. She lifted her face to the heavens, thanking God for putting him in her way yet again.

A snap as loud as firecrackers hit the still air. "America!" Mother's voice shrilled as their wagon came to a stop.

The wagon lurched to one side, followed by a barrage of thuds as objects hit the ground. When she climbed down, she saw that a disturbing pile of belongings had fallen from the wagon. The back wheel stood, unbroken, sunk into a mud pit under its rim. Thrown to the side, a spoke had flown free from the wheel.

Father assisted Mother off the wagon, and she appeared uninjured. The boys jumped to their feet, coated in mud but unhurt. America joined her parents to review the boxes that had fallen to the ground. Her heart dropped when she saw a burlap sack full of flour poking through the slats. If the foodstuffs spoiled in any way, their future in this new land was all the more precarious.

Strong arms lifted the box, mud making sucking noises as it lifted up. Rick—she had given up trying to think of him as Mr. Eady—had come to their rescue once again. She blinked away the tears forming behind her eyelashes. "Thanks."

Mother caught sight of the box and ran forward with a little scream. "The flour. And where's the sugar?"

"It looks okay to me," Rick said. "Do you have a pallet where I can lay out your things while we figure out how to free the wheel?"

Soon they separated the boxes of the badly soaked boxes from the untouched. Father did little but look through the contents of one box, picking up one object then another.

Rick walked in Father's direction, and America followed. She came to a stop when she recognized the objects in his hand: the family Bible, passed down from her great-grandparents. He held it in one hand, the brittle pages opened to the book of Psalms. When she took a step closer, she saw a clutch of papers scattered around the ground. Her breath froze in her throat.

"Don't move," Father said. "We need. . .I need. . ." He didn't finish. His face said it all.

Down in the mud. As far as she could tell, of all their books only the Bible had dropped pages from the binding. They were fragile, a precious heirloom she couldn't bear to lose.

They tiptoed through the mud, finding five separate pages, all of them wet and muddy, some of them torn as well. Mother laid out a bedsheet, where they placed each section separately for a chance to dry.

By the time they finished, Rick had freed the wheel. "The wheel should get us there where we can fix the spoke. We can't wait too long. We gotta get back by sundown, at the latest."

"You staked a claim?" America's voice squeaked.

"I did," Father said. "Rick here did as well."

America clasped Rick's hands, and he spun her around as if in an impromptu dance.

Chapter 2

For two nights after the land run, Rick didn't get to sleep until late in the evening. Even so, he had little to show for it. He had spent his days with the Bartons.

The Bible said to love your neighbor as yourself, and Rick tried. After they arrived at their claim, he checked the boxes with Mr. Barton. The damage to the pages from the Bible disturbed him the most. For sure, the Bible was God's Holy Word, but Rick couldn't understand why anyone wanted so many other books when he was starting a farm from the ground up.

Rick didn't have a single book in his bags, for the best of reasons. He couldn't read. The raven-haired beauty sleeping across the creek wouldn't give an unschooled man a second gaze.

He stared into his cup of coffee long enough for it to cool down, while he decided what to do first. He had to prepare and plant a small vegetable garden. An even patch of ground near the creek seemed a promising place for it.

Before spring, he would fashion a plow, but for now elbow grease and a hoe would do the work. His hand hovered over soap and a razor, but he decided against that. His stubble could grow into a beard, although he might shave it off on Sunday.

After adding a clean shirt and soap to his stack, he whistled on his way to the creek. He removed his dirty shirt before lathering his hands with soap and scrubbing his chest and arms, getting rid of a week's worth of dust. While he bathed, he sang. "Praise the Lord! Praise the Lord! Let the earth hear His voice." The words of praise lifted his heart. Slipping his clean shirt on, he turned around before he had finished with the buttoning.

Openmouthed, America stared at him. The hand covering her mouth couldn't quite hide her smile. "Excuse me, I should leave."

"I'll just be a minute." Rick whirled around, buttoned up the shirt in record time, and tucked it into his waistband. He slowed down a tad, giving his face a chance to return to its normal color. Behind him, he heard water splashing and a crackling fire. How he had missed them on his way to the creek made him feel foolish.

Without turning around, he tilted his hat back on his head. In September's still-warm weather, it provided a welcome measure of protection. He pictured America, the sun highlighting the auburn glints in her dark brown hair. If she intended to spend much time out of doors—and she had to stay outdoors twenty-four hours a day until they built a shelter—she should wear some kind of bonnet to protect her skin.

The more he saw of the Bartons, the more he wondered if they would survive their first year. Mr. Barton studied a handbook he had brought with him like a Bible, but it left so many skills unmentioned.

"Good-bye, Mr. Eady," America said.

Rick turned around and waved. "Call me Rick."

She held full buckets in both hands. "Monday is laundry day, so I'm fetching the water." She set down one bucket. "If you give me your shirt, we'd be happy to wash it for you."

No. Did they think he was dirty? Perhaps they wanted to give back, exchange services, the way neighbors did for each other. He threw the shirt into the air, but it landed about a foot from shore and followed the ripples downstream.

Rick found a long stick and took a couple of steps downstream. Luckily, the shirt had caught on a stone that kept it from floating farther away. "Maybe I should just hang it on a tree until it dries. A lot of the dirt has already washed away."

She shook her head even before he chuckled at his foolishness. "Cold water can't take the place of hot water and soap. Let me do this much for you." She reached for the end of the branch and draped the shirt across the top of the water buckets she was bringing for the laundry.

Rick hated to see her leave, but it was best. If she stayed on the creek bank, he'd be tempted to join her instead of working. After setting pegs in the four corners of the garden plot, he dug up the topsoil with his hoe. It was a good place to work. Prince had plenty of water and grass if he was hungry.

If the Bartons washed his clothes and gave him milk, he should continue to offer his assistance. They were destined to be good neighbors.

❦

America wanted to keep Rick's unexpected appearance at the creek to herself, but Mother guessed as soon as she saw his shirt. Nodding with a smile, she said, "Invite Mr. Eady to give us all his laundry for washday on Monday."

Father returned the laundered shirt to Rick early Tuesday but didn't say anything about the visit. Had he learned any details about their neighbor? If he did, he didn't share them with his daughter.

As the family ate their way through biscuits—not quite hard enough to break a tooth this morning—and dry, scorched eggs, Father swallowed a spoonful of eggs with a generous swallow of coffee. "When I saw Mr. Barton this morning, he said he had snared a brace of rabbits and invited us to his camp for supper tonight."

"Rabbit stew—grand." Bert grinned.

Freddy rubbed his stomach without saying anything.

Relief loosened America's shoulders, and she almost dropped the dish on her lap. Her interests lay in sewing more than in cooking. As a child, their cook had taught her a few things. Before long, she lost interest. Now that she and Mother did all the cooking, she wished she had paid better attention.

She poked through the food, forcing it down. With the heavy physical labor each day, they needed plenty of food. At least the coffee had improved. Father lifted his cup in salute and winked at her. "Can I have another cup?"

"Gladly."

"The bacon was good. Just crispy enough." Bert stuffed another slice in his mouth. Bless her brother. He could be kind when he wanted to.

"I accepted his invitation, of course, and asked him for secrets on snaring rabbits. Better in our stomachs than eating our crops."

A twitching nose and long ears leaped into America's imagination, and her heart fluttered with the need to see them as a food source. Rabbits reproduced rapidly, didn't they? Maybe they could capture a male and female and raise their children. At least they'd always have pets. The guide to the life of the homesteader couldn't begin to cover all of their concerns.

She set aside her questions about the evening until she saw Father heading back from the land he was plowing. Time to milk Daisy, a chore she enjoyed both morning and evening. A few minutes alone gave her time to talk to God, or sometimes to Daisy, about how the day had gone.

As they walked toward Rick's campsite, her stomach growled in anticipation of supper. How many rabbits came in a brace? More than enough for him alone, but that didn't mean it would stretch for four adults and two children. How did one cook rabbits? On a spit over a fire? How long? Or boiled in a stew? A wonderful aroma tickled her nose, and her stomach rumbled. They hadn't eaten well for a week.

When they arrived at the campsite, Rick welcomed them, offering them seats on blankets he had spread around the fire pit. Curious, she looked around his camp. A tarp protected a number of belongings, perhaps his bedroll and saddlebags. She was tempted to peek and see what belongings he had brought with him.

Rick paused to say grace before serving the food. He must know the Lord, and America rejoiced.

Father cleared his throat. "If you'd like, we always read from the Holy Bible before we eat. We'd love to hear you share your favorite passage with us." He sat back while America leaned forward, eager to hear Rick's choice.

Rick's spoon clattered against his bowl. "You want me to read, from a Bible?" His voice sounded as squeaky as Bert's.

"We'd love to hear it."

Not moving, Rick cleared his throat. "I can't do that. I don't have a Bible."

America's heart dropped to her stomach.

Rick swallowed once, then twice, looking at the ground. Speaking in a low voice, he said, "I carry God's Word in my heart, like the Good Book says, but I don't have a copy of the Bible myself." He looked up at that point. "It wouldn't do me any good. I can't read."

Rick read the shock on all five faces of the Barton family, from Mr. Barton all the way down to little Freddy. Freddy looked too young to know how to read. He sneaked a glance at America. Sympathy softened the shock on her face.

Goodness, he didn't want her sympathy. She needed his help, and he intended to offer it.

But first things first. "I love those verses in Revelation that talk about what it's going to be like in heaven. No more tears, no more death, no more pain. That bit. I believe it's from chapter twenty-one. I'd love for one of you to read it, if you have your Bible with you."

Mr. Barton shook his head, but America opened her purse and pulled out a miniature book. "I carry this copy of the New Testament with me everywhere I go." She thumbed through the book to the final pages. "It is in chapter twenty-one." As she read the familiar words, the beauty of heaven filled Rick's heart. Imagine one of those forts the army built, with the walls made out of precious stones and the gates one big pearl.

America ended with the last verse. "And there shall in no wise enter into it any thing that defileth, neither whatsoever worketh abomination, or maketh a lie: but they which are written in the Lamb's book of life."

Mr. Barton leaned forward. "In our family Bible, we write down the day each one of this family had their names written in that book of life. Mr. Eady, is your name there as well?"

"Amen!" Rick told them about the day he accepted Jesus as his Savior during a tent revival, when he was eight years old.

The boys ate the stew as if they hadn't seen food for weeks. Maybe they hadn't had a hearty meal since before the land run. America dished up different bits in her spoon and studied them before eating them. In spite of her hesitation, she ate the food with a good appetite. The stew stretched for double servings, along with corn bread he had made in his skillet.

"I confess I have never eaten rabbit before," Mrs. Barton said. "I have the recipe for it, and now I shall have to try it. It is delicious."

"Once I learn how to snare them," Mr. Barton said.

Uncertainty laced the family's laughter. Their lack of experience was evident, but Rick didn't want to embarrass them. "Are you folks interested in a trade? There's not much I don't know about farming and living off the land, and I'm thinking I could help you out. And me, I've wanted to read since I first saw pictures of Jesus in a Bible. I bet even Freddy could teach me my ABCs."

Freddy grinned and ran through a list of letters so fast that Rick couldn't understand, even if he had known what they were.

"America here would be the right person for the job," Mr. Barton said. "She taught the children's Sunday school, and that included some English lessons, too."

Spend time with America? He couldn't dream of anything he'd rather do. "Only if she's willing."

"Oh yes." A brief smile fluttered across her face. "I love to teach. I was planning to become a teacher before. . ." She cleared her throat. "Before we changed our plans."

"We do not need to hide the facts. Our fortunes took a dive in the bank failures earlier this year," Mr. Barton said. "The store I managed closed, and when we prayed for answers, God led us to Oklahoma." He shrugged. "I don't know much about farming, but I am willing to learn, and now God brought you to us. I accept your offer." He shook hands with Rick.

"What about you, Mr. Eady? What brought you to the Cherokee Strip? Do you have family waiting to learn of your good fortune?" America's cheeks turned pink as if embarrassed for asking personal questions.

"Call me Rick, please. My ma and pa raised ten of us down in Texas. We never had much, but we always had enough to eat, even if I wore my brothers' hand-me-downs. I'm right dab in the middle, ready to leave out on my own. I thought about taking part in the last land run, in '91, but saved up a bit of money, bought Prince, and look what God did for me." He grinned.

"We have never properly introduced ourselves. I'm Henry. And this is my wife, Harriet." Mr. Barton put his hand on her shoulder. "America is our eldest, and our sons, Bert and Freddy."

"*Harriet* America," Mrs. Barton—Harriet—said. "She was born on the centennial of the United States. America seemed like the perfect name."

"And one Harriet in the family was enough," Henry said.

Rick was still stuck on *centennial*. Something like century? "July 4, 1876. You must be—" He counted the numbers in his head. "Seventeen."

"Yes." She paid attention to her nails, probably dirtier than she had ever seen them in her life. When she looked at him again, her brown eyes were clear, determined; the kind of woman this country was built on.

Rick could spend the evening staring into her eyes. "I think America is a fine name." Night was creeping from the west, and tomorrow would arrive early. "Do you have a plow, Mr. Barton?"

Chapter 3

America pulled her shawl around her, a chill wind whistling through the chinks in the walls of their soddy. At least they had a shelter over their heads, thanks to Rick. It seemed like everything good since the land run three months ago came with the help of Rick Eady. From God, she reminded herself, but through Rick.

Rick's latest gift, a pheasant, waited for her by the fire pit. Holding the carcass, she began plucking the feathers, setting them aside for pillow stuffing. Rather than frying separate pieces, she'd roast it whole. They had to stretch food as far as possible these days. Mother hadn't adapted to life on the prairie very well, and the family was struggling.

America thrived on the challenges. While Mother looked for ways to cram their possessions into the small soddy, America cooked, cleaned, and did farm chores. Rick estimated they wouldn't get to a more permanent dwelling place for a year or more. Everything Mother asked for seemed destined for "maybe next year," and she wanted it now.

After each long day, America sat with Rick and her brothers around the table, teaching them how to read. Rick knew most of the letters when they started, and he was flying through their lessons. How precious those evenings had become.

Since he often arrived at this time of day, she went to the door for a peek. Rick's red jacket flashed in the stand of trees by the creek. The red disappeared, and she stood on tiptoes, willing him to reappear.

"America?" Mother's voice intruded on her thoughts.

Cutting a sigh short, America flung her arms wide, letting the air puncture her skin, and she scurried into the dugout. "How can I help you, Mother?"

An open crate sat on their makeshift table. "I found our Christmas decorations. This is the star you made when you were Freddy's age."

The paper showed the wear and tear of years, but the yellow star, striped with red and a trail of sparks following it, still brought tears to America's eyes. Mother had wrapped it in linen cloths that protected it year after year.

"And here is the yarn ball Bert made that Kitty liked to bat around." Half the ball had lost its yarn, claw marks evident on the ball's surface. Kitty had disappeared a few years ago. No pet had made the trip to Oklahoma with them.

"Where are we going to get a proper tree?" Mother held up one ornament then another. "Does seed corn pop? I want strands around the tree."

The contents of that barrel represented their future, but America had an idea. "I've seen trees with lovely white berries. Perhaps we could string those. The boys love to climb trees, and perhaps Rick would help."

"Rick." Mother harrumphed. "I'm not comfortable with how close the two of you have become."

"He's a good man." America could fill a dictionary with his good qualities, but Mother clung to the differences that would have separated them in the past—money, his lack of education.

"I don't doubt that. I hoped for more for you, that's all." Mother packed the decorations back into the crate. "You are too young to become serious with anyone."

Here in Oklahoma, they had met women her age who were married and mothers. If America reminded her mother, she would count it as one reason why they should never have left St. Louis.

"I have seen those berries as well. Your idea is a good one. Perhaps we can gather extra berries, enough to decorate and to cook."

America's stomach contracted with the thought of a berry cobbler, or a jam. White berries would look strange, but taste mattered the most. They put the decorations back into the crate, in hopes of finding a Christmas tree.

Saturday, the family threw themselves full-hearted into holiday preparations. Mother and Father headed to the closest store, in Pawnee, the proposed county seat, with a shopping list. The day was pleasant, with no hint of storm clouds, a perfect day for frolicking. Best of all, Rick had agreed to help. America donned her red hat and mittens, since he had once mentioned he liked her red hat.

Rick wore his usual black hat. Without it, she didn't know if she would recognize him. Of course she would. His sun-streaked hair grew darker as the days grew shorter. He wore his hair a little long, combed back from his face with bangs that escaped and dangled over his eyes.

As they approached the stand of trees, Bert shouted, "There's one with the white berries."

"Mistletoe," Rick said. "That's not the name of the tree. It attaches to other trees and borrows what it needs to grow."

"Mistletoe." America's cheeks burned as she said the word. What did Rick think when they asked for his help to hunt for the kissing berry?

∞

America looked cute, her cheeks a bright red when he mentioned mistletoe. What would Mr. Barton do if Rick dangled a piece over their heads and caught America in a kiss?

He shoved that thought aside. "The Oklahoma legislature named mistletoe as the state flower earlier this year."

"Mistletoe?" Freddy twisted his mouth in confusion.

"Do they want everyone in Oklahoma to go around kissing?" Bert said.

"Bert." America's face grew even redder. "Maybe they chose it because it's so beautiful, like the land here."

"That's not what I heard," Rick said. "They chose it because it survives no matter what bad things happen to it. It's strong, like the people of Oklahoma."

"I like that." Red had drained from America's face, leaving only her hat and mittens as reminders of Christmas.

They stopped under the first tree with mistletoe. Although the branch was within reach, the bundle resisted Rick's attempts to tear it off. "This is going to need a knife." He looked at the two boys. "Can I trust you with my pocketknife?"

America's face blanched, as if her brothers had never handled a sharp blade before. Perhaps they hadn't. He cut the bundle and dropped it into America's waiting arms, resisting the temptation to lean in for a kiss.

During the next few minutes, he demonstrated how to use the pocketknife as they cut the bundle into smaller clusters of berries. "But don't eat any of the berries. They'll make you sick."

Freddy spit out the berry he had popped into his mouth. "It didn't taste good, anyhow."

America ran her fingers through the berries, sucking a finger where the slivered edges pinched her skin. She held one up against the sunshine to study it. "What a beautiful pearl of God's creation." She held it out to Bert and Freddy. "It reminds me of Grandma's ring."

"Yup." Bert flicked the knife open and closed, more interested in harvesting more berries than in a family story.

"Are you boys ready?" Rick asked. As they scampered to the next tree with mistletoe, Rick spoke to America. "I bet it was a beautiful ring."

"It is. A single pearl in a setting with two rubies." America sighed. "Mother and Father saved it for me to wear"—a faint pink flashed across her cheeks—"when I am married."

Her husband would be one lucky man.

They reached the next tree. Once again, the mistletoe dangled tantalizingly close. He could probably reach it, but instead, he turned to Freddy. "Can you climb on my shoulders and cut this one down?"

"Can I?"

"May I," America corrected.

Freddy flicked the knife open and shut before Rick knelt down. With a gleeful shout, Freddy climbed on Rick's neck and threw his legs over his shoulders. The boy squealed as Rick stood, securing Freddy's feet with his arms. "I won't let you fall. You don't have to hold on to my neck."

America circled in front of him, worry written on her face.

"It's okay," Rick said, and a smile reappeared on her face.

"I've got it!" Freddy said. The bundle flashed past Rick's face and landed on the ground. He bent and helped Freddy to the ground. In his enthusiasm, Freddy stomped on some of the berries until America rescued them and dropped them into the basket.

Freddy jumped up and down. "Can I do it again?"

America's face changed expressions half a dozen times before she said, "You can, but give Bert a chance next."

Instead of placing Bert on his shoulders, Rick gave him a step up to climb the tree, standing guard in case he should fall. Bert cut the first bundle quickly. Before Rick could call him down, he had scampered up one more branch and taken another.

"Come down." America glared at her brother.

"Ah, Sis." Bert climbed down. "I see a tree over that way that would make a good Christmas tree. I can show it to Father tomorrow."

Rick bit his tongue to stop himself from offering to chop down the tree, since they were already there. But even if Bert couldn't find the tree he wanted, they would choose another.

"Isn't this a redbud tree?" America said. Dry leaves dangled lifelessly on the tree.

"Yup. This spot will be right pretty, come spring."

"I didn't know we would have redbuds here in Oklahoma. Their pink flowers are the first breath of spring." America patted the tree trunk. "And here is mistletoe that I can reach." She smiled at Rick. "If you trust me with your knife, that is."

He held out the knife, palm up, and she reached for the mistletoe. When she found the spot where it attached to the tree, she opened the knife and caught the bundle in her arms before dropping it into the basket. Grinning, she handed the knife back to Rick.

Before long, mistletoe filled the basket. America said, "That's enough berries. Mother and Father should be back from shopping by now." As they retraced their tracks to the soddy, she said, "Thank you for such a wonderful day. I know you have work to do on your own farm."

Not much. His dugout was snug for the winter, and he had fashioned a shelter for Prince as well. The garden plot hadn't yielded as much as he had hoped, and he had canned the meager crop already. With so little he could do outside, he spent his hours crafting farm tools. Stacks of wood awaited his attention for a table and a chair. While light permitted, he worked on the homework America had assigned in the evenings.

They exited the stand of trees, the creek rippling a few feet away, their homes in opposite directions. "I'll see you folks at the church gathering tomorrow."

∞

America sat with Mother and the boys, stringing the mistletoe. "Ouch." Freddy stuck his pointer finger in his mouth. The berry fell onto the floor, and Mother reached for the needle to return it to her needle case. "Freddy, if you would rather play outside instead of stringing the berries together, you may."

"Me, too, Mother!" Bert jumped up and ran out the door after his brother, taking a ball in his hand.

Mother stuck her needle in the berry. "That's enough. We'll have Christmas here, if it's the last thing I do." She disappeared behind the curtain to their sleeping quarters.

America's hands were shaking, but she made herself gather the four needles, clean and dry them before sticking them into the pincushion. Ever since they had returned from their shopping trip, the atmosphere in the sod house had lowered to the freezing point. In spite of their earlier plans to cut down a tree, Father disappeared.

In spite of—because of—the unhappy mood, America decided to start decorating. The string of white berries would look best against the dark green of a Christmas tree, but until then, she would drape the garland around the walls of the soddy. She anchored the string at the door and continued to the right. Every few feet she nailed a plug into the sod blocks to hold the garland above the floor. Her parents' bed gave her pause, but she decided they needed cheer more than anyone.

When it came to the rest of the decorations, America wanted to consult Mother. A short, three-shelved bookcase held happy reminders of earlier times. Books crowded the bottom shelf: the family Bible, the complete works of Shakespeare, *David Copperfield* by Charles Dickens, Mark Twain for the boys, and *Pride and Prejudice* for America. Thoreau's *Walden* for Father hinted at a lifelong dream for a simpler life. *McGuffey Reader*s were essential for schooling the boys and now Rick as well. How hard they had struggled to choose that one perfect book to bring with them.

One final book rounded out their library, which they read every year along with the Christmas story: Dickens's *A Christmas Carol*. Oh, she hoped Rick would join them while they read the book. Would he love the transformation of Scrooge's "bah, humbug" character the way she did?

Rick would love it, she knew it. The thought of sharing it with him made her smile. Maybe the beautiful story would help him understand why they "wasted" so much space on books. Taking a deep breath, she packed half the books in a crate until after Christmas. That gave her a little space for decorations.

The remaining shelf space mostly held necessities for schooling, personal hygiene, and cooking. Her hands hovered over the paper supplies, remembering her own joy at the Christmas break. No lessons, but the paper stayed.

A tintype of her grandparents sat on top of the shelves. America wiped the surface of the glass free of grime that coated everything in their home, and clutched it close to her heart. *Oh Grandma, are you looking down on us from heaven? You would like Oklahoma. The adventure. The land, pretty much the way God created it.* She wouldn't remove the portrait, so Grandmama could enjoy Christmas with them.

Other items had been added as they discovered unexpected problems. Who knew snakes would slither through the roof over their heads? Or rain would seep through the roof? She would be glad when they could build a house.

But who had money for lumber, nails, or ladders? Who knew how to keep the walls and floors even and what kind of foundation they needed? Rick? Surely he had helped with barn raisings, or whatever they were called, at least.

Perhaps he would wait until he married to build a proper house. Why did marriage jump into her mind? America blushed. Her girlfriends in St. Louis teased her about the lack of eligible bachelors in Oklahoma. Mother had dismissed the taunts, saying at seventeen America was too young to worry about such things. How could she avoid it? Molly Green, who was homesteading with her husband, Mark, and baby girl, was younger than America by a month.

America shoved those thoughts away. If she wasted time thinking about Rick, she wouldn't finish her job. Rummaging through the Christmas crate, she chose two items for display. A star-shaped crystal candleholder would go on the kitchen table.

Her second choice was a music box that played "Silent Night." Where should it go? Her hand hovered, until she took down a small chest that held their pennies and other change. Mother and Father could keep it safe in their room until after Christmas.

When she reached for it, it flipped out of her hands to the floor, flying open.

America groaned as she bent over to pick up the change, but she didn't see any. Impossible. The last time she had seen it, the chest was half full, a lot of pennies as well as nickels, dimes, and quarters, and even a golden eagle. She ran her hands through the dirt, convinced her fingers would find what her eyes could not see. Not a one.

She set the empty bank on the table and set the music box in its place.

But who had emptied the bank—and why?

Chapter 4

Sunday was Rick's favorite day of the week. From the beginning, people from nearby farms came to the communal plot to worship and enjoy a meal together, weather permitting.

Christmas Eve fell on Sunday, a special time for celebration. The chilly air couldn't harm the joyful sounds filling the evening. Among the men, they had crafted simple plank benches, which they brought back and forth each week.

A few other families arrived before the Bartons. Mrs. Barton and America sat on the bench nearest the front, wanting to see their boys in the pageant. Instead of looking his way, America talked with her brothers, as if rehearsing for the pageant. When she did see Rick, she waved her hand in a brief greeting, but her usual smile was missing.

The Green family would play the roles of Joseph, Mary, and Jesus, the obvious choice since they had a new baby, but Rick bet America had played the role in her childhood. On this day, with all the joyous music and the replaying of the most familiar story in the Bible—when God became a man—what had happened to make America unhappy? After she settled her brothers on the bench, she gestured for Rick to join them. Maybe that meant she wasn't mad at him.

Their music leader, the one settler who had brought a hymnal with him on the land run, led them through every Christmas carol in his book. Everyone knew some of the carols. When he ran across something unfamiliar, he sang a line, which they repeated. Beautiful words, all of them. Tears glistened in America's eyes. She knew more of the songs than Rick did.

They closed the hymn sing with "Amazing Grace," five verses of it, which they all seemed to know. What they didn't, they made up.

While their preacher reminded them of the precious gift God had given to them, His only Son, the children disappeared among the wagons and slipped on costumes. Towels and nightshirts worked well with imagination.

Mark and Molly Green were compelling as the young parents. Next up, Freddy and Bert, with a few girls, came in with family dogs as substitute sheep. Three wise men came forward with glass jars filled with money, designated for the church's charity fund. When the tableau ended, oohs and aahs went up from the congregation. As they all clapped, the elderly Mr. Jackson shouting hallelujah, America turned a trifle sad again. Rick sent up a quick prayer that God would comfort whatever was worrying her on that day.

After the service, they traveled home together. When they reached Rick's soddy, Mr. Barton repeated the invitation to spend Christmas with them. Rick took comfort from the invitation.

Before sunrise on Christmas morning, Rick headed for the Bartons's. If Freddy and Bert were anything like he was as a child, they'd already be awake, demanding presents.

Faint candlelight shone through the grease-papered window, so he knocked lightly on the door. America's face peeped around the door, and she waved him in. "I was about to milk the cow and then start breakfast."

Rick grabbed the buckets. "I'll milk Daisy." He grinned. "Unless you want me to cook for you?"

Her cheeks flared pink. "You've already fixed us breakfast a dozen times or more. Johnnycakes this morning—I can cook them, thanks to you."

How dumb to embarrass her on Christmas morning. "It sounds good. I brought a cake for us to share with the meal." He unbuckled the saddlebag and pulled out the cake he had wrapped. "Now I'm going to milk the cow."

She lifted the cake plate and inhaled deeply. "It smells delicious. Cinnamon and nutmeg and—what fruit is that? Dried apples?"

He nodded and held a finger to his lips as he walked to the door. In the lean-to, he started the milk flow. When the bucket was about half full, he heard a soft yelp. A furry black head peeked at him from a box in the corner, a red ribbon tied around his neck.

America came in with a cup. "I need some cream."

The puppy yelped and scratched its way out of the box.

"You've made a new friend," Rick said. Daisy mooed softly and Rick resumed milking her.

The puppy licked America's face, and she ran her hand down his back, ruffling behind his ears. He jumped out of her hands and ran to the corner.

Rick sprang into action, scooping him under his arm before he ran away from the lean-to and got lost. "Is it okay if I bring him inside with us?"

"Not yet." America kissed the puppy on the nose.

When they reached the door, it flung open. Freddy and Bert blocked the entrance. "Look overhead," Bert demanded.

A sprig of mistletoe Rick hadn't noticed before danced before his eyes.

"Kiss, kiss, kiss," the boys chanted.

Behind them, he spotted the parents, looking shocked.

When he turned to America, her mouth had opened in the tiniest, most kissable bow, and he leaned in for a kiss.

❦

Rick's lips lifted from America's, but she was no more able to move than a fish out of water. Her eyes remained closed, hiding the memory deep in her heart.

"Are you all right?" Rick asked. When she opened her eyes, his kind brown eyes twinkled at her.

She touched her lips, and they curled in a smile at the memory. "Merry Christmas,

Rick. Come on in." She shook her finger at her brothers. "But I'm not done with the two of you."

America blocked out the chatter in the background while she beat the mixture for the johnnycakes. Before long, each plate sported a stack, with more on the stove. She munched on her share while she cooked.

Bert punched Freddy in the arm, and he reached into his pocket and stood behind his parents. Before America could speak, Rick pointed to the mistletoe in Freddy's hand. Father smiled and gave Mother a kiss on the cheek. The boys cheered, and America relaxed, pleased at the show of affection.

Even the coffee tasted better than usual, as if God had sprinkled Christmas spirit in with the coffee grounds. The food disappeared with appreciative grunts and fast bites. When they finished, America set the dishes in soapy water to soak and joined the others around the Christmas tree. Father had found the tree late Christmas Eve, and every ornament brought back memories. Mistletoe berries gleamed like pearls on the branches, the garland draped around the tree as the final decoration.

Bert wound the music box, and the tinny sound of "Silent Night" played as the manger scene slowly rotated. Father brought out a burlap sack packed as tight as Santa's would be on his sled. America had added a few items for the sack, leaving the puppy outside, still.

With so many presents, America worried they had used the missing coins on Christmas presents. She prayed not.

Father took the Bible from their bookshelf. "I see you put *A Christmas Carol* up here. I suppose you expect us to read it later today."

"Of course." She grinned.

Father opened the Bible to Luke, leaving a marker in Matthew. "Rick, part of our tradition is to read the Christmas story, all of it, from the birth of John the Baptist to the visit of the wise men. So I weave back and forth between Matthew and Luke to get the whole story."

With a story that filled her with such wonder, why did America's mind keep wandering? She kept glancing at Rick, while he sat forward, as if captivated by every word.

What would Rick have done if he learned his fiancée was pregnant? If he was the father, they both would be ashamed. But how much worse if he knew he wasn't the father? From what she had seen of Rick, she suspected he would be like Joseph, quiet, noble, loving his wife to an extraordinary degree.

She wrenched her mind back to the reading, when Mary and Joseph presented Jesus at the temple. When Father read of Simeon and Anna, America longed for her grandmother. She rubbed her ring finger, remembering it on Grandmama's ring finger.

Reading the full story took an hour. By the time Father read, "And Jesus increased in wisdom and stature, and in favor with God and man," her brothers jumped to their feet.

"Can we open the presents now?"

Mother nodded yes, and America wondered if she should bring in the puppy now or later. Better now, she decided. "I need to fetch one more gift. I'll be right back."

The puppy had escaped his box again, but she found him buried in a bundle of hay amid the cattle. She brushed the hay from his coat and tugged him close. In the few feet between the lean-to and the house, she shivered as a strong wind blew from the north. Next time, she'd put on her coat before heading out.

The door opened, and the puppy yipped. Freddy saw the black head in her hands and jumped in the air. "A puppy!" When America handed him the puppy, he licked Freddy's face.

"What are you going to call him?" Rick asked.

"Rover," Freddy said without thought.

Rover was the name of their last dog. Maybe he thought all dogs should have the same name.

"Do I have a dog, too?" Bert asked.

America looked at her parents. "You and Freddy can take turns taking care of him. And, if Mother and Father agree, the Greens still have one puppy. If you promise to take care of both of them."

"Can we?" Bert asked.

The smile on Father's face told him he knew he was fighting a losing battle.

⬥

Rick returned to his sod house that night with a full stomach and one overriding memory.

Mistletoe encouraged couples to kiss. He had played that trick a few times himself. He should have expected the boys' trick in a house they had deliberately filled with the berries.

How sweet that brief brush of the lips. If only the boys had tried again, he would have given her a proper kiss. By the shy pink of her cheeks, she wouldn't have minded.

A surprising number of presents filled his saddlebag—a new shirt, sewn by Mrs. Barton; a lathe he had borrowed from Mr. Barton; small, rough carvings made by the boys.

America had given him not one, but two presents, which pleased and puzzled him at the same time. She had written a letter for him to send to his parents, and the depth of detail revealed a lot about her. She included extra pages, as well as an addressed envelope, so he could copy the letter in his own handwriting if he wanted. Would Mom and Pop be glad he was learning how to write—or would they be embarrassed that they needed someone else to read it?

At the end of the day, before he left, she handed him her tiny New Testament. He refused.

"I know how you want to read the Bible for yourself." He couldn't refuse her, so he

79

opened to the index to find the page where the Gospel of John started. Feeling good he could manage that much, he looked for words he could pick out.

*In the. . .*a long word. A memory jumped into Rick's mind. John and Genesis started with the same words. *In the beginning.* He slowly made out the rest of the first verse, and that made the second verse easier.

America had turned out to be a tough teacher, but good. He had learned a lot. He couldn't decide if the letter to his parents was a writing assignment or a personal gesture. In the letter she wrote to them directly, she spoke of him and his kindness in glowing terms. Did she see him that way?

Maybe she did. The boys' trick had given them the opportunity he had longed for since they cut mistletoe from the trees. Every time he remembered their kiss, he grinned.

The writing material and the Bible went in his saddlebag to protect them from the elements. He bet Rover was sharing a bed with Freddy and Bert tonight. He wouldn't mind a dog for a companion, himself.

He woke up in the morning, cold to the bone, so when he poked his head out the door of the soddy, he wasn't surprised to find the ground frozen. No snow or sleet had fallen yet, but by the look of the skies, they were due for a storm like none he had ever seen. In south Texas, he had only seen snow one time.

As long as he stayed in his soddy, he would stay relatively warm and well fed—dried meat, water enough, the chinks of the sod plugged in, a good fire pit and plenty of wood to keep it burning. The shed provided shelter for Prince, and with his hide, he would withstand the cold.

The Bartons weren't so lucky. Oh, they had more cooking supplies—fluff—but little dried meat and no canned vegetables. How well the cattle would survive an onslaught of frozen weather, he couldn't guess. They hadn't filled the holes in the sod as well as needed, and their fire pit was too shallow for a good-sized blaze.

He had to go to their home. If the storm delayed, he hoped to convince them to come to his soddy and bring the two animals. In case he couldn't, he packed essential items into the largest bag Prince could carry. He threw the heaviest blanket over the horse and added one from his bed as well.

By the time he mounted Prince's back, a light rain was falling. Rain didn't describe it well. It was water with a bite of ice in it. He tugged the collar of his coat around his neck and pulled his hat forward on his face. For one last prevention, he tied a kerchief on his face that covered his nose and mouth, leaving only his eyes uncovered.

The driving rain doubled the time to reach the Bartons's home. The rain had already changed to sleet when he left his soddy, air white and heavy in all directions. When he reached their yard, snow began to replace the sleet. Snow carpeted the ground quickly, not the slow-falling snowflakes Rick remembered from childhood.

The fog was so thick Rick didn't see Mr. Barton and America until he led Prince to the lean-to. They were strengthening the structure in an effort to better protect their animals from the storm, in addition to the blankets already draped on their backs.

"Rick." America breathed his name into the air. "You came."

Rick nodded. "You've done a good job with the animals. How about inside?"

Mr. Barton headed for the soddy without answering. Praying for wisdom, Rick placed a protective arm around America as they followed. With his other hand, he grabbed his bag. In his hurry to leave, he hadn't brought a single page of homework America had assigned.

Surviving the storm mattered more than reading and writing.

Chapter 5

America felt safe with Rick's arm around her. Harsh winds blew snow in every direction, but she could make out the soddy. The animals required care twice a day, regardless of the weather. On days like this, losing her way only a few feet from the door seemed possible. Rick would know what to do.

Snow showered St. Louis several times each year, but this storm was unlike anything she had ever experienced. Without buildings that offered shelter from the wind and snow, each flake stung her face like a rose's thorns. Wind whipped across the empty plains and drove snow onto every exposed surface.

"Is our soddy safe during this storm?" With the wind, America wondered if Rick could hear her.

Snowflakes fluttered to the ground as Rick shrugged. "We'll find out." When he dropped her hand to push the door open, she felt abandoned. "Ladies first."

America hustled through the door and hung her outer clothes on a peg on the wall before squatting by the fire. Rick said hello to Mother before walking around the soddy, examining the walls. He even went behind the curtain, where her parents slept.

A frown marred his face when he joined them by the fire. "It's going to get much colder. We need a larger fire."

Father shook his head. "A bigger fire is a fire danger, without a vent."

Rick accepted a cup of coffee from Mother. While the wind made its way through the chinks and the fire flickered, he looked around the walls again without speaking. In spite of his advice and the directions given in the manual for homesteaders, America knew Rick's soddy was better constructed. She knew better than to mention it. Father took pride in his ability to provide for his family.

Father studied Rick now, his gaze none too happy. "Something is on your mind. We're listening."

Rick took a deep breath, released it, and leveled his shoulders as he sat up straighter. "There are several things you can do to make the soddy warmer. One is to patch the chinks with any materials at hand. You've got dirt on the ground here. Make mud pies with it, and examine the walls for every sliver of light or wind gust for the holes." He chuckled. "The way this wind is blowing, it should be easy to find them."

Rick's next suggestion struck America as audacious: cut a small hole in the ceiling to draw smoke upward while allowing minimal wind into the soddy. "Get the mud for the chinks from the fire pit. Dig it deeper, and ring it with whatever rocks you can find."

No one said anything for a few seconds. Freddy reached between his feet and let the ground drip between his fingers.

"Freddy, Bert, this is the only time you will hear me tell you to make mud pies."

America joined the men in the search for rocks for the fire pit. Rick found one a yard from the front door. His fingers brushed away dirt and snow as if they would never meet an obstacle he couldn't overcome. She found the next one, about the size of their mixing bowl. She couldn't manage anything bigger on her own. It pulled away easily and she dropped it into the bag at her feet. The next one proved more difficult. After scraping snow and slush from around the rock, her hands couldn't grasp it.

"Let me." Rick worked next to her, digging deeper and wider. A minute later, they had dislodged the rock. He added it to the pile by the door.

Father found another good-sized rock. The semi-daylight, lessened by the heavy clouds, lingered as they continued accumulating rocks. Smaller rocks were covered with a thin layer of snow, and they had cleared most of the rocks when they built the soddy. America had found three more rocks and the men, two more, when Rick called a halt.

While they dragged the rocks inside, the new puppy ran outside. He stuck his nose in the snow and did his business, yowling when the cold air and flakes pinched his skin. He ran back in, tail tucked between his legs. Freddy stared outside. "I want to build a snowman."

"No." Mother and America spoke in unison. "It's too cold."

"You could get lost," Rick said, pointing with one finger.

"Not me," Freddy said. "And Rover can always find his way back home." The boy broadened the distance between his legs, adopting Rick's slightly bowlegged stance before he squirmed into his jacket.

"Me, too." Bert plunged past America to join Freddy.

Father pulled the boys back by the scruff of their necks. "Give me a few minutes to warm by the fire and I'll go outside with you."

Freddy jumped up and down, Rover circling him. America glanced at her mother. She had pulled her lips together, upset, but she wouldn't confront Father in front of the rest of them.

⚭

Sometimes Henry Barton didn't have the sense God gave to baby chicks. If he went outside again, he couldn't help with fixing the inside of the soddy. Worse, he might overwork himself, get too wet and too cold, get sick. Then what would the Bartons do?

America was sweet and good willed, but like her parents, she didn't know much about farm living. Building a homestead from nothing required more than a willingness to learn. If Rick wanted to marry, he would need a wife ready to stand by his side, not someone as helpless as America.

At the moment, America and her mother busied themselves with filling every chink they could find. He joined them as they fitted and smoothed out the mud. Although they did a decent job, they should have done it months ago, but they had ignored his warning. They were always so busy and tired, and Rick couldn't run both homesteads. No matter how captivating America Barton was.

When they finished with the walls, they sank by the fire, exhausted. The small blaze didn't give out much warmth. If they didn't finish the job, the night could reach to unbearably cold. "We need a bigger fire."

Harriet rose to her knees, surveying the room in a quick glance. "If we do that, there will hardly be room to move." She wiped at her eyes, leaving a dirty smear on her cheek.

In Rick's opinion, Mr. Barton had no business bringing his family to Oklahoma. Like the problems with the soddy—people lived shoulder to shoulder in the biggest soddies. He wanted to tell them to throw away things they didn't need but figured they would learn the hard way.

Love your neighbor as yourself. If that meant getting the fire pit ready and logs burning, he would do it. They smothered the fire with a thick quilt, cleaned the pit, and together dug the hole until he declared it deep enough. America flashed a tired smile. He pinned the largest boulder between his knees and shifted it to the right, as the center point of the ring. She nestled her rocks around the boulder like he had shown her, and he added other big stones to the east, north, and west, until the circle was compete.

"I will start the fire." Harriet held an armload of kindling and some matches.

"Wait until we have the hole in the roof." Rick took a chair, sturdy enough, and used the blade he had packed in his saddlebag to cut a small square and ease it from the roof. While they rebuilt the fire, he circled the room a second time. They had taken out the Christmas tree, but the ornaments remained unpacked, and the garland of mistletoe berries looped around the pile.

America started with a few pieces of kindling, sneaking glances at Rick, her dark eyes bright with light in the darkening room. She lit the fire and fed it small branches until the fire had grown to the point where she could add a log.

He fingered the garland, smiling at the memory of the kiss. It fell apart in his hands, the string broken. Something had chewed the string in half, most likely Rover. To avoid a repeat of the accident, Rick threw the string into the fire. Neither woman commented as he separated ornaments into two piles. By the time he finished, he had cleared enough space for lying on the floor to sleep and their other needs, and the storm shouldn't keep them inside for more than two or three days. Job done, as best as they could.

Rick added a second log to the fire.

"Thanks." The slump of America's shoulders showed how much the day had taken out of her. "I'll get some water warming." She struggled to stand.

"Let me do it." Rick took the bucket from her hands. "Rest for a few minutes." She sank to the floor gratefully, her head slumped over her chest. Her breathing slowed as she fell asleep.

Her rest was short-lived, however. The boys bounced into the soddy, Mr. Barton stumbling along behind, a bucket of fresh milk in one hand.

America watched the boys remove their gloves and stretch their arms over the fire pit, water from their snow-soaked coats dribbling into the flames. They'd had too much fun to realize how cold they must be, wet to the skin. She stripped the boys to their long johns.

"Let me help." Rick held clean clothes over his arms. "Your mother gave me these." He huddled them into the corner, hiding them with his broad back. Father went behind the curtain to change. When they gathered around the fire, it blazed brightly, warm air circling the room. Mother poured tea for all of them, the drink warming them from the inside out.

America didn't want to move, but soon the boys would demand supper. She forced herself to her feet. Rick joined her as she moved toward the pantry corner. "Want help?"

Even shrugging hurt. "I'm going to make those dumplings you showed me. We have chicken stock."

Rick smiled. "I look forward to eating it, but my offer of help still stands."

Yes. America closed her eyes. *No.* She wanted to demonstrate how much she had learned. *Yes.* She would welcome help, and he offered. She tied on her apron. "I need flour and lard and. . ."

As she listed the ingredients, Rick set them on the table. Last of all, she mentioned the chicken stock. "I should have said that first, so we could warm it before we add the dumplings."

"It's all right." Rick smiled. "How much do you want in the pot?"

America's aching arms appreciated his help. "Half. We need some for tomorrow."

Tasting the broth, he smacked his lips. "Good." He added a dash of salt and a couple of carrots and potatoes then set the kettle over the fire. He felt for another carrot in the sack, but it was empty. What must he think of how little food they had in their pantry?

Mother and Father had indeed spent all the coins they had saved on Christmas presents they didn't need, on farm implements recommended in the homesteader's manual, bolts of cloth, and only a small amount of food. America didn't know how they would manage until their first harvest, months away. Sending up a prayer, she set aside her worries.

Conversation lagged as the family gobbled up the food—better than ever, the bottom of each bowl scraped clean. While America washed the dishes, Rick talked with her parents about the state of their pantry and preparing for the remaining winter and next year's crop.

She glanced over her shoulder, her hands staying busy in the sink. Father took Mother's hands in his. "My employer promised a final check once they settled their obligations, but they have written that they have no money left to disburse."

America drew in her breath. Without that money, how would they buy seed to grow next year's harvest? How would they survive until then? Worries ran through her mind as she put away the dry dishes. Every bone in her body screamed for rest. They gathered around the fire, the boys on one side, America and Rick on the other. Father read from the Bible, from the end of Revelation, about the final bloody battle, but America couldn't keep her eyes open. With his final "amen," her eyes flew open, and her head was lying on Rick's shoulder.

She jerked up and knocked a hot rock with her foot. "Poor dear," Mother said. "You've worked so hard today."

Rick laid out a pallet for her, close to the fire. Her legs trembled beneath her as she sank onto the bed, grateful the fire had dried the hem of her skirt. Rick busied himself with untying her boots and removing them. She wiggled her toes then pulled the quilt over her.

Two days passed before they could head outside for anything more than caring for the animals. They passed the time with Bible reading, singing, storytelling, and lessons. Sometimes Rick joined the lessons, but other times he joined Father for the outside chores.

No homework had made its way into Rick's saddlebag. Any number of reasons could account for its absence, but she wondered if he had given up on reading and writing. At church, she had met several people who couldn't read. She sighed. Had moving to Oklahoma destined her to marrying a man who couldn't even sign his name on their wedding certificate?

Rick left on the third day, and when he didn't return for lessons in the evening, America felt sorry for herself. Rover grabbed Freddy's slate board from the table, and it clattered to the floor. They couldn't afford to replace it. However, it fell on a bed pallet, and only a small corner was nicked. But the night left them all somber. Mother and Father spoke in low tones late into the night. Her bed was closest to their corner, where she couldn't help eavesdropping. While they argued, she prayed.

After a lengthy argument, they came out. America's eyes flew open.

"Good, you're awake." Mother drew a deep breath. "We have run into an emergency." She stretched out her arm, Grandmama's opal and ruby ring in her open palm. "I know we promised we would give you this when you married. But—" She looked at Father helplessly.

"We have two problems. Expenses have been higher than I expected. And I was counting on receiving the final check from the store."

"No." America's hand flew to her ears, not wanting to hear what they had to say.

"We have to sell this ring, if we are to survive the winter."

Chapter 6

Rick had never known such long, dark nights. Of course, nights didn't last longer in Oklahoma than in Texas. But at home, kerosene lamps added cheer to times of family fun. Maybe he felt drawn to the Bartons because they were a family. Spend two days with only himself for company and he was ready to pack his bags and return home.

Tonight he couldn't sleep. *"Whenever the good Lord keeps you awake, He wants to talk with you."* Pa's oft-repeated advice spurred Rick to action. He sat at the table that America had loaned to him. After a few attempts to read from John, he gave it up as too difficult.

The Bartons offered to repay his neighborliness in the best currency they had— knowledge. Instead of learning from them, he had avoided the school lessons around the table. Pa would be disappointed.

Tonight he would try John again. He recognized maybe two words in every five or six. When the boys ran into a word they couldn't understand, America made them use a dictionary. Words were listed in alphabetical order.

Even if Rick owned a dictionary, he couldn't find the words or read the definition. He could make a list of the hard words and ask America for her help at his next lesson.

Rick stumbled through the first four verses but came to a stop in verse five. He wasn't sure of *darkness*, but he guessed the first part read *dark*, like the night sky. Sin was dark, and Jesus was the Light of the world. But he couldn't decipher *comprehended*, no matter which way he scratched his head. *Com* was like *come here*, but the word was too long to guess its meaning.

After he wrote down words he couldn't read, he read the first four verses aloud. Tucking the Bible with his notes in his chest of clothes, he laid down and prayed for the Bartons. Instead of blaming them for foolish choices, he should have been praying for them all along, so he asked for forgiveness as well.

Rick stayed with reading John, but the words got harder. He had a long list by the time he joined the Bartons for Saturday dinner and lessons. America praised his work, showed him how to use the dictionary—not that he could find the word on his own— but he still didn't understand the verse.

"The dark couldn't understand the light?"

America giggled. "Maybe it's one of those words that has changed meaning since they translated the Bible. Like 'Suffer the little children to come unto me.' "

Since the boys were restless, they went outside while daylight remained. The ground had dried enough so their feet didn't sink into mud. A skeleton of the snowman they had made remained but wouldn't survive another week of sunshine. With gray clouds gathered to the west, another storm headed their way. "We got more weather coming."

"What did you say?" America turned her attention to where he pointed. "More snow?" She kept her voice low, the boys ignoring them.

"Can't say." Rick shrugged. "Where we lived in Texas, we almost never got snow. It feels too warm for snow, but the temperature can go down right fast when a storm hits. It might be an ice storm."

Her nose wrinkled. "Ice. That's worse than snow. Do we need to do anything else to get ready?"

He gave her a few suggestions.

"We should have an ice ax," America said. "Maybe you could talk with Father. He doesn't always take me seriously." She looked at her hands. Hard work had roughened her hands, her fingernails broken and edged with dirt. No one would mistake her for a city girl any longer.

He only hoped her spirit grew stronger, not harsher, along with her body. "If you ever want to speak with someone your age— " He paused. Why would a seventeen-year-old woman talk over her problems with him? "Your parents are wonderful people, but nobody's parents always understand."

She stared at her fingernails for a few seconds before she answered. "They sold the ring that was supposed to be mine one day. It belonged to my grandmother, beautiful white gold with an opal, like the mistletoe berries, but even prettier. A ruby on either side. I know we need the money, but it's like losing Grandmama all over again." A few tears sprinkled down her cheeks.

Rick thought of the mementos he brought with him. A quilt from Ma, a knife from Pa, and a few things from his brothers and sisters. "Aw, America, it's hard to leave your family behind. I'm sorry about the ring."

Money had never meant much to Rick, but the ring had value beyond dollars and cents. He pulled America close, silently vowing to find the ring and return it to her.

After the service on Sunday, Rick approached Bill Adams, the man who had stepped in as their preacher while working his own land. Since the picnics had ended when cold weather hit, families headed home quickly. Adams brought Rick to his plot, on the opposite side of the communal acreage.

Mrs. Adams was stirring a pot of beans over their fire. "Bill, I'm glad you brought us company for lunch today."

The two men sat around the fire. "Do you mind if my wife listens to what we have to say?"

"No." Rick swallowed, his throat dry. Mrs. Adams might offer romantic advice. "I find myself in need of cash."

The Adamses exchanged looks. Did his request sound like a plea for charity? "It's for a friend, but I feel like God wants me to help. Do you know anyone who is looking for hired hands?"

Adams rubbed his chin thoughtfully, and Rick prayed that the impossible would become possible, that someone needed a hired hand in the middle of the winter lull.

"Can you leave your claim for a few months?"

Rick calculated the costs. Leaving now meant leaving his goals for his farm unfinished. He wouldn't see America. *The Bartons*, he corrected himself. He had known a job might take him away. "I think so. As long as I'm back in time for spring planting. March, at the latest."

"My brother is a shopkeeper in Guthrie. He broke his leg and can't move around much. He needs help driving his wagon, moving products, and all those physical tasks involved with a store."

A store. "I don't know numbers. I can do them in my head, well enough, but I can't keep the books."

"He doesn't need help with that," Adams said. "His arms and fingers work just fine. And the doc says he should be back on his feet in about six weeks."

The next morning, Rick was on his way to Guthrie.

∞

When Rick barely said hello to America at church on Sunday, she was puzzled. When he didn't come to their usual Saturday lesson, she grew so unsettled that Mother shooed her away and taught the boys herself. The soup America cooked suffered from her inattention, and a few chunks of potatoes got burned.

Sunday morning, Rick arrived at church late, a smile lighting his face. During the hymn sing, he joined the Bartons on their pew. When Mr. Adams gave them time to greet each other, Rick leaned close to America and her mother. "Can I join you for dinner? I have news I'd like to share with you."

"Of course," Mother said.

America wasn't so sure. After his unexpected absence all week, she deserved an apology—or at least an explanation. Maybe he decided to stay away after she confided all their family problems.

Rick acted like no time had passed when they gathered around the table. Last night's soup stretched for a second meal, with the burnt bits removed and adding biscuits. Father asked Rick to say the blessing.

"Before I do, I have some news of my own to report." Rick waited for silence. "I'm working in a store between here and Guthrie for a few weeks. I'll come home on weekends. Do you mind if we still spend Sundays together?"

Mother and Father murmured, "Of course."

He pointed to the window. "I can't stay long. I need to leave before nightfall to get back to Guthrie in time." He said grace and ate the food with relish.

"What about your claim?" Father broke the silence after they all had eaten a few bites.

"I'm helping a shopkeeper who broke his leg. As soon as it's healed, I'll come home. Gotta be here in time for spring planting. It'll keep me plenty busy, but I've never been afraid of hard work."

America had never seen anyone who worked as hard as Rick. How he had ever managed his own claim while helping them so much had always mystified her.

"I wish I could pay you for all the things you did to help us." Father must have thought the same thing.

"I told you. Sharing your family with me helps me not miss my family so much. And learning how to read is something that I can use for the rest of my life. I could use some learning on numbers, too." He grinned at America. "I think I've been looking at the verses where John baptized Jesus. Another list of words to look up."

A smile jumped to America's face in spite of her determination not to care. Now was a good time to use her idea for the Gospel of John.

Mother took over washing the dishes and enlisted Bert's help in drying them and putting them away. "The boys don't need to study today. We've had lessons every night."

Did embarrassment cause a light pink to cross his face? She would accept it. "That's okay, because I had a special lesson plan for you this week. I was disappointed when you didn't come."

"I'm sorry. I couldn't send a letter, and I left in a hurry." He opened his Bible to John, his paper filled with his awkward letters, his dedication to his studies obvious. "Reading the Bible slow like this makes me think about it. I keep thinkin' on how the dark can't understand the light. Made me think how people who don't know Jesus make fun of Christians."

The light in his eyes warmed her all over. "That's good. I have a challenge for you tonight." Instead of saying chapter three, verse sixteen, she said, "Turn to the next page."

When Rick turned the page, she pointed to the verse she had circled with her pencil and wrote down the date she had become a Christian—*April 10, 1887, Easter Sunday.*

"I bet you already know this verse. Back in St. Louis, our preacher quoted it every time he gave an invitation at the end of the service. See if you can tell what it is."

❧

Rick looked at the print, focusing on the print and not on America's bright eyes that brimmed with delighted surprise. *F-o-r.* He held up four fingers. "*Four?* The number?"

"No. It's what teachers call a preposition."

The next word he had memorized already, it showed up so often. *God.*

S-o. He grinned at the thought of God with a needle and thread. Maybe it was another one of those prepositions or whatever.

L-o-v-e-d. He sounded it out slowly. *Loved.* When he reached that point, he knew exactly what verse it was. He held the Bible before him, pretending to read it word for word. "For God so loved the world, that he gave his only begotten Son, that whosoever believeth in him should not perish, but have everlasting life."

America clapped. "You recognized it!"

"*For God so loved.* Who could forget words like that? It must be one of your favorites."

He loved the way pink flushed into her cheeks. "Our pastor preached on it on the day I was saved. I never forgot." America leaned in, close enough that he could kiss those lips if he stretched forward by merely an inch. He cleared his throat and returned his attention to the reading lesson.

By the time America had explained how to read the more difficult words in the verse, the time had come for him to leave. Rick gathered up his courage to approach Mr. Barton. "May I take America for a walk?"

Henry's look showed he suspected Rick's reason for asking permission. A half second passed before he nodded his approval.

Rick offered America his arm, and they walked over the ground. Ahead of them, the trees by the creek were stripped of leaves, a travesty for the music singing in his heart. He told America amusing stories from the store, without mentioning the young ladies who tried to catch his eye. America talked about the calf Daisy expected in March and Rover's latest antics. She had changed from the woman he had met last September, more at ease on the prairie now.

For all he knew, the only interest Harriet America Barton had in him was a man in the need of reading 'n' writing 'n' arithmetic. No, they shared something more—friendship.

A week later, Mr. Barton led Rick aside before the Sunday service. He led him to a grove of trees, where no one could overhear. "What are your intentions toward my daughter?"

Rick held the breath he wanted to blow through his mouth, and sent up a quick prayer. "I wish to court her, sir. With your permission."

Mr. Barton nodded without speaking. He stuffed his hand inside his coat, where the top button was undone. "My wife and I have talked about this." He smiled through thin lips. "We had to make a time when America couldn't overhear us."

When Mr. Barton said no more, Rick felt compelled to break the silence. "I know at the moment I have little to offer. But I work hard, and I promise to love, protect, and provide for her and any children the good Lord might give us." Flames burst onto Rick's face at his honesty, but America's father deserved the truth.

Mr. Barton heaved a sigh. "I know, young man. You are loyal and generous and hardworking. More so than many men I know. But you. . .this. . .is not the life I hoped for my daughter. She is so young, with so much ahead." He bowed his head for a moment. "My sister offered to let America live with her while she goes to a teachers' college. To live the life she could have had. And in the Lord's time, to marry a man with similar interests."

Not an ignorant farmer. "I understand." Rick turned away.

"Come back, Mr. Eady." Mr. Barton's authority had returned. "America has refused. My little girl has grown into a strong woman before my eyes, and it scares me."

Rick waited, tamping down the hope that flickered in his heart.

"This was our decision: other qualities are more important than the amount of education a person has accumulated. The decision is up to America. But one thing my wife and I agree on." He pointed his finger at Rick.

Rick froze, wondering what obstacle Henry was about to throw his way.

"America is too young to marry. If you ask, and she says yes, you must wait a year before you wed."

Rick's heart took flight. "Jacob waited seven years for Rachel. I figure I can wait a year."

Chapter 7

When Rick ground-tied his horse as the Bartons dismounted from their wagon, America took an involuntary step in his direction. Father took him aside, and Mother took her hand, a simple pat that told her to stay still.

When the men disappeared among the trees, America's heart hammered. They startled a pair of birds with long black tail feathers who circled in the sky for a minute. As the flycatchers returned, she wished she could take their place and listen to the conversation.

"Don't stare," Mother whispered. " 'Tis unseemly."

Together they headed for their usual bench in the front, Mother's hand at her elbow as effective as a puppet's strings. If America's legs were covered by pants—perish the thought—everyone could see how her legs jerked forward as if dragging a weight behind her.

The boys raced ahead to talk to friends they had made in the congregation. Bert came back. "Ma, can Freddy and I sit with Johnny and Pete during the service?"

Ma? Can, not may? Would the boys forget good English?

Before Mother answered, Freddy said, "We promise we'll be good."

"Very well." Mother stopped a couple of rows behind their usual spot. "You must sit in front of us. If you misbehave, Father will act."

"Yes!" Bert jumped in the air. The newfound friends continued a game of marbles.

"Sit down when the music starts," Mother said.

Bert nodded as if he heard.

America and Mother sat next to each other while the benches filled and their neighbors greeted them, asking about Father and Mr. Eady. Between the boys playing a game on a Sunday and Father and Rick in a private conversation, America didn't know how to answer. At last the music began, and the boys scooped up their marbles and ran to a bench up front. The men returned, smiling, and America relaxed.

As they rode to the soddy after the service, America wondered if he would ask her for another walk. In case he did, she planned for a shorter lesson to make sure they had time.

The afternoon proceeded the same as last week, America pointing out another verse, from chapter six, what Jesus had to say to the disciples after feeding the five thousand.

"That's a short one." Rick quickly read, "I am." He took a second with the *that*. "Breed?" he asked. "It's spelled like *read*."

"Read the rest of the verse. Then I bet you can guess."

"Of life." Rick grinned. "The bread of life. The more I read, the more hungry I get for more of His Word."

The lesson wound to its conclusion. At a nod from Father,. Rick invited her for another walk outside.

"God has been good to us, giving us such good weather on Sundays." A storm would bring a halt to their walk as well as Sunday worship.

Rick looked around as if he hadn't noticed the sunshine. The soddy fell behind them as they strolled through the dead grass toward the creek, Rover romping along. Man and dog played fetch with a stick.

When they reached the creek, Rick held on to the stick. Rover whined, placing his paws on the knees of Rick's pants. At that point, he reached into his pocket and gave the dog a piece of jerky. "Maybe that will keep him occupied for a few minutes. I've got more."

"Bribing Rover, I see." America's heart beat faster.

He smiled. "I'm having a hard enough time getting together my courage to talk to you without Rover's help."

America held her breath. Did Rick mean what she thought he did? Her head said she was too young, that she didn't know what she wanted. Her heart had a different opinion.

"Your father asked about what my intentions toward you are." Rick looked at the ground.

He didn't sound happy. Did Father say no? America's heart plummeted.

"And I told him I wish to court you, if you agreed."

Courtship. What would her friends back in St. Louis say about a farmer standing in an empty field in the middle of winter offering romance? But she was no longer one of those girls.

"What did he say?" She wouldn't reveal her heart, not until Rick had spelled it out.

"He said yes."

America closed her eyes and leaned in for a kiss. His finger touched her lips then left.

"No kissing. Your father was very clear on that point." He shifted his feet. "He also said we have to wait for a year before we can get married."

Was he going to propose? Confusion and delight wrestled within America.

He looked straight at her, his eyes dark brown pools where she could drown. "Unless you object, I want to spend as much time together as we can, Miss Harriet America Barton. What do you say?"

America didn't hesitate. "I would like that very much."

Before he could say anything more, Rover broke the moment. Rick threw the stick in the direction of the soddy. "We'd better get back before your father comes hunting for us."

America laughed. Nothing could ruin this beautiful day.

The next week, Mr. Barton asked to speak with Rick again. He opened a cash box, with only a few bills and coins. A piece of paper with letters and numbers lay on top. "That's all I have left of three generations of hard work by the Barton family. I hoped I'd be a better farmer than a businessman, but so far I'm not doing well at that either." He shrugged, resigned but not despondent. "I've made my peace with it and am trusting God for our future."

He tapped the piece of paper. "I had to let go of my last earthly treasure, my mother's ring, to take care of my family. I want you to have it."

"Why?" Rick asked.

"Take it as a reminder. You're making money now. Tuck this in your Bible, and ask yourself where you want your treasure—on earth or in heaven."

Rick didn't have a chance to study the paper until he returned to Guthrie. *John* leaped off the page at him, and it was repeated twice, the man's first name and part of the last name. *John John*—oh, he knew this word. *Son. John Johnson.* The following letters and numbers might be an address or a business name. Thanks to Mrs. Adams's help, he could puzzle out the numbers, although he still didn't know how to find the place.

Below that, he recognized columns familiar to him from the store. When he worked out the price of the ring, he whistled. Even if he spent every penny of his salary, he wouldn't have enough to buy back the ring. Since Mr. Johnson would want a profit, he'd charge more than he paid for it.

Rick prayed about it as he delivered lumber for new buildings. He prayed about it as he stocked the shelves and helped customers find merchandise. He prayed for insight when he joined the Adamses for their daily Bible reading. He prayed about it through the long hours of the night. His prayers hit the ceiling so often, he thought maybe God's answer was no.

The Adamses had given Rick a bed in the back room at the store. They had settled in the 1889 land run. In the four, almost five, years since then, they had built a home and opened a thriving store. Mrs. Adams treated him like the son they had lost to typhoid as a child.

The cramped space didn't bother Rick, not after growing up in a large family. The Bartons's crowded soddy felt more like home than his own place.

To make things easier for Mrs. Adams, Rick kept his belongings neat, his bed made, and tucked his Bible and notes under his pillow for easy access. So far he had reached chapter three of John. He guessed the strange words had something to do with Nicodemus the Pharisee, but he would ask America for certain. He opened the Bible to the bookmark, Mr. Barton's receipt.

Someone knocked on the door. "Come in."

Mrs. Adams carried a plate with her. "I brought you a slice of pie."

"Any time." He closed his Bible and took the plate in his hand. The receipt fluttered to the floor.

He and Mrs. Adams bent over at the same time, their heads almost colliding. She reached it first. Surprise crossed her face as she read the heading. "What a small world. John Johnson is a good friend."

Rick's stomach snarled as he bit into the buttermilk pie.

She handed the receipt to Rick, and he slipped it into place in the Gospel of John. "I didn't know you had business with Mr. Johnson. He's a good man."

The sweet pie slid down Rick's throat like honey, and he wondered if Mrs. Adams held the answer to his prayers all along. "Not yet, but I hope to."

"Your unspoken request." She opened the door. "Come over to the house. Maybe my husband can help."

Walking the few feet to the Adamses' one-room house, Rick asked God to give him a sign. Step by step, he felt more at peace.

"What business do you have with Johnny Johnson?" Mr. Adams asked.

Before Rick finished a single sentence, he found himself talking about an opal ring and America. Chunk by chunk, they pulled the story out of him, until he revealed every detail: his desire to return the ring to the Bartons and his lack of money.

The Adamses looked at each other, and Mrs. Adams nodded as if her husband had asked a question. He said, "We've been praying, too, asking God if we should follow our hearts. God's brought us to the same place, so we can help each other."

Mystified, Rick nodded. "I'm ready to hear it."

Mr. Adams tapped his leg. "This old peg of mine isn't healing the way it should. Doc warned me I may hobble a bit till the end of my days."

I can't stay here. My claim. Rick wanted to protest, but he had promised to listen.

Mr. Adams swept on. "You promised to work for me until the second week of February."

"I wondered if that had anything to do with Valentine's Day." Mrs. Adams's cheeks dimpled.

"I am hoping to see America on Valentine's Day, but I can work until the beginning of March if you need me."

"That's not what we mean." Mrs. Adams waved his suggestion away. "By mid-February, my husband should be ready to clerk in the store. But we still need your help with deliveries. We wondered if you would switch your schedule: stay on your claim five days a week, and help us out for two days a week. We'd appreciate it."

"I'll think about it." A salary would guarantee an ongoing source of cash and give him time to make his farm profitable. "I would consider it." Unfortunately, it wouldn't solve his desire for immediate money, leaving his dreams in the cold.

"I will speak with Johnny Johnson on your behalf." Mr. Adams smiled widely. "I am certain we can come to an agreement which will answer your heart's prayer."

∞

February 14, 1894. America wrote the date on the slate board she used with the boys when teaching their classes. Bert was sweet on a girl at church—she knew it when he showed her the worms he had dug up for fishing—and Freddy thought the world of his teacher at church. After she told them about the history of the day, they made valentines to deliver next Sunday.

Her valentine for Rick was almost finished. One of America's hair ribbons outlined a heart shape, and she made a flower with a handful of mismatched buttons. She had written *Happy Valentine's Day* in her best script, but she couldn't decide how to sign it. Did she dare say "I love you"? Should she sign it "Your friend"? Should she give him a valentine at all?

When Rick came home last weekend, he didn't say a word about Valentine's Day. Maybe she shouldn't give him a valentine.

Bert copied the valentine greeting in his best script, a skill she had taught him since their arrival in Oklahoma. "You did a good job," she said. "Betsy will like it."

Red jumped to Bert's face. "It don't matter." He stayed busy, adding pictures of Rover and a field of flowers.

"It *doesn't* matter." America feared she fought a losing battle.

Freddy's pencil scratched across his paper, teeth biting his lip. He had lost his first tooth. America remembered when he was a sickly baby. Now he was a strong, healthy boy, loving the time he spent in the meadow and among the trees. "Do you ever miss our home in St. Louis?"

What would happen if someone in their settlement needed a doctor? Molly Green, her friend, had said a few months ago that trusting God was the same wherever you lived.

Freddy shook his head. "We never had a dog in St. Louis." By the time he grew up, St. Louis would only be a hint of a memory.

Bert picked up a yellow crayon to add a sun to his meadow scene. "Do you miss St. Louis?" he asked.

Did she? "I miss our house." Her friends stopped writing after a couple of letters. "But God is here, and my family is here. And I can't wait to see Oklahoma in the springtime. People say it's beautiful."

As soon as Freddy finished forming the *y* on his paper, he ran to the door. "The sun is shining. Can I take Rover outside?"

The puppy, twice as big as he was at Christmas, ran in circles, barking and waving his tail.

"Let me check your schoolwork." America kept a serious look on her face, but both her brothers had done a good job. Almost as good as Rick's efforts.

She had to stop thinking about Rick.

"You did well. And, yes, you may both go outside."

America put away the study materials and joined Mother by the fire pit, ready to take out the seams in Bert's clothes. Her brother was growing out of clothes faster than they could keep him in pants.

"Keep an eye on the boys." Mother's smile was kind. "And thank the Lord that He loves you so much that He sent Jesus to earth, just for you. Any other kind of love just makes life sweeter."

America slipped into her coat and opened the door, welcoming the warming air. An hour of daylight remained before sunset. In St. Louis, she'd look at a clock for the time of day, not for a sky blocked by buildings.

Here, daylight made the difference between inside and outside, without streetlights or lanterns glowing through windows. A bobwhite issued its call, and another answered.

Her ears remained cued to the boys' chatter, but her gaze focused to the west, waiting for God's daily masterpiece of the setting sun. The store where Rick worked lay to the west.

When Columbus sailed west, people feared he would drop off the edge of the world. Instead he found the New World. What did Oklahoma resemble more—the edge of the world or a new world? Her thoughts circled back to Rick, one of the fixtures of her new life.

In the distance, a figure on horseback galloped across the prairie. A featureless, tall, dark figure, he could have been anybody. But her heart knew it was Rick.

Oklahoma was definitely a new world.

Chapter 8

Rick and his brothers had teased their sisters when they played dress-up; they'd put on Ma's old dresses, pretending to be princesses in need of rescue.

Today, he wished he had paid more attention to their play. If he ever saw a princess, she would look like America. In the dim light, her red woolen hat circled her dark hair better than a crown. Her sturdy blue coat suited her better than a royal robe. She was a prairie princess, ready to hold a child in one arm and a weapon in the other.

She could command an entire army, and they would obey. Although he was one man, this soldier would do everything in his power to protect and serve her, to love and honor her. If only she accepted his hand.

Time stood still. His horse had stopped moving, awaiting a sign from Rick before plunging into battle. At this distance, he couldn't read the look on America's face. He touched the pouch that held his deepest dreams. With courage born of love and faith, Rick signaled Prince to move.

The pounding of Prince's feet broke the tableau. Rover ran the distance, tail wagging tall.

"Rick!" Freddy ran after the dog, Bert keeping pace.

America took a couple of steps then stopped. The darkening sky hid her eyes, her expression unreadable, uncertain. He dismounted and said hello.

"It's Wednesday." She looked more puzzled than happy.

"They let me take a few extra days this week." He dismounted and led Prince to the lean-to. Daisy mooed in welcome, her sides bulging with the soon-to-be-born calf. He noticed improvements to the building and their equipment and felt relieved.

The boys followed Rick around like dogs on a hunt, but America stood immobile by the door. The time had come to put act one of his plan into motion.

The boys pulled his arms, leading him to the door. Mrs. Barton stood at the entrance. "May I have a moment alone with America?" Rick asked the boys, but he looked at Mrs. Barton for permission.

"Certainly. Boys, come inside. Supper is nearly ready."

"So." Rick looked at America.

"So." She smiled shyly.

"Let's head for our favorite cedar tree." He linked their arms together as they walked toward the tree. He loved this time of year, when the first hints of the coming spring could be felt. Night no longer lasted after the rooster crowed, and green showed up now and then, until another cold spell stepped in. Did America appreciate the beauty of the land?

"I was just thinking today how much my life has changed since we came to Oklahoma," America said.

"For the better—or for the worse?" He thought—he hoped—he knew her answer.

She touched a tiny bulb at the end of the tree branch, the promise of leaves and fruit and harvest to come. "Oh, for the better. No doubt."

His last hesitation flew away with those words. "I had to come today." He reached inside his coat for his homemade valentine. "Happy Valentine's Day, America." He handed her the card that had taken hours to read, write, and correct a dozen times before he had it perfect.

She unfolded it and started crying.

"Don't cry. The ink will run."

She laughed through her tears, clutching the page to her chest. "I don't care. If it stained my blouse, I would cherish it until I die." She held the card open and read the words aloud. *Happy Valentine's Day.* "*Charity. . .beareth all things, believeth all things, hopeth all things, endureth all things,*" *1 Corinthians 13:7. I love you.* Her voice faded even as her face burst into flame.

"Mrs. Adams found the verse for me. Our preacher in Texas taught about the 'love chapter.' He said *charity* is one of those old words, that today the right word is"—he hesitated.

"Love. Charity means love," America finished.

"And that's the way I feel about you."

Tears tickled her ears. "When you didn't mention Valentine's Day last weekend, I thought you didn't want to do anything for Valentine's Day." A single tear slid down her cheek. "And I couldn't stand it." A hiccupped laugh interrupted her words. "I was so confused. . ." Her voice trailed away. "Promise me you won't disappear while I go inside."

"I'm ready to come in now." He swung his saddlebag across his shoulder, his hand touching his chest, reassuring himself that his other surprise was still there.

"You have to wait." She twirled, her skirt sashaying as she walked toward the door.

"If you're not back in ten minutes, I'm coming in," he said.

She moved her fingers, letting him know she had heard. Rick wanted to gather the animals and stampede the soddy, breaking it down to claim his bride. Instead he counted *one-Mississippi* until the number reached three hundred, and he started again.

If one valentine made America so happy, Rick felt encouraged about his other surprise. His heart didn't agree, pounding his chest until it hurt.

∞

America looked at her homemade valentine. After the extravagant touches Rick added to his, not to mention his perfectly formed letters, her simple card felt inadequate.

If Rick worried about that, he wasn't the right man for her.

Stop dillydallying. She took her freshest quill, dipped it in ink, and added the message her heart whispered. *With love, America.* While the ink dried, she drew a heart with red-and-white stripes filling the bottom, along the point, and solid blue on the top half: symbolizing her name and her heart.

She heard a light tap on the door and flew to open it.

Rick removed his hat and held it across his heart, offering himself as a gentleman caller. "May I come in, m'lady?"

The boys had the good sense not to speak, their eyes wide and dark as if they didn't recognize their visitor.

"Of course." She took his coat and hung it on a peg by the door. All eyes fixed on her, awaiting the next scene in this play.

Freddy pulled on her arm. "When are you going to give him your valentine?"

She swallowed the giggle that threatened to escape, a remnant of the schoolgirl she had left behind in St. Louis. "I made this for you but didn't know when I would see you again. It's nothing fancy." Enough excuses—she handed him her card.

His fingers ran around the ribbon-wrapped curve of the heart. "I loved the way the yellow ribbon looked in your hair, a ray of sunshine over a cascade of shining coal. And this button." He pointed to Bert. "You lost it when you climbed the tree when we were collecting the mistletoe." He ran his finger over the letters. "Happy Valentine's Day." He read it with ease, although he must have known what it would say.

He had taken such care with adding the Bible verse, she wondered if she should have added something more. No, keeping it easy to read was the right decision.

He came to her signature, and his ears turned bright red. He cleared his throat. "I love it." The valentine went into his pouch.

Hope and love and something she didn't dare to name beamed from his eyes. Before he had a chance to say anything else, Mr. Barton came in. "Rick. I didn't expect to see you today?" The sentence ended as a question.

"No, sir. I have news for all of you."

"You can tell us while we eat." Mrs. Barton served them each with a bowl of beans.

"Mr. Adams offered me a job."

America held her breath, fearing he would say the Adamses wanted him to move there permanently.

"He wants my help with deliveries."

America's heart plummeted to her feet. Rick said he loved her, but he was moving away.

"I'm afraid you'll be seeing more of me." He grinned. "I'll work for the store two or three days a week, but I'll be right here most of the time."

America released her breath in a smile.

"Not only that." Leaning forward, he traced lines on the table like a map. "He wants to open up stores in the new towns springing up along the Cherokee Strip. I told him about your background, Mr. Barton. If you are interested, he'd like to speak with you about opening a store here." He glanced at America. "When I go back, on Monday."

"A store?" Father sat stone-still, like he did when he was thinking hard. "Did you tell him what happened to the store I managed in St. Louis?"

"He don't care. Oklahoma is all about second chances and new beginnings."

Father leaned across the table to shake Rick's hand, and Rick met him in the middle. The pouch beneath his shirt fell to the floor by America's feet. When he reached for it, he dropped to his knees and removed a small box from the bag.

Breath fled from America's body, her toes curling inside her boots in anticipation.

"Harriet America Barton. Your beauty captured my heart the day I met you, and my love has grown every day, as I have come to know you in good times and bad, at work and at play."

America wriggled on the inside, her eyes drinking in his earnest expression and the burning light in his eyes.

"I have dreamed of this day for weeks, and with Mr. Adams's help, I have what I hoped to offer you." He opened his hand, revealing a small black box.

A ring box, tied with ribbon.

She waited for the question that didn't come. Instead he handed her the box. "Untie the ribbon before you open it."

The ribbon looked like gold-colored satin. A scrap of paper was folded beneath the ribbon. Written in clear block letters, she read the message aloud. WILL YOU MARRY ME? Her mouth dried, and she couldn't speak.

"Will you? Marry me?" Rick reached for her hand.

"Yes!" Her answer burst from her.

His smile spread across his face like the coming of dawn. "Open the box."

"Ooh, he bought you a ring." Bert leaned against America's arm to see better, but Father lifted him straight in his chair with the back of his shirt.

America didn't care who was watching or whether the ring was plain or fancy. Any ring was a symbol of Rick's love.

What lay in the box was so much more.

A perfect opal set between two bright rubies, held in place by twining gold filigree. *Grandmama's ring.*

"America, I give you this ring as a symbol of our promise, for a wedding and a life together." He slipped the ring on her finger.

He helped her to her feet and swung her in a circle. When they stopped, he leaned in for the kiss. Her joy knew no bounds as past and present collided, the ring a symbol that connected them, now and forever.

Bestselling author Darlene Franklin's greatest claim to fame is that she writes full-time from a nursing home. She lives in Oklahoma, near her son and his family, and continues her interests in playing the piano and singing, books, good fellowship, and reality TV in addition to writing. She is an active member of Oklahoma City Christian Fiction Writers, American Christian Fiction Writers, and the Christian Authors Network. She has written over fifty books and more than 250 devotionals. Her historical fiction ranges from the Revolutionary War to World War II, from Texas to Vermont. You can find Darlene online at www.darlenefranklinwrites.com.

PROVING UP

by Carla Olson Gade

For ye shall go out with joy, and be led forth with peace: the mountains and the hills shall break forth before you into singing, and all the trees of the field shall clap their hands.

ISAIAH 55:12

Timber Culture Act, March 3, 1873
"An Act to encourage the Growth of Timber on the Western Prairie."

Chapter 1

I'm ready to prove up, Nettie." Nils Svensson spoke out loud, his only audience his grove of trees. . .and God. The hearty cottonwoods, with their leafy branches, reached into the skies above in agreement.

This grove was living proof of his success at raising his acreage of trees in accordance with the Timber Culture Act. He'd planted a section of his hundred-and-sixty-acre timber claim in compliance with the original stipulation that forty acres be planted, only to meet with a loss of a fine crop the first few years. But once the act was revised and he was required to cultivate only ten acres on his claim, he had a better rate of success. Yet, he still managed to grow trees on almost thirty acres, *Gud* be praised, though Nils was the one with the aching back.

Prove up. *Ja,* it was time, only Nettie wasn't here to see it. He'd written her again. Asked her to return to Nebraska. She'd see his thriving claim. He'd prove himself to her. Prove it could be done, prove he could build a lumber mill, the first in the precinct. The county, even. The location was prime, with the Chicago and Northwestern Railroad running right through the village of Swedeburg. He'd build a name for himself. One she could be proud of. If she'd only come to him.

Nils tromped over the low brush between the cottonwoods then the green ash. The tangle of brush and vines between the narrow rows made it so he had to leave his large Percheron horse behind and travel by foot through the shady grove. He'd need some help taking inventory of the thousands of trees now inhabiting his land.

He blinked and wiped the perspiration from beneath the brow of his slouch hat as he neared the western boundary of his claim. He hadn't been this far out on his claim since early March, between tending his livestock and building his new stick house.

He made it out to the clearing by the wagon road. On the other side of the wide dirt trail lay golden fields of unbroken land, the abandoned claim of an old homesteader gone west. Nils walked along the road for a stretch, sizing up the wide-open space that he coveted for his own. *It wasn't a sin to want it, Lord, was it, since the land hadn't been proved up in due time?*

Nils blinked in disbelief when he neared a long patch of freshly harrowed soil. A moderate row of saplings revealed that either Hans Hokanson had returned or someone was squatting on his land—the land that Nils intended to purchase once the old man relinquished his homestead.

Nils had been saving for this opportunity to obtain the land adjacent to his own for some time. That property on the tail of the Wahoo Creek was what he needed to help expand his lumber business. By law he could enter only one timber claim, so he'd have to purchase it outright at $1.25 an acre. But it would be a *gott*—good investment. Now he'd have to investigate—go to the Land Grant Office in Wahoo. No one was going to intrude on his dream. It had already been trampled on enough.

He turned around in frustration and trudged back into his thickly forested acreage. He located a footpath worn between rows of ash trees that cut through the corner of the acre to the road back to his ranch. The dappled light filtered through the foliage, illuminating the silhouette of a woman. Was he seeing things? Nettie? Nettie! She'd come back to him!

Stubborn woman, she hadn't even sent him a telegraph so he could pick her up at the train station.

He stared at the vision of her lovely form in disbelief. *Gott Gud*, it was lonely out here without a woman. The wide brim of her poke bonnet tilted upward, and she turned with grace in her long bustled dress, standing in almost the same place she had left him in a fury that last day. He hastened his steps, astonished at the sight of his wife after all these years. He knew she'd return to him. She must have received his last letter.

Nettie wove between the trees, inspecting his work and Gud's blessing. Nils trotted down the path, but the trees now concealed his alluring wife. Just like her. She probably noticed him and baited him to follow. Toying with him, manipulating his affections, as she had often done. Even in her absence.

Nils moved through the dense grove, staying hidden behind trunks and new foliage as he followed her once again. At last, he snuck up behind her and spun her around, pulling her into a tight embrace. He pressed his mouth against hers, and she trembled. Her lips tasted like sweet nectar.

But his thumping heart gave way to pounding fists against his back. Her arms flailed, and he grabbed her wrists. When he looked into the woman's horrified face, she kicked him in the shin and yelped, "Mr. Svensson!"

Nils leaned down and rubbed his throbbing leg. Through his gritted teeth he ground out, "You're not *min fru!*"

"You beast!" The woman before him clutched the sides of her long dress. She ran several feet, only to trip over a tangle of gooseberry briars, falling to the peaty earth.

Nils hobbled after her and hollered, "*Vänta*—wait! You are not Nettie!"

She looked back over her shoulder as she scrambled to get up on her feet. "Stay away from me, you troll!" she hollered at him with an unmistakably Swedish lilt.

Upon reaching the woman, he grabbed her by the waist, and she kicked her legs in the air. "I am no troll." *Though I surely am a* dumbom—*idiot!* "You are safe here. . .but you are *intrång!*"

He plopped her down, and she looked at him, aghast.

"Trespass! Hmph!"

"Ja, that is what I said. You are trespassing on my plantation."

"And **you** were trespassing on my person."

"I thought you were min fru—my wife."

Strands of dark blond hair spilled out from beneath a brown straw hat that sat askew on her head. "I understood what you said. I am *Svenske,* too. Isn't nearly everyone in Saunders County?"

"If you mean Svedeburg, Malmo, and Mead. . .ja." He tossed his palms up. "I can tell you are Svenske, but how am I to know who you are?"

Then, through her mask of consternation, he realized that she was his elusive neighbor from a homestead some miles away. He'd seen her only on occasion, the last being when he went by to pay his respects after her husband had been killed, offering to help her if there was a need. She'd assured him that she would be fine with the help of her brother and brother-in-law and seemed offended by his asking.

"Mrs. Lindstrom? Truls Lindstrom's wife?"

Dirt was smudged beneath one of her high cheekbones, her deep-set blue eyes ablaze.

"I am. . .was." She straightened, smoothing her skirts. "Am."

"Ja, I know you now—despite the dirt on your face." *Who could forget such striking beauty?* He managed a slight grin, hoping to allay the awkward conversation.

Mrs. Lindstrom released an exasperated breath. She slipped a handkerchief from beneath the cuff of her jacket and swiped at her face.

"You, ah, you missed." He hesitantly reached out but then brought his hand to his own face, signaling where she should wipe.

She took a step back, obviously still intimidated by him, and duly wiped the bit of earth from her face.

He found himself distracted by the light spattering of freckles across her nose, until she spoke again.

She took a breath, and at last her countenance softened. "You must miss her very much."

Nils narrowed his eyes in question.

"Your wife. I take it you were expecting her, ja?" She pushed loose tendrils of hair beneath her bonnet.

Nils looked at the ground, and his jaw tightened. He looked up, stiffly. "Ja, it did not occur to me that it might be any other woman."

Mrs. Lindstrom blinked.

"Please accept my apology for frightening you."

"That is not all you did, Mr. Svensson." She hiked her chin with a chastising pause. "But I will consider your apology."

"Will you also consider telling me what brings you to my tree claim?"

"I will." She gave a quick nod.

He inclined his jaw, beckoning her answer.

"I am interested in your trees. I went first to your soddy, but you were not there."

"So you came out here to find me?"

"I believe it was *you* who 'jumped in the mad barrel,' Mr. Svensson." She covered her mouth with her kid glove, her lips curving slightly beneath it.

Nils laughed at the old-time Swedish expression about the man who chose wrongly and ended up in a barrel of tar. He placed his fist over his mouth and cleared his throat. "Ja, I suppose I did. You must call me Nils."

She nodded. "Likewise, call me Elsa. . .since now we are so intimately acquainted." She looked heavenward, a sparkle of mirth still in her eyes—and the tinge of pink in her cheeks belied her affront.

"I beg your pardon, Mrs. Lind—Elsa, but it is not wise for a *kvinna* to venture alone in this wild country." The muscles in his jaw grew taut. Perhaps he should not push his opinion on this woman, but he would feel responsible if anything should happen to her while she was on his land.

"I am not alone," she said. "My *broder*, Olaf, and *svåger*, Einar, are around somewhere. We are on our way home from Wahoo. Our spring wagon is out yonder on the wagon road."

"May I walk you out then? I would hate to have anything else happen to you on account of me."

She murmured something, then her voice rose. "I can manage on my own, Mr. . . . Nils." Her slender neck turned as she surveyed the uniform rows of trees. She released a deep sigh, and her eyes darted to his.

He scratched his beard. "Is something wrong?"

Her brow lifted. "If you could point me in the correct direction. . ."

Nils held forth his arm. "This way, ma'am."

"*Tack så*—thank you." Elsa nearly tripped trying to keep up with his long strides, so he slowed his pace.

"You have done quite well, despite the hardships of growing trees in Nebraska," she said as they passed by tree after tree.

He looked about proudly and smiled. "Ja. It has taken me over ten years to do so."

"Will you be ready to prove up soon?" Her blue eyes lit with interest.

"I am soon to file my papers." Nils pushed a branch out of the way and let her pass. "I could show you around if you have the time. You did say that you came to inquire about my trees."

She drew in her lips a little, and a pretty blush brightened her cheeks. "Although I'd like to hear more about your trees, Mr. Svensson, I believe I have seen more than enough for one day."

Nils swallowed a groan. "Another time then."

"Um, perhaps."

Elsa walked along in an uncomfortable silence until she tripped on a root and released a sharp squeal.

Nils caught her arm before she fell. "I've got you."

She turned her head toward him, and again their faces were closer than they should have been for a recent widow and a man who still had a wife. She released a tiny breath.

"Is everything all right here, Elsa?" a deep voice snorted. "We heard you scream."

Nils pivoted around as two beefy young men came toward them like riled buffalo. Elsa's brother and brother-in-law. He'd seen them around the village. Nice boys but a bit ornery.

"Easy, boys. As you see, I have found Mr. Svensson." Elsa offered him a weak smile. "Nils."

"Move away from her, Svensson," one of them growled.

"*Lugna ner*—calm down, Olaf and Einar! I merely tripped. Nils kept me from falling."

"Nils, is it?" Einar narrowed his eyes at him, the muscles in his neck strained.

"You know who I am." He was not in the mood for this.

Elsa turned toward Nils again. "I didn't scream, did I?" Her quick wit deflected the friction.

Nils shoved his hands in his pockets and shrugged. "Maybe a little."

She cast an exaggerated wince.

"C'mon, Elsa. We've been looking for you. The wagon is through that clearing." Olaf pointed toward the old dirt wagon road.

Nils trailed behind the Lindstroms out to the road, where the team of horses was nibbling prairie grass. As Einar checked the team and Olaf secured the tailboard, Nils followed Elsa around to help her onto the front bench.

Olaf stepped between Nils and the wagon. "That won't be necessary." Without waiting for her reply, her brother-in-law lifted her up.

Einar joined Olaf, and the young men crossed their arms over their broad chests. "You may leave her alone now."

Nils squinted in the bright afternoon light. "She was the one on my property, boys."

Elsa clutched the long ribbons beneath her bonnet. "And now, you are on mine."

Nils looked at the plowed acres, incredulous. "This isn't your property. This claim belongs to Hans Hokanson."

The sun shone down on Elsa as she scanned the golden prairie. "As of this morning, this claim belongs to me."

Chapter 2

"Any person who is the head of a family, or who has arrived at the age of twenty-one years, and is a citizen of the United States, or who has filed his declaration of intention to become such as required by the naturalization laws of the United States, may make a timber culture entry without regard to how much land he already owns."
— Timber Culture Act, *Copp's Land Owner*, 1874

She should have run.

Lord, she tried, but her legs felt like gooseberry jam after that kiss!

Of all the outlandish situations Elsa Lindstrom ever found herself in, this topped them all. Mercy, she hadn't been kissed like that since her late husband—her *man*—had kissed her good-bye nearly two years ago. And for land's sake, she couldn't tell which remembered kiss was giving her that crinkly feeling running up her spine.

If Elsa hadn't recognized him as the owner of that tree claim, she'd have been more alarmed. But she knew Nils Svensson to be as gentle as a prairie breeze and as stable as a rock bluff. He had come to her to pay his respects and offer his services after Truls died. Although they attended different congregations, she at the Mission church and he the Lutheran, reports around town were frequently heard of this respectable tree farmer. She'd seen him last August at the Saunders County Old Settlers Picnic in Mead. People came from miles around in covered wagons, spring wagons, on horseback, and on foot to celebrate their Northeast Nebraska settlement, with bounteous food and old pioneers telling of their early experiences. How could she not have noticed the stalwart man who stood like a Viking god among the throng? She recalled when his piercing gaze had locked with hers, but for a moment, and she'd quickly looked away, embarrassed for staring.

Just as she was now.

Over her shoulder, Elsa cast her discreet gaze farther down the boardwalk at Nils, engaged in conversation in front of the Saunders County Land Grant Office. J. B. Davis, the local land agent, puffed on his pipe while Nils paced like a caged animal. As if in surrender, Nils tossed his arms upward and marched down the boardwalk.

Toward her.

Had he seen her standing there spying on him?

Elsa turned and looked out at the dirt street, nothing more than an alley dividing a singular row of storefronts from the wide-open prairie. Perhaps she was mistaken and he hadn't seen her after all, but if she didn't hurry along he would most certainly run into her. She spun around and looked toward the hardware shop. Ja, she could duck in there.

112

Scurrying away like a scared jackrabbit, Elsa stepped toward the door of Solheim's Hardware. The door swung toward her as Olaf and Einar pushed their way through, arguing about some petty thing, their arms filled with cartons of farm supplies. She let out a screech as she tripped backward toward the edge of the boardwalk, the heel of her boot caught in the hem of her long skirt. Her brothers lunged forward, spilling the contents of their cartons on the ground.

But once again, the strong arms of Nils Svensson were there to save her as he landed on one knee and she fell into the cradle of his rigid embrace.

∞

Nils stared into Elsa Lindstrom's mortified face as she looked up at him, sparks in her eyes like blue speckled tinware. "Mr. Svensson! I'll thank you to release me!"

Boot heel ground into the dirt, Nils struggled to keep his balance. Elsa's corseted rib cage nested within the grip of one hand, the other buried deep within the folds of her gown, clutching some unknown body part. A thigh perhaps. He contemplated how to rise without compromising this exasperating woman's virtue—or his. Olaf and Einar instantly appeared on opposite sides of her, each snatching an arm and yanking her to her feet in a quick swoop. Nils was knocked onto his back into the street with a thud. A poof of dust rose around him, and he could feel it settle over his face.

Elsa's brothers roared with laughter as Nils stood, fists clenched at his sides. Angling his neck, he spit into the road behind him and wiped at his mouth with his sleeve. His dusty sleeve. He released a low growl beneath his breath.

Elsa's pretty brow wrinkled. "Mr. Svensson. . .Nils. I—"

He held up his hand, halting her words. The air swooshed through his nostrils as he looked down and raked both hands over his thick mop of hair.

She reached beneath the cuff of her sleeve and handed him her handkerchief. "Here."

Nils took the pristine square of linen and wiped it over his face and beard. He looked at the dirt-covered cloth and frowned. "Sorry, ma'am."

"Keep it, Nils." She offered a weak smile. "At this rate, you may find it useful again someday."

"Let's hope not." Nils stepped out of the road and onto the boardwalk, beneath the shade of the porch roof. Olaf and Einar reloaded their cartons with the spilt goods.

Einar, the more serious of the two young fellows, set his cartons on a bench. "I know you are respected in town, Svensson, but you aren't proving it by Elsa. Since my broder, Truls, is gone and Elsa has no man—no husband, it is up to us to see she is treated with respect."

"Ja, treat my *syster* the way she deserves," Olaf said. "She is a gott kvinna. No finer woman is there in all of Nebraska."

Elsa looked fondly at her brothers.

"I do not disagree." Nils cocked his head. "But maybe she can explain why she stole the property I was ready to stake a claim on right out from under me?"

Einar and Olaf scowled.

"Go load the wagon, boys, so I may have a word with Nils," she said.

Her guard dogs didn't budge. "You have no right to know Elsa's business dealings," Olaf said. "Leave her now."

"We're asking you nicely, Svensson." But Einar's face reddened.

Nils's jaw tightened. "Maybe you boys ought to show your syster some of that same respect that you want others to show her."

Olaf slammed his hat against his thigh. Einar muttered an oath.

Glaring at her brothers, Elsa planted her fists on her hips. "Enough!" Her lower lip quivered, her voice rising. "Load the wagon."

Elsa glanced meekly at Nils, and the softness budding in her eyes made his rapid heart rate relax.

"Tell me, Nils. What has you so up in arms?"

"Hans Hokanson's property."

"I told you the other day, the property is mine."

"Ja, and it has taken me two trips to Stocking to see the land agent, since he was not in his office the first time." Nils tried not to glower at the lady.

"I came to town today to pick up the certificate to my land, since it was not available the other day."

"What do you mean, 'certificate'?" Nils narrowed his eyes.

"I own the property outright, Nils. I did not have to enter a claim."

It felt like one of her brothers socked him in the gut. "How did—you can't—"

Elsa place her gloved hand on his dirty sleeve. "I'm sorry, Nils. I had no way of knowing about your plans for Mr. Hokanson's land. Didn't Mr. Davis explain?"

Nils lowered his eyes. "Don't know if I gave him the chance."

"Mr. Hokanson sent me a letter telling me he relinquished his claim with the hope that I would file a Timber Culture Act entry in his stead."

"Why would he do that?"

"Truls and Mr. Hokanson had invested in a mining scheme together in Wyoming Territory. Our investment was gone—my man was gone—and all Hokanson had left was the title to a small mine and his claim on section thirty, adjacent to my homestead." Elsa wet her bottom lip as he stared in disbelief. "He could not return our investment, but I accepted his recommendation. Was I to reject his benevolence? I'm a widow—the head of my household—with two younger bröder to consider. I believed the opportunity was an answer to prayer."

What about the answer to my prayers? Nils shifted his feet. "J. B. Davis told me the circumstances of ownership were confidential. I insisted that he show me the land tract records, but he refused. Now I understand. He did not want me to contest."

Elsa's countenance waxed apologetic.

Nils tilted his head, meeting her gaze. "Tack så, Elsa. You did not have to tell me." He shook his head.

"Didn't I?" She smiled at him sweetly. "You caught me from falling once again. Now we are even, ja?"

Nils clamped the back of his neck and looked up as the sun rolled behind a large cloud, reminding him of a great fluff of cottonwood seeds. "We may be even, but my plans just scattered to the winds."

∞

Elsa shifted on the bench as she sat in front of Solheim's Hardware waiting for her brothers to load their wagon. Nils insisted on keeping her company, the gentleman that he was. But they remained in awkward silence, save for a few idle pleasantries following their discourse regarding Hans Hokanson's property. Two older woman strolled by, and Nils nodded politely. They whispered in each other's ears before peeking back over their shoulders for another look at them. Couldn't a gentleman and a lady carry on a business discussion in public without raising eyebrows? But she was a widow, and the handsome farmer was a married man—though word was that his wife left him over seven years ago and he'd not heard from her since. Elsa shook off a chill, startled at her straying thoughts.

Olaf and Einar trotted up to the boardwalk, sporting triumphant grins.

Elsa eyed them with curiosity. What were they scheming now? "Wagon ready?"

"Ja, but we have a change of plans," Einar declared.

Olaf cocked his head. "Eh, if you do not object."

Einar continued, "Hendrik Gunderson needs our help on a lean-to he's adding to his house and some repairs on his barn."

"We would be gone for two days' time," said Olaf. "And the pay is gott, Elsa."

Her burly brother squinted. "He wants us to deliver his lumber, so we need the wagon."

Elsa crossed her arms. "How do you propose I get home?"

Their eyes darted toward Nils and to her again in an awkward dance. They weren't thinking. . .no. . .

"We are neighbors, Elsa. I can bring you to your place," Nils's deep voice interjected. "It will be gott for your bröder to have the extra work."

"Ja, see? A gott plan," Einar said.

Her eyes flitted toward Nils, and then she frowned at her brothers. "A few minutes ago you were ready to bite this man's head off."

Olaf shrugged. "We were only protecting you, syster."

"Ja, sure. Showing your pride, you mean." Elsa's lips curved into a smile. "Go on. I shall go home with Mr. Svensson." Her neck warmed beneath her calico collar. "Er, ride back to Svedeburg with him.".

After they transferred their supplies onto Nils's wagon, Olaf and Einar were on their way.

Nils glanced up, the sky filling with clouds. "C'mon now. It looks like we might be in for some rain. Hopefully we are not heading into it."

Nils escorted Elsa to his buckboard and handed her up to the front seat. She liked the way his strong hands felt around her waist. She missed that feeling—feeling attractive, being attracted to a man. How could Nettie Svensson ever have left this man?

Nils spoke, startling her out of her musings. "Looks like you will have a little break from your bröder," he chuckled.

"What break? I will have extra work to do," she quipped. "Nevertheless, they deserve an opportunity to earn some money. They have their own futures to consider."

Nils snapped the reins, and the team of horses picked up their speed. "How old are they?"

"My broder, Olaf, is twenty, and Einar, my husband's youngest sibling, is yet nineteen," Elsa said. "They are hard workers. If only they would get along better, they might be more productive."

"It is gott they have this work for Hendrik Gunderson. He won't put up with any horseplay." Nils turned his head and offered her a nice smile.

"Truls promised them that the three of them would each do equal shares of work on one another's claims. First on ours then on theirs when they came of age," Elsa said.

"So they are motivated."

"Ja, but I am anxious to get started with my plans for Mr. Hokanson's property." She offered a meek smile. "My property, I mean."

Nils stared straight ahead, looking out over the open prairie, and released a deep breath. A crack of thunder resounded in the distance, and a muscle in his jaw twitched.

Elsa squeezed her hands together. "Nils, I'm sorry your plans won't work out the way you anticipated." Why did the blessing of her new land have to come at the cost of Nils's happiness?

"*Människan spår, men Gud rår.* Man proposes, God disposes."

" 'A man's heart deviseth his way: but the Lord directeth his steps.' Proverbs 16:9."

"Is this what you believe?" he asked.

"Don't you?"

"I believe the part about Gud taking away. It takes a lot of hard work for man to achieve his goals, but it can all disappear at Gud's whim."

The wagon jogged Elsa in her seat, and then it steadied into a more even rhythm. "Perhaps there is another way of viewing it? We set our hearts on our own ideas, but sometimes Gud redirects us to give us something better."

"Is that what He did when you lost your man? When I lost my fru?" Nils's tone was curt.

Elsa nibbled her lip. *Oh dear.* "My husband's life came to an untimely end due to his discontentment. Perhaps he would be alive today if he had trusted Gud. What I do know is that I must trust Gud for my own life, regardless of the decisions of others." She'd never spoken that way about her Truls before. She looked down and wrung her hands, trying not to cry.

"Aw, I did not mean to upset you."

Elsa peeked over at Nils, his expression full of sorrow.

"There is truth in what you say," he said. "I know that discontentment wreaks havoc in a person's soul, as it did for Nettie. She could not bear to stay on the prairie, despite her promises. I tried giving her everything she wanted. I kept her in fashion and fripperies. I even bought her a piano. Imagine, a piano in a soddy."

"Perhaps she wanted more."

"Ja, a baby. But she had trouble that way." Nils's earlobes turned red beneath his hat. "It was too hard for her to stay, so she returned to Illinois with her parents."

"Hmm. . .a baby. I understand." Elsa, too, had longed for a child, but now without a husband, those dreams were also gone. "Did she intend to ever return to Svedeburg?"

"Ja, once I proved up. That's when I. . ." Nils groaned. "What an oaf I am!"

"Correction, I believe I called you a troll." Elsa grinned at him, and he returned a tight-lipped smile. "My family is from Trollhätten, so I know all about trolls. And you?"

"My parents were from Kristianstad Lan. We arrived here with a group from Illinois, led by Reverend Larson, a few years after the first settlers came in '71."

Elsa scanned the fields of prairie grass and wild spring blooms. The sun and clouds created a canopy of varying shades of green, gold, and gray over the land. "So you were born in America."

"Ja. I came from Illinois with my new bride." Nils shook his head. "She was not cut out for this life."

The clouds completely enveloped the sun now. Elsa pulled her crewel-work shawl, of Swedish lamb's wool, snug around her shoulders. "Do you hear from her at all?"

"*Nej.* I write and write, and all my letters are returned. I wonder if she ever receives them, nor has she written to me." Nils's voice became gravelly. "After seven years apart, we may not even be legally married. I am not sure."

"What does your heart tell you?" she asked softly.

"My heart deceives me, Mrs. Lindstrom." His cobalt eyes darkened as he regarded her. The wagon jolted, and she clutched the seat board beneath her. His hand flew over hers to secure her. Encompassing. Warm. Like a wild prairie fire.

Thunder cracked above, and a bolt of lightning zigzagged through the western sky. Nils grabbed both reins and snapped them over the Percherons' backs. "Ye-ah!" The team of horses bolted down the wagon road toward Swedeburg. "We might outrun the rain."

Elsa inspected the sky as her father—a man of science—had taught her to do. Dense vertical clouds towered over the horizon like cannons ready to shoot down the afternoon sky. "Those are cumulonimbus clouds. We'd better brace for a storm."

Nils pulled over to a tree break lining the side of the road. He jumped down and tied the team. "Get in the wagon," he called out.

Elsa pivoted around to crawl into the back of the wagon beneath the canvas bonnet, but barrels and crates and tools blocked her way. She'd have to get in from the back. She turned to step down from the wagon, but her shawl caught in the sideboard. As she hastened to release the beautiful mantel, lovingly woven for her on her mother's loom back in Sweden, Nils came to her aid and swooped her into his strong arms. He rushed her out of the pouring rain and slipped her inside the wagon, beneath the arched canvas tent.

April rain pelted over their heads in an unsteady staccato as the horses' restless stirrings shook the farm wagon. Elsa's and Nils's breaths mingled in the cramped space.

Elsa looked at him, pulling her damp shawl around her shoulders. "We need the *regn*," she said softly.

He removed his hat and shook off the rainwater. "Not today."

Chapter 3

"The refusal of the wife to live on a homestead provided the husband complies with the law will not injure his rights."
— Homesteads, *The American Settler's Guide*, 1885

Nils's bulky frame filled a good amount of space as he crouched beneath the canopy of his buckboard. Arms wrapped around his knees, clasping his wrist, he peered out the back where the sudden rain came down in torrents. Elsa huddled near him in the tight confines of the canvas shelter, the faint scent of her hair wafting over him like sweet Nebraska wildflowers. He breathed in her freshness, allowing himself the liberty of enjoying such a rare moment in the presence of a female. Releasing a low groan, he reminded himself that he probably smelled like a horse, and the sentiment was most likely not reciprocated. Nor should it be.

He angled his head, looking over at the pretty lady with her blond braid spilling over her shoulder. "You never did tell me what was so important that you sought me out on my timber plantation the other day."

She offered a tiny shrug. "Trees. I thought I told you."

"Ja, trees." He took the small silver notebook from inside his jacket pocket. "You mean like the ones you were sketching in your little notebook along with your notes."

Elsa's eyes lit with a smile in the dim space. "You found it!" She took the notebook from his hand and rubbed her thumb over the embossed metal.

"It was in my grove of cottonwoods. You apparently dropped it during your visit." Nils recalled how the sun glinted off the silver cover, catching his eye. But when he opened the small notebook, he never expected to see such scientific notations and botanical sketches.

Elsa flipped through the pages of the tiny pad no larger than a pack of playing cards. "Tack så *mycket*, Nils. You don't know how important this is to me."

"Why don't you tell me then?" He narrowed his eyes at her. "It appears that you have been taking notes on my tree cultivation. What is your scheme, Mrs. Lindstrom?"

"I have no scheme." She opened her mouth and then closed it, releasing a little breath of frustration. "This is personal property, and you had no right looking at it. What if it were a private journal?"

"I suppose you would have preferred not to have it back, ja? I had to see who it belonged to," he said, shifting on the crate beneath him.

Elsa wiped a stray eyelash from her cheek. "But you did not need to examine its pages so thoroughly."

Nils tossed his palms up. "I was astounded to find such scientific documentation inside. And documentation of my tree farm. Do you care to explain? And how do you fit so much into your little notepad?"

"First of all, Nils, this notebook broke off my chatelaine."

"Chat-e-what?"

"It's a French word meaning 'mistress of the castle.' Many housewives carry one of these." Elsa lifted a brooch pinned at her waist with several chains dangling from it. "See, this one is my sewing case, here is my pencil, this one holds the key to my sugar box, and this chain should be attached to my silver notebook, but is in need of repair."

"Handy little thing."

"Ja, that is why I wear it. For convenience. I find myself often in need of recording my thoughts and studies, especially of the prairie horticulture, which interests me. Primarily wildflowers. . .and trees."

"My trees."

"Nej. . . Ja." Elsa winced. "Not exclusively your trees. Although I have taken notice of your success, and that is why I was hoping to interview you on your cultivation methods. When I did not find you, I, um, took the liberty of sketching part of the timber grove. I added notations of the space between your plantings with estimations of trunk width and height, and branch span."

Nils looked into her intelligent eyes, too fascinated to complain.

She continued. "I saw that you had planted *fraxinus lameolata* as well as *populus delfoidee*. Green ash and cottonwood. And you also have *maclura pomifera*, Osage orange, out at your homestead."

"The Osage orange is a gott windbreak. Bull-strong. Makes a gott hedge for my livestock." Nils looked at her, incredulous. *Did she always speak like that, in Latin, with scientific terms?*

"The *popul*—I mean, cottonwood, greatly outnumbers the green ash on your plantation. Any particular reason?"

He dragged his palm over his bearded jaw. "I lost several acres of green ash the first few years, hazards of the dry prairie. The cottonwood is more resilient and has cultivated well. It's a useful hardwood for posts, siding, and fuel."

"Hmm." Her brow pinched with interest. "The green ash appears very healthy now, and the cottonwood is a prime example of your progress. You must have had to experiment much through the years for you to have found such success with your forestry, ja?"

"Not as many experiments as hard work and experience."

"But didn't you have to work out your experience through trial and error?"

"My error was not all that inhibited the growth of my trees. I obtained extensions three times due to prairie fire, grasshoppers, and drought. Like I said, Gud disposes. My crops were doing fine until then."

The woman looked perplexed.

"Is something the matter?"

"Nej. I was just thinking about the trials of growing trees on my own homestead. I use a scientific approach to cultivate the crop. I tend to think of the hardships simply as natural events occurring within our environment. The rest I attribute to poor choices or lack of information."

"I didn't say my methods are not scientific. But I work hard and stick with what works best."

"For instance?"

"Planting trees the recommended twelve feet apart will never form a forest. Too much space to cultivate, too many weeds to choke out the nourishment. So I thinned them out and planted them four feet apart each way." Nils lowered his chin. "But you already noted that in your little book."

"Surely it isn't a secret? Why, anyone can see your dense grove as they drive down the wagon road from Lincoln to Wahoo."

Nils shook his head. "No secret. I'm proud of my work."

"As you should be." Her lips curved. "Imitation is the greatest form of flattery, they say. I'd like to know more about your methods."

"After three years of cultivating the soil between the rows of trees, they have done fairly well with little maintenance. The narrow plantings provide short branch spans and dense shade to keep the weeds from stealing the nourishment from the ground." Nils stretched his arms out in front of him. "Initially, the green ash provided that shade and a windbreak for the cottonwoods I later planted. Those cottonwoods were to provide the windbreak for new timber on Hokanson's land." He stared blankly out the end of the wagon.

Turning back, Elsa's eyes met his, and she wiggled uncomfortably on a sack of grain beside him. He narrowed his eyes, squeezing his fist. "You knew that, didn't you? That you could use my plantation as a wind- and firebreak. Are you intending to grow trees?" Dash it! Did those freckles scattered over her pert nose have to distract him every time?

"I intend to develop a tree nursery."

"On Hokanson's land?" He frowned. "Pardon, *your* new land. So convenient. My cottonwood seeds will float over to your fields and plant themselves."

A gust of wind and rain blew in between the flaps of canvas and doused them with a light spray. Elsa wiped the moisture from her face. "I don't think it will be as easy as that, Mr. Svensson. The government distributes free seeds to anyone planting timber claims, and they must get them somewhere. But the cultivation of saplings is much more productive. I have experimented with this on my homestead with several varieties, including fruit trees, nut trees, and berries. There is no reason why I should not expand on my new property and capitalize on the opportunity to operate a nursery."

"I've every right to contest your claim, Mrs. Lindstrom. I've had my eye on that property for many years."

"Contest!"

"Ja, contest."

"And I had every right to file my own timber culture claim as the head of my family when the property became available." She crossed her arms and stared daggers at him. "Don't you already have enough land?"

"I have three hundred and twenty acres. My homestead and timber claim."

"As I now do. So, again, we are even." She pouted. "Besides, it is not within the law to file two timber claims, so you wouldn't have been allowed possession of his land anyway."

"But I could have purchased that land outright at the government price when Hokanson relinquished it, had I known about it." A drip of water seeped through the canvas overhead and trailed down the side of his nose. "It wasn't even published."

"It was, and you needn't sob, Mr. Svensson." Her lips curved into a tiny smile.

"So we are back to formalities again, ja?" He wiped the drip away from his face. "And I am not *snyftning!*"

They stared at each other for a long moment. Hand over her mouth, Elsa covered a giggle. Her eyes twinkling. Mocking.

"I see no humor in it," he murmured. He tugged on his jacket and recalled the letter he'd picked up while in town. He reached inside his pocket and opened the envelope. Maybe the insensible woman would remain quiet for a while if he occupied himself with something else.

The postmark was from Illinois. When the postmaster handed him the letter, he'd assumed it was just another of his returned correspondences to his wife and stuffed it in his pocket. But now he saw the return address of Nettie's father. As he read through the brief missive, shock jolted through him like a bolt of lightning. His hands dropped to his thighs, trembling.

Elsa clasped his sleeve. "What is it, Nils?"

"My wife is dead."

❧

Elsa's heart sank at the word—so familiar—that Nils spat out of his mouth like a bitter seed. Dead. His spouse was dead. Just like hers.

Without even looking at her, Nils pushed back the canvas flaps and leaped from the buckboard into the pouring rain. She lunged forward, watching out the tail of the wagon as he dashed like a pronghorn antelope into the tall prairie grass and fell to his knees.

Her mind reeled, not knowing what to do or how to comfort a man like Nils

Svensson. *Gud above, meet this man in his grief and loneliness. Comfort him in his loss, I pray. Help him to draw near to You and find the peace that You gave me in my own time of grief. Blessed be the name of the Lord.*

Before she realized what she was doing, she was there with him, in the field of grief, kneeling beside him in the wet grass. She said nothing. But apparently her heart spoke everything he needed to hear at that moment. The moment he turned to her and wept.

Chapter 4

"A woman may commute her deceased husband's entry and receive a patent in her own name, and afterwards may make another homestead entry in her own right."
— Timber Culture Act, *Copp's Land Owner*, 1884

Elsa trickled water from her tin watering can into the pot of geraniums set on the deep windowsill of her sod house. A beam of sunlight peeked through the square opening, spilling its blessing onto the bright red flowers. The geraniums thrived from the sunlight of the open prairie; if only her trees would grow so well. But on her new land, trees would have the potential to thrive, and she relished the thought of it.

She pulled back her white lace curtains, thankful for the real glass windows Truls had installed in their modest home made from the earth. While some prairie dwellings used oilcloth instead of glass, over time, Truls had provided her with the best he could afford to aid her comfort on their rural Nebraska homestead. With whitewashed walls papered and plastered, a ceiling covered with cheesecloth to keep out the insects, ample furnishings, and a fine hay burner cookstove with which to feed her hungry brothers, she could not complain. She also had bountiful quilts and a fine feather tick mattress to rest comfortably upon after each long day of work on her homestead.

The many tears spilt upon her pillow after Truls had left in search of greener pastures in his scheme with Hans Hokanson had magnified tenfold when she learned that Truls had been killed in a mining accident, making her a young widow. Elsa thought of Nils, whose own grief had increased through the loss of his wife. What measure of sorrow must he be going through to have lost her once when she returned to Illinois after only a few short years on their claim, and now to learn that she would never return to him again? The poor woman was dead, and Nils was now a widower.

Did God really take away so freely, as Nils thought? Or did He bless and give life? A time for everything the *Helig Bibel* said. A purpose for everything under heaven.

En tid att dö—a time to die.

Elsa wiped the tears that pooled in her eyes. Were her tears for herself. . .or for him? How shameful that she had fleeting feelings of attraction for this man. After his kiss, she had not been able to dismiss the surge of life that infiltrated the core of her being. Yet he was a married man. A married man that tasted of salt and spice. Smelled of the sweet earth and hard work. A man, now, no longer married. And she felt miserable about it.

Elsa placed her watering can on the small oak table beneath the window. Looking past the potted geranium, she viewed the belt of trees her man and brothers had planted.

En tid att dö; en tid att plantera—a time to die; a time to plant.

A time to plant! What had Nils been planning to do with Hokanson's acreage? It was not Gud who took that away from him, it was she!

Elsa stirred the *Kalops*—her traditional Swedish beef stew—simmering on the burner of her stove. The boys would be in soon for the noonday meal. She lifted the towel off one of the loaves cooling on the table, but even the yeasty aroma of the rye bread did nothing to ease the unsettling feelings flitting through her. She flipped the loaf onto the table and placed it on the cutting board. As she worked, she could not help but be reminded that Jesus was the Bread of Life. Hope warmed her heart the way the promise of spring warmed her cold Nebraska winters. The way the Svenske people looked forward to the new sun of May. Before she knew it the old Swedish song "*Sköna maj*"— "Beautiful May"—was upon her lips.

"Beautiful May, welcome, our playful friend!
Godlike flame of feelings awakes at your light.
Earth and sky are filled with love and delight.
Sorrows flee in springtime, happy smiles from tears.
Now from the bosom of a grove, and from the flower's fragile bud,
Rise to meet you, happy victims up."

When Elsa reached the last two lines, deep male voices joined in her cheerful melody. She looked up, smiling with glee as Einar and Olaf joined her at the table, singing heartily. Her voice nearly caught in her throat when Nils entered the soddy behind them.

"Nils, how nice to see you."

"And you, Elsa." He dipped his chin and removed his felt hat, revealing thick brown hair that hung just above his collar. "You have a fine voice. Nettie used to sing that one. It is gott to hear it again."

She smiled sympathetically and continued to hum the tune.

Einar peeked into the pot of stew. "And it is gott to hear our syster singing. She is our own Jenny Lind, but she has been melancholy for days."

Elsa averted her eyes from Nils, knowing it was thoughts of him and his situation that troubled her so and had her moping around. She finished slicing the loaf and retrieved several bowls from the cupboard.

"Nils, you are welcome to join us for lunch."

"Tack så. It does smell delicious."

"What brings you by?"

"I came to see if your bröder could help me with a project. Just for a few days." Nils hung his hat on the hook by the door. "I will pay them a fair wage."

Elsa worried her lip. More time away from their farm meant more time away from getting the new fields plowed. But how could she say no to those three eager faces? "Well. . ."

"Olaf and Einar can leave after their morning chores and will be home each evening," Nils offered.

"Say ja, syster," Olaf pleaded with his best charming smile. "He needs us to help count his trees."

"Ja, sure." Elsa sighed and ladled the Kalops into the bowls.

"She will agree to anything to get us out of her pretty hair," Einar said to Nils.

"And pretty hair it is," Nils said.

She looked down, pretending not to hear his compliment. "All right, men. Wash up. Einar, fill the pitcher with fresh water for washing, and fill the bowl."

Einar took the porcelain pitcher to the sink and cranked the pump. "There is no water!"

Elsa and the others gathered around.

"Let me try." Olaf gave it a few cranks. "The pump's broken!"

Nils headed to the door and stepped out into the yard.

Elsa followed him. "What are you thinking?"

He said nothing, proceeding to their Aeromotor windmill like metal drawn to a magnet.

Elsa scurried after him, trying to keep up with his long strides. She stopped beside him and looked up at the metal blades, shielding her eyes from the bright noonday sun. A slight gust of wind blew her skirts, and loose tendrils of her hair whipped at her cheeks. But the windmill did not spin. Instead it rocked back and forth in an awkward fashion. One of the blades had come loose and dangled precariously.

Olaf and Einar joined Elsa and waited for Nils's assessment of the towering mechanism that powered the water supply for their well. What would they do without it?

∽

"Okay, boys," Nils said, "looks like you have a windmill that needs repair."

"Not sure how to do that," Olaf said. "And don't look at Einar, he can't do it either."

Nils offered a reassuring grin. "Gott thing I stopped by then. It won't be my first, and it won't be your last, either."

"Perhaps they can barter their wages with you for helping with the repair," Elsa suggested.

Her brothers glared at her.

"Not necessary," he said. "But if it can wait until after lunch, that will be payment enough for me."

"My Kalops!" Elsa hiked up her skirts and ran for the soddy, her long blond braid bouncing against her back.

By the time the three of them walked back to the Lindstroms' modest abode, Elsa had the stew served and was pouring fresh lemonade into glass tumblers. The smell of the meal made Nils's mouth water, and it tasted just as fine. He smacked his lips after having another piece of warm bread. "This homemade currant jelly sure is delicious on your fresh baked bread."

Elsa stood to clear the table. "I have an arbor off to the side of the house where I grow *underbart*—wonderful currants."

"You ought to sell your jellies in town. You'd get gott business, for sure," Nils said.

"I do." She smiled, wiping her hands on her apron. "The Svedeburg Mercantile sells my jellies after I make them in the fall. I also make gooseberry jam and buffalo-berry preserves. Fru Jeppson also uses my jellies at her café. I'll send you home with a jar or two to thank you for your help on the windmill."

"Tack. I won't say nej." Nils wiped his mouth and rose from the table along with Olaf and Einar. "C'mon boys, we have a windmill to fix." On their way out, he looked back over his shoulder and grinned at the pretty *Svenska flicka*. The lovely Swedish lass peeked up at him from beneath her lowered lashes, and he thought he saw her blush.

Chapter 5

"The object of the timber culture law is to promote the growth of timber by providing a method of acquiring title to public lands on condition that timber shall be grown thereon to an extent and to a period of time therein specified. The wisdom of this law is seen in the increased annual rainfall in regions heretofore subject to frequent droughts."
— Timber Culture Act, *The American Settler's Guide*, 1882

Elsa sat in her cane bentwood rocker in the shade of her sod house reading Hodges's *Forest Tree Planters' Manual.*

"In the study of forestry, nature is our greatest and best qualified teacher. To the close observer, the pages of her great book are spread wide open through the primeval forest, over the wide-spreading prairies—everywhere—covered with characters so legible, that the way-faring man, though a fool, need not err."

She was not a wayfaring fool, though at times she thought that of her late husband—Gud rest his soul. No, Elsa Lindstrom was a woman of science, like her botanist father in Sweden. She studied horticulture and forestry, and her agricultural pursuits would reflect her knowledge as far as it depended on her. Yet, it did not all depend on her, she'd learned. Nature had a way of impacting her plans, and so did Nils Svensson. He was a force to be reckoned with. Would he really contest her claim to Hokanson's property?

"That must be interesting reading there, ja?" Nils towered over her, looking down at the book in her lap.

Elsa glanced up at him. "Ja. The new *Forest Tree Planting Manual* for 1885 by Leonard Hodges."

"You seem quite absorbed." Nils wiped the perspiration from his brow.

"I am. I never tire of reading, and find the instruction useful." Elsa stared at the earth house, as if she could see through the thick sod walls. "I have a shelf of publications in the house on agriculture, horticulture, and forestry. I have copies of the *American Settler's Guide* and *Model Farms and Their Methods*, and several other books and magazines."

He cocked his head. "Sounds like you are quite a student of the topic."

"The roots run deep," she said with a chuckle. "My *fader* is a botanist for the Svenska government. He is always interested in hearing about my studies and experiences with agriculture here in America. I sent him a copy of the *United States Report on Forestry* last fall."

Nils nodded.

Elsa glanced at the small table beside her and looked up at him. "Sit and have some *citronsaft*, or if you prefer, there is *kaffe* boiling on the stove inside."

"Lemonade sounds gott." He lowered himself onto the old ladder-back chair.

Elsa poured him a cup of lemonade from the pitcher.

"Tack." Nils took a sip of the cool liquid. "It looks like you were expecting company."

"I know my bröder, and I suspected that the three of you would like some refreshment after your hard work." She passed him a plate of cookies she'd baked that morning. "May I offer you some Brunscrackers?"

"For sure." Nils grabbed a few of the flat, diagonally cut Swedish sugar cookies.

Elsa took one for herself and then looked down at the planting manual. "Horace Greeley's advice here might interest you. He says, 'Plant thickly and of diverse kinds so as to cover the ground promptly and choke out weeds and shrubs.' That is what you told me the other day."

Nils brushed crumbs from his beard. "Ja, and I learned that from my own experience."

"So did you plant more than 2,730 trees per acre on your plantation?"

"I have planted close to 4,000 on each acre."

"How many acres have you planted?"

"I entered my timber claim before the amended law in 1878 allowed ten acres, so I originally planted forty, as required, with 2,730 trees. Despite the great loss I suffered the first few years, several acres were salvaged. With the additional trees I planted, I now have twenty-eight acres, with varying amounts of trees on each, not including the timber and hedgerow on my original homestead." Nils braced his legs like sturdy elms and crossed his arms. "That is why I need the help of your two bröder to count my trees so I can file my final proof."

"It makes me tired thinking about it." Elsa smiled. "Yet you need more?"

"As I said, I have plans." Nils's jaw stiffened, but then he relaxed, letting out an easy breath. He looked out toward the treed acreage past her barn. "You have a fair stand of timber out there."

"Tack. We have a few rods of *Juglans nigra, Acer negundo*, and—there I go again, reciting their Latin names." Elsa's face warmed. "We grow black walnut, box elder, and Osage orange, but not in any great quantities. I've had my own troubles with growing a successful crop. I've experimented with many species, and now I mostly foster saplings. The rich, loamy soil and the springs in Saunders County generally make it a fine place to grow trees and—"

"Ja."

He cut me off. He cut me off! Schooling her expression, Elsa tried not to appear insulted, though she was.

But of course he cut her off, with her incessant chatter about trees. Why did she always feel wound up like a twister when she was around this man? Was it his rugged looks? His stalwart presence? His broken heart. . .that she longed to heal but couldn't imagine how?

Nils stared into the distance. Was he thinking of Hokanson's property again and his annoyance that she now had claim to the land? Perhaps a turn of topic. She handed Nils the magazine resting beneath the book in her lap. "Would you care to review the new volume of *The Prairie Farmer*?"

Nils accepted the quarterly journal with interest and flipped the pages. "Ah, here's an article about Percheron horses."

"You may borrow the magazine if you'd like," Elsa said. "There is an advertisement for rain gauges. I was thinking of purchasing one to record the rainfall in our area as a volunteer observer for the Smithsonian Institution. My fader is interested to hear if the planting of trees has indeed made environmental changes on the Great Plains by providing more rainfall to this arid climate as the Timber Culture Act boasts it will."

Nils raised his dark eyebrows. "On account of the storm we encountered earlier this week, I suspect it has."

"I have yet to see reports documenting any actual increases over the years. The Weather Signal Service of the War Department says that it will take many years to be able to draw any valid conclusions."

"You can see the evidence for yourself," he said, the corners of his lips curving.

"You are making fun of me." Elsa frowned. "I see no reason why I cannot conduct my own scientific experiments and track measurements of the rainfall in service to arborculture."

"I did not say it was a poor idea."

Elsa arched an eyebrow. "You did not say it was a gott one."

⤤⤣

Nils tossed his palms upward. This woman was so direct, he doubted her brothers got away with anything. She was as bright as one of Thomas Edison's carbon filament lamps that he'd seen at the Nebraska State Fair in Lincoln. A woman of science, and she could cook, too. He licked his lips, tasting the sweet golden syrup of the Brunscrackers. Suddenly Nils's thoughts wandered back to the day in his grove when he kissed her by accident.

"Speaking of rain, water, and such. . . How is the windmill coming along?" Elsa asked, breaking him out of his wayward thoughts.

"You'll be pumping water again soon," Nils said. "I showed your bröder how to make the repair to the damaged wheel arm. Then they will reinstall and tighten the bands." They were attentive to his instruction, once they stopped arguing about who was going to climb the tower to put it back in place. Nils stalled the quarrel when he informed them that they had to complete that task together.

"I appreciate your help. They've been doing fairly well since Truls has been gone, but they are still learning."

The woman's hands were full, for sure, but he was glad that the young widow had the help of her strong young broder and broder-in-law to help her on their farm. "They are gott young men. They just need a little guidance."

"And a lot of food." Elsa giggled. "Here, have another Brunscracker. When Einar and Olaf return, they will consume them in seconds."

"Tack. They are gott." Nils took a bite of the crisp cookie and stretched out his legs.

Elsa leaned toward him, resting her elbows across her knees. She looked at him from beneath her feathery blond lashes. "Nils—"

He swallowed, his Adam's apple bobbing up and down in his throat. "Mmm?"

"How are you doing?" she asked, her eyes taking on a calm shade of the blue sky above. "You had quite the shock the other day."

The sound of her soft voice and Swedish lilt warmed him to his toes. And he almost fell off his chair. He caught himself by digging his boots into the sod. How could his thoughts be at such odds within himself? Consumed in sorrow these past days, and troubled that his thoughts so often turned toward Elsa instead of Nettie. He betrayed his own grief. How could he answer Elsa's question?

"Forgive me, I shouldn't have pried." Elsa looked down at her lap.

"I. . .I appreciate your concern." *Oh Gud, You sent me such an angel that day when I learned my wife had died.* "You are not prying, Elsa."

She offered a tiny smile. The sympathy in her eyes entreated him to open up to her.

"It was a tremendous shock. I fear that my affection for my wife has been absent of nurturing for so many years that I almost forgot I once loved her. But then when I saw her—saw you—on my timber plantation, my hopes reignited." He stared down at the dirt beneath his feet and then looked back up at Elsa. "It took me only eleven days with the help of some neighbors to assemble my first homestead here on the Nebraska prairie all those years ago, and ten more years to build my future—but without her in it. Now the hopes of her ever joining me are gone, but this is a truth that I resisted for many years when she told me she could never return to me. After that, every letter I ever sent to her in Illinois has been returned—if not by Nettie, by her parents' interference."

Nils slid his hand over his face and shook his head. "I am ashamed to say, but some of those tears I shed in the field the other day were for myself. I have long grieved the loss of my wife. My heart has been numb for so long, Elsa." He stood and looked away but jerked back and stared at the evocative woman. "Until you."

Elsa's mouth drew open, but her words seemed to be stuck to her tongue. Her lower lip quivered and her eyes glistened as she absorbed the meaning in his words.

Nils knelt in front of her and took her sun-kissed hands in his. She remained still—speechless—her eyes searching his.

This woman, like a prairie storm, set his emotions whirling around inside him. She excited him, charmed him, maddened him, and awoke his feelings of manhood.

"*Hujeda mig*—dear me, Nils. *Jag anar ugglor i mossen*—I sense owls in the moss!" The Svenske and English words tumbled over one another like wrestling gnomes. Elsa reclaimed her hands and pushed at his chest.

Nils jumped to his feet like someone had poured ice down his back. "There is nothing wrong here. I am sincere, Elsa. Gud help me, I am drawn to you."

"Me, or my land?" Elsa stood, and her book and magazines tumbled to the dusty earth. "Would you really go this far to obtain Hans Hokanson's land? My land! I will not give it up. I have *ett framtida*—a future of my own to cultivate! I have two bröder to consider."

The muscles in Nils's jaw bunched. "Calm down, Freydís Eríksdótter—you are terribly mistaken. I am not a man to do such a thing!"

She scowled at his reference to the Erik the Red's fiery daughter. "You just did!"

"It is not like that at all." A gust of wind swooped the magazine away, and he chased it a few feet. He clutched her precious publication before it was gone forever.

Elsa snatched it from his grip and placed it beneath her *Forest Tree Planters' Manual*. She planted her fists on her hips and continued her tirade like a Viking gone berserk. "Tell me, Nils Svensson—"

In a cloud of dust, Einar ran to them, shouting, "Come quickly, Olaf has fallen from the windmill tower!"

Elsa grabbed the sides of her calico skirts and bolted across the clearing toward the windmill, Nils following on her heels. He'd never seen a woman run so fast, nor heard one pray so hard as she shouted into the prairie sky, "Gud in heaven, save my bröder!"

Nils uttered his own prayer, "Ja, and Gud in heaven, save my wits."

Chapter 6

*"Yet Nebraska accords all honor to her noble women, who in her pioneer days
endured the discomforts of these primitive habitations in the hope of future competence,
and if any people on earth should be richly rewarded for patience, which was sublime,
for faithful endurance and arduous toil it is the wives of the pioneers."*
—*Annual Report of the Nebraska State Horticultural Society for the Year 1897*

Elsa looked down into Olaf's ashen face as she knelt on the hard ground beside him. *Gud, do not take him from me, too!* She cupped his face in her hands and patted his cheeks. "Olaf, Olaf! Wake up, bröder, I insist!"

Olaf's bright blue eyes blinked open. He coughed. "You do not need to be"—he coughed again—"bossy about it, Elsa."

Elsa released a deep sigh. "Olaf! You ornery cow!" She leaned over and kissed his forehead, brushing his straggly blond hair away from his brow.

Olaf groaned as she gently lifted his head, feeling for bumps.

Elsa looked over her shoulder at the sound of Nils's deep voice. "Looks like you got the wind knocked out of you." He squatted down beside Elsa, gently patting Olaf's limbs, sides, and belly. "How far did he fall?" he asked Einar.

"About halfway down. His boot caught on one of the rungs." Einar shaded his eyes, looking up at the top of the windmill about twenty feet in the air. "At least he didn't fall from the top. He'd be a goner, or his back would be broken."

Nils offered his firm hands as Olaf rose to a sitting position. "I wouldn't have fallen at all if you hadn't been hollering at me."

Elsa glared at Einar. "What were you hollering at him about?"

"You and Mr. Svensson here." Einar narrowed his eyes. "I told him I saw you two arguing about something, and he looked to see what it was about."

Elsa squeezed her eyes shut and shook her head. "Pay attention to your own business next time, Einar."

Nils and Einar helped Olaf to his feet, and Olaf brushed the dust from his trousers.

Olaf nodded at Nils but then angled his jaw toward Elsa. "So what about it, Elsa? What were you arguing about with this man?"

"This man and I were having a private conversation."

"I hope it is settled then," Einar said.

Elsa and Nils exchanged disappointed glares. Had she jumped to the wrong conclusion about his interest in her property? Had he jumped to a wrong conclusion about her? What would make a new widower become so quickly attached to another woman? But here on the lonely Great Plains it happened all the time. Sometimes for a matter of convenience. . .sometimes for love.

Dismissing the thoughts, she took her brother by the arm. "Let's go to the house so you can rest. Though nothing seems to be broken, I suspect you will have some aches and pains for a few days."

"I will be fine, Elsa," Olaf insisted.

"Perhaps, after you have some Brunscrackers and lemonade," she said, brushing some dust from his back. "Come now, you must rest."

"And I have overstayed my welcome." Nils turned on his heel and headed toward the corral for his horse.

"Don't forget to take the magazine with you, Nils, if it hasn't blown from here to the badlands."

He tipped his hat, and under his breath she thought she heard him say, "Ja, like my dreams."

∞

Nils walked around to the front of his barn, wiping his brow after stacking a bundle of green ash cordwood under the lean-to. What a fool he'd been to think that he could tell Elsa how he felt about her. She had seemed so caring, so—he slapped his hand against the barn door—so sympathetic. But that's all it was. Sympathy.

When he'd told the young widow that his wife had died, she had followed him out into the field. . .in the rain. . .during a thunder and lightning storm! Elsa was familiar with the loss of a spouse, as hers had died not two years before. But had he mistaken her compassion for something more?

He recalled the way she stayed there with him, until he found his breath again. Until the rain stopped and his tears—and hers—had ceased. He'd never known a person with that kind of a heart. Nor that kind of a mind. A brilliant mind. But the young lady's moods changed direction like a wildfire on the dry prairie.

He hadn't thought to consider that Elsa had dreams of her own. He'd only thought of his own plans. And the loss of them, now that Nettie no longer was part of his future. But he never meant to suggest that he could so easily exchange one woman for another or that he had any intention of gaining her affections for the purpose of gaining her property. What kind of man did she think he was?

Dang it! He grew incensed at the thought of how he'd now damaged any hope of becoming better acquainted with Elsa. Though at this point, he felt as though he'd seen—and experienced—a good portion of her personal qualities. Qualities he couldn't help but be fascinated with. Elsa Lindstrom was extraordinary!

As Nils trudged toward his soddy, stripes of red and orange painted the western sky as the sun lowered itself on the horizon. Best forget about any aspirations he had toward Elsa and focus his attention on his plan of expanding his timber business. With the population of Nebraska ever increasing, he stood to make a good name for himself in the timber trade. But he needed water access on Hokanson's—Elsa's—land to build the lumber mill to support his dream.

Inside his modest home, he tossed his jacket over the back of a chair. He splashed water from a bowl on a small stand over his face. Drips of water fell from his beard as he grabbed a small towel and dried himself. Kicking off his boots, he plopped down onto his straw tick. Hands clasped behind his head, he contemplated his options for expanding his plantation. But as he drifted off into slumber, there was only one thing on his mind. . .and she had the bluest eyes in Nebraska.

∞

Elsa scanned the books on her shelves in the sitting area of her earthen home. She ran her finger down the spine of *Copp's List of Patented Mines*—the book that put the notion in Truls's head to go farther west with Hans Hokanson.

She heard a scuffle across the floor and pivoted around, hoping a prairie dog or another small animal hadn't invaded her home. But as she turned, she found Olaf stumbling from his bed in the corner of the room.

Elsa rushed toward her injured brother. "What are you doing up, Olaf?"

"I am fine, Elsa," he said, gripping the back of a chair.

She eyed him with concern. "Are you still dizzy?"

"Nej. I feel a little weak, though, from lying around these past few days." He grimaced. "All I need is to get back to work before I lose my strength completely."

Elsa placed her hand on Olaf's sturdy shoulder. "I doubt that will ever happen. You are built like one of Nils Svensson's Percherons."

Olaf stretched and clasped his brawny hands in front of his chest. "Ah, someone on your mind, syster?"

Elsa set a tin cup of coffee on the table. She'd roasted the coffee beans that morning in the hay burner stove, and the aromatic scent filled the soddy. "Here, sit."

"I've been resting long enough. Here is your chatelaine. I fixed it for you." He took a swig of the hot liquid.

"Tack så mycket!" Elsa inspected the silver notebook now securely hanging from the chatelaine, recalling when Nils had returned it to her. "How is your headache, Olaf?"

"My head is fine. So is this kaffe." He lowered himself to the bench and took another sip of his coffee.

"Gott thing you have a hard head." Elsa grinned as she served him a currant and cardamom muffin then planted a kiss on her brother's stubbled cheek.

"It runs in the family," he said, winking.

"What did you say?"

"You heard me." Olaf smirked. "I am not the only one in this house with a hard head."

"What do you mean by that, dare I ask?"

"Nils Svensson."

"What about him?"

"You tell me." Olaf leaned back in the chair. "From where I sit, it looks like he has a soft spot for you. But you push him away."

"He is a brand-new widower. He should not have such thoughts." Elsa looked away, wiping her hands on her apron.

"It is sad that his wife died, but she has not been in his life for many years. Don't you think he has grieved long enough?" Olaf angled his chin. "Haven't you?"

Elsa pushed a loose lock of hair behind her ear and rested her palm on the side of her face. "He is just interested in my land for his trees."

"Ja, and he cares nothing for his pretty neighbor?"

"Pretty?" Elsa tilted her head. "Why, Olaf, I didn't know you think I am pretty."

"You are the prettiest *kvinna* in Svedeburg. But I think it is you who do not think of yourself as pretty." Olaf's brow lifted. "It is about time that you do."

"Don't be *fjollig*."

"I am not foolish. One day Einar and I will be gone from here with wives of our own. It would do you no harm to consider marrying again someday."

"But certainly not Nils Svensson." Elsa huffed. "I have never heard of anything more outrageous." *Though Nils did imply that I affected him somehow.*

"Elsa, you cannot see the forest through the trees. That man is smitten with you."

"Me? Really?" Elsa wrinkled her nose.

"Ja, syster. Really."

She arched her eyebrow a tad. "*Tappad bakom en vagn?*"

"Nej, I did not fall from a wagon." Olaf chuckled at the Swedish proverb. "But I did fall from a windmill."

Elsa placed her hand on her hip. "That must explain this fjollig notion of yours."

Olaf shrugged his broad shoulders and chuckled. "By the way, Nils asked Einar and me if we could give him a few more days to help him with a contract to plant trees on land owned by the railroad."

"You mean after you help him count the trees on his plantation?" Elsa turned her palms upward and released a sigh.

Olaf nodded confidently. "Ja."

Elsa emitted a tiny growl. The little forest monster inside her, aching to come out. "You see! This is what he does! He is deliberately trying to take you and Einar away from your work on our farm and on our new timberland!"

"It is not timberland yet, Elsa," Olaf placated.

Elsa frowned. "And it won't be, at this rate."

"He is just trying to give us an opportunity to earn some extra money, Elsa."

"Nej. . . I can see what he is up to." She shook her head. "That man infuriates me!"

A sly grin emerged on Olaf's face. "That is because you are in love with him and won't admit it."

Elsa's mouth opened wide in shock.

"Be careful, syster, you might catch some flies like that." Olaf lifted his arm to shield his head, feigning protection from her wrath.

Elsa crossed her arms and tapped her foot on the tamped-dirt floor. "If you hadn't just gotten out of bed, I'd wring your neck."

"You would not be so angry if I weren't speaking truth, ja?"

His jesting struck a chord. "Truth! Hmmph!"

Could it be? Was she falling for Nils as her brother said? Nonsense! Besides, whether she was or not, the man had schemes, and she wouldn't be a part of it.

Elsa rattled off another proverb. "Nils Svensson *kommer inte dra mig på en tallpinnevagn*—he won't drag me on a pine-twig wagon behind those Percherons of his!"

Chapter 7

"The filing of the application and affidavit with payment of fees are essential prerequisites to the allowance of a timber culture entry and he who first complies with the conditions obtains priority of right. A prior verbal application unaccompanied by the written application etc. gives no preference right, as it is not the duty of the local officers to prepare the necessary papers."
— Timber Culture Act, *Copp's Land Owner*, 1883

Nils leaned against the clapboard siding of the Swedeburg Mercantile as he perused his proving-up notice of intent in the current week's edition of *The Wahoo Independent*.

LAND OFFICE AT WAHOO, NEB., APRIL 10, 1885
Notice is hereby given that the following settler has filed notice of his intention to make final proof in support of his claim, and that said proof will be made before the Register or Receiver at Wahoo, Nebraska, viz, Nils Svensson, who made Timber Culture entry No. 9590 for the southeast quarter of section 28, Range 4, Swedeburg Township, Saunders County, Nebraska.

The comfort of the warm wooden slats against his back, baked by the sun on this warm April afternoon, was in stark contrast to the situation that deflated his pleasure over this long-awaited moment. Sure, he could prove up on his tree claim, but to satisfy his goal of expanding his timber business and building a water-powered sawmill on the section of land next to his, he'd need to contest Elsa Lindstrom's new land patent. At what cost? His happiness for hers? No. Nils hadn't made any improvements on the land in Hokanson's absence. But hadn't he had the intention of obtaining Hans Hokanson's property if he should leave, as some homesteaders were in the habit of doing, long before the Lindstroms ever settled on their homestead claim in this town?

Nils murmured under his breath. Truth be told, he didn't know if he had it in him to do that to her.

A pair of petite gloved fingertips drew his newspaper down in the center.

"Ahem." The loveliest eyes in Saunders County, above a nose kissed with freckles, looked up at him from beneath her feathery lashes.

"Elsa."

"Nils." The pert lilt in her voice contrasted with his own flat greeting. "What do you find so interesting in *The Independent?*"

"I've filed my intent to prove up. Just checking the publication." He rolled up the newspaper and swatted it against his palm.

"Something upsetting you?" Elsa arched an eyebrow and offered a meek smile. "If you are upset with me due to the way I treated you last week, I would like to apologize."

"Treated me? Ah, your accusations." His jaw tightened. "I suppose I deserved them. I haven't exactly earned your trust."

"You deserved none of that. I jumped to conclusions." She clamped her lips together, tilting her head.

"As did I." He looked down at the boardwalk, and his own lips pulled taut within his beard.

He caught Elsa blushing when he looked back up at her. She turned away uncomfortably and fidgeted with her chatelaine. How could he have been so foolish to offer any affection—affection she misunderstood for manipulation—especially so soon after Nettie died? Having lost her own spouse so recently, she must have found him coldhearted. An insensitive philanderer. It was not the first time he had made unwelcome advances toward her, even if it was an accident on the first occasion, when he'd kissed her. No wonder it incited her rage when he implied that she meant something to him. But to further suspect that he would woo her to gain her land—it confounded him that she would think such a thing. He could never do that to a woman, and especially a woman like her.

His eyebrows dipped in apology. "I am sorry, too, Elsa."

Her eyes beseeched his, and she offered a little grin. "Truce?"

"Ja, truce." He looked past Elsa's shoulders, peering down Main Street for a glimpse of her brothers. "How is Olaf? Is he with you?"

"Nej, I've come alone today. But he is doing well. He was back to work on the farm within a few days." She shook her head. "I tried to keep him in bed longer, but he insisted that he was fine."

"I am glad he was not more seriously injured. I feel somewhat responsible."

"Whatever for?"

"I left Olaf and Einar to finish repairing the windmill on their own. I should have stayed and supervised."

"How else will they learn? They are more than capable of following your instructions."

"But then Olaf was distracted by our. . .quarrel."

"If that be the case, I share the responsibility."

Nils looked across the road at Mrs. Jeppson's café. "Would you care to have some kaffe with me and some of Fru Jeppson's famous *äpple pannkaka*?"

Elsa's face brightened. "Tack. That sounds nice."

Nils escorted Elsa across the street and entered the board and batten café, washed in typical Swedish red milk paint and trimmed with white gingerbread. The kind of wood he could provide for such buildings, as well as clapboard like the mercantile.

Fru Jeppson took their orders, returning with their food a short time later. She placed dishes of Swedish apple pancake on the table and poured egg coffee—the Scandanavian kind, boiled with egg and strained to remove the bitterness—into their porcelain cups. "*Varsågod*," she said, inviting them to enjoy the meal.

Nils licked his lips at the sight of the äpple pannkaka and then took a sip of the rich black brew. "*Smakar* gott."

Elsa held her steaming cup to her lips. "Ja, tastes gott. It is best this way."

Fru Jeppson nodded with a satisfied smile and went away humming the tune to "*Kaffevisa*," the Swedish coffee song. Elsa softly sang a verse, "Coffee the best of all earthly potions is." She covered her mouth with her fingertips, a grin tugging at her high cheekbones. "Sorry, I could not resist!"

Nils knew just what she meant, as he, too, was having a difficult time resisting this lovely woman.

⌇

Elsa glanced down at her newest issue of the illustrated monthly magazine *The Century*, eager to bring it home and delve its topics. Of course, she'd already skimmed through the table of contents and begun reading an article of interest while she waited for a meeting with the bank manager this morning.

Nils looked at her magazine with curiosity. "What do you have there?"

"It is the February 1885 volume of the *Century Magazine*. I've been waiting for this edition to arrive so that I can finish reading the last five chapters of a novelette by Grace Denio Litchfield."

"A novelette?"

"Ja, a short novel."

"You do not strike me as the type of woman who would read fiction."

"There is nothing untoward in the story of *The Knight of the Black Forest*."

"I did not mean to imply that there was. I simply meant that I thought you might be more apt to read scientific journals and nonfiction books like the ones you were telling me about when I visited your farm."

"I do enjoy being entertained on occasion."

"It must give you a break from your heavy reading. I see nothing wrong with it."

"Gott, then, I am glad to have your approval." Elsa sipped her coffee, smiling over her cup.

Nils took the last few bites of his apple pancake and leaned back in his chair. He brushed a few crumbs from his beard and said, "Tell me about this 'The Knight of the Black Forest.'"

"It is a tale of love and adventure about a German prince disguised as a knight."

Nils arched a dark eyebrow. "Love always makes a gott adventure. Don't you agree?"

Elsa's stomach fluttered as he spoke. "Sure." Suddenly self-conscious, she patted her mouth with her cotton napkin, woven with blue and yellow.

Nils placed his hand on the table, pointing toward the magazine, and the tips of his calloused fingers grazed hers. "You will have to let me know how it turns out. Perhaps I can read it sometime."

A little shiver slipped up her spine, and she found herself wondering what it would feel like to welcome his touch, not like the last time she saw him, when he took her hands in his.

"May I?"

"Oh, ja, certainly." Elsa straightened as Fru Jeppson came to the table and asked if they were in need of anything else.

Nils looked at Elsa, inquiring also. She looked up at the stout, white-haired woman with a smile. "Nej, tack." But Nils asked for a refill of his coffee.

Elsa's eyes widened as she recalled another exciting piece in the magazine. "There is a brand-new serial story by Mark Twain in the magazine."

Nils tipped his chin. "Mark Twain, ja? What is it called?"

"*The Adventures of Huckleberry Finn*," Elsa announced with glee.

"Another adventure tale."

"It is! And they say that children and adults will all be delighted to read it." She smiled. "The story is the sequel to *The Adventures of Tom Sawyer*. Have you read it?"

"Ja, I read it last winter." Nils smiled up at Fru Jeppson as she served him another cup of egg coffee. When she returned a grin his way, her cheerful gaze flitted toward Elsa. Fru Jeppson gloated like she was the keeper of a great secret. What did she think she knew?

No matter. There was nothing between Nils and Elsa except a forming friendship and a coveted piece of land.

⁂

Nils listened to Elsa prattle on about an article called "Progress in Forestry" in the *Century Magazine*. He never grew tired of listening to her sweet voice. The topic was interesting, and she was so easy to look at.

"You're staring," she said, pink tinting her cheeks.

"I'm looking at you. I could always look at Fru Jeppson while you talk. . ." Nils cast his eyes across the room at the rotund hostess of Jeppson's Café and back again at Elsa. He shook his head with a little scowl. "Nej. I like this view better."

She lowered her chin, giving him a mildly chastising look. "Let's see, the article says. . ." She picked up the magazine and found the page she was referencing. "Due to the Timber Culture Act, 'The uninhabited plains of the West described in the old geographies as the Great American Desert are fast filling up with an enterprising and prosperous population. Tree planting is becoming almost universal on the great prairies of Minnesota, Dakota, Kansas, and Nebraska, where it once was believed no tree would grow. The old notion that trees could not be grown on the great oceanic prairies has been thoroughly exploded.' " She looked up from the publication. "Oh, I'm spoiling it for you by telling you all about it."

"Nej, go on."

Elsa continued scanning the article. "It reports that over ninety-three thousand entries have already been made, with nearly fourteen million acres covered with trees. It says that many settlers have planted far more than the required ten acres, like you! Isn't that exciting?"

"That is exciting." And he loved seeing the enthusiasm on her face.

"A Nebraskan," she continued, lifting her eyebrows, "is quoted here saying, 'We have thousands of trees thirty to forty feet in height and eight or nine inches in diameter grown from seedlings or cuttings planted less than ten years ago. The fuel problem is settled for many farmers. The trees and land are already worth three times their cost. The cottonwood is a prime favorite on account of the facility of its propagation and rapid growth.' "

Nils crossed his arms over his chest with a satisfied grin but remained quiet.

"What?" Elsa's eyes widened as knowledge dawned. "Did you? You didn't!"

Nils nodded. "I did."

"You are the Nebraskan quoted here?"

"A reporter from New York was out here last fall and interviewed me about my tree plantation and participation in the Timber Culture Act."

Elsa narrowed her pretty blue eyes, lifting her chin in question. "What was the reporter's name?"

"Not sure if I recall." Nils drummed his fingers on the table for effect "Norton. . . Nordling. . . Northrop. Ja, Bryant Northrop."

Elsa placed the magazine on the table and traced her finger to the bottom of the article then looked up at him, astonished. "B. G. Northrop. You haven't already seen this article, have you?" she asked, doubting.

"How could I? Isn't it a new volume?"

"It is February's issue." She offered a smile. "But it does take some time to get here from New York."

"Then why don't you trust me when the proof is right in front of your eyes?" he asked, casting her a daring look. A woman like her needed to be held accountable. She was too smart for her own good. . .and if he wasn't careful, for his own good.

Elsa gave him a little shrug, waxing apologetic. She offered him her hand in a polite gesture. "It is truly a pleasure to know someone who has been quoted in *The Century*, Mr. Svensson. I am impressed."

"Enough to trust me?" Nils held her warm, slender hand—devoid of glove—slightly longer than necessary.

She slipped her hand from his, confusion clouding her bright blue eyes.

"Elsa, I want you to know that I've decided not to contest your patent on Hokanson's land."

"Tack så mycket, Nils." She was quiet for a minute but then tilted her chin. "You were really thinking of contesting my patent?"

"I did consider it," he admitted. "But only because of the understanding I thought I had with Hokanson. Hans knew I was interested in his land. He as much as gave me his word that if he ever were to relinquish or sell, that I could have first refusal. It took me off guard when you told me that you were the new owner of his claim. Even when you explained why."

"It was Hans's prerogative to transfer his claim to whomever he so desired," Elsa said.

So desired. His stomach did a flip. Nils couldn't tell what he desired more, this remarkable woman or her property. Was it wrong to desire such things?

Just then Reverend Larson of Grace Lutheran Church came into the café with his wife on his arm. The white-bearded gentleman, who brought the first group of Swedish pioneers to Swedeburg and began the first congregation preaching on an upside-down wagon box as a pulpit, nodded at him with a twinkle in his blue-gray eyes. Although Nils's faith could stand a little cultivation of its own, he did make an effort to attend church each Sunday. A sudden remembrance of the Ten Commandments shot into his mind.

"Thou shalt not covet thy neighbour's house, thou shalt not covet thy neighbour's wife. . ." Oh Gud, help me. I complain because You take away, when I wish to do the same.

"Nils. You do agree, ja? I did not obtain the land by illegal appropriation." Elsa's eyebrows pinched, her tone defensive.

Nils shifted in his chair, and it made a little screech across the planked floor. "I did not accuse you of that."

"Yet, that is your contention." She stiffened. "I am well aware of the land laws."

"I have no doubt that you are, with that library of yours."

"I cannot tell if that comment is meant to insult me or not."

"There is no insult. Just stating a fact," Nils said flatly. "If Hokanson relinquished his property, it should have gone up for public auction. These laws are flagrantly violated so often that soon the Timber Culture Act and other homesteading laws will be repealed. "

"I agree. Therefore, Einar, who is also interested in the land laws, and I looked into the matter diligently before we acted." Elsa fiddled with her fork. "When Hans wrote to me of his intention to relinquish his homestead, he expressed his hope that I would file an entry of a timber claim. He sent me a banknote to get me started. He said it was his way of returning the investment Truls made with him for the mining scheme. Hans Hokanson is an upright man, despite his idealistic notions. Everything was legal."

Just as Elsa peeked inside her empty coffee cup, Fru Jeppson came by the table and gave them each a refill. Elsa looked up at her, saying, "Tack," with a smile.

Nils breathed in the rich aroma of the coffee and took a sip.

"More äpple pannkaka, Mr. Svensson?" Fru Jeppson asked in her singsongy Svenske accent.

"Nej, tack. It was delicious."

Dabbing her mouth with her napkin, Elsa said, "Mmm. I agree."

Fru Jeppson said a cheerful, "Tack så mycket," before skittering away to serve another customer.

Elsa resumed their conversation. "Mr. Davis, the land agent in Wahoo, said there was no waiting period. He also commended Einar for his diligence in looking into the matter on my behalf and said he stands a chance for a promising future as a land attorney. Einar intends to go to Luther Academy in Wahoo next year if he can raise the funds. I intend to help him pay for his college education with any means I have access to."

Nils absently rubbed his beard. "That would not include selling out to the railroad, would it?"

"Now who is lacking in trust?" Elsa's voice rose an octave.

"You must have heard that the Chicago and Northwestern Railroad plans to run a line through Svedeburg. If they haven't already contacted you, they will soon enough. Before long they'll be buying up land under their employees' names and having them commute it back to them." Nils released a deep sigh.

"I have plans for my property, and despite your accusations and misgivings, it may include negotiations with you."

Nils leaned forward, resting his elbows on his knees. "Negotiations? What kind of negotiations?"

"First, I'd like to hear what you had in mind to do with section thirty?" Her lips curved into a mischievous grin. "Tell me about your dream, Nils."

Of all the. . . What did this kvinna have up her pretty calico sleeve?

"Nils Svensson! Nils Svensson!" Nils turned to see an adolescent boy in too-short trousers rushing into the café.

Nils raised his hand and stood from the table. "I am Nils Svensson. What is the matter, pojke? Is it my Percherons at the livery?"

"No, sir. The overland stage came through and made a delivery for you," the lad said, still catching his breath.

Nils looked at him, confused. "I'm not expecting anything on the stage. I pick up all my orders myself."

"She is waiting. And crying. Postmaster Brodahl said you must come at once."

Elsa put her hand on the boy's shoulder. "Who is this 'she' you are talking about?"

"The girl he ordered from the orphan train is here." The boy's eyes darted back up to Nils.

"I ordered no girl from the orphan train. It is some mistake," Nils said with a chuckle, shaking his head.

Elsa looked at Nils with concern. "Regardless, you cannot leave her there alone. You'll have to go see what this is about, ja?"

Nils shrugged and left some money on the table for Fru Jeppson. He trudged after the boy then paused, turning back and looking at Elsa. "Tell me you're coming with me, please. I don't know what to do with a girl."

Chapter 8

"The entry must be made for the cultivation of timber and for the exclusive use and benefit of the person making the entry. It must be made in good faith and not for speculation nor for the benefit of another."
— Timber Culture Act, *Copp's Land Owner*, 1883

Elsa skipped along on the heels of Nils's boots as he strode toward the Swedeburg Post Office, dually the Swedeburg Overland Stage Office. Thankfully, Reverend and Fru Larson followed them for support after overhearing the predicament about Nils's special delivery.

Mr. Brodahl scurried down the steps to greet them. "She's inside," he said. "I found a hard candy in my desk drawer, so at least she isn't *snyftning* any longer. She sure can wail."

"Who is she?" Reverend Larson asked. "Nils insists he hasn't ordered an orphan."

"I sure have not. If I needed an orphan, I might have sent for a boy to help me on my farm, but what would I do with a little girl?" Nils took his hat off and raked his hand through his thick hair. "Brodahl, what makes you think that she is for me?"

Mr. Brodahl handed him a torn slip of paper. "This was pinned to her dress."

Nils grabbed the paper and read his name and town in bold print as clear as the spring day.

Mr. Brodahl looked at Elsa and then at Fru Larson. "I don't know much about fashion, ladies, but she doesn't look much like an orphan to me. She is wearing a fine little frock and patent leather boots."

"Where did she come from, Brodahl?" the minister asked.

"Does she have a name?" his wife added.

"Her own name must have been ripped off the bottom of the paper, so I asked her." The postmaster/stage agent looked at Nils. "She won't tell me who she is, but the stage driver said that she arrived on a train from Illinois with instructions to deliver her here. To you."

Elsa looked up at Nils and could see a squall of thoughts running through his mind at the speed of her windmill during a prairie storm.

"Illinois? That is where your Nettie was from, ja?" Fru Larson asked Nils.

Nils's shoulders lifted. "Ja. Her family still lives there, last I heard."

"Perhaps the girl is a relative of the family," Reverend Larson suggested, his mouth drawing into a straight line between his long white whiskers.

Elsa placed her hand on Nils's sleeve and looked up into his eyes, roiling with confusion. She gave him a tiny nod and turned toward the small office building. She hitched the sides of her skirts as she scurried up the steps and made her way through the front door. There on a bench against the back wall, a little girl sat hugging her doll, a small valise on the floor near her feet.

The girl looked up at Elsa, her eyelashes damp with tears. Elsa offered her a gentle smile. "Is it all right if I sit here?"

The frightened girl looked at her doll and nodded.

"Tack så. That means 'thank you' in Swedish." Elsa tilted her head. "Do you know Swedish?"

"No, but my father is Swedish."

"Oh? I am Swedish, too." Elsa looked at the girl's doll and smiled. "Who is your father?"

"I don't know him. But his name is Nils."

Elsa's breath caught in her chest, but she at last released it. "I know someone named Nils. Would you like to meet him?

"Is he my father?"

"I don't know, but we can try to find out, ja?" Elsa smiled. "Your dolly, does she have a name, too?"

"Her name is Nettie, like my mama. But I don't have a mama anymore." The girl sniffed and buried her head in Elsa's side.

Elsa's heart ached for the little one. She brushed her fingers over her soft hair and pulled her close. "Oh, there now. You are not alone." After a moment the flaxen-haired girl looked up into Elsa's face with her sweet molasses eyes.

"I'm not?"

"No, why I'm right here with you. And so is your doll." Elsa smiled. "She has a pretty name. My name is Elsa. What is yours?"

"Leah."

"My surname is Lindstrom. Do you have one, too?"

Leah smoothed her doll's fancy dress and looked up. "Svensson."

Elsa swallowed. "You have a nice-sounding name. It is a pleasure to meet you, my new friend."

Nils filled the doorway, staring at the child, speechless. He approached the bench, and Elsa could see the trepidation in his eyes.

The girl wiggled closer to Elsa.

"Who is she?"

Elsa's brow wrinkled as she looked into Nils's inky-blue eyes. How else could she say it? "Her name is Leah Svensson. I believe she is your *dotter*."

∞

"I don't have a dotter." The words spewed out of Nils's mouth like he'd bitten into the bitter fruit of an Osage orange.

Elsa chastised him with her glare. "Now, Nils. . ."

He eyed Elsa in silent question. *Can she read my mind? What makes her think she is my daughter? What is this girl doing here? Why does she look so much like. . .like Nettie?* His chest squeezed, and he almost forgot to breathe. He glanced down at the blond little girl whose dark brown eyes pierced his heart with innocent inquiry. *Does this lamb think that I am her fader?*

"You say her name is Leah? Leah Svensson?" *And she is from Illinois. Delivered to me.* Nils struggled to assemble the clues.

"You may speak to her directly, Nils."

But what would he say? He stared at her rag doll.

"The doll's name is Nettie," Elsa said softly.

Nils's worried eyes widened. He swallowed hard and swooshed out a breath caught in his throat. *Breathe, man, breathe. This is only a child. My child? How can it be? I was never told.* He looked back over his shoulder and could see Postmaster Brodahl and the Larsons waiting outside on the porch. It looked like they were praying.

"Hello, Leah," he started, but even as he spoke, the muffled sound of the words felt like they were stuck inside a hot-air balloon. "I'm Nils." He stiffened. "I'm Nils Svensson."

With eyes as big as black walnuts, the little *flicka* asked, "Are you my papa?"

"Well, you see, I'm not sure."

"You don't like me!" The girl frowned, and then the tears came. Loud tears.

Nils looked at Elsa with terror.

She rolled her eyes and put her arm around Leah. "He did not say that. Why don't we all see if we can learn a little more about each other? We can even have a picnic. Do you like picnics, Leah?"

Leah looked at her doll's face. "Nettie does."

Ja, Nettie liked picnics. And apparently Elsa does as well. What did this woman have in mind? A picnic. . .at a time like this?

"We have some friends outside, a minister and his wife. Do you think we could invite them to join us?"

Eyes, the color of Fru Jeppson's coffee, landed on Nils's beard and then flitted to his eyes. "All right. Can Nettie come, too?"

"Ja, sure," he said. "As long as she promises to behave." He offered her a grin, but she didn't smile back.

"That settles it then," Elsa said, her voice cheerful. "A picnic it is. But first we will stop by the café and have Fru Jeppson pack us a basket." She looked at Nils. "Perhaps we can have the picnic in your grove of trees. Then we will already be on our way home."

"Home?" Nils asked, Leah's little voice echoing his.

"Of course, everyone needs a home."

∞

The girl could eat. Leah popped another berry tart into her mouth after already devouring a serving of ham pie, a hunk of cheese, and buttermilk biscuits from Fru Jeppson's café. Didn't they feed her on the train? Poor child. His child. Nils tried to reject the idea, but the more he looked at the girl, the more he saw her mother in her. Her blond hair—though lighter than Nettie's—her dark eyes, the shape of her nose. Even some of her facial expressions.

Nils gazed at the sweet girl sitting in the center of the old quilt that Fru Larson and Elsa spread out in a sunny clearing in his grove of green ash trees. Who'd have thought that the barren land, obliterated by a prairie storm long ago, could now provide such a sublime setting for this simple gathering of friends. . .and family. He hoped Elsa's idea would help Leah feel more comfortable with them and transition more easily, while the adults put their heads together to figure out what to do with her.

Leah looked up at him, licking her lips. "Grandfather likes berry tarts, too."

"I'm glad you like them," Elsa said. "Fru—ah, Mrs. Jeppson uses my preserves to make them."

"Is your grandfather from Illinois, Leah?" Nils asked.

"Oh, he isn't in Illinois anymore. He went to heaven with Grandmother and Mama," the little girl said matter-of-factly. "Didn't Great-Uncle Wilson tell you in the letter?"

Letter? He'd received no such letter. Nils shook his head. Elsa and Fru Larson made little sighs. At least Leah didn't burst into tears again.

Leah wrinkled her nose. "Uncle Wilson said Grandfather died of 'aruptsy.' "

"Do you mean apoplexy?" Elsa asked.

The girl scrunched her nose. "No. . .it was at the bank."

Nils scratched his beard. "A bankruptcy?" He covered his mouth, trying not to chuckle, though there was really nothing humorous in the situation. Reverend Larson made a little snort then tried to cover it with a cough.

Leah frowned. "Mmm-hmm. His ticker went out."

"Oh dear," Fru Larson said, patting her on the arm.

Leah picked up a small cookie and pretended to feed her doll. "No more after this, Nettie. I think you've had enough already."

"I am sorry that you have lost so many people that you love, Leah," Reverend Larson said. "You are a brave girl to come all this way by yourself."

"My dolly came with me," Leah said. "And Miss Elsa told me that I am not alone anymore."

Nils looked across the quilt at Elsa, mottled sunlight from the trees nearby dancing over her shoulders. This woman, so amazing. She even had a way with this little sojourner.

Leah looked around the grove at his trees. "I like it here." She lay back on the quilt, looking up through the burgeoning trees into the blue sky dotted with puffy white clouds.

"I am glad to know it, Leah." But as Nils spoke, the girl scooted closer to Elsa and laid her head down on Elsa's lap. Was she shy of him or simply tired after her long journey to Swedeburg?

Within moments, Leah had fallen fast asleep. Elsa stroked the girl's hair, looking down at her with tenderness while softly humming a Swedish folksong. It did something to Nils's insides to see his daughter nestled against the woman he loved. . .the woman he loved! Somehow, he could not even imagine Leah in Nettie's arms. He did not doubt she had been a fine mother, though her controlling parents had shown little affection toward her. Why had he never been told that he was a father? Leah had to be at least six years old. Here he had been raising trees when he should have been raising a daughter!

"What are your plans, Nils?" Reverend Larson asked quietly. "Gud has given you a precious gift."

Nils looked at Leah, and his eyes stung. He swallowed hard. "I never imagined. I thought I had lost everything."

"You will take the girl home, ja?" Fru Larson looked from him to the sleeping child and smiled.

"My soddy is not set up for a child, a girl no less." Worry pinched his brow, and he tried to keep his voice low. "Though I was hoping to build a frame house in the near future." He glanced at Elsa. He'd wanted to build it on Hokanson's land, but that was impossible now. He'd have to rethink his whole scheme.

"I have a suggestion, Nils," Elsa said in a hushed tone, talking above the child in her lap.

Nils cocked his head. "Ja?" The Larsons looked from him to Elsa, listening with interest.

Elsa enunciated her words to ensure he could hear her over the breeze rattling through the leaves. "I can take her home with me for a few days, until you make preparations."

"It is a generous offer, but do you have room with your bröder there, too?" he asked.

"I thought perhaps Olaf and Einar could bunk at your place while they work for you. They could also help you get your home ready while they are there. While she is with me I will see to her other needs, such as clothing and bedding."

"It sounds like a wonderful idea," Fru Larson said, smiling at Nils and then at her husband. "Gud is intervening already, as we prayed. He put this on Elsa's heart."

"I have been praying, too." Elsa released a peaceful sigh. "There is more, Nils. Earlier I mentioned negotiating with you, but we were interrupted." She glanced down at little Leah. "I am willing to relinquish eighty acres of my new timber claim—including water rights—so that you may purchase that half section, if you will act as my overseer and instruct my bröder in the proper planting and cultivation of my tree nursery."

Dumbfounded, Nils's bearded jaw dropped open. Whatever it was that had kept him from feeling like he had a stone bluff crammed in his mouth all day disappeared.

What an ingenious solution! "I do not know what to say, Elsa."

She offered him a brilliant smile. "Say ja!"

Chapter 9

"If at the expiration of eight years from the date of entry or at any time within five years thereafter, the person making the entry, shall prove, by two credible witnesses, the planting, cultivating, and protecting of the timber for not less than eight years, according to the provisions of the act of June 14, 1878, he or they will be entitled to a patent for the land embraced in the entry."
— *The Forest Tree Planters' Manual*, 1883

Nils exited the Wahoo Land Grant Office, Olaf and Einar—his two witnesses for offering final proof in accordance with the Timber Culture Act—with him.

Olaf extended Nils a hearty handshake. "Congratulations, Nils, you now own your tree plantation free and clear."

Nils perused his land patent certificate with a huge grin. "It was a long time coming." It had cost him the original eighteen-dollar entry fee, the final proof filing fee of six dollars, and a lot of sweat and hard work. But he did it! By Gud, he did it.

"Mr. Davis said as soon as he files your affidavit with the county courthouse they will send it to the General Land Office in Washington," Einar said. "It will go in the records that you are an official owner of a piece of the United States of America."

Pride filled Nils's chest. "I already own my homestead, but it is sure nice to double my acreage."

Einar smirked. "And now you can start paying taxes on your land, since you've been exempt from the time of your entry."

Nils glared at him. "Don't remind me."

Olaf pushed his hands into his pockets. "I hope to enter my own claim once I turn twenty-one. A homestead first and then a timber claim, like you and like Elsa."

"I'm sure you will be successful, Olaf. You and Einar are hard workers and ambitious."

"Ja, and as soon as Elsa files relinquishment, you can purchase your additional acreage for your sawmill and new home."

"That might not be necessary," Einar mumbled under his breath.

Nils narrowed his eyes. "What do you mean?"

"Why make a purchase when you can marry her instead?" Einar's cheeks rounded with mirth.

"Now, there is one thing Einar and I agree on, Nils." Olaf chuckled.

Nils lifted his eyebrows, not knowing what to say. Just then he saw Reverend Larson coming toward them, dressed in his usual dark suit and preacher's hat, giving him an excuse to dismiss their nonsense. "You two go over to Jeppson's Café and order a sarsaparilla. I'll be right along and treat you to lunch to thank you for helping me prove up." Olaf and Einar promptly trotted across the dusty street.

"*Bra dag*—good day, Reverend. I am surprised to see you here again," Nils said.

The elderly pastor clutched his lapels. "I had a clergy meeting."

Nils glanced past his shoulders. "Is Fru Larson with you?"

"Ja, she is doing some shopping. In fact, she is now purchasing some fabric. She is going to make a new dress for your dotter, and a little one to match for her doll."

"Tack så mycket." Though grateful, Nils could feel the creases of his forehead deepen as his smile faded. "I have been so busy with my work and preparing my house for her, I haven't given much thought to such things. I guess I have taken it for granted that Elsa is taking care of her other needs."

"There is one particular need that Leah has that cannot be met by anyone else but you, Nils," Reverend Larson said.

Nils returned the minister's serious gaze.

"She needs the love of her fader," the reverend continued. "I know you are making an effort to provide for her, but that little flicka has a tender heart, and she needs to be assured that you love her."

"I care about her deeply. But doesn't love take time?" Nils asked.

"It must be cultivated."

"Like my trees."

"Ja, but people are not trees, my friend." The reverend's white eyebrows lifted. "It requires more to nurture a child than it does a sapling."

Nils rubbed his beard with the end of his thumb. "I imagine it does."

"I did not ask you what brings you to Wahoo today, Nils." The minister glanced at the door sign of the Saunders County Land Grant Office from which Nils had just exited.

"I finally proved up on my timber claim." Nils showed the man his certificate.

"That is a great accomplishment." Reverend Larson smiled. "Now, have you anything else to prove up on?"

∞

After a hearty lunch at the café, Nils, Olaf, and Einar were on the wagon road back to Swedeburg. Nils couldn't help but be preoccupied with the conversations of the day. Proving up, raising a daughter, marrying Elsa. Could it be that with all of his loss, he had failed to notice his gain?

Looking out over the rolling prairie, he uttered a prayer, *Lord, give me eyes to see,* but he never expected the plume of smoke that suddenly appeared in the distance. Nils yelled to Einar and Olaf in the back of the wagon, "A fire, in the hedgerow by your soddy!"

He snapped the reins over his Percherons' solid backs, and they bolted toward the fire. The three jumped from the wagon and ran to the well, all thankful for the repaired windmill.

Elsa ran over to meet them, carrying shovels and trying to catch her breath. Leah trailed behind her with a pail of water. "Lightning struck the hedgerow!" Elsa explained, while thunder rumbled in the distance and dark clouds moved through the sky.

As they doused the low fire with barrels of water and dirt, the smoldering ground soon turned to a blanket of soot. Only a small portion near the tree line was damaged.

Elsa wiped ash from Leah's face with her apron. "We could have lost everything," she said, looking into Nils's face.

His voice cracked. "I am glad you both are all right."

"We are fine. Praise Gud it was only a small fire and could be contained."

Nils wiped the soot and perspiration from his brow with his handkerchief. . .her handkerchief.

"You still have that?"

"Apparently so," he said with a grin. He took his proof certificate out of his pocket. "I proved up today, Elsa. But there is something else I must prove." He pulled her into his embrace and claimed her sweet lips. When she pulled away, breathless, he whispered, "I adore you, Elsa."

Elsa's eyes misted, and she stroked the sides of his face, gazing at him with affection and admiration. "It has taken me too long to admit it, but I love you, Nils Svensson."

He slid a loose tendril of her blond hair between his fingers. "I cannot believe that I once thought you sabotaged my dreams and that Gud was in the business of destroying them, too." He shook his head with remorse. "Now I understand that you are my dreams, and He is the giver."

He drew her fingers to his lips, kissed them, and held her hand in his against his chest. " 'There is never happiness for me if the heart I love beats not with mine, pulse for pulse. All its pleasures must be my pleasures, its pains my pains.' "

" 'Where there is not true sympathy, there can love be never,' " Elsa whispered. "Oh Nils, you've been reading *The Knight of the Black Forest.*"

"A man has to relax somehow."

Leah scooted up beside them. Nils looked into his daughter's precious face and slid his fingertip over her nose.

He addressed his girls. "While I was in the city I heard that Governor Furnas has decided to make Arbor Day an official holiday. It will be held on April 22, the birthday of J. Sterling Morton, Arbor Day's founder." He looked back down at Leah. "There will be a big celebration in Wahoo, with a parade and everything. With plenty of trees to be planted in Nebraska as well."

His daughter looked up at him with sweet lamb eyes. "Can we go, Papa?"

Papa. She called him Papa.

"I hope that we can all go together. Olaf and Einar, you, me, and Miss Elsa. Reverend and Fru Larson will meet us there also."

"For another picnic?" Leah asked.

Nils took Elsa's hand in his and looked into her eyes. "I was hoping for a wedding."

Elsa's eyes brightened with surprise.

"Would you do me the honor of becoming my wife?" Nils wrapped his arms around Elsa and Leah. "*Jag älskar dig*—I love you, Elsa. And I love my Leah, too. I wish to be a family."

"I would be proud to be your wife, Nils." Elsa looked down at his little flicka, and her misty eyes again met his. "But as for a family, I think we already are one, ja?"

Nils chuckled. "Ja!"

Elsa tilted her chin. "What about those trees to be planted on Arbor Day?"

"Trees can wait, but love cannot."

"A single woman, duly qualified, who has made an entry under the Timber Culture Act, and subsequently marries, is not thereby debarred from acquiring title to the land."
— Timber Culture Act,
Sweat's Sectional Map and Settlers' Hand Book, 1884

Native New Englander Carla Olson Gade writes adventures of the heart with historical roots from her home in rural Maine. With twelve books in print, she is always imagining more stories and enjoys bringing her tales to life with historically authentic settings and characters. Carla is an avid reader, amateur genealogist, photographer, and historical research enthusiast. Though you might find her tromping around an abandoned homestead, an old fort, or interviewing a docent at a history museum, you can always connect with her online at carlagade.blogspot.com.

PRAIRIE PROMISES

by Ruth Logan Herne

Chapter 1

S tate your business or get shot. Your choice."

The woman's voice shouted the warning from the grass-walled hut that should belong to Jack's widowed mother if his hand-drawn land map was correct. A slight quiver said she might not be as tough as she wanted him to think. Or it might mean she was downright trigger-happy. Taking a chance on the former, Jack O'Donnell set the brake on the wagon and started to climb down.

"If'n I shoot, I'm likely to scare that pretty team, and that would be a shame." The sharp metallic *click* said the shotgun was ready. "Whereas if it's you I hit, then I've got me a new wagon and a team, once I round them up. A sensible man would see how that narrows my choices."

Jack put his hands up. "Is this Mary O'Donnell's place?"

"Who's asking?"

"I'm her son. I've come to take her home."

A sharp laugh came from inside the walls. Built of layered grass, the soddy seemed solid compared to a few he'd passed. He was pretty sure he'd traveled by a couple of dugouts, too, and the thought of holing up in a virtual earthen cave with earthworms and vermin made his skin crawl. What in the name of all that's right and holy had his parents been thinking? And now, with his father gone, he owed it to his mother to rescue her from this endless stretch of waving grass and take her back to civilization.

"What's your name?"

"Jack. Jack O'Donnell. My mother's Mary, and my father was William." He choked on that last part. He hadn't seen his father in over ten years. His parents headed West, war raised its ugly head, and he'd served in the Union Army while his parents and brother tackled the western plains. But when his brother, Michael, brought his wife and two kids back East, leaving their widowed mother alone on the forsaken prairie, well—

Jack left his holdings in Philadelphia with his younger brother, Tim, packed what he might need, and grabbed a train west. "Where is my mother?"

"Jack?" A voice hailed him from behind, a familiar voice, sweet and hearty. "Jack, is that you? Oh, thank God, you've come!"

Jack swiveled about.

This was the greeting he'd expected, happy, heartfelt, ready to be saved from the rigors of settling an unsettled land. "Mother!" She raced his way from a slight rise to the south. He met her halfway and grabbed her into a hug that felt wonderful and long overdue. "Let me look at you, you're all right? You're okay? I could have killed Michael

159

when he showed up back home without you."

"There'll be no talk of killing, of course," she scolded as she stepped back to see him better. She reached a hand up to his face and smiled. "So grown-up and even more handsome than the last time we were together, so long ago! Every day I thank God for that new railroad and how it will bring us closer together even though we're miles apart. And don't be too hard on Michael. He tried to make it here. The prairie's tough on women. And Susannah—"

"Had the common sense to insist they return to something with a measure of refinement," Jack interrupted. "But leaving you here to fare for yourself was the height of foolishness. I decided then and there—"

"That you'd take over your brother's claim."

"That I'd get out here in time to gather you up and take you back home where you belong before winter sets in."

They spoke in unison, and reason dawned on Jack as his mother's words registered. *She thinks you've come to take over Michael's claim.*

Jack had traveled west via the most mixed-up network of railroad lines one could imagine, with one goal in mind: to take his mother home to Pennsylvania, a place of civilized propriety. And that was exactly what he intended to do. She, however, seemed to have a different plan in mind.

"Jack, this is home." She waved a hand around her as if thatch-covered, unimproved land meant something. Clearly, it did not. "We have a stake here. Your father and I worked hard to get this going, to be landowners."

"Except Dad's gone." He said it softly, the pain of the loss still fresh. "And this is nothing a woman can do on her own."

"And yet, I am, and I'll continue to do so because this"—she swept the widespread, waving grass prairie a look of respect—"is our legacy." She smiled up at him, patted his cheek as if he were a little boy, and moved toward the house. "Come in and I'll get us a drink of water. We'll unhook that fine team and set them to pasture. The creek runs through part of our spot and Michael's, so there's water aplenty, and that's a blessing, isn't it?"

He remembered being on battlefields for long, hot hours in the scorching southern heat. He'd learned to respect the availability of water in those times when the wrong move to quench a thirst could get you killed. "It is." He put a hand to her arm to pause her as she moved closer to the house. "Mother, there's someone in there."

"In where?"

"The house."

"Of course there is!" She smiled up at him and hugged his arm with her free hand. The other held a basket of wild berries. "That's Bridget, my friend. Oh, she's the sweetest thing, but not so soft she won't make it out here."

"She wanted to shoot me."

"Well, a woman can't be too careful, can she?"

"Would you be this glib if she'd done it?" he wondered out loud, but he followed her into the low, long dark house.

Cool air bathed his skin, a contrast to the late summer heat outside.

It took a moment for his eyes to adjust, and when they did, he looked around.

Disappointment filled him. He recognized a few items from his youth, but most of what filled the dark home was rustic-style roughed-in furniture, essential and basic. The thought of their old, quaint wood-sided farmhouse in lower Pennsylvania made him shake his head. They'd gone from that to this, and the reasoning behind his parents' change made little sense.

"Stop judging, and give this a chance." His mother's practical voice made him wince. "Yes, it's kind of bare bones compared to Grandpa's house in Pennsylvania, but we have land here, Jack. A lot of land. And with Michael's claim, that's over three hundred acres. You don't need to put land in a bank, you don't need to doll it up, you don't need to hide it under a floorboard to thwart robbers. It's here, it's proved up, and it's ours. And by the time my great-grandchildren walk these bluffs, this place will have meaning. You mark my words."

With Michael and Susannah back in the heart of civilization, there most likely wouldn't be any grandchildren, great or otherwise, walking the thick, empty grasslands, but he wisely bit his tongue as the back door swung open. The triangle of light gave him a quick glimpse of blond hair, a stout body, and a scowl. The scowl made a perfect match for the "how 'bout I shoot you now and keep the horses" voice he'd heard earlier.

"Bridget!" His mother hurried across the dirt floor and grabbed the bucket. "Here, honey, let me get that. It's heavy."

"I brought two; actually, they're easier to carry when they're balanced." She handed a bucket to his mother then went back outside and lugged in another. "I couldn't handle the door latch and both buckets. I figured if we were doing a washing today, we'd need more water to heat."

She turned slightly as Jack started forward.

He stopped dead, staring.

This woman—Bridget—wasn't stout or fat. She was going to have a baby, and from the look of her, sooner rather than later. His mother, alone on the prairie, in a grass hut, with no one to help her but a pregnant woman?

He hadn't thought the situation could get worse.

It just did.

"Bridget, this is my middle son, Jack."

The blond didn't look all that impressed. "We've met."

"Not exactly," Jack returned smoothly. "All I saw from the trail was the business end of a shotgun poking through a crack in the door. Nice to meet you, Bridget."

She frowned, thumped the second bucket down, and moved toward the back door again. "I'm going to pick down those beans, Mary. We can shuck them later. And I put the fresh milk in the storage dugout to chill it quicker. This heat's good for nothin' but cheese if we aren't careful."

"Perfect."

Jack turned toward his mother and stared straight at her as Bridget strode out the door, then he waved a hand toward the door and the departing woman. "None of this is perfect," he hissed. "Not this house, not this situation, and certainly not the woman clomping around in men's boots about to have a baby."

"Her feet are swollen so her old shoes don't fit, not that they were much to talk about anyway." His mother faced him, firm and straightforward as always. "She's a widow, she's alone, and she's proving up her claim just like we did. Another year and she'll be set, so I'll thank you to be kind. Her circumstances are troubling, but we're coping. And as you can see"—she moved to the back door and swung it wide—"we've got a nice little garden here, we're self-sufficient for most things, and while we could use some sugar and flour and a bit of this and that, we're getting by until we make a trip into Omaha."

"Omaha?"

She nodded, swung the door shut, and turned back to him. "It's the closest place for supplies and trading."

"Bawdy men, loose women, and saloons on every corner!" Jack knew his mother. He thought he understood her desire to be independent, but Omaha?

Out of the question.

"I don't look left or right, I just go about my business," she assured him.

Jack was anything but assured. "You've got no business going into a town like that, a place where all kinds of things could happen and most likely do."

"Lots of places start out rough." Mary drew water from the bucket, put it in a teakettle, and walked out back with it. "And then faith and good women demand better. Omaha just needs a hearty dose of both." She called over her shoulder, "We cook outside in the summer so the house doesn't heat up. No sense making things uncomfortable when the good Lord's given us such a cool respite from the summer sun."

"I'll say," Bridget added from the stand of green beans two dozen feet away. "A place with no trees, or barely any. My parents would talk about the rolling green grass of Ireland, how the grass just went on for mile after mile, perfect for raisin' sheep and goats and cattle, a sight they loved until the potatoes all soured. The minute I saw this land, stretchin' out before me?" She turned, and Jack was surprised again but not by the pregnant shape.

Beautiful.

Freckled skin, evened to a soft gold from months of working in the sun. Big blue eyes that tilted up at the outer edge, framed by dark lashes. With her hair pulled back, the outline of her face reminded Jack of the fashion models he'd seen in Philadelphia city. The shape, a perfect oval. Thick brows, a strong chin, and a wry gaze said she didn't appreciate his scrutiny.

"What did you see, Bridget?" His mother's question took him back to the commentary.

"A chance to come home." She pointed to the rectangular garden carved out of thick grassland. "Food aplenty. Water for us and the cows."

"You have cows?" Jack turned back to his mother. "Where?"

"Along the back swells." She pointed north. "Thirty-two of them, and I think most of the heifers will prove up with a new calf in the spring. And then we'll have fifty or more. And the year after that—"

"With the train runnin' smooth and cattle cars taking beef East, we hope." Bridget chimed in, smiling at his mother.

"We'll be looking at a hundred, depending on whether they're bulls or heifers."

"And a milk cow." Bridget pointed to a small grassed shed on the far left. "Now if we could only talk those chickens into laying more winter eggs, we'd be set to bake, with some sugar from town."

"Light and heat help."

Bridget eyed him curiously. "Light and heat help what?"

"The chickens. Laying eggs. That's what we were talking about, wasn't it?"

"Among other things." She glanced at Mary.

"My mother always said a snug chicken is a happy chicken. I wonder if we build them a sod shed. . ." Mary supposed thoughtfully.

"With a thick roof," Bridget added.

"And face it south." Mary nodded, as if the decision was made. "Bridget, we'll get on that as soon as the weather cools. Cutting sod is hard and—"

"We'll get on no such thing," Jack exclaimed. "I came to bring you home, Mother. Not make more work."

Mary turned, surprised.

Bridget's eyes went wide and even bluer, if such a thing was possible. She opened her mouth, seemed to think better of it, and turned back to pulling pods, but a quiet "hum" from the bean area said staying quiet didn't come naturally to the Irish girl.

"Jack, I'm not going anywhere." His mother had set the pot on the fire rack and now sat alongside the thin coals, waiting. "If I went back East with you I'd be sitting around, waiting for folks to take care of me." The shake of her head said that wasn't possible. "Or I can stay here, on the place your father and I dreamed of. Our own place, our own land, not a shared farm with two brothers who fought your dad on every little thing. You know how it was with the uncles, Jack. They second-guessed every decision your father made, and naysayed his suggestions. There he was always the younger brother, a show-off, and they never let him forget it. Here?" She gazed right and left then tipped her head back to smile up at him. "I'm home, Jack. I'm only sorry it didn't work out for Michael and Susannah, but I understand. It takes a different sort to make it out here."

It sure did, Jack thought. Plum crazy, that's what it took, but he was pretty sure his opinion wouldn't be appreciated by his mother or tolerated by her stand-your-ground pregnant friend.

"Mother." He sat alongside her on a berm of land situated just right of the cleared fire area. "It was different before. And while I know that Uncle Walter and Uncle Will aren't the easiest people to deal with, coming way out here, taking a chance. . ." He gazed off to the west and shrugged. "It was a gamble, one we lost when we lost Dad. There's no way—"

She put a hand up to silence him, and he paused, but not because he wanted to, no sir. He paused because he respected and loved her, because she was the one person who believed in him all along. None of his highly acclaimed accomplishments would have been possible if Mary O'Donnell hadn't pressed and pushed him each step of the way. He owed her so much, but that meant he was responsible for her now, in his own way. Wasn't that what faithful children did? Take care of the surviving parent?

She doesn't seem all that inclined to let you do that, his conscience warned. *And you might want to remember that she wasn't afraid to speak her piece with your father as needed. Which means she won't be shy about lambasting you.*

The mental warning hit home.

A breeze swept in from the northwest, a breeze that hinted coolness.

"Feel that?" Mary turned her face into the gentle wind.

"It feels nice," Jack admitted.

"It feels like fall," his mother announced.

"It's barely September," he argued but then paused when she and Bridget exchanged glances. "Don't tell me fall comes early here? Because that doesn't make a lick of sense."

"I can't explain it, but it's true." His mother poured hot water into the teapot and then covered it to let the fragrant leaves steep. "Tea is our guilty little pleasure."

Bridget smiled and nodded but kept right on working, long enough and hard enough that guilt crept up Jack's spine for sitting with his mother. "We'll have to make a supply run before the weather turns serious," she noted from the garden.

"And that will be easier with Jack here," his mother agreed.

Jack clapped a hand to his knee because he wasn't in the least bit agreeable about helping them stay here when his mission had been to retrieve his mother. "I'm not *here*. I'm there." He jerked a thumb east and frowned at his mother. "In Philadelphia. Tim's already keeping watch on my properties and looking after my affairs while I'm out here. I promised him I'd bring you home—"

"I am home," she insisted. "Although once they've got the train connections a little smoother, I'd love to bring Bridget back to see Pennsylvania. In the nice weather, of course, no sense tempting fate in winter."

"Bridget is cordially invited to come back East with us. I'm sure she must have family there, don't you?" He directed the end of the sentence to Bridget, and she promptly skewered him with a look that said he wasn't all that quick on the uptake.

"I have no family 'ceptin' my unborn child. My husband was lost in the April blizzard, and your mother and I have agreed to work together to maintain all three claims. Hers. Mine. And Michael's. And although you look ten shades of city-pretty, I expect we could toughen you up enough to make it on the prairie. Or not." She added the last over her shoulder, a challenge, and a good one, because right about then Jack was tempted to roll up his sleeves and show her how he could make quick work of her garden harvest, handle a band of roaming cattle, and butcher a hog on the side. All in a day.

Better yet, he thought, make that *two* hogs. All that thought of beans and pork made his stomach growl. Since he wanted to growl right along with it, he had to work to keep his mouth closed.

"You're hungry!" Mary jumped up, dismayed. "Oh Jack, how foolish of me. Of course you must be starved. Bridget, I'm going to pull those soaked beans out of the dugout and set them to cooking. And some of those salted grouse would be lovely! Did you start a rising of bread?"

"Inside on the fancy worktable."

Mary clapped her hands together. "Perfect! Jack, if you can give Bridget a hand in the garden, I'll go see to getting things done. Land sakes, I plum forgot about cookin' and doin' the moment I laid eyes on you!" She reached out as he stood, gave him a hug he desperately needed, and smiled. "Bridget will tell you what needs to be done, and I'll get us some food going. In the meantime, we've got some hardtack in the house. Would you like some?"

He'd rather die, but he bit back that exclamation. He'd eaten more than his share of hardtack during the war. Too many days in ditches and not enough food had put him off hardtack forever. "No thanks, I'm fine."

"You're sure?"

Oh, he was sure, all right. He nodded.

"Bridget, let's dig a couple of those young onions, too, don't you think? They'd go so nice with beans and bird." She indicated a small patch of pungent onion stems, and Bridget nodded.

"That will be a feast, Mary."

"It will!" His mother smiled wide and hurried toward the house.

Chapter 2

Jack drew a deep breath, exhaled, and moved toward the garden. "How can I help?"

Bridget's hands paused. Her chin dropped. And for just a moment, he thought she might give him a mouthful of sass for coming out here and breaking up their little hen party, but then she surprised him by turning and handing him the basket of beans. "If you could start at that end of the row, grabbin' all the dried pods, it will help the plant develop the last beans on the stalk. I'm fearin' that cool wind means harvest will be done sooner instead of later."

"Sure." He'd helped with his share of farm and garden chores as a boy, so picking and shucking beans was no big deal, but as he worked along the row, it seemed the beans weren't as lush and full as he remembered. "Is this the second picking?"

She grimaced. "First."

"A little scarce, aren't they?"

The grim look deepened. "Dry summer. We carted water, but it's not the same. And we should have put the beans in the land your parents cleared a few years back. We put other stuff in there, squashes and the like, and they came fine. We broke more sod this year, but I'm afraid it took too much energy from the soil."

That made sense to Jack. He'd never had to break sod at the family farm in lower Pennsylvania. Their land had been cleared of forest and brush long before, but he'd heard his father and uncles talk about sod corn and sod potatoes, measly, spindly things barely worth the trouble. "Did you plant more beans somewhere else? Like, on your property?"

Her face darkened. She shook her head. "No. We should have, but no. It's a fair piece to travel, and takin' care of a garden there would have been too much trouble. Now?" She looked at the meager vines and made a face of dismay. "I wish we'd a done it."

"You're determined to stay?" He wasn't sure why he dared ask the question. It wasn't his business, and the woman was plenty prickly and seemed to find his decently tailored clothing a nuisance, but she was still a woman, great with child, alone on an endless patch of ground that stretched forever west in wave on wave of growing grass. "Because this can't be what you hoped for."

"It's exactly what I hoped for." She stared west then north, and breathed deep. "Not losing Jedediah, that wasn't part of my plan, and he wasn't one to listen to anyone, anytime, anyhow. Women didn't know much, and even other men weren't all that bright or brave, according to him. And that was his undoin' at the end. That, and not havin' faith in the Lord, our God, to provide as needed."

Jack pondered that. He'd had some seasons of doubt himself, facing month after month of war, gunfire, cannon shot, and lack of food. He'd about gorged himself for a week when he got back to Philadelphia and still hadn't filled up the emptiness within. So he could understand a young husband's need to strike out on his own. Kind of.

"He'd have been so excited about this child."

"He didn't know?"

She shook her head. "I suppose, bein' gone and all, it doesn't much matter now, but he'd have been right pleased. For all his bullheadedness, he was a good man. And a kindly husband. He had a dream." She glanced his way and shrugged. "We had a dream, like your ma and pa. We wanted land, the land my parents couldn't have in Ireland, the land Jed's family lost in a poker match when he was knee-high. A place of our own."

"How many years in are you?"

"Two, plus two earned up by Jed's time in the war early on. And I aim to see it through. Bein' a widow, I have the right to stay and keep my claim, and with your mother's help I can do it. Which means if you talk Mary into goin' East, I might as well catch a ride west and start again. I think this prairie will be worth a fair bit one day. But I can't stay here alone."

"Pay heed to the land and the good Lord, son, and everything else will fall into place."

His grandmother's words, an old woman's teaching to a young man, determined to make his way in the world. She'd offered that advice nearly twenty years back, not long before she died. He'd held tight to her insight and now was part owner to several Philadelphia properties, a partner with his younger brother, Tim. They made enough on rent to bring in a decent living and keep buying. An old mother's wisdom brought to fruition.

Well, the first part, anyway. You've been plenty lax on the second.

Jack shoved that thought away. He wasn't all too sure about the God notion these days, he'd felt pretty abandoned on the field of battle, so he and God hadn't been on speaking terms in a bunch of years. Kind of like hardtack, he'd pushed God aside and moved on.

The breeze lifted again, and this time Jack felt the distinction. The soft wind carried the promise of chilled, starlit nights and thick-dew mornings. And then winter.

He couldn't leave his mother here for long, cold months of a desolate northern winter. And he wasn't about to stay in this perpetual grass wasteland.

But as he bent to gather the pods from the lower reaches of the vines, the scent of fresh soil, bean leaves, and soft cotton gingham took him back to a simpler time. Boys chasing frogs. Girls playing catch-the-hoop, braids dancing, skirts swirling.

Life had been predictable then.

It was anything but foreseeable now. He and Tim had deals in the works, and the last place he should be was in the middle of nowhere, trying to protect his mother from who knows what might come wandering across the bluffs.

"You set on taking her back?"

Jack nodded. "I am."

"Well, then."

She didn't harangue or lambaste him. No, she squared those narrow shoulders, drew up her chin, and kept working with fierce determination. Her stoicism made it worse. If she lashed out at him, he could point out the logical reasoning of his position and then take his mother calmly back East, although she seemed to need a fair bit of convincing. Good thing Tim was set up to take care of things for a while, as needed.

"You're welcome to come with us." He made the offer quickly, before he rethought his choices. What would she do in Philadelphia, a woman alone, with a child, with no means of support except an unproved claim in the wilds of Nebraska?

"Nothin' for me there. And everything for me here." She shook her head, chin down, her profile set tight. "But if I portion out the supplies and stay holed up through the winter, I could do okay."

"When is—?" Despite his longtime experience at war, treating wounds, bandaging limbs, and rescuing fellow soldiers, he couldn't wrap his tongue around the thought of addressing the woman's pregnancy.

She glanced his way, and her expression said he was a ninny. And that was kind of how he felt when he got tongue-tied asking about something as normal as a baby.

"Eight weeks."

"Oh."

She shrugged off his look of regret. "Women have borne children since the dawn of time. We won't be stoppin' now because you've got a bee in your bonnet about livin' in a big city surrounded by walls someone else built. Me?" She gazed around the small garden in the middle of land that rolled forever, and her chin softened. "I like bein' part of God's country."

It suited her with her cornflower-blue eyes, wheat-toned hair, and gold-tinged skin. It would never suit him.

In the distance, a train whistle pierced the cooling air. She raised her head, looking west, and Jack got a new glimpse of Bridget. Longing filled her gaze, the set of her jaw, as if wishing she were on that train, and for just a moment he wondered if she felt as trapped as he did.

"All right, I've rinsed the grouse, and I've got new potatoes to boil. It will be a feast like old times, Jack!" Mary's voice interrupted his thoughts. He turned and smiled at her as Bridget picked up her basket and carried it around to the other side of the garden.

A strange voice hailed from the front of the long, low soddy, and then a stocky man trudged through the thick grass and came around back. "Mary? Bridget? Came to check on you."

"Leroy, thank you." His mother strode forward and clasped the man's hand. "You rode all the way over here?"

"Anna said she spied an unfamiliar wagon coming this way, and I wasn't sure if it meant harm or good, and she couldn't tell, neither. So I thought I'd head over. See what's going on. Make sure you ladies were safe."

"How kind of you." Mary motioned Jack forward, while Bridget stayed completely out of sight on the far side of the beanpoles. "Jack, this is one of our neighbors, Leroy Cooper. He and his sister have a claim about a mile east."

"A pleasure to meet you." Jack stuck out his hand. The middle-aged man grasped his hand, nodded, but his eyes seemed to be searching for something else.

Or someone else.

It hit Jack that Leroy was scouting the area, looking for Bridget.

A niggle of unrest climbed his spine. It was no business of his, but was a pretty, young thing like Bridget interested in this guy?

The fact that she stayed behind the cover of the garden beans said no. But Leroy hung around too long, as if hoping to see her, and that said his interest was more defined.

A new mental picture bombarded Jack. Bridget alone, a long winter, a newborn child, and a neighbor she seemed bent on avoiding, trying to court her.

"Leroy, Jack and I were just going to check out a few things with the cattle out back. You'll forgive us for hurrying, won't you?" His mother's smile made the easy dismissal seem downright nice. "And thank you so much for riding right over here. We're grateful."

"It seemed neighborly." Looking put out, he gave the brim of his hat a rather gruff one-finger tip, walked out front, mounted his horse, and headed up the road.

"You can come out now," Jack called the words in the general direction of the tall, staked beans.

Bridget marched from behind the patch, her basket full to overflowing. "I wasn't hiding. I was taking my time. There's a difference."

"Either way, he's gone." Jack turned to walk over the closest rise with his mother but then swung back. "He won't come back, will he, Bridget?"

She shrugged. "No. He's not that determined. Yet." She wrinkled her brow on that last word, and that meant she knew he'd get more determined as time went on.

"We need a gathering," Mary said as she took Jack's arm. "We don't have a proper church yet, but a fall gathering would be good. That way Leroy can see there are plenty of other possibilities out there."

Bridget looked up quickly. "That's a downright good idea, Mary. And with Jack here, we can get word out. Although I think the pickin's are slimmer than you make out."

"I'm not staying." Why weren't they hearing him? "I've got plenty to do in the city."

"I'm sure Timothy has everything under control." Mary drew him away from the sod garden, past a more abundant one farther back, and over the small rise.

A small herd of crazy-looking cattle roamed the area, but as they moved contentedly around, unbothered by the two encroaching humans and happy with the lush grassland, Jack glimpsed the truth of his mother's words. "I have to admit, cattle and grasslands make a winning combination."

" 'When I consider thy heavens, the work of thy fingers, the moon and the stars, which thou hast ordained; what is man, that thou art mindful of him? and the son of man, that thou visitest him?' " His mother quoted the psalm softly. "I look at how far and wide these prairies roll, and I consider the natural order of things, the cows, giving birth, raising their young, and giving more heifers. And as the cycle continues, I see the opportunity your father saw, stretching before me. Unfettered, unbothered, able to make our own decisions at long last."

Jack glimpsed the truth behind her words.

He'd always been a numbers guy. His affinity for math and reasoning did him well in school and the service, and he could see the equation before him: *Cattle + grass = rising values.*

But a sod house?

A sod shed?

The very idea made him yearn for Market Street, row houses, and wood floors. He loved the quick pace of horses clomping, traders calling, the speed of the merchants' market, the gathering crowds. He and Timothy had put an offer in on a significant plot of land above the Schuylkill River. He'd heard whispers that the university might relocate. Common sense told him the broad expanse above the Schuylkill would be the most likely spot, and he and Tim were willing to take a chance. Given time and the university's change of address, that plot of land would be worth ten times what they'd offered the owner in a decade or two.

But standing here, in the middle of widespread prairie with a cool breeze beating back the heat of the day, the air so fresh he thought he could inhale forever and never quite get enough, a certain peace touched him. Though fleeting and light, the emotion held its own draw.

"Let's get that food going." His mother turned to go back down the rise. "Everything looks better after a good meal."

Jack wasn't sure the situation could look better as they approached the dull-toned grass-and-thatch house. The very thought of willingly living in the thing made him itch.

Weren't there bugs? Critters? Snakes? Of course there were. He added "mind reader" to his mother's attributes, because her next statement touched on that very thing.

"If I'd known you were coming, I'd have had you bring a couple of cats along," Mary told him as they reapproached the yard. "Remember how Gran's barn cats loved to capture pesky things and leave them on the side porch?"

"They were good mousers." He tipped his gaze down. "I expect a house made out of grass and dirt doesn't do much to keep the burrowing wildlife on the outside, does it?"

"Not as well as wood, no, but with the railroad connections going through, we'll have lumber out here before you know it."

"And then we'll bake in the summer and freeze in the winter," Bridget noted as she set a pan full of chopped onion and meat on the low fire. "But we wouldn't wake up to mice and snakes and mosquitoes, and I can't say that wouldn't be a blessing." She cut up a hunk of peeled squash and sighed. "An apple would be just the thing to go with this."

"Really?" Jack looked from her to the pan. "Apples, onions, squash, and meat?"

"Best stew I've ever had," she said softly. "My mama used to make it all the time, and when meat was scarce we still had a good meal on it. Tasty and filling."

Jack excused himself to gather his bags from the wagon. He pulled them off the wagon seat and toted them around back. He lifted the leather flap, reached in, and withdrew three large red apples and handed them to Bridget.

Her eyes went wide, putting him in mind of those dancing blue flowers that grew each spring, clutches of them here, there, and everywhere. Her mouth open, she squealed and jumped up. "You brought apples?"

"I thought some traveling food would be prudent."

"Mary!"

His mother came out of the house, saw the fruit, and laughed out loud. "Jack, how did you know? We've been pining for fruit. We've done some berry jams, but the taste of fresh tree fruit is a treat beyond belief!"

Jack added *apples* to his mental list for Omaha then struck the word away when he reminded himself they wouldn't be staying.

"I'll get a knife."

"Wonderful!"

Jack plunked himself back onto the natural grass berm that flanked the south side of the fire and stared at Bridget. "I wish I'd brought more."

"Oh, this is good right here." She stared at the apple then smiled in delight when Mary came back with a knife. "We can use one tonight—"

"Or all three," Jack cut in. "We can get more in town, can't we?"

"It's a day's ride there and back, and no way of knowing what they might have in the general stores and what they're out of," Bridget explained, but the sight of the apples seemed to soften her tone. "Out here we try to make do with what we have the best we're able."

"And getting a tree to grow in this sod is a true test of patience," his mother added. "It seems the thicker the grass, the weaker the tree. So Jack, these truly are a treasure. And I'm going to save each seed and plant it next summer. I'd love an apple grove, and maybe with the proper care, we can get some going."

"I wish I'd thought to bring more," he told her. "Of course, apples are a common enough occurrence in Philadelphia, Mother."

"Goes hand in hand with throngs of people," she replied, ignoring his hint that Philadelphia was a better choice.

Bridget chunked the fruit into the pan, and as the apple pieces hit the warming onions, the mingled scents of good food helped cover the smoke of the cottonwood and dried grass fire. "Is Philadelphia really busy?"

Mary's frown said she wasn't moving back to Pennsylvania, no way, no how, but she kept her silence and let him speak. "Yes. Always people coming and going. It lies at the juncture of two rivers leading into the ocean. Roads come down from as far north as Massachusetts and then head south to Florida, although I've heard the bugs drive the horses near mad down there. Philadelphia is beautiful, in my humble opinion."

"You don't mind so many folks around?"

He did, kind of, and he couldn't lie. He shrugged. "Sometimes."

Bridget poked a long forked stick into the pot, gently turning the simmering grouse breasts. "I can't rightly imagine it. Going into Omaha riles me enough, so many things, noises, smells. People. Men." Her face said she didn't think real highly of his gender, and that didn't surprise him after the brawling and bellowing scenes he'd seen in Omaha. "It's a confusion. Here—" She flicked a glance to her surroundings. "It's just so blamed peaceful that I feel like God's walkin' 'longside me most days. As if He knows what Nebraska's all about and loves it, just like I do."

"That shoots down your thought of this as godforsaken country, I suppose," his mother teased.

"Although we do need a church," Bridget admitted. "It's tricky business out here, all unsettled, and a body needs that communion of the spirit to get by, don't you think?"

"Um. Yes?" He answered as a question, saw his mother's sharp look, and confessed, "I haven't been going to church since the war. Watching all those men die took church right out of me."

"Men are born to trouble as the sparks fly upward." Bridget paraphrased the quote from Job. "I don't see war as God's fault. Men like power, always wanting more." She made a face that said she disagreed. "Sometimes less is more."

"Do I get a lecture on women wanting to vote, next?" Jack wondered aloud, only half teasing.

"The right to vote and the right to hold land in their name," Bridget shot back, and her expression said she might talk like a country girl, but she had Yankee stamina. "I lived in New York when I was young, before my parents moved to Ohio. There was plenty of talk up there about rights for women, and they all made perfect sense. When you look around this fire, the two folks you see making do on three claims are women, and we're a hearty lot."

"You're a suffragist?" That amazed him for two reasons. First, because the only suffragists he knew were somewhat cryptic and unattractive women who carried signs in the streets and created a traffic tie-up for wagons. And the other?

He hadn't thought of Bridget as educated enough to have political opinions, and that realization shamed him.

"I am an independent woman who wants the best for her children." She placed a hand on her rounded belly. "Boy or girl, this baby will grow up knowin' a woman's place in this world should be to stand side by side with man, not in his shadow and not leadin' him 'round by a nose ring."

Mary smiled as she set a tin pan with a rounded loaf of bread off to the side of the fire and placed a large domed lid over it. "Bridget, just being around you makes me pray for change in the world and peace on earth. And it gives me the backbone to do what I can to help that change along."

Jack stared at his mother.

This wasn't the strong but docile woman he'd grown up with. This woman didn't fear to voice the strength of her convictions. Was that because of Bridget or being in the Wild West, working among the loners and recluses seeking a different way? "We talk about women's rights in Philadelphia."

Bridget's snort said talk was cheap. And the sound of it told Jack she was absolutely right.

Why shouldn't women vote? Why shouldn't they have open rights to property and not relinquish everything to their husbands?

The sound of a train whistle in the distance brought him back to his senses.

Half of Philadelphia would blackball him for such notions. Property was important in the city, and ownership equated power. A man could leverage a lot of things from a position of power.

Bridget's words came back to him. *"Sometimes less is more."*

The words flooded him as a soft, chill breeze bathed him again.

"We started by talking about a church, and moved to politics." Mary shook her head. "The two should never go together, but freedom for both is crucial. Jack, while you're here, do you think you could help us come up with an idea for a church?"

"Not if that's your sneaky way of getting me back into one," he retorted.

She sighed and rolled her eyes.

Bridget stabbed that stew so hard with the long fork, Jack was pretty sure she was taking her frustration at him out on the food, but the sight of the sharply forked spear said that was for the best. "I wasn't planning on staying around, Mother. I figured I'd head out here and take you home. End of story."

But as he said the words and swept a gaze toward the pregnant blond opposite him, he hauled in a breath. "Clearly this is not as cut-and-dried as I originally thought."

"And since it's not, why don't you stay a week or two, just long enough to help us settle in for the winter?" Mary met his look, and despite his original intention, he couldn't refuse her commonsense request. "Then you'll feel better about leaving us behind, and you can enjoy the winter in Philadelphia, knowing Bridget and I—"

"And the baby."

"Of course!" Mary clapped her hands, laughing. "Oh the thought of holding a baby, watching him or her grow. Smile. Crawl."

"In the dirt with the vermin," Jack muttered, and the very thought of Bridget's sweet, innocent baby crawling around in the muck of the house made him cringe.

"By the time this baby's crawling, we'll be about able to go outside again," Bridget corrected him. "He'll crawl in God's green grass, surrounded by property his mother owns, once I've proved up next year. And he'll know I was willing to sacrifice a little comfort for his future, and what baby would trade that for a drafty city floor filled with splinters?"

"My floors don't have splinters." Saying that, Jack knew he was wrong. Some of his rentals probably did have splinters, and suddenly his head was filled with visions of peoples' babies, crawling around his row houses, getting slivers in their tiny baby knees. What in the name of all that was good and holy was happening to him? If folks didn't have sense enough to put down a rug to cover old wood, was that his worry?

He stood, excused himself, and strode away to gather his thoughts. Right then he didn't care what the women thought of his quick departure. He needed a few minutes to wrap his head around the few choices he had. He'd come west on a clear and defined mission, the way he handled everything, and to be thwarted by two women. . .

His gut clenched as he saw the path his thoughts jumped to. He was more upset because he was being shrugged off by *women* than by being shrugged off, and that made Bridget's words hit home with greater ferocity.

He wanted the best for his mother, but he wanted it on his terms because—he sighed in realization as he approached the summer-narrowed creek—he was a grown man, and she should listen to him.

Shame bit deep.

His father had always treated his mother as an equal. The uncles hadn't liked that, but Jack was raised to see women as equals. When had that changed?

When you surrounded yourself with men seizing every opportunity they could find, his conscience reminded him, *you embraced their philosophies and turned your back on God.*

He scrubbed a hand to his neck, stared into the creek, and listened to the lowing of contented cattle just upland of where he stood. Quiet surrounded him. It made him half-nervous and half-happy, as if he'd been waiting to drink up some quiet for a long, long time.

He turned back and saw the women in the distance, tending food and the small fire. No matter what else happened, he had to stay long enough to see them settled for winter if they refused to come East. He owed his father that allegiance and more. And if they insisted he help with a church?

He sighed, rubbed his neck one more time, and stared up at the deep blue sky, wishing he felt something other than nothing.

He'd do it. He wouldn't be one bit happy about it, but to help his mother and her very pregnant young friend?

He'd do it.

Chapter 3

Bridget hadn't given a thought to her appearance in months.

Today she did, and that made her spittin' mad, to think that just because Mary's handsome son showed up out of the blue, she'd start thinking about combing her hair out, putting on a clean dress. Nothing fit right anyway, and she'd refused to spend a bunch of money making clothing she'd never need again, what with Jed gone. She and Mary had refitted a few of Jed's old shirts to work for Bridget's smaller height, and though they might be pieced, they did the job.

Well, they look ridiculous, her conscience scolded. *Patchwork clothes and messy hair. Ain't a thing wrong with taking care of yourself even in times of grief. Didn't Jesus spurn those who made a big show about their sacrifice and loss? And He blessed those who went quietly on. Wash your hair and your clothing. Remember what Paul told those Philippians, how things that are just and virtuous and lovely are good. Well, you ain't all that lovely of late.*

Now was as good a time as any to clean up. Today had become washing day, since Jack's arrival put the chore on hold the day before.

She lugged more water from the creek, snatched up a bar of last spring's lye, and went to town on the clothing then laid the various pieces on clean patches of sunny grass to dry.

"A clothesline would be a help, wouldn't it?"

She hadn't heard Jack come out of the soddy, and the sound of his voice, gentle but questioning, put her heart into a swift motion that couldn't be good for her or the baby she carried. Still, he was right. A clothesline would be a thing of amazement. "It would, but wood's so scarce here that using some for a convenience like that seems wasteful. But I won't deny that shakin' bugs from my clothing is an annoyance."

"There's still wood along the creek bank."

"We keep that for shade for the cattle so the summer sun doesn't drive them batty, and for emergency use. We've had to chase poachers off more than once, and the little timber that grows hereabouts gets harvested too quick."

"And keeping cattle from gnawing on young trees is tough."

"Pretty much impossible, less'n you fence it, and there's only so much time." She turned fully then and noticed he didn't look like he'd just gotten up and ready for the day. "Did you go someplace?"

"Took a ride to check things out."

"This early?"

"Days get wasted too quick if you don't harness them. And I had plenty of time sitting and waiting in the war, so ever since then, I'm quick to get up. Get a start on the day."

She was, too, and it had irked her that Jed let so much time slip past him each day when hours of light and good weather were short-lived. She caught herself up because it wasn't right to think ill of the dead, but lagging about when there was work to be done never sat right with her. "See anything?"

He half frowned, half smiled, and that crooked face made her insides churn up like fresh-turned butter, a little lumpy but good.

"I didn't, not really, but that was kind of a nice surprise in itself. It's a long way between claims here."

She nodded. "Mostly these are full claims, except where folks have sold off, and it makes a fair distance."

"Which could mean trouble if you women have a problem." His gaze dropped to her expanding belly, which seemed unreasonably huge to her since he showed up yesterday. "Birthing doesn't always go easy or right."

"Don't be scaring her, Jack," Mary's voice scolded as she moved toward them from the far side of the house.

"I've got God's hand and your mother's wisdom and the reality that creatures have young'uns regular. I think I'll be fine, but I am grateful for the concern." She went to turn a few half-dry items on the grass, but Jack's hand to her arm made her stop.

"I'll get them. Please."

Her heart stuttered. So did her tongue. For the life of her, looking up, seeing the utter sweet intensity of this man's eyes made her almost want to be cared for. He smiled, ever so gently, released her arm, and then flipped the clothing to the other side, letting them bake in the warming sun. "This has to be a trick in the winter."

His mother made a face. "Everything's a trick in the winter. We've heard natives tell of winters where there was no snow, mild all year, but our winters have told a different story. And with no wood to burn, we've been baking chips in the fields and harvesting them."

"Chips?"

"Cow droppings." Bridget's opinion of Jack almost soured when his jaw dropped, but then he paused and shrugged.

"Does it work?"

"Burns too quick and hot, like soft wood. And we do hay ticks, too, but with a growing cattle herd, we don't want to use too much hay."

"And twisted hay burns quickly, too, without much in the way of heat," Jack noted.

"We put on lots of layers and expect our feet to get mighty cold. In the house."

His expression said that was unacceptable, but he didn't argue. He worked his jaw, pointed east, and said, "Wagon's coming."

"The Thumm family." Delight softened his mother's face. "Oh Bridget, look how much Millie has grown!"

"And wee Mary, too!" They hurried to greet their visitors, and when the toe of

Bridget's too-big boot caught on the edge of a swell of grass, Jack's hand steadied her.

And then he didn't let go.

She tried to shrug him free, although it felt mighty nice to have someone watching out for her for a change, but his grip stayed firm, gentle, like the man. He released her arm once they drew close to the young family, but the spot he touched and held clung to the warmth and strength of his grip.

She chanced a glance up, only to find him looking down.

Heat swept upward. She was silly, ridiculous, maybe crazy like some said, thinking an educated city fellow like Jack O'Donnell would be making eyes at a barrel-shaped woman. He was being kind because, well, he was kind. . .

And that's the whole of it, she assured herself as she hugged Pansy Thumm. "What a nice surprise! And I can't get over how these children have grown, Pansy! Before you know it, I'll be lookin' Young John in the eye."

"And you've grown, too," Pansy replied, smiling at Bridget's rounded shape. "Oh Bridget, I didn't know for sure, and time got away from us. I feel foolish for not coming by sooner. How can we help?"

"It's been a busy spring and summer, and Bridget's been keeping to herself, understandably," Mary reminded them. "But we should have this baby in about eight weeks, give or take, and what a gift for winter that will be."

"If we can keep all three of you warm," Jack offered. He reached out a hand to John Thumm. "I'm Mary's son Jack. Michael is my older brother."

"And no doubt you've come because you're worried about the women being on their own."

Jack shot Bridget and his mother a look of triumph. "Exactly. Finally someone with some common sense about women alone on the prairie."

John laughed out loud. "Don't be settin' words in my mouth that my wife will sear me for later. I've been thinkin' of this, too, and with a babe on the way, it's more thought-provoking than it was. Ladies, we were wondering if you'd like to winter over at our place. We'd be tight on room, but it makes a lot of sense when there's no way of knowing how tough the weather will be."

"That is a nice offer," Bridget began.

"And we don't dare accept it because of our responsibilities here," Mary continued.

"But considerin' what all that's been said, I'm so grateful." Bridget hugged Pansy again. "I know folks don't always understand one another—"

"Women do what must be done, and don't you think another thing about it, Bridget Murphy." Pansy softened her rebuke with two gentle hands on Bridget's shoulders. "And if men are too stubborn for their own good, then it's up to us women to help them see the way."

"We've been talking of a church," Mary told them as the children chased off to explore the back field. "Mind you stay clear of those cows," she called after them.

Young John turned back. "I'll watch 'em, Miz O'Donnell."

"I'm beholding, John."

The teen smiled at the use of his rightful name then followed the younger children over one of the endless small rises.

"Will they be okay?"

Pansy nodded. "Young John will keep them in hand. Now, about this church business."

"It's time," Big John agreed.

"We thought a gathering to get talk going would suit." Mary looked from John to Pansy. "Sunday maybe? Before the weather takes a turn to wet?"

"Our place is in the middle," Pansy noted. "Let's meet there around noon; we can each bring a dish to pass, and we can talk amongst ourselves and get a plan going."

"We need to get word out, and I need to cut hay for the winter." Big John frowned but turned and smiled when Jack said, "I can ride and do that today. Then tomorrow I'll turn that hay lot I saw up the road and start raking it into windrows."

Bridget's heart opened further. She'd intended to do the hay lot herself today, but the washing interfered, and that was her fault for not getting to it yesterday, visitor or no visitor. "It's our second cutting, and it was a good one, but we usually hope for a third."

"That long winter and late spring robbed weeks," Big John said. "But two good cuttings and an early spring can build hope, for sure."

"Well, I can help with the first and let nature—"

"And God," Bridget added.

"—handle the rest." Jack moved toward the timber-supported sod barn, facing east, its thick back blocking the prevailing west wind. "I'll ride now so I've got time to pull the rake later. How far west and east?"

Mary explained things to him as he saddled his horse. He nodded several times, and Bridget watched from her spot next to Pansy Thumm. Finally Pansy leaned close and whispered, "A mighty fine team there. Horse and man."

Caught out, Bridget flushed. "Well, he's a city slicker and no place for him here on the prairie."

"Seems tough enough to me." Pansy placed her hands around her middle and smiled. "And it's not a bad thing to have the strong arms of a man around when you're with child."

Bridget turned. "Are you?"

Pansy nodded. "About three months or so after you, so our children will grow up in Rolling Bluffs together. They'll see changes you and I can't imagine. Who'd have considered a cross-country railroad twenty years back? Now it's almost a reality, and we'll have access to everything."

A railroad whistle pierced right then, at the same time an eastbound wagon bumped its way along the worn trail. The overloaded cart said this family had given up and was packing it in, much like Mary's oldest son had done in the spring. As they drove by, Pansy waved. "God's blessings to you!" she called, and Bridget wanted to hang her head.

Would these folks be insulted?

Would they feel like losers for leaving while it was clear their group was staying? What kind of hardships had they faced that made them turn their back on all this free land?

"And you." The man tipped his broad-brimmed hat as the wagon rolled by. From the back, three pigtailed girls peeked out at them. Two smiled. The other stuck her thumb in her mouth, glum as a November storm cloud, and Pansy laughed. "That little one's a handful, I expect."

"Are we foolish for staying?" Bridget turned to Big John and Pansy as the wagon rolled eastward. "Are we stupid? Because this prairie isn't always kind to children."

"Wandering children and dangerous prairie don't mix," Big John agreed. "But that same wandering child could be hit by a wagon or drowned in a river back East. Life never has come with guarantees, Bridget. Your own history shows that."

It had. She'd lost her parents to illness and then Jed to a late blizzard, despite her attempts to keep him home then save him when he couldn't resist the urge to test the storm. "How can a parent be in two places at once?" She gazed toward the rise the children had crossed earlier. "How do you do it, Pansy?"

"God helps. And a firm hand to mind. But mostly, I face things knowing only so much is in our control. Instead of worrying about each day, I thank God for the blessing of the day. And that helps."

Jack mounted the horse just then. He looked their way and tipped his hat in a way that made Bridget's heart go quiet then dance in a flutter of activity.

He smiled. Just that, a sweet smile, as if directed at her, and she didn't want to but she smiled back and darned if her hand didn't raise of its own accord to wave him off.

His smile deepened, and that was even better than a wave in return, and right about then she wanted to kick herself for foolish notions.

She marched off, determined to not get sidetracked any more than she already had. She'd finish the washing and then start pulling the ripe squash. Green squash put to storage would rot, so she'd leave the unripe ones to develop further. She heard Pansy call the children's names. As the small crew came running up, over the rise, her heart lifted. Their joy?

Palpable.

Their strength? Of the Lord and good health and glorious.

If Pansy and Big John could handle four children, surely she and Mary could keep this baby safe. If Mary stayed.

"Bridget, look what Pansy brought." Mary moved forward once the Thumm wagon pulled away and she held out her hands. "Feel how soft this is."

"Oh, it is!" Bridget didn't dare touch the sweet yellow flannel with her dirty hands, so Mary laid it against her cheek. "We can make a couple of baby gowns out of that."

"And we need to get some flannel when we go to town. Jack said he'll go with us next week. We'll make a day of it, gather everything we need into the wagon and be set for winter before he leaves."

"Mary." Bridget hated to face this, hated to say the words, but Mary O'Donnell had been more than a second mother to her. She'd been a friend in time of need, at a time when others spurned her as foolish and crazy. "If you want to go back with Jack, no one will blame you. Least of all, me. I can understand that a warm home and having your children around could pull you back to Pennsylvania. I don't want you thinkin' you need be stayin' here for me. You've got family that loves you. This"—she placed her hands atop her ever-widening belly—"is all the family I've got, but I understand the powerful urge to be with them. Help them. So if you decide—"

"I've already decided." Mary's voice stayed firm, and then she gave Bridget's tummy a serious look. "And I'm staying right here. There's more than one way to have a family, Bridget, and you and this baby mean a great deal to me. We made a pact."

They had, months ago, but with the change of seasons looming, the time to have this conversation loomed as well. "A promise can be broken if needed."

"Are you staying?" Mary met her gaze point-blank and waited for her answer.

"I am."

"As am I. And if we don't stop gabbing about it, nothing will get done, and then we'll look like a couple of ninnies when Jack rides back this way. I'm already looking forward to meeting with folks on Sunday, and it's days away."

Bridget wasn't looking forward to it at all, not after folks shunned her last spring. Chin down, she went back to pulling squash and piling them up in the thick green grass. Mary paused as if wanting to say something, then didn't. She reached down, gave Bridget's shoulders a brief hug, and moved on to pull carrots farther down the row. She had a wobbly shovel to help pierce the ground, but the shovel was no match for the hard-crusted earth. "These will have to wait until we have a rain to soften things up."

"Potatoes, too."

"Yes."

"With a good plow and a fair team of oxen, we could plant a small field next year."

"A cash crop?" Mary turned, surprised. "Could one of us handle a plow, Bridget?"

"We can find out." Bridget tipped a smile up. "If the team works well, I think hangin' on is the rule."

"It's an idea worth talking about, for sure." Mary took up the piece of yellow flannel, draped it over her shoulder, and then shook out the various clothing from the warm grass. "I intend to cut the shape of the little gowns from this flannel while the sun is bright, and then we can sew in the evenings."

"That sounds good."

Mary moved off to the soddy, and funny, with Jack gone, it felt lonely to be just her and Mary again, when two days ago it hadn't felt empty at all. It had been just plain normal. But normal changed when Jack's wagon clambered up that last rise to the east and paused, and a part of Bridget wasn't sure anything would ever be normal again.

Chapter 4

*M*y mother is living with a certified crazy person, and something's got to be done about it.

Jack could have ignored the warning from one settler, but when three out of twelve said his mother's young companion was "titched" in the head, he couldn't shrug it off. He'd ridden west to three settlers' homes then doubled back east and hit two places along to the south, and in the end, folks seemed to like the idea of a get-together, but several shared their concerns about the yeller-haired girl livin' off Mary.

By the time he'd finished the route his mother specified, Jack had never seen a less likely bunch to succeed. Coaxing a living off thick-thatch land seemed to appeal to a handful of people, including his mother and Bridget, and he couldn't say his mother's reasoning was bad. Cattle should thrive here, he saw the logic in her stand. It was, in fact, farsighted.

But as he rode the circuit of here-and-there homes, he saw several wagons aiming east, folks looking downright worn. Few seemed to travel west in lower Nebraska, although he'd watched two wagon trains follow a more northbound trail out of Omaha in his brief stay there. Which meant folks were still pushing west but not across the lower, rolling prairies west of the noisy town.

Did they know something he didn't? Or were his parents part of the few who saw a different kind of gold in the Nebraska soil? Rich grass, four seasons, and a hearty breed of cattle spelled profit to Jack, but more than that?

He paused the horse at the top of a knoll overlooking his mother's wide expanse of land and breathed deep.

Nothing but fresh air and green grass assaulted his nose, and that was a big change from crowded Philadelphia in the hot, humid summer he'd left a week before. The press of people in a busy city made its own stench.

He hauled in another breath and tried to pretend it didn't matter, but it did. It felt more than good, it felt wonderful, and if he wasn't careful he'd be caught up in his parents' crazy notions of new land, new hope.

But first, he had to tackle the problem at hand, and he didn't have an inkling how to do it, because asking a young woman if she was crazy, especially one who knew her way around the business end of a shotgun, might not be the smartest move he'd ever make. He directed the horse to the tethered area west of the sod barn and dismounted.

"You're back!" His mother's voice hailed him from the far side of the grass house. "When you're done with the horse, come tell me how things went."

He half dreaded walking to the house, not sure how to face the pregnant young

183

woman, then stopped dead in his tracks when he turned to the back corner of the house. Bridget sat just outside the back door, in the shade of the low roof, her fingers working a fine needle through a pile of yellow flannel. The beauty he'd glimpsed yesterday seemed more pronounced today. "Your hair."

She looked up and touched the twisted hank as if embarrassed he noticed, but how could he not notice? The pinned-up hair made the classic beauty of her Celtic features more obvious. "It's easier when it's up, and I didn't want it in my face while makin' clothes for the baby."

His ears buzzed like a swarm of bees approaching, but he looked around and saw nothing.

"Coffee, Jack? I've been saving this last bit, but if we're going to town next week, we could celebrate your visit this afternoon with some hot coffee. Unless you'd prefer tea?"

He shook his head, trying to figure out what to say, but now? Face-to-face with the woman some called crazy? He knew it wasn't so, no matter what they thought, and he'd trusted his instinct before. He'd trust it again now. "No, I'm good, Mother. I'm—"

Bridget's gaze tightened. Her chin quivered so slightly he almost didn't see it, but he did, and that made him feel worse.

"I think folks have told Jack about me, Mary."

His mother turned more fully, her gaze appraising, and what could he do? Pretend they hadn't raised his concerns?

Yes. That's exactly what you do.

He crossed the short expanse of prairie yard, took a dipper of water, and shrugged. "Folks say lots of things. I come from a place where talk is constant, and most of it's worth nothing but the air it moves. And that's how I see things wherever I go, Bridget."

He faced her full, and she met his eyes with hers, assessing him, then dipped her chin but not before he saw the sheen of tears. "Thank you, Jack."

"You're welcome. Mother." He shifted his attention to his mother, and he'd have to be blind and foolish not to see the gratefulness shining through her smile. The look of approval felt real good. "I've got hours of daylight left, so if you could show me your rake, I'd like to start those windrows."

"I'll show you." Bridget stood and handed off the sunny flannel to Mary. "I get tired of sitting real quick, and a little exercise is good for me. It's alongside the barn." She walked him to the far side of the barn and grabbed two rakes.

"I can do this." Stubborn, he put one rake back.

Just as obstinate, she picked it back up. "I aim to help."

"Making clothing is a help, otherwise that baby's going to be mighty cold come winter."

"Plenty of time to work on such things at night. And raking goes a lot faster with two, although I can't say I'm good at finishing the piles to shed water, and we don't want the rain soaking into them, spoiling the feed."

"Too short."

She started to glare up at him but then laughed instead, and to hear her laugh made him feel even taller. "I can't deny it. And now, round to boot."

A sweet sort of longing made him want to tell her she was downright pretty, even with the rounded shape, but she moved ahead and the moment was gone, which was a good thing. Neither one of them needed to complicate things with thoughts like that, but when she peeked up at him now and again from where she raked, his mind poked fun at his heart.

∞

"We've got everything we need?" Jack asked as Bridget approached the wagon on Sunday morning.

"We do."

Jack took her arm to help her up, and the momentary sweetness of his grip was dimmed by the expectation of seeing neighbors again. Jack held tight until she claimed the seat alongside his mother then waited until she looked down.

"It'll be fine."

Easy words for him to say. He wasn't the one the locals called crazy, but his steadfast gaze strengthened her. "Yes."

He smiled, released her arm, and climbed onto the wagon seat on the other side of Mary. He clicked the team into action with his tongue and headed them east at an easy pace. They'd no more than climbed the second rise, when a covered wagon heading west moved toward them at top speed.

"Jack! Runaways!"

His mother's cry carved a grim picture. The approaching horses raced their way on the narrow path as Jack guided their team to the right. "Mother, take the lead."

Mary grabbed hold of the reins then stared. "Jack, you—"

He stood, holding his ground carefully as their team shied in the disturbance, and when the racing wagon was almost abreast, Jack shot into the air, toward the galloping horses.

Bridget's heart froze.

Stern faced, Mary held tight to the reins and spoke in a strong, steady voice. Her reaction helped keep their team calm, and as Bridget turned, she saw Jack fumble for a grip, one leg up, the other hanging low, dangerously near the ground. "Help him, God, help him get on up, grab that harness."

She reached out and gripped Mary's cold hand, and as she did, Jack's right hand found a better grip and he wrenched himself astride the near horse, bent low. He straightened as they watched, his strong arms pulling the harness back hard. His mouth moved, but she heard nothing other than the shrieks of the people in the wagon and the thunder of hooves against dry, hard ground.

She prayed. She prayed that Jack would be fine and that the people would fare well. The sight of their faces, so thoroughly frightened, made her remember those cold blizzard-filled days, when she sat alone in her tiny, dark soddy and knew she'd never see Jed again.

Scared to death then but doing all right now, and that's what she hoped for these folks.

Mary turned as the other wagon finally slowed then stopped. She murmured to their team, her low voice softening the moments, and when Jack finally climbed down from the frightened horse, Bridget saw pride and satisfaction in Mary's eyes. She turned toward Bridget and touched her hand. "He could make it here. Fast thinking and hardworking."

"He's made it plain he's not stayin'." Bridget smoothed her shirt over her plain skirt and refused to join in Mary's optimism. "Gettin' our hopes up is like askin' for trouble."

"You're right. But he saved five lives just now, and those folks would be ending their day differently if Jack O'Donnell didn't happen to be driving this wagon. And that's not chance. That's God's plan."

Two boys and a teenage girl climbed out of the wagon's back. As the father shook Jack's hand repeatedly, the mother grabbed her children in a fierce, protective hug. For short seconds, Bridget doubted their combined intelligence. What were they doing, bringing innocent children to a place laden with unseen dangers? A place with little food or fuel. Were they all mad?

Jack moved back to their wagon as the family resituated themselves. He climbed aboard, grabbed the reins, and clucked to the team as if it was any old day.

"Nice work."

He slid a sideways grin to his mother. "I thought for a minute you were going to stop me."

"And I was sorely tempted, but I saw that look in your eyes, Jack Patrick O'Donnell, a look I've seen since you were a tiny boy, chasing after Michael, running just as quick, jumping just as high, no matter that you were two years younger almost."

"A show-off." Bridget said the words mildly, and when Jack chanced a look her way, she hooked a thumb to the family-filled wagon behind them. "But a fellow who acts as needed is a blessing, for sure."

"A show-off *and* a blessing." Jack's cheeks softened into a smile. "Well, I'll be rubbing down some bangs and bruises later, but that's a short price to pay for halting that team. And the Thompsons will be new neighbors. They bought a claim to the west of Bridget's and north of Michael's. They mentioned there's another one to be claimed up there, away from the creek, and mighty good land, but they couldn't afford both."

"Saul Miller's place. He and his brother Merton had those claims originally, and then his family laid claim to two more, but it was too much to keep and stay on over winter. I heard he was merging two."

"The upland is prime growin'." Bridget pointed north. "It's windswept, but grass grows free and strong up there, and it's a different sort of grass than the lowland and the creek banks. And in the hot weather, the mosquitoes can drive you crazy along the water."

"So you think it's good land?"

"The best." Bridget folded her hands in her lap lest they give her away. Was Jack really thinking of staying?

No.

"Does it abut Michael's land or Bridget's?"

"Mine along the back," Bridget answered. "There's a cutout where they thought to put a town on the original maps, but towns have a way of finding themselves out here. And then they redraw the maps."

"There's the Thumm place up ahead." Mary pointed to the left. "And we could always use that cutout for our church spot if folks are willing."

Bridget nodded but stayed quiet.

In short seconds she would be surrounded by folks who thought her actions last spring were the mark of a crazy woman. And on the prairie? Folks had been known to go crazy.

She hadn't been crazy ever, not then and not now. Desperate? Yes. But if she had a chance to do things over again, she'd do the exact same thing. A barn and two cows were little price to pay to save a human life, and if folks couldn't add up the reasoning of that, well, too bad for them. The baby stirred as she moved to climb down, and a new reality hit hard.

Did she want to raise her baby in a place where folks thought badly of her? Wouldn't that disregard rub off on her child?

Heart heavy, she longed to turn the team about and head back to the obscurity of Mary's place, bury herself in work and ignore the world.

The touch of Jack's fingers on her arm made her look up, into his eyes.

He smiled, and in that gentle smile she saw a hope she'd given up a long time ago. A spirit of faith and hope and love, despite his admitted absence from church. Presence in church wasn't what marked a person's soul for God, that was all in the heart. And right then she figured Jack O'Donnell's heart was in the right place at the right time. Seeing him risk his life to save others had confirmed her belief.

She let him take her arm and help her down. Her heart beat fast and strong against her chest, the thought of facing these folks pushing her pulse into overdrive, but as she stepped down and looked up, two quick-talking women moved her way.

"A baby!" Minnie Samples put a hand to her mouth as if the very idea of a baby was too wonderful to believe, and when her sister Cora did likewise, Bridget's heart calmed.

"Oh, dear child, how special! We haven't had a baby in three years out here, what a wonderful blessing this is! Oh, and I know we're not supposed to speak of such things."

Cora rolled her eyes as if that rule was about the stupidest thing she'd ever heard. "But if God didn't want us to talk about babies, He'd have taken care to make them less obvious." She took Bridget's arm and led her over to the lone tree where a long board table had been set up. "You come and sit in the shade, Bridget, and let us take care of you. We might be on in years, but Minnie and I both know how much work comes with making do out here on the grasslands, and if you get a day to have someone wait on you, then best grab hold and let it happen."

Someone caring for her. Helping her. Being outright kind and open with her.

Softness stirred Bridget's heart. She hadn't had anyone but Mary to look after her in so long, she'd forgotten how good it felt. Jed had cared *for* her, but he wasn't the sort to take care of anyone, and after seeing Jack in action the past few days, a difference dawned within her. She felt instantly ashamed for comparing the two men. Jed had been good to her. She knew that.

But did he ever look after someone besides himself first?

She chased the thought back, because Jed's impetuous nature had led to trouble more than once, but it was wrong to think badly of the dead.

Honesty and ill are two different things, and a person needs to think to make decisions. That's the way of it, man or woman.

"Try this, dear, see what you think." Minnie brought her a small chipped cup of pale creamy liquid, cold and fresh.

"It's cold."

Cora laughed. "Irv built our icehouse last summer, and I shamed him for taking the time away from farm duties, but I'd have been better off staying quiet because what a convenience this is! To have ice in September, and fourteen cakes of it remaining. A wonder, isn't it?"

Oh, it was, and when Bridget tasted the foamy cream, she sighed, delighted. "Eggnog."

"My mother's recipe. Daniel's two young cows have both come into calving, and there's milk aplenty. As long as we keep them healthy, this will be the first time we've had milk all year long."

"The grandchildren will be thrilled." Minnie smiled as two of her grandkids raced along a nearby bluff, their hair blowing in the cool breeze.

"How did you build the icehouse?"

Jack's voice took Bridget by surprise. She nearly spilled her drink, but too many of these people already thought she was odd. Best not to test their beliefs any further.

"Well, Clive and Irv backed it into a bluff," Minnie explained. "They made the entry on the level so's they could walk right in as needed, but they made a short tunnel entry to help catch the heat."

"Is it dirt sided?" Jack asked, and his sincere interest made Bridget wonder why he wanted to know. Was he thinking about staying?

She didn't dare suppose such a thing, but as Minnie explained Irv's process, Jack's intensity ran deeper than polite conversation and idle curiosity. He squatted low as Minnie finished her explanation and faced Bridget. "I can see how that would be mighty helpful for you gals for next summer, can't you? I'm wondering if I start it now, if I can get it done before I have to head back to Philadelphia. But then who could cut the ice come winter?" Questions deepened the W-shaped furrow in his brow.

"My sister's daughter lives in Philadelphia." Cora's bright voice gave Bridget time to hide her disappointment. "She's upriver a bit, in one of the newer neighborhoods. She tells her mother that crime is less rampant there."

"There's a rough contingent in parts of the city," Jack acknowledged. "And no small number of outbreaks among the children, especially."

"She noted that as well, whereas here, we've been blessed so far with good health." Cora's gesture took in the prairie as a whole. "I wonder if less congestion and more air makes a difference? If folks get sick here less often and better in quick fashion, but it's been so long since I've been to a city, I'd scarce know what's normal and what's not."

Chapter 5

Jack had been wondering the same thing.

Most everyone out here seemed thin but hearty, by comparison to his city counterparts. And the sanitation of a broad expanse of land for so few, versus narrow streets and row houses for so many, made the grassland parcels distinctive.

Clean air, clean grass, less noise and confusion. . .

Despite his misgivings, he could no longer say his parents chose poorly.

"Jack, take a ride over to our place soon, and see what Irv's got going," Minnie urged. "Now that the boys are big enough to put up hay and break sod, he's got plans for this, that, and the other thing."

"I'd like that." Jack smiled down at her then noted Bridget's cup. "Can I get you more?"

She shook her head kind of quick. "No, but thank you."

"Oh, I remember that, all right." Cora made a noise of sympathy at Bridget's expression. "When there's precious little room left for food, you know baby's drawing near."

Her words opened a new reality for Jack. It must take some time to recover from bearing a child, didn't it? And that meant his mother would be doing everything on her own. Could she handle it?

Well, sure, she handles everything, doesn't she?

But should she have to?

Not if you stay.

The thought met with instant resistance but bore some merit. Tim could handle anything that came up in Philadelphia, Jack was financially secure, and his mother needed him. Could he stand a long, cold winter surrounded by nothing?

Mary laughed as a new wagon pulled up, and the sound of her laughter made his decision easier. His parents had done everything for their children, minding their education, their needs, their desires. With nothing but property to tie him to Philadelphia, why couldn't he stay here awhile and offer his help? Tim would understand.

A tall, thin man called the neighbors to order. Bridget hung to the back, tucked under her tree, as the group discussed the option of a church.

"You put up a church, then you need a pastor." The newest arrival joined the group and frowned as he caught the gist of the conversation. "That's a lot of doin' and promise money for somethin' we might not get to half the year."

"Everything starts somewhere, Simon."

"Nothin' sayin' a body's got to start at the top, is there? Not when we could start havin' prayer meetin's right here in our homes for no money, nothin' but the cost of time."

"That's actually a good idea."

Folks turned to look at Jack, and when his mother nodded, he stepped forward. "I've seen what each year out here has brought in the way of improvements at my mother's place, then some of you shared similar stories. So if you put off building a church for a couple of years but start tucking a bit by for that day, then you're working ahead of the game."

"And we'd be building the feeling of community that so many of us miss," Pansy added.

Simon's snort said he didn't miss community all that much, but everyone ignored him. "We could make up a schedule," Mary said.

"And them that can come, will come," added Cora.

"Should we stop coming in December and the next months of winter?" Minnie wondered. "The weather's awful unpredictable that time of year, and to be caught out in a storm—"

An awkward silence reigned as a few people shot quick glances toward Bridget. She sat tall, her face averted, and Jack's heart ached for the tight set of her jaw.

"It's a dangerous thing, for sure." Mary's words should have been enough, but Simon had caught sight of Bridget when folks turned, and now he scowled.

"I won't be takin' communion with crazy folks, nor will my family be party to such things."

"Simon!" His wife stared up at him, her cheeks red with embarrassment.

"In my house, a woman knows her place." His dark tone matched the shadowed lines of his scowl. "And that place is to do what she's told by the man of the house."

"And if she loses that man, Simon Bradshaw?" Mary took two steps forward, and Jack knew what was coming and almost felt sorry for Simon, but the narrow-minded man deserved whatever Jack's mother was about to dish out. "What's she to do then? Wait for others to throw her scraps like a stray dog or do what proves necessary to take care of herself and her children? And while a man is working the field, who do you think takes care of the children? Or the food, the drink, the house, the washing, the teaching, the raising, the preserving, the sewing, the mending? Why do you think menfolk are in a right hurry to find a replacement if they lose a woman on this prairie, Simon? Because we have value far above rubies, a biblical phrase you might want to reacquaint yourself with. 'She considereth a field, and buyeth it: with the fruit of her hands she planteth a vineyard.' " Face firm, she quoted the old proverb to make her point and took one step closer. "Pay heed, Simon. If you come to church meetings, Bridget Murphy and I will be there, and I'll not take disparaging talk lightly."

"Nor will we." John Thumm came and stood next to Pansy in a second show of support. "Folks do what they need to do to get by out here, and fightin' amongst ourselves sets up nothing but trouble. We meet enough of that along the way."

Simon stomped off, and his thin little wife made a face of regret before following.

The angry interchange put a pall over the neighborly proceedings. Mary, Minnie, and Cora gathered the women and set up a schedule of Sunday meetings, but the talk among the men had lost its sheen of optimism.

"No one likes to think of death hereabouts," Mary explained as they rode home an hour later. "And that's understandable to a point."

Bridget's huff said she didn't agree, and Jack almost smiled to hear it.

"Losing someone you love affects folks different," Mary went on. "A softer sort might not be able to grab hold of what's left to make it alone under these circumstances. We've got no lumber, little fuel, and we fight the sod for every scrap of food. But I don't believe it will always be that way, and what we do have is land, hundreds of acres of good, thick land for growing, for tilling, for raising cattle and sheep. With a broad base of land, eventually, you can do anything."

"But—"

His mother fought a yawn then shook her head. "I look at what the first people did in this country. They trusted enough to cross a great ocean then carved farms out of the thickest forest imaginable. Some starved, some froze, and others died of illness or caused the illness of others. In all that, the reason they succeeded was because folks trusted in the Lord and didn't give up. And that's the way I see things here. We just can't give up." She yawned again and passed a hand to her brow, clearly uncomfortable.

"Mary"—Bridget leaned closer and touched a hand to Mary's brow—"you've got a fever."

"I don't, of course, I'm just overtired."

"No." Bridget's firm voice left no room for argument. "You've got fever. You need to rest once we get home."

"Bridget—" Then, instead of arguing like she normally would, Mary sat back slightly and nodded. "Actually, I think that sounds like a good idea."

◈

I can't lose you, Mary. Not you, too. Bridget laid another cool cloth against Mary's brow as the second night wore on. She'd hoped the fever would break that morning, but it hadn't, and keeping Mary comfortable took all her time.

"I'll do the chores," Jack had announced first thing. "I'm going to make the haystacks in that front field then cut the far field. There's still time to dry and rake it if the weather cooperates and the nights don't hold too much dew. That will take a fair time, but if she gets worse or you need me, I'll be close enough."

"All right. And we should move the cattle to the next feed ground. If you look at how your father did the ditch-and-swell to keep them boxed in, there's a spot on the northeast side that he would fill to make a dirt ramp then drive the cattle to the next area."

"Clever."

"It is that," Bridget agreed. Mixed feelings threatened to strangle her. Jack's work ethic filled a huge gap while she tended Mary, but the thought of being here alone, with her mentor. . . What if she lost Mary? What if she died, here on the prairie, with most of her family back East?

Cling to the Lord. Believe in His tender mercy, and don't borrow trouble!

The stern internal scolding helped. She shifted slightly to see Jack. "When folks first get here, backbreakin' labor is about all you can do to get a leg up. Your mother said those first two years were mostly drudge work like that, diggin' ditches to hold cattle they wouldn't even buy for two more years, but with each job done, they felt closer to the. . . dream." She stumbled over the last word then fought the swift rise of emotion.

Jack started to move forward, but she held him off with an upraised hand. Sympathy would put her over the top. Right now she needed to focus, like Ruth had done with Naomi in the Bible.

Mary had been gently nice to her when Jed was alive, but when he'd died, she'd taken a firm hand and invited Bridget to stay with her and work the claims together. Having lost her own husband a few months before, she knew the dark emptiness of those early days, the solitude of the soul. Waking up alone in a grass shack, surrounded by inhospitable land and a host of problems had loomed indomitable at first. Mary's strong faith and willingness to teach helped bridge that gap.

Jack set a hand on her shoulder.

She couldn't turn and face him. If he looked as scared as she felt, she'd lose it, and Mary needed her to be strong. Jack gave her shoulder a light squeeze then hurried outside. Through the long day she bathed Mary's cheeks, her forehead, and packed cool cloths beneath her arms, but the fever paid no heed to her ministrations. By nightfall, with Mary's obvious discomfort and refusal of even a wet cloth to her parched lips, fear mounted.

Jack took a seat on a rough-sawn stool after dark. The cool night kept mosquitoes at bay, and the small lamp burning offered slight light but fading hope in the darkness.

Bridget shifted on her bench and motioned Jack over. "Sit by her. I've been holdin' her hand all day, I expect she'd like the feel of her son sittin' close, standin' guard."

Half-shadowed, he hesitated then moved closer and took the spot on the bench next to her. He clasped his mother's hand, and oh, the look on his strong face. As if faith and fear forged an awesome war within him.

He reached out. Touched his mother's face. The sight of his strong, blistered hand against the smoothness of his mother's skin tipped Bridget's emotions into a tailspin.

Could God be this uncaring as to take Mary now, when Bridget needed her most? Was this a sign that she should move on, go west on her own, abandon the folly of the prairie? If Mary recovered, should Bridget encourage her to go back East where she'd be surrounded by family? Was it selfish of her to want another person's mother here, with her?

A tear snaked its way down her cheek. One was bad enough, but then it was followed by another and another, until Jack couldn't help but notice.

"Hey." He let go of his mother's hand and reached out, pulling Bridget in for a hug. "Hey, don't cry, Bridget. Don't cry."

"I can cry if I want to, I expect."

"No." He shook his head against her hair, and the feel of his arms, his strength, his warmth, poured into her. "No, because if you cry I'll think hope is gone, and I can't even bear to think that. So don't cry. Please?" He tipped her face up with one finger, and when he did, the gaze he settled on her wasn't just a kindly man with a distraught woman.

It was the kind of look that sought permission. He glanced to her mouth, as if wondering, and then leaned in to answer his own question.

The kiss was light and warm, a summation of sweetness and wonder, but then he deepened the kiss, drawing her closer, his arms a haven.

"Jack, I—"

"Jack?" Mary's voice, calling Jack's name. They turned at the same time. "Mother?"

"Mary?"

"So thirsty." Mary's voice sounded sandpaper rough, but she was talking and asking for water.

"I've got it." Bridget lifted the tin cup while Jack helped his mother sit up a little to sip. "Jack, I think her fever's broke!"

"I'm thanking God if it did," Jack declared. "I might not be a churchgoing man, but I did my share of begging in that field today."

Mary's weak smile said she appreciated the prayers. She took one more long swallow then settled back against the goose-down pillows. She drifted off to sleep, but this time her breathing didn't sound hard and harsh, and the steady rise and fall of her chest had no sound at all. "I think she's going to be okay."

"Really?" The joy in Jack's voice matched hers. "She does sound better."

"Just waking up and drinking is a good sign," Bridget assured him, but then she stood up and moved several steps away. "Jack, I've been thinkin' on this a fair bit, and I've decided you need to take her back East."

Chapter 6

Jack pretended to clean out his ears. "Say what?"

"I'm serious." Her voice sounded solemn, but in the darkness, he couldn't see her face. "You've got kin there. There's nothing for you here but hard work and trouble, and it was wrong of us to try and keep you here."

"Especially when I made it clear I'm not staying."

"Exactly." He saw the bob of her head in agreement. "We thought we could do this, but it's clear we can't, and if Mary goes East, I'll grab a train to the end of the line and start over."

"A woman alone, and pregnant to boot?" Her hesitation said she hadn't quite gotten that far in her thought process. "What kind of life would you have in the unknown, Bridget? And what kind of life would that baby have?"

If she blushed when he mentioned the child, he couldn't see it, and he figured out the first day that getting squeamish over a woman's issue wasn't going to stand good ground on the prairie. There were different proprieties at foot here and maybe not bad ones at that. "What if I stayed?"

She didn't say a word, not one word, but if hope had a sound, it would be the soft change in her breathing as she pondered the meaning of his words.

"I wasn't real fond of God on those battlefields, Bridget." He sat back down on the bench, alongside his sleeping mother. "I didn't like man or God for some time. I expect it was the same for a good many, but we didn't talk about it. Talk would do nothing but make us more unhappy, and there was a job to be done."

"And you did it." She moved closer, listening.

"We did what we had to do, and in the end?" He shrugged, thinking hard. "We held a nation together. I don't know what that will mean in the long run, but I know we felt good, and bad, about the whole mess."

"Bein' united is sanctified by God," Bridget whispered. She took another step and sank down beside him. "Paul told those Corinthian folk that they needed to be joined in hand and judgment, to push away division. And if more folks did that, our country would stand tall and strong. Fightin' for justice isn't wrong, is it?"

"I don't know. Parts of it felt wrong, but then it was war. And the end was the right end, I'm convinced of that." He sat silent, letting the rise and fall of his mother's calmer breaths fill the night, then he turned. "Why does Simon accuse you of being crazy, Bridget?"

She sat still and quiet for so long that he thought she might have fallen asleep, but then she clasped her hands over her swollen middle and sighed. "Jed didn't listen to anyone, ever. He got it in his mind to go hunting that day, even though the snow had already started falling. He said it was too late for much of a snow, but the air had a strange nip, a surge of cold so deep and wet that I felt it to my bones. I begged him not to go, but he was hungry, and Jed didn't do sacrifice all that well."

She paused, and Jack waited, unsure what to do, so he thought up a rusty prayer for the second time that day and used it.

"He was gone a long while, over a day, and the storm got worse and worse. Howling wind, blowing snow, everything going slantwise and swirling till you couldn't see the little shed barn from the house or vice versa. I'd tied a rope from one to the other in the fall, just in case we had a bad day. We only had two cows, both in calf, and a donkey team stubborn as any you'd find. When he didn't come back that day, I prayed he holed up somewhere, but I. . ." She stopped, and her hands clenched tighter. "I sat there alone in that howlin' storm and thought, what could guide him back to the house? What kind of light could pierce this storm? And then I knew."

Jack waited again.

"We'd used creek wood to shore up the sod barn. I went out there, hoping to guide him in. I tried to turn the animals loose, but not all of them left, the storm had 'em spooked, just like me. I used lamp oil and my lit lamp to set that small barn on fire, and when the wind took hold, it lit up the night. I thought surely Jed would see that glow and come to it."

"He didn't."

"No." She shook her head, chin down. "Most likely he was already gone, and I just couldn't believe such a thing was possible. I thought I was with child, but I hadn't said anything to Jed because we'd been disappointed before." She stared downward, her cheek curved in sadness. "I couldn't stop thinkin' that if I'd just told him about the baby, maybe he'd have stayed. Maybe he'd have chosen safety over danger."

"You think that likely, Bridget?" Jack kept his voice soft, because he'd already figured out that Jed Murphy probably wasn't the think-first type.

"Not now." She raised her chin and faced Mary's low bed. "When so many thought I was touched in the head for setting that fire, Mary O'Donnell came by and put her arms around me, and she made me look her right in the eye, Jack. Firm as can be she smiled down at me and said I was about the gutsiest thing livin' this side of the Mississippi, and bein' without a man herself, she'd be honored if I'd take up home with her and face this prairie together. In all that darkness and sorrow and sadness, she rode over by herself and showed me the light of hope."

"That's my mother." Jack could see his mother making that trip to comfort another widow. "She's the sort that turns good intentions into laudable actions. Always was that way."

"And that's why you've got to take her back home, Jack." Bridget turned fully. Her earnest gaze danced in the flickering shadows. "She should be safe and sound. Cared for proper."

"Like you did the last two days?"

Bridget huffed. "I did nothing but offer comfort, and that was little enough."

"Well, let me explain a few things to you. In Philadelphia, I'd have been lost about what to do, as would Tim, neither one of us being a nursing type."

"But Susannah. . ."

"Is a nice woman, but she'd have never sat here for two days, sponging Mother's forehead, holding her hand. She'd have hired someone to do it if money was available, but she's not like you, Bridget. I think my mother's got the best care possible right here."

⬡

His words confounded Bridget. Wasn't he listening? But deep tiredness made argument useless. Jack reached out a hand to her cheek, the very cheek he'd nuzzled and kissed a short while ago.

Or had she dreamed the kiss in her exhaustion?

The warmth of his hand against her cheek and the slight smile he sent her way said the kiss had been real enough, it just *felt* like a dream come true. "Get some rest. That baby needs you to be strong."

"What about you?"

"I'll sit by Mother and watch her. I'll wake you if she takes a bad turn, okay?"

She hadn't realized how spent she was until his offer came, and that, combined with relief at Mary's improvement, made sleep sound real good. She stood, and when it felt like she could fall asleep standing straight up, Jack stood, too, took her arm, and led her to the other makeshift cot. "Lie down before you fall down, then I've got two patients to watch."

She took his advice, and by the time she awoke in the morning, the front door was wide open and warm sun streamed in. She sat up, confused, because sleeping in was an uncommon occurrence.

"Good morning, sleepyhead."

Mary's voice.

She turned fully and saw Mary sitting up in her bed, with two pillows supporting her against the broad wooden chest Jack's father had made her, the only piece of furniture she'd brought west. "You look better!"

"I feel better." She smiled as Bridget stood and moved her way. "I don't remember much of the last few days, but Jack said you sat by me, day and night." She grasped Bridget's hands between hers. "God bless you for that, dear one."

"Oh, it was an honor." She looked around, surprised. "Jack's out working? Of course he is," she answered her own question. "I slept way later than usual, of course he's working."

"He's gone, Bridget."

The words broadsided Bridget.

Gone? Jack was gone? But that made no sense, and yet, in a way, it made perfect sense. No man in his right mind wanted to saddle himself to a big empty prairie filled with nothing but trouble and someone else's child. She was only surprised he hadn't taken his mother with him.

"He took the wagon to Omaha to fill up on supplies. I didn't want to wake you, so I used the list you and I had and then added to it. I hope that's all right. You looked so very tired, lying there."

"He's gone to Omaha?"

Mary nodded and took up the knitting needles lying in her lap.

"He's coming back?"

She nodded again but this time raised a brow of interest. "Late today, as long as there's no problem. I know he needed to get word to Tim about some things, make arrangements, but we should see him later."

Make arrangements.

Arrangements to take Mary back home to Pennsylvania? He'd have to go to Omaha to do that, and the thought of him gathering winter supplies for her showed the kind of decent, caring fellow he was.

Mary coughed, and once she started, she couldn't seem to stop. Bridget pushed her worries aside and jumped into the day. "I'm going to get water for a sponge bath for you, and then I'm going to make you a poultice for your chest like you did for me last spring. That will help the cough. And if you get tired, you put that knitting down. You've been real sick, Mary, and I want nothing more than to get you better."

"Thank you, dear." She reached out, gave Bridget's hand a quick squeeze, and picked up the needles again. "A pesky cough is often a sign of returning health, but it can be tiresome. But Jack told me all he'd accomplished while I was sick, and I realized what a blessing it is to have a man around. Things they can do in an hour take you and I all day."

And when he took Mary back East? How would Bridget manage on her own with a newborn child? She couldn't, and the thought of going west, moving into some rough new town, made her heart quake. She'd always been tough, but risking her baby, her child?

That didn't sit right. Still, what choice did she have?

None, really.

Chapter 7

She hurried through the day to make up for time spent sleeping, and when the late-day shadows said evening was near, the sound of horse hooves drew her to the front door.

Jack sat atop the wagon seat, much like he had two weeks before, but this time she had no urge to greet him with a shotgun.

Her heart leaped, remembering his kiss.

Her soul stirred, thinking of his words, the years-long struggle of battle. The pondering, heartsick sound of his voice made her long to protect him, and what nonsense was that, a small woman offering protection to a big, strong man?

Plain foolishness, but as he lifted his head and saw her watching, he smiled, and oh, that smile made her pulse dance. He pulled the wagon off the path, circled it closer to the soddy door, set the brake, and jumped down. "A pretty sight, you in that doorway, Bridget Murphy."

She was big, round, and cumbersome, and she knew it, but his words and his expression made her feel beautiful as she surveyed the wagonload of supplies. "You've spent a good deal."

He laughed and started lugging barrels inside. "Winter's a long season hereabouts, from what I've heard, and we can't have you and that baby going hungry, can we?"

She shook her head, because really, what did she expect? "I can't repay you for all this, Jack. There's not money enough."

He frowned and kept unloading. "I wasn't looking for payment, Bridget."

"Just so's you know." She reached into the wagon bed and started to lift a crate.

Two strong hands reached over her and relieved her of the crate. "I'll unload. You put things where they need to be. And keep my bullets and powder near enough the stove to stay dry but far enough out to avoid a disaster. No time to dry things out if we need them, so best to be prepared."

She obeyed the direction, but figured there'd be little time left for his ammunition to get wet. She had her own cache tucked aside, and while her gun gave a powerful kick, she'd learned to live with a few bruises in return for fresh meat.

Fear threatened once more. This baby would arrive in a matter of weeks, hand in hand with rough weather.

Could she make it through a long, cold winter alone? Was she doing right by her child, or was she selfishly chancing her baby's life against her dream of owning her own piece of land? And if Mary sold her place and returned East, could Bridget and the baby survive in her smaller, darker dugout? And shouldn't a baby be born into the light?

The thought of a tiny child, crawling on the floor of the cavelike home made her wrap her arms around her expanding middle and hold tight.

"Are you okay?" Jack was by her side in an instant. Worry deepened the sweet, crooked line between his brows. "Come here, sit down. Are you in pain?"

"What is it, dear?" Mary pushed up, off the bed, and Bridget waved her back.

"I'm fine, no pain, not a thing wrong. I'm just bein' a dunderhead, so ignore me."

"You're no such thing," Mary began but paused when Jack squatted low beside Bridget.

"You're worried."

She tried to shrug that off, but Jack took her hands in his, and oh. . .

The feeling of her hands being enrobed by the strength in his made her feel happy and sad all at once. He'd be gone soon, and the strength would ebb with him, but for this moment he was here, and she'd rely on the joy of that.

"Why are you fretting, Bridget? And you might as well be honest with me because I'll get it out of you eventually."

He thought that, did he? She straightened her bowed head and stared him right in the eyes. "I expect I can keep my own counsel for the few days left you'll be hereabouts, Jack O'Donnell."

He studied her, slow and easy, and then a broad, infernal smile spread across his jaw. "You don't want me to go."

"I was hopin' your mother would stay," she corrected him. She moved to get up, but his hands on hers kept her right there, in her chair. "But her illness made me realize I was downright selfish and Mary should be back East with her kids."

"You decided that?" Mary inquired, laughing.

"I reckoned it would be best," Bridget corrected her. "When you really, truly love someone"—she half choked on the next words, the truth of them making conversation more difficult than she ever imagined—"you put their needs first."

Mary's soft smile said Bridget's declaration brought her joy.

Jack squeezed her hands and laughed. "That's it, exactly! You're not as hardheaded as I thought at first, Bridget Murphy. Good."

"Hardheaded?"

He nodded and went back to unloading an amazing amount of stuff from the wagon. "Stubborn as a mule, I'd say."

"Oh really?" She watched as the pile of supplies grew, and when Jack thrust several bolts of flannel and cotton her way, she stared down, amazed. "You thought to buy cloth?"

"And yarn, until we have sheep enough someday to spin our own." He handed off a tied bundle of various yarns to his mother. "I thought the softest stuff would work better for a baby. Was I right?"

Tears pricked Bridget's eyes. "Yes, of course, but such fine things." She picked her words with care, not wanting to hurt Jack's pride. "They'll get ruined in my dugout, Jack."

"Well, there'll be nothing but chickens or pigs allowed in that dugout, so that's not a worry," he advised as he brought in the last of the household supplies. The western end of the soddy was chock-full of barrels and sacks. Lamp oil, flour, brown sugar, coffee, tea, saleratus, new boots, oh, countless things! And then more fabric, this time in floral print and solids. "I thought there'd be time for you ladies to sew this winter, while I take care of the animals and the baby."

Mary choked.

Bridget gaped. "What?"

"I can't sew," he went on as if he hadn't dumbfounded the pair of them. "I have no intention of learning how, and if you ladies need clothing, you'll have to be making it. I thought that blue might make a fine wedding gown come spring, Bridget." He handed her a bolt of blue calico with sprigs of yellow flowers, soft green leaves, and tiny dots of white brightening the sky-blue background. "If you don't mind marrying an O'Donnell, that is."

"Jack!" Glad surprise brightened his mother's face. "Oh Jack, that would be most wonderful!"

"Are you—?" Bridget passed a hand over the pretty fabric, swallowed hard, and looked up. "Are you thinkin' about marryin' me, Jack?"

"Praying on it, actually. And hoping you'll say yes when you get to know me better."

She weighed her next words carefully. "Ruth knew as soon as she saw Boaz ridin' in the field that God put him before her, wanting love and safety for Ruth and Naomi."

Jack's gaze softened. He reached out and laid a firm hand against the soft curve of her cheek. "Are you sayin' you don't want to wait until spring, Bridget? Speak clear because there are several new preachers in Omaha, and I'm willing to make a ride back if it gets me the bride of my dreams."

Bride of his dreams?

Oh, his pretty words touched her in a way that made her cumbersome body and swollen ankles seem not so bad. "Well, I—"

"Will you marry me, Bridget?" Jack didn't drop down on one knee, but he put his hands on her shoulders and waited until she raised her eyes to his. "Marry me next week, when Mother's well enough to make the trip. If we do that, this baby will start off his life knowing a father who will love him forever."

"I thought you were leaving."

"Well"—he angled a quick grin to the supplies piled up behind him—"it appears I'm not. I wired Tim to watch over things, I'll travel there in the spring to take care of business, but odd as it sounds, I decided I'd much rather stay here with you. And Mother," he added, with a quick grin over his shoulder. "Say yes, Bridget, yes that you'll marry me sooner than later, and then if that's soup I smell, I'd be real happy to eat some.

Unless you'll allow me to kiss you first."

Jack didn't wait for a response, and she liked that about him. He reached down, grabbed her up, kissed her soundly, then set her back down with hands so strong and gentle they seemed at odds.

Married. To Jack.

The very thought brought such joy that she was at a loss for words.

The baby kicked and stretched, and sweet realization washed over her. This baby wouldn't be born in the depths of a dugout. He or she would be born here, in the O'Donnell soddy, with a mother, father, and kindly grandmother to welcome the precious life into the world.

Fear thou not; for I am with thee. . . . Isaiah's words, God's reassurance. She'd forgotten to trust for a bit, but hadn't God provided each step of the way?

Yes. And when Jack caught her attention from across the room, and his broad, open smile of affection took hold, Bridget Murphy blushed like a schoolgirl to think such a fine man could love her. She stood, brushed off her dress with quick hands, and ladled up a fine big bowl of soup. On the side, she sliced up a crisp, fine-fleshed apple from the sack Jack had carried into the house.

He took care of the horses, and by the time he got back inside, the soup had cooled just right. He sat down, grabbed her hand, and bowed his head. "Dear Lord, we thank You for this food, this land, and this chance to start a new branch of the O'Donnells here on the prairie." His quick smile toward Bridget made her go weak in the knees, so it was good that she was sitting. Less chance of falling, that way. "We ask You to bless this new family, to bless this baby, and to watch over us during the winter ahead. And Lord, thank You for bringing me here for *one* purpose, only to discover another."

"Amen." Three voices chorused together, then Jack turned toward Bridget, his eyes soft, his chin firm, and he crooked his little finger beneath her chin. "I love you, Bridget Murphy. And I aim to be a fine husband to you. But I'd be lying if I didn't admit I'm real glad you can cook."

"Seein' as how you did such a fine job rakin' that hay and roundin' those stacks, I think we'll make a mighty fine team, Jack O'Donnell. And Jack?"

"Hmm?" He took a taste of the thick soup and looked as happy as she'd ever seen a man look.

"I love you, too."

He paused, smiling.

"I wouldn't have thought such a thing possible, nor dreamed it, but it's so, and I wanted you to know that."

"Well, that kiss was a pretty good clue," he acknowledged.

His mother's eyebrows shot up from her cozy nest across the room. "Kiss?"

Bridget blushed, chin down, but Jack just laughed, hauled her in for a hug, and then kissed her cheek before he went back to his food. "I thank you for this food, Bridget.

And the love that goes alongside."

"You're welcome, Jack." She sat, watching him eat, poking tiny stitches through the yellow flannel baby gown as he told tales of Omaha and new merchants and pretty houses being built overlooking the town.

She didn't need a fancy house, although a wood-sided one would be nice eventually. And she didn't want to live in a town. Everything she ever longed for was here in this room and the broad expanse of unfettered prairie surrounding this solid, thatched home. Two people she loved who loved her in return, encircled by land, hers and theirs, a blessing she'd never expected that was suddenly real.

Blessed by God, yes. And happier than she'd ever thought she could be again.

Multi-published, award-winning, and bestselling novelist Ruth Logan Herne has over 50 novels and novellas and is living her dream of being a published novelist on a busy pumpkin farm in Western New York. A mother and grandmother, Ruthy loves God, her family, her country, dogs and mini-donkeys, and can generally be seen with coffee and/or chocolate. She loves to hear from readers through her website RuthLoganHerne.com, via Facebook, or through email at loganherne@gmail.com.

THIS LAND IS
OUR LAND

by Pam Hillman

Chapter 1

The wind howled around Lasso McCall, biting through his sheepskin coat clear down to his bare skin.

Lasso jerked his hat low over his eyes and hunched against the wind. His horse stumbled, and he grabbed for the pommel of his saddle with clumsy fingers, half frozen inside his gloves.

"Easy, girl, easy." He patted the mare's trembling neck.

The early snowstorm had caught him by surprise, or he would've already been well on his way to Morehead's Double M spread to bunk down for the winter. As it was, he'd be lucky if he made it by Thanksgiving.

The thought that he could be snug at home in a few hours niggled at him, but he pushed the notion away. His pa and stepmother wouldn't want to see him. They had enough mouths to feed without adding another one to the table. He'd be better off riding out the storm at the old abandoned cabin just up the road then heading for the Double M as soon as the storm let up.

Big, fat snowflakes whirled around him, and he squinted at the faint outline of the road. It wouldn't be long before the wagon ruts would disappear completely underneath the layer of new-fallen snow, and he'd lose his way for sure.

His mare lifted her head, ears pricked forward. Lasso squinted through the whiteout, searching for what had caught her attention. He could barely make out the hulking frame of a covered wagon, not twenty feet in front of him, the horses' backs hunched against the wind.

He edged his mount closer, not wanting to catch anybody off guard. A surprised man could react any number of ways, not all exactly friendly.

"Hello, the wagon."

A double-barreled shotgun snaked out the back of the prairie schooner and trained unerringly on his chest. "Hold it right there, mister."

The high-pitched voice brought him up short. A kid, maybe? And that worried Lasso more than if the voice had been the deep, slow drawl of a grown man. Even a nervous kid couldn't miss with a shotgun at ten paces.

"I don't mean any harm." Lasso rested his hands in plain sight on the pommel of his saddle.

"That's good to know." The steely edge that crept into the voice sounded older than he'd first thought, but still higher pitched than a man's. He frowned. A woman, maybe?

He took a stab at it. "Where's your husband, ma'am? Is everything all right?"

"Everything's fine. We. . .we just decided to stop here. . . ." The wind snatched the words away.

"I see." But he didn't see. Not at all. The voice on the other end of the shotgun hadn't denied being a woman and hadn't said a thing about a husband.

But there'd be time enough for that later. Right now they needed to get out of the storm. He kneed his horse closer and locked gazes with a pair of dark eyes, a thick shawl obscuring the rest of the face behind the gun. But those eyes. . .

Big, brown, and ringed with dark lashes against pale cheeks.

His pulse kicked up a notch.

Definitely a woman.

"You'd best find shelter." He raised his voice to be heard over the howling wind. "I'm from around these parts, and a storm like this could last for days. There's an abandoned cabin up ahead. It's not much, but you can build a fire and get the horses out of the wind."

She blinked, and the shotgun inched back a mite, easing his mind by a long shot. "Much obliged, mister. We'll think about it."

We. At least she wasn't alone. "You'd better think fast. If the snow gets too deep, your horses will have a hard time pulling that wagon. And I'd hate to see them freeze to death."

Lasso edged his horse around the wagon. The draft animals lifted their heads slightly as he passed. As his mare fought the wind and blinding snow, he heard the jingle of harness and the creaking of the wagon as it inched along behind him.

When the dilapidated cabin came into view, he swung down and stripped the saddle from his horse. As quickly as he could, he led the mare out of the wind into what was left of the barn and headed back to help with the other horses.

The wagon rolled to a stop at the edge of the cabin, the woman handling the team. An uneasy feeling hit him square in the chest. She'd said *we*. Did she have a husband? A father? He wanted to ask again, but questions could wait until they were inside. Snow fell so hard and fast, he could barely see ten feet in front of him.

Lasso reached up to help the woman down from the high wagon seat. Once on the ground, the top of her head barely reached his chin. The heavy man's sheepskin coat cinched tight around her waist dwarfed her small frame. "I'll unhitch the horses, ma'am," he yelled over the wind. "Get inside."

She nodded but headed to the back of the wagon instead. He didn't take the time to figure out what she wanted out of the wagon, but set about unbuckling the harness.

Once the horses were settled, he hurried back out into the raging storm. A bulky burlap sack lay on the ground at the back of the wagon, but there was no sign of the woman. What was taking her so long?

"Ma'am?"

She stuck her head out. "We're ready."

She lifted her full skirt and clambered over the back of the wagon, and he offered a steadying hand.

"Thank you." A gust of wind tugged the shawl away from her face, and Lasso got his first good look at her. Strands of dark hair tore free from her braid and whipped wildly about her face. The cold painted her pale cheeks with a pink glow, and she had the biggest, brownest eyes he'd ever seen. But right now, they were filled with caution as she took in his measure.

Apparently he passed muster, because she turned back to the wagon. "Hurry up, Jedediah."

A gangly boy tossed another sack out of the wagon then handed off a small child to the woman. The kid's sleepy eyes popped open as he spotted the snowflakes swirling around them. He reached out a chubby hand. "Fowers!"

"Not flowers, William. Snow." She let him slide to the ground and turned back to the older boy in the wagon. "Help Grandpa."

Before Lasso could offer assistance, the two of them helped an old man carrying a Bible almost as big as a saddlebag to the ground. The frail old man shuffled to the side, the wind buffeting him. Lasso snagged him by the arm to keep him on his feet.

Behind him came three small figures, all girls by the flurry of skirts under the layers of coats and scarves they wore. The young woman helped them down one at a time, and they huddled around her, stair steps in size.

The smallest, not bigger than a mite, stared at him, her trembling lips turned out in a pout. She snubbed then started whimpering, and fat tears rolled down her cheeks. The young woman tucked her closer. "*Shh,* Marie, it's going to be all right. You'll be warm soon."

Lasso swallowed, afraid to ask what was on the tip of his tongue. "Is that everybody?"

"Not quite. Jennie?"

"I'm coming!"

"Bring the lantern."

Another girl, about the same age as the boy, appeared at the back of the wagon, a mound of quilts in her arms. The young woman with the big brown eyes ringed with dark lashes took the quilts, passed them off to the tallest stair-step, then glanced around, panic on her face. "Where's William?"

The little boy was already halfway to the barn, battling the blustery wind with a determination that made Lasso laugh. The wind tossed the youngster on his backside, but he just giggled and struggled to stand up again. The young feller she'd called Jedediah took off after the boy, grabbed him around the waist, and hauled him back.

Lasso surveyed the motley group before him. Jedediah stood with the kid on his hip, a burlap sack thrown over his shoulder. The girl called Jennie fussed with her shawl, muttering about the cold. The three stair-steps huddled together, gazing at him as if he could tread on water. Grandpa clasped his big black Bible against his chest with both hands.

And the young woman who seemed to be in charge lifted her chin, her stance, and the shotgun cradled in her arms, daring him to mess with her little chicks.

He took a deep breath. Just what had he gotten himself into?

Chapter 2

When the door closed against the howling wind, darkness engulfed the cabin. Mollie Jameson fumbled to light the lantern. As the feeble light chased the shadows into the corners, she counted heads, something she did almost as an afterthought these days.

Her sisters, Emily, Samantha, and Marie all snuggled close to Jennie, who held tight to William's hand, lest her little brother wander off again. Grandpa shuffled to sit on the lone cot in the room, cradling his Bible. Her younger brother, Jedediah, dumped their belongings in a corner. She bit back the urge to tell him to be more careful but was too relieved to be out of the gusting wind and biting cold to chastise him.

"I'm cold," Samantha said, her teeth chattering.

The stranger headed straight for the wood box, where the last traveler had left a decent supply of wood and kindling. He motioned Jedediah over and handed him a knife. "Shave off some of that kindling, and we'll get a fire going."

Mollie fumbled with their bedding, spreading an oilcloth on the floor, then covered it with a quilt. "Girls, huddle together, and I'll wrap you up. It'll keep you warm until Jedediah and Mr.—" At a loss, she broke off, trying to remember if the stranger had mentioned his name in the rush to get out of the storm.

"The name's Lasso McCall, ma'am."

"I'm Mollie. Mollie Jameson."

The flickering shadows of the lantern and the muffler that covered the lower part of his face hid his features, but he tipped his hat, acknowledging her, even as he built the fire. "Pleasure, ma'am."

Being in such close quarters with a stranger made her a bit uncomfortable, but what choice did she have? The storm hadn't left them many options. At least Mr. McCall seemed friendly enough. She covered the girls with another quilt and tucked them in, offering them a reassuring smile. "Mr. McCall will have a fire started in no time."

Five-year-old Marie would have none of it and reached for Mollie instead. Mollie took her sister in her arms, hugging her close. Marie laid her head on her shoulder, and Mollie smoothed her silky, light brown hair away from her face. *"Shh."*

She unbuttoned her father's coat and pulled Marie close, rocking her from side to side, patting her back, while she took stock of her surroundings in the dim light cast by the lantern. The moldy cot Grandpa had claimed, a few pegs on the walls, and a broken chair were the only furnishings in the small room. Wasn't much, the owners had taken everything when they left, but they couldn't take the fireplace, and for that, she was grateful.

A cold gust of wind hit her from behind, and she turned to see William heading through a door between the cot and the fireplace. Mollie made a grab for him and hauled him back into the room. "Oh no you don't."

A firm hold on William, Marie dozing on her shoulder, Mollie peeked through the open door into an even smaller room built on the back side of the cabin. A tree had crashed through the wall on the far side, and gusting winds tossed swirling snow through the gaping hole. Spotting an overturned bench, she handed her sister and brother off to Jennie, dragged the bench into the room, and closed the door against the cold.

"Do you think the chimney's safe?" she asked, positioning the bench between the children and the fledgling fire.

"Don't see why not. It's been used recently." Mr. McCall hunkered in front of the fireplace, nursing the fire into existence. Flames licked at the wood, blazing higher and burning brighter, casting a comforting glow over the dreary room, and driving out the bone-numbing chill.

Jedediah rolled into one of the quilts. "Don't get too close, Jedediah. You'll singe Mama's quilt."

Her brother ignored her and settled deeper into his cocoon. She sighed, deciding to let him stay there for now. Jedediah would move when he was good and ready. Stubborn as the day was long, just like Pa, and resentful that she'd been born first. She plopped down on the bench and closed her eyes, weary with trying to keep them all together, body and soul.

Her head lolled, and she jerked awake, only to find Mr. McCall still hunkered in front of the fire, his forearms draped across his knees. She hadn't had a chance to get a good look at him, and she couldn't see much in the faint light given off by the fire. He wore a bulky coat, a cowboy hat, and a weatherworn bandanna covered the lower half of his face. His gaze caught hers before sweeping the room, landing first on Jedediah then on the girls, watching from their cocoon of quilts.

"Looks like everybody's settled in." He tossed his hat to the side and pulled the faded neckerchief down, revealing several days' growth of whiskers on his jawline. He squinted at her. "Hungry?"

She shook her head. "More cold than hungry right now. We had some leftover biscuits and ham earlier."

Samantha's eyelids began to droop, and she burrowed deeper inside the mound of quilts. Marie had stopped crying now that she was warm and safe. Even William lay snug and warm in their midst, hopefully too tired to wander off for the time being. It took the whole family to keep the child out of harm's way.

The warmth cast off by the fire finally started to penetrate her chilled bones. "Is that your real name?"

"Lasso?" He quirked a brow at her, and she nodded.

A half smile cocked up one corner of his mouth, and he shrugged. "It's not the name

I was born with, but I'm a fair hand with a rope, so it stuck."

Her grandpa left the cot and shuffled toward the fire, hands extended toward the warmth. "Grandpa, this is Lasso McCall. Mr. McCall, my grandfather, Reverend Rupert Vincent."

In one fluid movement, Lasso stood, his size dwarfing her grandfather. He nodded in greeting. "Reverend."

"Grandpa's memory fades in and out sometimes. You'll have to forgive him if he forgets who you are." She pointed out the rest of her family. "Jedediah and Jennie are twins. They're fourteen. Then there's Emily, Samantha, Marie, and William. He's the last of the bunch."

"If you don't mind my asking, what happened to your parents?"

Mollie hugged her father's sheepskin coat close and turned her face into her mother's thick woolen shawl. "Mama died when William was born, and Pa died in"—she closed her eyes, thinking. How long had it been? Three months, four?—"in July."

Two years of trying to hold the family together without Mama had been tough, but losing Pa had magnified the chore, and Mollie wondered if she was up to the task. She blinked back tears.

She didn't have time to mourn the loss of her parents, not now, maybe not ever. Maybe someday she could take out her memories and thumb through them, but not until she had her family safely settled. Grandpa wasn't much help. Sometimes he was as much a child as William. Jedediah scowled and gave her fits, but there were times when he and Jennie made her heart swell with pride.

"Traveling mighty late, aren't you?"

"Pa took sick in May. Before he passed, he insisted we head to Nebraska and claim our land."

"Lincoln?"

"You've been there?" She struggled to keep her eyes open as the fire chased the chill away.

"My pa and stepmother live right outside of Lincoln."

Mollie bit back a yawn, feeling warm and cozy. Grandpa dozed on the cot, the sound of his soft wheezing growing in volume. Jedediah's snoring soon rivaled their grandfather's. Even their snoring wouldn't keep her awake tonight. "Then you're headed that way?"

"No, ma'am. Headed north."

"You don't want to see your family?" She frowned, wondering what she'd missed. Why wouldn't he be headed to Lincoln with winter setting in?

He looked at her, the firelight flickering over his face, his dark eyes serious. He turned away, picked up a poker, and stabbed at the logs. "It's late. Get some sleep."

"You. . .you'll be here come morning?"

"I'll be here."

Chapter 3

Lasso tended the fire while Mollie covered her grandfather with the last quilt. Then she lay down beside her sisters, fully clothed, the heavy men's sheepskin coat her only covering. The entire Jameson family had quieted down. It hadn't taken long for the lot of them to fall asleep, after being stranded in the snowstorm.

His attention swung back to the oldest sister, Mollie. Her shawl had fallen back to reveal a mass of long dark hair caught in a messy braid that reflected the flickering light from the fire. Her cheek cushioned against a rolled-up shawl, her lips quickly parted in the gentle rhythm of slumber. She'd been just as tired as the rest of them. He grunted. Probably more so.

The boy rolled on his back, dead to the world, except for the constant rasp that cut through the cabin with every breath he took. Lasso grabbed the quilt and slid boy and all away from the fire, before finding a spot on the floor next to the door.

As he settled down for the night, he pondered the situation. He didn't want to be responsible for the Jameson family, and he certainly didn't want to escort them to their destination. He wasn't too fond of how this horde of children reminded him that his father had made a new life for himself.

But the blizzard outside hadn't taken his plans into consideration. As soon as the storm blew itself out, he'd bid pretty little Mollie Jameson and her family good-bye and skedaddle toward the Double M.

∞

Mollie woke with a start. The roaring fire had burned down, leaving the cabin in shadow but still comfortable enough.

She pulled her coat close and padded to the shuttered window. The gusting wind battered against the cabin, but she couldn't see enough to determine if it was still snowing. What time was it? Still night? Almost daylight? She thought the sky seemed a bit brighter, but the storm-laden clouds kept it too dark to tell for sure.

Her gaze swept the dim room, and her heart stuttered in her chest. Lasso McCall was gone. She took a deep breath, willing herself not to panic. She tamped down the disappointment that he'd left without saying good-bye after promising to be there. Her face flamed. She didn't even know why she'd asked him to stay in the first place. She'd managed to take care of the children just fine in the months since Pa had died, and she'd keep doing it with Jedediah and Jennie's help.

A new resolve in her step, she strode to the fireplace and stoked the fire, put coffee on to boil, and then set about gathering the ingredients for a batch of sourdough biscuits. As soon as this storm let up, she wanted to be ready to roll, and a batch of biscuits would keep them until they arrived in Lincoln.

She'd just located the flour when the door opened, letting in a gust of cold wind and a flurry of fat snowflakes. Lasso stepped inside, a thick layer of snow covering his coat and cowboy hat. He dropped a pile of pine boughs just inside the door, snow falling in heavy clumps to the floor.

"I thought you were gone." Mollie winced, regretting the accusing tone in her voice.

He removed his hat and hung it on a peg, his dark brows drawn into a scowl. "I told you I'd be here."

She dumped flour into a bowl, unwilling to admit she was relieved that he hadn't ridden out and left them alone. She nodded at the pine boughs. "What are those for?"

"Bedding."

"Bedding?"

"For tonight. No need in the young'uns sleeping on the floor again."

Mollie froze, the realization that they were stuck in this cabin as chilling as the storm raging outside. "We can't stay here another night. As soon as it's daylight, we'll take stock."

"It is daylight, ma'am, and nobody's going anywhere until this storm lets up."

"How far are we from Lincoln?"

"Three to four days. Possibly longer, depending on how much snow we get." He shrugged. "We'll just have to wait for the storm to blow itself out."

"I don't have time to wait it out." The churning sensation in her stomach intensified, and she forced her fingers to move, kneading the mixture of lard and flour, wishing she could bend the storm to her will as she did the dough.

Lasso hunkered down and snagged the coffeepot from the fireplace. Steam rose from his cup as he poured. "Maybe it's time you tell me why it's so all-fired important to get to Lincoln."

"In May, my father filed on a Nebraska homestead. As a Union soldier, he had six months to take possession of the land." Mollie made quick work of the biscuits as she talked, stuck a lid on the Dutch oven, and covered the whole thing with hot coals.

"And then?"

An ache stabbed Mollie between the ribs, and she faced him, wrapping both arms around her waist. The firelight flickered over his face as he waited for her answer. "He took sick and died."

"When's the deadline?"

"Next Thursday."

"These early storms tend to blow over quickly. You've still got time." He took a sip of coffee, studying her over the rim.

"Won't do any good."

Mollie whirled. "Grandpa. You're awake."

"I've been awake the whole time, missy, and I'm telling you it won't do any good." Her grandfather's piercing blue gaze shifted from Lasso to her, the old familiar, determined jut to his bearded chin in evidence.

"What do you mean?" Lasso straightened, his stance wary. "What won't do any good?"

"Ain't nobody going to give all that land to an old preacher like me with one foot in the grave, and—" Even in the dim light of the fire, Mollie caught the flush that rolled up his neck. "And my memory's not so good anymore. Even I have sense enough to know that."

Mollie rested her hand on his arm. "Grandpa, we've been over this time and again. We have to try."

"They won't give me that land, no matter what your pa thought." He flipped open his Bible and extracted a piece of paper. "If there was one good thing that came from your pa fighting for the Union, it was being able to file a claim on that land in Nebraska. Lot of good it did him in the end, though."

"Grandpa, please. Mr. McCall doesn't want to hear about that." Her grandfather and her father hadn't seen eye to eye on the recent conflict between the North and the South, and she'd hoped that when her father died, her grandfather would put the old grievance to rest.

"I'm sorry, Mollie girl. You're right. What happened twenty years ago is neither here nor there." Her grandfather's chagrined smile asked for her forgiveness. Then he waved the piece of paper in the air. "And even though I've heard they let women file for these homesteads, this flyer says you still have to be twenty-one, and your birthday is. . ." He paused, frowning. "When is it again?"

Mollie's heart sank at the befuddlement that shuttered across his face. His lapses in memory sometimes came on so suddenly that she scrambled to keep up. "January, Grandpa. It's in January."

"Mr. Vincent—"

"Call me Reverend." Her grandfather clapped Lasso on the back. "It's all I've ever answered to."

"Reverend." Lasso nodded. "As head of the household, there shouldn't be any reason why they won't deed the land to you."

"No, they won't because. . ." Her grandfather trailed off in midsentence and gave Lasso an uncertain smile. "And who might you be, sonny boy?"

Mollie took her grandfather by the arm and led him to the bench. "That's Mr. McCall, Grandpa. You remember—"

"Lasso will do," Lasso interrupted, his voice soft and compassionate. She threw him a grateful look. Not everyone understood or was as accepting of her grandfather's addled state.

"You remember the snowstorm, Grandpa? Mr. McCall—Lasso—helped us find this nice cabin to wait out the storm."

"It is a nice cabin, nice and warm. God was surely looking out for us, wasn't He?"

Her grandfather smiled and patted his Bible, not really acknowledging that he knew who Lasso was or what role he'd played in finding shelter for them. Sorrow squeezed Mollie's heart. How long would it be before her grandfather slipped into that shadowy place in his mind and never came back?

How long before full responsibility of her brothers and sisters fell to her and her alone?

A stirring on the pallet drew her attention as Jennie threw back the covers and sat straight up, her eyes wide with alarm.

"Where's William?"

Chapter 4

Who was William?

Lasso tried to remember which of the children had been William. There'd been so many and the cabin had been so cold and dark that he hadn't really gotten a good look at all the youngsters last night. He'd just known there was a whole passel of them. The tall, lanky boy—the one called Jedediah—rolled out of his blanket, hair standing on end. Hadn't there been only one small boy among all the girls? The one who'd taken off for the barn during the storm.

Yes, he remembered. They'd called the little tyke William.

Pandemonium erupted as the Jameson family scrambled to their feet, even the little girls wide awake now. The littlest one, maybe five or six, started sniffling again. The two oldest, twins, if he recalled, Jedediah and Jennie, bolted for the door, straight toward the storm raging outside.

"Hold it right there!" Lasso yelled. The two halted in their tracks, Jennie with a wide-eyed expression of terror, Jedediah mutinous as if he would charge out into the storm regardless of the danger. "Nobody's going anywhere in this storm."

Mollie already had her coat on and was busy buttoning it up, shaking fingers bungling the task. "He was there just a few hours ago. I checked on him."

She headed toward the door, Jedediah right on her heels, but Lasso cut them off, grabbing Mollie by the arm. "You can't go out there. You can't see your hand in front of your face, and you'll be lost five feet from the door."

"That's my little brother out there." Her eyes flashed with purpose. Jedediah moved to stand beside her, the stubborn jut of his chin a mirror image of his sister's.

Lasso held Mollie's gaze, recognizing the resolve of a mama bear determined to protect her cubs. He took a deep breath. "I'll search. Jedediah, you come with me. I strung a rope between here and the barn, and we'll tie off that to keep from getting lost. He couldn't have gone far. But you have to promise me that you and the children, and your grandfather, will stay here."

Tears spiked her eyelashes. "But—"

He gave her arm a little shake and gritted out, just loud enough for her and Jedediah to hear, "It won't do any good for you to get lost in this storm. Your family needs you." He paused, and the sounds of the little girls' sobs penetrated the silence. "Your sisters need you right now. Me and Jedediah will find your little brother."

⚭

Mollie's stomach clenched as she peered out the single oilskin-covered window, the shutters allowing her only a glimpse of the storm raging outside. The wind clawed through the cracks, stinging her face, but she barely noticed. Her baby brother was lost in that storm, and only her promise to Lasso to keep the other children safe kept her from wrenching the door open and rushing out to search for him.

The entire family had plenty of experience hunting for William, and they usually found him without difficulty, but this—this was different. The odds of finding him safe in the middle of a blizzard was something they'd never encountered before.

Lord Jesus, keep William safe. Help Lasso and Jedediah find him. Keep him safe. Keep him safe. Keep him safe. . . .

The prayer repeated itself over and over inside Mollie's head even as she straightened the tiny cabin and sorted through the meager supplies they'd brought inside in their rush to get out of the storm. Jennie and the girls helped her spread the blankets over the pine boughs, anything to stay busy and keep the panic at bay.

When there was nothing else to clean, nothing else to organize, nothing else to keep her hands and her mind busy, she turned to her grandfather. She knelt beside him as he sat on the bench and read from his Bible. Grandpa might not know where he was or who she was half the time, but he knew who God was.

He smiled at her and patted her on the head as her tears overflowed. "There, there, child. What's the matter?"

"William's lost in the storm, Grandpa, and I need you to pray."

"William?"

Her heart broke that Grandpa didn't know who William was this morning, but it didn't matter. Grandpa's heart was as tender as ever. "He's just a little boy, Grandpa. Please help me pray."

"Of course I'll pray, child. Lord, please take care of this little one. Return him to safety and to his family." He rested a gentle hand on Mollie's head. "And bless this young lady. Teach her not to fret, but to trust in You. Amen."

He smiled and patted Mollie's shoulder. "Everything will be fine. You'll see."

Mollie smiled through her tears, praying he was right.

"Mollie?" Emily sidled up to her side, her brow drawn down in a frown way too severe for a nine-year-old. "Is William going to be all right?"

She crushed her sister to her side to hide the worry pinching her face. Guilt stabbed at her. How William had gotten away from all of them when she'd thought he was snug on the pallet between his sisters gnawed at her. "Yes, sweetie. He's going to be fine. Lasso and Jedediah will find him."

"Are you sure?"

Don't fret.

"I'm sure." She held Emily away from her and gave her an encouraging smile. "Now, let's eat before our breakfast gets cold."

Emily bit her lip. "I don't think I can eat with. . .with William gone."

Mollie smoothed her hair back and sent a quick prayer heavenward, her gaze meeting Jennie's over Emily's head. "All right. We'll wait a few more minutes, then we can all eat together. How about I braid your hair and Jennie can do Marie's?"

She'd finished braiding Emily's hair and was brushing Samantha's when she heard pounding at the cabin door.

Mollie rushed forward and lifted the bar. The howling wind slammed the door open and Lasso and Jedediah fell inside, tied together with a length of rope. Even as Lasso grabbed the door, shoved it closed, and dropped the bar into place to hold the wind at bay, a chill swept Mollie from head to toe.

They hadn't found William.

Chapter 5

Stiff from cold and near frozen, Lasso removed his gloves and fumbled with the buttons on his coat. Jedediah stood just inside the door, staring at his sister, numb disbelief on his face.

All color drained from Mollie's face as she realized they hadn't found the child. Lasso had a sudden urge to fold her in his arms and hold her. The weight of this entire brood of little children and one dotty old man rested on her slim shoulders. She took a deep breath and pinned him with a look. Stark pain creased her brow. "Did you find anything? Footprints? A hat? Anything at all?"

"Nothing." Lasso shook his head and reached for the buttons on Jedediah's coat. The boy had to be frozen, and helping him would take her mind off her little brother. "Let's get Jedediah out of these wet clothes."

"Of course." That galvanized her into action, and she grabbed a quilt off the pile spread over the pine boughs. Jedediah didn't resist as they removed his wet clothes. "I've got coffee. That should warm you both. Jennie?"

"Mollie, I tried—" Jedediah's voice cracked on a sob.

"*Shh.* I know." Mollie wrapped one arm around her brother and led him to the bench in front of the fire. She wrapped the quilt around his shivering form and held a cup to his lips, blue and trembling. "Drink. Careful, it's hot."

Lasso nursed the cup Jennie handed him, letting the warmth of the fire soak into his bones. But nothing could warm the chill that permeated the Jameson family. One by one, the little girls sidled up to the bench and huddled around Mollie and Jedediah, like chicks to a mother hen, apprehension stamped on each small heart-shaped face.

"He couldn't have gone far. I'll go back and search for him again." The offer was futile, but he had to make it.

Mollie shook her head, the despair on her face gut-wrenching. "It's too late. He couldn't survive out there this long."

"He could if he made it to the barn, or—" His gaze fell on the door to the other room, and he slammed his coffee cup against the mantle. In two strides, he reached the door and wrenched it open.

Please, God.

Mollie joined him, the rest of the Jameson family crowding in behind them, quiet. The remains of a giant oak lay across the roof, broken, rotting limbs reaching inside. The smell of decay and something like wet dog permeated the room. The wind wasn't so bad here, but it still gusted through the far side of the room where one wall had collapsed upon impact.

"Call him," he whispered.

"William?" Mollie's voice trembled.

A thump interrupted the quiet.

She clutched Lasso's arm. "What was that?"

They waited. Silent, straining to hear the sound again. For a long moment, there was nothing except the wind whistling through the tree limbs that brushed against the rough-hewn walls of the cabin. Then they heard another *thump*, a scratching, scrabbling sound, and tiny whimpers, followed by a giggle.

Mollie surged forward. "That's William."

The children started yelling, calling for their brother.

"*Shh. Shh. Shh.*" Mollie held a finger to her lips and shushed her brother and sisters. "Listen."

Lasso found himself holding his breath as they waited. Then he heard it, a faint scratching sound but no more little boy giggles. He motioned with his fingers. "The lantern."

"Here." Jennie passed the light forward, until it reached Lasso. He ducked under a protruding limb and led the way farther into the room, Mollie and Jedediah on his heels. His eyes adjusted to the gloom, the hole in the roof letting in scant light, the moisture-laden skies filled with snow blocking the sunlight.

He held the lantern high, the flickering light casting eerie shadows over the walls, the broken tree, and the swirling snow. Mollie stood next to him, her arm brushing his. Then he heard it again.

Tiny, satisfied whimpers came from the back side of the fireplace. Mollie stood on tiptoe, one hand on his shoulder, the other pointing to the far corner. "There."

Lasso pushed a rough-hewn table out of the way, bent down, and squinted into the gloom at a brightly colored patchwork quilt.

"That's Mama's quilt," Jedediah exclaimed.

Lasso reached out and peeled away the heavy quilt to reveal a mound of puppies snuggled against a shaggy-haired mutt.

Along with a little dark-haired boy, wide-eyed, warm, and none the worse for wear.

Chapter 6

Uppies cold, 'ollie."

William held one of the puppies in his chubby little arms and gave Mollie a sidelong glance that melted her heart. "I know, sweetie. But you can't run off like that. Do you understand?"

He buried his face in the puppy's fur. "I 'stand."

"All right." Mollie hugged him to her, her heart filling with gratitude that he'd been found safe and sound. "Are you hungry?"

"Yesth."

"Give me the puppy, then, and come eat."

"No." William jutted out his bottom lip and shook his head. "Mine."

She didn't have the heart to take the pup from him and return it to its mother. There would be time for that later, when he fell asleep. She herded the children to the side as Lasso and Jedediah manhandled the rickety table into the cabin along with an old keg that would serve as extra seating.

William ate precious little then squirmed out of her lap to play with the puppy. Mollie let him go, knowing he'd be back for more later. Quiet, shy Marie tugged on Mollie's sleeve. She bent down and her sister whispered, "Can I play with the puppy?"

Mollie bit her lip. Taking the pup away from William to give to his sister would certainly cause a ruckus, but hadn't there been a whole litter of puppies in the other room? And the mama dog had seemed friendly enough. She hugged Marie. "Let's see about finding you a puppy of your own."

Emily's and Samantha's hopeful expressions nearly did her in. Her gaze met Lasso's across the table. "Mr. McCall, how many puppies did you see back there?"

One corner of his mouth quirked up, and he winked at her. Her stomach did a slow roll even as Emily and Samantha giggled. The urge to join them slammed into her like the wind howling outside the cabin. Flustered at her reaction to an innocent wink designed to amuse the children, she stood and began gathering the dishes from their meal.

"Well, let's see. I think I saw at least one more." He scratched his jaw, frowned, and scrutinized the ceiling, as if pondering an extremely important problem. "Is that enough?"

The girls shook their heads no, still giggling.

"Maybe we'll get lucky, then. Come on, girls. Let's go see." Lasso stood. His tall, broad-shouldered frame loomed large in the small confines of the cabin. He held out his hand to Marie, and she took it without hesitation, her face turned up to his with nothing short of adoration.

"Do you think it's safe?" Mollie worried her bottom lip. "The mama dog won't hurt them, will she?"

"She was fine with William." He jiggled Marie's hand. "But we'll be careful, won't we, squirt?"

Marie grinned and nodded.

Five minutes later, the cabin was filled with the sounds of snuffling puppies, giggling girls, and one shaggy-haired black-and-white mutt ensconced in the far corner. Mollie kept her eye on the dog, but she seemed more than happy to share her litter of pups with the children.

The children occupied, the remains of breakfast cleaned up, a pot of stew with a salt pork ham bone for seasoning simmering over the fire, Mollie's thoughts returned to the delay in their trip. Anxious, she pulled back the corner of stiff oilskin and peeked through the cracks between the shutters. The storm still held them prisoner.

Lasso sat on the bed of pine boughs covered with a thick layer of quilts, his back to the wall. William had climbed up on the makeshift bed and had promptly fallen asleep against Lasso, one of the puppies cradled in his arms.

Mollie let go of the oilskin and turned to Lasso. "How long do you think it'll last?"

"Who knows?" He shrugged, one hand toying with the puppy's soft fluffy ears, his touch gentle. "Since it's a bit early for a blizzard, hopefully it won't last long."

"A day? More?" She pressed, needing reassurance that they would make it to Lincoln in time.

"Storms like this have a mind of their own." He shifted William to the pallet, and her little brother stretched, yawned, and then relaxed into slumber again. "There's no sense in worrying how long it'll last until it's over."

"I'm sorry." Mollie removed her shawl, sat down on the edge of the bed, and covered William with it. "If we don't make it to Lincoln in time, our entire trip will be for naught."

"What did your grandfather mean when he said they wouldn't give the land to him? He might be a bit addled, but that wouldn't stop them from giving him the land."

Mollie took her time tucking the shawl around William, before looking up to meet Lasso's gaze head-on, a challenge on her face. "They won't give him the land because Grandpa fought for the Confederacy."

Chapter 7

Lasso stilled. He'd heard of families being split down the middle during the war, but he hadn't ever met a family who'd lived through such a rift. He'd been a child when the war ended, and he didn't remember much, other than the day his pa had come home. And Mollie would have still been in diapers, but the standoff between her father and grandfather still haunted them. This morning's conversation had proven that.

He studied Reverend Vincent, calmly reading his Bible. Every so often, the old man would read a passage of scripture out loud, or hum a few bars of a hymn. And when he wasn't reading, he watched the children, an indulgent smile creasing his face. It was hard to believe the gentle old soul had fought and killed men in the war.

"Can't you file another claim when you get there?" he asked.

"We could, I suppose, but ours has a creek running through it, a soddy, and a barn, and we'll need that to get through the winter." Her fingers plucked at a loose thread on the quilt. "When Pa took sick, we delayed our trip, hoping he'd get better. He urged us to go on without him, but I just couldn't do it. It wasn't right to leave him sick and alone, and I kept praying he'd get well and could make the trip with us."

"You did what you thought was best."

"But was it the right thing to do? By disobeying him, I risked losing the very thing he'd dreamed of for so long." Pain laced her voice, and Lasso wanted to reach out and smooth the worry off her brow, to tell her everything would be all right.

But what right did he have to promise her anything? He was just a cowpoke who rode roughshod over a few cattle now and then. Other than his horse and his saddle, he didn't even have a place to call home. And he liked it that way. No responsibilities meant he didn't have to worry about losing anything when hard times came. And hard times would come. They always did.

"When. . .when he knew the end was near, he made me promise to take Grandpa and the children and head West. We pulled out as soon as the last shovelful of dirt covered his coffin."

She ran her hand over the quilt, her fingers absently tracing the pattern as she related the events leading up to her father's death. Lasso covered her hand with his, the warmth of her fingers shooting fire through his belly. She stilled but didn't pull away. "You're going to make his dream come true."

"But what if I don't? After everything Pa went through. After what we've been through to get here. What if we don't make it?"

He tried to concentrate on the conversation, but the soft warmth of her hand beneath his did funny things to his thinking. "If the weather breaks today, you can still make it to Lincoln in time."

She eased her hand out from under his and rested her palm against his knuckles. The brief touch hit him with the force of the storm raging outside. "Thank you. For. . . everything."

With those words, she stood and moved away, toward the fireplace across the room, skirts swishing against the rough plank floor. Lasso watched her go, wondering how he'd walk away from Mollie and her brood of brothers and sisters when the time came.

Chapter 8

The soothing sound of Pa's bow saw from the other room calmed Mollie's nerves as the wind continued to howl around the cabin. The dead tree was a welcome source of seasoned wood, and Lasso and Jedediah had kept busy all morning chopping up broken limbs.

Snowdrifts blocked the front door overnight, and Lasso had taken to coming and going to the barn through the other room. Mollie shivered, more from the incessant wind than the cold. Would Nebraska always be like this? She opened one of the crates and peered at the dwindling contents. The longer they delayed their trip, the lower their food stores would get.

Jennie set the table for the noon meal while Grandpa read from his Bible and the children played with the puppies on the floor. As much as she hated to admit it, the puppies had been a godsend while cooped up in this cabin with nothing else to do.

Grandpa looked up from his reading and took an appreciative sniff. "Is that coffee I smell, Mollie girl?"

"I just made a fresh pot. Would you like some?"

"That sounds good." For a change, his eyes were clear, bright, and he seemed like his old self. "Where's Jedediah? And that feller with the funny-sounding name?"

"They're outside, cutting firewood." She poured him a cup of the steaming dark brew and placed it in front of him.

"Mollie? Jennie? Open up!" Jedediah banged on the door that led to the room where they'd found the puppies. Jennie hurried to let him inside, his arms full of firewood, the mama dog right on his heels. Jedediah dropped the pile of wood into the wood box next to the fireplace, and the dog padded over to the children and sniffed at her offspring before settling down beside them. The puppies started scrambling toward her, anxious to nurse.

Mollie eyed the overflowing wood box. "That's a lot of wood."

Jedediah warmed himself in front of the fireplace. "Lasso says if we don't use it, whoever stays here next will."

"Lasso? What kind of name is that?" Her grandfather snorted, his bushy eyebrows drawn down in a frown, a lot like when he used to preach fiery sermons in their small country church back home in Alabama. But those days were long gone. His forgetfulness had relegated him to sitting out services on a pew while a new, younger preacher had taken his place.

"It's a nickname, something his friends call him." Jedediah turned a half circle in front of the fire.

"Lasso, huh? He must be one of those no-account cowboys then, wandering all over the country." He wagged a finger at Mollie and Jennie. "You girls stay away from him. No good will come from the likes of him."

"Yes, sir." Heat swooshed to Mollie's face as the feel of Lasso's work-roughened fingers gently touching hers came rushing back. Thankful for the dim light in the cabin, she ducked her head, hoping nobody noticed. "But, Grandpa, he did lead us to this cabin and has stayed with us during the storm."

"Well, girl, he ain't going out in the storm, now, is he? But mark my words. As soon as the storm lets up, he'll take off. We don't know anything about him, or where he's from."

"Sure we do," Jedediah said. "His pa and stepma live close to Lincoln, and he's heading to a spread up north to winter. I'm going with him, too."

Mollie whirled, sweet thoughts of Lasso's touch flying away on the blustery wind. "What did you say?"

"I'm going with Lasso." Jedediah jutted his chin, daring her to defy him. "He's going to teach me how to be a cowboy."

"But, Jedediah, we need you."

He shrugged as if the matter was settled. "You and Jennie can handle things on your own. And, besides, when I get a job working cows, I can send money to help out, just like Lasso sends money to his family."

Mollie turned away, knowing that now wasn't the time to argue with him. She donned her coat and marched to the door, suddenly needing answers to the questions swirling inside her head.

Lasso had cleared a wide swath to the barn, making it easier to keep a close eye on the horses. She hurried that way, holding on to the rope as the wind buffeted against her. His back to her, he swung the ax, the *thwack* loud in the close quarters. Jerking the ax free, he swung it again, and the wood split all the way to the ground. He reached down to set up another piece of firewood, and spotted her.

"Is something wrong?"

"Yes, something's wrong." She stalked closer, crossed her arms, and glared at him. "Jedediah said you're taking him with you when you leave."

"I never said that."

"What did you say then?"

He swung the ax, and the sharp blade dug into the wood. "He asked me about riding the range, herding cows, and roundups. And I told him."

"You filled his head full of nonsense."

Lasso's gaze snapped to hers. "I did no such thing. He already had it in his head to take off on his own as soon as the family is settled in Lincoln."

"He's just a boy." Mollie wrapped her arms around her waist, quenching the foreboding feeling that her family was falling apart and she couldn't do a thing to stop it.

"He's fourteen." Lasso moved to stand in front of her and rested his hands on her shoulders. "Mollie, give him a chance to grow up. Let him prove he's a man."

"I don't know if I can." Her gaze searched his, and she shook her head.

"If you don't, he'll leave for sure."

She took a deep breath and nodded. "All right. I'll try."

"Good. In the meantime, I'll talk to him. He needs a horse, an outfit, and a stake before he strikes out on his own. And he needs to wait until springtime for sure." Lasso smiled, a crooked little grin that twisted her insides. "Who knows, some pretty little filly might change his mind before then."

"He's too young for court—" She broke off in midsentence when Lasso's brows drew together in a frown. "Sorry. I'll do better, I promise."

"See that you do."

His gaze flickered, shifted, and focused over her shoulder. He nodded toward the barn door, propped open to let in a bit of sunlight.

"Look. It's stopped snowing."

Chapter 9

Even though it stopped snowing, the wind continued to whip the snowdrifts into a frenzy.

Mollie chafed at the delay as the day wore on, but she could see the wisdom of waiting until the wind died down. By nightfall, Lasso and Jedediah had packed everything in the wagon except the bedding and a few cooking supplies. Mollie cooked a batch of corndodgers, potatoes baked in their skins, and beans that would see them through the next couple of days of travel.

As she worked, she worried about what would happen when they left. Would Lasso ride along with them? And what about Jedediah? The two of them had been in and out all afternoon. Surely Lasso had managed to talk some sense into her brother.

Lord, please don't let Jedediah go off half-cocked without the means to survive.

For the first time in ages, Mollie was alone, except for the puppies all curled up together in the corner and Grandpa dozing on the cot, his soft snores making her smile. After being cooped up in the cabin for two days, the children had donned coats and hats and were playing on the far side of the cabin out of the wind. The sounds of their laughter brought a smile to her lips.

Lasso came inside, stomped the snow off his boots, and hung his hat on a peg. "Is that everything?"

"One more crate, but it can wait until morning." Mollie packed her spices and seasonings in the box, cushioning them with flour-sack hand towels. "Are the children all right?"

"You mean William?" He laughed. "Yes, he's fine. Rolling around in the snow with the dog. Oh, by the way, the girls named her. They've been calling her Stormie."

Mollie pursed her lips. "I don't know if that's a good idea."

"Why?"

"If they name her, then she becomes a part of the family, and then we'll have to take her—and the puppies—with us."

"You're going to have to take her with you, regardless." He brushed by her, his nearness causing her breath to hitch in her throat. "You know that, don't you?"

She sighed. "I suppose."

He hunkered down in front of the fireplace and poured a cup of coffee. She kept packing the crate, resisting the urge to turn but finding it impossible to ignore the sound of his movements behind her, the rattle of the coffeepot as he plopped it back on the flat stone just inside the fireplace, the rustle of his clothes as he straightened.

"Did you talk to Jedediah?"

"Yep. He agreed that it's not a good idea to head out on his own until the weather warms up and he saves up a stake." Her hands froze in their task as he moved up behind her, leaned down, and whispered close to her ear, "Happy now?"

Her stomach flipped as his breath tickled her cheek, but she casually smoothed a hand towel and folded it before turning slightly to catch the glint in his dark brown eyes, the teasing smile on his face. Butterflies took flight in her stomach.

"Yes. Thank you."

Chapter 10

Without discussion or question, Lasso mounted up and led the way toward Lincoln the next morning. Mollie drove the wagon, pleased he'd decided to ride along. She had no idea how long he'd stay with them, and she couldn't bring herself to ask.

The wagon slogged through the half-frozen muck left by melting snow, the horses struggling to pull the weight up and down the hilly terrain, mud sucking at the wheels. Mollie set the brake and motioned for Jennie. "Here, take the reins. I'll walk."

"In this mess?" Jenny clambered over the seat back, looking surprised.

"We need to lighten the load. You, too, Jedediah."

Jedediah and Mollie kept pace with the wagon, knocking clumps of mud off the wheels with hefty sticks, Stormie trotting along beside them. Finally, the road leveled out, and they made decent progress for a couple of miles, before dipping down into a tree-studded hollow. The road wound down and around the trees, branches and limbs blocked from the wind still heavily laden with snow. Mollie and Jedediah dropped back as the wagon eased down the steep grade.

The shaded area at the bottom of the hill proved to be more difficult to navigate, and the distance between them and the wagon grew. Mollie slogged through the slush, her boots caked and growing heavier with each step. She groaned as she rounded the bend and saw the road winding up a steep hill. A thick stand of trees blocked the wind and the sun, and a blanket of wet snow still covered the ground. Jennie wasn't up to the task of forcing the horses to pull the wagon up the steep incline.

"Jennie, wait!" Mollie picked up her skirts and stumbled forward, but her sister kept urging the horses forward. When they balked and started backing up, the wagon jackknifed, and raw terror slammed into Mollie's stomach. She rushed forward as the girls screamed her name.

Mollie and Jedediah reached the horses just in time to keep them from becoming entangled in the traces. They grabbed the harness, and Mollie called to Jennie, "Set the brake."

"I'm sorry, Mollie." Jennie's pasty face rivaled the off-white canvas cover on the wagon.

"It's all right, you didn't do anything wrong," Mollie assured her sister, soothing the frightened animals. "Let them rest a bit before we attempt this hill."

As her pounding heart slowed, Mollie patted the horses and eyed the steep, snow-covered hill. Would the horses be able to pull the load up the steep incline, slick with half-melted snow? She didn't any experience forcing the horses up a steep hill in snow, and she wouldn't let Jedediah or Jennie attempt it. Lasso had gone on ahead to scout out a campsite for the night, or she'd ask him to do it.

No, she'd drive the wagon herself, as soon as the horses rested, and she worked up her nerve. *Lord, please help us up this hill. Help me to be strong.*

When the horses' sides stopped heaving, she took a deep breath. Lasso was depending on her to follow with the wagon, and she'd waited long enough. "Jennie, get the children and Grandpa out. Go on to the top of the hill while the horses rest a minute, then I'll bring them up."

"I'll do it." Jedediah's defiant gaze met hers across the backs of the horses. "You go on with the others."

It was on the tip of her tongue to tell him no, that she would do it by herself. But she bit back the words when Lasso's words came back to her. She'd treated Jedediah like a child for so long that she'd missed the subtle cues that he was turning into a man, that he needed more responsibility. And if he planned to strike out on his own, it was time to start treating him as an equal. "We'll do it together, once the children and Grandpa are all out of the way. Hold the horses while I help Jennie."

"Puppies?" William asked as she lowered him to the ground and took his hand.

"No. The puppies can ride."

Just as they topped the ridge, Lasso rode into view. Mollie had never been so glad to see anyone in her life. Lasso had been raised in this country and would know if the hill was too dangerous for the horses and wagon. He dismounted. "What's wrong?"

"The horses didn't want to take the hill. I told Jedediah to wait until I got back." Mollie led the way back, and her heart nearly stopped when she spotted Jedediah climbing up onto the wagon seat. She stepped forward. "Jedediah, no."

Lasso reached out a hand and stopped her. "Let him be. He'll be fine."

"But—"

"Trust me." He squeezed her hand and winked before letting go and crawfishing a few steps down the steep hillside. "Jedediah? Once you start for the top, don't let up. Keep 'em coming."

"Yes, sir." Jedediah grinned and slapped the reins against the horses' backs. "Giddyup."

Of course the horses balked, but he kept urging them to take the hill. And once they started, Jedediah did exactly as Lasso had said and didn't give them any quarter. Her brother's commands and slapping leather rang in her ears even as Mollie held her breath.

When the wagon topped the rise and rolled onto level ground, Jedediah set the brake and jumped down, swaggering with pride.

"Good job." Lasso slapped him on the back then started scraping mud and snow off the horses' hooves, Jedediah following his lead, his grin wide enough to rival the sprawling Nebraska prairie.

Pride swelled inside Mollie as she watched the two of them together. Her younger brother was turning into a man right in front of her, and most of the credit could be laid at Lasso McCall's boots.

Chapter 11

Lasso leaned back against his saddle, full of beans and corn bread. The fire had died to embers, and while the temperature wasn't as warm as he'd like, the night wouldn't be unbearably cold. And he was thankful for that, especially for the old man and the children's sake.

Mollie and Jennie settled the children inside the wagon, puppies and all. Stormie whined to be allowed to sleep with the children, and Mollie finally relented. Earlier, they'd rigged up a canvas skirt around the wagon for Mollie, Jennie, and Reverend Vincent, while another piece of canvas staked alongside made a serviceable lean-to for Jedediah and himself. All in all, the entire lot of them would pass the night in comfort as long as the weather cooperated.

Once everyone was settled, Mollie sank down beside him with a weary sigh. Lasso reached for the coffeepot and refilled her cup.

She nursed the tin cup between her hands. "We're not making very good time."

"On horseback, I could make it, but another day or two like today will make it iffy." He sipped his coffee, wanting to offer reassurance, but he couldn't lie. "What if your grandpa and I ride ahead?"

"It'll never work." She shook her head. "Grandpa couldn't ride that far, and he's convinced they won't give him the land anyway."

"He's also convinced they won't give it to you, either."

Mollie didn't answer, just stared at the fire, lost in her own thoughts. Lasso added a couple of sticks of wood to the fire and banked it for the night. Mollie tossed the remains of her coffee to the side, stood, and pulled her shawl close to ward off the chill.

"Get some sleep, Mollie. We've got another long day ahead of us." Lasso brushed past her, intending to check on the horses before turning in.

"What if he's right?" she asked, her voice barely a whisper. "What will we do if they won't let us have the land?"

Her eyes sought and held his, tears shimmering in their depths.

Unable to stand the sight of her tears, Lasso tugged her to his side. She came willingly, her head cushioned against his coat. He wrapped his arms around her and held her close, resting his chin on the top of her head. Nothing had ever felt better than holding Mollie, comforting her. But holding her wouldn't solve the problem.

And he was fresh out of ideas.

Chapter 12

I've been thinking."

Bright and early the next morning, Lasso pulled Mollie to the side while Jedediah and Jennie loaded the wagon. Her heart tripped as she remembered the feel of his arms around her last night. She'd lingered longer than was proper, but knowing he was there helped ease the fear and worry that had dogged her day and night for months.

"There's a cutoff up ahead. It'll shave at least a day off the trip."

A glimmer of hope shot through her worry. "That sounds wonderful."

He smiled, and for a wild moment, she wondered what it would be like if Lasso stayed, if he decided to court her and they could farm the land together. He kept talking, lashing his bedroll into place. With an effort, she concentrated on what he was saying.

He leaned a forearm on his saddle, nodding in the direction of the crossing he'd mentioned. "I think we can make better time. The trail's more exposed to the elements, so the wind should have dried it out by now."

"Why don't people use it then?"

"The crossing's too dangerous in the spring and early summer when the river runs high, but come late summer, many of the cattle drives use it." He squinted at her. "It's our only chance."

Mollie worried her bottom lip. Did they dare leave the main trail? But Lasso had already proven that he had their best interests at heart, and she trusted him to keep them safe. She nodded. "If you think it's best."

"I would never do anything to hurt you or the children, Mollie."

"I know." She smiled.

After a long searching look, his gaze flickered and dropped to her lips. Mollie's heart raced in anticipation. The rattling of the wagon intruded and he broke eye contact, before tossing her a crooked smile that let her know he regretted the interruption. Mollie stepped back, heart pounding, feeling a bit of regret of her own.

He helped her onto the wagon seat, before mounting his horse and heading out. The temperature rose with each passing mile, and only patches of snow remained here and there. For the first time in weeks, really, for the first time since her father had died, happiness bubbled up inside Mollie. Just as Lasso had said, the road was easy to follow, windswept and packed hard from thousands of cattle passing through during the summer months.

. God had blessed them in the most unexpected way. They'd easily make it to Lincoln at this pace. Jedediah handled the reins and she sat beside him as the entire family rode in the wagon for a change.

Her gaze lingered on Lasso's broad back, and her heart turned over at the ease with which he rode, capable and confident. Lulled by the rocking motion of the wagon, she let herself dream of a future on their land. A future that included Lasso. She'd never been in love, but a few beaus had called on her. Even though she wasn't well versed in courting, the feelings developing between her and Lasso were beyond anything she'd ever felt for anyone else. But did he feel the same? Surely she hadn't imagined the look on his face as they broke camp this morning, and the tender way he'd held her in his arms last night.

Soon, they'd stop for the noon meal, and. . .and what? And maybe he'd kiss her? Mollie pressed a hand to her stomach to quell the butterflies that erupted at her silly flight of fancy. She was acting like a love-struck schoolgirl. Other than an almost kiss that she may or may not have imagined, Lasso hadn't given any indication that he planned to stick around long enough to do more than make sure they arrived in Lincoln safely. She'd do well to remember that.

Noon came, and they stopped to rest the horses in a flat expanse of prairie that stretched for miles. Not a shade tree in sight, but it felt good to bask in the sunshine after the bitter cold winds of the last few days. Mollie spread a quilt on the grass. On a whim, she hurried to the wagon and unearthed a jug of sorghum molasses that she'd been saving for a special occasion.

Today was a special occasion. Tomorrow they'd be in Lincoln, and God willing, they'd have their own land.

She kept an eye on Grandpa as he strolled a short distance away, stretching his legs. Lasso and Jedediah picketed the horses on the tough prairie grass that seemed unaffected by the recent snowstorm. Lasso strode toward her, saddle over his shoulder, and she looked away, pretending to watch the children, but she was acutely aware of every move he made. He dropped his saddle at the edge of the quilt, took off his hat, and stretched out beside her, near enough to touch.

Instead, she kept her attention on Jedediah and the children as they romped in the grass with Stormie and her litter of fat puppies. William fell, face-first, into the grass, his giggles floating on the breeze as the puppies crawled all over him. Lasso laughed, and it was all Mollie could do not to reach out and caress the dimple creased beside his mouth. She clutched her hands in her lap, tamping down the bubble of joy that threatened to erupt.

She loved him. She didn't know how it had happened, or even why. But she did. And that was all that mattered.

He plucked a strand of prairie grass and nodded at William's antics. "I wish I had that much energy."

"What was your childhood like?" The question slipped out, but she didn't regret it. She wanted to find out everything she could about him before they reached Lincoln, in case she never saw him again. Her stomach dropped. No, she wouldn't think about that right now. She'd savor this time and then tuck it into a corner of her heart to remember him by.

"Much like yours, I reckon." He shrugged. "Except I didn't have a horde of younger brothers and sisters underfoot."

"What, no brothers and sisters?"

"My mother and baby sister died in childbirth when I was twelve. Ma had been sickly, and the doctor advised her not to have more children."

Mollie shook her head. "I can't imagine being an only child."

"Well, Pa remarried, so I've got a whole passel of stepbrothers and stepsisters." He grinned at her. "I imagine they could give your bunch a run for their money."

"Probably." She laughed, before turning serious. "Lasso, I meant to thank you for everything. If you hadn't come along when you did, I don't know what we would have done."

"You're welcome." He dipped his head, and a slow smile turned up one corner of his mouth, his lazy regard doing funny things to her insides.

Heat rushed to her face, and she lowered her gaze and toyed with a loose button on her coat. "What are you planning to do after we get to Lincoln?"

"I'd planned to winter at a spread a bit north of here. Ol' Man Morehead likes to get an early start in the spring and doesn't mind having a few of us on hand at the get-go."

His words had the effect of being doused by a bucket of cold water. "So. . .he's expecting you?"

"No. Not really. But he won't be surprised when I show up."

"I hope you'll stop in and see us when you can. I'll miss—" Her face flushed, but she had to know if she'd see him again. "I mean—the children will miss you. Especially Marie."

"Just Marie?" His voice was low and husky, tinged with amusement. "What about you, Mollie? Will you miss me?"

"Of course." She reached for the Dutch oven where she'd stored the baked potatoes. Anything to keep him from recognizing what was in her heart. "We've all grown to. . . to care for you."

His hand covered hers, large and work-roughened against her smaller one. "Mollie?"

She turned toward him, heart pounding with fear and excitement all mixed together so much that she thought she'd take wings and fly. He reached out and tucked a strand of hair behind her ear, his warm fingers lingering against the side of her face. His dark-eyed gaze flickered over her face then dropped to her lips.

Then, slowly, like molasses poured out of a jug on a cold winter's morning, he dipped his head and captured her lips with his. Mollie's eyes slid closed as she savored the sensation of her first kiss.

It was all and more than she'd dreamed it would be. All too soon, he eased back, his breath a whisper on her heated cheek. He tipped up her chin, and she met his gaze, feeling a bit more brazen than was proper. He smiled and leaned toward her again.

A waterfall of sensation trickled through Mollie as she waited for the feel of Lasso's lips against hers again.

"Where's William?" Jennie called out, her voice penetrating the soft, rosy glow surrounding Mollie.

Lasso groaned, and Mollie peeked at him through half-closed eyelids. The frown on his face brought a bubble of laughter to her lips. He grabbed his hat, stood, and pulled her to her feet. His thumb rubbed lazy circles against her wrist, and she shivered at his touch.

Plopping his hat on his head, he growled, "I'm going to tie that boy to the wagon."

Chapter 13

Lasso rode ahead of the wagon, trying to untangle the knots in his brain. In the span of a few days, he'd gone from being a Good Samaritan doing a good deed, to wanting to protect and provide for Mollie and her family for the long haul.

If William hadn't wandered off again, he would have told Mollie that he wasn't going anywhere any time soon. They'd need help through the winter, wouldn't they? They'd need food, fodder for the horses, firewood, protection. No telling what kind of shape the soddy and the barn were in, and Reverend Vincent, Jedediah, and the girls wouldn't know how to chink a soddy against the harsh Nebraska winters. Someone would have to show them.

He scowled, knowing there were plenty of men in and around Lincoln who'd jump at the chance to lend a hand to the Jameson family once they got a good look at Mollie. And then there was Jennie, Emily, Samantha, and Marie. Someday, they'd all need a man handy with a shotgun.

He'd never understood why his pa had married his stepmother with her houseful of young'uns. There'd been plenty of other suitors seeking her hand back in Arkansas, so it wasn't like she hadn't had options.

Oh, his stepmother was a godly woman and treated him kindly, but even as a youngster, Lasso had known the difficulties that lay ahead, and he'd figured that he and his pa could make it better alone than with a woman and a bunch of young'uns underfoot. And he'd been right. Their first winter in Nebraska had been tough. They'd almost starved, and the next year hadn't been much better. They'd been poor, still were, and Lasso sent money when he could, but it was never enough. But his pa didn't seem to mind. He'd just smile and say they were rich in other ways.

Pa said he'd understand someday. Understand the need to care for a woman and provide for her regardless of the hardships that lay ahead. And since Lasso had met Mollie, he had an inkling of what his father had tried to tell him.

Even as he longed for the freedom of the open range, the satisfaction of a successful drive, it was plain as horns on a bull that Mollie was going to need help. Jedediah was already talking about taking off for parts unknown as soon as the family was settled, and Lasso expected the boy to make good on his plans. He'd done the same thing at that age, sowing his wild oats, getting out of a house packed to the gills with children and more on the way.

But one taste of Mollie Jameson's lips made him forget all about his aversion to being tied down with more responsibilities than he could shake a stick at. All he could think about was coming home to her smile every night, seeing her eyes shine with joy when he walked in the door, wrapping her in his arms and running his fingers through her long, silky hair.

And someday having a houseful of little children the spitting image of their mother.

Laughter pealed out, and Lasso glanced back to see Mollie strolling along beside the wagon, Marie and Samantha running ahead of her. And right then and there, he decided he'd stick around Lincoln for a while. He wanted Mollie for his bride, and he wouldn't risk some yahoo coming along and stealing her away from him.

Chapter 14

The river rushed past, and Mollie tamped down her alarm. The water was a lot higher than she'd expected, probably due to the recent rains and melting snow. "We should go back." She pulled the wagon to a halt beside Lasso, worry knotting her stomach. "Isn't there a ferry at the other crossing?"

"There's not enough time." He gave her a reassuring smile. "It's not as bad as it seems. Wait here."

He urged his mare down the bank, his attention on the water, and the rocks lurking beneath the surface. His horse picked her way across, mapping out the best route for the wagon. To Mollie's relief, the water didn't reach the mare's belly, even though the fierce rush of it worried her. Lasso backtracked and trotted his mount up to the wagon.

"See. It's safe enough. I'll lead the way back across, so just follow along behind me."

He wheeled away, and Mollie slapped the reins against the horses' backs, determined to see this task through and get her family safely to the other side. "Giddyup!"

"Mollie? Let me—" Jedediah reached for the reins, but it was too late for her to rethink her decision. The horses were already in the water. Her heart pounded as the water drew closer and closer to the wheel hubs, and she cringed every time the wheels slipped off rocks she couldn't see. She kept her attention centered on Lasso's back, praying they'd make the crossing without incident.

The wagon jolted as it rolled across a rock along the bottom of the riverbed, and her heart lurched right along with it. Jedediah glared at her. "Let me take the reins."

"I've got it. Just hold on. And keep your eye on the rocks." She gritted her teeth, praying under her breath. She wouldn't put this responsibility on Jedediah, and it was too late now anyway. They were committed to the river whether she liked it or not.

As they drew near the opposite side, she began to breathe easier. They'd almost made it across.

Thank You, Lord.

The front end of the wagon rolled off a large rock into a depression, almost unseating her. Jedediah wrapped one arm around her waist, the other holding on to the wagon. She drove the horses forward as Lasso had taught her, and they surged against the harness, jerking the wagon forward. But the next thing she knew, they balked and started backing up. The wagon lurched sideways, along with her stomach.

Not giving the horses a chance to stop, she braced her feet against the floorboards and slapped the reins hard against their backs, forcing them to move forward. "Hiya! Hiya! Giddyup! Giddyup!"

In that instant, she felt the wagon lurch sideways with a sickening *pop*. The girls screamed as the rear end fell into the water with a splash. Mollie twisted on the seat, lost her balance, and fell headlong into the river.

Chapter 15

The screams pierced Lasso's heart. He wheeled around, took in the situation at a glance, and spurred his horse toward the river.

He yelled at Jedediah, who'd grabbed the reins. "Keep coming. Bring 'em on out of the water."

"Giddyup!" Jedediah lashed the horses and pulled the crippled wagon out of the water.

Lasso jumped off his horse and waded into the water where Mollie struggled to get a foothold on the slick rocks. The water wasn't deep, but it was swift. If the current carried her away before he reached her, she could be swept into deeper waters downstream. He grabbed her and hauled her out of the water to safety. When they reached the bank, he held her at arm's length and raked his gaze over her, head to toe, heart pounding from the near catastrophe. "Are you all right? Are you hurt?"

"No." She shook her head, already twisting in his arms. "The children!"

"They're fine."

"Thank You, Lord."

She slumped against him then, and Lasso picked her up and strode toward the crippled wagon. Reluctantly, he set her on her feet as everyone came rushing toward them, Jennie carrying one of their mother's quilts. She wrapped it around Mollie, and the little girls crowded around her. Mollie assured them she was fine, and Jennie hustled her toward the wagon and dry clothes, clucking like a mother hen.

Lasso watched them go, breathing hard. When his heart rate returned to normal and his mind accepted the fact that they were all safe—that Mollie was safe—he turned his attention to the problem at hand.

He glared at the broken wheel, disgusted with himself. He'd given Mollie hope, and not only damaged the wagon but put the entire family in danger. What little time they'd gained by taking the shortcut was now lost. Even if he could get the wagon going, they'd have to take it slow and easy.

And they didn't have time for slow and easy.

But, regardless, they needed to move. He considered and rejected options as he examined the wheel. All of them couldn't ride on three horses, and short of abandoning the wagon, there was only one thing to be done at this point. He strode to the horses and grabbed the harness.

"Jedediah, lend me a hand. Let's get these horses unhitched and picketed. Then we'll fix the wagon."

Jedediah started unbuckling a harness. "How're you going to fix it? We don't have a spare wheel."

"We're going to make a crutch."

Chapter 16

A crutch?"

In dry clothes and wrapped in a quilt while her coat dried out, Mollie stared at Lasso. Had he lost his mind?

"Trust me." He climbed into the wagon, Jedediah dogging his heels. They started moving things around, shifting the heavy items to the front of the wagon on the off-side of the broken wheel.

"That should do it." He jumped out of the wagon and handed Mollie a length of leather strapping. "Soak this while we're gone. I'll need it to lash the crutch to the axle."

Then he said something about a stand of lodgepoles a mile or so back, and he and Jedediah took two of the horses and headed out for the thicket, ax in hand. Mollie shook her head as she watched them go. The whole thing sounded like a wild goose chase to her, and she had a passel of hungry children to feed. With Jennie's help, she built a fire and draped her wet clothes nearby to dry out. As they prepared supper, she tried not to worry about what this delay meant.

Grandpa sauntered over to the wagon and squinted at the broken wheel, a frown on his face. "A crutch, huh?"

"That's what he said." Mollie warmed the last of the beans and whipped up a fresh batch of corndodgers. "Do you think it'll work?"

"I've heard of such a thing, but I've never actually seen it done. But I reckon it's worth a try. And besides, what other choice do we have?"

Grandpa was right. They didn't have a choice. Mollie searched the horizon but didn't see any sign of Lasso and Jedediah returning. If Lasso could get the wagon moving again today, they still had a slim chance of making it on time.

But Mollie gave up hope of travel as the day wore on. The children had already eaten and the sun hung low in the sky by the time Lasso and Jedediah came back, dragging a fresh-cut lodgepole, three times longer than the wagon. Mollie eyed the long, slender sapling, trying to visualize what he had in mind.

Whatever it was, she hoped it worked.

Lasso took an ax and notched the larger end of the pole, then he and Jedediah jacked up the wagon. Grandpa was right in there with them, working to get the wagon serviceable again. Lasso nodded at Jedediah. "All right, run the pole under the rear axle toward the front, and I'll lash it to the front axle."

As Lasso tied the notched end to the axle with the long strip of damp leather, his intentions became clear. The pole stuck out behind the wagon and supported the rear axle, much like the poles the Indians used to make a travois. They eased the weight of the wagon down onto the crutch, being careful not to jar it to the point of breaking it. The supple sapling bent beneath the weight but didn't break.

Even Mollie could see that by placing the heaviest items in the front of the wagon on the opposite side and leaving the rear empty, the green sapling would bear the weight of the rear axle on the left. The wagon still listed, but at least it cleared the ground.

Lasso slapped his hand against their handiwork then nodded at Jedediah and Mollie. "Keep a close watch on it. If it breaks, we'll have to do it all over again."

Mollie marveled at the contraption. "Where'd you learn to do this?"

"Same thing happened to the chuck wagon on a trail drive a couple years ago." He hunkered down and used a leftover strip of leather to loosely secure the crutch so that it didn't slip off the rear axle. "We should be able to limp along for a few days."

"A few days?" Mollie's earlier excitement popped like a bubble in a pot of boiling water. "The deadline is day after tomorrow."

"Can't be helped. Too much jolting and the pole will snap." He pushed his hat back and squinted up at her. "There's one other option."

"What's that?" Mollie couldn't see anything that would get them to Lincoln in time.

"I can make it on time on horseback."

Chapter 17

W hat good would that do?"

Lasso stood and leaned against the wagon, trying to gauge Mollie's reaction. "The land agent might extend grace if I'm there with the papers."

"And if he doesn't?"

"It's our last hope." Lasso winced. He hadn't meant to include himself as part of the family. But he agreed with Reverend Vincent. The odds of the land agent deeding the land to an underage woman were slim to none, and even less for an ex-Confederate soldier.

"But"—she frowned, working through the plan—"the paperwork's not in your name."

"You'll have to sign everything over to me. I'll make it right by you and your family as soon as you get there." His heart pounded, but he knew he was doing the right thing. He reached for her hand. "And, Mollie, if you're willing, we'll get—"

"He's right." Lasso jerked his head up as Reverend Vincent approached, Bible in hand. "You know that I've felt this entire trip was in vain because they wouldn't let either of us prove up on your pa's claim. But I went along with it because you promised your pa, and God kept telling me to trust Him to provide." He eyed Lasso. "Seems like He's provided in ways I couldn't have imagined."

Reverend Vincent took Lasso's measure, his countenance more clear and aware than it had been all week. He nodded as if satisfied with his decision then turned to shuffle away. "Let's all get cleaned up now. As soon as you two are hitched, Lasso can head on out."

"Hitched? As in married?" Mollie's shocked expression hit Lasso square in the stomach. Was the idea of marriage that surprising to her? Before he could reassure her, she hurried after her grandfather. "Grandpa, Lasso wasn't proposing marriage. He was just going to Lincoln to get the land for us."

Her grandfather patted her hand. "I know what he meant, girl, and I appreciate his willingness to do what it takes. But we didn't come all this way to just sign our claim away to a stranger." He dipped his chin, an apologetic smile on his face. "No offense, son, but what proof do I have that you won't lay claim to that land for yourself, leaving my grandchildren high and dry?"

"Grandpa!"

"He's just protecting your interests, Mollie." Lasso stepped forward, his gaze taking in Mollie's disheveled state. Seeing her plunge into that river had scared the very life out of him. In that instant, he'd known that he couldn't live without her. And if she'd have him, he'd do whatever he could to make her happy. He squared his shoulders and faced her grandfather.

"I'm willing, sir. I'll marry Mollie."

Chapter 18

In a daze, Mollie let Jennie fuss over her. She'd been content to change into dry clothes and pull her damp hair into a tight bun, but Jennie would have none of it. Mollie gave in when the younger girls pleaded with her to let them wear their best dresses for the occasion. The quick ceremony uniting her and Lasso McCall as husband and wife turned into an afternoon of primping.

Finally, they were all ready, and Mollie glanced around the wagon at her younger sisters. The girls' faces glowed with excitement, and they wore their Sunday best, their freshly combed hair in neat pigtails. Jennie had even cut up two of her blue ribbons so that there would be enough ribbon to tie the ends of each braid.

Little Marie's face broke into a shy smile as she glimpsed herself in the tiny mirror Mollie held out. Mollie hugged her and tapped her nose with the tip of her finger. "Don't lose your ribbon. As soon as the wedding is over, we'll put it back in the trunk, so you can wear it again."

"When I get married?"

Mollie and Jennie laughed. "Yes, when you get married."

Samantha popped up at the back of the wagon, her arms filled with long stems of dark gold, brown, and pale cream prairie grasses. A few dried wildflowers in faded purple and pink clung to the stems. "Look what I found. There aren't any fresh flowers, but I hope these will do."

"Oh, they're beautiful." Mollie smiled, touched at Samantha's gesture. Jennie and Samantha divided the flowers into five bouquets and tied each bundle with leftover blue ribbon and string pulled from the stitching of a flour sack. Samantha handed the largest to Mollie. "Thank you, sweetie. It's perfect."

She took a deep breath and moved toward the back of the wagon. "Well, looks like we're all ready."

"No, you have to stay in the wagon until it's time." Jennie clambered out and helped the girls down.

Mollie called after her, "Check on William."

"He's fine. Lasso's got a hold of him."

Lasso.

Just thinking of him made her go weak in the knees. She'd be a married woman in a matter of minutes. Remaining in the shadows inside the wagon, she peeked out. The sun rode low on the horizon, casting purple, red, and golden rays into the sky. It was if God decorated all of Nebraska for her wedding in the waning hours of daylight. She spotted Lasso amid her brothers and sisters, and her heart fluttered against her rib cage.

He'd shaved and wore a string tie and a faded print shirt that looked suspiciously like one of her pa's. Probably more of Jennie's doing.

Soon, he'd be her husband. She held her hand to her stomach to quell a nervous flutter.

Jennie was busy instructing everybody where to stand, then she ran back to the wagon and whispered, "It's time."

"Grandpa?"

"He's all right, but you'd better hurry."

Mollie climbed down, smoothed her blue calico, and nodded. "Let's go."

Jennie motioned for Jedediah, and he loped to her side and offered the crook of his arm. Mollie blinked back tears. Pa should have been the one to escort her to her groom, but Jedediah, standing straight and tall, and taking his role very seriously, was more than up to the task. Jennie led the way toward the small party, walking so slow it seemed as if they would never get there.

But Mollie etched the scene in her mind, wanting to remember every detail down to the hum of the river rushing over the rocks. God had even provided music. Her baby sisters, all so pretty, made her heart ache with pride. William stood beside Lasso, holding a puppy. For once, he seemed to understand the importance of the occasion—or they'd bribed him by letting him hold the puppy. Regardless, they all knew not to turn their backs on him, not for a second. And her grandfather, wearing his faded black suit, waiting to join her in marriage to Lasso McCall.

Finally, her gaze swept over Lasso, and her step faltered. He stood, legs braced apart, hat in hand, his hair damp and curling. A slight smile lingered on his face, and his dark eyes shone with something she didn't recognize. Something meant for her and her alone. Could it be love? Or was the girlish excitement of the occasion causing her to see him through rose-colored glasses?

She'd always longed to marry for love, but love hadn't been mentioned. But he wouldn't have agreed to the marriage if he didn't at least feel something for her, would he? She blushed and lowered her gaze, on the pretense of watching her footing.

Her pulse was thrumming in her veins by the time she and Jedediah arrived at the pretty spot beneath the trees Jennie had chosen for the wedding. Lasso offered her one of his half smiles, and her heart tripped alarmingly in her chest.

"We're gathered together to join this man and this woman in holy matrimony," her grandfather intoned. Pausing, glanced at the assembly. "Who gives this woman to be wed?"

"We do," Jedediah and Jennie said in unison.

Grandpa grinned. "I do, too. So, now that we've got that settled, let's continue."

Jennie nodded at Jedediah, and he stepped away and let Lasso take his place at Mollie's side, her hand nestled in the crook of his arm. When his warm, calloused hand rested on top of hers, Mollie forgot everything but the way his fingertips rubbed the back of her hand. Somehow, she managed to say all the appropriate words at the right time.

As soon as her grandfather pronounced them man and wife, Jennie and the girls swarmed her with hugs and kisses. Her grandfather beamed like the proud grandfather he was, and Jedediah asked if it was time to eat.

Mollie clapped a hand to her mouth. "Oh, I forgot all about supper. I'll just change and whip up something real quick."

"Jedediah and I took care of supper." Lasso pulled her back as Jennie and Jedediah herded the little ones toward the wagon.

"You did?"

"It won't taste as good as anything you and Jenny could fix, but we won't starve." He winked, and her stomach flipped.

"I'm sure it'll be fine." Mollie turned to go, but Lasso stopped her with a hand on her arm. She glanced up, and he met her gaze, looking a bit sheepish.

"Mollie, I. . ." He stopped, glanced at her grandfather and siblings, then took her hand and led her toward the river. They stopped close to where she'd fallen out of the wagon. He let her go and faced the river, his back to her.

Mollie waited, growing more nervous as he just stood there. Finally, he rubbed the back of his neck with one hand and turned, his eyes dark and serious. "I just wanted you to know that I don't expect—I mean, it's not—well, what I'm trying to say is I'll—I'll bunk with Jedediah tonight and head out first thing in the morning."

Relief flooded over Mollie as he turned on his heel and strode off toward camp without a backward glance. She wrapped her arms around her waist and turned toward the river, the rush of emotions careening through her as fierce as the waters hurtling downstream. Tears pricked her eyes at the consideration Lasso had shown for her feelings regarding their hasty marriage. Yes, she cared about him, and she wanted to be his wife, but she was more than happy to have a bit more time to get used to being a married woman.

The sun had gone down by the time they'd eaten. One by one the children started yawning, and Mollie and Jennie got them all ready for bed. As she tucked away their wedding finery, she dug deep in the bottom of the trunk and pulled out a leather pouch that contained Pa's discharge papers, the letters, and the paperwork where he'd filed on the land, along with the extra cash they'd brought to pay the solicitor's fees. All her pa's hopes and dreams were in this one small pouch.

She ran her hand over the cool leather.

"Pa," she whispered, "Lasso will see that your dream comes true."

Chapter 19

The sun struggled up and over the horizon as Lasso caught up his horse.

Clouds roiled in from the west, battling with the sun, and it promised to be a cold, wet, dreary day. The sooner he left, the quicker he could come back for the Jameson family. He smiled.

For Mollie.

As he lashed down his saddlebags, he spotted her moving about the camp. She stirred the fire and started making coffee. While the coffee boiled, she unbraided her long, dark hair, running her fingers through the tresses to work out the tangles, then made quick work of braiding it back with nimble fingers. He rested his forearm on his saddle and drank in the sight of her.

She spotted him, and the shy smile that flitted across her face kicked his pulse up a notch. He grabbed the reins and headed toward her as it hit him that they were truly married, in name only, of course, but maybe that would change as soon as he returned.

Without speaking, she offered him a cup of fresh-brewed coffee. Lasso let his fingers linger on hers a moment longer than necessary, and the air crackled with tension before he took the cup and lifted it to his lips. Mollie moved away, reaching for a small oilskin pouch tied with string. She held it out. "Here are the papers, and there's some money there, too."

"You should keep the money."

"It's to pay the solicitor. Pa said there might be some fees."

Reluctantly, he took the pouch and the money. She stood in front of him, hands clasped, looking lost and alone in the oversized coat. He stuffed the papers into his saddlebags, strapped the flap down, then scanned the horizon before settling on her face, memorizing every feature. He wanted to reach out, pull her braid free, and run his fingers through her hair, much like she'd just done.

Instead, he muttered, his voice low, "Remember what I said. Take it easy on the horses, and just let 'em drag the wagon along. As long as you don't break that crutch, you'll make it to Lincoln without any problem."

She nodded, looking serious. "All right."

"And watch those clouds. If it starts snowing again, or if anything happens, find a place to hole up, and wait for me."

"Yes, sir." Her lips twitched, and those dark eyes of hers flashed to his as she struggled to hide her amusement.

"What's so funny?" He frowned.

"I got us this far, didn't I?"

"Well, only as far as the cabin—"

"True." She nodded, laughing. Fingering the horse's mane, she grew serious, and her gaze searched his, before skidding away. "Please be careful."

He studied her lowered gaze, the curve of her cheek in the early morning light. Slowly, he reached out and tucked a strand of hair behind her ear, letting his fingertips slide over the curve of her jaw. She shivered at his touch. He closed the distance between them, took her by the arms, and turned her to face him. He arched his eyebrows and scolded, "You worry too much."

"I can't help but worry." She sniffed, blinked a couple of times, and attempted a smile. "I'm afraid something's going to happen to you."

"Nothing's going to happen," he whispered and pulled her closer, his heart pounding double-time as he wrapped her in his arms. She tilted her face up, and he claimed her lips once more. Ever since he'd promised to love and cherish her until death parted them, he'd longed to see if she tasted as sweet as she had yesterday. How long he held her was anybody's guess, but when a light drizzle began to fall, he reluctantly pulled away and rested his forehead against hers.

"I'd better go."

Chapter 20

The drizzle turned to a steady rain within an hour of breaking camp, making travel miserable. Mollie insisted everyone ride in the wagon, even though she worried about the extra weight, but she'd didn't want the children getting sick. It was enough that she had to worry about Lasso riding through the downpour.

Jedediah drove, letting the horses plod along, careful not to jolt the crippled wagon too much. Every few miles, Mollie called a halt to check on the crutch. They weren't going to make it in time, so her first priority was to keep the wagon moving at all costs.

When the temperature fell and the rain continued to beat down on them during the afternoon, Mollie and Jedediah made the decision to stop. They picketed the horses and made a dry camp, spending a long, miserable night in the confines of the wagon. Daylight brought another cold, miserable day, but at least it wasn't raining—for the time being.

They hitched the horses to the wagon, and Mollie and Jedediah eyed the crutch that held the rear axle off the ground. It was bowed down under the weight. Jedediah added an extra layer of axle grease to the pole, hoping the extra lubricant would help keep it supple. "You think it's gonna hold?"

"I don't know." Mollie glanced at the sky, worried about the hazy clouds forming in the distance. "But we need to keep going. The closer we get to Lincoln before bad weather hits again, the better off we'll be."

They headed out, Jennie driving, Grandpa riding shotgun, with Jedediah, Mollie, and Stormie walking. It was too muddy for the little girls and William, even though Emily pouted, wanting to do her part to lighten the load. It took some doing to convince her she was needed in the wagon to take care of the little ones.

Mollie slogged through the mud, trying not to think about Lasso, where he was, or if he'd made it to Lincoln yet. But hard as she tried, it was all she could think about. The clouds rolled in around noon, dark and ominous, obscuring the sun. The heaviness that sucked at her feet, sucked at her thoughts as well. What if he didn't make it? What if. . .

She wanted to run to the wagon, call out to her grandfather, and ask him to pray, pray against the worry and fear that threatened to consume her on this dark and dreary day. Suddenly, his words to her when William was missing flitted into her mind like a feeble ray of sunshine.

"Don't fret, my child. Don't fret."

The heavy load that pulled at her heart and mind eased, and she concentrated on praising the Lord for bringing them this far, for bringing Lasso into their lives when they needed him most. He should have made it to the land office by now and had the deed transferred. They still had hope, and all she could do was fret.

If things went as planned, he could easily make it back on horseback by the end of the day, and then they could all continue on straight to their land. Not just Jameson land, but McCall land.

"Our land," she whispered, and the day seemed brighter just by saying the words out loud. The thought of seeing Lasso again and starting their new life together on their very own land encouraged her.

Just a few more miles and the journey would be over.

Chapter 21

Got to help Mollie. I can't let her down.

Lasso groaned, feeling like his head might explode. He opened his eyes, determined to get up, to get help for Mollie and the children. Where were they? Were they all right? He'd promised to return for them, to take care of them.

The ceiling spun, and he tried to focus, frowning up at the tongue-and-groove ceiling even as it registered that he lay on a soft mattress, covered by a warm quilt.

Where was he? He'd left Mollie and the children in the broken wagon, and now he was in a strange place while they were stuck somewhere in the cold, abandoned, struggling to make it to Lincoln. He had to get to them, make sure they were safe.

The room tilted as he pulled himself upright. Where were his boots? His hat? Abandoning the search, he focused on the door. He had to get to Mollie, had to help her. The distance to the door seemed like miles, and the floor heaved like a shimmering desert mirage. He reached for the doorknob, missed, and fell flat on his face.

The last thing he heard was the sound of someone rushing to his side before everything went dark again.

Chapter 22

Lasso hadn't returned, and they'd been forced to make camp yet again.

The rain had slacked off for the time being, and Mollie was thankful for the respite. She tried to keep up a brave face in front of the younger children, but Jedediah, Jennie, and their grandfather knew that things were bad. After the children were asleep in the wagon, the four of them huddled around the campfire.

"He should've been back by now." Jedediah fidgeted. He'd grown up the last few weeks, especially after Lasso had treated him as an equal. No longer the sullen youngster he'd been when they started this journey, he'd proved to be as strong and capable as she was, and she'd learned to depend on him more than she ever thought possible.

"Maybe the land office was closed." Mollie grasped at straws.

"Mollie girl, it's the middle of the week, and the deadline for us to take possession of the land has passed." Her grandfather speared her with a look. "We have to consider the fact that Lasso isn't coming back."

"Grandpa, we don't know that." Mollie's stomach clenched, and she closed her eyes. As the afternoon had waned, she'd begun to fear that very thing, but her heart didn't want to believe it. She couldn't believe that the man who had held her close, the man who'd kissed her so tenderly, the man who'd stolen her heart, was also the man who might have stolen her family's future.

"I hope and pray I'm wrong, but we need to be prepared. That young man has the deed to the land, as well as what little money we had." He sighed. "I shouldn't have agreed to this plan."

"It's not your fault, Grandpa." Mollie grasped his arm, her gaze begging him not to blame himself. "We both did what we thought was best. Let's try to get some sleep. We've got a long day ahead of us."

They rolled up in quilts underneath the wagon, and Mollie stared at the pitch-black sky, as dark and foreboding as the future stretched in front of them. Long into the night, she wrestled with a host of reasons explaining why Lasso hadn't come back to them—to her.

And none of them were good.

❧

Each passing mile that drew them closer to Lincoln pulled Mollie deeper and deeper into panic at what she'd find when she got there.

The sun was setting by the time the wagon limped into town. There'd been no sign of Lasso or anyone else on the trail all day. Gray overcast skies wept on the gray weathered boards of the town and on the dead, gray vegetation of winter.

Jedediah stopped the wagon in front of the land assayer's office, and Mollie just stared at the building, too weary to really comprehend that they'd arrived a day late, penniless, and no paperwork to back up their claim to the land.

It didn't even faze her when Jedediah tried the door and found it locked, a small hand-lettered sign informing them the office was closed for the day. Even Grandpa had forgotten his ire from last night and smiled at her as if nothing was amiss.

Jedediah pulled himself back to the wagon seat and sat there for a minute. Mollie focused on the horses' backs, knowing she needed to think, to figure out what to do for her family. Her pa's hopes and dreams for their future had blown away with the blizzard that had trapped them in the cabin. What were they going to do? And what had happened to Lasso?

She remembered the way he'd smiled at her, the feel of his lips on hers, his thoughtfulness the day of their wedding. She refused to believe that he'd abandoned her.

"I'll find him," Jedediah gritted out, his stance stiff with anger. "I'll get Pa's gun, and I'll—"

"No." Jerked from her stupor, Mollie rounded on her brother. "We'll find someplace to rest outside of town then come back in the morning. We'll file another claim."

"He took our money."

She shook her head. "It doesn't matter—"

Stormie jumped out of the wagon and rushed forward, barking. She ran straight for the livery stable across the street. William tumbled out of the back of the wagon and took off after the dog.

"William, get back here," Jedediah yelled, but the boy paid him no mind. He handed Mollie the reins and jumped down, chasing after William and the dog. Jedediah scooped up his little brother and made a grab for the dog, but she dodged and kept going.

Mollie urged the horses forward as Stormie disappeared inside the livery, Jedediah right on her heels. Moments later, he rushed outside, William bouncing against his hip. "Lasso's horse is here—in the livery."

Mollie's heart pounded. "That means—"

"Lasso's *here*. In Lincoln."

Chapter 23

I'm so thankful you're here, missy. I've had the hardest time keeping that feller in bed."

Mrs. Truhitt, the proprietor of the boardinghouse, bustled about, placing clean hand towels and a basin of water on the vanity. "Practically had to tie him down the last two nights. All he could talk about was finding his Mollie and the young'uns."

Mollie ran the tips of her fingers over Lasso's chapped lips, and blinked back tears. "What happened?"

"Fool man rode all that way in the rain and got soaked to the skin. Then somebody waylaid him in the street from what I heard."

Mollie's heart lurched, and she clutched a hand to her stomach. "He was robbed?"

"Wal, I don't know if them scalawags got anything. Saddlebags are there in the corner. The sheriff came along about that time, or it woulda been a lot worse, I'm sure." Mrs. Truhitt headed for the door. "Just holler if you need anything. Maybe now that you're here, he'll settle down and get himself well."

"Thank you." Mollie brushed Lasso's hair back, her heart breaking at the heat radiating off his forehead. She sponged his face, his lips, and blushing, eased the sheet down a few inches and sponged off his heated shoulders. Mrs. Truhitt said tonight would tell the tale. If his fever broke, he'd likely make it. If not. . .

Don't fret.

She closed her eyes, letting peace flood her soul.

As night fell, she lit the lantern and ate a few bites of the meal Mrs. Truhitt brought in. Mollie asked if there was anything she could do to help, wanting to repay the woman for her kindness, but she smiled and replied that Reverend Vincent was turning out to be a big help in the kitchen while Jennie watched after the children.

Mollie managed to get a bit of broth into Lasso, before placing the tray on the table by the door. As she turned, she spied the saddlebags in the corner. With shaking hands, she unbuckled the flaps and searched for the pouch that held the papers and the money.

It was gone.

Her heart withered inside.

They had nothing left. Except each other.

Lasso moaned, and she dropped the bags and hurried to his side. She leaned over him, touching his face, murmuring soothing words. His eyes flickered open. "Mollie?"

"I'm here." She blinked back tears.

"You. . .you made it."

"Yes. It's going to be fine. You just get well."

He struggled to sit up. "The land—"

"*Shh*. It's all right." She placed both hands on his shoulders. "I know all about the land. It doesn't matter."

A fit of coughing hit him, and he fell back to the bed. Mollie bathed his face and changed the onion poultice Mrs. Truhitt had prepared. She prayed, offering reassurances as he fought against the fever. After too many hours without sleep, Mollie rested her head on his chest, her heart breaking at the deep rattle. She made no effort to stop the tears that trickled from the corners of her eyes. Instead, she let them flow, slid her hand down Lasso's arm to the back of his hand, and laced her fingers through his.

Lasso hadn't abandoned them. He hadn't abandoned her. He'd risked everything—his very life—for her and her family. Mollie didn't care about the land anymore. It didn't matter. The only thing that mattered was that he get well.

Chapter 24

Lasso woke feeling like he'd been trampled and left for dead. He ached from head to toe, but whatever had happened, at least he was alive. He moved his feet and flexed his fingers. And other than the pressure on his chest, it didn't seem as if anything was broken.

He lay there, trying to remember what had happened.

Mollie. The children.

The land.

Feeling feverish.

Then a couple of shadowy figures rushing him and dragging him into an alley.

Slowly, he became aware of his surroundings and the sweet-scented weight pressing against his chest. Not an injury, but a woman. His breathing hitched, and he moved his arm and touched her hair, caught in a long, thick braid down her back. Moisture pricked his eyes, and he breathed a sigh of relief. She was there.

Mollie had made it to Lincoln, and all was well.

She stirred, lifted her head to focus on him, her beautiful face going from sleep-filled, to concerned, to happy in a heartbeat. She rested one hand on his forehead, and a smile trembled on her lips. He closed his eyes, relishing the feel of her soft fingertips stroking his brow.

"Praise the Lord. The fever's gone. How do you feel?"

"As weak as a newborn calf."

She laughed, the sound doing funny things to his insides. "Mrs. Truhitt's chicken broth will put that to rights in no time."

"Mrs. Truhitt?" He frowned.

"She owns the boardinghouse. That's where we found you when we got to town."

He nodded. "I remember her. Barely."

"You need to eat something. Get your strength back."

She started to stand, but he grabbed her hand. "Later. Where's the deed?"

A pained expression crossed her face, but she masked it quickly. She moved across the room, picked up his saddlebags, retraced her steps, and sat on the edge of the bed. "The paperwork and the money's gone. You were so sick when you got here that someone stole it from you. Mrs. Truhitt said that if the sheriff hadn't come along when he did, they might have killed you."

Lasso frowned. "But—"

"*Shh.* Don't fret." Mollie placed the tips of her fingers on his lips, silencing him. A tiny smile pulled at the corners of her mouth, and she shook her head. "It doesn't matter. We'll file a new claim. The land might not be as good as what Papa found, but it'll be ours." She lowered her gaze, and a rose-colored blush flooded her cheeks. "That is, if you—if you want to."

Lasso cupped her face with one hand. "Ah, Mollie girl, I want to."

Her hopeful gaze lifted and met his. "You do?"

"I do." He slid his fingers to the back of her head and urged her toward him. She came willingly, her lips sweet as honey. He closed his eyes and thought about all the years that stretched before him, bound to this woman. A sigh of contentment and longing escaped his lips, and he deepened the kiss. He couldn't think of anything he wanted more than to be surrounded by Mollie and a houseful of young'uns all their own.

He eased back, drinking in the sight of his beautiful wife. "I know we didn't have a proper courtship, but I meant it when I said those vows. I love you, Mollie Jameson McCall."

She blinked, moisture glistening on her long lashes, her dark eyes shining with joy. "And I love you, Lasso McCall."

"But there is one thing."

Her smile faltered. "What?"

"Stick your hand there, between the mattresses." He patted the edge of the bed.

Mollie gave him a curious look but did as he instructed. A smile bloomed on her face as she pulled out the leather pouch she'd given him three days ago.

"Open it."

She pulled out a thick sheet of paper and clapped her hand to her mouth to smother a quick indrawn breath. "The deed! Oh Lasso. How—"

Lasso tapped the deed with his finger, enjoying the delight spreading over his wife's face. "I made it to the land office in time and got the deed transferred. This land is our land, fair and square, Mrs. Mollie McCall."

 Award-winning author Pam Hillman, a country girl at heart, writes inspirational fiction set in the turbulent times of the American West and the Gilded Age. She lives with her family in Mississippi. Contact Pam at her website: www.pamhillman.com.

FLAMING STARR

by DiAnn Mills

Chapter 1

Starr never believed in luck until she saw the full house in her hand. She masked her emotions—soiled doves always do.

"Come on, Starr. Let's see your hand," Clem said. "I'm ready to clean up this table and take you upstairs."

She studied his face, smoke curling from his mouth and joining the gray haze above his head. Did Clem have a good hand like he claimed? She'd never won a thing in her life. Fought and scraped for everything, but—

"Show me your cards. It's late." His voice bristled, causing her to reconsider her cards.

He could be a brutal man when angered. She'd seen the broken men and women when he'd finished. A dead man, too.

But she held a full house.

Hope wrapped its shawl around her.

Inhaling to control the steady pounding of her heart, she spread her cards on the table: three kings and two tens.

Clem swore, and his face turned as red as her dress. "You cheated." His words thundered through the saloon.

"I play an honest game." She didn't know how to swindle at cards.

"Liar. Your kind is out for what a good man earns."

Clem Nabors was a gunslinger and poker player. He didn't know the meaning of good. "What are you holding?" she said and dug deep for courage.

His left hand wrapped around his Colt.

"There's no need to use that." If only her voice would steady or she had a derringer tucked in her bodice.

He tossed his cards on the table, all of them spades. A flush.

"She got ya," an older man said from a chair between them. "Looks like Starr has herself a Texas homesteadin' plot."

She kept her attention fixed on Clem. He'd cut down the last man he accused of cheating. Maybe she should have folded and let him win. At least then all she'd have lost was an hour behind a closed door.

"She won fair and square," the man said. "Hand over the certificate."

Clem raised his gun, but the man drew first and fired at his left wrist, grazing it. "That coulda been your heart, but ya got lucky. Be glad I didn't destroy your shootin' hand. Now pull out those papers and give 'em to Starr."

Blood dripped from Clem's wrist, and judging from the strained muscles in his face, it had to hurt. "She cheated, and I'm going to the sheriff."

"Just 'cause he's your brother-in-law don't mean you're right. She played fair. This is the last time I'm tellin' you to cross off your name on that certificate and write hers." The hammer clicked.

Clem stood and pulled an envelope from inside his tattered jacket, pulled out the certificate and made the changes, replaced it, and slapped it on the table.

Starr opened it to make sure he'd done what the old man said. She touched her lips. One hundred sixty acres north of Houston. All she had to do was live there three years, and it would be hers. A dream come true. A way to leave this shameful life behind.

"Miss Starr, you look real happy," the old man said.

She glanced into the gray eyes of the toothless man who was older than her father. "I am," she whispered. "Thank you for helping me."

"Glad to see you win."

"It won't be yours for long." Clem swore. "I'll have my land certificate back as soon as I talk to the sheriff." He leaned closer to her. The stench of his whiskey-laden breath sickened her. "I'll see you dead. No one cheats me and gets by with it. Not even a pretty face."

"Told you, I play honest." She held up the papers giving her a new life. "This man will testify for me."

"That's 'cause you take care of 'em." Clem swung around and headed toward the door. "I'll be back."

Starr sensed her heart dip to her stomach. Clem and the sheriff were as close as real brothers, and the sheriff had tried to run her and the other girls out of town. He might have a motive with Clem accusing her of cheating. The man who'd defended her stayed close.

"Miss Starr, do you have a horse?" he said.

"No." Fear clamped its fangs into her heart. "Are you thinking I'm in trouble?"

"Yes ma'am. You need to leave town before Clem comes back with the sheriff. It's near midnight, and Clem will have to wake him. But it's your only chance. Clem and the sheriff will get caught by the Yankees, but I know a way out of town that avoids the army." He shook his head. "I have an extra horse and saddle. All yours."

"Why?"

He pressed his lips together, accenting the lines in his face. "Had me a daughter once. You remind me of her. Miss Starr, you're made of better stuff than the other women here."

She held her breath while her thoughts raced. "Won't it look like I cheated?"

"I know you didn't. But it doesn't matter, 'cuz you'd be dead."

He was right. She had no choice. "I thank you for your kindness. I can pay you."

"No ma'am. It's for you. I'll bring my mare around to the back door. Hurry now."

Starr nodded and headed to the steps leading upstairs to her room. How many nights had she climbed them with some man who was drunk and filthy? Like her. Never again. She had no idea how to till the earth or build a house, or even cook. But she'd learn or die trying.

⤬

Texas

Aaron wiped the sweat from his face with a dirty bandanna and lifted his ax to split another log, piling it atop several others stacked nearly twelve feet long and five feet high. He ran his tongue across parched lips. His children would not be cold again. The wood would have all summer to dry. To the west, the sky darkened from streaks of violet to deep gold. Time to call it a day.

"Papa, dinner's ready," Anne called from the cabin's porch, waving a bar of lye soap. "I didn't burn the corn bread."

Aaron sank the ax into a log and smiled at his oldest daughter. "You're going to be the best cook in Texas. I knew I smelled something good. My stomach's roaring like a bear."

Anne giggled, her dark curls dancing. She bounded down the steps and handed him the soap. "Rabbit stew, too, and the potatoes are tender."

"Wonderful." He planted a kiss on her forehead. "Give me a moment to wash up." Together they walked to the well, where he drew water. After a long drink he splashed his face and rolled the soap in his hands. If only the good Lord would give him more hours in the day.

"Do you feel up to hearing me read tonight?"

He was too tired to think, but he'd oblige. Had to pay more mind to her schooling. "I will. Ella and Parker like to hear you read from the Bible, too."

"Parker listens for a few minutes, then he wants to play."

"Little ones are like that." Aaron splashed water onto his face. Soon he'd need to make a trip into town for supplies. Other things were running low. He smelled coffee. "Sweet girl, better save the coffee for breakfast until I get more."

"We're nearly out of sugar and flour, too."

How long would his money hold out? The garden would provide plenty of vegetables for summer and fall, and he could spare a cow if necessary. Mostly, he counted on chickens for eggs and game for food. But not for the extras, those things that put joy on his children's faces.

"Are you sad, Papa?"

"Only tired."

"I miss her, too."

Little got by Anne. Her mother's death walked with him like a dark shadow. The homestead was to give all of them a new beginning, but images and memories of Margaret were branded on his heart.

"It's not Parker's fault, is it?"

"Not at all." Her little heart shouldn't be frettin' on such things. Aaron bent to her level. Water dripped from his face and hands, but still he touched her little face. "God took your mama to heaven because He had a special job for her. Birthing your brother had nothing to do with it. He's a gift from your mother and the Almighty."

Anne blinked back the tears. "All right. I was only wondering. Just—"

"What?"

"What could be so important He had to take her? Don't seem right."

He agreed but wouldn't tell her so. "God-things can be hard to understand."

"Do you know why, Papa?"

He blew out a weary breath. "No, I don't. But I know we'll get past this, and we'll all see her one day." He peered into the face that reminded him of Margaret.

"I can help with more work."

"You do enough by taking care of your brother and sister. Tending to the cooking and such is more than any eight-year-old should do."

"I don't mind."

He opened the door of the cabin and motioned for her to step inside. "But I do. Are the two behaving?"

"As much as you can expect from children."

Aaron laughed. His precious daughter needed to be a child, not a substitute mother. Inside, Ella and Parker were already seated at the table. They jumped from the bench into his arms, as though forgetting he'd been within eyeshot all afternoon.

"I'm hungry," he said. "Let's eat, then we'll hear Anne read." He helped the two younger ones back onto the bench.

"It's my turn to pray, Papa." Ella bowed her head.

"Of course. I haven't forgotten."

"Dear God, we thank You for our food and all our blessin's. Help Papa not to be so tired. Anne, too. Teach me how to peel taters without cutting my thumb. Help Parker to talk better. Oh, and help Papa find a lady to be our mama so he won't be sad. Amen."

Aaron's gaze flew to his five-year-old. Where had she gotten the idea he needed a wife? He did his best to remember how their mama had taken care of them. He must be doing a poor job, for Ella to pray for a new mama.

The last thing he wanted or needed was a woman interrupting his life. He'd learned his lesson the hard way. Loving a woman meant getting abandoned and losing a piece of your heart. He shook off the misery of loneliness. Anne, Ella, and Parker were his light and his reason for putting one foot in front of the other, every morning, every day, for as long as it took.

Chapter 2

Three Weeks Later

Starr patted the neck of the mare she'd ridden over land that gave beauty a new meaning. "Goldie, we're nearly there. I figure by nightfall we'll be looking at the site of our new home." She'd spent too many nights on the hard ground, but the bed she'd left behind was far harder than Louisiana and Texas soil. As soon as New Orleans escaped her, she'd bought suitable clothes—a wide-brimmed hat, britches, and a shirt. Burned the red dress and kicked the ashes into the night. She tied her unruly curls with a piece of leather and sealed the death of the soiled dove.

During the long, lonely hours riding to Texas, she'd wondered why Clem had been so quick to put up the land certificate as a bet. Of course, he didn't plan on losing.

She'd been saving money for a long time. Had plenty to buy whatever was needed to make her homestead a fittin' farm. The supplies and the skills required for the work was what bothered her. Forcing the apprehension out of her thoughts, she told herself it couldn't be so difficult. Folks had been building homes, raising cattle, and planting crops for centuries. Spring sprouted life, ensuring her dreams of tomorrow and the next day and the next. Nearly half her life had been spent on her back, and the other years were lost, a little girl who fought those who wanted to abuse her until she gave in. No more. Sometimes in the recesses of Starr's mind, she remembered days that fear took a step behind her. But not many.

Forget the past. It served as lessons learned.

Maybe she could hire a neighbor to help her. If there were any around. She'd stopped at a town called Last Chance and hadn't seen a soul for the last hour. Hope the name wasn't a premonition.

Years ago with her mama, she'd worked in a Louisiana brothel over a saloon called Last Chance. Mama got a beating there, one that killed her.

The future is ahead. You're twenty years old and strong.

Following the landmarks given to her by the storekeep in Last Chance, Starr lifted the brim of her hat. In the distance she saw smoke rising from a small cabin. Who'd built a cabin? Who was on her land? Fear snaked up her spine. The storekeep had eyed her strangely when she asked for directions. At least his scrutiny didn't equal the men's who'd paid for her services.

"Do you know someone there?" he'd said, not giving her eye contact.

"No sir." Could be he didn't like the idea of a woman homesteading, thinking she couldn't make it thrive in three years. "Can you tell me how to get there?"

He'd done so, but he'd been gruff.

Did he have a friend living there? Perhaps the same friend who'd built a cabin and now cooked his dinner? She touched her rifle, hoping she wouldn't need it. The land certificate lay in her saddlebag.

This was her life. No one would take her land from her without a good fight. Urging Goldie toward the cabin, she pulled the rifle across her lap. Killing a man wouldn't be the same as a rabbit. The latter meant satisfying hunger, while the former gave her nightmares.

Life will be better. This is your new home.

A man stepped from the cabin onto the porch. Muscular. Dark hair hung to his collar.

Starr reined in Goldie and aimed her rifle. "What are you doing on my land?"

"Hey, put down the rifle," he said. "This is my homestead."

She patted her saddlebag. "I have a Texas land certificate right here that proves otherwise."

He folded his arms over his chest and stood square. "I'd be obliged if you'd put down your weapon, ma'am. You're scaring my children."

Children? But he was still on her land. "Then let me see your land certificate."

"When you put down the rifle."

A little girl about eight or nine stepped from the doorway. "Papa, what's wrong?"

"Nothing, honey. Just a mistake. You go on inside while I talk to the lady."

Starr had never been called a lady before. A small girl and yet smaller boy joined the man. Where was his wife? Caution seized her senses. The woman could have a gun pointed at her. Starr kept her rifle aimed at the man.

"We want to be with you," the middle girl said, clinging to the man's pant leg.

"Anne, take them inside." His voice sounded gentle but firm. "Ma'am, please put down your rifle, and I'll get my land certificate."

"What about your wife?"

A frown crossed his features. "Don't have one." He turned to the oldest child. "Now, Anne."

The fear and sadness on the older girl's face yanked emotions from Starr she didn't know existed. No mother? They were so young. She lowered the rifle while the child shepherded the younger two children inside the cabin.

"Your having three children doesn't change the fact you're on my land." She took a deep breath, her gaze on the empty doorway where the children had disappeared. "If you have proof this is yours, I'd like to see it."

He captured her attention with huge blue eyes. "Take me just a moment."

Would he fetch his own rifle? Shoot her in front of his children? She'd take a chance on him being an honest man who'd made a mistake. "All right."

While waiting, she took in the surroundings. A lean-to offered shelter to his horse and a wagon. Two oxen grazed inside a fence, along with three cows. Chickens pecked in front of her, and a rooster strutted. Typical male, always thought they were in control of womenfolk.

The man stepped out of the cabin, a folded piece of paper in his hand. No weapon, unless he concealed a knife. The wrong end of a knife was a bad place to be. She had a scar on her chest to prove it. Starr dismounted. Her fingers trembled opening the saddlebag and pulling out the envelope. She walked toward him and thrust the paper in his face. He handed his to her.

Starr read his deed. Aaron Conrad. . . Their certificates were different—his had a Texas seal and no cross-out of names. Foreboding rose in her. Surely after coming all this way, her land certificate was the legal document.

Chapter 3

Aaron's anger burned from his toes to the flames in his face. With control that came from his Maker, he subdued his fury so the woman wouldn't see him lose control of the situation. She was dead wrong if she thought she could ride in here and claim his homestead. He studied her certificate then his own.

God would not knock him off his feet again. Would He? These one hundred sixty acres were his home, the opportunity Texas offered to start over with his children. He inhaled sharply. He'd been here first, and his land certificate had been filed appropriately. He was certain of his legal right. Crops were planted, along with a promising garden. Any other man would have grabbed his rifle the moment this woman made her accusation.

Margaret believed kindness went further than any spark of anger. To honor her and their children, he'd not lose his temper.

"Ma'am, I'm Aaron Conrad. We have a problem here."

Huge brown eyes stared at him, eyes that emitted determination and a spark of something he couldn't discern.

"I'm Starr Matthews. You have the problem, sir. I'm within the law."

He searched for words instead of the ones that the good Lord wouldn't appreciate. "When did you receive your land certificate?"

"Less than a month ago."

"I've had mine for ten months. My certificate has a Texas seal."

"Doesn't make the homestead any more yours." She glanced at the paper in her hands. "Mine has a signature."

"We'll need to ride into town tomorrow and talk to the sheriff. He can wire the land office and rectify this."

"That seems fair."

He saw the uneasiness, but she promptly took a rigid stand. "We'll leave first thing in the morning."

Darkness closed in around them. As much as he wanted her off his land, sending her to Last Chance in the night was inhospitable. Dangerous, too. He hesitated, hating the words before he spoke them. "You can sleep in the cabin, and I'll bed down on the porch."

"I won't be beholden to you when you're already on my land. I'll take the porch. It will be more shelter than I've had since leaving home."

"Where is home?"

"None of your concern." She pulled a bedroll off her mare. "May I draw a bucket of water for me and my horse?"

The woman frustrated him. She was young, but her mannerisms spoke of suspicion. At least what he could see beneath the hat. "As much as you need. Plenty to graze in the pasture."

"I'll pay for what I use."

Aaron narrowed his gaze, the ire burning his face again. "I don't want your money," he said without taking his eyes off her. "Anne, bring Miss Matthews a plateful of the rabbit stew and corn bread."

"I'll pay for that, too."

"Told you, no. Tomorrow we'll right this situation so you can be on your way."

She walked toward the well with her horse then slowly turned. "I think you've built me a fine cabin and dug me a well. The lean-to will suffice. Thank you, Mr. Conrad. I'll help you pack once we talk to the sheriff."

He should have grabbed his rifle. "There are plenty of other places for you to homestead."

"Exactly what I was thinking about you."

Aaron clenched his fists, wanting to grab the woman by the neck and toss her back where she came from. He made his way to the outhouse, where Ella had complained about a wasp nest. Right now he'd get along just fine with the nasty winged creatures.

⧓

Starr gulped, horrified at the horrible things she'd said to Aaron Conrad. Had she grown so calloused that manners and respect no longer held importance? She lowered the bucket into the well, guilt pummeling her. A few moments later, Mr. Conrad stomped up the steps and slammed the door to the cabin. His children had heard her ugly words, and no child needed to be subjected to the fear of anger.

She drew the bucket and set it down for Goldie. While the horse noisily drank the water, her thoughts anchored on her prideful ways. The man deserved an apology. He was about to lose his home, and she gloated over the matter. How often had others knocked her down and laughed at her distress? How many times had she sworn she'd never do the same? Wiping away the tracks of the past meant treating others like she wanted to be treated. Someone said that to her once, and she never forgot it.

Before easing her thirst, Starr made her way to the cabin and knocked on the door. Her heart thudded like a nervous rabbit. "Mr. Conrad." Her raspy voice matched what she had to say.

The door flung open. The firelight behind him silhouetted him, making him seem like a giant. Sensing his anger, she stepped back.

"Could I speak to you outside, please?" Her words choked out.

He obliged, closing the door behind him. "What do you want, Miss Matthews?"

She deserved his anger. "I want to apologize for what I said earlier."

"Which time?"

He made this doubly difficult. "The things your children shouldn't hear. My words insulting their father."

He relaxed slightly. "Thank you. Have you changed your mind about trying to take my home?"

"Not at all."

"Sleeping inside instead of out there?" He pointed to her bedroll on the splintered wood.

"No sir. I'll be fine on your porch."

He leaned against the doorjamb. "What if I said rattlers crawled up here? I often have to kill 'em before my children can greet the morning."

She'd slept with worse rattlers than anything that could congregate on his porch. "I'll manage. Met a few scorpions in my day, so I can handle a pesky snake."

"Sleeping with your rifle, I suppose?"

"Always." So he'd better not get any ideas of eliminating her when she fell asleep, or beating her to a pulp.

"Then good night. If a coyote wanders toward my chicken coop, please use your rifle. He hides behind the outhouse. Had a dog until about two months ago. He tangled with the coyote and then got bit by a rattler."

"I'll be wary."

He went inside, leaving her irritated with his comments about his dog. Did he think she'd leave, afraid of the night and not able to take care of herself? He was wrong, very wrong. She hadn't come this far in the middle of a war to give up now.

Chapter 4

Starr tossed fitfully during the night, her fingers wrapped around her rifle. She'd always considered herself a good judge of character, and Aaron Conrad appeared to be a good man. His children were well behaved and beautiful. His wife must have been a lovely woman. She couldn't imagine being a woman alone with three little ones. How did a man do it? She'd never experience it, since her mother said their kind weren't the motherly type.

Once the sheriff probed, he might learn the truth about her. Her thoughts ground to a halt. She'd been too upset to think Mr. Conrad might be right. His land certificate held a Texas seal. Hers didn't. Had Clem been cheated? He wasn't known for his intelligence, only his quick temper.

She shot up just as the sun brought streaks of gold across the morning sky. What would she do if the land belonged to Mr. Conrad? She'd be forced to find work before her money ran out. What could she do? She only knew one profession, and she'd die before allowing her thoughts to wander in that direction.

Refusing to think on trouble any longer, she chose to concentrate on the rich land. Lots of thick pasture, and a winding creek flowed through it. The cabin nestled between large live oaks, providing shade for the hot months ahead. Picturesque. Perfect.

The aroma of coffee and bacon met her nostrils, causing her stomach to rumble. Little voices from the cabin sounded musical, and she smiled at the sweetness. Then the deep voice of Aaron Conrad.

"As soon as breakfast and chores are done, we're going into town."

"For supplies?" a little voice said.

"Yes, Miss Anne. We'll get a few things to make your cooking easier."

"Goody," another little voice said. "A peppermint stick?"

"Not this time, Ella. Maybe another."

"What about the lady who wants to shoot you?" Anne said.

"She's coming, too," Mr. Conrad said. "Y'all need to be on your best behavior. Ella and Parker, I mean you, too."

"Why?" Anne said. "She's mean, and she doesn't like us."

"Miss Matthews thinks we have something that belongs to her. But we don't."

"Our land."

"Yes. But we'll get it all worked out today."

"So the sheriff will run her off?"

"Anne, must you always say exactly what you're thinking?"

"You told me to be honest."

"That I did. And I also said to be respectful of others."

"Yes sir. I couldn't tell if she was pretty or ugly under her hat."

"Anne, what does God look at?"

She sighed. "The heart."

"Right. Now let's finish breakfast."

The children's chatting took over. Starr folded her bedroll and walked to the well for water to wash up.

"Mornin', Miss Matthews," Mr. Conrad said. "We have food ready."

Her stomach hadn't stopped protesting since she first smelled it. "I can pay."

He waved away her comment, with lines across his forehead. Anne carried a plate heaping with bacon, biscuits, a small bit of scrambled eggs, and potatoes. He held a mug of coffee out to her. How many people fed their enemies?

Starr stuck a fork into the eggs and into her mouth. Fluffy. "This is really good. For a man, you're a fair cook."

He chuckled. "Anne's the cook."

The little girl curtsied. "Thank you, ma'am."

Was this the child who wanted her father to run Starr off? "I can't cook at all, except for coffee and burned beans."

"Would you like to come inside? Leaving Ella and Parker alone for very long means trouble's brewing." Anne shook her dark head. "Children. Don't know what I'm going to do with them."

Starr laughed, and it felt like a burden had been lifted. Not much to laugh about for a long time, except the hope of a new life. Now her hope might be snatched away. "I'd be happy to join you for a little bit. Then I need to tend to my horse before we ride into town." By noon this family could be homeless. Perhaps she should keep her distance. "Still, maybe it's best I eat out here."

"You were invited." Mr. Conrad's authoritative tone shook her, and she followed them inside.

The children eyed her warily. Ella had lighter, wavy hair, more like spun honey. She didn't share the dark hair and blue eyes of her father, brother, and sister. Perhaps she resembled her mother. She was holding a straw doll, and Parker played with a whittled stick that resembled a rifle. He stayed close to Anne, who bustled about.

"When do you play?" Starr said to Anne.

"Sometimes the children wade in the creek or go fishing. Mostly I'm busy with other things. Sundays are rest days."

A child shouldn't have to work like an adult. How did her father feel about that? "How long has your mother been gone?"

Anne wrapped biscuits in a cloth. "Since Parker was born."

No wonder the boy moved with her as though attached like an arm or leg. She'd been the only mother he'd ever known.

"We get along fine," Mr. Conrad said.

She hadn't heard their father climb the porch steps. "Didn't mean to pry."

He narrowed his brows. "Well, you did. We'll leave shortly."

She understood what he didn't say. Could she blame him for trying to protect their home?

⤬

Late afternoon shadows fell before Aaron received word about his land certificate. Impatience had crawled up his spine and taken residence. Work awaited him at home, but he had to make sure the homestead was legally his. He'd been up most of the night trying to figure out how he'd take care of his children if they were forced to move. While they waited for the sheriff to hear back from Austin, he'd purchased a few supplies and loaded them into the wagon. Praying the good Lord spared him another tragedy.

He stood in the sheriff's office with his children and Miss Matthews. One minute the woman looked like she'd shoot him dead, and the next, she blinked back tears. Women were hard to understand. Except Margaret. And her daughters would never display this woman's peculiar behavior.

The sheriff walked in and waved a piece of paper. "I received the wire from Austin."

Aaron shook his hand. "I appreciate your looking into this."

"Glad to do it." The sheriff turned to Miss Matthews. "We have our answer. I'm sorry, ma'am. But your land certificate is a forgery, just as I thought. Without a Texas seal, it's worthless. The man's name on your certificate doesn't match our governor's signature."

Her face paled, and although she'd caused him to nearly forget his Maker, Aaron was sorry for the hopelessness in her face. "I see." She lifted her shoulders.

"Who sold you this?" the sheriff, a tall, leathered man, said. "The thief deserves to be behind bars."

"He's long gone. I'm sure of it."

"You could apply for another tract of land. Texas has plenty of it, but homesteading is hard for a man, even harder for a woman."

She pressed her lips together. "Thank you. Maybe you're right." She turned to Aaron. "I apologize for the trouble."

Anne opened her mouth, but he closed it with a threatening glance. "We were both upset."

"I'll get what I owe you." She walked outside with the look of defeat etching sorrow into her face.

Aaron bid the sheriff good day and joined Miss Matthews.

"I won't take charity." She dug through her saddlebag. "Or be beholden. What about your children? Surely they could use something."

"We have all we need."

She sighed and secured the leather flap. "I see. You're a stubborn man, Aaron Conrad."

"I'm in good company."

She half smiled, as though he'd complimented her. "Does the town have a boardinghouse?"

"No ma'am." He gestured around them. "Sheriff's office and jail, general store, livery, barber shop, saloon, and the church is all we have. Why don't you come on back with us, and you can leave tomorrow?"

"That's not fittin', Mr. Conrad."

"The name's Aaron. I'll take the porch, and you can help Anne cook tonight for a bed inside."

She shook her head. "More like Anne will have to show me. Remember, I can't cook. Nearly starved riding out here."

"You're thin as a fence rail," Anne said.

"Anne!"

"Sorry, ma'am. Can you do mendin'? We could swap."

"Anne!" Aaron couldn't believe his daughter at times. "Where are your manners?"

"I'm good with a needle, and my name is Starr."

"Like in the sky?" Ella said with a twist of her blond head.

"Guess so."

"Papa was named after a man in the Bible." Ella took his hand.

Starr bent to Ella's level. "Your papa is an honorable man, so I guess he lives up to his name."

Her soft words weren't at all like the ones she'd tossed at him last evening. If she'd take off her too-large hat, he could see what she looked like. From what he'd observed, she was nothing but a scrawny girl who needed a bath. But she had huge brown eyes the color of pecans, and lashes that seemed to hide something she didn't want anyone to see.

He urged the little ones onto the wagon while Starr mounted her mare. Aaron didn't care what she looked like or about the sadness in her eyes—haunting eyes that gave him chills. He had enough problems of his own.

Chapter 5

Starr fretted about taking advantage of Aaron Conrad's generosity, especially after the devastating outcome today. She'd made a fool of herself in front of him and the sheriff. Humiliation stung deep.

Why Aaron had resorted to kindness was beyond her, unless his generosity centered on pity. She hoped not. Pity sounded like a horrible sickness that placed the recipient on the same level as a wounded animal. Tonight she must earn her keep, and tomorrow she'd ride out. Possibly to Austin, where work would be more plentiful than in Last Chance. The homestead could have been a new beginning for a life destined for better things. Now all she had was a grave, with no one grieving.

She sensed his eyes on her, as though he was trying to figure out the woman who dressed like a man, tried to take his home, and then agreed to do his mending. Perhaps he wasn't like the other men she'd known. But it made no sense to trust a man. Even one to whom she had a peculiar attraction.

Pulling through one stitch after another kept her mind occupied. She wanted to break down into a river of tears but feared if she wept, she might never stop. Caution had always held her emotions intact, but this time she was losing the struggle. Since leaving New Orleans, she'd found light in each new day—not the kind from the sun, but the kind that linked arms with dreams. She'd managed to isolate herself from what she'd done in Louisiana and Texas and to remake Starr Matthews into a respectable woman.

She clenched her toes in her boots to combat the brink of disaster where tomorrow looked like yesterday.

I won't go back to a brothel. I'll secure my own land certificate or find a way to earn an honest living.

Disappointments were like huge rocks—but she'd find a way to push them aside. Right now she'd play a familiar role, hiding behind a smile. *Don't let anyone get too close.*

She threaded a needle and picked up a second sock that belonged to Parker. The little boy was built like his father, walked with the same swagger. He talked little, yet his gaze constantly followed either Anne's or Aaron's path.

"Miss Starr, you've been mendin' for the past two hours," Aaron said. "Looks to me like you've more than repaid us for a little food."

Starr peered into the basket, where a little girl's dress was torn at the sleeve and a little boy's britches were ripped at the seat. "Nearly done." She glanced up to find him smiling. A strong face.

"You sure seem happy," Anne said with a shake of her head. "When Papa or I have to mend, we're scrappin' like two roosters."

Starr laughed. "With the ham and fried potatoes you made for dinner, my full stomach is content, too."

Anne grimaced. "My fingers would be bleeding and I'd be crying like a baby by now."

"This is a way for me to rest." She'd sewn dresses for the other soiled doves since she was a little older than Anne. Made clothes for their children, too. The satisfaction of a job well done had filled her with confidence then and now. "I like working with my hands."

"Papa says the same thing," Ella said. "Do you like to pull weeds?"

"Why? Do you have another job for me?"

"Ella, please." Aaron's voice rose. "Both you girls are guilty of persuading Miss Starr to do your chores. She's a guest, not a hired hand."

"Yes sir," the girls said.

Parker stifled a giggle.

"Parker, would you like to tell us what's so funny, 'cause I'm sure it's not because your sisters are in trouble."

"No sir. Nothin's funny."

The most Starr had heard from the boy all evening.

She picked up the boy's britches and examined the tear. It needed a patch, so she sorted through the "patch basket," as Anne called it.

Aaron pulled the girls onto his lap. He had a difficult time covering up his love with a scolding. The children were fortunate to have a father who cared. She met her father once. At least, her mother introduced the drunk as such. But, considering her mother, who had Starr working on her back by the age of twelve, she probably didn't know who Starr's father was.

At least Starr had never been in the motherly way. Brothels weren't good places for children to grow up.

"Anne, Ella, Parker, time for bed," Aaron said. "I'll listen to your prayers when you're ready."

"Miss Starr, too?" Ella said.

Starr inwardly startled. She'd never heard anyone talking to God, other than cursing. Would she have to do or say anything?

"Not sure Miss Starr wants to hear your prayers."

"Please?" Ella had a way of ducking her chin that gave her an endearing look.

"I would be happy to listen."

Once the children were in their loft bed, Starr listened to Anne and then Ella thank God for the day, their father, and everything else in between. She imagined it was a way to keep from going to sleep. Parker listened to his sisters and echoed a hearty amen at the end. In the light of the kerosene lamp, staring into their sweet faces, Starr longed for something she couldn't quite name.

"Wait, I forgot somethin'," Ella said and squeezed her eyes shut. "Thank You, God, for answering my prayers about a new mama. I didn't like Miss Starr much last night, but today she's nicer. I'm sure she'll be even better tomorrow after a bath."

Starr drew in a sharp breath. Thankful the shadows masked the heat rising up her neck, she couldn't look at the children or Aaron. She'd never been an answer to anyone's prayer, and if their father understood what she'd done before her arrival, he'd have tossed her to the rattlesnakes.

A bath would never wash away her filth.

She slipped outside and onto the porch. Hot tears burned her eyes. She willed them to stop, but the dripping increased.

The door behind her creaked open and shut. From the weight on the porch, Aaron must be standing behind her. No doubt to offer an apology. One she didn't need. In fact, she should be giving him one.

"Aaron, I'd like to be alone." She crossed her arms over her chest.

"Can't blame you. This day hasn't gone like you expected, and you didn't need Ella insulting you."

She'd experienced worse. "If I take offense at what a child says, I'm not going to survive very long in this part of the country."

"She'll be disciplined."

Starr whirled to face him. "Please, don't. Why should she be punished for stating the truth? I need a bath, and she needs a mother. I'm simply not the latter."

He stared at her in the darkness. "Can we sit on the steps and talk?"

Why? "I guess so. If it's about me sleeping on the porch, I'm not moving inside."

He chuckled, such a pleasant sound. "No ma'am. As much as I'd like for you to have a soft bed, I'm not going to argue with you."

She eased onto the steps beside him. Singing cicadas reminded her of the nights she'd slept under the stars from New Orleans to Texas. "What's on your mind?"

"I'm thinking you should give the sheriff the name of the person who gave you the land certificate."

She hesitated. "I won it in a poker game, and the loser wasn't happy, which leads me to believe he didn't know it was fake. I had to leave town because he wouldn't admit I won it fair and square."

"I see," he said softly. "Do you have a place to go?"

"I'll be fine."

"Family?"

"No." This conversation was headed to the bottom of a river. "Look, I don't want your pity. I'm a tough woman. I know how to handle myself. Seen a lot of bad in this world and have the sense to deal with it."

"How old are you?"

"Twenty."

"Anne was born when I was twenty. Scared me to death that I had a child and responsibility. Just when I'd gotten used to her mother, I had a baby daughter."

"Now you have three children."

"Blessings. Every drop of sweat is worth the blessing they give me."

She hesitated before posing a question he might consider too personal, but he'd done the same to her. "How do you manage to mother and father them?"

"God's grace. Somehow it all gets done. Real difficult at times. Parker is too attached to Anne. Of course, she's taken care of him since he was born. Ella's a sweet girl, seems to wake up in the morning wanting to please. Schoolin' Anne challenges me. She's smart, reads the Bible, and does figures. Still, the older she gets, the more she needs a mother. Ella's right behind her. Womanly things that I'd rather wrestle a wolf than handle." He paused. "Excuse me for unloading on you."

Better she listen to his problems than deal with her own. "We all need a listening ear. You'll find the right woman someday."

"Don't think so. Don't want one. Losing Margaret drove me to drinking."

Surprised, she recalled what she'd seen of him—an excellent father and provider. "I find it difficult to believe you'd succumb to a weakness."

"I'm not proud of it. Drank night and day for five months. Then I saw Anne feeding Parker, dressing Ella, and trying to cook. This was while the preacher visited. Sobered me real fast."

"The preacher?"

"No, seeing my little girl taking on the role of her mama and papa. I claimed to be a follower of Jesus, but Margaret's death made me want to die, too. I'd grown selfish. Only cared about myself."

A preacher had tried to talk to Starr once. His words didn't make sense. "Looks like you're doing a fine job now."

"Thanks. So what is ahead for you?"

What could she say? "I'll find work."

"Not much around here until more people settle." He hesitated. "There's an empty house on the outskirts of town. Maybe you could make it into a boardinghouse."

She could more easily find a job at the saloon. But she wouldn't. "I can't cook. Might poison a few good folks."

He shrugged. "Can't be too hard to learn."

"I'll think on it." The idea gave her new hope.

Thunder sounded, and a flash of lightning zigzagged across the night sky. Within seconds, rain splattered in heavy drops. Starr and Aaron scurried back onto the porch.

"Looks like good fortune has hit the earth. We sorely need rain," he said. "Winter was dry."

Luck might be with Aaron Conrad, but not a down-and-out prostitute.

Chapter 6

Aaron listened to the rain beat against the roof and onto the ground. All night long, he'd sleep a little then check on the rainfall. Finally he gave up, looked in on his children, and waited out the rain on the porch.

The chickens were fine, but a cow and bull were missing. Still it continued to pour. A flash flood worried him—a whirl of water could sweep across the land and take his children with it. Dread clamped chains onto his heart. What had disguised itself as a blessing now looked precarious.

Starr sat on the bench, watching. Repeatedly he invited her inside where it was warm and dry. She refused each time, and he gave up asking. The woman was the most stubborn person he'd ever met. Long before dawn he made coffee and brought her a cup.

"I'm keeping an eye on the storm," she said. "Ever been through a rain like this before?"

"Not here. Just heard about them." He leaned against the porch post. "This gully washer will destroy my seeds, and I just planted my fields."

"Can you replant?"

"I'll have to." By now the seeds had washed away, and he didn't have the money to purchase more without asking for credit. An inquiry he'd rather not make.

"It's only nearing May. You have plenty of time with the warm temperatures."

"Seeds cost money." He startled. Why had he revealed his situation? Confessions like this were personal. Had it been so long since he talked to a woman that he didn't know what to say? "We'll manage. Always do. The good Lord provides." Now he sounded self-righteous.

She took a sip of the coffee and thanked him. "I'm surprised your children haven't wakened with the thunder and lightning."

He smiled, despite the fretting. "They're all like their mother. She used to say, 'If Jesus comes while I'm sleeping, He'll have to shake me.' " He stared out into the darkness, willing the sun to rise so he could assess the damages. "Margaret died in her sleep. Causes me to check on them during the night. Feel their breath against my palm." He shrugged. "That must sound ridiculous."

"Not at all. I'm sorry for your loss." She stood. "The rain's slacking off."

Aaron stepped to the ground into mud and held out his hand. "You're right." He blew out a sigh and pointed to the east. "Here comes the sun. I need it. Now I can check out my garden and fields." Like a child, he wanted to believe all was well. "Hope this is over. I have a feeling the creek is swollen beyond its banks."

"I'll stay with the children until you return. Doubt if I can ride very far with all the water."

He might have misjudged Starr Matthews. Last night and this morning had shown she wasn't the same person who rode onto his land and claimed it as her own. She offered to help. . . Should he accept? Would Margaret think he was using a stranger to make his life easier?

"I'm in no rush, Aaron. You're not the type to take advantage of someone any more than I am."

"I'd be mighty beholden if you could delay your leaving," he said. "Not sure how long I'll be. Two of my livestock are missing."

"I enjoy your children. It will be a pleasure for me to spend time with them."

Fingers of daylight proved his suspicions. The garden had washed away, taking any thoughts of vegetables with it. How would he feed his children? The idea of going into debt to buy more seeds clawed at his insides. How would he pay the debt back?

After breakfast and giving the children instructions to be obedient, he set out through the mud and water to check on the fields and his cattle. In some places he sank to the tops of his boots. The creek had risen to twice its size. Beyond that was the corn to feed the animals. Before the rains, his plans were to sell the extra for more cattle. Not anymore. In the distance he heard the cow bawling, then he spied her and the bull.

Thank You.

Aaron stopped and panned the area. All he could see was water. Only by the grace of God had his cabin and livestock been saved. What would he do now?

∽

Starr dumped a bucket of dirty dishwater outside with the rest of the mud. Parker had managed to cover every inch of himself with it. Ella joined him, and together they made mud houses, hills, trees, and anything else they could create. Their laughter echoed around her, and she was envious—of their innocence, imagination, and the ability to snatch moments of fun.

"Those children." Anne shook her head from the porch. "It'll take me the better part of an hour to bathe them."

Starr laughed. "I'll do it." She eyed the child curiously. "Why don't you join them?"

Anne touched her heart as though she were a hundred years old. "I don't have time for such nonsense."

"You mean play?"

She nodded. "Not sure I know how. Haven't played since before Mama died." She studied her brother and sister with a rosebud smile, maybe wondering if she could be a child again.

"Why don't you try. Every little girl needs to pretend."

She shook her head. "Oh, the mess, Miss Starr. Even hair washing."

"What if I joined all of you?"

"Then you'll need a bath and head washing, too."

Starr sat on the porch step and pulled off her boots. "Ella already told me I need a bath, and I have spare clothes in my saddlebag." She took Anne's hand. "Ready?"

Anne giggled and covered her mouth. "Yes!"

Starr didn't know any more about playing in the mud than Anne did, but for the first time, she'd enjoy three beautiful children. And pretend, too.

An hour later, after Parker and Ella showed Starr how to make mud angels, a task she'd done as a child in the snow, Anne relinquished her mama-attitude and did the same.

In the midst of playing with the children, the sound of male laughter caused Starr to gasp. Aaron stood over them, his eyes watering with one belly laugh after another.

"I'm so sorry." Starr stood, dripping in mud. What had she been thinking? "I'll get them cleaned up."

He gestured around them. "Take a look, Miss Starr, it's about to rain. Nature might do it for you."

She saw no signs of lightning nor heard the rumble of thunder, only the sky darkening to pale gray silk. She'd thought the watering trough would suit them for bathing, but that was before the threat of rain. Her gaze flew to his face. Their baths were not as important as his family's provisions. "What about your crops?"

"Gone." The lines around his eyes deepened. "I was asking for the good Lord to let me know He cared, and then I see all of you playing in the mud."

Her heart pounded. The poor man didn't need her indiscretion with his children. "I wasn't thinking clearly." She should have cleaned his cabin, asked Anne about chores. First she attempted to take his home, then she invited his children to drench themselves in mud.

Aaron raised a hand. "Don't look so sad. This is wonderful. They haven't had this much fun in a very long time. You are an answer to my prayer."

She blinked. This whole time she hadn't once worried about her future.

"Papa, you want to play with us?" Anne said.

He bent to her level. "Who are you?"

"Anne."

"My Anne never gets this dirty. Did you do something to her? Is she hiding?"

Laughter exploded from all three small Conrads.

"I'm Ella." The little girl tapped her mouth with a muddy finger.

Aaron looked amazed. "This couldn't be Ella. Neither could this short fella be Parker." He shook his head. "Miss Starr, you can stay as long as you like with these muddy three."

"We need to bathe," she said.

"I'll get the trough filled with clean water."

Rain started softly, a spring shower that quickly increased. Anne stood and held out her arms, lifting her face to the cleansing flow. With her eyes closed and the mud washing away, she seemed transformed. An angel if she ever saw one. Starr swiped at a tear, not sure of its origin.

"Thank you," Aaron whispered, his warm breath on her neck. "You've given Anne the freedom to be a child. The girls haven't been together like this since before Margaret passed. Parker, well, he's a little boy, and he loves anything that involves dirt."

Starr shivered, from a mix of Aaron's nearness and his gentle words. His kindness filled her with unexplainable joy. She treasured this precious family who were rapidly stealing her heart.

Chapter 7

Aaron studied Starr combing Ella's honey-colored hair. In the firelight, his little girl's curls glistened. She reminded him of her mother, and his heart ached. By now healing should have strengthened him for moments like these. But Margaret had been too much a part of his life, and everywhere he saw glimpses of her. When he and the children journeyed from Kansas to Texas, she traveled right beside him, often holding his hand and encouraging him to go forward. Her smile mirrored his children's faces, and he didn't want anyone to take her place. That degraded what she meant to him, his beloved wife and the mother of his children.

Yet, hearing Starr laugh with his treasures made him wonder if God planned for him to find love again. Seemed wrong, like a horrible sin, but he couldn't deny the attraction to a scrawny little woman who played with his children. She loved them, too. The hollowness in her eyes seemed to come from her soul, but she brightened in the children's midst.

Anne busied herself in rearranging wet clothes by the fire. Oh, his dear Anne, Ella, and Parker. Shiny faces and rosy cheeks meant health. . .and happiness. He'd hold on to these memories when life took a turn for the worse. Like trying to figure out how he'd recover from the flood.

His attention wandered again to Starr. She'd added fresh water to the trough after the children were bathed, and he'd ushered them inside for her privacy. Later, when she entered the cabin, dressed in clean britches and a blue chambray shirt, the sight of her had nearly stolen his breath. Pecan-colored waves flowed down her back. A comely woman, if he were looking.

While Anne cooked dinner, Starr kept busy asking his precious daughter what she could do next, even posing cooking questions. Parker crawled onto her lap once he'd eaten, and now he sat at her feet. Odd how she fit in, and how the children had taken to her.

Must be because she'd joined them in the mud.

No point in dwelling on her, or any of them getting attached to her. She'd be gone in the morning. And he'd go back to fretting about how to replant.

"Miss Starr, would you listen to me read?" Anne said.

"I'd be happy to."

"We'll all hear what the Bible says," Aaron said. A thin streak of jealousy whipped through him at Anne asking Starr to be her audience. "But I appreciate your including Miss Starr."

"What shall I read, Papa?"

Aaron smiled, sealing the image of Anne at this very minute. The years would go by fast, and one day she'd leave for her own home. He swallowed the lump in his throat. What was wrong with him?

Must be the worrisome thoughts about the flood damage.

"Why don't you have Miss Starr choose?" he said.

Starr flushed, her brown eyes silently pleading for help.

He hadn't considered she might not be familiar with scripture. "I bet she'd like the story of Ruth."

"Oh good. That's my favorite." Anne hurried to his bedroom to secure the Bible.

The moment the story of Ruth began, Aaron regretted his suggestion. Ruth was a foreign woman who'd traveled to Israel with her mother-in-law after her husband died. She was a foreigner and not easily accepted. Then she found a husband among those people and became part of Jesus' lineage. Would Starr think this was about her and him? Of course not. Foolishness.

Must be memories of days gone by with thoughts of Margaret eating at him.

Anne finished the story. Usually she looked at him for approval, but not tonight. Her sweetness flew to their guest.

"What a beautiful story," Starr said and wrapped her arm around his daughter's waist. "I especially enjoyed that Ruth's life became easier with her marriage to Boaz."

"Thank you. What's your favorite Bible story?"

Starr hesitated. "I believe the one you just read."

Anne beamed, but Aaron sensed the truth. How had the woman walked through life without knowledge of God?

"Miss Starr, if you could stay another day, I'd teach you how to cook," Anne said.

"We still have mud. Lots of it." Parker looked at her from his perch on the floor.

Ella moved to Aaron's side. "Papa, can she stay a little longer?"

"I have to go," Starr said. "We've had so much fun today, but tomorrow I must leave to find a job and a place to live."

"Must you?" Anne said, her little face in a frown.

"Yes, but I have a secret to tell you." Bright eyes turned her way. "Today has been one of the best days of my life."

"Maybe we can do it again?" Anne said.

Starr blinked. "Hard to say. Sometimes special moments are just once. But we can relive them over and over in our hearts."

"Have you thought about the boardinghouse?" Aaron said, marveling in Starr's wisdom. "I heard the terms were good. Probably pay for it as you took in business. Folks who travel through are forced to move on or stay at the saloon."

A strange look swept over her face, sad and distant. "I'll look into it. Thanks for the suggestion. Aaron, take care of yourself for the children's sake. You haven't changed your wet clothes."

"I'm fine." He'd miss her. Having her close by would be good for the children, since they were fond of her.

Must be something in the wind. Why else did he long for her beside him?

⸎

Starr unwrapped her bedroll on the porch. In the darkness, heartache clawed at her. She shrugged off the despairing thoughts of leaving the Conrads. Instead, she chose to remember the family as an example of decent people. How would Aaron react to her confession of how his children affected her? They'd stirred a longing for motherhood. How very peculiar for a woman who believed children were for those who could make a sensible choice in a husband. Not the poor excuses of mothers who had no idea who the father of their child or children was. She'd confessed enough to Aaron by admitting the land certificate had been won in a poker game.

Anne, Ella, and Parker. . . *Starr, forget this glimpse of happiness. This was but a short season in your life, another lesson to make you a respectable person.*

The door creaked open and Aaron joined her on the porch. "Sure wish you'd reconsider and sleep inside."

She laughed. "How many times are you going to ask me that?"

"I have no idea." He eased onto the bench on the far side of the porch. "You've brought gladness to my children, and I appreciate it."

"You already thanked me. My pleasure."

He rubbed his jaw. "Miss Starr, you brought light to my family, even me. I call you a friend."

How dear. If only she were the right kind of person, he might see differently. "I tried to take your land and used a rifle to prove my point."

"I've forgotten."

"But I haven't." She hesitated, forming her words. "Your garden washed away. Tell me about your crops. Is it as bad as it looks?"

He pressed his lips together, and she had her answer. "I have credit at the general store," he said. "I'll replant, and we'll have crops growing before long. Seems like life is a progression of always starting over."

"True. But when we work through hard times, we learn how to be a wiser person."

He chuckled, a low, pleasant sound. "If that's the case, by the time I'm old, I'll be real smart."

"Me, too."

He rose and stood on the edge of the porch and stared out into the night. "I hope the prospect of buying the boardinghouse works out. I'd like to see you again. For the children's sake, of course."

Her heart pounded against her chest. "I've been thinking on it. Who do I talk to?"

"Jacob Verishon, the owner of the general store. He built the house for his wife and children, but she couldn't handle the harshness of the land and moved back to Virginia with their children."

Now Starr understood why the man was surly. She could resort to bitterness if she slipped back into prostitution. "How misfortunate. Does he live there?"

"No. He's lived above the store since his family left, which is why I think he'd like to be free of the house."

"I have business sense. The idea has become more appealing."

"If it worked out, would you be willing to see us?"

She hesitated, torn between the truth and a life she longed to grasp.

"That's all right. I was just asking."

"My past is not honorable," she whispered.

"You already know I nearly drank myself into an early grave and ignored my responsibilities. Couldn't be worse than mine."

Oh yes, Aaron Conrad. It could be so bad you couldn't bear it. "Some things we do are worse than others."

"The Bible claims all sin is sin, not in degrees."

But not for her. "Good night, Aaron. I'll be leaving at daybreak."

He swung around to her, but she ignored him. Best this way. He entered the cabin and shut the door. A moment later the kerosene lamp went black.

A plan occurred to her, a way to repay him for his kindness.

Chapter 8

Starr and Goldie picked their way to higher elevation and skirted the creeks that had risen over their banks. Risking her life and the mare's by traipsing through high water didn't rank as smart. After all she'd told Aaron about hard times making a person smarter.

The sun glistened brighter than she ever recalled, its rays laying out a golden path. Perhaps it came from the light of three small children who loved to play in the mud and their father who loved them. Amazing how such a short time could give her inspiration for a better tomorrow.

Her thoughts were that of a little girl. She hadn't touched Aaron Conrad, but he'd touched her deeply. He deserved a clean woman, and because of her respect for him, she'd discouraged seeing any of them again. Yet like a child, she assured him she'd check into the property that could be a boardinghouse. Indecisiveness had never been a part of her before. She didn't like it, but the draw to Aaron and the children pulled stronger than her logic to leave the area.

In one breath she chased him away, and in another she welcomed him.

All around her, green growth and pink and yellow wildflowers flourished. Trees budded, and a doe and her baby scampered into a thicket. She marveled at a field of robins and relished in the songs of nature. On the way to Texas, she'd not been aware of the beauty and innocence for fear Clem followed her. She hoped the Yankees had stopped him cold. No place escaped the war. Not even Texas. Angst did that to her, made her blind to the here and now.

Without warning, the story of Ruth came alive in her mind, and she could hear Anne reading verse after verse of the young woman's tale. Ruth accompanied her mother-in-law into a land where she was considered an outcast by everyone except the noble who claimed her as his wife. Interesting. A beautiful story. Had Ruth ever wondered if she'd made the right decisions?

For that matter, did the God of the Conrads hear prayer and provide blessings? They'd lost a dear woman, and rain had destroyed their crops. Her original thoughts still proved true—no one looked out for those in need but the one suffering. Only courage and strength brought ultimate happiness.

If only a real God existed who cared, a God like the one who looked out for Ruth.

Last Chance came into view, the town's name settling into her soul. The saloon grabbed her attention first, as though the dilapidated building recognized her for what she was. Tossing the ugliness aside, she focused on the important matters and reined in Goldie at the general store. Tying her mare to the hitching post, she grabbed her saddlebag and entered the store. Mr. Verishon was stacking flour and sugar onto a shelf in a shadowed corner.

"Good morning, sir." She pushed her hat back so he could see her face.

He squinted and plopped a bag on top of another. "What do you need?"

"Did Mr. Aaron Conrad purchase his seeds from you?"

He turned toward her as if hard of hearing. "He did. I imagine it's all washed away with the rain."

"Yes sir. Do you still have the order?"

"Of course I do." He raised a brow as though she'd insulted him.

"I'd like to duplicate the order and pay for it."

He walked closer. "All right. Folks will be here soon enough to do the same thing. For sure I'll run out of seeds. This way, Aaron will have his fields replanted."

"Can I pay you extra to deliver it?"

He pressed his lips together. "Are you paying in gold?"

"Yes sir."

"No charge for delivery." He smiled for the first time. "Does this man's eyes good to see Aaron's children."

"Thank you. And please, don't tell him who paid for the seeds." She gave him her name and pulled out the pouch containing the gold. "Add peppermint sticks for the children, coffee, sugar, and flour to the order."

"He bought that yesterday."

"But not enough."

He smiled. "You're an angel, Miss Matthews. Bless you."

Not exactly. "I only want to help."

"Are you kin?"

"A friend." She drew in a breath for courage to ask about his house. "Sir, I hear you own an empty home on the edge of town."

"I do." His shoulders rounded, and he glanced away.

"I'm interested in opening a boardinghouse." There, she'd said it.

He stared out the window, as though his thoughts were far away. The poor man must have been incredibly lonely without his family. "I should do something with it. Not doing a person any good empty."

"Could I see it?"

"I haven't been inside for two years. Now's as good a time as any."

She didn't ask why he'd avoided the house, for she knew his bitter story. He locked the store, and the two walked past the barbershop, saloon, and church.

"We have a nice town," he said. "Don't care for the name. Always thought someone should change it."

"Maybe someone will."

They stopped in front of a white picket fence surrounding a two-story whitewashed home, hosting an upper and lower porch. It reminded Starr of homes in New Orleans. A grand home for any family, and her heart tore for Mr. Verishon's misery. He lingered opening the door. The memory of lively children and a wife who once greeted him probably yanked him back to a happier time.

"After you," he said and gestured for her to enter.

A painting of a pleasant woman and four children caught her eye the moment she stepped inside.

"My wife and children." He wiped the dust from the ornate frame.

"A lovely picture." The grandeur of the winding stairway, a mahogany side table, and golden candlesticks caused her to gasp. "Magnificent," she whispered.

"Thank you. There are five bedrooms, a water closet, dining room, parlor, and a separate kitchen in the back." He wandered through, and she followed.

She'd never seen such thick woven rugs nor a chandelier that sparkled even though laden with dust. The huge rooms would accommodate guests where once children roamed. "Oh Mr. Verishon. I can't afford this luxury."

He pulled back a gold drape in the parlor, allowing sunshine to explore a sofa, chairs, and bookcase. The furniture would fade with the light, although she preferred the openness.

"The house needs to be lived in, or it will decay," he said. "I have no use for it."

Starr admired the glassware, figurines, and books. Why had they been left behind? "I'm good with numbers, and I'm frugal." The prospect of maintaining a boardinghouse sent her into a panic. But she wanted to try, to be someone. "What if I worked for you here? I could take care of the guests and maintain a budget, and you'd still be the owner."

He crossed his arms over his chest and paced the floor. "Do you have experience working in a similar business?"

"I do." She cringed at the thought of him asking more questions. "I'm not afraid of hard work."

"Can you keep a ledger?"

"Yes sir."

"I should ask for references, but after your kindness to Aaron Conrad, I'll forgo that." She held her breath. "Thank you, sir."

He glanced about. "I always liked this room the best. A good place for people to gather after dinner." He sighed. "Having you here would keep the home. . .more like a memorial."

"And it would still be yours if you'd have need of it."

"Don't see that happening, but if so, I'd be fair. What would you do then?"

"I'd find another way to earn a living."

He picked up a photo of a young woman, a younger version of the woman in the picture. "You must be sent from heaven, Miss Matthews, for you've given me reason to believe in humanity." He dusted the photo with his shirtsleeve. "The Verishon Boardinghouse. Miss Starr Matthews, manager."

Chapter 9

Aaron watched Jacob Verishon drive his empty wagon back to town. His eyes blurred with fresh tears, not in watching the man disappear but from what the man had delivered. He'd almost given up, realized he'd have to sell all his livestock to buy seed or go into debt. He owed money to Margaret's parents, and that couldn't wait much longer. Now he wouldn't have to sell his cows to meet financial obligations when the children needed meat, milk, and vegetables to survive.

Thank You, Lord, for Your provision.

Now he could replant the garden and fields. An anonymous benefactor. Aaron wasn't fooled. Starr had purchased the seed. Anger swelled at the thought of taking charity from a woman he barely knew. He'd repay her as soon as harvesttime came. Or sooner.

In two days, he'd hitch up the wagon and drive into town for church. Jacob told him Starr had struck up a deal to manage his empty home for a boardinghouse. She'd begin living there tonight. Jacob's way of telling Aaron who'd purchased the seed. Why had she been so generous? They'd barely met, and initially tempers flew with the land squabble.

Although Starr hadn't appeared interested in seeing him again, he'd thank her proper on Sunday. If she didn't sit in a pew, he'd be knocking on her door. The children had talked of little else, and if he was honest, he missed her smile and musical laughter. How could a heart work so fast?

He hoisted a bag of seed corn onto his shoulder. The water should recede enough by the first of the week to replant. Until then, he'd keep the bags in his bedroom, safe from any more rain.

"Papa, why did Mr. Verishon bring us seeds?" Anne said.

"So we could have a garden and crops." Aaron laughed. "Brought us a few other things, too. Seems there are three children living here who like peppermint sticks." He nodded at a burlap sack, and she grabbed it.

"Mercy, more coffee, sugar, and flour, too."

His Anne needed to be roaming the pastures, wading in the creek, doing child things. "It's a bit heavy for you."

She lifted it with a pint-sized grunt. "I can carry it. Wish I could have thanked Mr. Verishon," she said. "I surely will on Sunday." She walked beside him. "Papa, we've been blessed this week. First Starr, and then you find a way to make our fields grow."

Starr. . . Where had she come from? What happened in her past that she couldn't go home? What caused the hurt in her brown eyes, a barrier between her and the world? Now she'd be living in Last Chance, and he planned to make a nuisance of himself. For his children's sake. They liked her company.

⚭

Sunday morning, Starr woke as though in a dream. One more night in a real bed, the finest she'd ever slept in. Fresh clean sheets, a choir of insects at night, and sweet birds to serenade her in the morning. The day before, Mr. Verishon had invited her to church, but she informed him she had nothing suitable to wear. When disappointment marred his rare smile, she purchased yard goods, thread, needle, and scissors to make a proper dress, a garment she'd never owned.

"Next Sunday I'll be there," she'd said. First time for everything, and it would be a good way to meet people.

"I have a daughter about your age." He seemed to grow taller with each word. "I'd like to think she's in church." He paused. "And thinking about visiting me with her sister and brothers. Maybe her mama, too."

What a dear man. "Could you travel there?"

He startled. "Hadn't thought about that. I suppose I could."

The man she thought was surly had been hurt. She understood protecting the heart.

Later in the day, Preacher Hawkins had stopped by the boardinghouse while she was outside beating rugs. Dust everywhere and mostly on her. The preacher was a nice man with a snow-white beard and a pink head. His clerical collar looked like it choked him. Definitely would cut off her breathing. Again she promised to be in church the next Sunday. She offered him coffee, reminding herself she needed to learn how to cook before a paying customer knocked on her door. Maybe she could borrow Anne for a few days, except that meant seeing Aaron.

A robin perched on the windowsill as if to say, "Time to get up. Plenty of work to do."

Starr closed her thoughts on the past few days and crawled out of bed, her body aching like she hadn't slept a wink. Cleaning and airing out the huge house had taken revenge on her. But so satisfying. A smile tugged at her lips. Her dreams were coming true.

With a log added to the stove, she brewed coffee and glanced at the backyard. Later in the week she'd pull weeds and tend to flower beds. Two rosebushes held her attention. She'd heard they took special care, a question for Mr. Verishon. Her stomach protested lack of food. The preacher's wife had sent bread, and a little was left. A thought occurred to her—could Preacher Hawkins's wife teach her how to cook? First thing tomorrow, she'd visit the woman with her problem, or she'd not have a job, and most likely, she'd starve.

She ventured outside with her mug of coffee to the front gate. A coat of whitewash and it would look like new. Sunshine warmed her. What could be better than this? Church bells pealed, and she remembered when the sound woke her from sleep after a long Saturday night, an annoyance. Not this morning. It was beautiful. Aaron and the children would most likely be among the churchgoers. She'd love to see them, but her conscience advised against it. Oh, who was she fooling? The womanly part of her wanted to see Aaron and his children every day.

She sighed and walked toward the house. Perhaps she'd cut out her dress. Hadn't thought about proper shoes. Looked like she'd need to pay Mr. Verishon another visit this week.

Closing the door to the sunshine, Starr sensed peace flowing through her. Her attention swept to the parlor and a Bible resting on a table. Curiously, she examined it and found the book of Ruth. She sank into a chair and read the story. How wonderful if all this was true.

Someone at the door grasped her attention. Could church be over so soon? She smoothed her hair in case it was Aaron. She hurried into the foyer. A tinny piano from church resounded in the distance, but she'd heard much worse.

She flung open the door.

The smell of the man took her back to a dark time.

"Well, hello there, Miss Starr. I thought it was you hanging on that gate." Clem Nabors lifted his nose. "You must be working out of a high-dollar place now."

"I gave that life up."

"Women like you have pleasin' a man in their blood."

"What do you want?"

"What's rightfully mine."

Chapter 10

Aaron left church humming "Abide with Me." Downright difficult to concentrate on Preacher Hawkins's sermon with visions of Starr swirling in his brain. He'd told himself repeatedly his children needed a woman for them to see occasionally, but guilt punched him in the gut when he dwelled on his fragile feelings for her.

Starr kept something hidden about herself, but most folks did. Whatever haunted her, she'd find him a listening ear if only he had the opportunity.

"Ready to see Miss Starr?" he said to his children. He and Anne had risen early to fry chicken, bake biscuits, and prepare greens and fresh berries for noontime in hopes Starr would join them for a picnic.

The three children looked as spit-polished as he could manage, and his thoughts pushed ahead to see Starr. Would Margaret approve? They piled into the wagon for the short ride, although if not for the food, they could have easily walked the distance. Once he pulled the horse and wagon to a halt outside the massive two-story home, he saw a man standing at Starr's door.

"You're a liar." The man cursed. "Give me what's mine, or I'll kill you."

"I don't have a thing that belongs to you. Now leave."

"Or what? You gonna pull a gun on me? Remember the last time you got smart?"

Starr touched her chest.

The man laughed. "Yeah, you go ahead and get all pale on me. You know what I can do."

Aaron grabbed his rifle. "Anne, take Ella and Parker. Hurry to the sheriff. Tell him there's trouble here. Then go stay with Preacher Hawkins and his wife until I fetch you."

Anne jumped from the wagon and pulled her brother and sister after her and on down the street.

"Hey, you," Aaron called as he approached the gate. "You best be getting on out of here."

The man jerked around, his left hand on his revolver. He whipped out the weapon and aimed it at Aaron. "Mind your own business. This woman stole from me."

Greasy best described the man. Smelled like he'd been rootin' with the pigs. Could this be the man Starr had played poker with and won the so-called land certificate? "Put your gun away. Leave her alone." Aaron spit each word, low and mean.

"Are you one of her new men? She's a good one for an hour, but feller, she ain't good enough to get shot for. Go find yourself another good time."

And in that instant, Aaron discovered Starr's secret.

"Aaron, he'll kill you." Starr's blanched face was stoic.

"The sheriff's on his way."

The man waved his gun between the two, as though not knowing who'd taste the first bullet. "The law's on my side. Where's my certificate? I need it to prove your thieving hide."

Starr's attention never left the man's face. "It's a forgery. Worthless. The sheriff contacted the land office in Austin. Ask him yourself when he gets here."

Aaron moved closer. "Put the gun down. The sheriff will hear your complaint."

The man's eyes narrowed. "If the certificate ain't legal, you owe me."

"I don't owe you a thing. I won the homestead fair, and now it's no good. If anything, you owe me." She crossed her arms over her chest. "So ride on out of here before the sheriff unloads his gun on you."

"You must be making big money here to have the sheriff and this man protecting you."

Her face was devoid of emotion. "This is not what you think. If I had anything that belonged to you, I'd hand it over." She sighed. "Aaron, would you stay with this man while I fetch what he wants?"

"Don't you try nary a thing," Clem said.

Pure hate poured from her eyes. "What would I do?"

She disappeared, leaving Aaron alone with Clem.

The man snorted. "New Orleans won't be the same without Flaming Starr. Best gal in the city. We lined up for her."

If Clem hadn't been holding a gun on him, Aaron would have taken a fist to his face. This couldn't be the woman who'd befriended him and his children. But he'd seen the emptiness in her eyes.

He'd made a terrible mistake. Never could he subject his children to a woman of ill repute. Or himself.

∞

Starr made it to the front door with the signed land certificate the same time the sheriff arrived. During the few moments it took to retrieve it, she thought about the gun under her pillow. Killing Clem would be easy, and she'd have no remorse. But she'd rather keep her vow to live respectable. She handed the folded paper to the sheriff.

"Sir, this man claims to own this homestead. Would you tell him what you learned?"

The sheriff eyed Clem. "If you sold her this, you're going to jail."

"I won it in a poker game," she said. Now it was twice that she'd admitted where it came from.

"She cheated," Clem said. "I want my land."

"There's no land for this paper," the sheriff said. "The certificate needs the state seal for it to be valid."

Clem reddened. "Why that thievin' pig. I'll find him and blow his brains out." He jammed a finger into Starr's face. "You're behind all this. I saw you with him before the poker game."

"You didn't see me with anyone."

"Enough," the sheriff said. "Leave now, or I'll lock you up."

"I'm going," Clem said. "Starr Matthews, you ain't seen the last of me. I'll get even. The likes of you belong in a grave."

"Three days in jail." The sheriff snatched Clem's gun from his hand. "You can cool off in my little homestead."

Starr stared as the sheriff and Clem walked away. The gate squeaked shut, like a jail door. Clem would be back, she had no doubt. Her heart crumbled. Everyone in town would know who she was. And the one person she wanted to protect from the truth stood in front of her. She lifted her gaze to meet his. Nothing registered on his face.

"I tried to tell you." Her lips quivered.

"You did. More than once. Guess I was the stupid one."

She clenched her jaw. "Right, Mr. Conrad. A lone woman looking to start over. Only a fool wouldn't see she was running from an ugly past."

"Seems that way."

Anger bubbled. "Thanks for your hospitality and coming to see me after church. Real Christian of you. Did the preacher talk about sin? Bet he did. Bet he told you to keep your children away from women like me."

Aaron's face hardened.

Starr should have ended the accusations pouring from her mouth. Here she thought this man might look at her differently. She'd even allowed a stone to loosen from her heart. Maybe two. But she'd not crumble.

Anne, Ella, and Parker raced from the preacher's house. Her stomach churned. The loss. The horrible loss.

"Papa, Miss Starr," Anne said breathlessly, "can we eat now?"

Starr's eyes moistened, and she hated for him to see her hurt. Blinking back the tears, she kneeled to the little girl's level. "I'm not feeling well, Anne. If you visit with me, you might get sick, too." She took a glimpse of Aaron. "Isn't that right?"

"I reckon so." He took Parker's and Ella's hands. "We need to get home."

The children's disappointment ended in Ella's tears. Poor baby. Starr wanted to pull her into her arms and dry her sweet face. Instead she stood, her hand on Anne's shoulder. "I'm sorry I spoiled things," she said.

Aaron nodded. "How long did you think it would last?"

"I never encouraged you."

"Are you still sick? Worried about us getting it?" Anne said.

"Yes. We want you healthy." Starr hurried inside without a farewell. Another moment with the Conrads and she'd have been in tears.

Chapter 11

On Monday, Starr dried her eyes and mentally listed the work inside and out for the boardinghouse to be presentable. Yesterday had crushed her, but disappointments weren't anything new. What was important was how she reacted.

Be strong. Learn how to endure. Make better plans. It'll turn out all right.

She never believed her own lies.

All morning she scrubbed and cleaned the upstairs. Even the corners, high and low, were whisked free of cobwebs. She wished she could do the same for her own life. Would Mr. Verishon change his mind about her managing the boardinghouse? Clem was sure to have told the sheriff about her, and he'd want the town's owner of the general store to know the truth about his employee. She couldn't blame anyone. She wasn't exactly a reliable, moral, upstanding citizen. Surely he'd heard from Aaron or the sheriff. And he hadn't stopped by to check on progress today.

Near noon, a light knock drew her attention to the inevitable. She descended the stairs, her insides bearing the guilt of deceit. The only person who would call was Mr. Verishon. Through the side window she saw a woman standing with a basket over her arm. Starr grasped the doorknob, wishing she'd taken the time yesterday to sew a dress. But with Clem's visit and Aaron's reaction, all she'd wanted to do was sleep.

A woman with blond and gray hair greeted her. Her eyes were too wide apart and her nose a bit pointed, but her smile could have outshined the stars on a clear night.

"Miss Matthews?"

"Yes ma'am."

"I'm Mrs. Hawkins, the reverend's wife. Wanted to stop by and welcome you to Last Chance." The woman looked behind her. "An appalling name for a town, don't you think? I'm sure you've heard the rumors."

Starr laughed, liking Mrs. Hawkins immediately. How many times had she heard adverse remarks about the town's name? "I agree. The name's depressing. Won't you come in?"

Mrs. Hawkins stepped inside. Her gaze followed the hallway, winding staircase, and furnishings. "Oh my. I've never been in this house. Simply grand. I imagine it's just like Mrs. Verishon left it."

"Mr. Verishon stated as much. Rather ghostly at times."

Mrs. Hawkins handed her the basket. "My dear, you are stunning. The single men in this town will be standing in line to court you."

Starr shook her head. "Dressed like this and up to my elbows in dirt?"

The woman touched her arm. "You're a blessing to Jacob. I was afraid he'd die of a broken heart. But you've given him purpose. Filling this house with guests will help heal his wounded spirit."

"Ma'am, I'm not a blessing." She took a deep breath. "I have fresh coffee. Would you like some? I don't have cream or sugar."

"Oh, I have those. Take a look in the basket." Mrs. Hawkins reached to peel back the cloth covering the contents—another loaf of bread, jam, sugar, a small jar of cream, and a bit of butter.

"Wonderful."

An hour later, Starr still listened to Mrs. Hawkins chatter. A wise, sweet lady.

"Tell me, is the cookstove simply heaven to use?" the woman said.

Starr might as well be honest. "I wouldn't know. I can't cook, and what I do make is disastrous."

The woman's eyes widened. "We must remedy that situation immediately. Especially if the boardinghouse is to be a success. Do you have anything for us to prepare?"

"No ma'am. We could go to the general store for beans and such."

"There's a farmer outside of town, one of our church people. We can buy eggs and a chicken, too."

That sounded like a feast. "Are you willing to teach me? I'm afraid Mr. Verishon will be sorely disappointed in me. I can pay you."

"Nonsense. We're friends. My sons are gone, living with their wives and children in Virginia. And I never had a daughter. You can help fill the hole in my life."

Starr melted in the kind words. A real friend. "I'm a good seamstress. Perhaps I can do something for you."

"We'll see. You could repay me by attending church."

"I'm sewing a dress for that very occasion."

The woman smiled, and her eyes held the light of something beautiful. Starr could only label it as peaceful.

"Are you going to be all right in this big house?"

"Yes. I'm enjoying it. Please, call me Starr."

"And I'm Winny." She nodded as though first names sealed their friendship. "Shall we commence to our errands so we can begin cooking lessons?"

"Let me wash up a little."

Moments later the two were on their way to the farmer Winny had spoken of earlier. She introduced Starr to everyone they met. Starr shuddered with each new face. Once the truth surfaced, her new friend would look foolish. Possibly be angry. On the way back to the boardinghouse, Starr resolved to tell her the truth as soon as they returned.

Once inside, they sat at a small table in the kitchen. Starr drew up her courage. "Winny, please sit down. I have to tell you about me."

"What about you?"

"I'm not the type you should be seen with."

"Says who?"

Heat prickled up Starr's neck and face. "Before I came here, I was a prostitute. In New Orleans."

"Did you leave it behind?"

"Yes ma'am. All of it. But I'm afraid it's caught up with me."

"Are you living for Jesus now?"

"I don't know a thing about Jesus, except He's in the Bible."

"Do you want to?"

She thought about Aaron and the story of Ruth in the Bible. "Depends on how He felt about soiled doves."

"Jesus had an opinion all right. He spent time getting to know young women who carried questionable reputations, telling them about God's love."

"That was then, and this is now. What would your husband say about your spending time with me?"

She laughed lightly. "Sugar, I knew all that man in jail claimed before I came. Doesn't change a thing about you and me being friends."

Starr's heart pounded. Winny had no idea how cruel people could be. "Think about how others will talk."

"Pshaw, Starr. The only thing in this world that counts is how God views me. No one else. Do you hear me?"

"Yes ma'am. What if folks stop coming to church?"

"Then they have no idea what it means to follow Jesus."

Starr hushed her confusion. Later she'd think on it. "Not today, but one day I want to know more about your way of thinking."

"You will. I'm sure of it. Do you have a Bible?"

"There's one in the parlor."

"Would you mind fetching it?"

Dread skittered over her. Visions of church ladies who made their way to the brothels only to point out their sins.

"I see the look on your face, Starr. I just want to show you a story."

She retrieved the Bible. Winny opened it and read aloud a story about a woman caught in adultery. The religious men wanted Jesus to condemn her, but He refused.

"Who is this Jesus?" Starr said.

"The Son of God. If you decide to read the Bible, I suggest the book of John."

"Are you asking me to?"

Winny patted her cheek. "If you are persuaded, that would be a good place to start."

"All right. For you."

Mrs. Hawkins laid the Bible on the table. "Aaron Conrad came by to see me and the reverend on Sunday afternoon. The children took a walk to the creek with our dog while we talked with him. Poor man nearly cried. Whatever you did for him filled a hollow spot in his heart, and now he's perplexed about it all."

"I deceived him," she said.

"Are you sure? Maybe he saw deep inside who you really are, a good, kind woman."

"I doubt it. No decent woman travels alone, dressed like a man."

"The heart has a special dress that outward signs can't disguise. Aaron has a choice to make, and it won't be easy for him."

Starr understood Aaron's decision had to be for the good of his children. That didn't include her. This had been her last chance. . .she'd come to the right town.

Chapter 12

Starr washed the last soiled cloth used to clean the boardinghouse. The clothesline was full, and her arms ached from all the reaching and scrubbing, but she felt so good. Winny had given her two more cooking lessons, and Starr caught on faster than what she'd imagined.

Not quite nine in the morning, and she had a few hours to sew on her Sunday dress. Then she'd read more. The book of John had captured her attention, which was a surprise. How comforting to think God loved her like the book said. She slowly grasped why others believed in Jesus, and questioned if God could have led the way for her to leave New Orleans. A smidgen of her had begun to believe. In other moments, doubt took over. Why had she been made to spend all those years with a mother who never cared and shoved her into prostitution? That was a loving God? Maybe someday she'd find an answer.

"Miss Matthews?"

Starr swung around to see the sheriff. "Morning." Her head pounded dread, as though he might run her out of town.

He waved from the side of the house and walked her way. "Wanted to let you know I ran that scoundrel out of town. Told him never to show his face again."

Relief swept through her. "Thank you."

He leaned on one leg and took off his hat. "Your secret is safe with me."

She swallowed the thickening in her throat. "Bless you."

"I hope everything turns out all right for you." He gave her a smile before leaving.

Perhaps God did care, and it took Him awhile to find her.

She lifted the empty laundry basket and stepped inside the house. She'd grown to respect this house and the love Mr. Verishon had poured into it. The finery was more than she'd ever want, but living here alone had given her time to think about the future.

Aaron often entered her thoughts. How very strange that in a few days' time she'd come to care for the small family. Her dreams were useless but still very present.

A pounding at the door secured her attention. She'd been expecting Winny. She hurried to let her in.

Mr. Verishon. . .

She pasted on a smile and opened the door.

He laughed and waved a folded piece of paper. "Miss Matthews! The Lord has blessed me indeed."

"What's happened? You look like a little boy with a fistful of peppermints."

"Much better than that." He nodded and laughed again. "After nearly four years, my wife and children are returning to Last Chance. Even my nineteen-year-old daughter. My wife wrote and said they were wrong to leave me. Asked me for my forgiveness. She said she'd live anywhere, if I'd take her back. It's a miracle, a beautiful miracle!"

Starr covered her mouth. The joy in his face was worth whatever she faced. "I'm so glad for you."

"Thank you." He sobered. "Now, don't worry about a position for you. I desperately need help at the store, and I'll want to spend time with my family. I'd like to fix the living quarters above the store to suit a fine lady like yourself. My family won't arrive for about six weeks, so you could stay here until I have things right." He frowned. "In my happiness, I forgot what this position as manager meant to you. I'm so sorry."

"Not at all. How wonderful, sir." And she meant it. "A family together is the way life's supposed to be. I'd be honored to work for you at the general store."

⬯

By midweek Aaron had pulled the bags of seed from his bedroom and replanted the garden. Anne helped, even Ella and Parker. What little soldiers. He took pains to teach them each seed's name, how to carefully bury them in rich soil, and cover them with a prayer. Tomorrow he'd sow corn.

"From these seeds will come a harvest that will feed our bellies during the summer, fall, and on into the winter," he said. "Beans, corn, squash, and tomatoes, too."

"I love watching things grow," Anne said. "I saw fresh greens growing near the creek. I'll make sure we have a mess for supper."

He watched her measure the distance from one seed mound to another. Her face and clothes were dirty—a little girl forced into adult work. It wasn't right, but he had no solution. Refusing to dwell on the worrisome matter, he completed the planting. His head ached, and he had chills. Weak, too. But he'd not let on. Too much work to do.

At supper, Aaron pushed back his uneaten food and announced he was going to bed. "Anne, do you mind getting your brother and sister in for the night?"

"No, Papa." Her little face twisted. "Are you not feeling well?"

He shook his head, and the movement sent a knife blade through his skull. "Just real tired. We all need rest to finish the planting tomorrow."

"I'll get them to bed and make sure they're quiet. Prayers will be quick," she said. "Your face is red. Did you get too much sun?"

"I imagine so, little one." A gnawing realization crept through him. . . He'd been soaked during the rains and hadn't gotten into dry clothes. The aching in his bones alarmed him. Worst of all, his chest hurt every time he took a breath.

He woke the following morning to the aroma of bacon and eggs. His Anne. He turned, and a jab of pain hit his head. He breathed deeply to steady himself and cringed with the chest pain. No, God. This wasn't a good time to be sick. Never would be.

Help me through this, Lord. My family needs me, and there's so much work to do. . .

He plastered on a smile and struggled to dress. His children were dressed and waiting for him to eat.

"I bet you're real hungry," Ella said, stroking his arm.

"I am, and this smells good." His words lacked strength, and he hated it.

Anne set a plate full of his favorite biscuits and sausage gravy before him with a steaming cup of coffee. Forcing himself to eat, he concentrated on his children and not the weariness tearing through his body.

After chores, he loaded bags of seed corn into the wagon, leftover bacon and biscuits, and two jars of water. The day would be long, but with the help of God, he and the children would get the fields planted. Then he'd rest.

Hours later, the pounding in his head and chest had grown worse. He attempted to hide his condition, stomping one foot in front of the other to finish the planting. At noon, he drank in the water and again ate when his belly didn't want it. Anne carried a worried brow, but he refused to admit how bad he felt.

When the last seed was laid to rest, he eased down onto the ground, afraid he couldn't get up.

"Papa," Anne whispered. "You look real bad. Maybe you got Miss Starr's sickness. But we're done now, and you need to rest." She placed a small hand on his head. "You're hotter than a cook fire."

Her voice sounded like a low hum, and her face blurred. "Yes, let's get back home. Do you want to drive the wagon?"

She bent to his ear. "Am I to drive because I know how, or because you're really sick?"

"My big girl needs to practice keeping the horse at the right pace." The way his weakened body alarmed him, he hoped Anne wouldn't need to fetch the preacher.

Lord, I haven't ever been this sick. I'm afraid it's pneumonia.

Back at the cabin, he stepped down from the wagon. Dizzy. Hurting. "Anne, just leave the horses hitched, and I'll take care of them later. I'm going to lie down for a little while."

Ella grabbed his hand, but he didn't have the strength to grasp hers. "Papa, what's wrong?"

"I'm tired. That's all."

"Hush," Anne said. "Let Papa be."

Aaron stumbled into the house, fearful his legs would give out beneath him. Through darkening vision, he collapsed onto his bed.

Chapter 13

Starr polished the silver from a delicately inlaid sideboard in the dining room. Everything would be perfect for the Verishon family. Oddly enough, she looked forward to their arrival. The idea of a boardinghouse had been Aaron's idea, and working at the general store suited her just fine. Living above it meant she could be at the store early and stay late whenever needed.

Needed. She liked the sound of it.

A faint knock at the door alerted her. She'd never had so many visitors. At times she considered not answering, but the caller might have something important to tell her. Starr flung open the door.

Anne stood before her, tears streaming down her dirty face.

Starr bent to her side. "What's wrong?"

"Papa's real sick. He's shivering and talking out of his head. I was afraid he'd gotten the same sickness you had. And hoped you could help me nurse him."

Digging her fingers into her palms, Starr swallowed what losing another parent to the children meant. "Does the town have a doctor?"

"No ma'am."

"I'll come with you. I know a little about taking care of sick folks."

"Thank you, Miss Starr. I'm so scared."

She wiped a tear from the little girl's face and drew her into her arms. "Your papa is a strong man." She looked to the road where an empty wagon and horse stood. "Where's Ella and Parker?"

"Tending to Papa."

"You drove here by yourself?"

She nodded.

Starr closed the door behind her. Aaron must be very ill. "We'll drive by the preacher's house and be on our way."

"I have herbs and medicine things, but I don't know how to use them." Anne burst into fresh tears. "Is Papa going to die?"

"Not if we can help it."

At the parsonage, Starr rushed in to tell Winny about Aaron. "Anne says there are medicinal items at the cabin, but—"

"I have some, too." Winny disappeared and returned with a small bag. "Feverfew and such. Go, and may God be with you. When the reverend returns from Dallas, I'll send him out there." She glanced behind her. "I'm keeping the five Jenson children for the next three days or I'd ride along."

"Anne and I will do just fine, and I have experience using herbs. You don't need to expose yourself or the Jenson children to whatever's ailing Aaron. Thank you for the herbs, and please pray for him."

"We all will."

Starr hurried to join Anne at the wagon, terrified that death stalked the Conrad family, those she'd come to love.

∞

At the Conrad cabin, Starr found Aaron more dead than alive. Ella and Parker kept vigil at his side, their attention focused on his pale face. He didn't respond when she whispered his name, and she masked her panic. His fever and labored breathing indicated pneumonia. A raspy cough rattled in his chest, confirming her suspicions. Her fear wrestled with anger. Hadn't she warned him to take care of himself? What would these children do without a mama or papa?

"I'd like to help"—Anne's voice quivered—"but I don't know anything about doctoring."

"Hot water to make a tea with the feverfew." She kissed the child's cheek. "I'll do all I can. I promise."

"I just have to do something. I used a wet cloth to wash his face before I left and told Ella to keep it up." She hesitated, no doubt to calm herself. "Doing nothing seems wrong."

Starr swung back to Aaron, his face venturing to gray. What dare she say when she was frightened out of her wits? She bit down hard to stop any flow of emotion. "Anne, you and your brother and sister can pray."

While the water boiled, Starr pressed a damp cloth onto Aaron's hot face. His shirt must be removed to cool him down, but the thought brought back memories from her past. She shoved them away and concentrated on how to lower his temperature. Back in New Orleans, she'd seen two people with pneumonia whose fever soared so high they slipped into unconsciousness. Before they died, she helped bathe them with hot and cold water. It made sense to use cool.

She'd do anything to keep Aaron alive.

Hours later, she watched his chest slowly rise and fall beneath a thin coverlet. The fever still raged like a wildfire, devouring every bit of life in its path. There had to be something she'd forgotten. Feverfew had been forced through his lips as well as a ginger tea. Cool cloths applied repeatedly, and still nothing changed his condition.

She slumped into a chair and stared at his rugged face, a man she could have loved deeply. Trusted, too. If she were the one lying there ill, what would he do? She took his limp hand into hers and entwined his fingers.

Pray.

The thought sent her heart pounding. Of course, pray as she'd instructed the children. Starr understood enough to believe God existed and He loved everyone. He longed for people to trust in Him. But understanding and believing were not the same. Standing, she walked to the doorway and looked into the kitchen, where Anne labored over fresh greens, with bacon and corn bread. If the child was not relieved of work soon, she'd grow old before her time. Aaron didn't want that, Starr was certain. But if something happened to him, Anne would be burdened with more responsibilities. Possibly separated from Ella and Parker.

God, please keep this family together. Heal Aaron. I'd gladly die in his place. Starr halted in her thinking. Belief had crept into her heart without realizing it. Bewildered, she turned back to Aaron. *Yes, Lord, I believe. Save this good man. No matter what You want from me, You have my soul. Take me if You must bring one of us to You.*

Had her words made sense to God? She hoped so, for He was all she had left. Aaron moaned. In his fever-infested state, had he pleaded for God to heal him?

She held on to his hand and slipped to the floor. Desperation had imprisoned her, and prayer hailed as the only way to save him. Three little people joined her on the floor, hands folded, and hearts melted into one plea.

Chapter 14

Aaron fought his way up a steep canyon wall, digging his fingers into crevices and dragging his body with him. When had he grown so weak? He struggled to open his eyes, but the more he tried the more difficult it became. He'd dreamed about Margaret and the days when they were first married. She dared him to chase her, with a flirtatious smile, and he raced after her toward a grove of trees, but when he reached for her hand, she disappeared, and in her place was Starr. Someone touched his shoulder and he spun to see Margaret again. "It's time," she said. "Don't let go of Starr's hand. Let her love you and our children."

He opened his eyes. Starr sat on the floor with her hand wrapped around his. Just like the dream. . . Just as Margaret stated. Wanted. Realization bolted into his heart. The feelings he'd fought were real. He'd been wrong to judge and turn from Starr. Shaking his head, he stared at her sleeping form. How long had she been there?

His movement wakened her, and she smiled. "You're awake. Praise God." She tugged at her hand, but he held tight. "I must tell the children."

"Not yet," he whispered. "What happened? The last I remember is falling asleep, my head and chest about to burst."

"Pneumonia," she said. "Anne fetched me from the boardinghouse. We were afraid you wouldn't make it."

Regret claimed him. "How long have I been this way?"

"Three days."

"And you've been here all this time, taking care of me?"

"Yes, Aaron."

"I'm so sorry."

She touched his face, tenderness nestled in hers. "There's nothing to be sorry for, except for not taking care of yourself and frightening your children and me. You need to rest so your strength will return."

"I'm sorry for hurting you."

A sad smile met him. "Thank you. But you were right."

"I was wrong. Forgive me?"

"Are you certain?"

"As sure as I breathe."

She nodded, and he dragged his tongue over his lips. "I'll get you some water."

"Promise me one thing." Weakness shackled his body but not his resolve.

"Of course."

He smiled into her pecan-colored eyes. "Don't ever leave me, Starr. You're my light, and I don't want to live another day without you. Took me being sick to know I love you."

Her eyes widened. "You must still be feverish."

"I am, with a flaming Starr. What's your answer?"

She trembled as though wrestling with her response. He'd hurt her once, and maybe she was afraid he'd do it again.

"I understand if you aren't ready to marry me."

"I love you and your children. God has blessed me far more than I could ever have hoped for. Yes, Aaron. That's my answer."

He closed his eyes. "I'd ask for a kiss, but I'm afraid I taste of death."

She brushed his lips with a feathery kiss. "You taste of forever."

Aaron would never let this woman go. Never.

"Papa?" Anne's shaking voice came from the doorway.

"He's awake," Starr said. "Get Ella and Parker."

Within seconds all three children were at Aaron's side. His dear children. "Thank You, Lord," he said. "For all my blessings."

"We prayed," Ella said. "A lot."

"Good girl." He took in her angelic face. "God answered your prayer."

"Yes, He made you well," Anne said.

"Your eyes are open," Parker said.

"God answered Ella's prayer, too. Miss Starr has agreed to marry me. You'll have your new mama."

A low laugh interrupted Aaron's next words. "Not if I can stop it." Clem Nabors stood in the doorway, rifle aimed at Starr. Greasy hair hung over his face beneath a hat. "Did you think you were free of me?"

"Clem, please. Think of the children."

"Stupid woman. That knife scar on your chest should have told you who you belong to."

Aaron remembered her clutching her chest the first time he saw Clem at the boardinghouse.

She shook free of Aaron's hold. "Can't you let us be?"

"Clem, what do you want?" Aaron said. "I haven't much money, but take my horse."

"Don't want your horse. I'm getting rid of all of you and taking what belongs to me." He raised his rifle. "Starting with you, Conrad." He sneered. "I'm gonna enjoy this."

Starr grabbed the children and pushed them behind her.

A shot rang out.

Clem staggered against the door and crashed to the floor.

The sheriff stood in the doorway. "The preacher was on his way out here and heard Nabors was back. He told me to ride out here fast, and I came. Some men never learn how to abide by the law."

Chapter 15

Five months later

S tarr set a venison roast on the table with green beans and fresh corn beside a cloth-covered basket of biscuits. She'd prepared it all. She walked to the doorway of the cabin and looked out on the children playing with a puppy that Winny and the preacher had given them the day Starr and Aaron were married. Anne, Ella, and Parker were her treasures. Anne no longer looked so thin and gaunt, but happy and healthy like an eight-year-old should. Ella and Parker loved having their big sister play, although she often reverted to a mama role.

Last Chance was a fitting name for the town, and she hoped no one ever changed it. Mr. and Mrs. Verishon looked so happy together, and their children appeared devoted to both parents. It just took time for some people to appreciate each other and let love blossom.

Starr felt a strong hand on her shoulder, and she leaned back against her husband. "I'm so happy," she said. "Thank you, Aaron Conrad, for loving me."

"That goes both ways. I wish the work wasn't so hard. Hate it for all of you."

"It's what we do when we love." She touched her stomach, where new life had begun to form.

"Shall we tell them tonight?"

Starr turned into his embrace and nestled against his chest. "Tell them what, Aaron? That their mama isn't going to be scrawny for long?"

He chuckled, a low rumble she'd learned to love. "You tell them however you want." He lifted her chin and kissed her deeply. "Then I'll tell them how much I love their mama."

DiAnn Mills is a bestselling author who believes her readers should expect an adventure. She creates action-packed, suspense-filled novels to thrill readers. Her titles have appeared on the CBA and ECPA bestseller lists; won two Christy Awards; and been finalists for the RITA, Daphne Du Maurier, Inspirational Readers' Choice, and Carol award contests. She is the director of the Blue Ridge Mountain Christian Writers Conference, Mountainside Marketing Retreat, and Mountainside Novelist Retreat with social media specialist Edie Melson. Connect with DiAnn here: DiAnnMills.com.

A PALACE
ON THE PLAINS

by Erica Vetsch

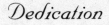

Dedication

To my husband, Peter, who teaches me more about love every day.

Chapter 1

All these yours?" The baggage handler spit a stream of tobacco juice toward the tracks.

Julia Farrington straightened her shoulders and took a steadying breath. "Yes."

"You could start a store with all this stuff. I've seen wagon trains that didn't have as much baggage." He scratched the hair over his ear and studied her, his battered hat tilting at a jaunty angle. "You got a wagon or something, or do you want it hauled over to the hotel? That'll cost you extra."

"No, thank you. I'm being met."

"Who by?" He spit again, swiping his forearm across his mouth to catch a drip.

She shuddered, but before she could answer, a voice piped up behind her.

"Is that the lady you said would be such a pain in the neck, Pa?"

"Hush, Titus."

"But, Pa, you said she'd be a fancy city miss with no more sense than God gave a sandhill crane. That's gotta be her. Anyways, she's the only one here besides old Booker."

Julia turned, her face warming. She encountered three sets of eyes, a man and two young boys. The eyes were all dark brown, a stark contrast to the blond hair she could see peeking from under their hats.

The man raised his hat a fraction of an inch with one hand and poked out the other, frowning. "I'm Cyrus Haskell. My brother, Walt, sent me to fetch you."

Julia studied his hand—large and work roughened, tanned with long, strong-looking fingers—and finally placed her fingertips in his clasp a bare instant before withdrawing. "Miss Farrington." *No more sense than a sandhill crane? Hmph.*

"Which one of these is yours?" He jerked his thumb toward the laden baggage cart.

"Well, all of them." Surely he hadn't expected her to show up empty-handed?

"All of them?" His voice went high, and his dark eyes widened. "Are you crazed?"

She blinked. "I don't believe so."

"Where do you think you're headed, missy? A palace? I'll barely have room for half this stuff in my wagon, and no room for any of it in the house. Just finding a place for you to sleep was trouble enough. You have more baggage than a circus." He settled his hands on his hips. "Pick out what you absolutely need, and we'll stow the rest here at the depot until you leave town."

Julia took a grip on her nerves and refused to back down. She'd had enough of being

317

made to feel small and ineffective by her father. She'd be blamed if she was going to put up with it from a stranger. "I assure you, I need all of it."

"Nobody needs that much stuff." He shook his head and looked at her as if she had cotton batting for brains. The smaller of the boys tugged at his father's pant leg, but he brushed the little hand aside.

The baggage handler slapped his thigh. "That's what I told her, Cyrus."

"I assure you, every one of those items is necessary." She set her valise on the platform and folded her arms.

The little guy tugged again.

"Not now, Cotton."

Another stream of tobacco juice splattered the edge of the platform. "Whatever you folks are gonna do, do it quick, 'cuz the sky's about to let loose, and I don't aim to stand here in a downpour while you argue."

"Pa!" This time it was the elder child. "Cotton's doing his dance."

The man's attention swiveled to his small son, who was hopping from foot to foot and holding the front of his little britches. "Titus, take him to the outhouse behind the depot. Quick!"

Titus grabbed his brother's hand and hauled him down the platform at a run, clattering down the steps and disappearing around the corner of the station. Once they were out of sight, their father fisted his hands, propping them on his hips again, and frowned at her from under his broad-brimmed hat. "Lady—"

"It's *Miss Farrington*. And I assure you, my hearing is quite sound. There is no need to raise your voice."

"Then listen carefully. There is *no room* for all those fripperies. Cull them to a reasonable pile, or I'll do it for you."

Julia stepped close to him, close enough to smell hay and earth and grown man. Close enough to see the gold flecks in his eyes and the pulse jumping in his throat. Close enough to notice that his top button was hanging by a thread and that his collar was frayed and in need of turning. "Sir, I have been hired to do a job. I brought the tools I need to do that job. I can no more leave them behind than you could do your work without a plow or harness or seed. If you cannot accept that fact, I will wait here in town until Mr. Walter Haskell arrives to transport me to his home. It was he, after all, who hired me."

"Walt's wasting enough money on you. He can't afford to waste time traipsing into town, too. I had to come in and pick up seed, so you'll go with me now, or you'll sit right here until the eastbound train comes through tomorrow to take you back to whatever big city you came from."

At that moment, lightning arced across the sky, and thunder shook the ground. A few scattered raindrops plopped around them, leaving silver-dollar-sized splats on the planks. Rolling his eyes, Booker jerked the handle on the cart and tugged it under the eave.

"You're on your own, Cyrus. Load her up or leave her, but I'm headed in where it's dry." He sauntered to the door, pausing in the doorway to spit before disappearing inside.

"Mr. Haskell." Julia adopted her most let's-be-reasonable voice. "I'm not trying to be difficult, but I cannot leave my belongings behind."

He yanked up her valise, took her elbow, and directed her out of the rain. With a jerk, he removed his hat and jammed his fingers through his hair, disrupting the streaky, blondish-brown locks. A sigh shoved out of his broad chest, and he resettled his hat. "I told Walt this was a cockamamie idea when he first voiced it."

His tone reminded her of her father's, and she pressed her lips together. If he left her here, she'd have no choice but to return on tomorrow's train. Humiliated, having to bear up under her father's I-told-you-not-to-strike-out-on-your-own smugness.

Mr. Haskell put his hands on his hips *again*—he seemed to do that a lot—and frowned. He seemed to do that a lot, too. "Fine. I'll see what I can do." With a shrug, he turned away from her and plunged into the curtain of water now pouring off the depot roof. "Boys, get under there and stay as dry as you can."

The youngsters tumbled through the rain and scampered toward Julia, skidding to a halt and scattering droplets from their hat brims and coats. The little one rubbed his nose with the heel of his hand, staring up at her with chocolate-drop eyes and ruddy cheeks. She couldn't help but smile, and he responded with a sunbeam grin and two perfect dimples.

His older brother regarded her skeptically, his features miniature versions of his father's. "Pa thinks you're an unnecessary expense that Uncle Walt is going to rue. What's rue mean?" He kicked the toe of his scuffed boot against the dark-red siding.

"It means to regret something or wish you hadn't done it." *Like hopping on a train and heading across the Nebraska prairie all alone.*

"That's what I thought. I reckon Pa already rues it."

It was perfectly unreasonable for her to feel guilty. After all, it wasn't her fault that her employer had pawned the job of transporting her off on his brother. Guilt settled on her shoulders anyway.

Thunder rumbled again, and the smaller boy sidled closer, his pudgy little hand finding a purchase in a fold of her skirt. She touched his shoulder, and a few tangled threads in her heart unraveled.

∽

Of all the useless bits of fluff ever found prancing across a train platform, *Miss Farrington* took the biscuit. Ruffles and flounces and fancy-styled hair. Impractical from head to toe. That pale-as-milk skin and those dainty little hands in their lace gloves would never stand up under the rigors of life out here. Good thing she wasn't staying long. If he'd have run into her back East, he might've thought her quite pretty. But out here, it took more than shiny hair, long eyelashes, and a pleasing figure to make a fellow take more than a passing notice. Out here, a man looked for a woman with some grit. Miss Farrington was all show and no stay.

Cyrus reached under the seat of his wagon and drew out his slicker, sliding into it and flipping the collar up against the rain. The trip home was going to be miserable if this didn't let up, and there was no question about waiting it out. His spring work was piling up like dirty laundry, and he was dallying in town.

Good thing he'd anticipated the possibility of rain and brought the canvas along. The boys could at least travel dry. Sacks of seed corn packed the whole bed of the wagon except for the small area behind the seat that he'd reserved for the boys and the woman's bag.

Her *single* bag.

Now he was going to have to reposition the load to fit in a bag, a trunk, a crate, and whatever it was she had wrapped up in that blanket. He tilted his head to let the rain run from his hat brim and scowled. If he didn't know for certain that Ma would blister him, he'd scoop up the boys and point the team toward home, leaving the starchy fusspot and her gear behind.

Not to mention how disappointed Walt would be if Cyrus ruined his surprise.

He blew out a breath and climbed up to restack the bags of seed, working awkwardly under the canvas to keep his cargo as dry as possible, muttering under his breath as he shoved the sacks. *She'd better be good at her job. No, check that. She'd better be amazing at her job.*

With the sacks piled up, he hopped down, his boots splashing into a mud puddle. Though it was inconvenient just now, they could use the rain. Winter had been so dry, the soil was begging for some moisture. This was by far the mildest winter they'd had since moving here two years ago.

Much easier than the winter that had taken his Hester.

Cyrus stomped through the rain, turning the team around to position the wagon alongside the platform.

"Wait up there till I get this gear loaded, boys." He levered himself onto the wet boards and reached for the crate first. It wasn't as heavy as he feared, but its size made it awkward.

"Would you like me to help?" Miss Farrington asked.

"Nope." He adjusted his grip and toted the box to the wagon, letting it drop into the bed with a thump. Her gunmetal-gray eyes regarded him from under the edge of her ridiculous hat, and the way her prissy little mouth tightened, he knew she was just dying to say something about his treatment of her belongings.

The trunk and the valise landed in the wagon next, and he tugged the canvas up to cover them. "There's hardly going to be room for the boys."

"Mr. Haskell." She spoke as if talking to a toddler. "I would ask you not to be so cavalier with the last object. If you break or damage it, I will be forced to seek recompense. It's quite valuable, and I won't have it harmed."

Cavalier? Recompense? Had the woman swallowed a dictionary? Why didn't she just say "Don't be so ham-fisted with my stuff or I'm going make you pay for it"? He grunted and jerked his chin, but she wasn't finished.

"And I shall have to insist upon helping you load it. If you'll carefully lift from that end, I will take this end." She threaded the strings of her little bag over her wrist and positioned herself on one end of the rectangular bundle. "And don't knock it against the wagon."

He clenched his jaw. *How on earth had anyone managed to haul any freight out here on the prairie before she arrived?*

"Fine." Anything to get on the road. He gripped the blanket, feeling corners under his hands. Backing away from the depot with it, he took small steps, knowing she couldn't make much time carrying her end of the bundle. It was surprisingly heavy, and he barked his shin on a black metal leg sticking out from beneath the blanket. Biting the inside of his cheek, he carefully stepped into the wagon, lifting the cargo over the side.

She teetered on the edge of the platform, straining to hold her end up. Before he could adjust his grip, she lost hers, letting the bundle crash to the bed of the wagon and startling the horses. They jerked and hit the end of their traces, rolling the wagon a few feet as Cyrus dove over the seat to grab the reins and pull them to a stop.

"Whoa there, boys. Easy." He glanced over his shoulder. "Thanks for the help. That went great." He swiped the rain off his face and sat down, adjusting the reins. "C'mon, boys. Scamper aboard and get under that tarp."

His sons shot into the wagon like little jackrabbits, diving under the heavy cover. Miss Farrington, her hat feathers dripping water and sagging onto her shoulder, gathered her skirts and moved to the edge of the platform.

She lifted her hem to about mid-shin, giving him a glimpse of white petticoats and a shapely ankle, raised her foot, then set it down again. Frowning, she turned to the side and repeated the maneuver.

"Well, are you going to get in, or is this some newfangled dance you learned back East?"

The glance she shot him was supposed to be withering, but he felt a tickle of laughter forming in his chest.

"I cannot make it into the wagon without landing even less gracefully than my possessions did. At least not without hiking my skirts up well past where a lady should." The prim look of her mouth wobbled, and she blinked fast.

The laughter died, replaced by remorse. What kind of example was he setting for his boys? Ma would have his hide for treating a lady so poorly.

Before she could do more than squawk, he leaned over and scooped her into his arms, depositing her on the seat. She took a moment to settle, adjusting her skirts and hat, her chin set at an outraged angle.

Touchy, wasn't she? All spit and vinegar. Whoever landed her as a life partner had better be ready for a right lively time.

Cyrus checked to make sure the boys were under the tarp, picked up the reins, and slapped the wet backs of the team. The wagon lurched ahead, and Miss Farrington grabbed her hat and the side of the wagon seat.

He tried not to notice how the rain had gathered her eyelashes into long points, and how she smelled of perfume.

∞

Julia flicked the sodden feathers off her shoulder and adjusted her damp shawl. Her hat was doing next to nothing when it came to protecting her from the rain. And her winter coat lay securely at the bottom of her trunk, out of reach.

Not for all the cotton in the Carolinas would she ask Mr. Haskell to stop so she could retrieve it. The rain had slackened to a steady drizzle anyway. She could survive. As long as her baggage stayed dry.

She swiped her cheeks with her free hand and studied the landscape. They were headed south, away from the Platte River and the tiny town, and into a great expanse of nothing. For as far as she could see, nothing but open, flat land lay before her. No trees, no houses, no barns, nothing but this faint, two-wheeled track cut into the tall prairie grass. After a lifetime of cities and bustle and crowded streets, all the openness disquieted her—and yet, it soothed, too.

She took a deep breath of the sodden air and relaxed a fraction. She had managed to get herself and her belongings this far, she was on her way to her first real job, and she was out from under the exacting strictures of her father.

"How far is it to the settlement? And does it have a name?"

"Nine miles. Folks call it the Haskell Settlement, I guess, if they call it anything at all. There are three Haskell quarter sections that abut, and the houses are just within sight of one another. At least, they will be when we finish building Walt's place. He filed on the land just last month when he came of age. Right after he asked Allison to marry him."

His tone made her curious. "You don't like Allison?"

He jerked. "I never said that."

"You sounded disapproving."

"I like Allison just fine. But she's a city girl, like you. Kinda dainty and fragile. Her pa is a banker over in Lincoln. That's where Walt met her. When her folks found out she was marrying him, they washed their hands of her, sent her on out here with nothing more than a satchel of clothes. I guess they had higher aims for her than to be a dirt-farmer's wife, and if she wasn't going to play along, then good riddance. I guess that's what led Walt to hire you. To give her some of the things she's missing out on by marrying him."

"They must be very much in love to persist in the face of such opposition from their families." She sliced a glance at him, wondering if he caught that she was including him in the opposition. Her romantic nature was ignited by the notion of two lovers willing to risk disapproval to be together. Who did Cyrus Haskell think he was, judging people like that? Just because a woman wasn't built like a plow horse ready to step into the traces, he thought she wasn't fit to live out here. His wife must look like a teamster and have the constitution of a buffalo.

Giggling and thumping came from under the tarp, and the older boy, Titus, whom she judged to be about six, wormed his way up like a gopher. "Is it still raining, Pa? Can we get out now? It's awful close in there with all that stuff. Cotton's getting squashed."

"You can come up for air. The rain's about stopped for now."

Cyrus swung around and lifted the smaller boy up and into his lap, giving him the ends of the reins to hold. Cotton grinned, his dimples denting his round cheeks as he settled back against his pa's chest and pretended to drive. Titus hung over the back of the seat between Julia and his father, hopping every now and again and making the bench lurch.

"What's that smell?" Titus sniffed the air like a puppy.

"Is it the rain?" Julia asked. "The air is so fresh here, like it's been washed clean."

"Naw, that ain't it. It's something I never smelled before." He sniffed his father's sleeve then leaned close to Julia, inhaling quickly, his eyes narrowing. "It's you." He wrinkled his nose.

Mortification quaked through her, and in spite of the chill, her cheeks grew hot. She looked at the horizon, away from Cyrus and his outspoken son. Suppose she did smell like soot and travel? That was only to be expected after coming all the way from Omaha.

To make matters worse, Cyrus started to laugh. He reached up and tweaked Titus's nose. "That's perfume, Troop. Ladies wear it."

"Gramma don't wear it." He looked skeptically through his lashes. "It smells like. . . like. . .flowers." The word came out loaded with disgust, as if he'd just claimed she smelled like a pigsty.

She couldn't help but laugh, relieved at so simple an answer. "It's called lavender water." Opening her handbag, she withdrew the little vial and opened it. "Here."

He took one whiff and toppled off the seat back onto the wagon floor as if he'd been poisoned, gagging and snorting before dissolving into giggles. Cotton laughed along with him, twisting around and under his father's arm to see.

"Maybe someday you'll like it." Julia let Cotton smell the perfume before returning it to her bag, and the little boy—perhaps four years old?—rubbed his nose and grinned.

"I doubt he'll get much of a chance to fall for fancy perfume. He's more likely to be attracted to the clean smell of lye soap and starched cotton." Cyrus slapped the reins again. "We're almost home, boys."

Julia straightened, rising a fraction from the bouncy wagon seat, but she saw nothing except gray skies and sodden, brown grass. The two-track road headed around a small mound. . .too small to be called a hill. . .and came to an end in front of the oddest collection of structures she'd ever seen. Cyrus pulled the horses to a stop, and the boys scrambled down. A shaggy dog shot toward them, barking and wagging, tongue lolling.

She sat still, blinking, trying to process what she was seeing. A door sat square in the middle of the side of the mound. That must be the storm cellar. A few dozen yards away, what appeared to be a large haystack had another door. A fence enclosed a livestock area nearby.

"You going to sit up there all day, or are you going to get down?" Cyrus stood beside the wagon, hands on his hips and his hat tilted back on his head.

"Where's the house?"

His eyebrows bunched. "Right here." He jerked his thumb over his shoulder to the storm cellar.

"I mean where you live."

"Miss Farrington, this"—he jerked that thumb again—"is the house. It's a dugout with a sod front. We live here—my grandmother, my two boys, and me. And for the next six weeks, you live here, too."

She swallowed hard, her resolve as limp as her hat feathers.

Chapter 2

Cyrus, you fetch her?" A tiny woman with grizzled hair and a dried-apple face burst from the doorway. Her apron fluttered in the slight breeze, and she looked up at Julia, her eyes like dark pips in her face.

"Hiya, Nan." Titus jumped into a puddle, scattering muddy droplets. "We brung her home. You should see all the stuff she has. We're gonna have to build a new soddy."

"Mind your tongue, young man, and stop jumping in those puddles. There's mud enough around here without you rolling in it like a piglet." She swatted the youngster on the seat of his overalls and bent to tweak Cotton's nose.

Julia remained frozen on the wagon seat. She hadn't expected the Palace of Versailles, but she had anticipated at least a frame house. A stovepipe jutted from atop the earthen mound, trickling a damp wisp of smoke from under the conical rain guard. Two square holes, one on each side of the doorway, must be the windows, but they didn't have glass panes. Oiled paper covered the openings.

"Come on down from there, dearie. Cyrus, what are you waiting for? Give her a hand, will you?"

Cyrus stopped wrestling with the canvas and rounded the wagon. He reached up and plucked Julia from the seat, swinging her down as if she were no more a burden than Cotton. She glanced up at him, trying to grab on to something intelligent to say, but the solid muscle under her palms as she braced herself distracted her.

Puzzlement reflected in his eyes, as if he wasn't quite sure what to do with her either. His brows, darker than his hair, came down, and his hands fell away. Julia busied herself with straightening her shawl and brushing her skirts.

"You'll be thinking we don't have a lick of manners." The older woman took her elbow. "I'm Nan Haskell, Cyrus's grandma. You can call me Nan. Everybody does." She drew Julia through the doorway.

Julia had to duck under the lintel, and even so, knocked her hat askew. The smell of dank earth hit her like a wet cloth to the face. Gloom didn't begin to describe the interior. She'd been right. Oiled paper covered the "windows." What light managed to filter through hovered near the openings as if trying to get back outside.

I don't blame it.

As her eyes adjusted, she realized the truth of Cyrus's words on the train platform. Two sets of bunk beds lined the walls, a small table with four stools pushed underneath took up one corner, and a stove took up another. Rather than true cupboards, open-sided crates hung from the ceiling to hold plates and cooking utensils. A door had been cut into the back wall. Why, her father's front parlor took up more space than this entire family had to live in. Where on earth was she supposed to work? Where was she supposed to sleep? Where were her things going to go?

Mrs. Haskell busied herself at the stove. "Just lay off your wraps. The top bunk is yours." She pointed to the beds on the east side of the room. "Usually Walt sleeps up there, but he's going to bunk in the barn until his new house is done. Titus and Cotton double up on the lower bunk."

The door bumped wider, and Cotton tottered in, both fists wrapped around the handles of her valise, barely keeping it off the ground. He grinned and dropped it on the—dirt!—floor at her feet.

"Thank you."

He nodded and scampered outside.

"Does he ever talk?"

Cyrus's boots klunked on the doorsill, and he edged into the room with her trunk over his shoulder. "When he has something to say. Just like Titus, except Titus always has something to say. Ma, where can we stow this stuff? She brought enough to stock a mercantile, and this is only half of it."

Mrs. Haskell tapped her upper lip. "I never thought. . .it's already so tight in here you practically have to go outside to change your mind."

"That's what I told her, but she said she needed all of it." He swung the trunk down in the only available floor space and sat on it, removing his hat and running his long fingers through his hair.

"What else is out there?"

Julia didn't know whether to be amused or annoyed that they spoke as if she wasn't standing right there.

"There's a crate and a blanket-wrapped bundle that's heavier than sin."

"Excuse me."

Their heads swiveled toward her.

"Is there, perhaps, somewhere else I could stay until I finish my job? Someplace with more room?" *And better light? And more congenial company? And not so much. . .dirt?*

"Not close enough to be practical. Walt's bunking in the barn, and Allison is staying over at my parents' place until the wedding. There are some neighbors, but nobody's got room." His disapproval of the entire enterprise was as plain as if he'd stitched it on a sampler and hung it on the wall. "And we haven't even started Walt's house yet."

"Cyrus, why don't you put her stuff in the cool room for now? She can get out what she needs a little at a time. I shoulda thought of her needing to bring supplies and the like."

"I'll have to move the rest of the potatoes to the barn. With the seed corn I bought today, I'll be lucky to have room for the team out there."

"Why should they have more room than us? Put the potatoes in the barn and picket the horses. The dog will keep an eye on them overnight." Her practical approach soothed

Julia's heart and made her feel not such a bother. The little woman stood on tiptoe to take down a couple of tin cups. "You'll be planting potatoes soon enough anyway. A few days in the barn won't hurt them."

With a sigh, Cyrus planted his hands on his knees and levered himself upright. He hefted the trunk onto one of the bunks to clear a path and opened the short door in the back of the room.

"Sit up to the table and have some tea. It will be a real pleasure having another woman here. My daughter-in-law isn't well, so she doesn't come to visit very often, and Allison's only been here a few days. She and Walt met when he went to Lincoln for some posts and wire to fence the garden plot, and they've been sparking by mail ever since."

Julia took one of the stools, conscious of Cyrus trudging back and forth with sacks of potatoes. It amused her that he, who looked so strong and hard-hewn, would bend so easily to his grandmother's wishes. She picked up her tin cup, trying not to compare it to her stepmother's fine china. Inhaling, she let the fragrant tea soothe her. Nothing was as she had thought it would be, not her reception or her accommodations. Were they really expecting her to sleep in a room with four other people—one of them a grown man—with nothing between them but four feet of dirt-tainted space?

"I don't want you to worry about the sleeping arrangements." Mrs. Haskell must've read her mind. "Cyrus will put up a curtain before bedtime. I was hoping he'd get to it before he left this morning, but don't you worry, he'll have it up as soon as he moves the potatoes and unloads the corn."

"What about. . .Mrs. Haskell, Cyrus's wife?" Nobody had mentioned her.

"Gone over a year now. Took sick a couple of winters ago." A shadow passed over her wrinkled face. "Cyrus don't like to talk about it."

The little boys ran in and out, giggling and playing with the dog. Titus shouted as the sound of a wagon rattled through the yard.

"It's Uncle Walt and Miss Allison!"

Mrs. Haskell hopped up from the table. "Ah, it's time for the surprise. You wait here until Walt calls."

Voices drifted through the door. Julia smoothed her skirts and hair, her hands encountering the bedraggled hat. She quickly removed her hat pin and plucked the millinery disaster off her head. Noticing a small square of mirror hung at what was probably Cyrus's shaving height, she stood on tiptoe and tried to right her appearance.

"Come on out." That must be Walt.

She emerged from the soddy. Titus scampered over and grabbed her hand. "Here she is. We brung her from town. Just for you, Miss Allison."

"Hush, Titus. Let Walt tell it." Nan shook her head.

A pretty girl with carrot-orange ringlets and freckles scattered across her nose looked bewilderingly at a young man who bore a striking resemblance to Cyrus. "Walt?"

Walt grinned and took her hand. "Ally, this is Miss Farrington. I brought her out here to sew up your wedding dress and one of those trousseau things you were talking about, and anything you need for the house, like sheets and curtains and towels and the like. She's a seamstress, works at a shop in Omaha. It's my wedding gift to you."

Allison's eyes widened. "Oh Walt, that's. . .but. . ."

He laughed. "You're gonna ask if we can afford it. Don't you worry. Now that I'm twenty-one, I came into some money my grandfather left me. I want to spend it on some of the things you're missing on account of me."

Allison threw her arms around Walt, who didn't seem to mind.

Julia glanced at Cyrus, who stood with his arms crossed, leaning back against the side of Walt's wagon. His face was unreadable, but his stance said he thought this was a waste of time and money.

Allison finally turned Walt loose so she could greet Julia. "I'm happy to meet you. Walt is always doing such thoughtful things. I was all set to get married in last year's summer frock, but now I guess I'll have a wedding dress."

Julia smiled. "I brought lots of yard goods for you to choose from, and I have several catalogs and pattern books, too." Her dressmaker's eye took in Allison's build and coloring while taking note of the dress she wore, hoping to pinpoint a style to build on. Her dress was girlish, light and ruffled. Now that she was going to be a married woman, she'd want something womanly, without being matronly.

Nan got everyone moving. "Cyrus, Walt, get the rest of those potatoes moved, and get Miss Farrington's belongings stowed. Gals, we should stand back and let them work, then you can get started on picking out material and such."

The potatoes were soon moved, and the crate of supplies toted into the soddy. Julia held her breath as Cyrus and Walt lowered the last bulky object to the ground. The minute it was safe, she exhaled, and Titus and Cotton crowded close around the blanket-wrapped bundle.

"What is it?" Titus asked.

"Guess." Julia loosened the first rope.

"Is it a corn sheller?"

"No. Not a corn sheller." She unknotted the second rope and raised the edges of the blanket to reveal the curved cast-iron legs.

"Is it a piano?"

"No. Guess again." The ropes tangled as she tried to coil them, and two large hands reached around her to take them. With no effort, Cyrus wound them into a neat bundle.

"I give up."

With a tug, she removed the blanket. "Ta-da!" The wooden box shone dully in the overcast light. She inspected the tabletop and the treadle, thankful that the journey didn't seem to have damaged it.

Titus blinked. "What is it?"

Julia reached up to her neck, withdrew a key on a chain, and used it to unlock the cover to reveal the contents. "It's a sewing machine. Isn't it beautiful?" She ran her hand over the honey-satin finish of the oak and the curved black metal of the machine itself.

"Is that all?" Titus scoffed. "Nan don't need no machine to sew. All she needs is a needle and thread."

Julia put a smile on her face. She'd saved for two years to buy this machine, her first step in getting out of her father's tailor shop. "I do that sort of sewing, too, but a machine is faster for some work."

Titus squinted up at her skeptically and crossed his arms. Cotton squatted to study the pedal, touching the shining black metal with one pudgy finger.

Walt and Allison came to admire it, and even Nan admitted it was a beautiful piece, but Cyrus said nothing, his mouth a straight line.

He took the cover from her hands and settled it over the machine. "You'd best pray for fine weather. Something like that, you're going to have to use it in daylight hours right in the doorway or else out here on the lawn. Be too dark in the soddy of an evening."

The pride in her chest dissolved. Why was it that every time this man weighed her up, he found her wanting? And why did she care? He wasn't the one who hired her, he wasn't paying her, and it wasn't his approval that mattered.

And yet, for some reason it did matter. She turned her back on him.

"Allison, would you like to see some of the fabrics I brought and talk about what you might need and like? I thought I should do the wedding dress first then work on the trousseau."

"Oh yes. I'd love that." Allison smiled at her fiancé, and he winked at her. "I can't believe Walt did this, but I'm so glad."

Walt squeezed her fingers. "You deserve it, honey. You're going to be the prettiest bride in the whole state. That wedding day can't get here soon enough to suit me. Six weeks is a long way off."

"Are you two gonna get mushy again?" Titus rolled his eyes. "That's nasty."

Walt laughed and tousled his nephew's hair. "You won't always think so, young man."

"Oh yes I will. I'm going to be like Pa. He's never mushy."

"Ha! He was, too. When he first met your ma, he acted like a lovesick bull calf."

Cyrus frowned. "Enough, Walt. That was a long time ago."

Julia followed Nan and Allison into the soddy and opened the crate of material, but she kept trying to get her mental tape measure around what Cyrus might've been like in love. He must've had powerful feelings for his wife if he didn't like to talk about her at all.

Chapter 3

I t's time to go." Titus swung from the doorknob. "We got all your stuff loaded. The plow's in the wagon, and all Nan's food."

"I'm almost ready."

"You're taking forever." He shot away, talking over his shoulder, a blur of constant motion and sound that Julia, after a week in his company, was becoming used to—that, and his devastating candor.

Cotton, on the other hand, was a silent little mouse, fascinated by Julia, especially when she was using the sewing machine. He liked to squat and wrap his arms around his knees to watch her work the foot pedal, and he could stand for hours, his nose on the same level as the work surface, watching the needle pump up and down. Thus far he hadn't said a word to her, but she'd seen him whisper in his father's ear, and he was full of giggles and squeals when playing with Titus.

Julia shuddered as a small chunk of dirt let go from the ceiling and plopped to the floor. She kicked it under the edge of the curtain surrounding her bed. The thin barrier didn't keep her from being aware of the others in the room as she lay in her narrow bunk each night—especially Cyrus. The soddy was so small, they couldn't really avoid each other. Each night after supper, Nan would light the lamp, and Cyrus would take a book from a trunk under the bed and read to the little boys while Nan crocheted and Julia worked on hand-sewing.

He read well; history, fiction, scripture. Often, Julia found her hands growing idle as she fell into the story, swept away by the timbre of his voice.

She nearly collided with him in the doorway as she hurried out, tying her bonnet strings as she went. His chest was a solid wall, and her gaze flew up to his as her breath deserted her. He reached out to steady her, his hands warm on her upper arms. "I thought maybe you got lost in this big house and couldn't find the door. Wagon's waiting." A rare, fleeting smile touched his lips, and her heartbeat quickened.

He assisted her into the wagon bed to sit with the boys. Titus squirmed and shifted, bouncing up to lean on the wagon seat between Cyrus and Nan then plopping down beside Julia before worming his way through the load to the picnic basket to see what Nan had prepared for later in the day. Cotton sat quietly, playing with an inchworm he'd found. Julia kept her knees bent to avoid the wide share of the plow tied upright in the back of the wagon.

They rattled across the prairie a mile or so to join a cluster of wagons and teams and people. She glanced at the sky, glad it was mild and sunny for the house raising.

Wagons were soon unloaded and horses hitched to the sod plow. Julia ignored her sewing machine, fascinated as Cyrus chose a likely spot, thrust the point of the plow into the dirt, and slapped the reins of the four-horse team. A long ribbon of earth peeled up and back, flipping over onto the grass stems. This action was accompanied by a tearing sound, as if someone were ripping a bedsheet in half.

"Howdy there." A tall, weathered man offered his hand. "You must be the seamstress. I'm Jed Haskell, Cyrus and Walt's pa. Sorry we didn't make it over to meet you sooner. My wife's feeling poorly these days."

"I'm sorry. Is she here today?"

He leaned on his shovel. "She is. Over yonder in the rocking chair. She isn't strong, but she wanted so much to be here. She's got the lung disease, and the prairie cure doesn't seem to be taking."

His shoulders straightened, and he peered at the sky. "That rain the other day sure did us a favor. Ground's soft but not muddy. We'll have a good start on the house by nightfall."

Julia asked, "Will you tell me how it works? I've never seen a sod house being built before."

He seemed happy enough to oblige. "First you need the right kind of grass, something that has dense roots to hold all the dirt together. This is good buffalo grass, perfect for building a sod house." He tapped the ground with his spade. "Cyrus will plow a strip, then the men behind will chop it into lengths about two feet long. It takes a strong man and a steady eye to keep the plow at the right depth to peel back a layer of sod. Too thick and you can't handle the bricks, too thin and they break and tear. Cyrus is the best plowman around here."

"What's that thing there?" She pointed to another team standing ready, hitched to an odd-looking low contraption.

"That's a stone boat, a kind of sled. They'll haul the sod bricks to where they're going to build the house. Each brick will weigh about fifty pounds, and they'll need about three thousand of them in order to make a sixteen-by-twenty cabin."

"Three thousand?" Her mind stopped, and her respect grew.

"Don't worry, there's plenty of grass. And this way, Walt gets a good start on his cornfield, too." He chuckled and tipped his hat before sauntering off to help out.

Julia made the acquaintance of Catherine Haskell, a pale, thin woman wrapped in a blanket, despite the warm weather.

"I'm good with a needle, though I'm not very fast these days. Maybe I can lend a hand." She coughed into her handkerchief, two red spots appearing in her white cheeks. Julia set her to hemming a set of napkins, grateful for the help and glad for the company.

The men labored all morning, hauling and stacking bricks, and at every stage, Julia asked questions. Jed continued to tutor her as he laid the sod and trimmed it into the shapes he wanted.

"I'm laying the bricks grass-down so the roots will continue to grow up into the brick above it and create a really solid wall."

Julia sought out Cyrus, a fair way out on the prairie. He had turned the team and started back, the horses leaning into their collars.

Jed continued. "You have to reverse the direction of the bricks every so often to lay crossways from each other. That makes the walls more stable."

And later, "We only cut as many bricks as we can use today. If you leave them overnight they dry out and crumble apart."

Jed wiped his face with his kerchief, watching Walt unload a crate with care. "The windows are the most expensive part of a sod house. Walt bought real glass windows from the lumberyard in Lincoln. When we get the walls high enough, we'll set the windows and put a couple of cedar logs across the tops, leaving a gap between the windows and the logs. That way, as the house settles, it won't break the windows. They can stuff the gaps with rags or straw until the house settles all the way.

"I'm making the base of the wall thicker than the top so as the house settles, it won't collapse. You have to remember that a sod house is a living thing—it's going to move and breathe, and you'd better make allowances, or you'll find yourself staring up at the stars through a collapsed roof some night."

Midmorning, a wagon arrived with a load of clay. After a coffee break where Nan served rich slices of fruitcake, two men shoveled the clay into the rectangle of sod bricks that had already been laid.

When it had been spread in rough clumps, Nan stepped inside with a bag of salt and began scattering the salt over the clay floor.

Jed took a dipperful of water. "The salt's to keep the insects down and to keep weeds from growing before the floor gets hard-packed enough to repel water."

At every turn, their precision and forethought impressed her. "Will they put boards halfway up the walls inside like Cyrus did?" She had noticed the makeshift wainscoting in Cyrus's half-dugout house and had come to appreciate how it helped keep the dirt at bay. She only wished it lined the walls all the way up. "Or will they plaster?"

"Eventually, they'll plaster, but again, you have to wait until the house has settled, or the plaster will crack and break off. This soddy will be 'green' for a year, then it will be ready for improvements like plaster. And in five years, Walt will have proved up on the land and it will be his. Cyrus only has one year left to prove up. They both figure to build frame houses once the land is truly theirs."

"But I thought you all had only lived here for going on two years. Doesn't he have three years left?"

"No, Cyrus is a veteran of the war. He gets to deduct the time he served from the proving-up time."

So Cyrus had been a soldier. "My father served in the war, too, but he never saw combat. He was stationed in Washington in the quartermaster's office."

"He was lucky. Cyrus saw too much combat. That, and losing Hester the first winter we moved out here, changed him. He was always on the reserved side, like his mother, but those things made him pull in even more."

Her eyes strayed to Cyrus driving the team and turning the earth, his muscles straining to hold the plow straight, the reins knotted over his shoulder, his boots braced. Powerful, yet gentle with his boys; quiet, yet not afraid to voice his opinion; self-sufficient, yet providing for his grandmother. Such a paradox. One that Julia wished to understand more fully.

Walt smiled so much, Julia wondered if his cheeks hurt, and she noticed he made plenty of trips over to the water barrel and the coffeepot, each time whispering something to Allison or giving her a wink. The unmarried men—save for Cyrus—seemed to have plenty of excuses to stop and visit with Julia as well, until Nan sent them back to work with a few pointed words.

Eventually, Julia felt compelled to focus her attention away from the ever-growing soddy and onto the work she'd been hired for. She began running pieces of blue fabric through the sewing machine. Allison had chosen the lightweight wool for a winter dress, and Julia had cut the pieces from a newspaper pattern she'd created using her dressmaker's chart and Allison's measurements.

Cotton sidled over, and she lifted him into her lap. Leaning over his shoulder, she whispered, "Do you want to help me sew?"

His head bobbed.

She placed his little hands on either side of the fabric, well away from the needle, and covered them with her own. "I'll pump, and very slowly, we'll feed the fabric through, all right?"

Another nod.

Together they sewed the long skirt seam. When the fabric ran out, she let him snip the threads.

"Thank you, Cotton. You're very good at sewing. Maybe you'll be a tailor someday." She gave him a squeeze.

To her surprise, he twisted in her arms and planted a moist kiss on her cheek.

"You're pretty, Miss Julia. I like you."

His voice was as clear as a church bell on Easter Sunday.

Before she could respond, he hopped off her lap and ran to play with Titus. Julia's eyes followed him, and when she looked away, she noticed that Cyrus had brought the team in for a rest and Nan and Allison were setting out the noon meal. His eyes studied her as he took a long drink from a canteen. A curious scurrying feeling ran under Julia's skin and raced through her chest, and she lowered her gaze, shy and exhilarated at the same time.

∞

Cyrus took the sandwich his grandmother handed him and bit through the dark bread. His stomach rumbled. Plowing was exhausting work, especially virgin prairie grass. The horses could barely get the plowshare through the tough roots. Oxen would be better, but none of his neighbors had a yoke of oxen.

"Eat up, boys, then get back to your stomping." Nan gave Titus and Cotton each a slice of her fruitcake, moist and spicy. The boys had been given the job of stomping the clay floor and pounding it with the backs of shovels. Their little feet would help get the process of smoothing and packing the floor started and work off their high spirits.

Julia slid her bonnet off her hair, and the brown strands glistened in the sun. The single men who had come to help sat on the ground around her chair, trying to get her attention.

Cotton wedged his way in and let Julia lift him to her lap. Cyrus hid a smile. Attaboy. His son leaned back against Julia, and her arms came around him. Something sharp twisted in Cyrus's heart for his son, for the softness the little guy obviously craved, for the mothering he wasn't getting. Nan was a fine woman, but she had an abrasive way about her. . .more rod of correction than milk of human kindness.

Julia's fingers came up and feathered through Cotton's white-blond hair over and over, and his son's eyelids grew heavy. His sturdy little body relaxed, and his mouth opened as he drifted off to sleep in her arms.

Lucky Cotton.

A nudge at his elbow yanked him off that ridiculous track.

"Think we'll get the roof on her today?" Walt held out a cup of coffee.

"Thanks. We should with all this help. Weather's holding, too."

"I'm glad the extra help showed up. I thought it might be just you and me and Pa, what with all the spring work everyone has to do, but word got around that we had a pretty single girl here." He grinned. "Allison's already making plans for where the furniture and things will go. I think by the time the day finally gets here, we'll be all set." He sipped his coffee.

"You can be prepared for marriage, but you're never really ready." The words came out absently as Cyrus watched his neighbors vie for Julia's attention.

"How's that?"

Cyrus shrugged. "Just that you can have the house and the furnishings and the ceremony and all that, but until you're really married, you can't know what it's like, you can't even imagine how it will change you. Not that the changes are bad."

Walt chewed that over for a while. "Must be like becoming a pa for the first time. You can have all the baby clothes and the name picked out and such, but until you have a kid of your own. . ."

"Just like that." Cyrus sought out his elder son marching around and around the interior of the half-built soddy, flattening the high spots of the new clay floor. "Being married, being a father, makes you see things different. Somebody else's welfare comes first. It's your job to protect and provide, and if you don't do those things, it's more than just you that suffers." Ache and guilt clashed in his chest. It was a familiar sensation, and while the ache had eased some over the last year and a half, the guilt hadn't abated a bit.

"You know that Hester getting sick wasn't your fault."

"Dragging her out here on the prairie away from doctors was."

"I didn't notice anyone dragging Hester. As I remember, she's the one who encouraged you to file on a claim. She's the one who read up on Nebraska, about the 'prairie cure' for Ma's sickness, the one who talked the folks into joining us, the one who said it would mean having something to give to the boys when they grew up. Us Haskells, who never owned a square foot of ground before, would have our own land, acres and acres of it. Hester's dream didn't die when she did. It lives on in you and the boys and me and the folks."

She *had* been the driving force behind the initial idea, but he could've said no. He could've kept saving and planning and hoping to buy a livery stable of his own someday. He could've made sure they stayed in a warm house—rental though it might be—close to doctors and medicines. Maybe if he had, she'd still be alive. As it was, the prairie hadn't cured Ma, and it had taken Hester. Proud as he was to own his own land—or at least he would own it when he proved up on it—the cost had been too dear.

He downed the rest of his coffee. "If you're going to have a house to pass on to your own kids, we'd best get a roof on it. Let's get back to work."

Slowly, the walls went up, the door was hung, and the rafters laid. Over a thatch-work of tree branches hauled down from the Platte River, the men laid strips of sod and shoveled dirt to fill the cracks.

As the sun lowered on the horizon, Walt leaned the ladder against the soddy and helped Allison climb to the roof. Nan passed him a bag that he handed up to her. Cyrus stood back, his hands cupping his boys' heads.

"What are they doing?" Julia came to stand at his elbow.

"Sowing wildflower seeds. In a few weeks, the roof will be covered with wildflowers and grasses."

"That's beautiful. Their house will bloom with life and color." She brushed a strand of hair off her cheek. "And love."

∞

When the last seed had been sown, a ritual that charmed Julia to her core, the men walked down to the creek to wash off the sweat and dirt. Nan stoked up the campfire, and Cyrus's father took out a violin and rosined the bow.

Tools were laid aside, the sewing machine loaded into the wagon, and Julia found her hands grabbed by Greg—or was it Gary?—Phelps, one of the men who had come to help. He hustled her to the makeshift dance floor, a bare patch of ground in front of the new soddy. The fiddle sang out "The Irish Washerwoman," and she was gathered up and swung around in a lively jig that had her breathless and laughing. That song rolled right into the "Jenny Lind Polka," and another pair of arms swept her along.

Walt danced with Allison until the men protested and demanded that he share, which he did, graciously and with a big smile. Julia's heart constricted a bit. What would it be like to matter that much to a man, that he would send such tender looks, hold her so gently, be willing to give her anything and everything he could just to make her happy?

Someone tugged on her hand, and she looked down into Titus's eyes. "How come you ain't danced with my pa yet? You've danced with everybody else."

She blinked. Had he been keeping track? Of course he had. Titus kept track of everything. Her eyes went to Cyrus on the far side of the fire. "He's not danced with anyone tonight, and anyway, it's manners for a lady to wait until she's asked."

"Pa!" Titus's voice cut across the chatter between dances. "You gonna ask Miss Julia to dance? She says she's gotta wait till you ask."

Her cheeks felt hotter than the campfire flames. Cyrus's eyes bored into hers, and she wanted to melt into the ground. Did he think she'd instructed Titus to ask him?

Someone slapped Cyrus on the shoulder, and Walt laughed. Cyrus never took his eyes off her, setting his cup on the tailgate and circling the fire toward her.

Something in his approach made her think of a predator approaching its prey, and she stood rooted to the spot like a rabbit before a hawk as he came to stand before her. "I'm sorry. You don't have to do this. I don't know why he said that. . ."

"No worry." His voice rumbled in his chest.

Her mouth went dry as dust as his hand went to her waist and drew her into his embrace. The violin began the strains of a waltz, and she followed his lead on the uneven ground, unable to break his gaze.

This was so different from dancing with Walt or one of the Phelps boys. Cyrus's hand clasping hers sent sparks shooting through her fingers and up her arm. His firm grip on her waist made her feel secure and yet like she was falling through stars. Every fiber responded to his closeness, the smell of sunshine and smoke, earth and sky that seemed such a part of him.

The firelight, the other dancers, even the prairie disappeared as they turned to the music. An invisible thread, strong and vibrating, seemed to come from her heart to wind its tendrils around them, holding them together.

A soft bump against her leg broke their gaze. Cotton stood looking up at both of them, and without a word he held his arms up. Cyrus laughed, and her senses, attuned to every nuance of his voice, sensed relief as he scooped his son into his arms. Had he felt that pull, too? Had he wanted to break free, or like her, run eagerly toward it?

Before she could move away, he put his other arm at her waist and continued the dance with Cotton between them, but as sweet as that was, and as warm as Cotton's giggles sounded, she missed how they'd been before, caught in a world of two.

Chapter 4

A week after the house raising, Julia put the final stitch on the wedding dress. She wrapped the snowy satin and organza beauty in a sheet and stored it in her trunk rather than keeping it on the dress dummy. She wrestled the dressmaker's form into the root cellar with a smile. Titus loved the dressmaker's form, which he had named Gertrude, but Cotton was afraid of it and woke up screaming several nights until Cyrus patiently showed him it wasn't a headless woman but wire frame and canvas. Julia kept "Gertrude" in her supply crate after that unless she was using her.

Allison came over from Jed and Catherine's soddy often, and Julia gave her basic lessons in dressmaking and mending. Nan began instructions on how to cook. Allison took to it eagerly, and Julia, who had little enough cooking experience herself, listened and learned.

"I don't know why Walt loves me. When I lived in Illinois, before my father's bank failed and we had to move to Lincoln, we had a big house and servants, and I never had to lift a finger. I never gave housekeeping a thought, but now I *want* to cook for Walt and wash his clothes and mend his shirts."

Nan cackled and stirred some salt pork in a skillet. "In a year or less, you'll find that desire might start fading, buried under the everyday, but"—she pointed her wooden spoon at the girls—"don't you let it. You have to work at a marriage. Right now it's all butterflies and rainbows, but the truth is, you're marrying a human being, and you aren't always going to feel like being loving. Right now those loving feelings are first and the action follows, but as you go along, you'll find that sometimes the action has to come first and the feelings will show up after. That's how you have a long and happy marriage." She whacked the spoon on the skillet. "There, my sermonizing is done for the day. You add the green beans to that salt pork and give it a pinch of salt and a pinch of sugar."

Julia took off her thimble and clipped her thread. "There, what do you think?" She stood and shook out the folds of the lawn nightgown.

Allison wiped her hands on her apron and fingered the lace at the cuff and the delicate drawn threadwork at the yoke. "It's so beautiful. I don't know how you make such pretty designs so quickly."

"I've worked since I was a little girl in my father's tailor shop. Especially after my mother died and before my father remarried. We moved around a lot, never spending more than a couple of years in a town before my father would pack us up and take us somewhere farther west. But now he's remarried, and my stepmother insists on staying put in Omaha." She folded the nightgown and laid it on Nan's bunk.

"That must've been hard on you, moving so often." Allison took one end of the sewing machine that sat just inside the doorway, familiar with the routine of putting it away each night before dinner.

"I didn't know any different then. I guess that's one of the things I admire about you and the Haskells. You're putting down your roots, establishing yourself in one place, planning for the next generation to have something solid and permanent. You can't get much more permanent than the land."

After supper, Walt walked Allison back to his parents' soddy, a dark spot on the prairie, half a mile away. The boys went to jump in what was left of one of the haystacks, and Cyrus settled in with a newspaper.

Restless, Julia wrapped her shawl around her shoulders. "I think I'll take a little walk. I'd like to work some of the knots out of my shoulders after all the time I spent bent over my needle today."

Cyrus barely looked up, but Nan nodded. "Nice that the twilight is lingering now. Come summer it will be light until near nine o'clock. But don't be gone too long. There were clouds coming in from the north, and it's not too late in the season for a blizzard."

"I won't be gone long. And after a beautiful day like today, snow is the furthest thing from my mind."

Her footsteps took her south and west, away from the settlement. Here the ground rose a little, and she thought she might be able to get some distance and perspective on all that had been happening to her.

For the first time in her life, she battled envy. Allison had everything that Julia wanted. Not Walt in particular, but someone who loved her, who was making a future for her. Titus and Cotton had the security of knowing that their family was grounded here, with a permanence that Julia had never felt. Even Nan had the surety that her family cared about her, that she was useful and necessary.

Julia had never felt any of those things. Always living in rented rooms, always moving on after a few months, and now, with her father remarried, she felt unneeded and unwanted. She hadn't known the depth of her longing for love and security until she'd come here.

Her steps grew longer in the twilight, carrying her up the rise and down the other side, out of sight of the homesteads. A few faint stars peeped out of the dusk on the eastern horizon, and brilliant pink and salmon and orange and golden rays streaked the western edge of the world.

When she'd taken the edge off her restlessness, she sat in the high grass and wrapped her arms around her knees. As she rested, her thoughts, as they had developed a habit of doing over the past three weeks, went to Cyrus.

Since the night they had danced together, she had been altogether too aware of him. She listened for the sound of his voice or his step when he came in from the fields. She knew every time he turned on his bed at night, and the cadence of his breathing when he'd fallen asleep. She knew he liked corn bread but didn't like turnips, had a nice reading voice, and was firm when his sons needed discipline, kind and indulgent at all other times. When he'd ripped the sleeve on one of his shirts, she'd delighted in patching it for him, treasuring the opportunity to caress the flannel.

The wind sighed through the grass, echoing the sigh in her heart. Julia admitted to herself what she'd been resistant to acknowledge.

She was falling in love with Cyrus Haskell.

Bounding up, she hiked her skirts, and for the first time since she was a girl, she ran. Willy-nilly, spinning in circles, arms outstretched until she was so dizzy she fell back in the grass, gasping and laughing. Hugging herself, she let the giddiness of first love wash through her until she was spent.

She squirmed, becoming aware of something poking into her back, and she rolled over, running her hands through the grass to see what it was. Her fingers encountered a sharp, cool stone and curled around it. Holding it up in the almost dark, she touched the point of the arrowhead, raspy instead of smooth. Flint.

Her skin warmed the stone nestled in her palm. A souvenir, a keepsake of her time on the prairie. She dropped it into her pocket for safekeeping.

Pushing herself to her feet, she paused then turned in a slow circle. She took a couple of steps, felt instinctively that direction was wrong and turned around. Which way was the soddy?

Feeling small and not a little uneasy, she tried to find the North Star, but the clouds Nan had mentioned had rolled in, obscuring half the sky. Ah, but she'd said the clouds were coming in from the northwest, so the house must be somewhere ahead of her.

She began walking, wrapping her shawl around her shoulders. What a silly thing to do, running and twirling and getting disoriented. But she wasn't truly lost. Was she?

In the distance, a coyote yipped, something that, from the safety of her bed, she'd thought charming, but out here by herself with no thick wall of sod protecting her, seemed menacing. A rueful chuckle worked its way up her throat. As horrified as she had been about the soddy, and as much as she didn't like the dark, dank earthiness, she'd call herself blessed to be within its walls now.

Grass tangled around her skirts and legs. She looked up again to get her bearings. The clouds had covered quite a bit more sky, increasing the darkness and making her doubt her sense of direction. Perhaps she should angle more to her right? The grass was longer here, and she didn't remember passing this way.

Worry clamped eager fingers into her skin. That humble sod house would look like a palace if she could just find it right now.

∞

Cyrus went to the door once again, looking out at the gathering darkness. The boys fussed and bickered getting into their nightclothes. Well, Titus bickered. Cotton just stuck out his lower lip and pouted because Julia wasn't there to tuck him in and sing that funny little good-night song she had.

Nan returned from outside and shook her head. "Didn't see her."

Cyrus rubbed his hand down his face, feeling the rasp of stubble. "She's been gone more than an hour, and it's blacker than the inside of a cow out there."

The lines around Nan's mouth grew deeper. "You boys stop squabbling and get yourselves into bed." Her sharp tone cut across their noise and made their eyes go round. Without a word they got under the covers, and Cotton pulled the blanket over his head. A tiny sob leaked out.

Cyrus shrugged into his coat and lit the lantern. "I'll go look for her. Maybe she sprained her ankle or something and is hobbling back. Stay here, and keep the lamp close to one of the windows." He went back in for his coat.

"Pa?" Titus leaned precariously out of the bed.

"What?"

"You going after Miss Julia?"

"Go to sleep, Titus."

"I seen her out by the cornfield before we had to come in for bed."

"Thanks, Son."

He headed to the barn for his saddle horse. Too bad Walt was over visiting Allison again. He could help look. The bay stomped and snorted, jerking his head to avoid being bridled.

Once past the barn and the newly planted cornfield, Cyrus raised the lantern high. "Julia!"

What was she thinking, straying so far from the homestead? And at night? Here he'd been entertaining the notion that maybe, just maybe, Julia Farrington had what it took to live out here, that maybe she could settle in. . .

She was so good with the boys, the neighbors, and his family liked her. She knew her way around that sewing machine better than he did his plow, and after her initial horror, she didn't even seem to mind the soddy too much.

At Walt's house raising, she had asked so many questions, seemed so interested in everything and everyone. . .

Not to mention how it had felt to hold her in his arms while they were dancing. He hadn't felt that way toward a woman since Hester.

"Julia!" He directed his horse up the rise, holding the lantern high. Plumb foolish to think you could take a city girl like her and expect her to survive out here on the prairie. Wandering off like this—who knew what had happened to her? Was she lost? Injured?

Or had she walked over to his folks' house for a chat with Allison and his mother? Walt might be bringing her back right now. Why hadn't he thought of that? That's probably what she'd done, gone to the rise for a look-see then circled back to his parents' place.

"Julia!"

He flipped up his collar against the brisk north breeze. She wasn't even wearing a coat, just that little shawl, the one she'd had on when he'd first seen her at the depot, as out of place as a rose in a pea patch. More than pretty enough for a second look, she'd been all prickles and bravado, standing up to him in the rain and arguing her case. She'd invaded his house and his thoughts ever since.

"You're almost thirty, a war veteran, a widower, a father, and a homesteader. Too old to have your head turned by a pretty little miss who's not right for life out here. If she was, you wouldn't be traipsing after her in the dark."

His horse plodded on.

After another half mile, Cyrus pulled up. She couldn't have gotten this far, not in the time she'd been gone.

Maybe he should circle back. Check at his folks' place and get some help.

Looping around, this time a bit farther west, he continued to call her name. The wind picked up, blowing from the north, and the darkness deepened as the clouds continued to thicken. He'd have to be careful, or he'd get lost himself, though if he gave his horse his head, the animal would most likely return to the barn.

"Julia!"

He paused as something faint came toward him on the wind. Had he imagined it? No, there it was again. Dismounting, he led his horse north. "Julia!"

"Cyrus?"

Swinging the lantern, he advanced. "Where are you? Are you hurt?"

Her slight form emerged from the darkness, and she all but fell into his arms. "Oh Cyrus, I'm so glad to see you."

Relief made him clasp her close, careful with the lantern, but after a moment, he stood her away from him. "What were you doing out here?" He was so happy to see her safe, he wanted to shake her. "You can't go wandering all over creation. This isn't the city, you know." His voice came out harsher than he'd intended, but he didn't apologize. She needed to realize the danger she'd been in, the trouble and worry she'd caused.

She let her hands fall away from his biceps. "I didn't intend to lose my way. Dark came before I knew it, and the clouds rolled in, and I couldn't remember which way was home."

"Home is two hundred miles that way." He pointed east toward Omaha before grabbing her hand to lead her to where his horse waited. "You know, I thought you might have the makings of a pioneer, but tonight's little escapade has reminded me just how unsuited a woman like you is to frontier life. The sooner you're back in the city where you belong, the better."

She blinked her big, round eyes in the lantern light, and he felt like a heel scolding her when she'd been so scared. Her hand was icy, and her cheeks and nose were red with cold. Worse yet, moisture gathered along her lower lashes, making him feel more terrible than ever. He handed her the lantern and shrugged out of his coat, wrapping it around her.

"You're freezing. You should be inside." Taking the lantern from her, he extinguished the flame and looped the handle over the saddle horn. He mounted then reached down and swung her up behind him, sidesaddle. "Wrap your arms around me and hold on."

Sweet torture to have her pressed against his back, holding on to him, depending on him to keep her safe.

Not that he was very good at keeping a woman safe. He'd let his wife die, and he'd let this one wander off in the dark.

No matter how appealing she was to him, he couldn't risk it. Better to do the best he could to look after her for the next three weeks and then put her on the train back to civilization.

Chapter 5

Following her adventure on the prairie, Julia felt she walked on tissue paper around Cyrus. He was out of the house much of the time, working in his fields, plowing and harrowing and planting, and when he came in, he avoided her as much as possible in the cramped space.

"The work's hard, but not as hard as last year." Nan punched down the clothes rolling in the boiler in the yard. "The sods have had time to rot and break down into the soil, so he's not battling all those tough roots this year." She wiped her brow and pressed her hands to the small of her back. "I feel like I've been trampled by a draft horse, the way these old bones are aching."

Julia turned the leg of the trousers she was making. Allison had asked her to make new suits for Titus and Cotton, and a new shirt for Cyrus for the wedding. Since she had never tailored anything so small, she had to concentrate. Cyrus had grumbled about the impracticality. The boys needed overalls more than suits. It was a waste of money.

But he'd stood still to be measured for his new shirt, and Julia had fought the desire to let her touch linger across his broad shoulders or to stand staring up into his eyes as she determined his cuff and collar size.

Allison was at the soddy every day and had begun taking the towels and sheets and curtains to her new house. Walt had moved into it last week once they got the cookstove installed and the bedstead made. He and Cyrus had made a trip to town to get lumber for a cupboard and table.

Julia tamped down her envy, the idea of creating a little nest for two, hanging curtains, putting dishes in the cupboards, filling the straw ticks, and spreading new sheets and blankets on the bedstead that she would share with her husband. It wouldn't matter that it was a humble soddy, as long as love was there.

"I imagine," Nan said, using a stick to lift a sheet from the boiling water and dropping it in the washtub, "that you must have a couple dozen beaus back home?" Her strong little hands grabbed the sheet and began rubbing it on the washboard, her words coming out in little jerks as she scrubbed.

Laughing, Julia pinned the waistband onto the pants. "Hardly. We moved around so much, there never seemed to be time for anyone to find me. And this winter, the shop in Omaha was so busy, I hardly got out of the sewing room. Young single men don't often go to a tailoring shop."

"Well, someone's missing out on a gem like you." Nan paused, leaning on her washboard. "I don't know why, on a beautiful spring day like today, but I can't seem to get warm, not even working over these steamy clothes." She coughed and tugged her hankie from her sleeve to blow her nose. "I must be starting a cold."

Julia laid the trousers over the sewing machine and rose. "Let me help you. I'm well ahead with the sewing."

"Now, you aren't being paid to do my chores." Nan's protest was feeble, and she coughed again, her thin frame racked with spasms.

Julia put her hand on Nan's forehead. "You're burning up. Go get into bed. You don't want to be sick for the wedding. It's just ten days away."

"I've never gone to bed in the middle of the day in my life."

"Then you're past due to try it. I'll get these sheets on the line, and then I'll come in and make you some tea."

Julia spent the afternoon sewing, folding clothes off the line, and tending Nan. In between, she kept an eye on the boys, who were trying—with little success—to train the dog to roll over. They finally gave up and decided to use the wagon as a fort. This seemed to involve lots of marching, Titus barking orders at Cotton, and sword fighting with cattail stalks.

By late afternoon, Nan could barely speak without a paroxysm of coughing. Her skin was dry and papery and her eyes dull.

Cyrus came in at dusk, covered in dirt and sweat. He held a grubby boy under each arm. They'd given up playing soldiers to make mud pies in front of the barn door.

"I'm thinking we should drop them in the boiler out there in the yard then rub them on the washboard. What do you think, Nan?" He spoke as he stepped through the doorway and stopped when he saw Julia at the stove and Nan in bed. "What's this?"

Nan started to sit up, but Julia, who moved to perch on the side of the bed to bathe Nan's hot face with a damp cloth, gently pressed her back against her pillow. "Lie still, young lady."

"But I need to fix supper."

Julia wrung out the cloth into a basin. "I'll cook supper."

Nan chuckled. "You said you didn't know how to cook." Coughing overtook her, and she held her chest.

"I've been watching you teach Allison for a month now. I'd be ashamed of myself if I couldn't rustle up something after all that. You're going to rest, and no more talking. It makes you cough."

Cyrus set the boys down and rested his hands on their heads. Concern clouded his eyes.

"Cyrus, would you take the boys outside and give them a bath? The wash water should still be warm. I'll get supper on the stove." It all sounded so domestic that if it hadn't been for her worry over Nan, she might've felt an even greater pang of longing for these men, big and little, to belong to her.

He nodded and turned his sons around outdoors.

"I'll bring towels out in a minute." When she'd gotten some tea into Nan, she laid out nightshirts for the boys from the stacks of clean garments on their bed and went outside for the towels now dry on the line.

∽

Cyrus sluiced the boys off with a bucket of cold water before he set them in the wash boiler. The fire had died out long enough ago for the water to be pleasantly warm. They splashed and played, and he soaped and scrubbed, his mind on Nan.

Her cough sounded just like Hester's had, tight and painful. Her skin had that same flushed-but-dry paper thinness. What scared him even more was that Nan, no matter how off-color she might be feeling, had never taken to her bed in his lifetime.

"Hey, now." He dodged a cascade of splashes. "Keep that water in the tub." He lifted Cotton and wrapped him in the towel Julia handed him, rubbing him from head to foot to keep him warm.

"Time to get out, Son." He reached for Titus as Julia took Cotton.

"Pa, not in front of Miss Julia." Titus ducked down in the tub, crossing his arms over his thin chest. "You can't be coming out here when men are taking baths, Miss Julia. We need privacy."

A smile tugged at her mouth as she turned her back. "I apologize, Titus. You're right. I'll just take Cotton inside."

Cyrus turned the stopcock to drain the boiler and wrapped a towel around Titus when he stood. Listening to the little guy prattle about his day, he rubbed him dry. "Let's get you dressed inside. It's getting nippy out here."

He ducked through the door and set Titus on his bed. "There you go, Troop. Get dressed while Miss Julia is at the stove." He held up his hand when Titus's mouth flew open to protest. "I'll hold the towel up for your privacy."

Cotton sat on the bed in his little nightshirt, legs crossed, leafing through a dog-eared catalog, turning down the corners on pages he found interesting.

Julia tugged on Cyrus's sleeve and motioned for him to join her outside. "I'm worried. Nan is very ill. I think that cough has settled in her chest. It might be bronchitis or even pneumonia."

The words struck fear cold and deep in his gut. Hester had died of pneumonia. Out of her head with fever, unable to take deep enough breaths, drowning in her own lungs. He scrubbed his palms down his cheeks. Why had he brought his family out here? "What can we do?"

"I don't know what grows around here, but have you seen any wild onion? Or do you think your folks have any onions? If I had some, I could make a poultice that would warm her chest and clear her sinuses."

"I'll get some." He turned away, grateful for something to do, grateful that Julia was there.

Rather than take the time to saddle up, he walked the half mile to his folks' place. Ma lay in the bed while Allison spooned hot broth into her.

She coughed, her thin frame shuddering worse than Nan's.

"Hey, Ma. I just stopped by to see if you had any onions left."

"I have a few, not many, why? Is Nan making something?" Her breath sounded thin and wispy.

"Nan's caught a bit of a cold. Julia thought she could make some kind of a poultice out of onions."

Allison headed for the door. "There are some in the storm cellar. I'll fetch them."

While she was gone, Cyrus helped his mother sit up against the headboard. "Is there anything I can do for you, Ma?"

She shook her head. "No, Son. It won't be long now for me, I fear. I just want to see Walt happily married before I go." Grabbing his wrist with her bony, hot hand, she drew him down. "I'm sorry."

"You have nothing to be sorry about." Cyrus's throat tightened.

"The prairie cure didn't work, and you lost Hester because of me. I wish we'd stayed back East."

"Don't talk like that. It wasn't your fault."

"If it wasn't mine, then it wasn't yours either. You need to let go of your guilt, Cyrus. It isn't wrong for you to be happy." Her faded blue eyes studied him, two red spots decorating her hollow cheeks.

He returned home with the bag of onions to find Julia with her arm braced around Nan's back as she coughed. Cyrus found himself taking deep breaths, as if he could help his grandmother inhale.

Julia made the poultice, filling the soddy with the overpowering smell of onion and mustard powder. When the onions ran out, she boiled kettle after kettle of water, turning the room into a steam bath. The thick sod walls held in the temperature and the steam, and eased Nan's cough. Through it all, Julia seemed tireless, caring for Nan as if the old woman were her family. She brewed tea, putting in a few drops of peppermint oil, and got Nan to drink it, spoonful by spoonful.

"You should go to bed, Cyrus. There's no sense in both of us being awake." She sat beside Nan's bunk, holding her hand and sponging her hot face.

He shook his head. "I wouldn't sleep." He couldn't. He feared that if he closed his eyes, he'd wake up and Nan would've died. "Anyway, I don't want you to be alone. There isn't much I can do, but I can be company."

He sat at the table, head in his hands, praying and watching by turns. Julia seemed so calm, so sure. When she wasn't tending Nan, she would check on the boys then pick up her sewing and join him at the table, working close to the lamp. She wore one of Nan's calico aprons over her dark green dress, and her hair was wound up in a knot with tendrils falling down. She looked as if she belonged there, and he was amazed at how seamlessly she'd fit into his life and home. Her departure would leave quite a hole in all their lives.

"I don't know how Nan does it. My back is sore from that washboard and my hands are achy from all that wringing. I never knew how big a bedsheet was until I had to wring one out by hand. We usually sent our laundry out. But I have to admit, there's a certain sense of satisfaction and accomplishment seeing all those clean clothes flapping on the line and knowing you did it yourself." She poked her needle in and out of the fabric, her hands quick and sure in spite of her claim of them aching.

"Do you think she'll die?" The words were out, and he knew how desperate they sounded, but he couldn't call them back.

"We're doing everything we can. It's in God's hands." A furrow formed between her delicate brows, and she bit her lower lip.

It was a tension-filled week, but by Friday, Nan was on the mend. Cyrus sent Julia to bed, and she slept right through Friday night and into a good part of Saturday. When she woke, Nan sat at the table with a quilt around her shoulders, sipping tea and listening to Titus talk in what he thought was a whisper. Cyrus nursed a cup of coffee beside his son.

"But how long? She's been sleeping forever. You sure she isn't sick?"

"Don't worry, boy." Nan's aged hand patted his young one. "She's just catching up on the sleep she lost while she was taking care of me. We're blessed she was here. I might not have made it without her."

"I wish she was staying. Pa says she has to go back to the city. Why, Pa?"

"This isn't her home. She has a life elsewhere." He took a sip from his cup.

"But I like her."

"I like her, too." Nan lifted Cotton up onto her lap and wrapped the quilt around them both.

"Then why can't she stay?"

"Titus, get your coat on. It's time to do chores." Cyrus pushed away from the table and stood, bringing him eye level to Julia.

Too late to pretend she was still sleeping, she stared back at him, afraid he could read her heart in her eyes. He studied her for a long moment before heading outside.

Chapter 6

Easter Sunday morning—the day of the wedding—finally arrived. Wagons and buggies began pulling in at Cyrus's homestead midmorning, and neighbors and family gathered around.

The preacher, who had ridden down from Denman, delivered a poignant sermon, reminding them of the great gift of their salvation. Julia loved the singing, the way the community came together to worship and to celebrate both the Savior's resurrection and the wedding of a neighbor.

Titus and Cotton looked so handsome in their new clothes, and her throat constricted at the sight of Cyrus in the shirt she'd made for him. Every stitch had been sewn with love, and she hoped it would last him for many, many years.

She opened her trunk and removed the sheet-wrapped wedding gown, gently shaking out its folds.

"It's so lovely." Allison touched the fabric, her eyes soft and glowing. "I can't wait for Walt to see me in it."

Julia helped dress her from the skin out—new underclothes, petticoats, corset, corset cover, dress, and veil. Nan slipped inside the soddy to fasten a cameo pin at Allison's throat, a gift from the Haskell family. Allison took her hands. "Thank you so much for accepting me into your family. I wish my parents weren't so stubborn about Walt. I wish they could understand that it isn't things that are important, it's people."

Nan smiled, brushing a wisp of hair off Allison's brow. "I couldn't ask for a better wife for Walt. I know you'll make him happy." She kissed Allison's cheek and went outside.

The wedding was lovely, with warm air, sunshine, and a couple so obviously in love it set up a sweet ache in Julia's heart.

Cyrus had held to his belief that Julia should return to her city home and city ways as soon as the wedding was over, and she didn't know how to get him to change his mind. She'd toyed with the idea of setting up a shop of her own in Denman, just to be closer to him, but if he didn't want her here, what good would it do? No, she would have to continue with her plan to be a traveling seamstress—procuring a wagon, loading it with yard goods, and forging her own path to remote homesteads in need of her skills.

After the wedding dinner, Walt and Allison drove away to their little house to begin their life together, and neighbors began heading to their homes. Soon the farmyard was empty save for Cyrus and the boys and Julia.

Nan leaned against the doorjamb of the soddy. "I believe I'll take a nap. It's been a big day, and I'm still a little wobbly." She smiled, her thin, wrinkled cheeks pink for the first time in days.

"Boys, how about if you go change into your everyday clothes, and we'll take a walk?" Julia lifted the last stool to carry inside. "It's been a long week, and I haven't gotten to see you much at all with Nan being sick and all the final sewing to do. I could use a walk in the sunshine to blow the cobwebs away."

They were quick to scamper in to change. Cyrus picked up the table they'd placed on the grass to hold wedding gifts and angled it through the doorway. When he reemerged, he took an envelope from his breast pocket.

"Walt wanted me to give you this and to say thank you for all your work. Allison is real happy with everything you made. Those clothes and linens and things will last her for years to come. Tomorrow morning I guess I'll take you to the depot."

She took the packet. The exchange pushed her out of the realm of friend and put her in the category of employee, reminding her once again that her time here was limited, that she would go away and they would stay, and the likelihood of their meeting again was flimsy, at best.

"You boys put on your coats." She forced the words past the lump in her throat.

"But, Miss Julia, it's pretty warm outside." Titus ducked into a somersault, a ball of energy after being on his best behavior all day.

"Nevertheless, I don't want you catching a chill on the way back when the sun's going down and the wind shifts. Coats, or we stay home." She tugged on her own brown wool coat. "You don't have to button them up, but you have to take them along."

Grumbling, Titus shrugged into his sturdy little coat. Cotton put one sleeve on and couldn't manage the other one, spinning in a circle with his arm behind him, trying to poke it into the elusive hole.

"Let me help you, buddy." Julia got him into the garment, patted his pocket to make sure his mittens were in there, and opened the door, determined to enjoy her last afternoon in spite of her heavy heart.

"Hang on, I'll go with you." Cyrus plucked his hat and coat from the pegs by the door. "Don't want you getting lost."

She couldn't deny the thrust of joy at his wanting to accompany them. A few more precious moments and memories to store up.

Cotton and Titus zigzagged like hunting dogs on a scent, forging ahead of Cyrus and Julia, toward the rise to the southwest. "Where do they get all their energy?"

Cyrus shook his head and warned the boys not to get too far away. "Hard to believe the grass is green this early. I've never seen a milder winter. I heard this morning that at least thirty new claims had been filed in the county, and folks are already throwing up shanties and busting sod. There's talk of starting a school and building a church. Titus can go to school next fall."

"He'll like that, having something to do, somewhere to go. He's so busy all the time. His mind is like a sponge; he wants to know everything right now."

"Gets that from his mother, always forging ahead, always wanting to see what's over the next rise. Cotton's more like me, I guess. We want to put down roots."

"You're both. . .steady. Thinking before you speak or act. Some folks find that restful and reassuring."

They were almost a mile from the soddy, poking around the deserted Indian camp, when Cyrus paused and stared at the southwest horizon. The air had gone completely still, gently blowing one moment, dying away to nothing in the next.

A long, flat bank of clouds approached from the southwest, gray and swift. The light changed quickly from friendly sunshine to an odd coppery-green. No birds chirped or rose up from the grass, no insects buzzed. Even Cotton and Titus noticed, standing still in the little hollow of the old camp.

Cyrus turned slowly to the northeast. From that direction, boiling, roiling, writhing clouds advanced. His face paled, and goose bumps broke out on Julia's skin at the uneasiness in his eyes. The hairs on the back of her neck rose. The two fronts advanced on each other like charging armies.

"Come on." Cyrus scooped up Cotton and took Julia's hand. "Grab hold of Titus and don't let go, no matter what."

She took Titus's hand, and together they ran, not northeast toward home as she had expected, but straight west. As they climbed up out of the basin where the camp had been, she spied a lone shack on the prairie, maybe a quarter mile away, much closer than the soddy.

The clouds raced faster than anyone could run, and before they'd covered half the distance to the shack, the wind slammed into them, cold and fierce. The storm fronts clashed overhead, and Julia's ears popped. The air sucked out of her at the rapid change in pressure. Rain fell in drenching sheets, blinding her. Her wet hand slipped in Cyrus's, and he changed his grip to her wrist, tugging her along.

Her skirts and coat dragged at her, and her lungs burned. Just when she thought she couldn't go another step, the pitch of the wind changed, and she felt a curious lightness, as if she weighed nothing. Cyrus shouted, but the storm tore his words away. In an instant, he'd tackled her and Titus, pressing them into the ground, wrapping his arms around her and the boys, covering their heads.

The noise was horrific, filling her ears. Rain splashed into the ground, falling faster than the earth could soak it up, falling so hard it stung the skin. She clung to Titus, praying, trying to shield him from hailstones that fell as icy bullets. Cyrus's arms remained around them all like bands of iron. The wind ripped her hair and clothes, a ravenous, clawing beast.

After an eternity, the worst roaring passed, and the light feeling went with it, leaving her pressed down into the soaking ground. She opened her eyes.

"Come on. We're almost there." Cyrus tugged her up and took her wrist again, lifting Cotton onto his arm. "Grab hold, Titus."

They ran the last few hundred yards to the wooden shanty. The door hung open, swinging wildly in the relentless wind, but they stumbled inside, and Cyrus slammed it shut.

They stood there, dripping, gasping, staring at one another. Cotton whimpered, his coat hanging open, his clothes sodden. Titus stared, white-faced and wide-eyed, at the rain-turning-to-sleet sliding down the broken window and spitting into the shack through the cracks between boards.

Julia tried to catch her breath, stunned at how quickly the weather had turned. Cyrus wiped his hand down his face, and the grave look in his eyes clued Julia in to the seriousness of their situation.

"Pa, can't we go home? I'm cold." Titus wrapped his thin arms around himself.

"I think we'll need to wait out the storm, Son." Cyrus shrugged out of his coat and dropped it around the boys' shoulders, pushing them together under the roomy garment. "Here, you two warm up while I see about getting a fire started." He drew Julia aside. "See what you can find to make us more comfortable. We might be here awhile."

He knelt in front of a battered monkey stove. "I hope there's no bird nest in the flue." The squat little stove with two stove plates bore a furring of rust all over, but it looked sturdy enough. "I remember when old Bennett hauled this stove from town. Was once used in a caboose, so he claimed. He thought it would make a good cookstove without being too big for the shanty."

Julia went to the single bunk in the corner, lifted the straw-tick mattress, and shook it. A mouse flew out and raced under the rickety table, and she shrieked, dropped the mattress, and hopped back, colliding with the wall and shaking dirt from the rafters.

"It's just a little old mouse." Titus hiked the coat higher around himself and Cotton.

Julia picked up the nasty mattress and tossed it back on the bed. Dust and bits of straw flew up, but no more rodents appeared. The one asset that she could see was an enormous buffalo robe hanging on the back wall over the bed. She wrestled it down, ripping it off the nails, and the dust cloud that erupted had them all coughing and fanning the air.

Gust after gust of wind buffeted the shanty, rattling the windows and driving sleet inside. Whoever had built this claim shack had known very little about weatherproofing. No tar paper, no battening strips; the place was a sieve.

She spread the buffalo robe on the floor, draping half of it over the edge of the bed, and gathered the boys to her. "Here, get out of those wet things, and we'll wrap you in this until your clothes are dry. You'll never get warm if you're wet." She stripped them as quickly as she could, handing Cyrus back his coat. Poor Titus. His teeth chattered too much for him to protest her invading his privacy, and Cotton stood as if made of wood, his eyes enormous in his pinched face.

The temperature was still dropping, and Julia's fingers fumbled the buttons and fastenings, numb with cold. She shivered, her own clothes still sopping. Her hair hung in hanks over her shoulders, muddy and sodden.

Cyrus turned from the stove. "There's some firewood here. Not a lot, but enough to last for a few hours. Trouble is, I don't have any matches. It might take me awhile to get a fire going if I have to rub sticks together." He withdrew a jackknife from his pants pocket and began feathering a stick for kindling.

"How long do you think the storm will last?" Julia's teeth chattered as she draped little pants and shirts and coats across the table, the cupboard, and the bed to dry.

"Hard to say. It hit so sudden, maybe it will burn out fast. The big problem is getting a fire going to dry us out a bit." He bored a hole in a scrap of wood, filling it with straw from the tick, and began rubbing another stick near the hole as fast as he could. His muscles bunched and heaved as he rubbed, faster and faster. After a couple of minutes, he leaned back, wiping the sweat from his brow with his thumb. "This wood's too wet, I think. I'm not even getting any smoke."

Julia wrung out her skirts as best she could then grabbed her hair and leaned over, wringing the water from the long strands. If only she had something to tie it back from her face. Her hand went to her throat, to the hair ribbon she'd used to turn the arrowhead into a necklace.

The arrowhead.

Icy fingers hindering her, she finally managed to drag the arrowhead over her wet hair. "Try this." She unwound the ribbon and handed him the flint.

"Where did you get this?"

"I found it near the Indian camp the night I got lost. Can you start a fire with it?"

"Yep. I sure can." He used his jackknife, more straw, and the kindling sticks, and in a moment, he had a blaze going in the stove. "Come over here, boys. We'll get you warmed up." He dragged them, buffalo robe and all, in front of the stove.

Another huge gust rattled the shanty, blowing cold and wet through the broken window. Pellets of ice pinged off the floor and hissed when they landed on the stove.

Julia opened her coat and tried to gather warmth from the fire to her core while Cyrus rooted around the shelves behind the stove and found a tattered bit of toweling. Stuffing it into the hole in the broken window, he tried to shut out some of the wind and sleet.

The boys huddled in front of the fire, teeth chattering, bodies shaking. Cotton's lips were blue, and Titus's face was drawn tight. Julia brought their clothes over and held them to the fire, trying to dry them enough that they could be worn.

Cyrus checked out the window, cupping his hand against the dirty pane. "It's going to be dark soon, and this isn't showing any signs of letting up. Looks like we'd better prepare ourselves to spend the night." His eyes held hers, sending her messages over the boys' heads.

Spend the night? Julia wanted to cry. Cold, wet, miserable, dark, mouse infested. . . She drew a shaky breath. It wouldn't do for the boys to see her crying.

"Imagine how surprised Nan will be when we show up tomorrow morning looking for breakfast." She forced herself to sound cheerful and unconcerned, but it was an effort. Cyrus nodded, winking at her, a gesture that sent a burst of pleasure through her that was better than an eiderdown duvet at that moment.

He dragged the bed frame in front of the fire to give them something to lean against, and threw the mattress on the floor for a cushion to give them a dryish place to sit. Taking the boys onto his lap, he patted the spot next to him. "We'll have to huddle together to stay warm."

She eased down beside him, drawing her legs up and covering her feet with her coat hem.

His arm came around her, gathering her into his side, and he wrapped the buffalo robe around them all. Who would've thought that getting stranded in a storm could be the best place she'd ever been? "Try to get some sleep, boys. It will make the night go faster. We'll watch over you."

Hearing his voice rumbling so close to her ear as she pillowed her head on his shoulder, Julia wasn't sure she wanted the night to go faster. Though she wasn't ignorant of the predicament they were in, she knew she would always remember this time with Cyrus.

Cotton stirred, and she lifted him into her lap. "You can help keep me warm, buddy."

"I'm hungry," Titus said.

"I know, Son, but there's nothing to eat tonight. We'll have a big breakfast in the morning when we get home."

The boys settled down and drifted to sleep, and Julia found herself growing sleepy in the warm cocoon of Cyrus's arms.

"Cyrus, do you think Nan is all right? You don't think she got caught out in this, do you? Or your folks?" She whispered so as not to wake the boys and scare them with her fears.

"I'm praying not. I imagine Nan's tucked up tight in the soddy worried sick about us and praying for our safe return. The storm came up so quick, there might be a lot of folks that got caught off guard. At least the wedding guests should've had plenty of time to get home before the weather turned." He tightened his arm around her. "Try to rest. It will help pass the time." Julia dozed against his shoulder, falling asleep in the middle of her own prayers.

Sometime after dark the sleet changed over to snow. Cyrus put the last of the cut firewood into the stove. In the light of the small fire, his lips moved in what she was sure was a silent prayer for his family. Had he slept at all? He closed the dampers and grate as much as he dared, to slow the consumption of fuel. Wind howled, and snow scoured the walls as if trying to scratch its way inside.

Julia lay on her side with the boys in front of her like spoons in a drawer. Her feet were numb, but the rest of her was passably warm beneath the shaggy, smelly pelt.

Cotton held her hand, and Titus snored softly under her ear.

Cyrus checked the window once more then crouched by the makeshift bed. She opened her eyes, trying to read his in the faint orange glow flickering through the narrow bars of the grate.

"You should try to sleep, too." She sat up, pushing her hair off her face.

He nodded but didn't move, and she knew why he hesitated.

"Stop worrying. If it will make you feel better, we'll put the boys between us. They'll be warmer that way anyway. When you're trying to survive, the proprieties need to be set aside. You can blush like a schoolgirl all day tomorrow if you want to, but for now, lie down and get some rest." She was surprised by her own temerity, and she must have caught him off guard, because he laughed.

"Does anything daunt you?" He tugged the boys toward the middle of the makeshift bed. When she started to scoot away from the fire, he took her hand. "Nope, I sleep farthest from the fire."

Julia lay with her back to the stove, pillowing her head on her bent arm. Cotton mumbled and kicked, catching her in the thigh before settling down.

"Yes."

"What?"

"You asked if anything daunted me. The answer is yes."

Firelight glistened in his eyes, and he propped his head on his hand. "Like what?"

"Lots of things. Taking a job that required me to live with people I'd never met. Traveling alone on a train. Confronting a rather stubborn farmer about my baggage." She smiled, remembering how intimidated she'd been that first day. "My future daunts me all the time. I am no longer needed or wanted in my new stepmother's home, so I must make my own way as a traveling seamstress. Will I ever have a place to call my own, a place to put down roots? Will I ever find someone to love and protect me, to give me a family and a home? Or will I always be sewing wedding dresses for other girls, fashioning clothes for other women's children?" Longing for him welled up in her throat and then her eyes. She rubbed her cheek against her shoulder.

He frowned, staring into the dark over her head. "You'll get married someday. You're pretty and smart and capable."

Julia wanted to grab him by the lapels and shake him. How could he be so dense? Didn't he realize how she felt about him? She didn't want anyone else. She wanted this stubborn, gentle, appealing, infuriating homesteader from the Haskell Settlement. If he thought she was pretty and smart and capable, why didn't he show it? Why did he seem so eager to send her away?

⸎

Cyrus watched her sleep—the gentle curve of her cheek, the fan of her lashes, the tendrils of hair at her temple—and it was all he could do to keep from touching her, seeing if her skin was as soft as it looked, if her hair would slide through his fingers like silk ribbons.

He wanted her, wanted her to stay here with him, wanted her for his wife. And he knew, from the way she watched him, the way her hand lingered whenever she had cause to touch him, the wistful sound in her voice, that if he courted her, she would accept his advances. Knowing she would react favorably put even more strain on his control.

The notion of some other man marrying her tasted bitter and twisted his gut. But she deserved someone who could give her a gentle, protected life. Someone who had more to offer than hard work, two rambunctious boys, a dirt house, and a dependent grandmother.

He flexed his numb fingers and hunkered into his upturned collar. Cold barged in from every direction through the gaps in the siding, sifting snow around them. The fire seemed to barely reach them with any warmth at all, and he eyed the table, the cupboard, the shelf, and the bedstead, the only wood left to him to burn. He'd have to be sparing with the fuel. This storm had all the earmarks of a three-day blizzard. If that was the case, they could run out of wood long before it was over.

Water wouldn't be a problem as long as they had a fire to melt snow. Food would be an issue. For himself, he could manage for a couple of days, and Julia could, too. It was the boys who would feel it the most.

The guilt that had been tugging at his soul rose up and smote him in the heart. He had one duty. To protect and provide for his family. And here he'd let them become stranded on the prairie in a blizzard. No woman in her right mind would put herself in his care.

He must've dozed off, because he awoke to thin light filtering into the shanty. Dawn. Cotton's hand lay on Cyrus's throat, as if the little boy had needed to touch him to make sure he was there all night. The boy's eyes were still closed, his breathing even. Cyrus touched his son's cheek, thankful to find it warm. The fire had died to a few embers, and the room outside the buffalo robe was freezing, but underneath the hide, they were passably warm.

The wind still howled, and snow clawed and scoured the little building. Occasionally, a gust would rock the shanty with its ferocity. Cyrus eased from the makeshift bed, careful not to let any of the heat escape.

Sleep would be the best thing for the boys, since when they woke, they'd be hungry. He'd break up the table after everyone was awake. He checked his pocket for the flint arrowhead. *Thank You, Lord, for directing Julia to find it.*

Swinging his arms, he tried to work blood into his hands. His breath hung in frosty clouds, even near the stovepipe. Poking around in the cupboard, he found a battered kettle and filled it with clean snow from the piles along the walls. Outside, on the northwest side of the shanty, snow had piled up as high as the windowsill. At least there was some respite from the wind along that inside wall. He'd just as soon the snow stacked up to the rafters. The room would be easier to heat that way.

In the very back of the rickety cupboard, he unearthed a treasure. A can of beans, unopened and undented. Again he had cause to thank the Lord. He wouldn't open it until he had to, maybe this afternoon, or even tonight if the boys could last that long.

Cotton sat up, fighting his way out of the heavy blanket, his cheeks flushed from sleep and his eyes blinking. His hair stood up every which way, and he yawned hard enough to crack his jaw.

"Pa?"

"I'm here, Son." Cyrus crouched and smoothed his hand over Cotton's head.

"Is the storm over?" He yawned again, giving an excellent view of his tonsils and reminding Cyrus of a baby bird.

"Not yet. Are you warm enough?"

He hunched his shoulders. "I'm all right, Pa."

Julia stretched and tugged the buffalo robe off her face. Her eyes found his.

"Stay under the blankets, still as you can. I'm going to stoke up the fire."

They passed one of the longest days of Cyrus's life, listening to the wind. Every hour or so, they got the boys up, had them march in place, swing their arms, clap their hands, get their blood flowing. When they were thoroughly warmed from the exercise, they'd tuck them into the buffalo robe again.

Darkness came, and Cotton held his tummy, tears leaking down his little face. "I'm hungry."

Julia held him on her lap, cuddling and crooning. "I know. I'm sorry. I wish I had something for you."

Cyrus unearthed the can of beans from where he'd hidden it behind the stove. "How about some supper, boys?"

"What?" Titus shot out of the blanket. "Food?"

"Just beans, but I figure they should taste pretty good right now." He opened the can and set it atop the stove. "We'll burn the door off the cupboard to heat them through."

The light of admiration in Julia's eyes made Cyrus feel as if he'd hung the moon. As he expected, she refused any of the beans, saying she wasn't hungry. He passed them up, too, though his stomach rumbled.

Cotton and Titus cleaned out the can, eating with their fingers for lack of a spoon, before falling asleep to the howling of the wind and the rocking of the shanty.

Chapter 7

Wednesday, at least she thought it was Wednesday, Julia awoke, stiff and cold, hungrier than she'd ever been, though the sharp pangs had dulled to a constant ache. Raising herself on her elbows, she listened.

The wind wasn't as desperate, was it? Stumbling up, she looked at the window. Snow had piled up against it, and she couldn't see out at all. During the night, Cyrus had put the last of the bedstead on the fire, and now the stove barely retained any warmth.

The past three days blurred together in her mind. Her internal clock was so off, and her thinking so muddled from the constant battle to stay warm, to ignore her hunger, to encourage the boys, that she couldn't even hazard a guess as to the time of day.

She peered through a crack in the southeast wall. Though the wind still scudded across the surface of the snow, the overcast seemed thinner, as if the sun might be fighting to get through. Her heart lifted. Perhaps they had made it after all.

Cyrus came to stand behind her, cupping her shoulders. "Looks like the snow has finally stopped." His breath warmed her cheek. "Does your head hurt like mine?" He rubbed his temples.

"Depends. Do you feel like someone is banging an anvil right behind your eyes?" A wave of weakness swept over her, leaving her dizzy and drained.

"I'm going to strike out for home. You and the boys wait here, and I'll be back with the team so you can ride home. There's no way the boys could walk through this snow—the drifts have to be above their heads in some places, and we're so weak, I'd hate to try carrying them."

"Do you have to leave us?" She clung to his arm. In her head she knew this was what needed to happen, but her heart quailed at being left alone with the boys. What if he got lost? What if he collapsed into a drift? What if the blizzard returned?

"I'll be as fast as I can." He dropped a brief kiss on her forehead, so quick she barely had time to realize what he'd done, before he wrenched open the door. A thigh-high wall of snow blocked his path, but he plunged into it, closing the door behind him.

She returned to the crack in the wall to watch him, a dark spot floundering in the white. *Please, God, watch over him. Give him strength to make it home, and I pray that Nan has weathered the storm.*

When the boys woke, they were listless, staying under the blanket. Titus's brow wrinkled when she told him his father had gone, but he said nothing.

She tried to mark time in her head. How long would it take him to break through the drifts? They were more than a mile from the soddy, probably closer to two. Then he'd have to check on Nan, hopefully eat something, then get the horses. Then he faced the long, cold trek back, this time into the wind.

Hours. They had hours to kill before he could get back to them.

Julia gathered the boys close under the buffalo robe, too tired to sing to them, too tired to do more than share body heat and pray.

A strange noise broke through the wool in her head, and she opened her eyes. Titus raised his head from her shoulder. "What is that?"

It sounded like. . . Had she fallen asleep? Surely not enough time had passed. . . Horses, and men's voices.

The door shoved open, and a snow-encrusted Cyrus came in, blinking. "Julia?" Walt and Jed crowded inside.

"You wouldn't believe it. Nan got on a horse first thing this morning and made it to Walt's house to tell them we were missing. Walt took off for Pa's, and they hitched up one of the stone boats and came looking for us. I met them about half a mile from here."

Jed and Walt took the boys, and Cyrus helped Julia. Together, all holding tight under the despised-yet-treasured buffalo robe, they returned to the soddy.

∞

Late that night, after the boys were fed and tucked into their bunk, and Nan had fallen asleep in her rocker, Julia and Cyrus sat at the table. The lamp burned brightly, chasing the shadows to the far corners of the room, and the stove glowed with warmth.

Julia pushed her shawl off her shoulders. "I never thought I'd say this, but it's almost too warm in here. I never thought I would bless this dirt house, but nothing can beat it for keeping out the cold."

Cyrus tapped the table then got up to check on the boys before returning to his stool. It was as if he couldn't stay still, but the confines of the soddy kept him from pacing.

"I'm sorry I couldn't get you to the depot. You must be going crazy to get out of here." He drummed his fingers.

"I'm in no hurry to go." She weighed her words. "The truth is, when I leave, I'm going to miss you all." The hard lump formed in her throat again at the idea of getting on that train.

He stood, this time thrusting his hands into his pockets. "The boys will miss you, too."

She slowly rose and stepped close to him, knowing she had to ask but fearing his answer. "Just the boys?" They stood barely a foot apart in the cramped space. A curious lightness opened just over her heart, and her pulse thundered in her ears. "Will you miss me?" Her eyes stung as she looked up at him.

He swallowed hard and sucked in a deep breath. "Julia, don't do this."

"Don't do what? Admit that I care about you? That I don't want to leave? That I think you care about me, too, but you won't let yourself do anything about it? Why?" Her hands came up and rested against his chest, feeling the thudding of his heart, the warmth seeping into her palms.

His hands came up and covered hers, and a look of anguish crossed his face. "Because I can't protect you out here."

"Protect me? From what?"

"Anything. Sickness, hard toil, blizzards." His hands tightened on hers.

"Cyrus, you've been protecting me from the moment I met you."

His brows darted together.

She nodded. "It's true. You brought me here, along with all my things, and gave me a place to stay. You've fed me and housed me, rescued me when I got lost, and as for the past few days, you got us to shelter, managed to keep a fire going, and deprived yourself of warmth and food so others could have them." She took one of her hands from his and waved toward the room. "You take care of everyone. Building Walt a house, taking Nan in, helping your neighbors and family. You can't help protecting people. It's your nature."

"I don't seem to be doing a very good job of it."

"That's because you're confusing who you are supposed to be with who God is. You're bearing a responsibility that isn't yours to tote. Your wife's death wasn't your fault. Nan says she was as eager as anyone to come to Nebraska and homestead. She got sick. There isn't anything you could've done to prevent that. People get sick back East all the time. People even die from sickness under a doctor's care. You didn't jeopardize her health by coming out here. You did the best you could. All you can do is the best you can do, and you do that every day."

He thought about her words. "Even if what you say is true, wouldn't you miss the city? Do you want to live in a soddy until I can prove up on the land and save for a frame house?"

A glimmer of hope ignited her senses. "Any place, even a sod house, is a palace if the person you love is there. Everything I could ever want is right here."

"A sod palace has everything you could ever want?" One eyebrow rose.

"I want a home, a family, someplace to set down some roots. . .but more than that, I want love. I want someone to love me so much, he would toil in his fields to provide for me but always have time for teaching his boys about horses and farming and how to whistle on a grass stem. I want someone to love me so much he would ride out on the prairie in the dark to find me if I got lost. I want someone strong and unselfish to love with all my heart, never counting the cost, only reaping the benefits."

His arms came around her. With joy exploding through her, she wrapped her arms around his neck.

"You realize the benefits will be few and far between until I can raise a few crops?" He brushed a tendril of hair off her temple.

"Nonsense. I'm thinking the benefits are starting right now." She gave him a squeeze.

"I love you, Julia. I didn't know how I was ever going to put you on that train."

"I love you, too, Cyrus. I don't know if I could've forced myself to board."

"I wonder what the boys will say."

Nan stirred. "They'll say the same thing as me. It's about time you came to your senses, Cyrus. The best thing to come along in an age, and you were about to let her slip through your fingers. Kiss her already so's I can go to bed. Chaperoning you two is exhausting."

Laughter lit Cyrus's brown eyes, and he shook his head. "Soon as this snow melts," he whispered in her ear, "I'm going to get to work on an addition to this so-called palace so we can have a room of our own." His lips came down on hers, and she fitted herself into his embrace, home at last.

Bestselling, award-winning author Erica Vetsch loves Jesus, history, romance, and sports. She's a transplanted Kansan now living in Minnesota, and she married her total opposite and soul mate! When she's not writing fiction, she's planning her next trip to a history museum and cheering on her Kansas Jayhawks and New Zealand All Blacks. You can connect with her on her website at www.ericavetsch.com where you can read about her books and sign up for her newsletter, and you can find her online at www.facebook.com/EricaVetschAuthor/ where she spends way too much time!

WAITING ON A PROMISE

by Becca Whitham

Dedication

To my fellow sisters-in-arms
who have learned the secret of bringing sunshine wherever they go,
and
To Kim and Gina (they know why)

Chapter 1

June 1890

M arta Christiana Vogel, you are shredding that dough."
Marta dropped the sheet of pastry on the cloth-covered strudel board and took a step back. "I am sorry, *Mutter*. It's just. . ." The same excuse for her various lapses in concentration over the past sixteen months raced through her mind and then died on her lips. With a flick of her head, she tossed her red braid back over her shoulder, unwilling to touch it with flour-coated fingers.

Mutter sighed. Her usual sympathy had disappeared days ago. "His letter is late. It does not make him dead."

"I know, but. . ." Karl Reinhardt was hiding something. Marta knew it more by what his letters didn't say than their actual content. "Why doesn't he send for me?" She twisted the brown cotton apron into a knot matching the one in her stomach.

"Perhaps he is waiting until I fulfill my promise to teach you how to make a proper *apfelstrudel.*"

"Yes, Mutter." Chastised, Marta pushed the dough back together and rolled it again with greater care. *"First you must use your rolling pin to make it even, yes? Then, pick it up and stretch the dough without making holes. It must be thin enough to see newsprint through it but not so thin it won't hold the apples, yes?"* Grandmother Ingrid lectured inside Marta's head. *"The secret ingredient to great apfelstrudel is patience, Marta girl. Patience."*

Why did everything come down to patience?

Mutter inspected an apple for worms. "Karl has gone to make a home for you. The Oklahoma Territory is not a civilized place. I honor him for wanting to make sure it is safe before he proposes marriage."

Marta honored him, too. But the absolute latest date he promised to send for her passed two weeks ago. No money came. Even worse, no letter arrived to explain why. Was he injured? Dying? Dead? Or simply unable to meet his impossible "ready for marriage" standards?

She pressed too hard with the rolling pin, creating a thin ridge in the dough. Mutter wasn't looking, so Marta folded it back together and tried again. She'd wanted to marry Karl six months after her father died, but Mutter said sixteen was too young. By the time Marta turned eighteen, Karl had left his father's clock shop to become a farmer. He couldn't support a wife until he had land and a proper house.

When the government opened the Unassigned Lands in the Oklahoma Territory for homesteading, Karl could claim one hundred sixty acres for free as long as he made improvements. Free land meant he had enough money saved to build a house so they could marry sooner. He promised it wouldn't be longer than fifteen months at the most. She'd counted every day. Fifteen months came and went seventeen days ago. Altogether, she'd been waiting three and a half years. How much more patient must she be?

Mutter came close with the bowl of apples mixed with raisins and her special blend of cinnamon, sugar, and walnuts. "You are working the dough too much. It is going to be tough as cowhide."

Unable to bear another reprimand, Marta tore off her apron. "Please, may I go check the mail?"

Resignation appeared in her mother's green eyes. "As long as you promise not to mope during dinner if his letter still hasn't arrived. Your brothers will be back from working soon, and I would like to make your last birthday with us special."

"I promise." Marta hugged her mother tight, tossed her apron on the sideboard, and grabbed her bonnet on the way out of the house. All the way to town, she chanted, "Please, please, please," at God, Karl, and anyone else with the power to grant her wish.

Ten minutes later, breathless, she reached Pfeiffer's General Store just as Mrs. Pfeiffer came outside.

The older lady pulled the door closed behind her. "Marta, dear. How did you know?"

Marta's stomach slammed into her lungs. "Know? Know what?"

Mrs. Pfeiffer dug inside her tapestry satchel. "Why, to come today. I was going to drop this by your home, since it's your birthday." Her forearm and elbow disappeared. "How old are you now, dear?"

Resisting the urge to snatch the oversized satchel and dump its entire contents on the boardwalk, Marta gripped the side seams of her blue calico dress. "Twenty."

"Well, then it is past time that boy sent for you, isn't it?" Mrs. Pfeiffer held up a tattered letter and squinted through her wire-rimmed glasses. "Is this the one? Let me see."

Marta squeezed her fingers so hard they tingled.

"No, this is for Pastor Ingvold." Mrs. Pfeiffer reached a little deeper. "What about this?" She pulled out a list of some sort. "No." The mutton leg sleeve of her blouse deflated as she dug around the bottomless pit of a satchel. "What about this?" She pulled out a letter with Karl's heartbreakingly familiar script.

Marta's fingers went numb.

"Yes, this is the one." Mrs. Pfeiffer held it out. Marta nearly tore it in half yanking it from Mrs. Pfeiffer's hand. The older woman smiled. "Go on. Tell me what that boy of yours says."

Grinning from ear to ear, Marta ripped open the seal and unfolded the paper. There was no money. And the letter was way too short.

With a heart thumping so hard it pulsed air from her lungs, she read the carefully formed words:

My beautiful Marta,

I'm sorry to ask for more time. Trust me. It won't be long before I can send for you. Until then, have a happy birthday and understand you are missed more than pen can write.

Yours always,
Karl

That was it? Nothing about why she needed to wait? No reason for the delay? Nothing?

The place in her chest reserved for a woman's intuition split open. Something was terribly wrong.

"Bad news?" Mrs. Pfeiffer leaned forward and squinted at the back side of the letter.

Marta crumpled the sheet of paper and stuffed it in her pocket. "Not bad, just not what I was expecting. Thank you, anyway." With a wave good-bye, Marta headed to the bank to withdraw every last cent. She was done waiting. Done writing letters. Done worrying because Karl was keeping something from her.

She and her hope chest would be on the next train to the Oklahoma Territory.

Before leaving town, Marta purchased a train ticket for the following afternoon, a tapestry satchel, and a few supplies to round out what was already packed in her hope chest. The bag—which seemed quite large when she selected it—could scarce contain her few items. As she lugged it home, she mentally packed the contents of her hope chest and bag into the travel trunk. Lighter or fragile items would go in her new satchel.

Fine and Dandy needed to come, too. Hens and roosters might be available in Guthrie, but Mutter had bred her flock until she had the perfect blend of egg layers and meaty birds. The extra cost in shipping was worth having reliable birds.

Mental list made, Marta entered the house and went straight to her room. She tossed her bonnet on the bed and bent sideways to ease the bag from her aching shoulder.

Mutter appeared in the doorway. "You were gone a long time. Did you get anything from Karl?"

Marta dug the crumpled letter from her pocket and handed it to her mother. "His letters used to be two and three pages long. They've been getting shorter and shorter, and now this." She backed up and slumped onto the bed. "I remember, after Papa died, you said you knew something was wrong the day of his accident."

Mutter finished the brief note and walked into the room to hand it back. "I did. It was here." She placed a fist over her heart. "Not that there was anything I—or you— could have done to save him."

"I know, but. . ." Using her hand like an iron, Marta smoothed the creased paper against her thigh. "If you could have one more day—even if you knew he'd be angry with you and it would break your heart to lose him again—would you go to him?"

Mutter sat on the quilt. "Of course I would. I miss him every day." She pressed two fingers under her nose. "Every day."

Laying her head on her mother's shoulder, Marta breathed in the scent of cinnamon and rosewater. "I miss Papa, too, but I also miss Karl. And I think he's in trouble. So I . . .I bought a train ticket. I leave tomorrow."

"Oh, my Marta." Mutter wrapped an arm around Marta's shoulder. "I understand, I truly do. But if Karl does not want you to come yet, there may be a very good reason for it."

Chapter 2

Karl Reinhardt reached for his Winchester as soon as he heard hoofbeats. One hand holding the plow handle and one on the rifle, he looked over his shoulder to see who approached. He relaxed his grip on the weapon when he saw the familiar gray horse and battered Stetson of his neighbor. He replaced the Winchester in the special holster he'd made for the plow and waited for his friend to get closer. "Good evening, Samuels."

"Evenin', Reinhardt." Joseph Samuels didn't call people by their first names, claiming the familiarity was reserved for good friends and good-byes.

It was difficult to figure how he and Karl could be on better terms. They spent so much time working each other's claims, it was hard to tell who made which improvements—except for the plowing. Karl made sure his rows were straight; Samuels weaved with the terrain or the whims of the oxen.

Samuels pointed at Karl's trampled wheat. "You thinkin' that's Walsh again?"

Karl pulled the kerchief from his neck and wiped sweat from his face. "Of course. I just wish I could prove it." The list of things he couldn't prove was growing longer: new plow handles splintering, bags of seed disappearing right before planting time when the stores in town were out of stock, and now a field ready for harvest crushed.

Maybe next time he'd get lucky and Walsh—or, more likely, one of his four henchmen—would slip up and leave a trail to follow.

Sunset burnished the clouds with copper streaks, reminding him of Marta's hair in the sunlight. It had been too long since he'd last seen her. Too long without her smile, her sparkling green eyes, or her terrible apfelstrudel. Missing her punched his gut anew. He swiped his face again and stuffed the rag into his pocket.

Samuels poked his hat brim higher. "I still don't think it's Walsh. A lawyer what's runnin' for mayor ain't got no need to farm. He'd be worse'n me when we first met. But I ain't here to argue with you. Not when you look like you're 'bout ready to drop into an early grave and take your oxen with you."

Stiffening, Karl patted the ox nearest him and checked for signs of exhaustion. Both Bruno and Ollie looked fine, albeit a bit tired. The one good thing Karl learned from his father was to always, *always* take care of his tools and animals. Karl wiped his hands on the front of his work shirt. Every muscle ached, and his only food since breakfast was the dirt collected in his teeth. "I suppose it's time to stop for the day."

Samuels pulled a canteen from his saddlebag and tossed it. "Here."

Karl caught the canteen and nodded his thanks. He took a swig of water and swished it around his mouth. When he spit it out, it was murky with red dirt. "I need to get this mess plowed under so I can plant a new crop before it's too late." And then he needed God to send rain.

"What you need is to send for that gal a' yours."

Karl took another swig of water and swallowed. "I'll not expose her to danger unnecessarily."

Samuels shook his head. "Now you're just imaginin' things."

"I didn't *imagine* being told I would do well to return to the safety of Pennsylvania by Walsh's head thug, whatever his name is." Karl thrust the canteen at Samuels.

"Yeah, yeah. I hear you, except I got me a suspicion about why that Milliken fella is so sore at you." Samuels corked the canteen and returned it to his saddlebag.

"Who's Milliken?"

Samuels stuck a pinkie in one ear and rotated it. "Walsh's head thug. He's sweet on Miss Annabelle Colchester." He withdrew his finger and flicked it against his thumb.

"He can have her for all I care." The woman was a nuisance. As Reginald Walsh's niece and substitute daughter, she was used to getting whatever she wanted when she wanted it. The first Sunday Karl walked into church, she latched on to his arm and wouldn't let go. Three weeks later, she proposed, because his blond "giantness" was the perfect complement to her brunette daintiness. Being proposed to was bad enough, but what man in his right mind wanted to marry a woman for such a stupid reason—not to mention one who thought "giantness" was a real word? "Milli—what did you say his name was?"

"Milliken."

"Right. He isn't the one with his name on a lawsuit against me. That's Walsh. He wants this land, so he sends his employees—who don't do a thing without his full knowledge—to threaten and sabotage me. That lawsuit is a sham. I'm no Sooner, and you know it."

Samuels shrugged. He wore his indifference like well-fitted denims. "Don't matter what I know, and it don't matter what you know. What matters is what a judge rules."

The reminder—even though it came from a friend—was like a slap. Karl licked his cracked lips and forced himself to calm down.

"Which is another reason to send for that gal a' yours." Samuels scratched his chest. "From what you've told me, people in town'll like her. Might make 'em less likely to testify against you if you can ever get Walsh into court."

Three neighbors had already lost claims because people lined up to accuse them of crossing the line into the Oklahoma Territory illegally.

The run had been a disaster from start to finish. Depending on which newspaper published the story, there were anywhere from twenty thousand to fifty thousand people racing for twelve thousand tracts of land. Most of them had been snatched up by "Boomers," who'd established homesteads before the land was opened for settlement and managed to avoid soldiers sent to clear them out, or by "Sooners," who crossed the line before noon the day of the great race. The numbers were hard to pin down, but too many people went broke trying to claim land by following the rules. With so much bitterness over the whole fiasco, it was no surprise people were willing to lie, cheat, and steal to grab land any way they could.

What Karl couldn't comprehend was senseless murder over a claim. Six people awaited trial in Guthrie, another eight in Kingfisher, and there were scores of rumors without enough evidence to prosecute.

Even though the land run was over a year ago, newspaper articles still appeared citing suspicious circumstances. Was he next? Would he be found with a bullet through the heart and rigid hands clutching the handles of his plow?

He hoped Walsh's threats and destruction would end once the lawsuit was settled. But hope wasn't enough. Karl needed to be *certain* before bringing Marta to Oklahoma. When she was sixteen, she found her father in a pool of his own blood after he slipped and hit his head on a rock. It took Karl years to console her, and she never quite got over the guilt she felt because she wasn't there to prevent the accident. If she found him murdered? Karl shuddered in the heat. He refused to bring her such grief, even if Joseph Samuels thought it mule headed.

Karl squinted against the sunset's last rays. "I thought you said you didn't come to argue with me."

"About Walsh, but I'm right about that gal a' yours. Now, to show there ain't no hard feelin's, whaddaya say we head into town?" Samuels grinned like a kid with his first peppermint stick, exposing the gap between his front teeth.

Since the crusty cowboy was the type who enjoyed losing money on whiskey, women, and wagers, Karl shook his head. "But I pity the female population of Guthrie tonight. Looks like you took a bath and even washed that poor shirt of yours."

Samuels picked at his blue flannel sleeve with the daintiness of a lady. "Why, thank you kindly, fine sir. You, I might add, look like you haven't seen clean water in a month. I can't even see that blond hair a' yours under that there grime."

"All the more reason it's not a good idea for me to join you tonight." As if he needed more than the promise he'd made to Marta and God to keep himself only for her.

Guilt made him cringe. His promise to send for her after no longer than fifteen months passed weeks ago. Common sense argued that, until the mess with Reginald Walsh was settled, she was safer in Pennsylvania.

Samuels pulled the reins left and started toward town. "I'll check on you next week."

"Unless you want to join me Sunday."

Samuels waved as he rode away. For fifteen months, Karl had asked and Samuels declined. It would probably take Marta a week to get the cowboy's tanned hide into a pew.

When the lawsuit was settled and Walsh gave up trying to force Karl off his land by sinister means—*please, God, let it stop*—he would send for her. But not until then.

The last streaks of sunset faded. Karl picked up his shovel, grabbed the plow handles, and headed back to the barn. His oxen had better living conditions than he did, but he had plans. Grand plans. A four-room clapboard house with real glass windows and a full-length front porch. It would have three bedrooms: one for him and Marta, one for their boys, and one for their girls. A kitchen with a Prairie Favorite stove for Marta to cook on while their children played at her ankles.

But plans took money, and he had precious little left.

He stabled Bruno and Ollie in the barn, rubbed them down, and got them some feed. He was giving them a final check before heading to his dugout when hoofbeats—coming fast—had him reaching for his Winchester again.

A boy of maybe thirteen galloped close, his elbows flapping like he was about to take flight. "Evenin', mister. You Karl Reinhardt?"

"I am."

"Telegram for you." The boy reached into his saddlebag.

Karl kept his hand on his rifle until he saw a piece of paper and nothing else in the boy's hand. He reached out to take the telegram. It was from Irmgard Vogel.

Marta coming.

Train arrives Guthrie June 19, 10:48 am.

Chapter 3

The train slowed. Marta gripped her satchel and tried to maneuver the rolling pin down a little farther. After fussing with the thing the entire trip, she wished she'd somehow found room in her trunk for it, but there wasn't an inch of space left. Something bumped against her foot. She leaned down, picked up a stubby pencil, and shoved it in her pocket.

As the train crawled into Guthrie station, Marta stood and lurched to the door so she could be the first to get off. The stale bread and shiny cheese she'd eaten for breakfast lodged between her throat and stomach.

Descending the train steps, her heart tumbled forward when she spotted Karl leaning against the small depot building and scanning disembarking passengers to her right.

He was alive. And healthy. And almost within reach.

Refusing to be daunted by his crossed arms and scowl, Marta slipped between groups of people on her way to him. She lost sight of him for a moment and, when she found him again, a woman leaned on his arm.

A gorgeous woman, wearing layers of fashionable pink satin, with a matching parasol. Her glossy black hair was topped by a white hat with feathers and roses resting on a brim so large it made the parasol redundant.

Was this why his letters were so short? Because he'd found a woman too beautiful for words to replace plain-as-potatoes Marta?

"Karl Avery VonFuerstenberg Reinhardt! You. . .you. Oh!" Marta flung the rolling pin before she realized it was in her hand. She squinted and watched the result of her temper somersault toward Karl Reinhardt's head.

The lady in pink satin shrieked but kept hold of Karl's arm.

He jerked away from the shriek but not enough to dislodge the woman.

The rolling pin arced down. Not sure if she was relieved or disgusted, Marta watched it bounce off his shoulder and land in the dirt two feet from his boots.

Karl picked it up and searched the crowd. When he saw her, his eyes narrowed and he marched toward her, dragging his attachment with him.

However mad he was that Marta came before he was ready, it paled in comparison to finding him with a woman latched to his side for the whole town to see. And see they did! Gawking faces encircled the three of them.

The shimmering pink lady finally let go of Karl's arm. She eyed Marta like a roach. "Who is *this*, Mr. Reinhardt?"

Marta gritted her teeth. If her skin got any hotter, they could use her to stoke the train's engine. "My name is Marta Vogel. And you are?"

The woman slid her eyes from Marta's face to her dress. "Mr. Reinhardt?"

Marta stood tall. She might be wearing an old straw hat and a brown wool suit cut down from dresses once belonging to her grandmother, but she'd be plumb-jiggered before she let it embarrass her.

His face blotchy red, Karl swiveled his attention between her and the other woman but remained mute.

Never—not even in her worst nightmares—had Marta imagined this. That other women would be attracted to Karl was not a surprise. That Karl would politely converse with women in town, also not a surprise. That Karl didn't rush to her side after their tender promises to one another. . .*that* was a surprise.

And not at all what she imagined.

The pretty woman tilted her chin and narrowed her eyes at Karl. "If you will excuse me, I'm late for an appointment." She picked up the corner of her voluminous skirt and gave a tight smile. The crowd parted to let her pass then began to disperse. A few watched until it became obvious there was nothing more to see. Children craned their necks, resisting the efforts of parents dragging them away, then gave up the fight.

Karl stepped close enough to touch. "What are you doing here?"

It was not the question—at least not in that tone—Marta wanted to hear.

Oh, how she'd longed to see him again. This moment, this reunion, had played out in her dreams a thousand different ways. In some scenarios, Karl even asked, "What are you doing here?" in a breathless I-can't-believe-you're-actually-here-because-I've-missed-you-so-much voice.

Marta almost hated him for crushing such loveliness under the dainty heels of a vision in pink.

She grabbed the rolling pin from his loose fingers and stuffed it inside her satchel as far as possible. Which wasn't very far. "I want to know who that woman is and why doesn't she know about me?"

Karl gripped her arm.

A different heat than the one coming from a wool suit on a summer day spread down to her toes. "Ow. You're hurting me." Though the pain was in her chest rather than her arm.

Instead of letting go, he pulled her around the back side of a nearby tree. He kept checking left and right, as if he expected someone to pop out and rob them.

"Answer me, Karl Reinhardt." Marta set her satchel on the ground in case she needed both hands free to either punch him or hold him close. "Who was that woman, and why were you escorting her around town? I would think, after all we meant to each other, you would at least do me the courtesy of telling me your affections had changed before I got on a train." Not that she'd given him a chance to object. She was on the train before her mother sent the telegram.

Karl let go of her arm. "You have to go home."

"Why? Because of that woman?"

"Of course not."

Marta stepped back and put her hands on her hips. "Then why aren't you happy to see me?"

Chapter 4

Karl checked the crowd again for Walsh or one of his henchmen before returning his attention to Marta. "Of course I'm happy to see you. I just need you to go home." Since what he really wanted to say was, *"You have no idea how happy I am to see you or how much I need you,"* the words came out harsh and icy.

Marta flinched and crossed her arms, rubbing her sleeve like she was chilled. "I'm not going anywhere until you tell me what's going on." Her skin was so pale, the freckles on her cheeks danced along the surface.

To keep from touching her, he shoved his hands in his pockets and felt a rip. He had to get her back on the train, and fast. Annabelle Colchester's appointment was most certainly with her uncle. In five minutes—seven tops—the four mercenaries who did Walsh's bidding would be using Marta to apply leverage. He wouldn't be able to withstand that.

"I'm waiting, Karl." Marta cocked her head. A shaft of sunlight snuck under her bonnet and found the corner of her lips.

Karl leaned forward. "You need to go." He didn't want her to leave. What he wanted was to find Pastor Nicholson, marry her, and never let her out of his sight again. "I'm not joking, Marta. You need to get back on the train before it pulls out."

She stepped closer and shook a finger under his nose. "And I told you I'm not going anywhere until you tell me what's going on."

Her lips were inches from his. Pink and moist and utterly kissable. He pulled his hands from his pockets and braced them against her shoulders. "Please, Marta. Please, trust me. Go home."

Tears formed in her eyes, making them glitter like emeralds. "It's difficult to trust someone who's hiding something, Karl."

The words embedded like splinters under his fingernails. She was right, but what would she do if he told her everything? Go home? Or believe her presence would somehow shield him from Walsh and his scheming? Karl didn't have time to find out. She needed to be on the train in the next three minutes.

Lord, please. Get her back on that train before I can't let her go.

"Who was that woman?"

Her life was in danger, and she was obsessing over something so trivial? He pulled her an inch closer. "No one."

Her nostrils flared. "No one is a no one, Karl." The words brushed his skin and made him shiver despite the heat.

Lord, help. He tried again. "No one of any importance."

Marta's chin dropped a fraction. "If she's of no importance, then why was she hanging all over you, and why didn't you say that when I asked the first time?"

"Because," he ground out between tight teeth, "in case you missed it the first four times I said it, you need to go home."

She made two fists and pressed them against his chest. "And I'm telling you I'm not budging until you tell me what's really going on. You've been hiding something—don't you dare deny it—and I am going to stand here until you tell me."

Part of him wanted her to simply trust him; another part wanted to pick her up and toss her on the train, whether she liked it or not. Somewhere between them was a compromise that began with telling her a bit of the truth. "It's not safe for you to be here."

Marta pounded her fists against his chest. "Trust me, of the two of us, *you're* the one in danger here."

Tremors shook his entire body. *"Trust me, Karl Reinhardt,"* her ten-year-old voice echoed in his mind, *"I might be smaller and younger than you, but of the two of us, I'd bet on me in a fight."* He'd fallen a little bit in love with her that day. At thirteen, he was taller and stronger than anyone else at school. No one stood up to him when he took out his pain on others. Then came Marta. She kicked his shins, punched him in the stomach, and cut him down to size with her tongue. It took him three years to win her friendship and three more to win her love. Six years of turning into the man he wanted to be rather than the man he feared he would become—all because an impish ten-year-old stood up to his bullying.

Was repeating the childhood threat a coincidence or on purpose? Did it matter? During their years in Pennsylvania, Marta became as necessary as air. Surviving these past fifteen months had been like living underwater.

He took a shuddering breath, tightened his grip on her shoulders to keep from crushing her into his desolate bones, and begged with what was left of his resolve. "Please, Marta. Please. Trust me. It's not safe for you here. You need to go home. Now."

The train whistled in the background.

Marta pushed him back. "Fine and dandy!"

In answer to his prayers, she grabbed her satchel and ran for the train, the rolling pin waving good-bye as it bounced in time with her gait.

Stunned, Karl watched the woman he loved run away. Which was what he wanted. It was.

Even if her footsteps trampled his heart on her way out of town.

And yet.

He tapped his index finger against his thigh.

Marta—or any woman, for that matter—would never rush off without hearing the whole story told in excruciating detail from start to finish.

He stepped from the shadow of the tree in case he actually did need to toss her over his shoulder and throw her on the train.

Two hulking shapes blocked his path. "Who's the girl, Reinhardt?" Walsh's head thug asked. The white scar on his left brow stood in sharp relief to the dirt gathered in creases beside the man's black eyes.

While keeping his attention on the two men, Karl watched Marta disappear inside the depot. He fought to make his tone neutral. "Someone from home who came a long way for nothing."

The second thug, his muttonchop whiskers so long the ends curled, spat tobacco juice at Karl's feet. "Nothin', huh? Ya oughta know by now that there ain't nothin' goes on in this town what don't concern the good citizens of Guthrie."

By "good citizens," the man meant Walsh, but there was no way to prove it. Neck muscles tense, Karl started walking toward town, the need to get them away from Marta more pressing than the one assuring she'd made it on the train. "To which good citizens do you refer? Because I see no one else but you two."

Eye Scar fell into step and placed the back of his hand against his forehead. "How very wounding to infer we are not good citizens."

Karl walked faster, trying to outdistance the two men, but they closed in tighter and surrounded him with the smell of something rancid.

"I asked you a question, Reinhardt. I have yet to receive an acceptable answer." Eye Scar's speech showed a level of refinement far above Muttonchops or Walsh's other two thugs.

Karl compressed his lips and kept walking. If he could get rid of them fast enough, he could double back to the depot and make sure Marta had left town.

As they passed the entrance of an alleyway, Eye Scar stepped back and Muttonchops shoved. Karl stumbled into the tiny space, his exit blocked by a pile of bricks. He righted himself and lowered his shoulder to force his way between them.

Muttonchops—a greasy man at least four inches shorter than both Karl and Eye Scar—pulled back his arm as if to strike.

Eye Scar grabbed him and whispered, "Let it go, Biggs." Then he smiled wide and clapped a genial hand on Karl's shoulder. "Glad we had this little moment, Reinhardt. Looking forward to seeing you come Sunday morning."

Two young ladies walked by, pointing at the men and whispering to each other. Eye Scar tipped his hat and elbowed Muttonchops to do the same. When the giggling women passed, Eye Scar twisted his torso to follow their progress. "If I didn't have other reasons for hating you, Reinhardt, I'd hate you for that alone."

The comment stunned Karl out of his strategic silence. "You have reason to hate *me*?"

A fist connected with his gut. Then another, and one more, until he was folded in half. Tobacco juice slithered down his temple. "Keep bein' stupid, Reinhardt, and I'll make ya so ugly not even yer momma'd want ya."

Bent over, Karl saw the scuffed boots of his attacker replaced by the snakeskin ones of the more refined brute. "What Biggs here is trying to say is that we aren't going to touch your pretty-boy face. Not yet. But keep holding on to what's not yours, and things might get—well—ugly is the least you need to fear."

Karl raised his head.

A harder fist connected with his stomach, knocking the air from his lungs. He fell to the ground, and after a steel-tipped kick in the ribs, the shadowed alley burst into black.

～

"Good thing you claimed these animals before they were halfway to Texas." The stationmaster checked the tags then handed Marta the hen and rooster cages. "Fine and Dandy, huh. What is it with women and naming animals that are just going to end up on the dinner table?"

Marta didn't bother to answer as he turned aside to assist the next passenger. All she wanted was to find Karl again.

She *knew* it would be okay as soon as she got here. It might not have been the reunion of her dreams, but Karl loved her. Everything except his words begged her to stay.

Next stop, a preacher.

She left the depot expecting to find Karl waiting, but he wasn't. She walked around the edge of the building. Maybe he was retrieving her travel trunk. But, no, it sat on the train platform. At least the people in Guthrie were an honest lot. Then again, it had taken all three of her brothers to lift it, so maybe it was simply too heavy to be stolen.

Holding Fine, Dandy, and her satchel at the same time proved impossible. She set Fine's cage down and scanned the street. If Karl was still around, she couldn't see him. Maybe he was off fetching a preacher. He couldn't think she'd leave moments after arriving, could he? *Could* he? No man expected a woman to listen to words saying, *"Go away,"* when his eyes devoured her the way Karl's had moments ago.

So where was he?

"May I be of some assistance, miss?" A well-dressed man stood a respectful distance away.

Dandy pecked at her hand, so Marta set him beside Fine on the red dirt. "I'm looking for my. . ." She couldn't call him her fiancé. Not really. Even though he'd practically kissed her. In public. "For a friend. Mr. Karl Reinhardt."

The man blinked and lifted his chin a fraction. "What a coincidence. I was just coming to find him myself." He took a step closer. The crease in his gray pinstripe pants could cut butter.

"You know him?" Marta looked around again, hoping she was wrong. Hoping Karl was taking care of some other business. Hoping her rising anger was unjustified. "I was just talking to him a minute ago, but I don't see him now."

Lifting his bowler to reveal black hair touched with distinguished gray—though it was a little too slicked down for her taste—he said, "I'm sure we can find him if we are both looking. If you will allow me, I would be happy to escort you up to town."

Though the town was only half a block away, Marta hesitated to leave the depot, especially in the company of a man she'd never met before.

"Would you be more comfortable if I told you that's my wife just there?" He pointed to a matronly woman in blue serge. She waved from her vantage point atop the small hill perched above the railroad tracks.

When Marta nodded, he extended his arm. She transferred the satchel to her right hand and placed her left one on his forearm. "Thank you."

"You can leave the hen and rooster." He snapped his fingers, and two men approached. "My men will see that no harm comes to them."

"Thank you, again. But would you mind asking one of them to look after my trunk? It's the big brown one with leather straps sitting there." No sense having two men guard the animals and leave her trunk defenseless. Like Karl had left her.

"Certainly." He turned aside and whispered something to the man guarding Fine and Dandy. "Shall we go meet my wife?"

"You're quite a knight in shining armor, Mr.— Oh dear. I'm afraid I didn't get your name."

His smile revealed crooked teeth. With everything else about him so polished, it came as a bit of a shock. "Reginald Walsh, at your service." He touched his gray bowler and bowed slightly.

Without taking her fingers from his arm, she dipped a curtsy. "Marta Vogel. I am so pleased to meet you, Mr. Walsh."

He patted her fingertips. "Not as happy as I am to meet you, Miss Vogel. It is Miss, isn't it?"

"Not for long, I hope." Marta kept scanning the area as they walked. Karl better hope she found him soon, because if he thought for one moment he could dismiss her without telling her what was going on, he had another think coming.

Mrs. Walsh proved to be as friendly as her husband. After a warm hug of welcome, she insisted on treating Marta to lunch.

As the three of them strolled through town, Mr. Walsh pointed out various shops and restaurants, many of which he leased to tenants, and his law office. A few structures were being built with brick, but most were of wood. In a little more than a year, Guthrie had gone from open land to a tent town and then a full-fledged city. There was even a perfumery shop amid the grocers, livery, and saloons.

They stopped their tour at O'Bannon's Restaurant. After they were ushered inside, Mrs. Walsh requested a table by the front window. "What do you think of our little town, Miss Vogel?"

Grateful to give both her feet and arm a rest, Marta set the heavy tapestry bag under the table. "It's much larger than I expected."

"And full of eligible bachelors." Mrs. Walsh winked and reached across the table to pat Marta's hand.

Mr. Walsh perused the menu. "I predict you will be snatched up in a month's time. Or did you have someone special in mind? One Mr. Karl Reinhardt, perhaps?"

If she had to drag him to the altar herself. "I'll need to find him first."

Mr. Walsh chortled. "We will find him, Miss Vogel, I assure you. I know right where he lives."

Chapter 5

By the time Karl came to, his rib cage screaming, Walsh's thugs were nowhere to be seen.

Neither was Marta.

He checked at the depot. The train was gone and few people were left. No one remembered seeing a woman like he described. The stationmaster didn't remember her, either, though he admitted baggage was more memorable to him than people. Karl asked about unclaimed baggage or anything being held until it could be picked up later, but there was none.

Knowing Marta, she would pack enough to survive the book of Revelation and wouldn't be able to lug a trunk around town.

Still, Karl spent almost an hour peering through restaurant windows, trying to find her. He breathed a little easier when he saw Reginald Walsh and his wife sitting at the front of O'Bannon's. It was just the two of them. No Marta, no Annabelle, and no satchel with a rolling pin sticking out of it resting on an empty chair.

Legs wobbling, Karl headed to the livery to get his horse. If Marta wasn't in town, chances were she hired someone to take her to the homestead.

He rode in at a gallop, searching for any sign of her, but she wasn't there. Not in the barn, not in the dugout, not anywhere.

Half-convinced she'd done as she was told, Karl took time to wrap his torso tight. He didn't think any ribs were broken, but he wouldn't be able to stay in the saddle if the pain got worse. He was mounting up to ride back into town and search again when he heard hoofbeats. After grabbing his Winchester from where it hung above the barn door, he walked into the open.

He pointed the rifle at the ground the second he saw Marta with Reginald Walsh in the approaching carriage. Fury fought with fear inside his stinging chest. Why was she with him?

"Good afternoon!" Walsh shouted from a distance. "I've brought Miss Vogel. I found her wandering in town, most anxious to find her Mr. Reinhardt."

Her Mr. Reinhardt? What had Marta said? Wishing he could smash a fist into Walsh's smug mouth, Karl looked at Marta to see if she was hurt in any way. "I'm sure Miss Vogel wasn't that anxious."

She tapped the rolling pin jutting out of the bag she held in her lap. "I was sure we had some unfinished business."

Walsh pulled on the reins of his matching blacks until they stopped then set the brake. "My wife and I took her to lunch at O'Bannon's to restore a bit of her equilibrium.

Our meal was quite delicious, I assure you."

Karl gripped the rifle harder. How had he missed that? Because he neglected to check the necessaries, that's how. "I thought she returned to Pennsylvania as we discussed."

"Return to Pennsylvania?" Walsh transferred the reins to his right hand. "Why would she want to do that when everything she wants"—he swung his left hand out to encompass the landscape in front of him—"is right here?"

Marta looked down at Karl. "Shall I get out of the carriage?"

Before Karl could answer, Walsh did. "Certainly. Please help her down, Mr. Reinhardt."

Karl couldn't very well leave Marta in the snake's den, even though it meant yielding his will. Determined to keep his injury from showing, he marched to her side with his rifle still clutched in one hand and stuck out his other.

Marta let go of Karl's hand as soon as her feet touched the ground. She gave him a you're-in-so-much-trouble smile.

He was in trouble? What about *her*?

"Shall I send Judge Parker your way?" Walsh asked.

Despite the fire in Marta's eyes, Karl turned to his bigger problem. "Thank you for the offer, Mr. Walsh, but you can't be sure Judge Parker is available. If we need a judge, I'm quite capable of getting one myself."

Walsh looked straight at Marta. "Probably not by this evening, though."

Marta stiffened. "Then I will return to town with you, Mr. Walsh."

Stepping close, Karl put his free hand on her back. "We'll figure something out."

"I'm sure you will." Walsh picked up the reins. "I almost forgot your belongings, Miss Vogel. Mr. Reinhardt, would you be so kind as to fetch the ones in back while I say my good-byes?"

Karl stretched his lips without smiling. "I most certainly wouldn't wish to detain you any longer than necessary."

Amusement danced in Walsh's black eyes.

The moment Karl let go, Marta stepped toward the carriage. She extended her hand to take her bag. "Thank you for your kindness, Mr. Walsh. I will forever be grateful for your warm welcome."

Relaxing his grip on the rifle before he accidently shot something, Karl strode to the back of the carriage and pulled down the hen and rooster, not sure who made him angrier—Walsh for being a snake or Marta for not recognizing a snake when she saw one. Karl set his Winchester on the ground because removing the trunk required both hands. The weight sent stabbing pain through him, and the trunk thudded to the ground before he could stop it.

"Everything all right back there?" Walsh didn't bother to disguise the hilarity in his voice. Nor did he wait for an answer. "Miss Vogel, it was such a pleasure to meet you. If you stay in Guthrie, I hope you will consider me your first friend—aside from

Mr. Reinhardt, that is—and call on me if you need anything. Anything at all."

∞

Marta waved good-bye to her first friend in Guthrie with reluctance. Karl's red-tipped ears and glowering eyes indicated he didn't wish to talk. Too bad, because they at least needed to decide where she would be spending the night and under what conditions.

"Do you intend to send for a preacher, Karl?"

Instead of turning toward her, Karl picked up his rifle and watched the receding carriage. "What did you tell Walsh?"

Had he always answered her questions with vague half answers or more questions? She didn't think so, because she couldn't remember ever finding him this frustrating. "I believe it's customary to answer my question before you ask one of your own."

"Do you realize who that man is?"

"Are you even listening to me?"

Karl turned. "What?"

Saints above, she was going to murder him with her bare hands. "I asked if you intend to send for a preacher, or even a judge. I'm still waiting for an answer."

"Of course not. I want you on the next train out of town, Marta. I mean it."

"Oh. You are the most exasperating man." Her hands fisted with the urge to punch some sense into his thick German skull.

Karl's shoulders raised and fell on an exhale. "Look. Can we. . .can we take a minute?"

Over their years together, they developed a simple rule. When one or the other needed time to think before saying something hurtful, they agreed to "take a minute."

Marta stomped to her trunk, sat down, and hugged her satchel tight. "All right."

"I'll be over there." Karl pointed to where the rumps of two oxen and a plow peeked around the edge of a sturdy barn.

As she sweltered in the baking sun, Marta breathed deep and exhaled a bit of anger into the wind while evaluating the homestead. The fields struggled to produce patches of wheat and scraggly cornstalks. A wide-open land with scrubby trees clustered along a muddy creek and a few meager hills, it felt harsh and vulnerable at the same time.

As did the dugout.

Shaped like an upside-down bowl with a slice missing, there was a grass roof and a stacked sod wall across the front. In the center stood a gray wooden door shrinking with embarrassment at its dilapidated condition. A stovepipe chimney poked up through the ground six feet back from the door. There were no windows anywhere. Four small plants in buckets bent in the wind beside the withered door.

Were those. . .? Marta leaned closer to study the leaves. Apple trees!

She smiled at the memories they evoked.

Karl eating her first and worst apfelstrudel. Mutter laughing because anyone brave enough to eat such a mess was brave enough to marry her daughter. Mutter pressing a small bag of apple seeds into Karl's hand before he left for Oklahoma and promising to teach Marta how to make a proper apfelstrudel while he was away. The bag had held at least twenty seeds. Either Karl was a terrible farmer or the land more unforgiving than advertised in newsprint.

Marta squirmed on the hard surface of her trunk. Visions of tall, waving wheat passing the train window for miles on end poked holes in her second theory.

She set her satchel on the ground and stuffed her right hand into her skirt pocket. The pencil stub she'd found on the train floor greeted her fingers. She pulled it out and rolled it between her thumb and index finger. Sweat beaded on her neck and under the band of her straw bonnet while brown wool pressed her limbs.

Back in Pennsylvania, she'd been certain Karl needed her. Certain he would be happy once he saw her. Certain the delay was because his standards were unattainable for mere mortals.

So much for certainty.

One of Karl's early letters had described the dugout as mute testimony of a Boomer chased off the property prior to the land run. Though he appreciated not having to carve one out from scratch, the rickety door, he'd written, was on his list to rebuild before winter. If he lacked funds for something so simple, no wonder he didn't send money for a bride.

She squirmed a little more. What she should do was pack herself and her belongings back home. Except she had five dollars and forty-three cents left after purchasing extra items to pack, extra shipping for Fine and Dandy, and extra food along the route just in case the train stopped somewhere without a restaurant nearby.

What a waste!

She kicked a rock into the tall grass. A snake head lifted, and the air filled with rattling. Fine and Dandy squawked and flapped inside their cages.

Marta tensed every muscle. "Karl!"

"I see it."

Footsteps crept close. The barrel of his long rifle appeared in her peripheral vision. She squeezed her eyes shut and prepared for the blast.

Bang!

The rattle faded to nothingness. Marta opened her eyes and was grateful clumpy grass hid what was left of the snake.

Karl lowered his rifle. "Let's talk inside."

Marta stuffed the pencil back into her pocket and followed him to the dugout. Inside was cool and dank. It took a moment for her eyes to adjust from the bright sunshine outside.

There wasn't much to see. A small bed, held off the ground by spikes driven into the back of the dugout and two posts underneath; bags of beans and food tins stacked beside the bed from floor to ceiling; a potbellied stove in the exact middle with a pan of soaking beans on top; a table and two stools; a shelf to hold a plate, cup, and bowl; and a writing desk. Dirt coated every surface, and a spider crawled across the table.

Marta moved closer to the table and gasped. Embedded in the dirt wall above it were seven rocks with painted portraits. She touched each face with reverence: her alone, Karl and her together, Mutter, all three of her brothers, Karl's mother, his sister and brother-in-law, and—at the very end—his father. "Did you paint these?"

There was a slight pause before Karl answered. "Yes."

Seeing the tender care of his work, hearing the loneliness in that one syllable, the rest of her anger dissipated.

"Where did you get the paint?"

"There's a clock shop in Guthrie. Sometimes the owner pays me to take on extra repairs or paint a bit. I did these with leftovers."

Marta swallowed hard.

With leftovers.

Those two words cleaved her soul with conviction. While she imagined him stubbornly refusing to marry her until his impossible standards were met, he'd been struggling to survive. While she'd been surrounded by her family and friends, he was keeping himself company with painted rocks. From the depth of his loneliness, he'd asked her to wait. To trust him. To be patient just a little longer.

Her fingers lingered over the portrait of them together. He'd painted a traditional wedding pose: him seated and her standing behind him with her hand on his shoulder. Karl's face wore a somber expression, but hers was beaming. He'd captured not only their faces but their personalities—all on the surface of a smooth rock.

With leftovers.

New conviction flowed into her soul. Dreams were lovely, but it was time to put them away and get to work. She would find a way to make up for her lack of trust, her impatience, and her spendthrift ways.

Vow made, Marta straightened and faced Karl. "Is there. . .maybe. . .enough work for two clock shops?"

He took a step back and hooked his thumbs through his belt loops. "What are you suggesting?"

She tilted her head toward the open door. "Your crops. They don't. . . They don't look very good."

The vein in Karl's neck bulged and pulsed. "It's not what it looks like."

Marta jerked her head upright. "What does that mean?"

"It means your first friend in Guthrie has been sabotaging me." The words burst from him like water breaking through a dam.

"Mr. Walsh? Why would he want to do something like that?" The man was both a sought-after lawyer and a landlord with enough properties in town it required four employees to collect rent. He was even running for mayor. Judging from the way people greeted him both in town and at O'Bannon's Restaurant, his bid for election would succeed. Which suggested he wouldn't stoop to sabotage. Yet Karl would never lie outright. Keep certain facts hidden to protect his pride, maybe, but never lie. "I think we'd better sit down so you can tell me what's been going on. And don't you dare leave out anything."

Chapter 6

How stupid of him!

Karl gauged his chances of getting Marta back home without telling her everything. From the look on her face, there was no chance at all.

He eased himself onto the stool beneath him as naturally as possible. A gentleman would wait for the lady to sit first, but a smart man—one who wanted to keep his beloved from doing something like marching into Walsh's office and making a scene—put safety over manners and sat down before he fell down. "I will tell you as long as you promise to go home when I'm done."

Marta sat on the creaky stool opposite him, crossed her arms on the table, and leaned forward. "And I will make no promises until I know the full story. It's unfair of you to ask otherwise."

He put his hands on the table and tapped his thumbs together. *Tap, tap, tap, tap, tap.*

"I'm waiting, Karl."

Tap, tap, tap, tap, tap.

She raised her eyebrows at him.

He sighed. "The thing is, I'm not sure I know the full story. There are so many things that don't make sense, it's like swimming through molasses in the dark."

She covered his hands with her own. "Then let's try and figure it out together, shall we?"

His hands turned to capture hers. How many times had he sat at this table and spoken to her tiny portrait while dreaming of the day she would be here—right across the table from him—making this hole in the ground a home with her mere presence? "It started nine months ago."

Beginning with Walsh filing the affidavit contesting the claim six months after the land run, Karl gave Marta a full account. She gasped when he told her about his new plow handles splitting and his disappearing bags of seed, squeezed his hands at the description of trampled fields, and turned fiery red when he recounted every threat whether veiled or delivered with fists. Every threat except the kick.

Marta pinched her brows together. "But why would someone of Mr. Walsh's standing need to resort to something so disgraceful? And why file a lawsuit if he intends to drive you out anyway? I can't believe Mrs. Walsh would be party to such a thing. She's far too gracious."

Having learned the hard way that her squinted eyes and downturned lips could either mean *"I think you're lying"* or *"I'm puzzling through this problem,"* Karl held his breath and waited for her to pronounce judgment.

"You're right. It makes no sense. If word got out, he'd be ruined."

The tension inside him eased. He'd been carrying this burden around for so long—part of him wondering if maybe Joseph Samuels was correct about making a mountain out of a molehill—that Marta's confirmation felt like healing oil on a raw cut.

Too bad it didn't help his smarting ribs.

Karl gripped her hand a little tighter, grateful for her understanding. "I'm going to tell you something else, but you need to know up front I was telling the truth when I said Miss Colchester means nothing to me."

She lifted her chin. "Which doesn't mean Miss Colchester feels the same about you."

Karl nodded. "She thinks my blond 'giantness' is the perfect complement to her brunette daintiness."

Marta withdrew her hands from his. "She *is* very pretty."

"Until she opens her mouth."

Laughter spurted from Marta's lips, and she started to cough. "Because she makes up words like 'giantness'?"

"Exactly."

Her green eyes twinkled. "What else did she say?"

Torn between relief at her amusement and irritation that she found anything about the situation funny, Karl made fists on the tabletop. "The woman proposed to me my third Sunday in church."

"She proposed?" Marta covered her cheek with a hand. "After knowing you three weeks?" She covered her lips then her cheek again. "Because you look good together? Oh. . .oh. . ." She laughed harder, coughed again, and patted her chest. "Nothing would have made you like her less."

"I grunted and sputtered like a *dummkopf* before telling her I had someone special back home."

Marta gasped for a full breath and beamed at him. "I'm sorry I ever doubted you. Though, I'm guessing she planned to change your mind with her sweet smiles and fashionable clothes?" She returned her hand to his.

"Exactly." Karl tightened his hold on her fingers. "I don't want to scare you, Marta, but the Walshes dote on their niece. I think Miss Colchester's misplaced regard for me might be the reason things haven't become violent." Except for a vicious kick, which he didn't plan to talk about. Ever.

"She wouldn't want anything to mess up your 'pretty-boy' face." Marta's eyes danced with humor. "Because then your blond 'giantness' would be of no use to her brunette daintiness."

"It's not funny, Marta." His ribs throbbed in time with the rapid beats of his heart. "I'm not sure how Miss Colchester will react to your arrival. Will she give up? Allow the attacks against me to get worse? Or send her uncle after you?"

"Hmmm." Marta pulled her hands away and stood up. She left the table to pace around the small dugout. "How can we get to the bottom of this fish barrel?"

"Hold on there." Karl stood so fast his head banged the ceiling. Dirt, spiders, and a centipede rained down. He swiped at what fell into his hair with impatient hands. "There's no we about it. You are going home, and that's final. I will figure this out and send for you when it's safe."

Marta stepped close and brushed debris from his cheek. "Do you love me, Karl?"

"Of course I do."

"And do you want to marry me?"

"When it's safe, yes."

"And when will that be?"

He was having difficulty breathing after his sudden movement. More words became impossible.

She patted his cheek and gave him an indulgent smile. "You can't answer, because there is no way to know. Even worse, you must attend to our homestead here while Mr. Walsh conducts business in Guthrie. Things would be resolved much quicker if there was someone working in town who overheard all sorts of gossip."

Karl grabbed her hand and pulled it away from his cheek. "No, Marta. Absolutely not."

"We are not married, nor are we even engaged, so I don't see how you can stop me."

"Then I'll marry you!" The words reverberated around the dugout like the walls were made of steel instead of dirt.

"But I won't marry you."

Chapter 7

Marta squeezed Karl's hand to keep herself upright. Had she really just turned down the long-awaited proposal? "Not yet, anyway."

His mouth fell open. Closed. Fell open again. "What?"

"I am well aware of the irony." She removed her hand from his grasp and took a few steps back. "You can't keep me safe from all harm, Karl. Such a goal is too lofty for any man. We've done this your way for over a year, and what is there to show for it? I mean no disrespect. You work hard and have good intentions, but your plan isn't succeeding. The Bible says two are better than one. Let me help you so we can marry without any mysterious threats hanging over us."

It was a good idea and would make up for her precipitate arrival. He might dislike her impatience, but she didn't like how he wanted things done his way all the time. Marriage needed compromise. Her plan—one that required sacrifice from both of them—would pave the way for their future together.

"Am I interruptin' anythin'?" A man strode into Karl's dugout like he owned it. His weathered skin contrasted with an almost childish gap-toothed grin. He wore a battered gray Stetson and leather chaps over faded denims. Point-toe boots with spurs peeked from below tattered cuffs. "Well, hello there, pretty lady." He bowed with surprising grace. "I'm Karl's neighbor. Name's Samuels. Joseph Samuels."

Liking anyone who called her pretty at first sight, she gave him her best curtsy. "Marta Vogel."

He cast a startled glance at Karl. "Really? Now ain't that an interestin' twist." Mr. Samuels grinned even wider. "Well, then. I'll skedaddle on outta your way. I only come 'cause I seen Walsh leavin' the place and wanted to see how Karl here was doin' before headin' to town."

Karl rubbed at his scalp like a centipede or spider still lurked. "I'm fine."

Marta smiled her brightest. "If you would be so kind, Mr. Samuels, might I prevail upon you to escort me back to Guthrie?"

His chest puffed. "I'd be right honored, Miss Vogel."

"And what are you going to do once you get to town, Marta?" Karl crossed his arms over his chest. "Where will you stay? Who will make sure you are safe?" He shook his head. "No. We will go find Pastor Nicholson, and—"

"We will not," Marta interrupted. The stubborn man was missing the whole point. "There was a HELP WANTED sign in O'Bannon's Restaurant—for a waitress—so you can quit your smirking, Karl Reinhardt. And I'm quite capable of finding a modest boardinghouse for however long our little project takes."

Leaning close, Mr. Samuels whispered in her ear loud enough for Karl to overhear, "He's worried 'bout a man named Walsh and his thugs hurtin' you if you're in town."

"I know," she whispered back at a similar volume. "However, I spent some time in town this afternoon with Mr. Walsh and his wife without harm. As for his employees, they took good care of my belongings."

Mr. Samuels wiped something from his eye. "Told him he fusses worse'n an old woman. Does he listen to me? No."

But fear lurked in the corners of Karl's blue eyes. She'd learned to recognize it after years of watching him deal with his father. Understanding why he needed to control things so tightly, Marta sobered. "Please, Karl. Let me do this. You must learn to trust God with me at some point."

The tilt of his head said, *I will when you will.*

"And if you don't trust that there God a' yours, you can at least trust me." Mr. Samuels interrupted their silent exchange.

Judging by the stunned expression on Karl's face, the words hit hard.

"Besides, ain't that a new bag a' seed settin' up against your barn?" Mr. Samuels pointed toward the open door. "You got another couple hours a' daylight. I'd think you'd wanna be plowin' and plantin' while you can."

Marta ached to lay her hand on Karl's tight jaw. "Mr. Samuels is a man of excellent sense."

The gruff man grabbed his shirtfront and stood tall. "After a compliment like that, you can't deny an old geezer like me the honor of escortin' a right pretty gal to town. Be downright criminal." He extended his arm like they were in a fancy hotel as opposed to a small dugout.

Marta latched on to it before Karl could object. "The honor would be mine, Mr. Samuels."

A blush appeared under his tanned cheeks. "Why, call me Samuels. Or Joseph, if you like. Call me mister again and I won't know who you're talkin' to."

"Then you must call me Marta, because I have a feeling we are going to be great friends."

They walked outside with synchronized steps.

"Lucky thing I brought the buckboard this here time. Usually it's just me an' my horse, Bob, hoofin' it to town." Joseph stopped by her trunk. "You want all a' what's in here to go with you?"

Marta sighed. Regret over past mistakes was worthless, and Karl could use some creature comforts. "No, we can unpack a few things." She unbuckled the leather straps holding the trunk pieces together and lifted the lid.

Karl stepped out of the dugout. "By a few things, she means enough to start her own general store." His smile was a mixture of fierce determination and teasing.

Proud of the effort he was making, Marta tamped down annoyance. Yes, her packing was excessive, but she was trying to make up for it. And it wasn't funny. *"Those who cannot laugh at themselves, Marta girl, miss many jokes,"* Grandmother Ingrid instructed from heaven. Well. . .maybe it was a little funny. Marta picked up a bag of dried apples. "Just for that, Karl Reinhardt, you can take this"—she tossed it at him—"and these." She grabbed five more bags and fired them at him in rapid succession.

He didn't drop a single one. "Anything else?"

When Karl was fourteen, he'd asked her the same thing after she yelled at him for being a *tyrann*, a *blödmann*, and a stinker. Once they started liking each other, he confessed that was the moment he determined to become the kind of man she'd want to marry someday. The question had become their abbreviated apology.

Marta stuck her tongue out to say he was forgiven.

He smiled all the way to his eyes.

How on earth had she ever captured the heart of such a handsome man? Longing to kiss him, she shooed Karl to the dugout and told him to come back for more.

While he carted off the apples, Marta loaded up Joseph's outstretched arms with two bolts of calico, a quilt, a tin of sugar, three bars of lard soap, two squares of pressed cinnamon, a bag of dipped candles, a bag of shelled walnuts, and some raisins wrapped in brown paper. He tottered to the dugout as she started sorting through her satchel.

By the time Karl returned, she'd piled together the rolling pin, a bunch of silk flowers she intended to add to a bonnet one day, two pieces of lace, a spool of brown thread that hadn't fit inside her sewing kit, a recipe box, and four jars of Mutter's homemade strawberry jam strategically placed to keep the flowers and lace from blowing away. Karl started to grab up the individual items, but she forestalled him.

"I have a straw basket in here somewhere." She bent over the trunk to block his view. Digging until she hit the bottom, she found the crushed basket beneath her nightgown and bloomers. She pulled it up and held it behind her while keeping herself between Karl and her unmentionables. "Here."

Out of the corner of her eye, she watched Karl head back to the tiny dugout. Certain she heard a snort of laughter as the men passed each other, she ignored it and hunted for anything else not worth carting back to Guthrie. Her somewhat haphazard packing left her memory fuzzy. Had she included the strudel board, or did Mutter convince her it would be easy enough for Karl to make a new one?

"You about done there, miss?" Joseph leaned over the trunk to observe.

"Yes, yes." Marta pushed him away to slam the lid down. Carting a few extras to Guthrie was worth avoiding the embarrassment of the man glimpsing her bloomers. She buckled the straps and stepped aside so he could load it onto his cart.

The grizzled man bent to lift the trunk. "Good night in the mornin'. . ." His remaining words were mumbled and indistinguishable as the trunk moved a mere inch.

Marta glanced to the dugout and back to Joseph. Dare she offer to help? No. Her truce with Karl hung by a tenuous thread. No use igniting his ire again.

Joseph grunted.

Marta stepped toward the wagon.

"Karl, you best get out here. This trunk ain't gonna load itself, and I don't want your pretty lady attemptin' to help."

Karl ducked out of the dugout door and hurried to help a struggling Joseph lift the trunk. Muttering a few jokes about aching backs, Joseph secured the trunk with rope and then told Karl to say his good-byes.

After a few steps, Karl stopped. His legs seemed rooted to the spot, and fear shone in his eyes. "Are you sure about this, Marta?"

No, she wasn't sure. And, seeing his distress, she wanted to scrap the whole plan. But she needed to be patient for once.

She stepped close enough to touch his beloved face. "We'll figure it out. I saw your church. Mr. Wa. . .uh, it was pointed out to me earlier. I'll see you there on Sunday."

The muscles in his jaw twitched, but nothing else moved.

She raised herself on tiptoe to kiss his taut cheek. He smelled of earth and sky and leather. "Until Sunday." Before she lost her resolve, she fled to Joseph's cart and clambered in.

Joseph walked to Karl and stuck his hand out. The air around the two men charged with the electricity of the moment. "I'll get her there safe and sound. You can trust me."

They clasped hands. Karl's knuckles turned white. "I know."

Nose stinging, Marta sniffed and willed down tears.

After pulling free of Karl's grip, Joseph rubbed his right hand. "Maybe I'll even join you for church." He climbed into the cart, flicked the reins, and stared at the horizon as they pulled away.

Marta strained to keep Karl in view.

He stood with hands pressed against his stomach like it ached.

"Don't you eat any of those apples," Marta yelled. She turned until her knees were on the seat. "Or any of the other ingredients I need to make an apfelstrudel. Because when I come back here for good, Karl Reinhardt, I'm going to bake you the best one you've ever eaten!"

❀

For a month, none of Marta's sleuthing efforts bore fruit, and life fell into a routine. Monday through Saturday, she waitressed at O'Bannon's Restaurant. Sunday mornings, Karl and she attended church with Joseph—who squirmed on the pew beside her—and Annabelle Colchester, who took every opportunity to compliment Marta's quaint style and remarkable ability to sew her own clothes. Dreadful woman!

Sunday afternoon, Marta and Karl picnicked and discussed the past week. Since their affection for each other had developed over squabbles in the school yard and crying over how one father inflicted pain with his presence and the other by his absence, Karl had never before courted her. Marta liked it.

Very much.

The weeks passed without any further sabotage on the homestead or anything resembling a threat coming Marta's way, and Karl reluctantly admitted he might have been a bit overprotective. Marta held her tongue. An "I told you so" would have done nothing but damage the fragile trust Karl had extended.

Every night, Marta prayed that tomorrow would be the day she uncovered the truth so she and Karl could marry. After a month of being courted, her patience was wearing thin.

On her fourth Tuesday at O'Bannon's, the cook came down sick. Marta volunteered to help in the kitchen and make a strudel. She needed to practice rolling and stretching pastry dough, and the dried plums Ellie O'Bannon had in the pantry would work as well as dried apples.

She was lifting the hot plum strudel to the kitchen window when she overheard Karl's name.

"You think we oughta rough up Reinhardt or his place again?"

Marta sucked in a breath and pulled the pan back before it clattered on the windowsill.

"How many times do I have to tell you? It's too risky. Walsh has taken a special interest in that Vogel woman. If we rough up Reinhardt and she happens to mention it to the boss, he'll figure out what we've been up to behind his back. He'll be so mad, getting fired will be the least of our worries."

"Speakin' of that Vogel woman, ya'd think Miss Annabelle woulda given up on Reinhardt by now."

Heat from the pan burned through the towels. Marta pressed her lips together and looked around for another place to set it without making noise. Every countertop was covered with her cooking mess.

"Reinhardt is the first man who hasn't fallen in love with her at first glance. Makes him downright irresistible."

"I still think ya oughta let me smash him till he ain't a pretty boy no more."

Face scrunched and leaning at the waist, Marta panted through the pain as quietly as possible.

"Don't be stupid, Biggs. I want him to look like a failure so Miss Annabelle gets over this childish infatuation, not make her feel sorry for him by turning him into a martyr."

"What's a martyr?"

The voices faded as they argued over who was dumber: a man who didn't know what a martyr was, or one who thought Miss Annabelle would ever look at him as a suitor even if he destroyed every man within a hundred miles of Guthrie.

Marta almost tossed the strudel pan on the sill in her haste to get it away from her burning palms. But, oh, it was worth it. She wanted to find Karl that instant.

Plunging her hands into a bowl of cool water, Marta gasped. Karl thought the sabotage was proof Mr. Walsh would never settle the lawsuit out of court. If Karl was wrong about who was behind the attacks, perhaps his gloomy predictions about settling the disputed claim were wrong, too.

Ellie O'Bannon lumbered through the kitchen doors. "Och! If this babe doesn't come soon, you'll have ta slick me with oil ta get me through a doorway." As petite as her husband was large, she looked like a bread stick that swallowed a pear. Her dark hair had come loose to frame her heart-shaped face with ringlets.

"What I dinnae ken"—Marta attempted a Scottish brogue—"is why you aren't resting like Dr. Gudger said."

Ellie shook her head. "Because what the doctor dinnae ken is the hardiness of a Scots lass married to an Irish laddie." She pointed at the plum strudel. "Is that one cool enough yet?"

"I just pulled it from the oven, so it will need another half hour." Marta removed her hands from the water and patted them against her apron.

"I have two pieces of the other one left." Ellie checked the clock. "Well, if I sell out before this one is ready, I'll just tell me customers they have ta be quicker ta come in next time." She leaned against the counter and rubbed her belly. "Mr. Walsh is askin' after ye. Go on and take a wee break. You deserve it."

Grabbing at the apron strings, Marta winced. "I'm afraid I burned my hands."

"Good thing I churned unsalted butter this morning, then, isn't it? Come here, I'll put it on ye." Ellie cleared some space on the counter and pulled a blue crock from the shelf above her head.

"Sorry about the mess." Marta held out her hands. "I'll clean up before I leave."

"Not with these hands, ye won't." Ellie slathered on butter and wrapped the burns with clean strips of linen. "I'll get me mister to clean up. Since you've come, all he does is chew the fat with customers. It'll do him good to get used to hard work again before the babe comes." She winked and tied off the last strip. "Take as much time as ye want for your break. It'll give the butter time ta work. Just promise me you'll return the favor if I ever *do* get stuck."

Marta kissed her friend's cheek. "*Danke.*"

"Och and away wi' ye."

As she made her way across the restaurant, Marta greeted everyone she knew by asking after their children or how they were recovering from various ailments. It took her five minutes to get to Mr. Walsh's usual table by the window, but it gave her time to figure out what to do about the conversation she overheard. She decided to tell him everything and watch for his reaction. If he was surprised—genuinely surprised—and as angry as Biggs and the other fellow thought, then she would at least bring up the possibility of dropping the lawsuit.

"You're quite the popular lady, Miss Vogel." Mr. Walsh stood as she approached. "Here, let me get that for you." He stepped to the opposite side of the table and pulled out the chair.

"Thank you, Mr. Walsh." She settled in and waited for him to be seated before describing what she'd heard.

He reacted as she'd hoped: surprised, shocked, and eager to assure her the scoundrels would be dealt with according to their offense.

Relief poured into her lungs. "I debated about telling you, but since you're a lawyer, I decided to tell the truth, the whole truth, and nothing but the truth."

The joke got him to smile.

"One point for me."

Mr. Walsh lowered his brows. "Excuse me?"

"Oh, it's just a little game I play whenever I see you. I like seeing a real smile instead of that halfhearted thing you usually do." Marta squashed her napkin between her wrapped hands. The fabric slipped but dropped fortuitously straight into her lap.

"I see. Do you play this game with others?"

Ellie arrived with a pitcher of sweet tea. "She doesn't have ta. She just beams her sunny smile and people can't help but smile right back. Someone started calling her 'Sunshine' awhile back, and it's catching on." She poured each of them a glass of tea without asking if they wanted it. "What would ye like for lunch?"

Mr. Walsh unfolded his napkin before placing it on his lap. "I'll take the roasted beef and fried potatoes."

Marta wrapped her hands around the glass of tea and ordered the same.

"I'll get that right out. But"—Ellie looked at Marta—"if ye hear yellin' from the kitchen, come a-runnin'. And bring butter."

Mid-gulp, Marta closed her lips before her drink spewed out. It took tremendous will to force the tea down while laughter gurgled up the same pipe. Not to mention the difficulty of holding on to a glass with bandaged hands. By the time she recovered, Ellie was gone.

"I'm curious, Miss Vogel. Why do you care about making people smile?" Mr. Walsh picked up his glass and took a sip.

Marta considered the question while she swallowed the tickle in her throat. "Two reasons, I guess. First, smiling lifts my spirits, so I assume it lifts those of the people around me. A smile is infectious and easy to give, so why not spread a little joy?"

"And second?"

She set her tea glass down then put her hands in her lap. "I think you can tell a lot about a person from their smile. In most cases, anyway."

Mr. Walsh lifted his chin. "And in my case?"

The pain in her hands forced her to unclench her fingers. "I think you sometimes give the wrong impression."

"Because of, how did you say it, that halfhearted thing I usually do?"

She nodded. "I think, maybe, Karl got the wrong impression of you."

"Ah." Mr. Walsh traced the rim of the tea glass with his fingertip. "And I got the wrong impression of Mr. Reinhardt?"

"I realize Karl hasn't made much effort to get to know people since he's been here, but he's a wonderful man. He would never lie or do anything dishonest. I went back over his letters just in case he might have done something without realizing it, but he didn't." Taking a deep breath to recover from the outburst, Marta gauged the reaction.

Mr. Walsh picked up his glass and sat back. "Let me see if I can sum up what I believe you are trying to say. You think Mr. Reinhardt and I have misjudged one another and, as a result, have a pending case which has no basis in fact. Is that correct?"

She bit her lip and nodded.

"I see. So, naturally, you are wondering if I would be willing to drop the case because I've misjudged Mr. Reinhardt."

Her heartbeat quickened. "Can you?"

He took a sip before answering. "It's not quite that simple. Once a lawsuit has been filed, there are certain procedures which must be followed. It can't just be dropped."

Her shoulders slumped.

"But. . ."

She sat straight again.

"I'll tell you what I can do."

Ellie appeared with two plates in one hand and a pitcher in the other. "Who's hungry?" She set the pitcher down first then the roast beef and potatoes. "Can I get ye anything else? More tea, perhaps?"

Mr. Walsh held up his glass. "Thank you."

With her stomach churning and teeth clenched tight, Marta shook her head and willed her friend to go away.

She didn't. After refilling Mr. Walsh's glass, Ellie placed the pitcher on top of her belly and said, "Be sure to save room for dessert. By the time you're done eating, Marta's famous plum strudel will be ready to serve."

"Famous plum strudel?" Mr. Walsh pursed his lips. "I've not heard of it, but by all means, save us two pieces."

The tiny thrill of baking success was overtaken by nausea. Marta was seconds away from stopping the sabotage and settling the lawsuit, and they were talking strudel.

"Two pieces it is." Ellie took a closer look at Marta. "You okay? Your hands hurtin'? I can bring some more butter, but I'm not sure it will help."

"I think Miss Vogel is anxious about something I was about to tell her before you brought our food."

"Well, why didn't ye say, 'Och and away wi' ye'? I'd 'ave legged it as soon as I served your hash." Ellie waddled toward the kitchen, still talking to herself.

Marta opened her lips enough to croak, "Please."

Mr. Walsh cut into his beef. "Ah, yes. Here's what I can do." He set down the silverware, leaving meat impaled on his fork. "I'm on good terms with all the judges in town. They often have cancellations. Though they like to take the next case on their docket, I'm quite sure I can convince at least one of them to try this little case ahead of schedule. I believe we can have it resolved quite nicely by the end of the week. Will that do?"

Joy bubbled through her whole being. "Yes. Oh yes." Karl would be so *pleased*! If not for the inherent rudeness of it, she would leave Mr. Walsh where he sat and hire someone to drive her to the homestead. Instead, she lifted her tea like a champagne flute, ignoring the pain in her palms, and saluted Mr. Walsh. "To getting things settled."

He raised his glass to meet hers and smiled, showing his teeth. "To getting things settled."

Chapter 8

It took every last shred of her patience, but Marta allowed Mr. Walsh to finish his lunch without pulling the plate from beneath his fingers and shooing him back to his office. The instant he left the table to pay, she grabbed the empty plates and headed for the kitchen. Her palms stung, but the pain was insignificant in comparison to the burning desire to tell Karl what she had learned. If everything went as planned, they could stand up at the end of church service on Sunday and be married. Five more days—just five more—and she would be Mrs. Karl Reinhardt!

Mr. Walsh hadn't promised a resolution by the end of the week. A man running for mayor had to be true to his word, he said, but he would do his best.

With a prayer of thanksgiving on her lips, Marta waltzed into the kitchen and nearly fell on top of Ellie, who was sitting by the door. "Oh! I'm sorry. Did I hurt you? Are you all right?"

"I'm fine. I think the bairn is comin'." Ellie laid her head against the wall and pinched the bridge of her nose while taking shallow breaths. Perspiration beaded on her forehead and dampened her dark curls.

Marta dropped to her knees. "Here, let me help you up so we can get you to Dr. Gudger."

"Get Thom." Ellie pressed her lips together and started to moan.

"Right. Right. Thom." Marta stood and rushed back into the restaurant area. "Thom!"

Thom, along with everyone else in the room, turned to see what the commotion was about. He smiled with his whole face. "If you'll excuse me, ladies and gents, I think it's time to welcome a certain wee lad into the world."

Applause broke out. Thom squeezed his bulk past tables, pausing to shake hands or accept a congratulatory word on his way to the kitchen.

Marta saw Mr. Walsh through the front windows. He was climbing into his carriage. She zigzagged through the restaurant and out the door just as he was about to snap the reins. "Mr. Walsh! Mr. Walsh!"

He struggled to control his horses. "Stop yelling, girl."

Stunned at the reprimand, even though it was deserved, Marta offered her apologies. "Ellie O'Bannon needs to get to Dr. Gudger right away. Can I trouble you to take her?"

Instead of acquiescing with his usual polite smile, he rubbed his index finger against his bottom lip. "Will you be staying with your friend until the child is born?"

Why did he care? "Yes."

"Then, let us get Mrs. O'Bannon to the good doctor."

Marta thanked him and rushed back to tell Thom and Ellie what she'd done.

"Good thinking, lass." Thom lifted his wife to her feet. "Come, love. Let's meet Mr. Thomas Patrick O'Bannon, the fourth."

"Or Aileen Margaret," Ellie and Marta said in unison, as they had for the past three weeks every time Thom insisted the coming babe was a boy.

Five minutes later, they had Ellie in the back of Mr. Walsh's carriage. Marta started to climb up beside her, but Ellie put up a hand to block the way. "Can you take charge of the restaurant?"

"But. . . I want to make sure you're all right." Marta stepped down onto the road.

Ellie frowned. "Make sure? Do ye think ye can make sure things turn out the way ye want them by bein' on the spot? 'Tis a foolish notion, for sure and for certain."

The carriage rocked as Thom climbed up beside Mr. Walsh. "We ready to meet Thomas Patrick?"

"Or Aileen Margaret," Ellie said, solo this time. "Will ye handle things here, or do I need ta ask Thom ta stay?"

Put that way, how could Marta refuse? "I'll stay. You just get Miss Aileen O'Bannon into the world safely."

Ellie nodded. "I'll do me best, but 'tis in God's hands, and you'd do well ta remember it."

For the rest of the afternoon and evening, as Marta waited tables, cooked, or did the thousand and one other chores needed to keep the restaurant running while her hands stung, the admonishment repeated in her ears.

The dinner crowd lingered until Thom came back beaming over the arrival of Aileen Margaret O'Bannon. By the time Marta made it to the boardinghouse, it was after eleven, and she was exhausted.

The room seemed messier than usual. She lit the oil lamp by the bed and wiped grit from her eyes. It didn't help. Clothes were still strewn about, her satchel wilted off one edge of the desk, and her sewing kit dripped thread from her latest mending project. All of it the mess of her own making, yet something was off.

Maybe she was so tired she was seeing double, which accounted for why her things seemed to have shifted.

A letter sat on her pillow.

My beautiful Marta,

Reginald Walsh came by the homestead to tell me we have a court date for tomorrow morning. I decided to get our letters to prove where I was and when. No need for you to come to the trial, I heard you had quite an exciting day with the new baby and taking charge of O'Bannon's Restaurant. Sleep well.

I love you,
Karl

Marta read the letter twice. Something about it was off, too. She held the page closer to the oil lamp then looked over at the desk where the pencil stub she'd found on the train sat next to the satchel.

Her weary brain pieced together what happened. Not wishing to disturb her during such a hectic day, Karl must have rummaged through the room looking for the letters and then didn't want her to worry about an intruder, so he left a note. The pencil stub was too small for his hands, so his penmanship was shaky instead of precise.

But still, something wasn't right. Why would he tell her not to come to the trial? Of course she would be there.

Except she had promised to work at the restaurant until Ellie could come back to work.

Her heart started to race. She couldn't do both.

"Do ye think ye can make sure things turn out the way ye want them by bein' on the spot? 'Tis a foolish notion, for sure and for certain." Ellie's words repeated like a phonograph playing the same song over and over again.

Taking a deep breath, Marta forced calm into her lungs. The simple solution was to be at the restaurant early, get through breakfast, prepare sandwiches ahead of the lunch crowd, and ask Thom for an hour off. A little court case—one where some formalities needed to be observed so it could be properly dismissed—couldn't take more than an hour, surely.

She undressed and tossed the food-stained shirtwaist and skirt on top of yesterday's outfit. After wriggling into her nightgown, she removed the pins from her hair and dropped them on the bedside table before kneeling beside the bed.

"Most gracious heavenly Father, thank You for Your many blessings today. I would count them all, but I'm afraid I'll fall asleep halfway through the list. That doesn't make me less grateful. And I hope You don't mind me skipping straight to asking for another blessing. It's about the trial tomorrow. Please. . ." The words *"let it turn out how I want"* died on her lips.

She would never say something like that to God. She was just tired. And Ellie's words got twisted up somehow.

Marta squeezed her hands tighter, intent on proving her sincerity by enduring the pain in her aching palms as she whispered, "Thy will be done."

She scrambled into bed, but sleep wouldn't come. At first she thought it was the nagging sense of "offness" about Karl's letter. He would laugh at her made-up word, but it was the best she could come up with in her exhaustion.

The more she tossed and turned, though, the more she felt the conviction of Ellie's question. Did she think she could control an outcome with her presence?

Recalling the months she'd spent apart from Karl as proof, she consoled herself she wasn't so foolish. But another voice nagged that her restraint only lasted as long as things were going according to plan.

She'd turned down Karl's proposal and left him to take care of the homestead. That was proof, right?

Except it was so she could manage things in town.

But everything worked out. By tomorrow, the men responsible for sabotaging Karl would be fired and on their way out of town, and the lawsuit would be dismissed.

Which confirmed—much as she hated to admit it—that she really did assume her presence could make things turn out how she wanted. Something she'd been guilty of thinking ever since she failed to prevent her father's accident. How many times had Mutter said it was no one's fault, and how many times had Marta nodded her head while her heart refused to let go of the blame?

She cringed, remembering her lecture to Karl about his controlling nature. It was time to take the log out of her own eye.

Tired as she was, Marta returned to kneeling beside the bed. "I can't promise I will be better at trusting You all at once, Lord, but I promise to try. To prove it, I'm going to stay at the restaurant tomorrow instead of going to court. I pray that, whatever happens there, it will be. . ." Oh, this trusting business was so much harder than how it sounded in sermons. She squeezed her hands tighter. "I pray it will be for my good, for Karl's good, and for Your glory. Amen."

She climbed back into bed wishing she had a wonderful sense of peace, but her hands were shaking, and her heart thumped so hard the bedcovers bounced.

Chapter 9

Karl didn't like it. Not one bit.

He sat behind the defendant's desk on a hard courtroom chair and waited for Judge Marlow to appear.

No, he didn't like this at all. But he wasn't sure if it was because he'd gotten everything wrong.

The attacks on his homestead had stopped.

Marta hadn't been harmed in any way. In fact, she was thriving.

Things were going well, when he'd predicted disaster.

Even his ribs had healed without a visit to the doctor.

And now Walsh—after months of saying he wasn't quite ready to present his case—was not only ready but eager to go before a judge.

Karl scanned faces around the room. He didn't recognize any of them. There was no jury; his fate rested with one man. One judge. At least it wasn't Judge Parker. Where was Marta? It wasn't like her to miss something this big. Not when it was the whole purpose for her coming to town. He'd sent Samuels to find her, and he wasn't back yet.

Karl tapped his thumbs together. It didn't add up.

He shouldn't have eaten breakfast. Much as he appreciated Fine's fresh eggs, they were rolling around in his stomach like he'd swallowed them with the shells still on.

"All rise for the honorable Judge Terrance Marlow."

Karl stood. His stomach didn't come with him. It stayed at the level of his knees and didn't return to its rightful place when he sat down again.

Walsh called witness after witness to testify that Karl had not been seen on the line running between the Oklahoma Territory and Kansas either before or on the day of the land run. Karl started to relax. Just because people didn't remember him didn't mean he wasn't there. Once he got to testify, he would recount the details of his time on the line.

God, let it be enough.

"I call Karl Reinhardt to the stand."

Praying for strength and wisdom, he came from behind the table and made his way to the witness stand, where he promised to tell the truth, the whole truth, and nothing but the truth. .

When he sat down, Walsh approached with an envelope in his hand. "Mr. Reinhardt. Is this your handwriting?"

It looked like his handwriting, but he was reluctant to say so. "May I see that?"

"Certainly." Walsh handed it over with a small smile.

The envelope was addressed to Marta. "Where did you get this?" Karl's heart thumped against his rib cage.

"I'll ask the questions, Mr. Reinhardt."

Judge Marlow leaned over. "Actually, since Mr. Reinhardt is acting as his own lawyer, I'm going to give him a little leeway here. But his question will be answered after yours, Mr. Walsh."

Walsh inclined his head in acknowledgment. "Certainly, Your Honor. Mr. Reinhardt, I asked if this is your handwriting."

The envelope was genuine, but Karl pulled out the letter to be sure it was, too.

March 21, 1889

Dear Marta,

I have arrived safely in Kansas. There are more people here than can fit in one place. I have purchased some—

"Well, Mr. Reinhardt. Is this your handwriting or not?" Walsh tapped the letter.

Why did he keep asking about the handwriting? Karl studied the penmanship. It was his, except it looked like the fifth-grade version when he had to work too hard to form each character. He remembered writing this on his thigh, which might explain the forced lettering. "It's my handwriting." Though he couldn't believe Marta would simply hand over a letter to Walsh.

"And do you remember writing to Miss Marta Vogel on March 21, 1889?"

Karl turned to Judge Marlow. "I thought you said he needed to answer my question now."

Walsh didn't give the judge a chance to speak. "So he did, so he did. My apologies. I obtained several letters from Miss Vogel. She didn't believe you were capable of willful dishonesty and wondered if perhaps you had done something illegal without realizing it."

"So she just gave you my letters?"

"May I ask my next question?" Walsh addressed the judge.

"It is his turn, Mr. Reinhardt." Judge Marlow held out his hand. "I'd like to see the letter, please."

Tamping down his temper, Karl handed it over. "Yes sir."

After the judge perused the letter for a moment, he gave it back to Walsh. "I assume you are entering this into evidence?"

"Yes, Your Honor." Walsh unfolded the paper. "Mr. Reinhardt, do you recall writing to Miss Marta Vogel on"—he checked the top page—"March 21, 1889?"

"Yes." The question was too easy. What was Walsh after?

"And do you remember the contents of your communication?"

Karl narrowed his focus. "In general, yes. But I wrote that over a year ago, as well as several other letters, so I might not recall my exact words."

Walsh's smug half smile made Karl want to smash something. Preferably that smug half smile.

"Then allow me to refresh your memory, Mr. Reinhardt." After unfolding the letter, Walsh began to read. " 'Dear Marta, I have arrived safely in Kansas. There are more people here than can fit in one place. I purchased some oxen and named them Bruno and Ollie.' " He looked up. "Did you write these words to Miss Vogel, Mr. Reinhardt?"

Again, the question was too easy. "Yes."

"And how about these?" Walsh returned his attention to the letter. " 'I took a train ride today. The land near Guthrie is perfect. I even saw a dugout.' " He looked up again. "Did you write these words, too?"

Karl searched his brain for some truthful reason to say no. It wasn't there. But he felt like he was being led by the nose down a long, narrow chute to slaughter. "There was nothing illegal about taking a train ride at the time."

Walsh took a step back. "I simply asked if you wrote to Miss Vogel that you took a train ride."

"Please answer the question as asked, Mr. Reinhardt." Judge Marlow smoothed the edges of his mustache.

Karl bounced his heel against the floor. "Yes, I wrote about the train ride."

"And seeing the dugout?" Walsh pressed.

Behind Walsh, Joseph Samuels entered the courtroom. He shook his head and mouthed, "She ain't comin'."

There was only one reason Marta wasn't coming. She'd handed the letters over to Walsh and knew Karl would be livid. Well, he was. "Yes."

"I'm surprised to hear you admit that, Mr. Reinhardt, considering what comes next." Walsh stepped closer.

"What?" Karl jerked his attention away from Samuels.

"It says"—Walsh ran his finger along the words—" 'I even saw a dugout. It's not much on the inside, but it is perfect for my needs. Bruno and Ollie are staying inside with me until I can get a barn built, so the stench is—' "

"Wait one second!" Karl jumped to his feet. He'd been so stunned, it took a second to register what Walsh was saying. "I didn't write that."

"You never described your dugout to Miss Vogel?"

"Well, yes, but not in that letter."

Walsh lifted the paper above his head like a banner. "Let me see if I understand you correctly. You admitted this is your handwriting. You admitted you wrote to Miss Vogel on March 21, 1889. You admitted writing to her about taking a train ride and seeing a dugout. And now you say you did write to Miss Vogel about the dugout but not in this letter."

"That's right."

Walsh's smile revealed his crooked teeth. "But didn't you also say you wrote several letters to Miss Vogel, and you couldn't recall exactly what information was in which?"

∞

"It is the ruling of this court that Karl Reinhardt illegally claimed Section 29 of Township 16 North of Range 2 West. He is hereby stripped of ownership and ordered to remove his personal property by sundown tomorrow." Judge Marlow whacked his desk with the gavel, and the courtroom erupted in cheers.

Karl sagged into the chair behind him. Everything that made him a man had been ripped from inside, leaving nothing but skin. He couldn't move. Couldn't think. Couldn't do anything but listen to every congratulations and "You've got my vote, Mr. Walsh," until his ears rang.

By the time Karl recovered enough to speak, he and Walsh were the only ones left in the courtroom. "Do you even want my land?"

"Want your land?" Walsh eyed Karl like he was the class dunce. "I had three offers to purchase it from me before I walked in here this morning."

"So this was about what? Votes?"

Walsh slipped papers into his briefcase. All but one. He tossed an envelope onto the table with Marta's address facing up. "An interesting theory. One that will be quite impossible to prove, I assure you." He buckled the top flap of his briefcase and took a step toward the exit. "I wouldn't be too hard on Miss Vogel for not being by your side this morning. She was only obeying your instructions not to come."

"What?" Karl lurched upright, his spine returning to its place by force. "What instructions?"

"Why, the ones you left in a note on her pillow when you went into her room last night to retrieve your letters." Walsh inclined his well-oiled head in mock courtesy before leaving the room.

Karl covered his mouth with his palm. He twisted to lean his elbow on the hard table before the weight of his head was too much to bear. Groans escaped from under his hand. No matter how hard he pressed, the gasping wheezed through his fingers and blew against his neck. He stared at the ceiling and blinked, but tears leaked from his eyes and pooled between his fingers and cheeks.

He tightened every muscle, compressed his lips and eyes, but the anguish built stronger and threatened to shatter his chest.

Since he was alone, Karl laid his head on the table and let the sobs shudder through his body.

He'd lost. Everything. And, if he understood Walsh's insinuations, the letters—the real letters—Karl planned to show a judge as grounds for an appeal had been stolen and no longer existed.

What was he going to do? He had no money to buy another farm or start a clock repair shop. If he sold Bruno and Ollie and everything else not sewn into the land, he might have enough to limp back to Pennsylvania and his father's rebuke.

All because Marta came to Guthrie and brought his letters.

He should have forced her to go home, if not that first day then every day after. Instead, he let her talk him into this cockamamie plan to stay and help.

"I'm so sorry, Karl." Her voice whispered in his ear.

He hadn't heard her come in over the sniveling filling his ears. Though it wasn't the first—or even the second—time she'd found him dripping from eyes and nose, he detested it whenever she saw him cowering. He wiped the proof of failure from his face and straightened his spine.

She sat in the chair beside his with red-rimmed eyes, flyaway curls, and flour-streaked cheeks. He hated her for being so beautiful, for comforting him with her presence despite being partially responsible for his grief, but mostly for the way he loved her too much. "Joseph told me what happened. I didn't give Mr. Walsh the letters, I swear. We had lunch yesterday, and I remember saying something about checking them. I never dreamed he would steal them and—oh, that. . .that beast! He must have forged the letter saying not to come today. I knew there was something wrong with it. The wording was too formal. Even if I hadn't been so tired last night I couldn't see straight, I don't know. . . I mean, how could I guess?" Her penitent eyes pleaded for forgiveness. "Mr. Walsh was always so nice to me. I thought he would help. I was just trying to help."

Hot anger poured into his torso and spread to his limbs. He used it to push against the table and stand.

She reached out to touch his hand.

He jerked it away. "If you wanted to help, you should have stayed at home and let me fix this my way."

Chapter 10

Marta reeled at the rebuke. A beating from his clenched fists would hurt less, yet her arms ached to absorb his shock and anger. She'd never seen that shade of steel in his blue eyes, and it killed her to be the cause.

There were no words to make up for his loss, so she offered her hand again. "Can we. . .can we take a minute?"

He stumbled backward, keeping upright by pushing his fingers against the table. "Leave me be, Marta. There aren't enough minutes for this one." He shuffled to the door but couldn't get past Joseph Samuels, who blocked his way with a scowl. Karl's shoulders hunched. "Get out of my way."

"Not until I blister your ears for bein' a fool."

Marta held her breath while the two men faced off like bulls in the same pasture.

"I mean it, Karl." Joseph growled and pointed a finger. "You go on and set your hindquarters back in that there chair before I make you."

Karl's shoulders inched down. "That's the first time you've called me by my first name."

"Then don't make me regret it." Joseph jabbed his finger toward the front of the courtroom.

After tapping his hand against his thigh for what seemed like a full minute, Karl turned on his heel and marched back to his seat beside her. He plopped down and crossed his arms on the tabletop.

Joseph tossed his Stetson onto the table in front of them. "How many weeks is it you've done dragged me to church and made me listen to the preacher man?" He stared down at them. "I'll tell you how many. It's four. Four hours a' sittin' and singin' and squirmin' to hear about how this God both a' you claim to follow can work all things together for good. Am I rememberin' that right? It is all things, ain't it?"

Marta nodded and angled her gaze to watch Karl's head bob once.

Joseph harrumphed. "Then I got me two questions, and I want answers from the both a' you. First, is somethin' good 'cause it turns out the way *you* want? And second, does all things workin' out mean *all* things or only the things you can figure out and do for yourself?"

"Do ye think ye can make sure things turn out the way ye want them by bein' on the spot? 'Tis a foolish notion, for sure and for certain. . .'tis in God's hands, and you'd do well ta remember it." At the memory of Ellie's lecture, Marta shifted on the seat. *"Ye brought birds? All the way from Pennsylvania? Didn't ye think God could provide ye with some here?"*

409

God could provide but maybe not the way Marta wanted. So she packed and picked up more and more stuff just in case.

God could watch over Karl but maybe not as well as He would if she hopped a train to help.

God could work things together for good but maybe not all—not a father dying or an honest man losing his land to a lying thief.

"I'm waitin' on you." Joseph scratched his whiskers, sending a shushing sound through the quiet room.

Karl heaved a sigh. "It's the essence of faith to believe God can do what you can't do for yourself."

"Alrighty, then. Marta," Joseph said, impaling her with his stare, "what about you?"

Her answer came from the place in her heart bruised by prodding. "I believe God always does what is good, but I struggle to let it reach my heart and turn into actions."

"Good girl." Joseph winked and gave her a gap-toothed grin. "Then I got me a solution to this whole mess, but it's gonna take some bendin' on your part." He pulled an envelope from his hip pocket and slapped it on the table. "Got a letter from my old boss in Montana. Seems his ranch is recoverin' after the '88 blizzard, and he needs ranch hands."

Karl sat back and rubbed his hands together. "I'd be worse at ranching than you were at farming."

"Then it's a good thing I weren't thinkin' about you." Joseph jutted his chin. "I still ain't no good at farmin', so. . .whaddaya say I go back where I belong an' you two take over my place?"

∞

Stunned, Karl braced his hands against his thighs. "Absolutely not." He was grateful for the offer, but it was too much.

Marta kicked his shin under the table and glowered at him. "Don't be hasty, Karl. This isn't about what you want, it's about what our friend needs." She gave him an interrupt-again-and-I'll-kick-harder smile before returning her attention to Samuels. "Go on, Joseph."

"If it helps, you can think of it as winnin' a case instead a' losin' it." Joseph pulled a chair from across the aisle and sat down like he was straddling a horse. "Or, better yet, as pullin' a fast one on Walsh."

Karl struggled to put pieces together. "What are you saying?"

Joseph shrugged. "I'm a Boomer."

The admission took a moment to sink into Karl's brain. "Why didn't you tell me?"

"Well, now, you ain't exactly been quiet about your views on Boomers and Sooners, have you? I'm guessin' that's how Walsh got so many people to speak against you." Joseph wagged a finger at the vacant benches behind them. "Three-quarters a' the folks in town are Sooners, maybe more. So are most a' the homesteaders close to town. Somebody like you, what done things legal like and ain't shy about sayin' so, makes 'em nervous."

Everything was starting to make sense. Perfect, horrible sense. Karl rubbed at the tension above his eyebrows. "So, getting rid of me garners Walsh votes from those who hate me for being legal and those who hate me because they think I claimed land illegally."

Marta gasped. "Votes? This was about votes?"

It was so close to what Karl said when he figured it out, the absurdity of it shoved against the anger trapped inside his chest. "Not that he will ever admit it." He recounted what Walsh said when the two of them were alone, including the veiled admission to stealing Marta's letters.

When he was done, Marta pounded a fist into the palm of her hand. "And I thought sabotaging your land to make you look bad in front of Annabelle Colchester was the worst it could get."

"Huh?" Karl and Joseph said in unison.

She explained what she'd overheard in O'Bannon's kitchen the day before and how it—stupidly—made her think Mr. Walsh was innocent of any wrongdoing.

Though he thought it naive, Karl at least understood her reasons for the misplaced trust. And it was what made Marta special. She always saw such good in people that she put everyone around her at ease. Made them like her. Made them remember her. If she had come with him from the beginning, there would have been at least one or two people to testify they saw the Reinhardts on the Oklahoma/Kansas line the day of the run. A little more anger escaped with his next breath. "What a mess."

Joseph propped his elbows on the chair back and folded his hands together. "Yup. But, like I said, I got a solution if you ain't too proud to take it."

Heel bouncing against the hardwood floor, Karl held his peace to avoid getting kicked again.

"Go on, Joseph." Marta reached over and put her hand on Karl's jumpy knee.

Tension shifted from his upper half to his lower half. He pressed his heel hard against the floor and did his best to ignore the freckled hand. "I'm listening."

Eyes lit with amusement, Joseph scooted his chair a little closer to the table. "Like I said, I'm what you would call a Boomer. I had my reasons at the time, though I ain't sayin' they was the right ones. After what I seen happen to my cattle during the '88 blizzard"—his eyes went dull—"I needed to see somethin' else for a spell." He coughed and rubbed the end of his nose. "But now I'm ready to go home."

Marta reached across the table to touch his forearm. "I'm so sorry, Joseph. It must have been terrible."

Gray tinged his skin. "Horrible. Beyond-words horrible. But it sent me here, and now I got a chance to make up for what I done. Look, Karl, you spent as much time sowin' my crops as you did your own. It ain't no charity. It might even be one a' them 'all things' that's gonna work for your good."

Karl nudged Marta's hand away so he could think. Accepting such a gift went against his nature. A man provided for himself. He took care of his own. He didn't rely on others.

"And it ain't just your good I'm thinkin' about." Joseph picked up the forged letter lying on the table between them. "This here ain't right. Walsh is a—" He broke off and grinned sheepishly at Marta.

"Shyster?" The way she said it made whatever cuss word Joseph cut off seem tame.

"—and I don't want him to get away with it. Maybe you can't convince people before this here election, but a man like him ain't gonna be satisfied bein' mayor for long. My guess, he's aimin' higher. I might be intent on leavin' Oklahoma, but I got enough loyalty that, once she becomes a state, I'd just as soon her first US senator not be a lyin', thievin' snake of a man. Now"—Joseph pounded a fist on the table, making his hat jump—"do you want my claim or not, Karl Reinhardt?"

"It is the essence of faith to believe God can do what you can't do for yourself. And," Karl amended his earlier thought, *"in a way mere mortals can neither comprehend nor accomplish on their own."* Because the essence of faith was also believing God turned sin into salvation for those willing to bend their knees to His sovereignty.

God used stealing, forgery, selfish ambition, and an illegal claim—as well as a bit too much German stubbornness—to provide land with better water access and a bigger dugout. If he wasn't too stubborn to take it.

Humbling his pride, Karl nodded. "I do."

"And do you want to marry Marta even though she don't know better than to pack for eight people instead a' one and trusts people what ought not be trusted sometimes?"

Mirth worked its way up Karl's throat. "I do."

"And do you promise to love, honor, and help her get the knowledge that God is always good from her head down to her heart and into her actions?"

Karl took Marta's hand and intertwined their fingers. Since he was saying his vows, he wanted the connection. "I do."

Joseph turned to Marta. "Do you wanna marry Karl even though he'll drive you crazy with wantin' things done just so?"

"Just a minute." She reached into her pocket and pulled out a scrap of fabric. "Ellie used it to bind my hand when. . .never mind." She dabbed at the corner of her eye. "I do."

"And do you promise to love, honor, and remind him that sometimes things work out in spite a' his fussin'?"

Marta laughed aloud. "I do."

"Alrighty then." Joseph stood and swung the chair under the table in one motion. "Let's get the judge so we can make this here legal."

"I think you forgot one thing." Karl rose and pulled Marta to her feet. Letting go of her hand, he faced her then put his hands on her waist. "I've been waiting to do this for a long, long time."

She wrapped her hands around the back of his neck. Her smile beamed warmth and light into the corners of his soul. "Me, too."

Awed by the holiness of the moment, Karl kissed his promised bride.

Epilogue

Karl came into the dugout to find Marta asleep in the new rocking chair, her hands resting on the slight swell of their new babe. Little Ingrid slept on the bed with her thumb tucked inside her mouth.

He tiptoed to the stove and poured himself a cup of coffee. Last night's strudel sat beside the coffeepot under a cloth. He cut himself a slice and crossed to the table to eat.

Marta had started a letter to her mother. So far, she'd written four pages full of news: Ingrid's latest antics; how well the crops were faring; how the leftover laundry water was hardening the floors and walls of the dugout; how much she enjoyed the new window she talked her stubborn husband into, especially since it allowed her to watch their home being built.

With a smirk, he turned the page.

As he suspected, she gave a detailed account of what it took to convince that same stubborn husband to add a parlor to his original house plans. Karl still didn't get it. The chances of entertaining were so small, why build a whole room for it? But Marta insisted it was the precise reason she needed a parlor. It made no sense, but he was done arguing with a pregnant woman. Besides, she'd become so thrifty, he could afford to make her happy.

Page three included the scandal when Annabelle Colchester ran off with Milliken, and Mr. Walsh's failure to be reelected as mayor.

Karl picked up the pen and added "which is better than the shyster deserved" above Marta's scrawl. Then he fixed the top loop of her *h* characters in Colchester and Walsh.

He finished the letter and his snack at the same time, not sure which satisfied more, the sweet strudel or the little descriptions summing up the richness of their lives together.

On the bottom of the last page, Karl added a postscript to his mother-in-law:

I know I've told you before, but thank you again for fulfilling your promise to teach Marta how to make good apfelstrudel. She baked one last night. Ingrid and I "helped," which made the whole process take longer, but it was definitely worth the wait.

Becca Whitham (WIT-um) Award-winning author, paper crafter, and Army wife, Becca currently resides in Washington State with her husband and a twelve-foot long craft cabinet she thinks should count as a dependent. So far, neither the Army nor the IRS is convinced. In between moves from one part of the country to the other, she writes stories combining faith and fiction that touch the heart. You can find her online at www.beccawhitham.com.

THE BOGUS BRIDE
OF CREED CREEK

by Kathleen Y'Barbo

Dedication

For the widows and orphans
And for those whose fears keep them living a lie,
May they all find freedom and provision in Him.

And the LORD said unto me, Arise, take thy journey before the people, that they may go in and possess the land, which I sware unto their fathers to give unto them.
DEUTERONOMY 10:11

Chapter 1

Creed Creek, Texas
June 20, 1880

With the wagon wheels rolling toward the home where she'd finally find some peace, Cora Duncan barely noticed the slow pace the trail required. Twice the nausea she put off to a combination of the summer sun and the nearness of her goal required her to stop.

The wagon reached Creed Creek, and suddenly the land she'd come so far to claim lay before her. The smattering of green along the edge of the creek gave way to an expanse of grassland swaying in golden waves in the breeze. Here and there rocky outcroppings punctuated the plains, but Cora saw no sign of the ranch house that factored heavily in her father's stories.

Her father built the two-story wood-frame house for Mama when they were first married, or at least he'd claimed to. And now she would finally live under its roof.

Cora flicked the reins and urged the horse forward. As she passed beneath the iron arch that proclaimed the entrance to McBride Ranch, she held her head high. Someday soon the name on the arch would be replaced with one that showed the world the property had been returned to its rightful owner. In the meantime, Cora would settle for knowing in her heart that she was home and that no man could take that home from her.

Not ever again.

The moment passed, and Cora set her mind on more practical thoughts. Indeed, she'd planned to reclaim the land her father had lost. That he'd chosen to use his last hours to write a letter stating she'd married the old codger who took it was beyond the pale.

She let out a long breath and studied her options. Telling the truth—that Israel McBride was dead and gone—came to mind. She could do that, but then she'd have to explain how she knew.

A bird's cry lifted her attention skyward where the warmth of the summer sun assailed her in unrelenting waves. She swiped at her brow and prayed for a breeze. Up ahead the trail wound through a scrub of low-growing trees, giving her a brief respite from the heat before sending her back into the June afternoon.

Drawing back on the reins, she negotiated the sharp turn then pulled back and stopped the wagon at the sight of the building directly ahead. This was no beautiful ranch house. Rather, the structure appeared to be made of bricks fashioned from dried mud, with bits of twigs and tree branches. A thin plume of smoke trailed from a makeshift chimney in the center of the structure, and an orange cat eyed her warily from an overturned bucket near the door.

Surely this was not the home her father had built. No, it couldn't be. The place seemed substantial despite the materials used to construct it, but in no way did it match her father's tales.

Perhaps the caretaker lived here. Or maybe one of the ranch hands.

Encouraged, Cora flicked the reins and set the wagon into motion. Just over the rise, she spied a smudge of black that gradually formed into the burned ruins of some sort of structure. As she neared the site, Cora's heart sank.

It was a house. Or what was left of one.

From what remained, she could see that the porch had been long and broad, the house generous in proportion yet not overlarge. *Just the right size for a family.* Cora pushed away the thought along with the desire to climb down and take a closer look.

Instead, she circled the wagon around and returned to the sod structure she spied earlier.

Other than the distant lowing of cattle, all was quiet. Even the orange cat was no longer around.

She knocked twice, and the door slid open on hinges that could use a good oiling. The interior was dim, the light slanting away from the door and bidding her follow. Though the exterior appeared primitive, the walls inside had been whitewashed to encourage a bright interior. Wood covered the floor beneath her feet, but a lovely rug colored in russets and blues hid most of it.

"Hello?" Cora called into the silence as she moved through the front room with its stiff rosewood furniture and the mantel clock that needed winding. A faint odor of chimney smoke permeated the room and threatened to cause her to lose what little she had eaten at her last meal. She looked around for a cookstove but found only a fireplace that appeared to do dual service, as witnessed by the cast-iron pot situated in the coals.

Something thudded against the wall, and Cora jumped. Before she could call out, footsteps came bounding toward her. She stepped out of the shadows in time to be greeted by a big brown dog.

"Well, hello," she said as she scratched the mutt's head. "Where's your owner?"

" 'Taint here."

Cora looked up to see a woman standing in the doorway. Her gray hair and weathered face belied the twinkle in her eyes. This she hadn't counted on. Did Israel McBride already have a wife? He was certainly old enough to have wed this woman, though the mayor hadn't mentioned that fact.

"You the new missus the boss wrote me about?"

Cora paused only a moment before nodding. How Pa managed this, she'd never know. "I'm sorry," she said, "but I don't know who you are."

The woman lifted a thin hand to her chest and chuckled. "Mercy, where's my manners? I'm Rosella, but you can call me Rosie. And that there's Buster. He don't do much but bark and beg for leftovers." She gestured toward the dog now making circles around Cora's skirts. "Looks like you've made a friend there, Miss Lavinia."

"Lavinia?" Cora shook her head. "No, I'm. . ."

She paused. A new life, a new name. Just like in the Bible. But the Bible never condoned a lie, did it?

"Cora," she said as she opted for the truth. "Cora Duncan."

"That'd be McBride, wouldn't it?" Rosie said.

"Y—yes, I suppose it would." The statement felt less well intentioned under Rosie's stare than it had when she'd made it to the mayor.

Another moment's scrutiny, and Rosie gave a curt nod before heading for the open front door. After peering outside she returned to stand before Cora. "Where's Iz?"

"Iz?"

"That's what I said." The housekeeper's eyes barely blinked as she once again studied Cora. "Israel McBride. Your husband. You sure you ain't named Lavinia? 'Cause I declare, he called you that in both the letters he wrote."

"I can't account for that." Cora shrugged then knelt to pet the impatient canine. The diversion served to give her a place to look other than into the older woman's miss-nothing eyes. "As for Mr. McBride, he's been delayed."

"Delayed?" The older woman's skirts appeared at the edge of Cora's vision. "He didn't mention any delays."

"Yes, well, I'm sure he will write you directly," she managed as she stood. "In the meantime, I don't suppose you'd tell me exactly what it is you do here."

If the change of conversation startled Rosie, she didn't show it. Rather, she grinned. "I guess you'd say I'm the day help. I feed the chickens, cook the meals, and clean up after the mister when it needs doin'. 'Course, it was easier done when Iz had a proper house. It burned back just before Christmas. Lightning strike."

"I see."

So the home had been nice. Once.

The scent of smoke still danced around her. Cora let out a long breath and prayed for her stomach to settle.

"Don't you worry none," Rosie said. "Iz, he's goin' to rebuild. You won't be livin' in this place any longer than it takes him to set that old home place back to rights."

With McBride buried back in East Texas, there would be no rebuilding of the old home place unless she saw to it. Until then, this oversized hut of grass and dirt would be her home. Somehow it seemed a fitting end to a trail filled with lies. The room swayed, and Cora grasped tightly to the back of a chair.

Seemingly oblivious to Cora's discomfort, Rosie nodded toward the parlor. "Don't judge my skills by the state of them rooms. It ain't needed doin' until someone came along who might sit there. First thing tomorrow I'll shine old Miz McBride's parlor setup nice and pretty. What's left of it, that is."

"Thank you."

"Don't need no thanks for what I do," she said good-naturedly. "Now, where are your things? And who have you got with you? I'll be needin' a head count so's I can know how many to cook for."

"It's just me," Cora said.

"Just you?" Iron-gray brows gathered. "What's a lady of quality doing traveling all by herself?"

Caught.

The word stuck in her mind and froze in her throat as she tried to decide on a response that might convince Rosie she was no pretender to the McBride name. The longer the woman's piercing gaze swept across her, the harder Cora found it to concentrate.

Finally she leaned against the door frame and gave up altogether.

Rosie crossed her arms over her chest as the dog's tail thumped against the sideboard. "That Iz. He's working up some sort of deal with the cattle, ain't he? Always looking for a way to make this place a little better off each year. Didn't inherit that from his pa, that's for sure."

"Yes, I suppose," Cora said, though she had no idea what the woman meant by the comment. His pa?

"I can't fault him for that," Rosie said as she linked arms with Cora. "Though I'd sure like to tan his hide for not thinkin' to send you with an escort. Just don't seem like somethin' he'd do 'lessen he had a good reason."

A moment passed, and Cora felt the silence acutely. Then Rosie patted her arm and led her into a kitchen that had not suffered the neglect visited on the rest of the house.

"Sit down," she told Cora, "and I'll see what I can find to feed you. It doesn't look like you've had nothin' worth rememberin' in way too long."

"Thank you," Cora managed as she watched Rosie shoo the dog outside. Exhaustion tugged at her the moment she settled onto the chair. She was home. The journey had ended.

Tonight she would sleep, and tomorrow she'd begin her new life as mistress of the Circle M. Or perhaps she would find a better plan, one that did not involve spending her days—and her nights—beneath a sod roof.

"Got some fried chicken left over from yesterday and some good buttered biscuits. Been soakin' a mess of peas for tomorrow, but I can throw 'em on to cook, if you don't mind waitin' awhile to enjoy 'em."

The idea of greasy chicken caused Cora's stomach to roil. "Maybe just a biscuit."

"Apple jelly, or some of the widow Smith's pepper jelly on 'em?"

"Apple, please." She fought the urge to close her eyes.

"Kitchen house is out back, so excuse me while I get on out there and get to work."

Cora watched her hurry out the back door and then cross the expanse of lawn to what appeared to be a wood-framed shed. Leaving the door open, Rosie bustled around inside while Cora moved to a chair nearer the window where she could take advantage of the fresh air. The dog kept a watchful eye on both of them, although he seemed much more interested in Rosie's kitchen activities.

The older woman made quick work of warming the biscuits. While Cora slathered on apple jelly, Rosie seated herself across the table. Slowly, a smile touched the older woman's lips. "I believe I see how it is," Rosie said. "You had a good reason for wanting to hurry home to the Circle M, didn't you?"

This, Cora could truthfully answer with a nod as she tested the strength of her flighty stomach with a nibble of the delicacy. Another bite, this one a bit heartier, and she knew she'd be tempting fate by finishing what was on her plate.

"I thought so."

Cora looked up from her meal. "I'm sorry?"

"I had my suspicions when I first set eyes on you, but watchin' how you piddle around with your food, well. . .I can see why Iz would send you ahead before it got too late and too far down in the fall for decent travel. Or have you told him yet?"

Cora's confusion must have answered for her. The housekeeper's gray brows rose.

"So you didn't tell him." She shook her head and looked away. "Figures you wouldn't want him to worry, but that was a mighty foolish risk you took, Miz McBride."

Lacking any more than distant memories of the company of women, Cora had to guess that Rosie was now either confused or irritated. When the older woman's eyes narrowed, she decided upon irritation.

Had she been any less tired, Cora might have engaged Rosie in further conversation on the topic. Instead, she managed a smile of her own then pushed away from the table.

"I know it's early, but I'm exhausted and—"

"Say no more." Rosie stood and swept Cora's plate into the dishpan then turned to address her once more. "Until the old home place is rebuilt, we're a bit sparse for rooms. Just have the one. Got roses on the quilt and a pretty bedstead with a canopy, though. Missus brought it all the way from New Orleans when she married, rest her soul, and the good Lord spared them from the fire."

"Sounds lovely."

She pointed Cora down the narrow hall. "Go on. I'll fetch your bags and have my boy see to the horses."

"Thank you." Cora paused at the staircase. "I just brought the one bag."

"'Course you did," Rosie said as she waved off any further comment. "Guessin' Iz'll see to the rest of your things."

"Yes, I suppose," came out softly, in the hopes Rosie didn't hear.

"You fetched us supplies," Rosie called from the parlor. "I know Iz'll be happy you thought to do that. We were runnin' low on our stores, but it looks like we'll be fine for a while now."

The old woman continued to speak as Cora put one foot in front of the other and made her way to the bedroom. The walls were mostly whitewashed the same as the front parlor; however, someone had hung a quilt, just to the right of the window, patterned in a lovely trellised rose pattern that climbed across the width of the spread. Holding a place of honor was a canopy bed draped in white gauze sprigged with tiny matching roses. The contrast of the meager room and the beautiful furnishings caused tears to threaten.

"I'm sure you'll be wantin' a bath," Rosie called from somewhere down the hall.

"Thank you," Cora said, though she had a difficult time imagining how she'd manage to stay awake long enough to accomplish the feat. Running her hand across the pink coverlet, she let out a soft sigh.

Thudding footsteps on the wood floor indicated she'd soon have visitors, so Cora moved from the tempting mattress to the window. A man carrying a copper bathtub stomped through.

"Just put it over in the corner," Rosie called, "and then hurry yourself to fetch water up afore it cools. Don't need to have the new missus catchin' her death before Iz gets home."

Cora leaned back against the window frame and slipped off her shoes then curled her feet beneath her skirts. The man soon filled the tub then hurried out without once making eye contact or greeting her. A moment later, Rosie arrived with a cake of soap and a length of toweling. Buster trailed behind her.

"I set out a dress for you to put on tomorrow, and it'll be freshened up and ready when you wake up in the mornin'. Now, get out of that one before you fall down from exhaustion."

When Cora made no move toward the tub, Rosie shook her head. "Modesty's a virtue, I'll give you that. How 'bout I just go see what I can find to do in the kitchen whilst you bathe? You can leave that mess of a dress you're sportin' outside the door, and I'll fetch it while you're nappin'. What say you to that?"

"Yes, thank you," Cora said, grateful for the alternative plan.

"Ain't nothin' I need to be thanked for, Miz McBride. It's my job to look after things. Been doin' that since I was younger'n you, and I reckon I'll keep at it till the good Lord calls me home." Rosie paused to smile as the dog settled down in a slice of sunshine and rolled onto his back. "I figure once I get to heaven, I'll just sit down and put my feet up and rest. Can't feature doin' that here. Not when there's daylight and chores to be done. Now, get on into that tub and wash the trail off you."

Cora almost thanked her again. Instead, she settled for a nod as Rosie moved toward the door. She'd almost made her exit when she paused to turn around and regard Cora with that piercing stare once again.

"Miz McBride?"

"Yes?"

"How far gone are you, exactly?"

"Gone?" Cora shook her head. "I have no idea what you're talking about."

"Sure you do." Once again Rosie crossed her arms over her chest while Buster ignored them both to let out a loud snore. "That baby you're carryin'. Iz McBride's gonna be a daddy come winter, ain't he?"

Chapter 2

September 21, 1880

At the sight of Creed Creek's main street, Israel McBride sat up a little straighter in the saddle. His shoulder still ached from the bullet, though it had been nigh on five months since he'd stepped in between an ornery mule of a cattle hand and the bandit determined to steal his best horse.

And while he'd won that gunfight, he'd lost the battle to return home with his bride, at least temporarily. He'd also lost the quick trip to the altar he'd hoped for. Somehow during his recuperation, the simple summer ceremony he and Lavinia Riley planned had grown to become a spring wedding in the cathedral with what sounded like the whole city of San Antonio in attendance.

The thought of being trussed up in his Sunday best and enduring a breakfast-to-bedtime celebration with several hundred strangers was only made palatable by the knowledge that Lavinia would finally be by his side. And while he could not yet say he felt a deep and abiding love for the woman, her sweet smile and soft-spoken ways made it easy for him to imagine building a life together.

A respectable life that would erase any lingering questions in the mind of the Creed Creek townsfolk about whether he would turn out like his father or not. For how could the son-in-law of the richest man in San Antonio be considered anything but an upstanding citizen—despite his parentage?

Iz nudged his horse forward and thought of how good a real bed would feel tonight. Most nights he hated to sleep anywhere but under the stars. His daddy called it the wanderlust, but he was wrong. Iz's need for wandering generally stopped at the edge of the Circle M Ranch. And though he occasionally had to travel on ranch business, he rarely enjoyed it.

He allowed—and then quickly discarded—a thought of how he would explain to Lavinia's father that he had no intention of leaving Creed Creek to work in an office in San Antonio, no matter how "auspicious" the opportunity. Surely once Lavinia saw what he planned to do with the Circle M, she would understand his reluctance to sit behind a desk and shuffle papers all day.

Up ahead he spied a lone rider coming his way. As the distance closed between them, he recognized John Griffin, Creed Creek's mayor and acting sheriff.

"You're a sight for sore eyes," Griffin called as he reined in his mount. "Where you been, Iz McBride?"

"Had a little dustup down in San Antone." He punctuated the statement with a grin as he shook hands with his old friend.

"You all right?"

"I'll live," Iz said. "Which is more than I can say for the horse thief who shot me."

The mayor swatted at the dust circling him and dislodged his Stetson in the process. Iz caught the hat as it tumbled past and handed it back. Griffin chuckled as he set it back in place.

"Well, that sounds fair. You take care now." Iz had already set his horse into motion when the mayor called his name. He glanced over his shoulder to find Griffin watching him. "And when you come to town, bring that bride of yours. She's something special, that one. The whole town thinks so."

So Rosie couldn't keep silent about his future bride. Iz chuckled.

By the time he'd tied his horse to the post outside Hilton's Mercantile, he'd made a list in his mind of items he needed. He held the door open for the preacher's wife and then tipped his hat and stepped inside. Likely Rosie had kept the staples decently provisioned, so he grabbed a few miscellaneous items and made his way to the cash register.

"Well, if you're not a sight for sore eyes, Iz McBride!" the proprietor called as he hurried toward him. A slap on the back punctuated his smile and sent a jolt of pain up Iz's shoulder. Still, he maintained his smile. In these parts, a man neither complained nor showed weakness.

"Glad to be back." He nodded toward the box where Karl Hilton kept his ledgers. "Might as well settle up accounts while I'm here."

Karl shook his head. "You've paid for these things. Nothing else to settle."

"You sure?" He leaned over to look at the page where an amount had been crossed out and marked "Paid in Full." "Guess Rosie decided I wasn't coming back."

The proprietor returned the ledger to the box. "Wasn't Rosie," he said. "You can blame that on your wife."

"My wife?" Iz stood a little straighter, his ire threatening. So Lavinia had been meddling in his accounts.

He gathered up his purchases and offered Karl a stiff nod. He'd known Lavinia's daddy spoiled her, but Iz had been quite clear that once she became Mrs. McBride, that would cease. Maybe he hadn't been clear enough that Hampton Riley's money wasn't going to pay a penny of Israel McBride Jr.'s debts.

Making note of the amount that had been settled, he determined to send the same amount back to the Riley account in San Antonio as soon as he could. The idea that Lavinia had gone behind his back to defy him dogged him as he passed through the gates of the Circle M.

A roll of his shoulders to release the tension gathering there, and Iz concentrated on the beauty that was his ranch. He'd missed spring and summer and, as witnessed by the coloring of the leaves, just barely arrived in time for the beginning of autumn.

Down by the river, the fields had gone fallow, but he hoped their crops had been generous enough for Rosie to put up food for the winter. If not, he'd be hard-pressed to feed the two of them as well as provide a decent meal for Rosie's grown son, Rafael, who helped with chores in Iz's absence. Stacks of wood lining the edge of the smokehouse and fences in no need of mending as far as the eye could see attested to Rafael's efforts.

On the other side of the barn, the foal that had been expected in the spring pranced around his mama looking half grown. Beyond the horse pen, fat cattle grazed as far as the eye could see.

His attention moved swiftly to the sod home and then to the remains of the ranch house. In place of the blacked-out smudge he'd left back in the spring, the wooden skeleton of a fine two-story home emerged. Piles of lumber and other building materials had been stacked neatly in front of a frame that appeared to mimic the original shape of the building.

At the sound of a hammer ringing out across the distance, Iz urged his tired mount forward, his temper spiking. The fellow doing the work was slight, his clothing more suitable to a lad twice his size, and his perch on the end of a beam jutting out where the second-floor porch used to be was precarious at best. His narrow shoulders bunched with his efforts as the sound of hammer hitting nail apparently rendered him unable to hear horse and rider approaching.

Or maybe it was the distance. Still, any man in these parts knew vigilance came before anything else.

When Rosie stepped in front of him, Iz had to rein in the mare. "What in the world possessed you to do that, Rosie?"

Ignoring the question, she surged forward to grasp his hand in hers as her son trotted toward them. "You're home! Come down here and let me see you for myself. Rafael, come and see to Mr. McBride's horse."

Iz slid out of the saddle and handed the reins over to Rafael as Rosie grasped him by the arms. She must have noted his grimace, for her smile quickly went south.

"What?" Just one word, and yet it spoke volumes coming from Rosie.

Iz pasted on his most casual expression. "It's nothing. Just a little dustup with a guy who didn't live to tell the tale. Now, tell me what's going on with the ranch house."

"It's nothing?" One gray brow rose. "You'll not get away with that answer, Israel McBride. You're late. Months late. And I was beginnin' to believe you wouldn't come back."

"Well, I did," he snapped and then thought better of it. "Look, I'm sorry, Rosie. I took a bullet to the shoulder, but the doc in San Antonio says I'm fine." At her look of disbelief, he tried again. "I am fine. Sore from the long ride and in need of a soft bed and a good night's sleep, but fine." He looked beyond her. Then he spied a dog. His dog. Iz whistled for his faithful companion, but Buster didn't move.

"What's wrong with Buster?" He whistled again, and the same thing happened. "Is he deaf?"

Rosie laughed. "Judgin' from how well he hears me rattlin' the pots and pans in the kitchen no matter where he is on the ranch, I'd say no. Why?" She followed the direction of his gaze. "Oh. Well, don't take it personally. You know how loyal that dog is."

Apparently not at the moment. He returned his attention to Rosie. "Is Pop here?"

"No, and I haven't seen or heard from him since before you headed south."

Iz shook his head. "But he headed south himself, back in February, soon as the roads were passable."

Pop had disappeared before, sometimes for months. Always he'd returned, usually with a story to tell. Never with a full explanation.

Not that Iz wanted one. He'd become far too well acquainted with Israel McBride Sr.'s reputation and had worked hard to see that the townsfolk's opinions on Pop hadn't been passed down to him. An absence as long as this, combined with the old man's age, did not bode well.

As if she guessed the direction of his thoughts, Rosie's expression softened. "Iz, don't go borrowin' trouble. He may come back yet."

"And he may not. Next time I go into town, I'll see what I can find out. Maybe the sheriff can make some inquiries on whether he's landed in jail somewhere again." He looked past Rosie, this time to watch the man reach for another nail and begin pounding it into the wood. "So Pop's not behind the rebuilding of the old home place, then."

"Oh no, he had nothin' to do with what's going on down there." She glanced over her shoulder and then back at Iz.

"Then who did?"

"Well, why don't you go down and see for yourself? I believe you'll find who you're looking for down there."

Iz shook his head. "I'm sorry, Rosie, but right now I don't have the patience for games. My stomach's empty, my eyes are ready to close, and I need some shut-eye."

Rosie's grin returned. "Well, of course. Now go on down there and see what's what. I'll have a plate warmin' for you on the stove."

"Thank you, Rosie. What would I do without you?" Iz set off toward the ranch house.

"Well, I certainly hope you never have to find out," she called with a chuckle. "Not with all the help you'll be needin' come the end of the year."

Iz halted to glance over his shoulder. "End of the year?"

"I'll leave you to find out." Rosie disappeared inside the sod house, her laughter trailing behind.

"Women," Iz grumbled. "Thank goodness I've only got one to deal with, at least for the time being."

But he'd have to deal with Lavinia and her penchant for using her money to interfere in Circle M business before long. Better to nip it in the bud now than to marry a woman who didn't care one bit about letting him be the man.

That sort of woman could never be Mrs. Iz McBride.

∞

Cora set the hammer down and watched the exchange between Rosie and the stranger with mild curiosity. When the man looked her way and then turned back to the housekeeper, she eased into a sitting position. Whoever he was, Rosie wasn't the least bit concerned.

Buster issued a low growl and then rose up on his back paws to nudge her with his nose. "Settle down now," she said to her constant companion of the past five months. "If Rosie likes him, then there's no reason to worry."

Not when Rosie was in charge of the worrying on the Circle M. Or so it seemed.

Rosie would be out soon to complain that Cora was working too hard, wasn't resting enough, or one of a dozen other fusses she made regularly. Indeed, she had been working hard, and rest was difficult at this stage in her pregnancy, but she was determined to do what she could for as long as she could.

One way or another, this child would grow up in a real home. Not one made of mud bricks, though that place would suffice until the new ranch house could be completed. And though she'd paid men to do most of the framing work, helping the project along using the skills learned by trailing behind her father meant that there would be less for those men to do when they returned.

Cora shifted positions to stretch her spine, and the baby protested with a firm jab to her ribs. "That'll be enough of that," she whispered as she rested her palm against the spot and felt the imp kick her again.

Apparently this child would be as ornery as Mama claimed Cora had been. Mama. At the thought of her mother, she sighed. While she was thankful for Rosie and the care she took, never had she missed Mama more than now that she was about to become a mother herself.

Another regret wrapped up in a blessing. One of many. She adjusted her borrowed straw hat and reached for another nail to set it into place as Buster began to growl.

"You there," a distinctively male voice called just as she raised the hammer. "Put that hammer away and come down from there."

Cora jerked around to see a man of decent size and ill temperament stalking toward her. Her fingers fumbled with the hammer. She reached to grab it and lost her balance, tumbling over the edge of the beam. A second later, with her fall broken by two strong arms, she looked up into a pair of eyes as blue as the Texas sky behind him.

Angry eyes, she amended as she slid from his grasp and stumbled to her feet. Buster surged past her and aimed his massive head for the intruder's midsection. The dog's bark, usually reserved for barn cats and squirrels, echoed around her.

The stranger took a step backward and rested his fists on his hips while his attention temporarily diverted from her to the big brown dog now circling Cora's legs. "Buster, it's me!"

The hound paused long enough to nuzzle her hand and then threw another warning growl in the man's direction. "Enough of that," she said as she leaned over to scratch behind the animal's ears.

"What have you done to Buster?" he demanded.

So the man knew Rosie, and he knew the dog. Well, good for him.

Whoever he was, he certainly could use a lesson in decent behavior. Cora grabbed her hat and stuck it back on her head and then reached for the hammer, but the stranger grabbed it first.

"You have no need for this," he said. "I'll explain to whoever you work for that. . ."

His gaze traveled from her face to the spot where her belly pushed out the front of the oversized workingman's shirt. Rosie complained Cora's choice of clothing wasn't proper, and this man's expression told her the same.

Buster growled again and then nudged Cora's hand. "Go on and find Rosie," she told the dog. He gave her a doubtful look then did as he was told and trotted off toward the outdoor kitchen.

"What have you done to my dog?" the stranger demanded again.

"Buster?" Cora shook her head. "That dog does what he wants. Now state your business here."

Squaring her shoulders, Cora gave the intruder a direct look that she hoped would let him know how little she cared for his opinion on this or any other matter. She then surprised him by snatching back the hammer.

Those blue eyes swept the length of her before returning to match her stare. "And just who might you be? Other than the woman who turned my own dog against me, that is."

"I am Mrs. Israel McBride, owner of the Circle M. Who are you?"

The man had the audacity to laugh.

Instinct told Cora his response did not bode well. Again she considered what he might know. Pushing the thought away, she stood a little taller. "I see no reason to find humor in that."

"Well, maybe you will when you find out who I am." He paused only just a second. "You sure you don't want to tell me your real name?"

Cora froze as instinct turned to dread. Her fingers tightened around the shaft of the hammer. A movement behind the stranger caught her attention. Rosie. And she was headed their way.

Pressing past the man, Cora straightened her spine and marched toward Rosie without giving him a backward look. Her mind raced. As far as anyone knew, she was Israel McBride's widow.

Wife, she corrected as she picked up her pace and offered Rosie something she hoped would pass for a smile. Until word came that the old crook was dead, she had to remember folks expected he was alive.

Cora closed the distance between her and Rosie. The older woman was beaming. Buster, however, still looked like he might take the man's head off, given permission.

"Well, you do look flushed, Cora," Rosie said. "Either you've spent too much time in the sun, or you're happy to see that rascal."

Rascal. Hardly.

The stranger caught up to them. "Who is this woman, Rosie?"

For a moment Rosie didn't speak. Instead, her gaze flitted between Cora and the stranger. Then she began to laugh.

"Shame on you," she said as she gave the stranger a playful jab then turned toward the door. "You almost fooled me. Now, you two get on inside and finish saying your howdies. Cora is already ignorin' my advice to rest. Maybe you can talk some sense into her. Come on, Buster, I've got a juicy bone waitin' for you in the kitchen."

"Cora, is it?" the stranger asked as he stepped between her and the retreating housekeeper and the easily swayed mutt.

She refused to answer, instead moving around him in an attempt to follow Rosie. The stranger was faster, and this time he grasped her arm to hold her in place.

"Look, *Cora*. I don't know how you've fooled my housekeeper, but you are not Mrs. Israel McBride."

Again she chose defiance over allowing any sign of fear. She had the papers to prove her status as owner of this ranch. All this man had was broad shoulders, an impressive swagger, and a smile that didn't quite reach his piercing blue eyes.

"And just how are you so certain of this?"

"Because I am Israel McBride."

Chapter 3

Cora yanked her arm from his grip, her heart pounding as she stormed away. Of course this man couldn't possibly be Israel McBride.

She stopped in her tracks, and the stranger nearly ran her down. Holding her hands out to stop him, her fingers collided with a chest that was surely made of cast iron.

"All right," she said as she took a step backward to put a decent space between them. "If you're Israel McBride, then Rosie will confirm that, won't she?"

One dark brow rose, as did the beginnings of what might have been a charming smile under other circumstances. "Oh, definitely." He called the housekeeper. "Rosie, what's my name?"

The housekeeper shook her dish towel at him. "You call me away from my work to play games? Shame on you, Iz. Now leave me alone, and bring that wife of yours indoors and out of the sun right now, or I'll set the dog on you. Again."

Iz.

Cora met his stare. Iz could be the shortened version of any number of names, couldn't it?

"Wife?" he said as her smile went south and his spine straightened a notch. "Wait just a minute. Did you tell Rosie you're my wife?"

"I did not," she managed.

"And yet you just said you're married to Israel McBride." He paused but only for a second. "That's me, lady."

His gaze fell to the spot where her growing belly pushed the old shirt out, and then rose to find her eyes again. Though he said nothing, his thoughts were obvious. As was his extreme displeasure.

"I never once claimed to be your wife," she managed, though the bravado in her voice might not have matched the fear she tried to keep from her eyes. "Not once."

This much was true. Had she somehow set up housekeeping at the wrong Israel McBride's ranch? Impossible. This was the Circle M Ranch. The land that Israel McBride had stolen from her father in a game of cards.

The land she'd been sent to reclaim.

"You did, unless the Israel McBride you're married to is my father."

His father. Cora's breath caught in her throat. Of course. She searched his face and saw the angry tilt of his chin, the way his mouth smiled when his eyes told a different story. Indeed, those were things she could remember about her father's former friend.

But those blue eyes. If he was Israel's son, those eyes came from his mother.

And if he was Israel's son, then the Circle M was legally his.

Her shoulders slumped.

"You running from the father of that baby?" he asked, none too gently. "Or are you just hiding out here to keep from letting on that you're in that state?"

His questions were impossibly rude. Far beyond the pale for decent folk. But then, she'd given up on being called decent by anyone who knew her. And arguing with him gave her a good reason not to think about the fact that she'd neglected to consider the dead man buried on her father's property had family who might wonder where he was.

She adjusted her chin so it jutted out just enough to let him know he'd offended her and then turned on her heels and headed for the front door of the sod house. What she'd do when she got inside was beyond her thinking, but she certainly wouldn't stand outside and let this man send her running when she'd only just found her real home again.

She refused to consider the odds that she'd be allowed to stay as she stepped inside and then blinked until her eyes adjusted to the shadowy darkness of the room. Though she fully expected McBride's son to follow, she turned to see him stalking away. Only when he was out of sight did she finally relax.

How long she stood in the doorway, her fingers gripping the rough wood frame, she couldn't say. From the expression on Rosie's face when Cora turned to find the older woman watching her, it had probably been awhile.

"I take it your reunion didn't go so well, Miss Cora." She closed the distance between them to place a motherly hand on her shoulder. "Don't you worry none. Iz's been shot. Did you know that?"

"No," she said softly.

"Well, he has. That'll make a man cranky on a good day, especially after a long ride and a lengthy lack of a soft bed and a good wife." She paused to give Cora an appraising look. "And unless I'm wrong, he didn't expect to find you here waitin' on a little one to come into the world, did he?"

She waved away any comment Cora might make. "You don't have to answer that. I'm not blind. I could see there's a bit of marital strife goin' on. But just give him some time. He'll come around." Rosie nodded toward the door and the kitchen beyond. "I cooked up a mess of those peas you picked this mornin', and I've got corn bread warmin'. Why don't you set a spell and I'll fix you a plate?"

"Thank you," Cora said gently, "but I think I'll go lie down."

Though she appeared concerned, Rosie only nodded. "I'll come and check on you later. You'll need to eat. If not for you, then for that baby of yours. You want Buster to come along and look after you?"

Cora looked down at the mutt she'd become attached to. "I think not. Better send him off to get reacquainted with his master."

Cora closed the door on any response Rosie might have offered and sank down onto the bed. Suddenly she was tired to the bone. She could blame the work she'd done over at the building site or perhaps the morning she spent picking vegetables from the garden before the birds ate them.

She could, but she wouldn't. This kind of tired came from dragging around a heavy secret far too long. Tucking her feet under her, Cora shifted to her side and rested her head on the feather pillow.

On the other side of the door, snatches of a conversation rose and fell. Cora pulled the quilt over her and closed her eyes. She'd made a promise to her father and another to the baby she carried, and she wasn't about to back down now.

No man would send her packing from the home that was rightfully hers. Especially not if that man carried the last name of McBride.

∞

Iz took another bite of corn bread and chewed it nice and slow. Indeed, it was the best corn bread he'd had in months, but his purpose in keeping his mouth full was to keep him from speaking before he'd thought everything through.

Right now all he could think about was a pair of green eyes and a look of panic that had almost caused him to back down on his decision to oust the little trespasser from the premises before nightfall.

That and the fact that the woman had somehow convinced his housekeeper to let her stay and then turned his own dog against him. The idea of either was intolerable. But both?

He washed the bite down with a glass of cold water from the well and then took in a deep breath. Rosie was picking at her peas and shoving them around like she wasn't even aware she was sitting at the table. Sure enough, that woman was trying not to speak her mind either.

Returning his mug to the table, Iz leaned back in his chair and fixed Rosie with a look. "All right, go on and say it."

She looked up, startled. "Say what?"

Iz wiped his mouth with his handkerchief then stuck it back in his pocket. "How long have we known each other?"

A smile touched her eyes. "Longer than you've been alive, and you know that good and well. Why do you even ask such a thing?"

"Because I need to remember how long you and I have been honest with each other." He shook his head. "Seems like that isn't happening right now."

Rosie set the fork aside and regarded him for a second. She seemed ready to say something she didn't really want to say.

"Say it," he repeated. "It's for my own good, isn't it?"

There. He caught her with the statement she generally prefaced any bad news or arguments with.

"Well," Rosie said slowly.

"Go on."

"All right." She nodded to the closed bedroom door. "Cora. What are you goin' to do about her?"

He bit back the words he preferred to say, choosing kinder ones instead. "You cannot possibly think she's my responsibility."

The woman's expression told him that was exactly what she thought. That, and possibly more.

Iz rose too fast, and his shoulder complained. Likely catching the trespassing female had undone whatever the doc back in San Antonio had fixed. He flexed his arm and then reached for his hat.

"Well, she's not. My responsibility, that is. She isn't my wife, and that child of hers, it's not mine. In fact, until today, I'd never laid eyes on the woman."

Rosie stood and moved around the table to stand beside him. Slowly she lifted her hand to touch his sleeve. "I know," she said softly.

"You do?"

She nodded. "But she has papers, though who knows what scoundrel signed them?"

"What do you mean?"

"I mean she could very well be as much of a victim in all of this as you are. Don't guess you stopped to think of that, did you? Or maybe she truly is married to Israel McBride. Senior, that is. Have you asked her that?"

Rosie seemed to be waiting just long enough to let that thought sink in. Something deep and protective in him rose up at the thought of a man using a good woman then throwing her away. Before he could think on it, Iz pressed the memory away.

"Pop?" Surely not. And yet she was pretty enough. Smart, too, and handy with a hammer and nail. It wasn't out of the realm of possibility, considering Pop had been thought to be quite a ladies' man in his younger years. But surely not.

"You don't really think that woman is carrying my. . ." He struggled to say it. "My brother or sister," he finally managed.

Rosie waved away the question with a swipe of her hand. "I'm sayin' it's a possibility, though I've asked enough questions over the past few months to think not. My guess is whoever the father of this baby is, it isn't that old scoundrel."

He relaxed a notch. "If she's not family, then what are we going to do about her?"

She looked back at the closed door and then leaned toward him. "I'd say this is a conversation best left until tomorrow, don't you think?"

"She's still sleeping on the feather mattress I've been dreaming of ever since I hit the trail back from San Antonio."

Rosie swatted him. "Just listen to yourself. You've got bigger problems than missin' that feather mattress."

"Like what?"

"Like the fact that the woman sleepin' on that mattress you're coveting has been livin' at the Circle M since June. She's been goin' to town and goin' to church and generally makin' friends and enjoyin' herself. As *Mrs.* Israel McBride."

His wife.

Iz groaned. No wonder the first two townspeople he'd seen on the trip back had mentioned his wife. Not Lavinia. Cora. If indeed her name was Cora. Because it certainly wasn't McBride. Or at least he didn't believe it was.

Rosie continued, ignoring his distress. "Whether she thinks she's married to Israel McBride or not, she's determined to make a home here for her and her child. She's a hard worker, that girl. And stubborn? Oh, but you two would be a good match." She hastily patted his good shoulder. "But yes, I know, she's not legally yours in any way. I never had a doubt. You're a good man, Iz McBride, and good men don't put women in situations like that one's in right now."

He let out a long breath and managed the beginnings of a smile. "Thank you, Rosie, for seeing the truth instead of thinking the apple didn't fall far from the tree."

Rosie frowned. "You and your father share a name and nothing else. His reputation and yours are completely different."

"If that's true, then why have I spent most of my life trying to prove the opposite?" Before she could respond, he shook his head. "Never mind. People will gossip. It's not ours to fix, only the Lord's."

"That's what your dear mama used to say," Rosie said. "And she's right, you know. You've always done the right thing. You're a good man, Israel McBride, and there's not a person who knows you who'd say different."

"Thank you, Rosie."

"Well, don't thank me yet, because I'm about to tell you that you can't just put her out. Not in her condition."

He crossed his arms over his chest. "She can't stay here."

"Where's she goin' to go?"

"Back wherever she came from," he snapped. "I'm sure she's got a home somewhere. I'll even pay to send her back, but I'm not sharing a home with a woman who isn't my wife. Especially since I've got a wedding planned with a woman I do want to make my wife. Like you said, I do the right thing, and harboring an unmarried woman here under my roof is not the right thing. Maybe before, but not now that I'm back."

"Well, congratulations on your upcomin' wedding, Iz, but your Lavinia might not understand once she hears you've got a child comin' here in Creed Creek."

"Lavinia will believe me." A thought occurred. "I don't want to sound indelicate, but considering how long I've been away, how could I possibly have managed to father a child due the end of the year with that woman?"

"The people in this town don't know that. There'll always be questions. You want that followin' you? It will. Just try and put her out and then bring some city girl home to marry, and see what folks say." She looked away. "I'm sorry, Iz. I've had plenty of time to think on this, and I can't see any way around it. Either you keep her here and keep your good name, or you send her away and let the town think you're just as bad as him."

After all he'd done not to be a man like his father. A man whose guile was as legendary as his ability to cheat at cards and land himself in jail. A man who left a good woman in the family way and didn't come back for almost ten years.

He could see the sense in her argument. He also saw the unfairness.

"Once this Cora woman is exposed for the fraud she is, the only thing that might follow me and any family Lavinia and I might have is the fact that I did the right thing and reported her."

"So you're going to the sheriff, then? Because John Griffin sure likes Cora, and so does his wife. When Elizabeth broke her arm, Cora stopped by and helped her cook up meals for the week and get her hair fixed for church. A thoughtful girl, that Cora."

"Thoughtful? Sounds like she knew just who to cozy up to so she wouldn't get thrown in jail. I think she's conned you and probably the rest of Creed Creek, even my dog. But she hasn't conned me. No, I see right through that helpful exterior. She wants my ranch, and this is how she plans to take it."

"Listen to yourself, Israel McBride." Rosie paused, though her attention never wavered from his eyes. "What would your mother think?"

Iz stalked over to the peg where his hat hung and snatched it up. "This has nothing to do with my mother."

But as he stalked away, he knew it had everything to do with his mama and how his father treated her before she died. And that made him even madder.

So did knowing that Rosie was right.

Chapter 4

Curled beneath the rose-strewn quilt, Cora closed her eyes, but sleep refused to come. The walls were closing in, jostling her with the reminder of the web of lies she had spun. Promising her father to reclaim Duncan land had seemed easy at the time. Now that promise rang hollow. Somehow even the fact that the Circle M had rested in the wrong hands longer than she'd been alive did not make up for the fact that she'd been no better than the crook Israel McBride in how she took it back.

Israel McBride, *Senior,* she corrected. She had no grudge against McBride's son beyond his current irritation with her. What man wouldn't be irritated to find his home now occupied by a stranger? There was no easy fix for this. McBride likely had nowhere to go.

She allowed the quiet to settle around her, offering her problem once again to the Lord her mama used to speak of so sweetly. "What am I to do?" she added when she'd finished her tale of woe. "This is Duncan land. My pa owned it free and clear until that criminal McBride stole it. All I'm doing is claiming it back for my own. Surely you can find Israel McBride a home of his own."

The baby shifted positions, and Cora did, too.

Then, simple as day, the words came to her.

"Israel McBride is home, and so are you."

She scrambled to a sitting position and nearly tumbled to the floor in the process. "What was that? Is there someone here?"

"Israel McBride is home, and so are you."

This time the words settled deep inside; not words she heard, and yet words she knew. She also knew where they came from. She'd heard that voice before, but it had been so very long ago.

"If we're both home, then what's the solution?"

This time He was silent, leaving her to consider the alternatives until she decided upon one. As soon as the ranch house was rebuilt, she would turn over this sod house to Israel McBride. The two dwellings were far enough apart to allow each privacy, and yet near enough that they could share Rosie.

With her time of confinement nearing, it would be a comfort to know that Rosie had someone besides her son Rafael to keep things running at the Circle M. Cora exhaled. She could find only one flaw in the plan, and that was Iz's current lack of cooperation.

There was only one way to fix that problem, and there was no better time than now to fix it.

Getting out of bed had become quite a trick, but her feet managed to find the floor eventually. A fresh chill had overcome the warmth of yesterday, so she reached for the warm shirt she'd found in the back of the wardrobe instead of her customary homespun cotton. The belt she'd made from a length of rope was getting less and less necessary to hold up the trousers she'd claimed months ago.

Wrapping the quilt around her shoulders, Cora slipped out of the bedchamber and across the moonlit main room to step outside. Buster spied her and came running. "You stay here," she told the mutt. "I'll be back in a few minutes."

The air was bracing, the September moon bright and almost full. A light shone in the barn, so she headed in that direction. She found the tack room empty and the door to the stables partially open. Golden light from the lantern spilled ahead of her and swept across the long legs of a man fast asleep.

Cora knew she should announce her presence, but the image of a slumbering Israel McBride stalled her. Adjusting the quilt so as not to drag the fabric across the straw-covered floor, she moved quietly toward him. Unlike her father, this man did not snore loud enough to shake the rafters. Instead, his soft intake and exhale of breath was barely heard over the sound of the horses shuffling in their stalls.

She moved closer to watch the soft puffs of breath as they emerged into the chill of the night air. He moaned and shifted positions to throw one arm back as if he were fighting some imaginary menace. Dreams, she decided, though definitely not pleasant ones.

He moved again, and this time she stepped back to keep his boot from making contact with her foot. Again the idea that she should wake him occurred. Instead, she slid the quilt from her shoulders and covered him gently then hurried away.

Buster met her at the barn door, his tail wagging and his cold nose nudging her hand. "I am such a coward, Buster," she said as she scratched the mutt behind his ears. "All I had to do was wake him up and tell him the plan."

"What plan?"

Cora whirled around to see Iz McBride standing in the doorway, the quilt slung over one shoulder. Silver moonlight slid over his handsome features as he seemed to study her.

"You said you had a plan."

Gathering her courage, Cora straightened her spine and tried to ignore the chill she felt now that the quilt wasn't keeping her warm. "Yes, I do, actually."

"Go on," he said evenly.

"All right." She crossed her arms and put on her most determined expression. "I thought that we could share this ranch, you and I. Of course, I'd prefer to change the name to reflect our shared ownership, but we can discuss that once the particulars are agreed to."

He opened his mouth to speak, but she held up a hand to stop him. "Before you go disagreeing, I think you should consider that I could be right in my claim. I am, actually. And once you've come to that conclusion, do remember that I am being generous in allowing you to remain here and take part in the profits this ranch will be generating."

Silence fell between them. Cora tried not to fidget as she watched the cowboy stand stock-still as if pondering her offer.

"And that's your plan?"

"It is." She felt something nudging her hand. Buster. Cora spared him an irritated glance then dried her hand on the tail of her shirt as Iz moved toward her.

"You keep this in the house," he said as he handed her the folded quilt. "My mother would have a fit if she knew it was in the barn. This one was her favorite."

"It's chilly out tonight," Cora said as she took a step back from the man and the quilt he offered. "It's not like she would know."

As soon as the words left her mouth, she wished to reel them back.

He draped the quilt around her shoulders, his fingers grazing the back of her neck as he settled the rose-strewn material in place. "No, but I would."

Their gazes met, and then Iz turned his back on her and walked back into the barn.

"Wait," she called before he disappeared inside. "The plan."

He turned around slowly. "Go on."

"Well," she said, "I know you think this ranch belongs to you, but—"

"It does."

Buster nudged her hand again and then issued a low growl. Cora hushed the dog and shook her head.

"Just listen, please. My plan is for us to share ownership of the Circle M. The ranch is rightfully mine, but I am willing to share."

His stance told her he did not think highly of this. "Is that all?"

"No," she managed while she sorted out the words she wanted to say. "Since it wouldn't be proper for us to live in the same house, I propose—"

"I think you gave up the right to worry about what was proper when you allowed whoever the father of that child is to have his way with you. Or are you going to stand there and tell me you married my father and are having his baby because you two fell in love and decided that's how things ought to be? And while I'm asking questions, where is my father? Or do you even know, *Mrs.* McBride?"

When she said nothing, he continued, "That's what I thought. If sharing my ranch with me is your plan, then you need another plan, lady."

Cora awoke to the sound of hammering. On a Tuesday. Lack of funds had limited her to paying for help one day each week, and that day was Thursday.

She tidied her hair in the mirror before slipping into boots she'd bought in town and heading for the kitchen, where Buster met her with an excited yelp. "You don't fool me, you silly dog," she said as she ruffled the spot behind his ears. "Likely you've already eaten at least two breakfasts."

His bark turned to a whimper, and then he nudged her hand. "Oh, all right. Let's see what we can find."

Though she hadn't been much for a big breakfast until recently, this business of being in the family way certainly stirred up an appetite. A fresh pan of biscuits sat on the stove beside a plate of sausages. She buttered up a few biscuits and then ate one. Oh, how she did love Rosie's biscuits. She would have another, but first she needed to see to the men working on the house. Tossing a sausage to Buster, Cora made her way back out into the morning sunshine.

If work was being done on her home, she'd not miss out on helping. After yesterday's near collision with the ground, she was less inclined to climb, but surely there were things she could manage, despite her condition. And after her conversation with Iz last night, she was in an even bigger hurry to get the house built. He might not like her plan, but he'd soon learn to live with it or leave.

Those would be the alternatives she offered next time he wanted to talk to her about what would be happening on the Circle M.

She rounded the corner of the barn and stopped short. Instead of the crew of two hired hands, there was Israel McBride pounding nails into the framing on the underside of what would be the second-floor porch. The hammering ceased. Even from this distance, she could feel those blue eyes studying her. "I brought breakfast," she said for lack of any better greeting.

"I see that."

Cora kept quiet and resisted the urge to pluck a piece of straw from his hair. Instead, she thrust the biscuits in his direction.

He gave her a wary look before taking the food. "Rosie said you had papers proving this ranch was yours." He paused to give her another appraising look. "That true?"

"Yes," she managed, though her throat was suddenly dry as cotton.

"I'll be up to the house later to take a look, then," he said, still watching her carefully.

"That's not possible."

"Thought so." He took a bite of biscuit and then wrapped the towel back around the food and set it on the pile of lumber. Then he turned his back to her and returned to his work without a word.

She moved around so that he could see her once more. "I'd be happy to show them to you, but the papers are in the safe at the Creed Creek National Bank."

"Then it looks like you and I will be going into town this morning."

The *ping ping ping* of hammer against nail followed her as she turned back toward the sod house. She found Rosie presiding over her domain with a frown.

"What's wrong?" Cora asked.

Rosie shook her head. "You and Iz. Must you fuss?"

"Fuss?" Cora glanced over in the direction of the hammering. "How could you tell when you can't see us from here?"

"You fussed this mornin' and you fussed last night." She leaned against the stove. "Am I wrong?"

"No," Cora admitted. "He's questioning the papers and demanding to see them. I told him I'd go with him to the bank."

Rosie dabbed at her forehead with the corner of her apron. "Wouldn't it just be easier for me to vouch for you? Seems like a lot of trouble to go all the way into town when I've seen 'em and can tell him that."

"That would be easier," she admitted. "Though I doubt he'll listen to you."

Rosie grinned. "Oh, he'll believe me. You just watch and see. Now how about you go sit yourself down and rest, while I try to talk sense into that stubborn man out there?"

"Rest? I've barely been out of bed long enough to get dressed and find a biscuit to eat." She reached past Rosie to pluck another one from the pan. "So how can I help you today, Rosie?"

"Since when do you want to help me when you could be out there hammering nails?"

"Since that man is working on my house." She took a bite of biscuit and waited for Rosie to comment. When she said nothing, Cora continued: "Why don't I go pick a mess of pole beans for our lunch?"

"You do that while I go talk some sense into him," trailed after Cora as she escaped the kitchen. She gathered up a basket and headed to the garden.

Midway down the first row of beans, Cora heard footsteps heading her way. Heavy footsteps. She set the basket aside and stepped between the rows to see who had come to find her, though she already felt as if she knew.

∞

Cora McBride—or whoever she was—looked even prettier with the morning sun slanting over her golden hair and the beginnings of freckles dotting her high cheekbones. Even in that ridiculous outfit, the too-big pants that were likely held up by a length of rope and the homespun shirt he'd long ago set aside, she outshined the best-dressed ladies anywhere. But then, she'd looked just as pretty in the moonlight with Mama's quilt wrapped around her.

If he hadn't already picked a wife, he might have been caught up in looking at her. But he was a man whose woman was waiting for him to claim her back in San Antonio, so he looked away. And while he was at it, he shoved any thoughts of how pretty she was out of his mind.

"We're going into town, you and I," he said. "Put on something decent, and be quick about it."

Rosie would have his head for the way he'd spoken to the woman, both now and last night when she'd found him in the barn. But Rosie wasn't here to have her say in the matter. He set off toward the barn and found Rafael already had the horse hitched to the buggy. Iz climbed up and took the reins then sat back to wait for the woman.

Only then did he allow his mind to wander back to his middle-of-the-night conversation with the Lord that still had him rattled. After he'd finished his moonlight conversation with Cora, he'd let the Man Upstairs know exactly how he felt about sleeping in a barn when he was the rightful owner of a nice bed under a solid roof. Other complaints followed, until Iz had poured out the last of his grudges against his unwanted houseguest and her ridiculous plan. Then he lay back on the straw and waited for God to tell him just how to rid himself of the menace to his sleep and his reputation.

Then waited some more.

And some more.

All he heard was the night sounds that fell around him, and the silence of the Lord. And then, just as he was about to fall asleep, something woke him up. Something loud and plain and unmistakably important.

Something that said these words: *Cora is home, and so are you.*

Iz shifted positions, trying not to consider what that meant. But he couldn't escape it. If only he could claim that he hadn't understood. That the once-in-a-lifetime encounter on the straw floor of the barn hadn't happened. But he couldn't. And it had.

He heard Rafael moving things around in the tack room and called to him. "Keep an eye on the horse, would you?" he said as he climbed down and handed the young man the reins. "This might take a few minutes, so if the lady wonders where I am, tell her she can wait in the buggy."

The Bible in his saddlebag held a pencil and some writing paper folded inside it. After two tries at putting the right words on the page, Iz gave up and settled for a simple apology that he'd found himself unable to marry Lavinia. He took the blame and wished her well and left it at that.

Iz stuffed the letter into his pocket along with the other letters Rosie had given him to mail and then stalked back to the buggy, where he found the woman waiting for him. She'd cleaned up quite nicely and now wore a pretty dress of pale green sprigged with flowers. Her golden hair was braided, a proper bonnet covering all but the coil that was pinned at her neck. Her condition was evident, and yet she still looked as pretty as any girl could.

He shook off the thought and settled onto the seat beside her then set off toward the town of Creed Creek without sparing her a glance or another word. He kept up his silence well beyond the point where he thought he could, and thankfully so did she. Only when he paused at Creed Creek's northernmost spring to water the horse did he speak.

"Rosie made me promise I'd stop halfway to let you stretch your legs."

She angled toward the side and then seemed uncertain as to how she would manage to find the ground. Iz went around and reached for her, easily lifting her down. "Thank you," she said softly as she made her way to the edge of the creek a few yards downstream. He ignored her as she knelt and cupped her hands for a drink, well mostly. And he ignored her some more when she rose and straightened the folds along the front of her dress, her fingers stalling on her belly as if considering the child she carried.

He thought of what he might be losing at her expense—and yet he still couldn't look away as she walked toward him. Their gazes met as he lifted her back up onto the seat. "Thank you," she said again, and he nodded in response.

Setting the buggy into motion once more, Iz slid her a sideways glance and found her watching him, her backbone ramrod straight and her expression neutral. To his surprise, she did not look away.

"Despite what you may have been told, the Circle M belonged to my father, and now that my father's dead, it belongs to me," she said.

"I'll look at the proof you've got, then we'll talk about that." They rode in silence for a while, and then Iz's curiosity got the better of him. "You never answered me last night about whether Israel Senior is that baby's daddy."

She stared straight ahead. "Of course not."

"And yet you claim to be Mrs. Israel McBride. That does make things interesting, doesn't it?"

His companion ignored the question. By the time Iz hitched the horse to the post outside the bank, he'd given up thinking she might answer.

When she didn't budge off the seat, he walked over to stand beside her. "Conscience bothering you?"

It had to be, but he doubted she'd admit it. Still, he stood there long enough to give her the chance.

Finally he gave up. "You go get those papers while I handle my business," he said as he handed her down from the buggy. "If you're not sitting here when I'm finished, I'll assume you came to your senses."

"I only want what's mine, *Mr.* McBride," she snapped as she turned her back on him and headed for the front door of the bank like her tail feathers were on fire.

"Then we both want the same thing," he said as he watched her disappear inside. He turned toward the post office located inside the mercantile.

Hilton's Mercantile was thick with people, but after jostling his way past what seemed like half the population of Creed Creek, Iz handed off the stack of mail to Karl and then headed for the sheriff's office. He found the lawman studying a telegram that appeared to perplex him.

When he looked up at Iz, John nearly jumped out of his chair. "You scared the life out of me, Israel McBride."

Iz let the door close by itself and crossed the distance between them. "Can't imagine why that'd be."

"Well, might be because I was just trying to decide whether to ride out to your place now or wait until later this afternoon to tell you the news."

"Guess you don't have to do either." He lowered himself onto the only chair in the room that didn't look like it needed fixing. "What news were you going to tell me?"

The sheriff sobered. "It's about your daddy, and it ain't good, Iz."

Chapter 5

Cora tucked the envelope of legal papers into her handbag and stepped out into the early afternoon sunshine. Iz had not yet returned to the buggy, so she took her time walking that direction.

She spied Harley Coleman, the blacksmith, watching from across the way, and offered him a smile.

"You looking for your husband, Miz Cora?" he responded.

"Have you seen him?" she said to the sweet man who sang such a lovely baritone in church every Sunday.

"Over at the sheriff's office." Harley stepped closer and pulled something white from his pocket. "I found this on the floor of the mercantile a few minutes ago. Looks like Iz must have dropped it. Or maybe one of Karl's little ones was up to mischief. Either way. . ."

Cora closed the distance between them and accepted the folded paper, now decorated with a few smudges of black that matched the blacksmith's fingertips and several lighter spots that looked like someone had walked on it. Upon further inspection, she determined the letter was indeed sent by Iz and was addressed to a Miss Lavinia Riley of San Antonio, Texas.

"Sorry about that," Harley said sheepishly when Cora brushed her finger across the dirt. "The fingerprints are mine, but the footprints were there when I found it."

"Oh, don't you worry about that. I'll see if I can't clean those off. I know Mr. McBride will be glad you found it." She offered him a smile. "Now, you tell your wife I'll be looking forward to seeing that new son of yours soon as I can pay her a visit."

"You're welcome anytime, Miz Cora," Harley called.

Cora pulled her handkerchief out of her handbag and dusted off the letter then waved good-bye to the blacksmith. A quick trip to Hilton's Mercantile and the letter was once again safely off to be mailed.

She'd almost reached the buggy when she spied Iz walking her way. His face was grim as he caught up to her and grasped her wrist.

"Come with me," he said in a tone that allowed for no refusal.

Cora had to step lively to keep his pace. When he stopped abruptly in front of the sheriff's office, she nearly stumbled into him. He caught her and set her on her feet again, but his hands remained on her shoulders.

"Do you have those legal papers?"

"I do." Cora looked past Iz to see the sheriff standing in the doorway.

"Afternoon," he said gently. "Elizabeth's been asking when you'll be coming to supper again. I do hope that'll be soon."

Cora smiled. "You tell her I'll come soon as I'm able. I do so enjoy visiting with her."

"About those papers," Iz said none too kindly. "I wonder if you'd take a look at them, John."

The sheriff gave Iz a look that indicated he was not pleased with the diversion in conversation and then offered a smile to Cora. "Yes, well, let's come on in and have a talk, shall we?"

Cora followed him inside and sat in the chair he indicated while Iz remained standing. Fear rose as she wondered if she would be caught in the trap she'd built for herself. The Circle M was Duncan land. The deed proved it. As to that awful letter from Pa saying she was married, she couldn't account for why he would put that in with the other paper, unless he was trying to give her baby a father, if in name only.

She let out a long breath and tried to pray that things would work out in her favor. Instead, she heard Mama's reminder that God doesn't ask us to go against what He says is right. And lying never was right. She inhaled again, and spots began to form before her eyes. Blinking, she chased them away, although the room still threatened to spin.

"First," Sheriff Griffin said as he reached to grasp Cora's hand, "Iz here's got some news he needs to pass on to you, and it might come as a shock."

Those spots danced before her again. "Oh?" she managed.

"It's about my father," Iz said evenly. "He's dead. Or did you already know?"

"Israel McBride," the sheriff chastised. "That is no way to talk to this young lady. I will excuse this as coming from a man grieving his father, but you'll be needing to speak kindly to her from here on out. You understand?"

"Understood," Iz said, though Cora doubted he was serious. "With all due respect, Sheriff, I wonder if you might take a look at those legal papers I mentioned before I have to get Cora back to the ranch?"

The sheriff swung his attention from Iz to Cora. "Only if she is amenable to discussing such matters today."

Temptation to use her pregnancy as an excuse to avoid this conversation arose, but on the issue of a deed to the Circle M, Cora knew there was nothing to hide. She gathered up her handbag and produced the envelope her father had given her. Those piercing blue eyes watched her as she handed the envelope to the sheriff.

The lawman pulled out the pages and began to read. After a few nods and a "hmm" or two, he handed the documents to Iz. "See those signatures there, and that seal? That deed's every bit as legal as the one your daddy filed with the county back when you were knee-high to a grasshopper."

Back when he stole the ranch from the Duncans, Cora longed to add.

She watched the younger McBride's eyes scan the first page and then stall. He looked up at her and then went back to reading until he'd finished. A look passed between the two men as Iz returned the papers to the sheriff.

Iz pointed to the pages on the sheriff's desk. "So if that deed's legal, too, then which one of us owns the Circle M?"

"Now Iz," he said slowly. "Does it matter?"

"It does," Iz said.

"Yes, it does," Cora echoed.

"Well, all right then." He leaned back, and the chair creaked in response. "Seems like whichever of you was to survive the other would be the one to own the place."

"And in the meantime?" Iz asked.

"In the meantime, you both do."

"That's not possible," Iz said.

"Sure it is. That's the law. A man and his wife, they own things together, although I will say that as long as you're her husband, you get the say in what goes on at the ranch and whether it can be sold. Things like that." The sheriff shrugged. "You don't like that, then take it up with the land office. They'd have the final say, but based on two deeds and the fact you two are married and both living at the Circle M, I doubt the answer would change."

"And if we weren't married?" Iz asked.

John Griffin's bushy brows went up at the question. "None of my business, of course, but why does it matter?"

"It's the funniest thing," Cora said sweetly. "Iz and I have been having a friendly discussion on the topic, and I'd be most obliged if you'd settle the matter."

"That's right," Iz added. "Cora here says that if we weren't married, her deed's the one that would settle who owns the ranch. I say the law's on my side, and I'd be the owner based on my Pa's deed." He paused just long enough to allow his gaze to sweep past Cora. "What do you say, John? If we were just two unmarried folks sitting in your office, which one of us would you declare as owner of the Circle M?"

His brows gathered as he appeared deep in thought. "Based on what I've seen so far and the law as far as I understand it, I'd say that'd be Cora."

∞

Iz managed to ride all the way to the creek without giving the woman beside him a single glance. Oh, he'd helped her up onto the buggy seat, because that's what a gentleman did. And he'd reached over to wrap an arm around her to be sure she wasn't in any danger of toppling over when the buggy wheel hit that rock a mile or so back. But other than that, he kept his attention on the trail ahead while his thoughts centered on just what he was going to do about the situation.

Instead of leaving him be, Cora followed him to the creek's edge and stood beside him while he watered the horse. "Did the sheriff say what happened to your father?"

"No." He watched her closely. "Why?"

"No reason." She turned to face him. "Will you miss him?"

"No."

He let out a long breath. Any other answer wouldn't make sense to anyone but him. Yes, he missed the old fool. The man hadn't been all bad, at least not to Iz's young eyes. Before his father lit out for parts unknown, the two of them would hit the trail for adventures that might include hunting or fishing or building or sleeping under the stars. Mama said that was where Iz got his wanderlust.

But it didn't take long for that awestruck boy to figure out that his daddy had another side to him. A side that was mean and spiteful and capable of all sorts of trouble. A side that made his mama cry. What puzzled Iz most was how Mama cried more after Daddy took off than she did when he was there.

By the time Iz McBride Sr. came back to the Circle M, Mama was buried in the church cemetery and Iz had turned the Circle M into a respectable ranch and the McBride name into a respectable name. They forged a truce and managed to live under the same roof, until lightning struck the ranch house. Iz Sr. stayed around just long enough to see the soddy built, and then he did what he always did. He left. And this time, Iz actually missed him.

But no, he didn't miss wondering what trouble his father would get into next or what else he would to do taint the family name.

He noticed Cora was watching him and shook off the thoughts with a roll of his shoulders. "We should go."

She allowed him to lift her back up into the buggy then watched him climb in beside her. "You and your father weren't close, were you?"

Iz flicked the reins and set the buggy in motion. "No."

"I'm sorry," she said softly.

He slid her a sideways glance. "Why?"

She shrugged. "Because I know what the loss of a parent feels like."

Not like this, he wanted to say. "Is that so?" is what he settled for.

Cora tucked a strand of hair behind her ear as she stared straight ahead. "After Mama died, it was just Pa and me. I was little, maybe eight or nine. He always talked about going home. I used to climb high as I could in whatever tree I could find and see if I could see home from there."

"Home as in the Circle M?"

She smiled. "Yes. I knew it was far away, but I didn't understand how something could be so far that I couldn't see it from up there." She paused. "I thought if I could just get home, then my mama would be there waiting. I didn't understand she wasn't coming back. Finally Pa told me she was dead, but I held on to believing that she was waiting for me at home for the longest time."

Her voice softened as she told her story, and so did her expression. It was all Iz could do not to offer a kind word. He knew what it was like to lose a mama. Why didn't he just tell her so?

They rode in silence for a while until Cora once again glanced his way. "You and I are in an interesting situation," she said as she toyed with the trim on her sleeve.

"How's that?"

"According to Sheriff Griffin, if you and I weren't married—"

"Which we're not."

"Which we're not," she echoed. "Then the Circle M belongs to me."

"He said it might," Iz corrected. "I disagree."

"But it was the likeliest outcome." She waited to see if he might challenge the statement, or at least that's how it appeared, and then shook her head. "The way I see it, you need to be married to me to be certain the Circle M is yours. I, however, do not need to be married to you to own it, and if I did marry you, then I would lose control of my land."

Again she met his gaze. Iz quickly looked away. "That's McBride land."

"Duncan land," she corrected.

Iz pulled back on the reins and brought the buggy to a halt. Cora had to grip the seat to keep from tumbling over.

He faced her, his temper close to snapping. "If you're so sure the Circle M is yours, why did you lie about a marriage to Israel McBride?"

"I had no idea my father put that letter in the envelope until Sheriff Griffin showed it to me the day I arrived in Creed Creek."

"But you went along with it," he said.

"Yes," she said, her eyes downcast. "It seemed the easiest way." She lifted her gaze. "How would it have looked to say that the deed was legitimate but my father's letter wasn't?"

"I'd say it would look like the truth," he said.

"Well, it seemed like the simplest way to handle things," she insisted.

"So you figured if you were married to Israel McBride, you'd get the Circle M."

"Yes," she said.

A hawk circled overhead as the horse pawed at the ground. "And you also figured if you were married to Israel McBride, nobody would be asking questions about that baby you're carrying."

Cora took her time answering. Just when Iz figured she wouldn't speak, she did. "At the time I didn't know there would be a child," she said. "But yes, once I discovered my condition, it was preferable to be known as Mrs. McBride, and I didn't see the harm in it."

"Until I arrived."

"Yes," she said softly. "Until you arrived."

He flicked the reins and set the buggy in motion again, then a thought occurred. "Didn't you wonder what would happen when my father came back to Creed Creek and found you living there?"

"No," she said, far too quickly.

He slid her a sideways glance. "And why is that?"

This time she didn't seem so eager to answer. "Because he and I both know the ranch belongs to the Duncans. The truth always comes out."

Something in that statement didn't seem to settle well with her. Interesting.

"Yes, it does. And speaking of the truth, where's the baby's daddy?" He paused just long enough to know he needed to ask the other question that was on his mind. "And does he know he's got a little one coming?"

Cora's low chuckle held no humor. "No, he doesn't know. As to what happened to him? I have no idea."

"I see."

"No, you don't see," she snapped. "I thought we were legally married."

Much as he hated to ask, Iz felt compelled to let her tell the rest of the story. "But you weren't?"

"No, we weren't," she said. "We stood in front of the justice of the peace and said our vows just as pretty as you please, then we had our honeymoon in the bridal suite of the Menger Hotel in San Antonio. It was a glorious two days." Again she paused. "Until his wife arrived."

"His wife?"

She nodded. "He neglected to mention that he was already married to someone else. She offered him the choice of going back to Dallas with her and never seeing me again or staying with me and going to jail. He chose Dallas."

Iz's heart sank. Much as he wished he didn't have the complication of sharing the Circle M with this woman, he hated that someone had hurt her so badly. And apparently so easily.

They rode the rest of the way back to the Circle M in silence. Try as he might, Iz couldn't imagine what sort of man would take advantage of a woman like Cora and then just toss her aside.

Then, as the sign for the Circle M Ranch came into view, Iz realized that was exactly what Israel McBride Sr. had done to his mama. He'd be no better than his father if he abandoned the woman on the seat beside him. If it was true that his father had taken land that rightfully belonged to another, then he was doubly guilty in not making that right.

And there was only one way to make this right.

Once again, he pulled the buggy to a halt. Cora's golden brows furrowed.

"Is something wrong?" she asked.

"There is," he said. "I don't want to lose the ranch, Cora. I've worked too hard to make it what it is." He paused. "But I want to do the right thing by you and your baby. I couldn't live with myself if I didn't offer to make you an honest woman."

The last thing he expected was for her to laugh. "An honest woman?"

"Well, you living out here with me and us not married and all. . ."

"As far as anyone in town knows, we are." She sighed. "Though maybe I need to correct that. I'm not very good at carrying on a lie, and this lie got away from me."

"No," he said. "Your baby needs a daddy, and I need to know my ranch won't be taken away should you decide to press your case."

"And so you want to make an honest woman out of me." She paused. "As in. . ."

"Marry you," he supplied.

"Thank you, but no."

"No?" He shook his head. "I don't understand. I'm offering you a home that you won't have to lie to keep. Your baby will have a roof over his head, and he won't have to know what it's like for people in town to whisper about him."

"Unlike you?"

Her question hit him square in the gut. "Yes," he managed. "Unlike me. Now be sensible."

Cora met his stare. "I am being sensible. I won't marry you, Iz, but thank you for asking. Now would you please take me back home?"

Home. His home. And hers.

"Of all the mule-headed. . ." he muttered.

He gave the reins a snap and set the horse moving at a decent clip toward the ranch. Buster raced to greet them then trotted along beside the buggy until Iz brought it to a stop. Rafael hurried out to take the reins, leaving Iz to help Cora down.

The mutt circled her skirts and nudged her hand until she leaned down to pet him. "Did you miss me, boy?" she said as she scratched his ears.

"Apparently he did."

She straightened. "He's your dog, isn't he?"

"He was. Seems he likes you better."

"I'm sorry," she said.

Iz looked back to see her still scratching the dog's head. He'd always thought Buster was a pretty decent judge of character.

"Don't be," he said, but Cora had already turned toward the house, and the dog trailed a half step behind. Just before the pair disappeared around the corner into the house, Buster stopped to look in his direction.

If he didn't know better, he might have thought the dog was trying to tell him something. Buster barked twice and then followed his new mistress inside.

Iz stood there a minute longer. If Buster liked spending time with Cora, maybe he could try it, too. After all, it appeared he was stuck with her.

But not married to her.

By the time he got to the door, the sound of laughter greeted him. Both women fell silent when they spied him. Buster, however, came directly to him to nuzzle his hand in a greeting he hadn't had since returning to the Circle M.

"Iz," Rosie said, "come on in here and join us. I was just tellin' Cora about how Mrs. Smith's pig got out. It's the funniest story." Her attention danced between Iz and Cora, and then she smiled. "You know what? I think I might have left a pot on the stove out in the kitchen. I ought to go see about that."

"Looks like you two have made up," Cora commented as she nodded toward the dog. "I explained to him that you're not such a bad fellow."

He met her tentative gaze. "I'm surprised you think so, considering how I've behaved."

She smiled. "You've behaved like a man protecting his property. I understand."

"And yet you've turned down my offer of marriage."

"Sit down, Iz," she said as she took a seat at the table and gestured to the one across from her. "I appreciate your offer, and I know it wasn't easy asking. But there's something else I want to talk to you about. The co-owner of the Circle M shouldn't be sleeping in the barn. Come sit down. I've got a proposition for you."

Iz lifted one brow in surprise. "Is that so?"

She laughed. "Don't go jumping to conclusions, Israel McBride. I've got a little money set aside, and I'd like to offer it to you to get that house rebuilt. Long as I'm sleeping there, you could sleep here."

He glanced around the room and then returned his attention to Cora. "I can see how that might appeal to you, but I'm not interested in living here any longer than I have to."

Cora sighed. "I was afraid you'd say that." She paused. "So I have another plan."

"As I recall, I've never liked your plans."

Smiling, Cora shook her head. "I don't think you'll complain about this one. What if we were to split the house right down the middle?"

He regarded her with a mixture of interest and disbelief. "How is that possible?"

"Oh, it's very possible." She spent a few minutes telling him just how the feat could be accomplished with two front doors and identical interiors on both sides split by a wall in between. Then she sat back and waited for his response.

"Cora, I think you've finally managed to come up with a plan I can agree to." He held up his hands to prevent her from responding. "However, I'm going to insist that we split the cost of this special house evenly between us."

"Agreed," she said.

"And one more thing."

She frowned. "What?"

"Marry me, Cora."

Cora pushed back from the table and then slowly got to her feet. "Don't be ridiculous."

"I am being practical," he said. "That baby needs a daddy, and everyone in town already believes that daddy is me. Why won't you see reason?"

She walked halfway to the door before turning around to face him. "People will think what they will think. Unfortunately, I've not done anything to correct the trouble I caused, but I will."

"I don't believe that's a good idea. What sort of life is that for your child?"

"Why does this matter so much to you?"

When Iz did not respond, Cora shook her head and walked out the door. "Because I was that child," he whispered as he stood and watched her go.

To this day he still wished his daddy had legally married his mama. It didn't matter that everyone believed he had. Iz knew the truth. And as long as he drew a breath, he'd see to it that never happened again on the Circle M.

Chapter 6

Last evening's chill had given way to this morning's frost, but the rising sun had already begun to burn away the icy sparkles left on the leaves. Cora had missed church again yesterday, but Rosie said it wouldn't be long until the baby came and she could travel again. Until that time, she wouldn't be leaving the Circle M for any reason.

Unlike Iz, who seemed to be gone more than he was home.

He'd already made three trips into Creed Creek in the past two weeks, and just yesterday he'd ridden off to parts unknown for some kind of business he preferred not to discuss. All he told Rosie was that he'd be back eventually.

Eventually. What sort of man just took off and didn't say where he was going?

A man like his daddy.

Cora shook off the thought. If she'd learned anything about Iz McBride, it was that he was a good man. A man who kept his word, as witnessed by the fact that the house they'd agreed to share was coming along nicely. At this rate, the roof would be on and the walls would be going up before the end of the week. After that, there would be nothing left but finishing out the interior.

None of it could happen fast enough to suit her. Rosie said it was the baby brooding that made her want to settle in and get everything sorted out for the child's arrival. Cora viewed it all in a more practical way. With the house complete, she could concentrate on trying to be the mama that her mama was.

She'd never manage it, but she certainly intended to try.

However, Iz had been clear that as much as she wanted the house done, she was not allowed to help with the building in any way. The only exception to this came in the form of food. For now that it was apparent that Cora would be staying on at the Circle M, Rosie had made it her business to begin teaching Cora how to cook.

And according to Iz, Cora had taken to cooking quite nicely.

Thus, twice a day, Cora brought meals to Iz and the crew down at the job site, and a time or two in between she would see that Rafael delivered fresh water and whatever treats she and Rosie had cooked up since the last meal.

In the evening, Rosie dismissed cooking classes. That's when she shooed Cora out of the kitchen and insisted the younger woman put up her feet and rest until supper was served. Iz made it his business to join her, and often the pair got to talking and laughing and almost forgot to eat.

Cora did enjoy Iz's company. And as much as she hated to admit it, she missed him something terrible when he was gone.

The sound of hammering punctuated the morning air. Cora cobbled together a breakfast for the crew from the food Rosie had left on the stove. Three weeks had gone by since she turned down Iz's proposal and offered one of her own.

One he had accepted.

And now the rebuilding of the ranch house was proceeding quickly. Winter would be closing in on them soon, as would the birth of her baby. Giving the last of the money she'd brought with her from East Texas to Iz to pay for supplies and a crew had been a risk she'd gladly taken.

Buster's bark diverted her from the kitchen. Spying a rider accompanying a man and woman in a buggy, she set down her pan of food and went to greet them. It wasn't often the Circle M had visitors, so she hoped these folks would bring news from town.

An older man dressed in his Sunday best climbed down from the buggy. "Are you the lady of the house?"

"I am."

He removed his hat and executed what amounted to a formal bow. "I am Hampton Riley." He nodded toward a pretty girl in a fancy pink dress and matching bonnet who was watching her closely from the buggy. "This is my daughter, Lavinia."

Lavinia. Where had she heard that name?

Cora froze. Lavinia Riley. The woman Iz sent a letter to.

The Riley fellow set his hat back on his head with a flourish. "I wonder if you could tell me where I could find Israel McBride?"

Dread gathered as she tried to sort through the actions she'd taken on that day several weeks ago. "I wish I knew."

The pretty lady leaned forward in the buggy. "Who are you?"

"That there's Cora," Rosie said as she walked toward the pair.

"They're looking for Iz, I mean Mr. McBride," Cora supplied. "These are the Rileys. Mr. Hampton Riley and Miss Lavinia Riley, his daughter."

Rosie's eyes widened, but only for a moment before she turned her attention to the third man. "And who is this fellow?"

Hampton Riley's eyes narrowed. "He's the man I hired to check up on you, Miss Cora Duncan."

Cora shook her head. "I don't understand."

"Well, it's simple," Mr. Riley said. "I was conducting business up in Amarillo when my daughter informed me the wedding she'd been much anticipating had been abruptly and rather cryptically called off. As you can imagine, this caused great distress for Lavinia and her mother, and propelled our family into a situation of no small measure of embarrassment."

While the elder Riley waxed eloquent on their current unsettled social situation in

San Antonio, Cora watched his daughter squirm. She might be wrong, but it sure didn't look like Lavinia Riley wanted to be here at all. Nor did it appear that her father cared for what his daughter might wish.

She knew too well what it felt like to be a girl who might even marry a man she didn't love to gain her freedom. Cora exchanged weak smiles with Lavinia then returned her attention to Hamilton Riley.

"Naturally I was concerned, so I asked Agent Woodward to investigate. His investigation led to you, Miss Duncan. He and I decided the best course of action was to come directly to the Circle M and see the situation for ourselves." He slid another glance at Lavinia. "My daughter insisted on accompanying us."

Again she watched Iz's former fiancée. What she saw only confirmed her suspicion that the Circle M was the last place Lavinia wished to be.

The other man dismounted and came toward her. "Pinkerton Agent Ross Woodward, Miss Duncan." He pulled back his coat just far enough to show the Pinkerton badge clipped to his belt and the revolver strapped to his thigh.

"Wait just a minute," Rosie said. "I don't know what's goin' on here, but there was no call to hire a Pinkerton agent to come and bother Miss Cora and Iz." She looked past the agent to the woman in the buggy. "He told you he couldn't marry you. Why don't you just let it be?"

At the woman's sharp intake of breath, her father stepped in. "I do not believe Mr. McBride realizes the woman he cast my daughter aside for is already married to someone else."

"Of all the nerve." Rosie whistled and Rafael came running. "Go fetch Sheriff Griffin," she told him. "Tell him there's trouble at the Circle M and he ought to come quick."

"No, Rosie, he's right. I am. Or I was." She met the agent's stare. "If you know about my marriage, you also know why he and I aren't together anymore."

Rosie stalled only a moment before dismissing Rafael. "Go on, Pinkerton man," she said. "What say you about all of this?"

Agent Woodward shrugged. "As far as the state of Texas is concerned, you and Rex Holley are legally married."

"That's not possible." Spots rose, and Cora's knees threatened to give way. "He already had a wife in Dallas. It's not legal to be married to two women at once."

"Did you tell the courts that?" Woodward asked, none too kindly.

"No," she managed as she felt Rosie's firm grip on her elbow. "I didn't realize I had to."

Pinkerton Woodward almost looked sorry he'd said anything. "I ought to mention, ma'am, that I also found that there was a claim filed on this ranch by you back in June of this year. Sheriff Griffin of Creed Creek registered the property in your name as wife of Israel McBride. Was that Israel Sr. or Israel Jr.?"

"Neither," she managed. "And I didn't seek that registration."

"Your father, ma'am, would he be named Josiah Duncan?" When she nodded, he continued. "Then it might interest you to know that the body of Israel McBride Sr. was discovered buried in a shallow grave a short distance from your father's house."

She let out a long breath as the spots gathered again and the horizon threatened to topple. Denying any knowledge of this would be so very easy. Just a simple untruth, and she could go on with the happy life she had created here at the Circle M.

Just a little lie. One small untruth. No one would know.

But she would. And the Lord would.

"It would not surprise me at all," Cora said. "I was present when Israel McBride shot my father. Pa returned fire, and unfortunately for Mr. McBride, Pa's aim was better."

The Pinkerton studied her for a minute. "I see."

"In case you want to ask my father himself, you'll find him in the Caravan Springs Cemetery. He was hit by McBride's bullet, but it took awhile before that killed him. Three weeks, if you're interested, and every day was agony."

Rosie patted her arm. "Does Iz know any of this?"

Lavinia Riley looked away as Cora leaned heavily on Rosie. "No," she said.

"Then you will tell him." Rosie nodded toward the trail leading to the Circle M. "For unless my old eyes deceive me, that's Iz comin' up the trail right there."

∞

Iz frowned as he spied the gathering of folks up ahead. He couldn't miss Lavinia seated in the buggy nor her father standing beside it. There was Rosie looking his direction. But who was the man talking to Cora?

Woodward.

He knew Woodward from his time spent in San Antonio. Though the Pinkerton man had claimed his interest in the shooting was professional in nature, Iz had suspected Woodward had designs on Lavinia that kept him coming around long after Iz had exacted his own kind of justice on the man who'd waylaid him.

And now here he stood on Circle M land.

"Afternoon, Ross," Iz called before settling his gaze on the Rileys. "Mr. Riley. Lavinia."

His former fiancée practically bolted from the buggy to embrace him. "Israel, I'm so glad you're here. I'm sorry we've bothered you and Cora. Daddy insisted."

Hampton Riley looked less than pleased at his daughter's display of affection. Iz held her at arm's length as his eyes found Cora. She looked as if she might keel over any minute. Like as not, good old Ross had delivered the news that Iz had hoped he might not have to share with Cora until he was sure she was strong enough to hear it.

Iz slipped out of Lavinia's embrace and closed the distance between himself and Cora. "You all right?" he asked her.

"I've had better days," she admitted.

He turned to Ross. "Guess you told her about her marriage to Holley."

"That it was still legal and binding? Yes, I did, although I haven't had time to mention that because of her marriage, her legal husband would be declared the owner of this ranch should a dispute arise. You do understand that's how property law works in this part of Texas, don't you, McBride?" The lovesick fool had the audacity to smile in Lavinia's direction.

"Yes, I do, but that's old news." Iz turned back to Cora. "I probably ought to start at the beginning and tell you where I've been going the past week or so."

Her smile was weak but encouraging. "All right."

"I've been chasing down a man named Simon Lavergne. Do you recognize the name?" When she shook her head, he continued. "You might recognize him by one of his aliases, Rex Holley."

She let out a long breath. "Has Rex claimed his ownership of the Circle M?"

"No, he hasn't, Cora, and he won't. His wife shot him dead not three days after he signed the license that caused you to believe you were married to him."

Cora shook her head. "Rex is. . ."

"Rex never existed, but yes, Simon is dead."

"So is your father, McBride," Ross said. "And this woman was there when he died."

"I know that, too." He glanced down at Cora. "Sheriff Griffin told me. The day he told me my father died, I asked him to investigate everything. His investigation led to the history of the man who claimed to be Rex Holley."

Iz turned to Lavinia's father. "Sir, I entered into an engagement with your daughter and intended to marry her right and honorable. I hope you understand why that is no longer possible."

The words seemed to strike the older man to the core. For once, he actually looked contrite.

Hamilton Riley stuck out his hand to shake, and Iz took it. "You're a good man, McBride. I am sorry we have caused a fuss." He motioned for Woodward to help Lavinia into the buggy. "We will be on our way, then."

When Hamilton and his daughter had turned the buggy back toward the trail leading out of the Circle M, Iz nodded toward the Pinkerton agent, who lingered behind. "Take care of her, Ross. Lavinia's a good woman."

He smiled. "I intend to. With her father's permission, that is," he added as he mounted his horse and set off to follow the buggy.

Cora touched his sleeve, and he turned toward her. "I'm sorry I didn't tell you," she said. "Will you forgive me?"

"I already have."

She shook her head as the dog nuzzled her hand. "But why?"

He smiled. "Because Buster is a good judge of character."

Epilogue

November 8, 1880

Be careful with her," Rosie admonished from somewhere nearby. "That baby coul[d] come any day."

Cora heard Iz's deep chuckle, but with a blindfold over her eyes, she could see nothing. His hand steadied her as he guided her forward. Then abruptly he stopped.

"I'm going to remove the blindfold, Cora. Are you ready to see the finished house?"

"More than ready."

She wouldn't mention that the baby seemed ready as well. Or at least that was her suspicion, given the fact she'd been awake most of the night with pains that had become more regular as the hours passed.

The blindfold came off, and there before her was the exact replica of the white house her father had described all those years ago. "Oh Iz, it's beautiful." She shook her head. "Wait, there's a door missing." She looked up at him. "I thought we agreed there would be two halves to this home and two front doors."

"We did agree on that," he said.

"Then why is there only one door?"

"Go on in," he urged as he helped her up the steps to the front door. "You'll see why."

She pushed open the door, and there stood Rafael and Sheriff Griffin, along with the pastor and his wife. Then she noticed there was no wall between what had been agreed upon as two separate living areas. In fact, there was nothing separate about this beautiful home.

Cora looked back at Iz. "I don't understand."

Buster's bark diverted Cora's attention. Several wagons rolled to a stop outside, each filled with a half-dozen or so citizens of Creed Creek. She moved past Iz to see that more wagons were headed up the trail, each carrying a number of friends from town. Most held baskets of food, and all were smiling.

"Iz, what's all this about? Is it a housewarming?"

"Not exactly, Cora. I only built one door to this house because this is your home. God's made that clear to me on more than one occasion. However, He's also made it clear that this is my home, too."

A pain hit her, and Cora clutched the porch post to steady herself. Buster hurried to her side and began to nudge her. "Iz, what in the world are you talking about?"

He reached for her hand. "Cora, this is our home, and I'd be honored to share it with you, but only if you'll marry me."

"Iz—"

"I won't take no for an answer this time," he said. "That baby needs a daddy, and unless I miss my guess, he's going to be coming soon."

"But, Iz," she said as softly as she could manage through gritted teeth, "if you don't stop asking me to marry you, the whole town is going to know we're not husband and wife. That was not part of the plan."

"Oh, they already know," the pastor said. "Iz here stood up in front of God and everybody last Sunday and told the whole story."

"Leaving out the part where your late husband was a bigamist," Iz whispered in her ear. "I figured that was best kept between us."

Cora searched Iz's face. "Why didn't anyone tell me?"

Rosie shook her head. "Your Iz had a plan, too, Cora, and telling you ahead of time wasn't part of his plan."

He winked at Rosie. "And there's one more thing."

Sheriff Griffin pulled a sheet of paper from his pocket and handed it to her. "What is this?"

"It's the deed to the Circle M," Iz said. "I also did some checking on who had clear title to this place, and I'm sorry to say that once you were declared a widow, my daddy's deed trumped your daddy's deed, at least in the eyes of the land office." He paused only a moment. "So I took care of that and had a new deed drawn up giving the Circle M to you."

She unfolded the document. Sure enough her name was right there on the deed. Duncan lands had been rightfully returned. Tears shimmered at the corner of her eyes, the pain temporarily forgotten.

"I made sure this is written up so that the Circle M is yours whether you marry me or not. However, I'd really like it if you'd marry me. So what do you say, Cora?"

Cora looked down at the good man now kneeling before her. And then she tore the deed to pieces. "Now I'll marry you, Iz, but only if you change the name of this place to the Duncan McBride Ranch."

Iz laughed. "Of course, but we'll need a new arch for the gate."

Harley pushed his way through the crowd. "And I'm just the blacksmith for the job. Consider it a wedding gift from me and the missus."

"Well, thank you, Harley."

Iz embraced her as yet another pain tore through her. "Pastor, you might want to hurry with the wedding," she said. "I believe the heir to the ranch is of a mind to attend the reception."

Sure enough, less than an hour after Cora legally changed her name, she gave birth to a healthy baby boy. His name?

Duncan McBride.